IRVING STONE

The Agony and the Ecstasy

A Biographical Novel of Michelangelo

Collins

FONTANA BOOKS

First published 1961
First issued in Fontana Books 1963
Thirteenth Impression May 1975

© Doubleday and Company, Inc., 1961

Made and printed in Great Britain by
William Collins Sons & Co Ltd Glasgow

The eighteen lines from Ovid's The Metamorphoses,
*translated by Horace Gregory, are reprinted by
permission. Copyright © 1958 by the Viking Press,
Inc. Forty-five lines from Dante's* Divine Comedy,
*translated by Lawrence Grant White, are reprinted
by permission of the publisher. Copyright 1948 by
Pantheon Books*

The Agony and the Ecstasy

Irving Stone's first biographical novel was *Lust for Life*, the story of Van Gogh. An immediate bestseller in 1934, it continues to attract readers all over the world. Now, fourteen bestsellers later, Irving Stone again portrays the life of a great artist—Michelangelo.

"Irving Stone has made a real and successful attempt to express the joy a great artist feels in the work of creation. The personality of Michelangelo, with his blunt way of speaking to his betters and the marble dust in his broken nose, breaks through an amazing amount of information to result in a book constructed with a great deal of art, in both senses of the word." *The Bookman*

THE BOOKS

THE LOVER AND THE SCULPTOR

The best of artists hath no thought to show
which the rough stone in its superfluous shell
doth not include; to break the marble spell
is all the hand that serves the brain can do.

THE ARTIST AND HIS WORK

How can that be, lady, which all men learn
by long experience? Shapes that seem alive,
wrought in hard mountain marble, will survive
their maker, whom the years to dust return!

BEAUTY AND THE ARTIST

Beauteous art, brought with us from heaven,
will conquer nature; so divine a power
belongs to him who strives with every nerve.

If I was made for art, from childhood given
a prey for burning beauty to devour,
I blame the mistress I was born to serve.

MICHELANGELO BUONARROTI

For my wife
JEAN STONE
Diaskeuast
Possibly, the
world's best

BOOK ONE

THE STUDIO

1

He sat before the mirror of the second-floor bedroom sketching his lean cheeks with their high bone ridges, the flat broad forehead, and ears too far back on the head, the dark hair curling forward in thatches, the amber-coloured eyes wide-set but heavy-lidded.

"I'm not well designed," thought the thirteen-year-old with serious concentration. "My head is out of rule, with the forehead overweighing my mouth and chin. Someone should have used a plumb line."

He shifted his wiry body lightly so as not to waken his four brothers, sleeping behind him, then cocked an ear towards the Via dell'Anguillara to catch the whistle of his friend Granacci. With rapid strokes of the crayon he began redraughting his features, widening the oval of the eyes, rounding the forehead, broadening the narrow cheeks, making the lips fuller, the chin larger. "There," he thought, "now I look better. Too bad a face can't be redrawn before it's delivered, like plans for the façade of the Duomo."

Notes of a bird's song came fluting through the ten-foot window, which he had opened to the cool morning air. He hid his drawing paper under the bolster at the head of his bed and went noiselessly down the circular stone stairs to the street.

His friend Francesco Granacci was a nineteen-year-old youth, a head taller than himself, with hay-coloured hair and alert blue eyes. For a year Granacci had been providing him drawing materials and sanctuary in his parents' home across the Via dei Bentaccordi, as well as prints borrowed surreptitiously from Ghirlandaio's studio. Though the son of a wealthy family, Granacci had been apprenticed to Filippino Lippi at the age of ten, at thirteen had posed as the central figure of the resurrected youth in St. Peter Raising the Emperor's Nephew, in the Carmine, which Masaccio had left uncompleted, and now was apprenticed to Ghirlandaio.

Granacci did not take his own painting seriously, but he had a sharp eye for talent in others.

" You're really coming with me this time?" Granacci demanded excitedly.

" It's my birthday present to myself."

" Good." He took the younger boy's arm, guiding him along the curving Via dei Bentaccordi which had been built on the oval site of the old Roman colosseum, past the high walls of the prison of the Stinche. " Remember what I told you about Domenico Ghirlandaio. I've been apprenticed to him for five years, and I know him well. Be humble. He likes his apprentices to appreciate him."

By now they had turned into the Via Ghibellina, just above the Ghibellina gate which marked the limits of the second wall of the city. On their left they passed the magnificent stone pile of the Bargello, with its colourful governor's courtyard, and then, after they had turned right on the Street of the Proconsul, the Pazzi palace. The younger boy ran his hand lovingly over the irregular roughhewn blocks of its walls.

" Let's hurry," urged Granacci. " This is the best moment of the day for Ghirlandaio, before he begins his drawing."

They went with unmatched strides along the narrow streets, past the Street of the Old Irons with its stone palaces and exterior flights of carved stone stairs leading to jutting penthouses. They made their way along the Via del Corso and saw on their right through the narrow slit of the Via dei Tedaldini a segment of the red-tiled Duomo, and after another block, on their left, the Palazzo della Signoria with its arches, windows and crownings of its tan stone tower penetrating the faint sunrise blue of the Florentine sky. To reach Ghirlandaio's studio they had to cross the Square ot the Old Market, where fresh beeves, cut down the backbone and opened wide, hung on pulleys in front ot the butchers' stalls. From here it was but a short walk past the Street ot the Painters to the corner of the Via dei Tavolini where they saw the open door of Ghirlandaio's studio.

Michelangelo stopped for a moment to gaze at Donatello's marble St. Mark standing in a tall niche of the Orsanmichele.

" Sculpture is the greatest art!" he exclaimed, his voice ringing with emotion.

Granacci was surprised that his friend had concealed this feeling for sculpture during their two years of friendship.

"I don't agree with you," he said quietly. "But stop gaping, there's business to be done."

The boy took a deep breath. Together they entered the Ghirlandaio workshop.

2

The studio was a large high-ceilinged room with a pungent smell of paint and charcoal. In the centre was a rough plank table set up on horses around which half a dozen sleepy young apprentices crouched on stools. In a near corner a man was grinding colours in a mortar, while along the side walls were stacked colour cartoons of completed frescoes, the Last Supper of the Church of the Ognissanti and the Calling of the First Apostles for the Sistine Chapel in Rome.

In a protected rear corner on a raised platform sat a man of about forty, his wide-topped desk the only ordered spot in the studio, with its neat rows of pens, brushes, sketchbooks, its scissors and other implements hanging on hooks, and behind, on the wall shelves, volumes of illuminated manuscripts.

Granacci stopped below his master's desk.

"Signor Ghirlandaio, this is Michelangelo, about whom I told you."

Michelangelo felt himself being spitted by a pair of eyes reputed to be able to see and record more with one thrust than any artist in Italy. But the boy too used his eyes as though they were silver-point pens, drawing for his mind's portfolio the artist sitting above him in an azure coat and red cloak thrown over the shoulders against the March chill and wearing a red cap, the sensitive face with its full purple lips, prominent bone formations beneath the eyes, deep cheek hollows, the opulent black hair parted in the centre and worn down to his shoulders, the long supple fingers of his right hand clasped against his throat. He remembered Granacci telling him of Ghirlandaio's exclamation only a few days before:

"Now that I have begun to understand the ways of this art, it is a grief to me that I am not given the whole circumference of the walls of Florence to cover with fresco."

"Who is your father?" demanded Ghirlandaio.

"Lodovico di Lionardo Buonarroti-Simoni."

" I have heard the name. How old are you?'"

" Thirteen."

" We start apprentices at ten. Where have you been for the past three years?"

" Wasting my time at Francesco da Urbino's school of grammar, studying Latin and Greek."

A twitching at the corner of Ghirlandaio's dark wine lips showed that he liked the answer.

" Can you draw?"

" I have the capacity to learn."

Granacci, wanting to help his friend but unable to reveal that he had been borrowing Ghirlandaio's prints for Michelangelo to copy, said:

" He has a good hand. He made drawings on the walls of his father's house in Settignano. There is one, a satyr . . ."

" Ah, a muralist," quipped Ghirlandaio. " Competition for my declining years."

Michelangelo was so intense that he took Ghirlandaio seriously.

" I've never tried colour. It's not my trade."

Ghirlandaio started to answer, then checked himself.

" Whatever else you may lack for, it isn't modesty. You won't become my competitor, not because you haven't the talent to do so, but because you care nothing for colour."

Michelangelo felt rather than heard Granacci's groan beside him.

" I didn't mean it that way."

" You're small for thirteen. You look too frail for the heavy work of this studio."

" To draw one does not need big muscles."

He realized that he had been baited into saying the wrong thing, and that in addition he had raised his voice. The apprentices had turned at this contretemps. After a moment Ghirlandaio's good nature asserted itself.

" Very well, suppose you sketch for me. What will it be?"

Michelangelo's eyes travelled over the workshop, swallowing impressions the way country youths break bunches of grapes in their mouths at autumn wine festivals.

" Why not the studio?"

Ghirlandaio gave a short disparaging laugh, as though he had been rescued from an awkward position.

" Granacci, give Buonarroti paper and charcoal. Now, if you have no objections. I will go back to my work."

Michelangelo found a point of vantage near the door from

12

which to see the workshop best, and sat down on a bench to sketch. Granacci lingered by his side.

"Why did you have to suggest such a difficult theme? Take plenty of time. He'll forget you're here . . ."

His eye and hand were good working partners, grasping the essentials of the large room: the worktable in the centre with its apprentices on both sides, Ghirlandaio on his platform under the north window. For the first time since entering the studio his breathing was normal. He felt someone leaning over his shoulder.

"I'm not finished," he said.

"It is enough." Ghirlandaio took the paper, studied it for a moment. "You have worked at another studio! Was it Rosselli's?"

Michelangelo knew of Ghirlandaio's dislike of Rosselli, who conducted the only other painters' workshop in Florence. Seven years before Ghirlandaio, Botticelli and Rosselli had been called to Rome by Pope Sixtus IV to create wall panels for the newly completed Sistine Chapel. Rosselli had caught the pontiff's eye by using the most garish reds and ultramarine blues and illuminating every cloud, drapery and tree with gold, and won the coveted prize money.

The boy shook his head no.

"I've drawn in school when Master Urbino wasn't looking. And I've copied after Giotto in Santa Croce, after Masaccio in the Carmine . . ."

Mollified, Ghirlandaio said, "Granacci was right. You have a strong fist."

Michelangelo held his hand in front of him, turning it from back to palm.

"It is a stonecutter's hand," he replied proudly.

"We have little need for stonecutters in a fresco studio. I'll start you as an apprentice, but on the same terms as though you were ten. You must pay me six florins for the first year . . ."

"I can pay you nothing."

Ghirlandaio looked at him sharply.

"The Buonarroti are not poor country people. Since your father wants you apprenticed . . ."

"My father has beat me every time I mentioned painting."

"But I cannot take you unless he signs the Doctors and Apothecaries Guild agreement. Why will he not beat you again when you tell him?"

"Because your willingness to accept me will be a defence.

13

That, and the fact that you will pay him six florins the first year, eight the second, and ten the third."

Ghirlandaio's eyelids flared.

"That's unheard of! Paying money for the privilege teaching you!"

"Then I cannot come to work for you. It is the only way."

The colour grinder was twirling his pestle idly in the air while he gazed over his shoulder at the scene. The apprentices at the table made no pretence of working. The master and would-be apprentice had reversed positions as though it were Ghirlandaio who, needing and wanting Michelangelo, had sent for him. Michelangelo could see the "No" beginning to take form on Ghirlandaio's lips. He stood his ground, his manner respectful both to the older man and to himself, gazing straight at Ghirlandaio as though to say:

"It is a thing you should do. I will be worth it to you."

Had he shown the slightest weakness Ghirlandaio would have turned his back on him. But before this solid confrontation the artist felt a grudging admiration. He lived up to his reputation of being a man "lovable and loved" by saying:

"It's obvious we shall never get the Tornabuoni choir finished without your invaluable help. Bring your father in."

Out on the Via dei Tavolini once again, with the early morning merchants and shoppers swirling about them, Granacci threw an arm affectionately about the smaller boy's shoulder.

"You broke every rule. But you got in!"

Michelangelo flashed his friend one of his rare warming smiles, the amber-coloured eyes with their yellow and blue specks sparkling. The smile accomplished the redesigning for which his crayon had groped earlier in front of the bedroom mirror: when parted in a happy smile his lips were full, revealing strong white teeth, and his chin thrusting forward achieved sculptural symmetry with the top half of his face.

3

Walking past the family house of the poet Dante Alighieri and the stone church of the Badia was for Michelangelo like walking through a gallery: for the Tuscan treats stone with the tenderness that a lover reserves for his sweetheart. From the time of their Etruscan ancestors the people of Fiesole, Settignano and Florence had been quarrying stone from the mountains, hauling it by oxen to their land, cutting, edging, shaping and building it into homes and palaces, churches and loggias, forts and walls. Stone was one of the richest fruits of the Tuscan earth. From childhood they knew its feel and smell, the flavour of its outer shell as well as its inner meat; how it behaved in the hot sun, in the rain, in the full moonlight, in the icy *tramontana* wind. For fifteen hundred years their ancestors had worked the native *pietra serena,* building a city of such breath-taking beauty that Michelangelo and generations before him cried:

"Never shall I live out of sight of the Duomo!"

They reached the carpenter shop which occupied the ground floor of the house the Buonarroti clan rented in the Via dell'Anguillara.

"*A rivederci,* as the fox said to the furrier," Granacci twitted.

"Oh, I'll take a skinning," he responded grimly, "but unlike the fox I shall come out alive."

He turned the sharp corner of the Via dei Bentaccordi, waved to the two horses whose heads were sticking out of the open-top door of the stable across the street, and climbed the rear staircase to the family kitchen.

His stepmother was making her beloved *torta*: the chickens had been fried in oil earlier in the morning, ground into sausage with onions, parsley, eggs and saffron. Ham and pork had been made into *ravioli* with cheese, flour, clove, ginger, and laid with the chicken sausage between layers of pastry, dates and almonds. The whole dish had been shaped into a pie and was being covered with dough, preparatory to being placed in the hot embers to bake.

"Good morning, *madre mia.*"

"Ah, Michelangelo. I have something special for you to-day: a salad that sings in the mouth."

Lucrezia di Antonio di Sandro Ubaldini da Gagliano's name was longer than the written list of her dowry; else why should so young a woman marry a forty-three-year-old widower with five sons, and cook for a household of nine Buonarroti?

Each morning she rose at four o'clock in order to reach the market square at the same time the *contadini* arrived through the cobbled streets with their pony carts filled with fresh fruits and vegetables, eggs and cheese, meats and

15

poultry. If she did not actually help the peasants unload, at least she lightened their burden by selecting while the produce was still in the air and before it had a chance to settle in the stalls: the tenderest, slender green beans and *piselli,* peas, unblemished figs, peaches.

Michelangelo and his four brothers called her *Il Migliore,* The Best, because every ingredient that went into her cooking had to be The Best. By dawn she was home, her baskets piled high with capture. She cared little about her clothing, paid no attention to her plain dark face with its suggestion of sideburns and moustache, the lacklustre hair pulled tightly back from her brow. But as Michelangelo gazed at her flushed cheeks, the excitement in her eyes as she watched her *torta* baking, moving with authority and grace from the fire to her majolica jars of spices to sprinkle a fine dust of cinnamon and nutmeg over the crust, knowing every second of the seven-hour morning precisely where she was on schedule, he saw that she exuded radiance.

He knew his stepmother to be a docile creature in every phase of her marriage except the kitchen; here she was a lioness in the best fighting tradition of the Marzocco, Florence's guardian lion. Wealthy Florence was supplied with exotic foods from all over the world: aloes, zedoary, cardamom, thyme, marjoram, mushrooms and truffles, powdered nuts, *galinga.* Alas! they cost money to buy. Michelangelo, who shared the bedroom with his four brothers next to his parents' room, often heard his parents' predawn debates while his stepmother dressed for marketing.

"Every day you want a bale of herrings and a thousand oranges."

"Lodovico, stop cutting costs with a cheese parer. You are one who would keep money in the purse and hunger in the belly."

"Hunger! No Buonarroti has missed his dinner in three hundred years. Each week don't I bring you in a fresh veal from Settignano?"

"Why should we eat veal every day when the markets are full of suckling pig and pigeon?"

On those days that Lodovico lost he gloomed over the account books, certain that he would not be able to swallow a bite of the *bramangiere* of fowls, almonds, lard, sugar, cloves and expensive rice with which his young irresponsible wife was ruining him. But slowly, as the fragrances seeped

16

under the door of the kitchen, through the family sitting-room and into his study, it would eat away his fears, his anger, his frustration; and by eleven o'clock he would be ravenous.

Lodovico would devour a prodigious dinner, then push his chair back from the table, slap his bulging viscera with widespread fingers and exclaim the one sentence without which the Tuscan's day is drear and futile:

"*Ho mangiato bene!*"

With this tribute Lucrezia put away the remains for a light evening supper, set her slavey to wash the dishes and pots, went upstairs and slept until dark, her day complete, her joy spent.

Not so Lodovico, who now went through the inverse process of the morning's seduction. As the hours passed and the food was digested, as the memory of the delicious flavours receded, the gnawing question of how much the elaborate dinner had cost began eating at him and he was angry all over again.

Michelangelo walked through the empty family room with its heavy oak bench facing the fireplace, the six-foot bellows propped against the stone, its wall chairs with leather backs and leather seats: all prodigal pieces that had been made by the family's founder. The next room, still overlooking the Via dei Bentaccordi and the stables, was his father's study, for which Lodovico had had built in the downstairs carpenter shop a triangular desk to fit into the forty-five-degree angle caused by the joining of the two streets at this end curve of the old colosseum. Here Lodovico sat cramped over his grey parchment account books. As long as Michelangelo could remember, his father's sole activity had been a concentration on how to avoid spending money, and how to retain the ragged remnants of the Buonarroti fortune, which had been founded in 1250 and had now shrunk to a ten-acre farm in Settignano and a house with a legally disputed title close by this one which they rented.

Lodovico heard his son come in and looked up. Nature had been opulent to him in only one gift, his hair: since it grew freely he sported a luxurious moustache which flowed into his beard, cut square four inches below his chin. The hair was streaked with grey; across the forehead were four deep straight lines, hard-earned from his years of poring over his account books and family records. His small brown eyes were melancholy with tracing the lost fortunes of the Buonarroti. Michelangelo knew his father as a cautious man who locked the door with three keys.

" Good morning, *messer padre*."

Lodovico sighed:

" I was born too late. One hundred years ago the Buonarroti vines were tied with sausages."

Michelangelo watched his father as he sank into his work-reverie of the Buonarroti records, the Old Testament of his life. Lodovico knew to the last florin how much each Buonarroti generation had owned of land, houses, business, gold. This family history was his occupation, and each of his sons in turn had to memorize the legend.

" We are noble burghers," Lodovico told them. " Our family is as old as the Medici, Strozzi or Tornabuoni. The Buonarroti name has lasted three hundred years with us." His voice rose with energy and pride. " We have been paying taxes in Florence for three centuries."

Michelangelo was forbidden to sit in his father's presence without permission, had to bow when given an order. It had been duty rather than interest that led the boy to learn that when the Guelphs took over power in Florence in the middle of the thirteenth century their family rose rapidly: in 1260 a Buonarroti was councillor for the Guelph army; in 1392 a captain of the Guelph party; from 1343 to 1469 a Buonarroti had ten times been a member of the Florentine *Priori* or City Council, the most honoured position in the city; between 1326 and 1475 eight Buonarroti had been *gonfaloniere* or mayor of the Santa Croce quarter; between 1375 and 1473 twelve had been among the *buonuomini* or Council of Santa Croce, including Lodovico and his brother Francesco, who were appointed in 1473. The last official recognition of the waning Buonarroti family had taken place thirteen years before, in 1474, when Lodovico had been appointed *podestà,* or outside visiting mayor, for the combined hamlets of Caprese and Chiusi di Verna, high in the rugged Apennines, where Michelangelo had been born in the town hall during the family's six months' residence.

Michelangelo had been taught by his father that labour was beneath a noble burgher; but it was the son's observation that Lodovico worked harder in figuring out ways not to spend money than he would have had to work in earning it. Within the Buonarroti fortress there had remained a few scattered resources, enough to let him eke out his life as a gentlemen providing he spent nothing. Yet in spite of all the skill and dedication Lodovico brought to his task their capital had dribbled away.

Standing in the recessed wall of the eight-foot window, letting the thin March sun warm his bony shoulders, the boy's image went back to their home in Settignano, overlooking the valley of the Arno, when his mother had been alive. Then there had been love and laughter; but his mother had died when he was six, and his father had retreated in despair into the encampment of his study. For four years while his aunt Cassandra had taken over the care of the household, Michelangelo had been lonely and unwanted except by his grandmother, Monna Alessandra, who lived with them, and the stonecutter's family across the hill, the stonecutter's wife having suckled him when his own mother had been too ill to nourish her son.

For four years, until his father had remarried and Lucrezia had insisted that they move into Florence, he had fled at every opportunity to the Topolinos. He would make his way down the wheat fields among the silver-green olives, cross the brook which marked the division of the land, and climb the opposite hill through the vineyards to their yard. Here he would silently set to work cutting the *pietra serena* from the neighbouring quarry into bevelled building stones for a new Florentine palace, working out his unhappiness in the precision blows in which he had been trained in this stonecutter's yard since he was a child and, along with the stonecutter's own sons, had been given a small hammer and chisel to work scraps.

Michelangelo pulled himself back from the stonecutter's yard in Settignano to this stone house on the Via dell' Anguillara.

"Father, I have just come from Domenico Ghirlandaio's studio. Ghirlandaio has agreed to sign me as an apprentice."

4

During the silence that pulsed between them Michelangelo heard one of the horses neigh across the street and Lucrezia stir the embers of her fire in the kitchen. Lodovico used both hands to raise himself to a commanding position over the boy. This inexplicable desire of his son's to become an artisan could be the final push that would topple the shaky Buonarroti into the social abyss.

"Michelangelo, I apologize for being obliged to apprentice you to the Wool Guild and force you to become a merchant rather than a gentleman. But I sent you to an expensive school, paid out money I could ill afford so that you would be educated and rise in the Guild until you had your own mills and shops. That was how most of the great Florentine fortunes were started, even the Medici's."

Lodovico's voice rose. "Do you think that I will now allow you to waste your life as a painter? To bring disgrace to the family name! For three hundred years no Buonarroti has fallen so low as to work with his hands."

"That is true. We have been usurers," angrily responded the boy.

"We belong to the Money Changers Guild, one of the most respectable in Florence. Moneylending is an honourable profession."

Michelangelo sought refuge in humour.

"Have you ever watched Uncle Francesco fold up his counter outside Orsanmichele when it starts to rain? You never saw anyone work faster with his hands."

At the mention of his name Uncle Francesco came running into the room. He was a larger man than Lodovico, with a brighter countenance; the working half of the Buonarroti partnership. Two years before he had broken away from Lodovico, made considerable money, bought houses and set himself up in style, only to be lured into a bad investment in foreign currencies, lose everything and have to move back into his brother's house. Now when it rained he scooped up his velvet covering from the folding table, grabbed his bag of coins from between his feet and ran through the wet streets to his friend, Amatore the cloth cutter, who allowed him to set up his table under cover.

Francesco said in a hoarse voice:

"Michelangelo, you couldn't see a crow in a bowlful of milk! What perverse pleasure can you derive from injuring the Buonarroti?"

The boy was furious at the accusation.

"I have as much pride in our name as anyone. Why can't I learn to do fine work that all Florence will be proud of, as they are of Ghiberti's doors and Donatello's sculptures and Ghirlandaio's frescoes? Florence is a good city for an artist."

Lodovico put his hand on the boy's shoulder, calling him *Michelagnolo,* his pet name. This was his favourite of the five sons, for whom he had the highest hopes; it was this affection that had given him courage to spend money for three years of schooling at Urbino's. The master had been too proud to report to the father that his seemingly bright son had preferred drawing in his notebooks to learning his letters from the collection of Greek and Latin manuscripts. As for rhetoric, the boy had been bound by his own rules of logic which the persuasive Urbino had been unable to alter.

" Michelagnolo, the things you say about artists are as true as the word of a bench-talker. I've been too angry at your stupidity to do anything but beat you. But you're thirteen now; I've paid for your training in logic, so I should practise logic with you. Ghiberti and Donatello began as artisans and ended as artisans. So will Ghirlandaio. Their work never raised their social position one *braccio,* and Donatello was so destitute at the end of his life that Cosimo de' Medici had to give him a charity pension."

The boy flared at this attack.

" That's because Donatello put all his money into a wire basket hung from the ceiling so his assistants and friends could help themselves when they needed. Ghirlandaio makes a fortune."

" Art is like washing an ass's head with lye," observed Francesco, for the Tuscan's wisdom is a web of proverbs; " you lose both the effort and the lye. Every man thinks that rubble will turn into gold in his hand! What kind of dreaming is that?"

" The only kind I know," cried Michelangelo. He turned back to Lodovico. " Bleed me of art, and there won't be enough liquid left in me to spit."

" I prophesied that my Michelangelo would recoup the Buonarroti fortune," cried Lodovico. " I should have spoken with a smaller mouth! Now, I'll teach you to be vulgar."

He started raining blows on the boy, his right elbow crooked stiffly so that he could use his arm as a club. Francesco, not wanting to fail his nephew in this critical moment of his youth, also began hitting the boy, boxing his ear with the heel of his palm.

Michelangelo lowered his head as dumb beasts do in a storm. There was no point in running away, for then the

21

argument would have to be resumed later. Deep in his throat he sounded the words of his grandmother:

"*Pazienza!* No man is born into the world whose work is not born with him."

From the corner of his eye he saw his aunt Cassandra bulking in the doorway, a big-boned woman who seemed to put on flesh from the air she breathed. Cassandra of the enormous thighs, buttocks and bosom, with a voice that matched her weight, was an unhappy woman. Nor did she feel it her duty to dispense happiness.

"Happiness," said Aunt Cassandra, "is for the next world."

The boom of Aunt Cassandra's voice demanding to know what was going on now hurt his ear more than her husband's palm. Then, suddenly, all words and blows stopped and he knew that his grandmother had entered the room. She was a retiring woman in black, not beautiful but with a finely modelled head, who exercised her matriarchy only in moments of family crisis. Lodovico did not like to give his mother offence. He slumped into his chair.

"That's the end of the discussion!" he announced. "I have brought you up not to crave the whole world; it is enough to make money and serve the Buonarroti name. Never let me hear again about this being apprenticed to artists."

Michelangelo was glad that his stepmother was too deeply involved in her *torta* to permit her to leave the kitchen; the room was too crowded now for more spectators.

Monna Alessandra went to her son's side at the account desk.

"What difference does it make whether he joins the Wool Guild and twists wool or the Apothecaries Guild and mixes paints? You won't leave enough money to set up five geese, let alone sons." Her voice was without reproach; had it not been her husband, Lionardo Buonarroti, whose bad judgment and bad luck began the downfall of the family. "All five boys must look to their living; let Lionardo go into the monastery as he wishes, and Michelangelo into a studio. Since we can no longer help them, why hinder them?"

"I am going to be apprenticed to Ghirlandaio, Father. You must sign the papers. I'll do well by us all."

Lodovico stared at his son in disbelief. Was he possessed by an evil spirit? Should he take him to Arezzo and have him exorcised?

22

"Michelangelo, you are saying things that make me swell up a dozen times in anger." He shot his last and crushing bolt. "We have not a scudo to pay for any apprenticeship to Ghirlandaio."

This was the moment for which Michelangelo had been waiting. He said gently:

"There is no need for money, *padre*. Ghirlandaio has agreed to pay you for my apprenticeship."

"He will pay!" Lodovico lunged forward. "Why should he pay me for the privilege of teaching you?"

"Because he thinks I have a strong fist."

After a considerable silence Lodovico lowered himself slowly into his leather chair.

"Except God keep us, we shall be destroyed. Truthfully, I don't know where you come from. Certainly not from the Buonarroti. All this must be your mother's side, the Rucellai."

He spat out the name as though it were a mouthful of wormy apple. It was the first time Michelangelo could remember hearing the name spoken in the Buonarroti house. Lodovico crossed himself, more in perplexity than piety.

"Truly I have conquered myself in more battles than a saint!"

5

Domenico Ghirlandaio's was the most bustling and successful *bottega* in all Italy. In addition to the twenty-five frescoed panels and lunettes for the Tornabuoni choir at Santa Maria Novella, which had to be completed in the two years remaining of the five-year contract, he had also signed agreements to paint an Adoration of the Kings for the hospital of the Innocenti and to design a mosaic for over a portal of the cathedral. Every few days he made a trip on horseback to a neighbouring town which wanted him to paint anything from a small altarpiece to the hall of a ducal palace. Ghirlandaio, who never sought a commission, could refuse none; on Michelangelo's first day in the studio he told him:

"If a peasant woman brings you a basket that she wants ornamented, do it as beautifully as you can, for in its modest way it is as important as a fresco on a palace wall."

Michelangelo found the place energetic but good-natured.

Twenty-eight-year-old Sebastiano Mainardi, with long black hair cut to imitate Ghirlandaio's, a pale, narrow face with a jutting bony nose and protruding teeth, was in charge of the apprentices; he was Ghirlandaio's brother-in-law, though not, insisted Jacopo dell'Indaco, imp son of a baker, through any willing of his own.

"Ghirlandaio married him to his sister in order to keep him working for the family," Jacopo told Michelangelo. "So be on your guard."

Like most of Jacopo's deviltries, this one contained a kernel of truth: the Ghirlandaios were a family of artists, having been trained in the workshop of their father, an expert goldsmith who had originated a fashionable wreath, called a *ghirlanda,* which the Florentine women wore in their hair. Domenico's two younger brothers, David and Benedetto, were also painters. Benedetto, a miniaturist, wanted to paint only the minute and precise aspects of a woman's jewels or flowers; David, the youngest, had signed the contract for the Santa Maria Novella along with his brother.

Domenico Ghirlandaio had moved on from his father's studio to that of Baldovinetti, the master of mosaics, where he had remained until he was twenty-one, leaving reluctantly to open his own studio. "Painting is drawing, and the true eternal painting is mosaic," he declared, but since few wanted mosaics any more he had turned to fresco, becoming the greatest absorber and eclectic in Italy. He had learned everything that the earlier fresco painters, from the time of Cimabue, had to teach. In addition he added something peculiarly and brilliantly his own.

Ghirlandaio had in truth embraced young Mainardi as a brother-in-law after the young apprentice had helped him paint his masterly frescoes in the church at San Gimignano, a neighbouring town of seventy-six towers. Mainardi, who now took Michelangelo in tow, was amazingly like Ghirlandaio: good-natured, talented, well trained in the studio of Verrocchio, loving above all things to paint, and agreeing with Ghirlandaio that it was the beauty and charm of a fresco that was important. Paintings had to tell a story, either from the Bible, religious history or Greek mythology, but it was not the painter's function to look behind the meaning of that story, to search for its significance or judge its validity.

"The purpose of painting," explained Mainardi to his newest apprentice, " is to be decorative, to bring stories to life pictorially, to make people happy, yes, even with the sad

24

pictures of the saints being martyred. Always remember that, Michelangelo, and you will become a successful painter."

If Mainardi was the major-domo of the apprentices, Michelangelo soon learned that sixteen-year-old Jacopo, with the monkey-like face, was the ringleader. He had a gift for appearing to be busy without doing a lick of work. He welcomed the thirteen-year-old boy to the studio by warning him gravely:

"Doing nothing else but hard work is not worthy of a good Christian." Turning to the table of apprentices, he added exultantly, "Here in Florence we average nine holidays every month. Add Sundays to that and it means we only have to work every other day."

"I can't see that it makes any critical difference to you, Jacopo," commented Granacci with a rare burn of acid. "You don't work on workdays."

The two weeks flew by until the magic day of his contract signing and first pay dawned. Michelangelo suddenly realized how little he had done to earn the two gold florins which would constitute his first advance. So far he had been used as an errand boy to pick up paints at the chemist's, to screen sand to give it a fine texture and wash it in a barrel with a running hose. Awakening while it was still dark outside, he climbed over his younger brother Buonarroto, sprang out of the bed, fumbled in the bed-bench for his long stockings and knee-length shirt. At the Bargello he passed under a body hanging from a hook in the cornice; this must be the man who, failing to die when hanged two weeks before, had uttered such vengeful words that the eight magistrates had decided to hang him all over again.

Ghirlandaio was surprised to find the boy on his doorstep so early and his *buon giorno* was short. He had been working for days on a study of St. John Baptizing the Neophyte and was upset because he could not clarify his concept of Jesus. He was further annoyed when interrupted by his brother David with a batch of bills that needed paying. Domenico pushed the accounts aside with a brusque gesture of his left hand, continuing to draw irritatedly with his right.

"Why can't you manage this *bottega,* David, and leave me alone to do my painting?"

Michelangelo watched the scene with apprehension: would they forget what day it was? Granacci saw his friend's expression. He slipped off his bench, went to David, murmured something in his ear. David reached into the

25

leather purse he kept hooked on to his wide belt, crossed the
room to Michelangelo and handed him two florins and a
contract book. Michelangelo quickly signed his name alongside the first payment, as stipulated in the Doctors and
Apothecaries Agreement, then wrote the date:

16 Aprile, 1488

Joy raced through his veins as he anticipated the moment
when he would hand the florins to his father. Two florins
were not the wealth of the Medici, but he hoped they
would lighten the murky atmosphere around the Buonarroti
house. Then he was aware of an enthusiastic hubbub among
the apprentices and the voice of Jacopo saying:

" It's agreed, we draw from memory that gnome figure on
the alley wall behind the *bottega*. The one who draws the
most accurate reproduction wins and pays for dinner. Cieco,
Baldinelli, Granacci, Bugiardini, Tedesco, are you ready?"

Michelangelo felt a dull pain in the chest; he was being
left out. His had been a lonely childhood, he had had no
intimate friend until Granacci recognized in his young neighbour a talent for drawing. So often he had been excluded
from games. Why? Because he had been small and sickly?
Because there was not enough laughter in him? Because he
communicated with difficulty? He so desperately wanted to
be included in the companionship of this young group; but it
did not come easy. At the end of his first week Granacci
had had to teach him a lesson in getting along with one's
contemporaries.

Thirteen-year-old, heavy-boned Giuliano Bugiardini, a
simple-natured lad who had been friendly to Michelangelo
from the moment he entered the studio, had done a practice
study of a group of women. Bugiardini could not draw the
human figure and had no interest in it.

" What's the use?" he demanded. " We never show anything except the hands and face."

Seeing the sacklike outlines, Michelangelo had impulsively
picked up a stub pen and made a number of quick strokes
which had put limbs under the heavy dresses of the women
and infused them with a sense of movement. Bugiardini
blinked his heavy eyelids a few times to see his figures spring
to life. He was free of envy and did not resent the corrections. It was the thirteen-year-old Cieco, who had been
apprenticed to Ghirlandaio at the conventional age of ten,
who had taken offence. The sharp-tongued Cieco cried out:

" You've been studying from a female nude model!"

26

"But there's no such thing in Florence," protested Michelangelo.

Tedesco, rawboned redhead, fruit of an early invasion of Florence, asked in a voice edged with hostility, "Then how do you know about the movements of a woman's breasts and thighs, that you can put real people under their clothes?"

"I watch the women picking beans in the fields, or walking along the road with a basket of faggots on their head. What your eye sees, your hand can draw."

"Ghirlandaio is not going to like this!" crowed Jacopo joyously.

That evening Granacci said confidingly:

"Be careful about raising jealousies. Cieco and Tedesco have been apprenticed for a long time. How could they see any justice in your being able to draw better instinctively than they can after years of training? Praise their work. Keep your own to yourself."

Now, at the apprentices' table, Jacopo was completing the details of the game.

"Time limit, ten minutes. The winner to be crowned champion and host."

"Why can't I compete, Jacopo?" Michelangelo cried.

Jacopo scowled. "You're just a beginner, you couldn't possibly win, and there would be no chance of your paying. It wouldn't be fair to the rest of us."

Stung, Michelangelo pleaded, "Let me join in, Jacopo. You'll see, I won't do too badly."

"All right," Jacopo agreed reluctantly. "But you can't have a longer time. Everyone ready?"

Excitedly, Michelangelo picked up charcoal and paper and began hammering down the outlines of the gnarled figure, half youth, half satyr, which he had seen several times on the rear stone wall. He could summon lines from his memory the way the students at Urbino's school had so miraculously brought forth verses of Homer's *Iliad* or Virgil's *Aeneid* when the master demanded them.

"Time limit!" cried Jacopo. "Line up your drawings, centre of the table."

Michelangelo ran to the table, put his sketch in line, quickly scanned the other sheets. He was astonished at how unfamiliar, even incomplete they appeared. Jacopo stared at him with his mouth wide open.

"I can't believe it. Look, everyone, Michelangelo has won!"

There were cries of congratulation. Cieco and Tedesco smiled at him for the first time since their argument. He glowed with pride. He was the newest apprentice, yet he had won the right to buy everyone dinner. . . .

Buy everyone dinner! His stomach sank as though he had swallowed his two gold florins. He counted heads; there were seven of them. They would consume two litres of red wine, soup-of-the-country, roast veal, fruit . . . making a sizable hole in one of the gold pieces that he had waited for so eagerly to turn over to his father.

On the way to the *osteria*, with the others rushing ahead laughing heartily among themselves, a loose thread began flapping in his mind. He ran the spool of his thoughts backward, fell in step beside Granacci.

" I was gulled, wasn't I?"

" Yes."

" Why didn't you warn me?"

" It's part of the initiation."

" What will I tell my father?"

" If you had known, would you have made yourself draw badly?"

Michelangelo broke into a sheepish grin.

" They couldn't lose!"

6

There was no formal method of teaching at Ghirlandaio's studio. Its basic philosophy was expressed in a plaque which Ghirlandaio had nailed to the wall alongside his desk:

The most perfect guide is nature. Continue without fail to draw something every day.

Michelangelo had to learn from whatever task each man had at hand. No secrets were kept from him. Ghirlandaio created the over-all design, the composition within each panel and the harmonious relation of one panel to the many others. He did most of the important portraits, but the hundred others were distributed throughout the studio, sometimes several men working on a single figure and on a one-day spread of plaster. Where there was an excellent angle of visibility from the church, Ghirlandaio did the entire panel himself. Otherwise major portions were painted by Main-

28

ardi, Benedetto, Granacci and Bugiardini. On the lateral lunettes, which were hard to see, he let Cieco and Baldinelli, the other thirteen-year-old apprentice, practise.

Michelangelo moved from table to table, doing odd jobs. No one had time to stop work to teach him. He watched Ghirlandaio complete a portrait of Giovanna Tornabuoni, painted as a separate commission, and then draw it for the cartoon of the Visitation panel.

"Oil painting is for women," Ghirlandaio said sarcastically. "But this figure will go well in the fresco. Never try to invent human beings, Michelangelo; paint into your panels only those whom you have already drawn from life."

David and Benedetto shared with Mainardi a long table in the far corner of the studio. Benedetto never worked freehand. It seemed to Michelangelo that he paid more attention to the mathematical squares on the paper before him than to the individual character of the person portrayed. Nevertheless he was an expert with the instruments for squaring up. He told Michelangelo:

"Remember that the face is divided in three parts: first, the hair and forehead, then the nose, then the chin and mouth. Now take the proportions of a man. I omit those of a woman because there is not one of them perfectly proportioned. The arm with the hand extends to the middle of the thigh . . . so. The whole length of a man is eight faces; and equal to his width with the arms extended. Always remember that a man has on his left side one less rib than a woman . . ."

Michelangelo tried drawing to Benedetto's geometric plan, with its plumb line and compass half circles, but the restriction was a coffin into which he could squeeze only dead bodies.

Mainardi however had an accurate hand and a self-assurance that breathed life into his work. He had painted important parts of both lunettes and all the panels, and was working out a colour pattern for the Adoration of the Magi. He showed Michelangelo how to tint flesh in tempera, going twice over the naked parts.

"This first bed of colour, particularly for young people with fresh complexions, must be tempered with the yolk of an egg of a city hen; the red yolks of country hens are only fit to temper flesh colourings of old or dark persons."

From Mainardi, Michelangelo learned to let the green tint under the flesh colours be just visible; to put highlights over the eyebrows and on the top of the nose with a little pure white; to outline the eyelids and lashes with black.

From Jacopo he received not technical instruction but news of the city. Nothing nefarious was safe from Jacopo. He could pass by virtue all his life and never stumble over it, but his nose smelled out the nether side of human nature as instinctively as a bird smells manure. Jacopo was the town's gossip gatherer and crier; he made the daily rounds of the inns, the wine- and barber-shops, the quarters of the prostitutes, the groups of old men sitting on stone benches before the *palazzi*, for they were the best purveyors of the town's yarns and scandal. Each morning he walked to the workshop by a circuitous route which enabled him to tap all of his sources; by the time he reached Ghirlandaio's he had a shopping basketful of the night's news: who had been cuckolded, who was going to be commissioned for what art project, who was about to be put in stocks with his back against the Signoria wall.

Ghirlandaio had a manuscript copy of Cennini's treatise on painting; although Jacopo could not read a word, he sat on the apprentices' table with his legs crossed under him, pretending to spell out the passages he had memorized:

" As an artist your manner of living should always be regulated as if you were studying theology, philosophy, or any other science; that is to say, eating and drinking temperately at least twice a day . . .; sparing and reserving your hand, saving it from fatigue caused by throwing stones or iron bars. There is still another cause, the occurrence of which may render your hand so unsteady that it will tremble and flutter more than leaves shaken by the wind, and this is frequenting too much the company of women."

Jacopo threw back his head and laughed froth bubbles at the ceiling, then turned upon the quite astonished Michelangelo, who knew less about women than he did of Ptolemy's astronomy.

" Now you know, Michelangelo, why I don't paint more: I don't want the Ghirlandaio frescoes to tremble like leaves in the wind!"

Amiable, easygoing David had been well trained in enlarging to scale the individual sections and transferring them to the cartoon itself, which was the dimension of the church panel. This was not creative work, but it took skill. He demonstrated how to divide the small painting into squares and the cartoon into the same number of larger squares, how to copy the content of each small square into the corresponding square of the cartoon, pointing out how mistakes that were almost unnoticeable in the small drawing became obvious when blown up to cartoon size.

Bugiardini, whose clumsy body made it appear that he would have trouble whitewashing his father's barn, nevertheless managed to get a spiritual tension into his figures for the Visitation, even though they were not accurate anatomically. He made Michelangelo spend one whole dinner period sitting for a sketch. After two hours Bugiardini said, " Have a look at your portrait. I have already caught the expression of your face."

Michelangelo broke into laughter.

Bugiardini, you have painted me with one of my eyes on my temple! Look at it!"

Bugiardini studied Michelangelo's face, then his sketch.

" It seems to me that your eye is exactly as I painted it, and so is your face."

" Then it must be a defect of nature," responded the boy.

Taking an indirect route home, Michelangelo and Granacci entered the Piazza della Signoria where a large crowd was gathered, and climbed the steps of the Loggia della Signoria. From here they could see into the *ringhiera* of the palace where an ambassador of the Turkish sultan, garbed in eggshell turban and flowing green robes, was presenting a giraffe to the councilmen of the Signoria. Michelangelo wished he could sketch the scene but, knowing that he could capture only a small part of its complexity, he complained to Granacci that he felt like a chessboard, with alternating black and white squares of information and ignorance.

The next noon he ate sparingly of Lucrezia's veal roast and returned to the studio, empty now because the others were taking their afternoon *riposo*. He had decided that he must study the drawing of his master. Under Ghirlandaio's desk he found a bundle labelled Slaughter of the Innocents, took it to the apprentices' table and spread out the dozens of sheets for the fresco. It seemed to him, poring over the finished fresco, that Ghirlandaio could not portray motion, for the soldiers with their swords upraised, the mothers and children running, created confusion and an emotional chaos in him. Yet these rough studies had simplicity and authority. He began copying the drawings and had made a half dozen

31

sketches in quick succession when he felt someone standing behind him. He turned to find a disapproving frown on Ghirlandaio's face.

" Why are you prying into that bundle? Who gave you permission?"

Michelangelo put down his charcoal, frightened.

" I didn't think there was any secret about it. I want to learn." He regained his composure. " The quicker I learn, the quicker I can help. I want to earn those gold florins."

The appeal to his logic served less to banish Ghirlandaio's anger than the intensity in the boy's eyes.

" Very well. I'll take some time with you now."

" Then teach me how to use a pen."

Ghirlandaio took his newest apprentice to his desk, cleared it and set up two corresponding sheets of paper. He handed Michelangelo a blunt-nibbed pen, picked up another for himself, started cross-hatching.

" Here's my calligraphy: circles for the eyes, angular tips for the nose, like this ; use the short nib to render a mouth and score the underlip."

Michelangelo followed the older man with quick movements of the hand, noting how Ghirlandaio in sketching a figure never bothered to finish the legs but tapered them down to nothing. Ghirlandaio could hang a convincing drapery on a figure with a few rapid strokes, do a woman holding up her dress with delicate grace, achieve a lyrical flow of the body lines and at the same time give the figures individuality and character.

A look of rapture came over Michelangelo's face. This was the happiest he had been. With pen in hand he was an artist, thinking out loud, probing his mind, searching his heart for what he felt and his hand for what it could discern about the object before him. He wanted to spend hours at this work desk, redrawing models from a hundred different angles.

Ghirlandaio was aware of the eagerness in the boy's face, the excitement in his hand.

" Michelangelo, you must not draw for its own sake. This figure is not usable in a fresco."

Seeing how well his apprentice followed him, Ghirlandaio took from his desk two more of his drawings, an almost life-size study of the head of a smooth-cheeked, full-faced, wide-eyed and thoughtful man under thirty, with robust modelling, the drawing of the hair finely decorative; the second, the baptism of a man within the choir of a Roman basilica, done with a beauty of composition.

"Magnificent!" breathed Michelangelo, reaching for the sheets. "You've learned everything that Masaccio has to teach."

The blood drained from Ghirlandaio's dark face; had he been insulted, judged a copier? But the boy's voice was full of pride. Ghirlandaio was amused: the rawest apprentice was complimenting the master. He took the drawings from him.

"Sketches are nothing, only the finished fresco counts. I shall destroy these."

They heard the voices of Cieco and Baldinelli outside the studio. Ghirlandaio got up from the desk, Michelangelo picked up his paper and new pen, quickly reassembled the bundle of the Slaughter of the Innocents, had it tied and back in its corner by the time the boys came into the room.

Locked in the big drawer of his desk, Ghirlandaio kept a folio from which he studied and sketched while he was conceiving a new panel. Granacci told Michelangelo that it had taken Ghirlandaio years to assemble these drawings of men he considered masters: Taddeo Gaddi, Lorenzo Monaco, Fra Angelico, Paolo Uccello, Pollaiuolo, Fra Lippi and many others. Michelangelo had spent enthralled hours gazing at their altars and frescoes with which the city was lavishly endowed, but he had never seen any of the working studies.

"Certainly not," replied Ghirlandaio brusquely when Michelangelo asked him if he might see the portfolio.

"But why not?" cried Michelangelo desperately. Here was a golden opportunity to study the thinking and techniques of Florence's finest draughtsmen.

"Every artist assembles his own portfolio," said Ghirlandaio, "according to his own tastes and judgment. I have made my collection over a period of twenty-five years. You build your own."

A few days later Ghirlandaio was studying a sketch by Benozzo Gozzoli of a nude youth with a spear, when a committee of three men called for him to accompany them to a neighbouring town. He failed to put the drawing back into the locked drawer.

Waiting until the others had left for dinner, Michelangelo went to the desk, took up the Benozzo Gozzoli sketch. After a dozen attempts he made what he considered a faithful copy; and an errant idea popped into his mind. Could he fool Ghirlandaio with it? The sketch was thirty years old, the paper soiled and yellowing with age. He took some scraps into the back yard, ran his finger over the earth, experimented with rubbing the dirt along the grain of the paper. After a while he brought his copy out to the yard, and slowly began discolouring his own sheet.

Old drawing paper had a smoky quality around the edges. He returned to the studio where a fire burned in the hearth, held his discoloured scraps over the smoke for testing, and after a moment his copy of the youth. Then he put the imitation on Ghirlandaio's desk and secreted the original.

During the weeks he watched Ghirlandaio's every move; whenever the teacher failed to return a sketch to the portfolio, a Castagno, Signorelli or Verrocchio, the boy remained behind to make a reproduction. If it was late afternoon he would take the sheet home and, when the rest of the family was asleep, make a fire in the downstairs hearth and stain the paper the proper colour. At the end of a month he had assembled a portfolio of a dozen fine sketches. At this rate his folio of master sketches would become as thick as Ghirlandaio's.

Chirlandaio still came in early from dinner occasionally to give his apprentice an hour of instruction in the use of black chalk; how to work in silver point, and then to intensify the effect with white chalk. Michelangelo asked if they might sometimes draw from nude models.

"Why should you want to learn to draw the nude when we must always paint it under drapes?" demanded Ghirlandaio. "There aren't enough nudes in the Bible to make it profitable."

"There are the saints," replied the boy; "they have to be nude, nearly, when they are being shot with arrows or burned on a grill."

"True, but who wants anatomy in saints? It gets in the way of spirit."

"Couldn't it help portray character?"

"No. All of character that's necessary to show can be done through the face . . . and perhaps the hands. No one has worked in nudes since the pagan Greeks. We have to paint for Christians. Besides, our bodies are ugly, misproportioned, full of boils, fever and excrement. A garden of palms and cypresses, oranges in bloom, an architectural design of a straight stone wall with steps running down to the

sea . . . that is beauty. And non-controversial. Painting
should be charming, refreshing, lovely. Who can say that
the human body is any of these things? I like to draw
figures walking delicately under their gowns . . ."

". . . and I would like to draw them the way God made
Adam."

7

With June the summer heat clamped down on Florence. The
boy packed away his *calzoni,* long hose, and stuck his bare
feet into sandals. He wore a light cotton shirt. The back
doors of the studio were thrown open and the tables moved
into the yard under the green-leafed trees.

For the festival of San Giovanni the *bottega* was locked
tight. Michelangelo rose early, and with his brothers walked
down to the Arno, the river which flowed through the city,
to swim and play in the mud-brown waters before he met his
fellow apprentices at the rear of the Duomo.

The piazza was covered by a broad blue awning sown
with golden lilies to represent heaven. Each Guild had built
its own cloud, high up in which sat its patron saint on a
wooden frame thickly covered by wool, surrounded by lights
and cherubs and sprinkled with tinsel stars. On lower iron
branches were children dressed as angels, strapped on by
waistbands.

At the head of the procession came the cross of Santa
Maria del Fiore, and behind it singing companies of wool
shearers, shoemakers, bands of boys dressed in white, then
giants on stilts six cubits high, hooded with fantastic masks,
then twenty-two Towers mounted on carts and carrying
actors who gave tableaux out of Scripture: the Tower of
St. Michael depicting the Battle of the Angels showed
Lucifer being cast out of heaven; the Tower of Adam presented God Creating Adam and Eve, with the serpent making
its entrance; the Tower of Moses acted out the Delivery of
the Law.

To Michelangelo the tableaux seemed endless. He had
never liked biblical plays and wanted to leave. Granacci,
enchanted with the painted scenery, insisted on staying to the
very end. Just as high mass was beginning in the Duomo a
Bolognese was caught stealing purses and gold belt buckles
from the worshippers jammed before the pulpit. The crowd

in the church and piazza turned into an angry mob shouting, "Hang him! Hang him!" carrying the apprentices
along with them to the quarters of the captain of the guard,
where the thief was promptly hanged from a window.

Later that day a tremendous wind and hailstorm struck the
city, destroying the colourful tents, turning the racecourse
for the *palio* into a marsh. Bugiardini, Cieco, Michelangelo
huddled inside the Baptistery doors.

"This storm came because that wretched Bolognese stole
in the Duomo on a holy day," cried Cieco.

"No, no, it's the other way round," protested Bugiardini.
"God sent the storm as punishment for our hanging a man
on a religious holiday."

They turned to Michelangelo, who was studying the pure
gold sculptures of Ghiberti's second set of doors, their ten
glorious panels populated layer upon layer by all the peoples,
animals, cities, mountains, palaces of the Old Testament.

"What do I think?" Michelangelo said. "I think these
doors are the gates of paradise."

At Ghirlandaio's the Birth of St. John was ready to be
transferred to the wall of Santa Maria Novella. Early as he
arrived at the studio, Michelangelo found himself to be the
last. His eyes opened wide at the excitement, with everyone
bustling about, collecting cartoons, bundles of sketches,
brushes, pots and bottles of colour, buckets, sacks of sand
and line, pointing sticks. The materials were loaded on a
small cart behind an even smaller donkey, and off went the
entire studio with Ghirlandaio at its head like a commanding
general and Michelangelo, as the newest apprentice, driving
the cart through the Via del Sole to the Sign of the Sun,
which meant they were entering the Santa Maria Novella
parish. He guided the donkey to the right and found himself in the Piazza Santa Maria Novella, one of the oldest and
most beautiful in the city.

He pulled the donkey up short: in front of him loomed
the church, which had stood uncompleted in its rustic brick
from 1348 until Giovanni Rucellai, whom Michelangelo
counted as an uncle, had had the good judgment to choose
Leon Battista Alberti to design this façade of magnificent
black and white marble. Michelangelo felt a quickening at
the thought of the Rucellai family, the more so because he
was not permitted to mention the name in the Buonarroti
house. Though he had never been inside their palace on the

Via della Vigna Nuova, when passing by he always slowed his pace a little to see into the spacious gardens with their antique Greek and Roman sculptures, and to study the architecture of Alberti, who had designed the stately building.

Gangling Tedesco was the unloading foreman, gustily bossing the thirteen-year-olds in his moment of command. Michelangelo entered the bronze doors, a roll of sketches in his arms, and stood breathing the cool incense-heavy air. The church stretched before him in the form of an Egyptian cross over three hundred feet long, its three pointed ogive arches and rows of majestic pillars gradually decreasing in distance from each other as they approached the main altar behind which the Ghirlandaio studio had been working for three years. Its lateral walls were covered with bright murals; immediately over Michelangelo's head stood Giotto's wooden crucifix.

He walked slowly up the main aisle, savouring every step, for it was like a journey through Italian art: Giotto, painter, sculptor, architect, who legend said had been discovered by Cimabue as a shepherd boy drawing on a rock, and brought into his studio to become the liberator of painting from its dark Byzantine lifelessness. Giotto was followed by ninety years of imitators until—and here on the left of the church Michelangelo saw the living, glowing evidence of his Trinity —Masaccio, arising from God alone knew where, began to paint and Florentine art was reborn.

Across the nave to the left he saw a Brunelleschi crucifix; the Strozzi family chapel with frescoes and sculptures by the Orcagna brothers; the front of the major altar with its Ghiberti bronzes; and then, as the epitome of all this magnificence, the Rucellai chapel, built by his own mother's family in the middle of the thirteenth century when they had come into their fortune through a member of the family who had discovered in the Orient how to produce a beautiful red dye.

Michelangelo had never been able to get himself to mount the few stairs leading to the Rucellai chapel, even though it contained the supreme art treasures of Santa Maria Novella. A grudging family loyalty had kept him out. Now that he had made his break from the family and was going to work here in Santa Maria Novella, had he not earned the right to enter? Enter without feeling an intruder on that side of the family which after his mother's death had cut all communication, caring nothing of what happened to the five sons of

37

Francesca Rucellai del Sera, daughter of Maria Bonda Rucellai?

He put down the package he was carrying and walked up the stairs, slowly. Once inside the chapel with its Cimabue Madonna and marble Virgin and Child by Nino Pisano, he fell to his knees; for this was the very chapel where his mother's mother had worshipped all through her youth, and where his mother had worshipped on those feast days of family reunion.

Tears burned, then overflooded his eyes. He had been taught prayers but he had only mouthed the words. Now they sprang to his lips unbidden. Was he praying to the beautiful Madonnas or to his mother? Was there truly a difference? Had she not been very like the Madonnas above him? Whatever vague memories he had of her melted into those of the Lady.

He rose, walked to the Pisano Virgin and ran his long bony fingers sentiently over the marble drapery. Then he turned and left the chapel. For a moment he stood on top of the stairs thinking of the contrast between his two families. The Rucellai had built this chapel around 1265, at the same time that the Buonarroti had come into their wealth. The Rucellai had recognized the finest practitioners, almost the creators of their arts: Cimabue in painting, somewhere around the close of the thirteenth century, and Nino Pisano in 1365. Even now, in 1488, they were in friendly competition with the Medici for the marble sculptures being dug up in Greece, Sicily and Rome.

The Buonarroti had never commissioned a chapel. Every family of similar wealth had done so. Why not they?

Behind the choir he could see his comrades loading supplies up on the scaffolding.

Was it enough to say that it had happened because the Buonarroti were not and never had been religious? Lodovico's conversation was interlarded with religious expressions, but Monna Alessandra had said of her son:

"Lodovico approves all the Church's laws even when he doesn't obey them."

The Buonarroti had always been hard men with a florin, sharing the native shrewdness about money and the fierce concentration in guarding it. Had the willingness to invest solely in houses and land, the only true source of wealth to a Tuscan, kept the Buonarroti from ever wasting a scudo on art? Michelangelo could not remember having seen a paint-

38

ing or sculpture of the simplest nature in a Buonarroti house. This took considerable doing for a family of wealth living for three hundred years in the most creative city in the world, where even homes of modest means had religious works that had come down through the generations.

He turned back for a last look at the frescoed walls of the Rucellai chapel, realizing with a sinking heart that the Buonarroti were not only stingy, they were enemies of art because they despised the men who created it.

A shout from Bugiardini on the scaffolding called him. He found the entire studio moving in harmony. Bugiardini had put a heavy coat of intonaco on the panel the day before, hatching a rough surface on which he was now plastering the precise area to be painted that day. With Cieco, Baldinelli and Tedesco he took up the cartoon, which they held over the wet panel. Ghirlandaio pounced the lines of the figures on to the fresh intonaco with a pointed ivory stick, then gave the signal for it to be taken away. The young apprentices scrambled down the scaffolding, but Michelangelo remained to watch Ghirlandaio mix his mineral earth colours in little jars of water, squeeze his brush between his fingers and commence his painting.

He had to work surely and swiftly, for his task had to be completed before the plaster dried that night. If he delayed, the unpainted plaster formed a crust from the air currents blowing through the church, and these portions would stain and grow mouldy. If he had failed to gauge accurately how much he could do that day, the remaining dry plaster would have to be cut away the following morning, leaving a discernible seam. Retouching was forbidden; colours added later needed to contain size, which would discolour the fresco, turn it black.

Michelangelo stood on the scaffolding with a bucket of water, sprinkling the area just ahead of Ghirlandaio's flying brush to keep it moist. He understood for the first time the truth of the saying that no coward ever attempted fresco. He watched Ghirlandaio moving boldly forward, painting the girl with the basket of ripe fruits on her head, the billowing gown then in fashion which made the Florentine girls look like carrying matrons. Next to him stood Mainardi, painting the two older, sedate aunts of the Tornabuoni family, come to visit Elisabeth.

Benedetto was highest on the scaffold, painting the elaborate cross-beamed ceiling. Granacci had been assigned the serving girl in the centre of the background, bringing in a tray to Elisabeth. David was working on Elisabeth reclining against the richly carved wooden bedboard. Bugiardini, who had been allotted the window and door frames, summoned Michelangelo to his side, flicking his fingers for him to sprinkle some water, then stepped back in admiration from the tiny window he had just painted above Elisabeth's head.

"Have you ever seen a more beautiful window?" he demanded.

"Brilliant, Bugiardini," replied Michelangelo. "Particularly the open space that we see through"

Bugiardini studied his work, puzzled but proud.

"You like that part too? Funny, I haven't painted it yet."

The climax of the panel was reached when Ghirlandaio, with Mainardi assisting, painted the exquisite young Giovanna Tornabuoni, elaborately robed with the richest of Florentine silks and jewels, gazing straight out at Ghirlandaio, not in the least interested in either Elisabeth, sitting up in her high-backed bed, or John, suckling at the breast of another Tornabuoni beauty sitting on the bed-bench.

The panel took five days of concentrated work. Michelangelo alone was not permitted to apply paint. He was torn: part of him felt that though he had been in the studio for only three months he was as qualified to work the wall as the other thirteen-year-olds. At the same time an inner voice kept telling him that all of this feverish activity had nothing to do with him. Even when he felt most unhappy about being excluded, he wanted to run out of the choir and the studio to a world of his own.

Towards the end of the week the plaster began to dry. The burnt lime recovered its carbonic acid from the air, fixing the colours. Michelangelo saw that his belief that the pigments sank into the wet plaster was a mistake; they remained on the surface, covered by a crystalline coating of carbonate of lime which fitted them the way the skin of a young athlete contains his flesh and blood. The entire panel now had a metallic lustre which would protect the colours from heat, cold and moisture. But the amazing fact was that each day's segment was drying slowly to the very colours Ghirlandaio had created in his studio.

And yet, when he went alone to Santa Maria Novella the following Sunday during mass, weaving his way through the worshipping Florentines in their short velvet *farsetti*, doublets, voluminous cloaks of camlet trimmed in miniver, and

high-crowned hats, he felt let down: so much of the freshness and vigour had leaked out from the drawings. The
eight women were still lives in mosaic, as if made of hard
bits of coloured stone. And certainly it was not the birth of
John to the modest family of Elisabeth and Zacharias; it
was a social gathering in the home of a merchant prince of
Italy, utterly devoid of religious spirit or content.

Standing before the brilliant panel, the boy realized that
Ghirlandaio loved Florence. The city was his religion. He
was spending his life painting its people, its palaces, its
exquisitely decorated rooms, its architecture and streets
thronging with life, its religious and political pageants. And
what an eye he had! Nothing escaped him. Since no one
would commission him to paint Florence he had made
Florence Jerusalem; the desert of Palestine was Tuscany, and
all the biblical people modern Florentines. Because Florence
was more pagan than Christian, everyone was pleased with
Ghirlandaio's sophisticated portraits.

Michelangelo walked out of the church feeling depressed.
The forms were superb; but where was the substance? His
eyes hazed over as he tried to formulate words to shape the
thoughts pushing against each other inside his head.

He too wanted to learn how to set down accurately what
he saw. But what he felt about what he saw would always be
more important.

8

He drifted over to the Duomo, where young men gathered
on the cool marble steps to make laughter and view the
passing pageant. Every day in Florence was a fair; on
Sundays this richest city in Italy, which had supplanted
Venice in its trade with the Orient, was out to prove that its
thirty-three banking palaces were providing wealth for all.
The Florentine girls were blonde, slender, they carried their
heads high, wore colourful coverings on their hair and long-
sleeved gowns, high-necked, with overlapping skirts pleated
and full, their breasts outlined in filmier fabric and colour.
The older men were in sombre cloaks, but the young men of
the prominent families created the great splash between the
Duomo steps and the Baptistery by wearing their *calzoni*
with each leg dyed differently and patterned according to the

family blazon. Their suite of attendants followed in identical dress.

Jacopo was sitting on top of an old Roman sarcophagus, one of several that stood against the jagged tan brick face of the cathedral. From here he kept up a running comment about the passing girls while his scandalous eyes sought out the ones to whom he awarded his highest accolade:

" Ah, how mattressable."

Michelangelo went to Jacopo's side, ran his hand caressingly over the sarcophagus, his fingers tracing out in its low relief the funeral procession of fighting men and horses.

" Feel how these marble figures are still alive and breathing!"

His voice carried such exaltation that his friends turned to stare at him. Now his secret had burst into the open of the Florentine dusk, with the sinking sun setting the domes of the Baptistery and cathedral on fire. His hunger had got the better of him.

"God was the first sculptor ; He made the first figure: man. And when He wanted to give His laws, what material did He use? Stone. The Ten Commandments engraved on a stone tablet for Moses. What were the first tools that men carved for themselves? Stone. Look at all us painters lolling on the Duomo steps. How many sculptors are there?"

His fellow apprentices were stunned by the outburst. Even Jacopo stopped searching for girls. They had never heard him speak with such urgency, his eyes glowing like amber coals in the fading light. He told them why he thought there were no more sculptors: the strength expended in carving with hammer and chisel exhausted mind and body alike, in contrast to the brushes, pens and charcoal which the painter used so lightly.

Jacopo hooted. Granacci answered his young friend.

" If extreme fatigue is the criterion of art, then the quarryman taking the marble out of the mountain with his wedges and heavy levers has to be considered nobler than the sculptor, the blacksmith greater than the goldsmith and the mason more important than the architect."

Michelangelo flushed. He had made a bad start. He studied the grinning faces of Jacopo, Tedesco and the two thirteen-year-olds.

" But you have to agree that the work of art becomes noble in the degree to which it represents the truth? Then sculpture will come closer to true form, for when you work the marble the figure emerges on all four sides. . . ."

His words, usually so spare, spilled over each other: the painter laid his paint on a flat surface and by use of perspective tried to persuade people that they were seeing the whole of a scene. But just try to walk around a person in a painting, or around a tree! It was an illusion, a magician's trick. Now the sculptor, ah! he carved the full reality. That was why sculpture bore the same relationship to painting that truth did to falsehood. And if a painter blundered, what did he do? He patched and repaired and covered over with another layer of paint. The sculptor on the contrary had to see within the marble the form that it held. He could not glue back broken parts. That was why there were no more sculptors to-day, because it took a thousand times more accuracy of judgment and vision.

He stopped abruptly, breathing hard.

Jacopo jumped down from his perch on the lid of the sarcophagus, extended his two arms to indicate that he had taken over. He was bright; he liked painting and understood it even though he was too lazy to work at it.

"Sculpture is a bore. What can they make? A man, a woman, a lion, a horse. Then all over again. Monotonous. But the painter can portray the whole universe: the sky, the sun, the moon and the stars, clouds and rain, mountains, trees, rivers, seas. The sculptors have all perished of boredom."

Sebastiano Mainardi joined the group and stood listening. He had taken his wife for her weekly walk, then returned to the Duomo steps and the company of his young men friends which, like all Florentines, he enjoyed more than that of women. There were spots of colour on his usually pale cheeks.

"That's true! The sculptor needs only a strong arm and an empty mind. Yes, empty; after a sculptor draws his simple design, what goes on inside his head during the hundreds of hours that he has to pound these chisels and points with a hammer? Nothing! But the painter has to think of a thousand things every moment, to relate all the integral parts of a painting. Creating the illusion of a third dimension is craftsmanship. That's why a painter's life is exciting, and a sculptor's dull."

Tears of frustration welled in Michelangelo's eyes. He

43

cursed himself for his inability to carve out in words the stone forms that he felt in his innards.

"Painting is perishable: a fire in the chapel, too much cold, and the paint begins to fade, crack. But stone is eternal! Nothing can destroy it. When the Florentines tore down the colosseum, what did they do with the blocks? Built them into new walls. And think of the Greek sculpture that is being dug up, two, three thousand years old. Show me a painting that's two thousand years old. Look at this Roman marble sarcophagus; as clear and strong as the day it was carved . . ."

"And as cold!" cried Tedesco.

Mainardi raised his arm for attention.

"Michelangelo," he began gently, "has it ever occurred to you that the reason there are no sculptors left is because of the cost of material? A sculptor needs a rich man or organization to give him a supply of marble and bronze. The Wool Guild of Florence financed Ghiberti for forty years to make the doors of the Baptistery. Cosimo de' Medici supplied Donatello with the resources he needed. Who would provide you with the stone, who would support you while you practised on it? Paint is cheap, commissions are abundant; that's why we take on apprentices. And as for the danger of working in sculpture and making the fatal mistake, what about the painter working in fresco? If the sculptor must see the form inherent in the stone, must not the painter foresee the final result of his colour in the fresh wet plaster and know precisely how it will turn out when dry?"

Michelangelo numbly had to agree that this was true.

"Besides," continued Mainardi, "everything that can ever be accomplished in sculpture has already been created by the Pisanos, by Ghiberti, Orcagna, Donatello. Take Desiderio da Settignano or Mino da Fiesole; they made pretty, charming copies of Donatello. And Bertoldo, who helped Donatello cast his figures, and was there to learn the secrets that Donatello learned from Ghiberti: what has Bertoldo created except a few miniatures reduced from Donatello's great concepts? And now he's sick and dying, his work done. No, the sculptor can do little more than copy, since the range of sculpture is so narrow."

Michelangelo turned away. If only he knew more! Then he could convince them of the magnificence of fashioning figures in space.

44

Granacci touched the boy's shoulder comfortingly.

"Have you forgotten, Michelagnolo, what Praxiteles said?
'Painting and sculpture have the same parents; they are
sister arts.'"

But Michelangelo refused to compromise. Without another
word he walked down the cool marble steps, away from the
Duomo, over the cobbled streets to home.

9

The night was sleepless. He rolled and tossed. The room
was hot, for Lodovico said that air coming in a window was
as bad as a crossbow shot. Buonarroto, who shared the bed,
was placid in sleep as in all other things. Though two years
younger than Michelangelo, he was the manager of the five
boys.

In the bed closer to the door, with the curtains drawn
around it, slept the good and evil of the Buonarroti pro-
geny: Lionardo, a year and a half older than Michelangelo,
who spent his days yearning to be a saint; and Giovansimone, four years younger, lazy, rude to his parents, who
had once set fire to Lucrezia's kitchen because she had disciplined him. Sigismondo, the youngest, still slept in a
trundle at the foot of Michelangelo's bed. Michelangelo
suspected that the boy would never be anything but a simpleton, since he lacked all capacity to learn.

Quietly he sprang out of bed, slipped into his *brache* loincloth, short drawers, shirt and sandals, and left the house.
He walked down the Via dell'Anguillara, the streets freshly
washed and the stoops scrubbed, to Piazza Santa Croce,
where the Franciscan church stood rough and dark in its
unfinished brick. As he passed the open-sided gallery his eye
sought the outline of the Nino Pisano sarcophagus, held up
by its four carved allegorical figures. He turned left on the
Via del Fosso, built at the second limit of the city walls,
passed the prison, then the house belonging to the nephew
of St. Catherine of Siena, and at the end of the street, at the
corner of the Swallows, the city's famous chemist shop.
From here he turned into Via Pietrapiana, Street of the
Flat Stones, which led through Piazza Sant'Ambrogio, in the
church of which were buried the sculptors Verrocchio and
Mino da Fiesole.

45

From the piazza he followed the Borgo la Croce until it led to a country road called Via Pontassieve, at the end of which he came to the Affrico River, an affluent of the Arno, its green banks covered with trees and luxuriant vegetation. After crossing the Via Piagentina he reached Varlungo, a little cluster of houses at what had been a Roman ford, then turned once again to the left and made his way up the slope towards Settignano.

He had been walking for an hour. Dawn flashed hot and bright. He paused on the hillside to watch the mammal hills of Tuscany emerge from their dark sleep. He cared little about the beauties of nature that so moved painters: the red poppies in the growing green wheat, the stands of almost black cypresses.

No, he loved the valley of the Arno because it was a sculptured landscape. God was a supreme carver: the lyrical hills, each range composed by a draughtsman's hand, complementing the succeeding ranges as they rolled back, with nothing the eye could see that was carelessly conceived. In the clarity of its air distant peaks, rolling ridges, villas, trees though miles away, stood out to be touched, their form tactile. Here nature's perspective worked in reverse: the more distant the object, the nearer at hand it seemed.

The Tuscan was a natural sculptor. When he took over the landscape he built his stone terraces, planted his vineyards and olive orchards in harmony with the hills. No two haycocks were shaped the same; each family inherited a sculptural form: circular, oblong, umbrella, tent, which stood as a sign for the farm.

He climbed the cart road into the hills, closed in by the walls that are the buttress of the Tuscan's life, giving him privacy and security and at the same time sustaining his land and his sovereignty; standing as much as thirteen feet high to hold the descending slopes, and built to last a hundred generations. Stone was the dominant factor: with it he built his farms and villas, enclosed his fields, terraced his slopes to retain his soil. Nature had been bountiful with stone; every hill was an undeveloped quarry. If the Tuscan scratched deep with his fingernail he struck building materials sufficient for a city. And when he built of dry rock, his walls stood as though masoned.

" The skill with which men handle stone tells how civilized they are."

He left the road where it turned off for the quarry at

Maiano. For four years after his mother died he had been left to roam this countryside, though it was the proper age for him to be in school. There was no master at Settignano, and his father had been too withdrawn to care. Now he climbed through land of which he knew every jutting boulder and tree and furrow.

His upward push brought him to the settlement of Settignano, a dozen houses collected around a grey stone church. This was the heart of the stonemason country, having bred the greatest *scalpellini* in the world, the generations that had built Florence. It was only two miles from the city, on the first rise above the valley floor, and an easy haul to town.

It was said of Settignano that its surrounding hills had a stone heart and velvet breasts.

As he walked through the tiny settlement towards the Buonarroti home he passed a dozen stoneyards scattered among the *poderi* or farms. Shortly, he came to the big yards that had produced Desiderio da Settignano. Death had caused him to drop his hammer and chisel at the age of thirty-six, but even by that time he was famous. Michelangelo knew well his marble tombs in Santa Croce and Santa Maria Novella, with their exquisite angels, and the Virgin carved so tenderly that she appeared asleep rather than dead. Desiderio had taken in Mino da Fiesole, who was just a young hewer of stones, and taught him the art of carving marble. Mino had wandered off to Rome in grief over the loss of his master.

Now there was no sculptor left in Florence. Ghiberti, who had trained Donatello and the Pollaiuolo brothers, had died some thirty-three years before. Donatello, who had died twenty-two years ago, had operated a studio for half a century, but of his followers Antonio Rossellino had been dead nine years, Luca della Robbia six, Verrocchio had just died. The Pollaiuolo brothers had moved to Rome four years ago, and Bertoldo, Donatello's favourite and heir to his vast knowledge and workshop, was fatally ill. Andrea and Giovanni della Robbia, trained by Luca, had abandoned stone sculpture for enamelled terracotta reliefs.

Yes, sculpture was dead. Unlike his father who wished he had been born a hundred years before, Michelangelo asked only that he could have been born forty years ago so that he could have been trained under Ghiberti; or thirty years, so he could have been apprenticed to Donatello; or even twenty or ten or five years sooner, so that he could have been taught

47

to work the marble by the Pollaiuolo brothers, by Verrocchio or Luca della Robbia.

He had been born too late, into a country where for two hundred and fifty years, since Nicola Pisono had unearthed some Greek and Roman marbles and begun carving, there had been created in Florence and the valley of the Arno the greatest wealth of sculpture since Phidias completed his work on the Greek Parthenon. A mysterious plague which affected Tuscan sculptors had wiped out the very last of them; the species, after having flourished so gloriously, was now extinct.

Sick at heart, he moved on.

10

Down the winding road a few hundred yards was the Buonarroti villa in the midst of a five-acre farm, leased to strangers on a long-term agreement. He had not been here for months. As always he was surprised by the beauty and spaciousness of the house, hewn two hundred years before of the best Maiano *pietra serena,* graceful in its austere lines, and with broad porches overlooking the valley, the river gleaming below like a silversmith's decoration.

He could remember his mother moving in the rooms, weaving on the broad downstairs porch, kissing him good night in his big corner room overlooking the Buonarroti fields, the creek at the bottom, and the Topolino family of stonemasons on the opposite ridge.

He crossed the back yard and the bone-textured stone walk past the stone cistern with its intricate hatching and crosshatching from which he had taken his first drawing lesson. He then scampered down the hill between the wheat on one side and the ripening grapes on the other, to the deep creek at the bottom, shaded by lush foliage. He slipped out of his shirt, short drawers and sandals and rolled over and over in the cool water, enjoying its wetness on his anxious tired body. Then he crouched in the hot sun for a few moments to dry, put on his clothes and climbed refreshed to the opposite ridge.

He paused when he came in sight of the yard. This was the picture he loved, one which meant home and security for him: the father working with tempered iron chisels to round a fluted column, the youngest son bevelling a set of steps,

one of the older two carving a delicate window frame, the
other graining a door panel, the grandfather polishing a
column on a pumice wheelstone with thin river sand. Behind
them were three arches, and under them scurrying chickens,
ducks, pigs.

In the boy's mind there was no difference between a
scalpellino and a *scultore*, a stonecutter and a sculptor, for
the *scalpellini* were fine craftsmen, bringing out the colour
and grain of the *pietra serena*. There might be a difference in
the degree of artistry, but not in kind: every stone of the
Pazzi, Pitti and Medici palaces was cut, bevelled, given a
textured surface as if it were a piece of sculpture: which to
the Settignano *scalpellini* it was. Lesser craftsmen were
confined to making routine blocks for smaller houses and
paving stones for the streets. Yet so proud were all Florentines of their simplest paving blocks that the whole town
bragged of the wretch who, being jostled in the cart that was
taking him to the Palazzo della Signoria for hanging, cried
out in protest:

" What idiots were these, who cut such clumsy blocks?"
The father heard Michelangelo's footsteps.
" *Buon dì*, Michelangelo."
" *Buon dì*, Topolino."
" *Come va?*"
" *Non c'è male. E te?*"
" *Non c'è male*. The honourable Lodovico?"
" He goes well."
Topolino did not really care how things went with Lodo-
vico: he had forbidden Michelangelo to come here. No one
got up, for the stonemason rarely breaks his rhythm; the two
older boys and the one exactly Michelangelo's age called out
with welcoming warmth.

" *Ben venuto*, Michelangelo. Welcome."
" *Salve*, Bruno. *Salve*, Gilberto. *Salve*, Enrico."
The *scalpellino's* words are few and simple, matching in
length the single blow of the hammer. When he chips at the
stone he does not speak at all: one, two, three, four, five,
six, seven: no word from the lips, only the rhythm of the
shoulder and the moving hand with the chisel. Then he
speaks, in the period of pause: one, two, three, four. The
sentence must fit the. rest count of four or it remains unsaid
or incomplete. If the thought must be involved it will be
spaced between several work counts of seven, filling two or
three counts of four. But the *scalpellino* has learned to con-

fine his thinking to what can be expressed in the single four-count pause.

There was no schooling for the stoneman. Topolino figured his contracts on his fingers. The sons were given a hammer and chisel at six, as Michelangelo had been, and by ten they were working full time on the stone. There was no marriage outside the stone ring. Agreements with builders and architects were handed down from generation to generation, as were the quarrying jobs at Maiano, where no outsider could find work. Between the arches hung an oblong piece of *pietra serena* with examples of the classic treatments of the stone: herringbone, *subbia* punch-hole, rustic, crosshatch, linear, bevel, centred right angle, receding step: the first alphabet Michelangelo had been given, and still the one he used more comfortably than the lettered alphabet with which he had been taught to read the Bible and Dante.

Topolino spoke. "You're apprenticed to Ghirlandaio?"

"Yes."

"You do not like it?"

"Not greatly."

"*Peccato.*"

"Who does somebody else's trade makes soup in a basket," said the old grandfather.

"Why do you stay?" It was the middle brother asking.

"Where else is there to go?"

"We could use a cutter." This was from Bruno.

Michelangelo looked from the oldest son to the father.

"*Davvero?*"

"*Davvero.* It is true."

"You will take me as apprentice?"

"With stone you're no apprentice. You earn a share."

His heart leaped. Everyone chipped in silence while Michelangelo stood above the father who had just offered him a portion of the food that went into the family belly.

"My father . . ."

"*Ecco!*"

"Can I cut?"

The grandfather, turning his wheel, replied: "'Every little bit helps,' said the father who peed into the Arno because his son's boat was beached at Pisa."

Michelangelo sat before a roughed-out column, a hammer in one hand, a chisel in the other. He liked the heft of them. Stone was concrete, not abstract. One could not argue it from every point of the compass, like love or theology. No theorist had ever separated stone from its quarry bed.

He had a natural skill, unrusted after the months of being away. Under his blows the *pietra serena* cut like cake. There was a natural rhythm between the inward and outward movement of his breath and the up-and-down movement of his hammer arm as he slid the chisel across a cutting groove. The tactile contact with the stone made him feel that the world was right again, and the impact of the blows sent waves of strength up his skinny arms to his shoulders, torso, down through his diaphragm and legs into his feet.

The *pietra serena* they were working was warm, an alive blue-grey, a reflector of changing lights, refreshing to look at. The stone had durability, yet it was manageable, resilient, as joyous in character as in colour, bringing an Italian blue-sky serenity to all who worked it.

The Topolinos had taught him to work the stone with friendliness, to seek its natural forms, its mountains and valleys, even though it might seem solid; never to grow angry or unsympathetic towards the material.

"Stone works with you. It reveals itself. But you must strike it right. Stone does not resent the chisel. It is not being violated. Its nature is to change. Each stone has its own character. It must be understood. Handle it carefully, or it will shatter. Never let stone destroy itself.

"Stone gives itself to skill and to love."

His first lesson had been that the power and the durability lay in the stone, not in the arms or tools. The stone was master; not the mason. If ever a mason came to think he was master, the stone would oppose and thwart him. And if a mason beat his stone as an ignorant *contadino* might beat his beasts, the rich warm glowing breathing material became dull, colourless, ugly; died under his hand. To kicks and curses, to hurry and dislike, it closed a hard stone veil around its soft inner nature. It could be smashed by violence but never forced to fulfil. To sympathy, it yielded: grew even more luminous and sparkling, achieved fluid forms and symmetry.

From the beginning he had been taught that stone had a mystic: it had to be covered at night because it would crack if the full moon got on it. Each block had areas inside where it was hollow and bent. In order for it to remain docile it had to be kept warm in sacks, and the sacks kept

51

damp. Heat gave the stone the same undulations it had in its original mountain home. Ice was its enemy.

"Stone will speak to you. Listen as you strike with the side of your hammer."

Stone was called after the most precious of foods: *carne*, meat.

The *scalpellini* respected this stone. To them it was the most enduring material in the world: it had not only built their homes, farms, churches, town, but for a thousand years had given them a trade, a skill, a pride of workmanship, a living. Stone was not king but god. They worshipped it as did their pagan Etruscan ancestors. They handled it with reverence.

Michelangelo knew them as men of pride: to care for their cattle, pigs, vines, olives, wheat, this was ordinary work; they did it well in order to eat well. But working the stone, ah! that was where a man lived. Had not the Settignanese quarried, shaped and built the most enchanting city in all Europe: Florence? Jewel of the stonecarver's art, its beauty created not by the architect and sculptor alone but by the *scalpellino* without whom there would have been no infinite variety of shape and decoration.

Monna Margherita, a formless woman who worked the animals and fields as well as the stove and tub, had come out of the house and stood under the arch, listening. She was the one about whom Lodovico had said bitterly, when Michelangelo wished to work with his hands:

"A child sent out to nurse will take on the condition of the woman who feeds him."

She had suckled him with her own son for two years, and the day her breast ran dry she put both boys on wine. Water was for bathing before mass. Michelangelo felt for Monna Margherita much as he did for Monna Alessandra, his grandmother: affection and security.

He kissed her on both cheeks.

"*Buon giorno, figlio mio.*"

"*Buon giorno, madre mia.*"

"*Pazienza,*" she counselled. "Ghirlandaio is a good master. Who has an art, has always a part."

The father had risen.

"I must choose at Cave Maiano. Will you help load?"

"Willingly. *A rivederci*, nonno. *A riverderci*, Bruno. *Addio*, Gilberto. *Addio*, Enrico."

"*Addio*, Michelangelo."

They rode side by side on the high seat behind the two beautiful-faced white oxen. In the fields the olive pickers were mounted on ladders made of slender tree stalks, notched to take the light crossbar branches. Baskets were tied around their waists with rope, flat against the stomach and crotch. They held the branches with their left hand, stripping down the little black olives with a milking movement of the right. Pickers are talkers; two to a tree, they speak their phrases to each other through the branches, for to the *contadino* not to talk is to be dead a little. Topolino said under his breath:

" Daws love another's prattle."

The road, winding along the contour of the range, dipped into a valley and then slowly climbed Mount Ceceri to the quarry. As they rounded the bend of Maiano, Michelangelo saw the gorge in the mountain with its alternating blue and grey *serena* and iron-stained streaks. The *pietra serena* had been buried in horizontal layers. From this quarry Brunelleschi had chosen the stones for his exquisite churches of San Lorenzo and Santo Spirito. High on the cliff several men were outlining a block to be quarried with a *scribbus,* a point driven against the grain to loosen the hold from the main mass. He could see the point marks in successive layers through the stone formation, layers of stone peeled off as though stripped from a pile of parchment sheets.

The level work area where the strata fell after they were loosed was shimmering with heat and dust from the cutting, splitting, shaping: by men wet with perspiration, small, lean, sinewy men who worked the rock from dawn to dark without fatigue and who could cut as straight a line with hammer and chisel as a draughtsman with pen and ruler: as concentrated in their hardness and durability as the rock itself. He had known these men since he was six and began riding behind the white oxen with Topolino. They greeted him, asked how things went: a primordial people, spending their lives with the simplest and most rudimentary force on earth: stone of the mountain, thrown up on the third day of Genesis.

Topolino inspected the newly quarried stone with the running commentary Michelangelo knew so well:

" That one has knots. Too much iron in this. Shale; it'll crumble into crystals like sugar on a bun. This one will be hollow."

Until finally, climbing over the rocks and making his way towards the cliff, he let out his breath sharply:

" Ah! Here is a beautiful piece of meat."

There is a way of making stone lift itself by distributing the tension. Michelangelo had been shown how to handle the density of the material without pulling his arms out of their sockets. He planted his legs wide, swung his weight from the hips; Topolino opened the first crack between the stone and the ground with an iron bar. They moved the stone over the boulders to open ground, then with the help of the quarrymen the block was fulcrumed upward through the open tail of the cart.

Michelangelo wiped the sweat from his face with his shirt. Rain clouds swept down the Arno from the mountains to the north. He bade Topolino good-bye.

" *A domani,*" replied Topolino, flicking the lines for the oxen to make off.

Until to-morrow, Michelangelo thought, to-morrow being the next time I take my place with the family, be it a week or a year.

He left the quarry, stood on the hill below Fiesole. Warm rain fell on his upturned face. The dark clumps of leaves on the olives were silver green. In the wheat the peasant women were cutting with coloured kerchiefs over their hair. Below him Florence looked as though someone were sprinkling it with grey powdered dust, blotting out the carpet of red tile roofs. Only the mammal dome of the cathedral stood out, and the straight proud upward thrust of the tower of the Signoria, complementary symbols under which Florence flourished and multiplied.

He made his way down the mountain, feeling fifteen feet tall.

11

Having taken a day off without permission, Michelangelo was at the studio early. Ghirlandaio had been there all night, drawing by candlelight. He was unshaven, his blue beard and hollow cheeks in the flickering light giving him the appearance of an anchorite.

Michelangelo went to the side of the platform on which the desk stood majestically in command of its *bottega,* waiting for Ghirlandaio to look up, then asked:

" Is something wrong?"

Ghirlandaio rose, raised his hands wearily to breast

height, then shook his fingers up and down loosely, as though trying to shed his troubles. The boy stepped on to the platform and stood gazing down at the dozens of incomplete sketches of the Christ whom John was to baptize. The figures were slight to the point of delicacy.

"I'm intimidated because of the subject," Ghirlandaio growled to himself. "I've been afraid to use a recognizable Florentine . . ."

He picked up a pen and flicked it swiftly over a sheet. What emerged was an irresolute figure, dwarfed by the bold John whom Ghirlandaio had already completed, and who was waiting, bowl of water in hand. He flung down the pen in disgust, muttered that he was going home for some sleep. Michelangelo went into the cool back yard and began sketching in the clear light that broke open Florence's summer days.

For a week he drew experimentally. Then he took a fresh paper and set down a figure with powerful shoulders, muscularly developed chest, broad hips, a full oval stomach, and a robust pair of thighs rooted firmly in big solid feet: a man who could split a block of *pietra serena* with one blow of the hammer.

Ghirlandaio was shocked when Michelangelo showed him his Christ.

"You used a model?"

"The stonemason in Settignano who helped raise me."

"Christ a stonemason!"

"He was a carpenter."

"Florence won't accept a working-class Christ, Michelangelo. They're used to having him genteel."

Michelangelo suppressed a tiny smile.

"When I was first apprenticed you said, 'The true eternal painting is mosaic,' and sent me up to San Miniato to see the Christ Baldovinetti restored from the tenth century. That Christ is no wool merchant from Prato."

"It's a matter of crudity, not strength," replied Ghirlandaio, "easy for the young to confuse. I will tell you a story. When Donatello was very young he once spent a lot of time making a wooden crucifix for Santa Croce, and when it was finished he took it to his friend Brunelleschi. 'It seems to me,' said Brunelleschi, 'that you have put a ploughman on the cross, rather than the body of Jesus Christ, which was most delicate in all its parts.' Donatello, upset at the unexpected criticism from the older man, cried, 'If it were as easy to make this figure as to judge it . . . Try to make one yourself!'

"That very day Brunelleschi set to work. Then he invited Donatello to dinner, but first the two friends bought some eggs and fresh cheese. When Donatello saw the crucifix in Brunelleschi's hall he was so amazed that he threw up his arms in resignation, the eggs and the cheese that he had been holding in his apron falling to the floor. Brunelleschi said laughingly:

"'What are we to have for dinner, Donato, now that you have broken the eggs?'

"Donatello, who could not take his eyes off the beautiful Christ, answered, 'It is your work to make Christs, and mine to make ploughmen.'"

Michelangelo knew both crucifixes, the one of Brunelleschi being in Santa Maria Novella. Stumblingly he explained that he preferred Donatello's ploughman to Brunelleschi's ethereal Christ, which was so slight that it looked as though it had been created to be crucified. With Donatello's figure the crucifixion had come as a horrifying surprise, even as it had to Mary and the others at the foot of the cross. He suggested that perhaps Christ's spirituality did not depend on his bodily delicacy but rather on the indestructibility of his message.

Abstract theology held no interest for Ghirlandaio. He turned back to his work, the automatic gesture of dismissal for an apprentice. Michelangelo went into the yard and sat in the baking sun with his chin resting on his chest. He had made a nuisance of himself.

A few days later the studio was buzzing. Ghirlandaio had completed his Christ and was blowing it up to full size with colour for the cartoon. When Michelangelo was permitted to see the finished figure he stood stunned: it was his Christ! The legs twisted in an angular position, a little knock-kneed; the chest, shoulders and arms those of a man who had carried logs and built houses; with a rounded, protruding stomach that had absorbed its quantity of food: in its power and reality far outdistancing any of the still-life set figures that Ghirlandaio had as yet painted for the Tornabuoni choir.

If Michelangelo expected Ghirlandaio to acknowledge him, he was disappointed. Ghirlandaio apparently had forgotten the discussion and the boy's drawing.

The following week the studio moved *en masse* to Santa Maria Novella to start the Death of the Virgin in the

crescent-shaped lunette topping the left side of the choir.
Granacci was pleased because Ghirlandaio had given him a
number of the apostles to paint, and he climbed the scaffolding singing a tune about how passionately he loved his sweetheart, Florence, the object of all Florentines' romantic ballads. Up the scaffold went Mainardi to do the figure kneeling to the left of the recumbent Mary, and David on the
extreme right, doing his favourite subject, a Tuscan road
winding up a mountainside to a white villa.

Santa Maria Novella was empty at this early hour except
for a few old women in their black shawls praying before
the Madonnas. The canvas screen had been taken down to
let fresh air into the choir. Michelangelo stood irresolutely
beneath the scaffolding, unnoticed, then began to walk the
long centre nave towards the bright sunlight. He turned to
take a final look at the scaffolding rising tier upon tier in
front of the stained-glass windows, dark now in the slight
western light; at the glowing colours of the several completed panels; the Ghirlandaio artists, tiny figures weaving
across the lunette; at the wooden stalls at the base of the
choir covered with canvas, the sacks of plaster and sand, the
plank table of painting materials, all bathed in a soft glow.

At the centre of the church were a few wooden benches.
He pulled one in place, took drawing paper and charcoal out
of his shirt and began drawing the scene before him.

He was surprised to see shadows climbing down the scaffolding.

"It's time for dinner," announced Granacci. "Funny
how painting spiritual subjects can give a man a carnal
appetite."

Michelangelo commented: "To-day is Friday and you'll
have fish instead of *bistecca*. Go along with you, I'm not
hungry."

The empty church gave him the chance to draw the architecture of the choir. Long before he would have imagined
it his comrades were climbing back up the scaffolding. The
sun arched to the west and filled the choir with rich colour.
He felt someone staring holes through him from behind,
turned to find Ghirlandaio standing there. Michelangelo
remained silent.

Ghirlandaio whispered hoarsely, "I can't believe that a
boy of such tender years can have received such a gift.
There are some things you know more about than I do, and
I have been working for over thirty years! Come to the

57

studio early to-morrow. Perhaps we can make things more interesting for you from now on."

Michelangelo walked home, his face suffused with ecstasy. Granacci teased:

"You look like a beautified Fra Angelico saint floating above the paving stones."

Michelangelo looked at his friend mischievously.

"With wings?"

"No one could call you a saint, not with your crusty disposition. But all honest effort to re-create that which God created originally . . ."

". . . is a form of worship?"

"Has in it a love of God's universe. Else why would the artist bother?"

"I have always loved God," replied Michelangelo simply.

The next morning he waited impatiently for the first grey ash to sift into the narrow strip of sky over the Via dei Bentaccordi. In the Via Larga the country people were dozing in their carts as the donkeys and oxen clop-clopped over the stones with their produce for the Old Market. He saw Giotto's Campanile standing pink and white in the first streaked dawn. Even in his eager rush through the streets he had time to marvel at the dome which Brunelleschi had had the genius to build after the vast space had stood open to the skies and the elements for more than a hundred years, because no one knew how to close it without the use of traverse beams.

Ghirlandaio was at his table when Michelangelo arrived.

"Sleep is the greatest of all bores. Draw up a stool."

The boy sat before Ghirlandaio, who pulled aside the curtain behind him so that the north light fell on them.

"Turn your head. A little more. I'm going to sketch you as young John leaving the city to go to the desert. I haven't found a satisfactory model until I saw you working in Santa Maria Novella yesterday. . . ."

Michelangelo swallowed hard. After his sleepless night's dream of originating whole cartoons with which to fill the still empty panels . . .!

Ghirlandaio had not meant to deceive his apprentice. He summoned Michelangelo, showed him the over-all plan for the Death of the Virgin, added casually:

"I want you to collaborate with Granacci in this scene of the apostles. Then we'll let you try your hand at the figures on the left, together with the little angel beside them."

Granacci had not a jealous bone in him. Together they sketched the apostles, the one bald-headed, the other supporting the weeping John.

"To-morrow morning after mass," said Granacci, "let's come back to the studio and I'll start you at bedrock."

Granacci had been speaking literally: he put Michelangelo to work on the rock wall at the back of the studio yard.

"Your wall has to be sound; if it crumbles your fresco goes with it. Check for saltpetre; the slightest patch and your paint will be eaten up. Avoid the sand that has been taken from too near the sea. Your lime should be old. I'll show you how to use a trowel to get a full smooth surface. Remember, plaster has to be beaten with the least possible amount of water, to the consistency of butter."

Michelangelo did as he had been instructed, but complained:

"Granacci, I want to draw with a pen, not a trowel!"

Granacci replied sharply:

"An artist has to be master of the grubbiest detail of his craft. If you don't know how to do the job how can you expect a plasterer to get you a perfect surface?"

"You're right. I'll beat it some more."

When the mixture was right Granacci handed Michelangelo a square board to be held in one hand, and a flexible five-inch trowel with which to apply the plaster. Michelangelo soon had the feel of it. When the plaster had dried sufficiently Granacci held an old studio cartoon against the wall while Michelangelo used the ivory pointing stick to outline several figures, then with Granacci still holding took up the little bag of charcoal to fill the holes, Granacci removed the cartoon, the boy drew a connecting outline with red ochre and, when this had dried, dusted off the charcoal with a feather.

Mainardi came into the studio, saw what was going on and forcibly turned Michelangelo to him.

"You must remember that fresh plaster changes its consistency. In the morning you have to keep your colours liquid so that you don't choke up its pores. Towards sundown they have to be kept liquid because the plaster will absorb less. The best time for painting is the middle of the day. But before you can apply colours you have to learn how to grind them. You know there are only seven natural colours. Let's start with black."

The colours came from the apothecary in walnut-sized pieces of pigment. A piece of porphyry stone was used as a base, a porphyry pestle to grind with. Though the minimum grinding time was a half hour, no paint was allowed on a Ghirlandaio panel that had been ground hard for less than two hours.

"My father was right," commented Michelangelo, his hands and arms blackened with the pigment: "to be an artist is first to be a manual labourer."

Ghirlandaio had entered the studio.

"Hold on there," he exclaimed. "Michelangelo, if you want a real mineral black, use this black chalk; if you want a slag black you'll need to mix in a little mineral green, about this much on your knife." Warming to the situation, he threw off his cape. "For the flesh colours you have to mix two parts of the finest sinopia with one part white well-slaked lime. Let me show you the proportions."

David appeared in the open door, one hand clutching a sheaf of bills, under his other arm an account book.

"What's the good of teaching him about colours," he exclaimed, "if he doesn't know how to make his own brushes? Good ones are not always available. Look here, Michelangelo, these hog bristles are taken from white pigs; but be sure they're domestic. Use a pound of bristles to a brush. Bind them to a large stick like this . . ."

Michelangelo threw his stained arms ceilingward in mock despair.

"Help! You're crowding my whole three years of apprenticeship into one Sunday morning!"

When Granacci's fresco was ready Michelangelo went up on to the scaffold to serve as his assistant. Ghirlandaio had not yet given him permission to handle a brush, but he worked for a week applying the intonaco and mixing colours.

It was autumn by the time he completed his own drawings for the Death of the Virgin and was ready to create his first fresco. The early October air was crisp and lucid. The crops were in, the wine pressed, the olive oil secure in big jars; the *contadini* were cutting back the trees and hauling home the branches for winter warmth, the fields were lying fallow as the foliage turned a russet brown to match the warm tan stones of the crenellated Signoria tower.

The two friends climbed the scaffolding loaded with buckets of plaster, water, brushes, mixing spoons, the cartoon and coloured sketches. Michelangelo laid a modest area of intonaco, then held the cartoon of the white-haired and bearded saint with the enormous eyes. He used the ivory stick, the charcoal bag, the red ochre connecting line, the feather duster. Then he mixed his paints for the *verdaccio*, which he applied with a soft brush to get a thin base. He picked up a finely pointed brush and with terra verde sketched the outstanding features: the powerful Roman nose, the deep-set eyes, the shoulder-long waving white hair and moustache flowing gracefully into the full-face beard. Free-hand, glancing only once at his sketch, he put in the old man's neck, shoulder and arm.

Now ready to apply paint in earnest, he turned to Granacci with big eyes.

"I can't be of any more help to you, *Michelagnolo mio*," responded Granacci; "the rest is between you and God. *Buona fortuna*. Good luck."

With which he scrambled down the scaffolding.

Michelangelo found himself alone at the top of the choir, alone on his perch above the church and the world. For a moment he suffered vertigo. How different the church looked from up here; so vastly hollow and empty. In his nostrils was the dampness of the fresh plaster and the pungence of paint. His hand clamped the brush. He squeezed it between the fingers and thumb of his left hand, remembered that in the early morning he would have to keep his colours liquid, took a little terra verde and began to shade all those parts of the face that would be darkest: under the chin, the nose, the lips, the corners of the mouth and the eyebrows.

Only once did he go to the master of the studio for help. "How do I mix the exact shade I had yesterday?"

"By the weight on your knife of the amount you cut off

the pigment cake. The hand can judge more accurately than
. the eye."

For a week he worked alone. The studio stood by to assist
if called, but no one intruded. This was his baptism.

By the third day everyone knew he was not following the
rules. He was drawing anatomical nude bodies of male
figures, using for models two men he had sketched unloading in the Old Market, then draping them with robes, the
reverse of the practice of suggesting a man's bones by the
folds of a cloak.

Ghirlandaio made no effort to stop or correct him, contenting himself with a sotto voce:

". . . I'll draw them the way God made Adam."

Michelangelo had never seen an angel, and so he did not
know how to draw one. Even more perplexing was what to
do about the wings, for no one could tell him whether they
were made of flesh or some diaphanous material out of the
Wool or Silk Guild. Nor could anyone give him any information about the halo: was it solid, like a metal, or atmos-
pheric like a rainbow?

The youngsters ragged him mercilessly.

"You're a fake," cried Cieco. "Those are no wings at
all."

"And a fraud," added Baldinelli. "They fade into the
. robe so no one can see them."

"That halo could be taken for an accidental marking on
the wall," contributed Tedesco. "What's the matter, aren't
you a Christian?"

"Haven't you any faith?"

Michelangelo grinned in sickly fashion.

"My angel is the carpenter's son downstairs of us. I asked
his father to carve a pair of wings for him . . ."

His two figures were a distinct picture by themselves,
located in the bottom corner of the lunette under a cone-
shaped mountain crowned by a castle. The rest of the lunette
was crowded with more than twenty figures surrounding the
Virgin's high-pillowed bier, the saints' and apostles' apocry-
phal faces set at slightly different angles of anguish. It was
even difficult to find Mary.

When Michelangelo came down from the scaffold the
last time, Jacopo passed David's little black hat and everybody contributed a few scudi to buy wine. Jacopo raised the
first toast:

"To our new comrade . . . who will soon be apprenticed to Roselli."

Michelangelo was hurt.

"Why do you say that?"

"Because you've stolen the lunette."

Michelangelo never had liked wine, but this cup of Chianti seemed particularly galling.

"Shut up with you now, Jacopo. I want no trouble."

Late that afternoon Ghirlandaio called him aside. He had said no word to Michelangelo about his fresco, either of praise or criticism; it was as though he had never mounted the scaffold at all. He looked up from his desk, his eyes dark.

"They are saying I am jealous. It is true. Oh, not of those two figures, they're immature and crude. If they stand out, it's not because they are better drawn but because they don't fit into our studio style. My six-year-old Ridolfo comes closer to copying the *bottega* method than you do. But let there be no mistake, I am jealous of what will ultimately be your ability to draw."

Michelangelo suffered a rare moment of humility.

"Now what am I going to do with you? Release you to Roselli? Assuredly not! There is plenty of work ahead in these remaining panels. Prepare the cartoon for the figures of the assistants on the right. And try not to make them stand out like bandaged toes."

Michelangelo returned to the studio late that night, took his copies of Ghirlandaio's drawings out of the desk and put back the originals. The next morning Ghirlandaio murmured as Michelangelo went by:

"Thank you for returning my drawings. I hope they have been helpful."

13

The valley of the Arno had the worst winter weather in Italy. The skies overhead were leaden, the cold had a creeping quality that permeated stone and wool and bit at the flesh within. After the cold came the rain and the cobbled streets were running rivers. Anything not cobbled was a bog of mud. The only bright spot was the arrival of Isabella d'Aragona on her way north to marry the Duke of Milan, with her large train of ladies and gentlemen sumptuously gowned by her father, the Duke of Calabria.

Ghirlandaio's studio had but one fireplace. Here the men sat at a semicircular table facing the flames, crowded together for warmth, their backs cold but their fingers getting enough heat to enable them to work. Santa Maria Novella was even worse. The choir was as icy as an underground cave. Draughts that blew through the church rattled the planks and leather thongs of the scaffolding. It was like trying to paint in a high wind, with one's nostrils breathing ice water.

But if the winter was intense, it was brief. By March the *tramontana* had stopped blowing, the sun's rays had a little warmth in them again, and the skies were powdered with a touch of blue. On the second of these days Granacci burst into the studio, his usually placid eyes blinking hard. Michelangelo had rarely seen his friend so keyed up.

"Come with me. I have something to show you."

Granacci secured David's permission and in a moment the two boys were in the street. Granacci guided Michelangelo across town towards the Piazza San Marco. They paused a moment as a procession passed carrying relics of San Girolamo, a jaw and an armbone richly bound in silver and gold, from the altar of Santa Maria del Fiore. On the Via Larga, opposite one side of the church, was a gate.

"We go in here."

He pushed the gate open. Michelangelo entered, stood confounded.

It was an enormous oblong garden, with a small building, or casino, in the centre; in front, and directly at the end of a straight path, was a pool, a fountain, and on a pedestal a marble statue of a boy removing a thorn from his foot. On the wide porch of the casino a group of young men were working at tables.

All four walls of the garden were open loggias displaying antique marble busts: of the Emperor Hadrian, of Scipio, the Emperor Augustus, Agrippina, Nero's mother, and numerous sleeping cupids. There was a straight path leading to the casino, lined with cypresses. Coming from each corner of the quadrangle and centring on the casino were other tree-lined paths curving through green lawns as big as meadows.

Michelangelo could not take his eyes from the loggia of the casino where two young men were working over a piece of stone, measuring and marking, while several others were carving with toothed chisels.

He turned to Granacci, stuttered:

"Who . . . what . . . is this?"

"A sculpture garden."

"But . . . what for?"

"A school."

". . . school?"

"To train sculptors."

His knees sagged.

"What sculptors . . .?"

"This garden belonged to Clarice de' Medici. Lorenzo bought it for her, to be her home in case of his death. Clarice died last July, and Lorenzo has started a school for sculptors. He has brought in Bertoldo to teach."

"But Bertoldo is dead!"

"No, he was only dying. Lorenzo had him carried here on a litter from Santo Spirito hospital, showed him the garden, and told Bertoldo he must restore Florence to its days of greatness in sculpture. Bertoldo got off the litter and promised Lorenzo that the era of Ghiberti and Donatello would be recreated."

Michelangelo's eyes devoured the garden, moving around the long loggias, consuming statues, Grecian urns, vases, the bust of Plato beside the gate.

"That's Bertoldo now on the porch," said Granacci. "I met him once. Shall I present you?"

Michelangelo shook his head up and down savagely.

They walked down the gravel path, circled the pool and fountain. Half a dozen men from fifteen to thirty years old were working at board tables. Bertoldo, a figure so slight as to seem all spirit and no body, had his long white hair wrapped in a turban. His red cheeks glowed as he instructed two boys in roughing a piece of marble.

"Maestro Bertoldo, may I present my friend Michelangelo."

Bertoldo looked up. He had light blue eyes and a soft voice that strangely carried over the blows of the hammer. He looked at Michelangelo.

"Who is your father?"

"Lodovico di Lionardo Buonarroti-Simoni."

"I have heard the name. Do you work stone?"

Michelangelo's brain stood numb. Someone called to Bertoldo. He excused himself and went to the other end of the loggia. Granacci took Michelangelo's hand and led him through the rooms of the casino, one displaying Lorenzo's collection of cameos, coins and medals, and other examples from all the artists who had worked for the Medici family: Ghiberti, who won Lorenzo de' Medici's great-grandfather's contest for the Baptistery doors; Donatello, who was Cosimo de' Medici's protégé; Benozzo Gozzoli, who had frescoed the chapel in their palace with portraits of the Medici in his Journey of the Wise Men to Bethlehem. Here were Brunelleschi's models for the Duomo, Fra Angelico's drawings of saints for San Marco, Masaccio's sketches for the church of the Carmine, a trove that staggered the boy.

Granacci again took him by the hand, led him down the path to the gate and out into the Via Larga. Michelangelo sat on a bench in the Piazza San Marco with pigeons thronging about his feet and the heel of his palm pressing his forehead bruisingly. When he looked up at Granacci his eyes were feverish.

"Who are the apprentices? How do they get in?"

"Lorenzo and Bertoldo chose them."

Michelangelo groaned.

"And I have more than two years left at Ghirlandaio's. *Mamma mia,* I have destroyed myself!"

"*Pazienza!*" consoled Granacci. "You are not an old man yet. When you've completed your apprenticeship . . ."

"Patience!" exploded Michelangelo. "Granacci, I've got to get in! Now! I don't want to be a painter, I want to be a marble carver. Now! How can I get admitted?"

"You have to be invited."

"How do I get invited?"

"I don't know."

"Then who does? Someone must!"

"Stop pushing. You'll shove me clear off this bench."

Michelangelo quieted. Tears of frustration came to his eyes.

"Oh, Granacci, have you ever wanted anything so hard you couldn't bear it?"

". . . no. Everything has always been there."

"How fortunate you are."

Granacci gazed at the naked longing on his friend's face. "Perhaps."

BOOK TWO

THE SCULPTURE GARDEN

1

He was drawn to the garden on the Piazza San Marco as though the ancient stone statues had magnets buried within them. Sometimes he did not know that his feet were carrying him there. He would find himself inside the gate, lurking in the shadow of the loggia. He did not speak to anyone, did not venture down the path through the meadow to the casino where Bertoldo and the apprentices were working. He just stood motionless, a hunger in his eyes.

Thrashing deep into the night, as his brothers lay sleeping around him, he thought, "There must be some way. Lorenzo de' Medici's sister Nannina is married to Bernardo Rucellai. If I went to him, told him I was Francesca's son, asked him to speak to *Il Magnifico* for me . . ."

But a Buonarroti could not go to a Rucellai, hat in hand. Ghirlandaio was patient.

"We must finish the Baptism panel in a matter of weeks and pull our scaffolding down to the lower panel, Zacharias Writing the Name of His Son. Time is growing short now. Suppose you start drawing instead of running the streets?"

"May I bring in a model for the neophyte? I saw one in the Old Market, unloading his cart."

"Agreed."

The boy sketched his roughhewn young *contadino* just in from the fields, naked except for his *brache*, kneeling to take off his clodhoppers; the flesh tones a sunburned amber, the figure clumsy, with graceless bumpkin muscles; but the face transfused with light as the young lad gazed up at John. Behind him he did two white-bearded assistants to John, with beauty in their faces and a rugged power in their figures.

Granacci hovered over him uneasily as the figures emerged.

"Ghirlandaio is incapable of drawing such figures."

"Bandaged toes, eh?"

Ghirlandaio was too swamped in designing the remaining half-dozen panels to interfere. This time when Michelangelo mounted the scaffold he no longer felt timorous before the wet plaster. He experimented with flesh tones from his paint pots, enjoying this culminating physical effort of bringing his figures to life, clothing them in warm-coloured lemon-yellow and rose robes. Yet always at the back of his mind he was crying:

"Two whole years? How will I endure it?"

Ghirlandaio was working him hard.

"We'll move you over to the other side of the choir now for the Adoration of the Magi. Prepare the cartoon for the last two standing figures here on the right."

The Adoration cartoon was already so crowded with figures that he derived little pleasure from adding two more. Returning from dinner, Granacci announced to the apprentices' table:

"It's just a year ago to-day that Michelangelo started. I've ordered a *damigiana* of wine brought in at sundown; we'll have a celebration."

Silence greeted him; the studio was crackling with tension. At the centre table the apprentices had their heads down over their work. Ghirlandaio was sitting at his desk as rigid as one of his master's mosaics, his scowl blacker than the base of his beard.

"*Il Magnifico* has summoned me and asked if I would like to send my two best apprentices to his new Medici school," he declared.

Michelangelo stood riveted to the planks of the studio floor.

"No, I would not like to send my two best apprentices," cried Ghirlandaio. "To have my *bottega* raided. And certainly not on the day that Benedetto is invited to Paris to paint for the King of France. I have half a dozen panels to complete!" He glared down at the assemblage. "But who dares say 'No' to *Il Magnifico*? You, Buonarroti. You would like to go?"

"I have been hanging around that garden like a starved dog in front of a butcher stall," pleaded Michelangelo.

"*Basta!* Enough!" It was the angriest Michelangelo had ever seen him. "Granacci, you and Buonarroti are released from your apprenticeship. I'll sign the papers at the Guild this evening. Now back to work, all of you! Do you think I am Ghirlandaio *Il Magnifico*, with millions to support an academy?"

Joy drenched Michelangelo to the skin like a *tramontana* rain. Granacci stood glum.

"Granacci, *caro mio*, what is it?"

"I like paint. I can't work with stone. It's too hard."

"No, no, my friend, you will be a fine sculptor. I will help you. Just wait and see."

Granacci achieved a wistful smile.

"Oh, I will come with you, Michelangelo. But whatever will I do with a hammer and chisel? I'll cut myself off at the knees!"

Michelangelo could not concentrate. After a little time he left the big table and went to Ghirlandaio's desk. He wanted to thank the man who only a year ago had taken him in; but he stood below the desk, stars in his eyes and silence in his mouth: how do you express gratitude to a man for letting you abandon him?

Ghirlandaio saw the conflict on the boy's face. When he spoke, it was softly, so no one else might hear.

"You were right, Buonarroti: fresco is not your trade. That neophyte you did for me looks as though it were carved out of rock. You have talent as a draughtsman; with years of training perhaps you can transfer it to stone. But never forget that Domenico Ghirlandaio was your first master."

In front of the Buonarroti house that evening Michelangelo muttered to Granacci:

"You'd better come in with me. With two of us in the same sack he's not so likely to drop it off the Ponte Vecchio."

They climbed the main stairway to avoid the kitchen and Michelangelo's stepmother, went quietly into the family room where his father sat hunched over the angular corner desk, dwarfed by the fourteen-foot ceiling. The room was cold; it took the Florentine sun the better part of spring to permeate the stone.

"Father, there is news. I am leaving Ghirlandaio's."

"Ah, splendid! I knew you would come to your senses. You will join the Wool Guild . . ."

"I'm leaving to become a student at the Medici sculpture garden."

Lodovico was caught between joy and befuddlement.

". . . Medici garden . . . what garden?"

"I'm going too, Messer Buonarroti," added Granacci; "we are to be apprenticed to Bertoldo, under the guidance of *Il Magnifico*."

"A stonecutter!" Lodovico threw anguished arms ceiling-ward.

"To be a sculptor, Father. Bertoldo is the last master left."

"One never knows the end of a piece of bad luck: it has more turns than a snake. If your mother hadn't been thrown from her horse you would not have been sent to the Topolinos to nurse; you would have known nothing of stone-cutting."

Michelangelo did not risk an answer. Granacci spoke.

"Messer Buonarroti, a dozen other children might have been placed with the Topolinos and never got stone dust in their lungs. Your son has an affinity for sculpture."

"What is a sculptor? Lower than a painter. Not even a member of the Twelve Guilds. A labourer, like a woodchopper. Or an olive picker."

"With one big difference," Granacci persisted courteously; "the olives are pressed for oil, the wood is burned cooking soup. Both are consumed. Art has a magic quality: the more minds that digest it, the longer it lives."

"Poetry!" screamed Lodovico. "I'm talking hard common sense to save the life of my family, and you recite poetry."

Monna Alessandra, his grandmother, had come into the room.

"Tell your father what Lorenzo, *Il Magnifico*, is offering, Michelangelo. He is the richest man in Italy, and known to be generous. How long is the apprenticeship? How large the wage?"

"I don't know. I didn't ask."

"You didn't ask!" sneered Lodovico. "Do you think we have the wealth of the Granacci, that we can support you in your follies?"

A flush mottled Francesco Granacci's blond cheeks. He spoke with unaccustomed bluntness.

"I asked. Nothing is promised. No contract. No pay. Just free instruction."

Michelangelo shifted his legs and torso to receive Lodovico's culminating burst of rage. Instead Lodovico collapsed on to a hard leather chair with a heavy plop, tears coming to his eyes. Detachedly Michelangelo thought:

"It's funny about us Florentines: not one drop of our blood is salted with sentiment, yet we cry so easily." He went to his father's side, put a hand on his shoulder.

" Father, give me a chance. Lorenzo de' Medici wants to create a new generation of sculptors for Florence. I want to become one of them."

Lodovico looked up at his most promising son.

" Lorenzo has asked specifically for you? Because he thinks you have talent?"

The boy thought how much easier it would be for everyone if he could tell a few simple lies.

" Lorenzo asked Ghirlandaio for his two best apprentices. Granacci and I were chosen."

His stepmother had been listening at the kitchen door. She came into the room. Her face was pale, the dark side hairs standing out in stark relief. To Michelangelo she said:

" I have nothing against you, Michelangelo. You are a good boy. You eat well." She turned to Lodovico. " But I must speak for my people. My father thought it would be an honour for us to be connected with the Buonarroti. What do I have left if you let this boy destroy our position?"

Lodovico gripped the sides of his chair. He looked weary. " I will never give my consent."

Then he walked out of the room, taking his wife and mother with him. In the lacerated silence Granacci said:

" He's only trying to do his duty by you. How can he conceive that a fourteen-year-old's judgment is better than his? It's asking too much."

" Should I lose my opportunity?" flared Michelangelo angrily.

" No. But remember he's doing the best he can, with a bull-headed son forcing him into a situation which he has not, forgive me, the intellect to understand."

Michelangelo blinked in silence.

" You love your father, don't you, Granacci?"

" Yes."

" I envy you."

" Then you should be kind to your father."

" Kind?"

" Yes, since you have no intention of being hurt by him."

2

The Medici sculpture garden was unlike Ghirlandaio's *bottega*; it did not have to earn its living. Domenico Ghirlandaio was always rushed, not only to earn money for a large family but because he signed so many contracts with completion dates.

Nothing could be further from pressure than the atmosphere into which Michelangelo stepped on the warm April day when he began his apprenticeship to Lorenzo the Magnificent and Bertoldo. The feel of the garden was:

"Take your time. Don't make haste. We have only one mission here: to learn. We have nothing to sell but training, nothing to push to completion but your own skill and artistry. You have only to grow. *Calma!* Prepare yourself for a lifetime of sculpturing."

The first person to greet him was Pietro Torrigiani, a powerfully built blond green-eyed beauty. He said with a flashing white-toothed smile:

"So you're the lurker. The Ghost of the Garden. You haunted these porticoes."

"I didn't think you noticed me."

"Noticed!" replied Torrigiani. "We were devoured by your eyes."

Bertoldo loved only two things as well as sculpture: laughter and cooking. His humour had in it more spice than his chicken *alla cacciatora*. He had written a cookbook, and his one complaint at having moved into the Medici palace was that he had no chance to celebrate his recipes.

But sculpture he could and did celebrate: for this frail person with the snow-white hair, red-cheeked face and pale blue eyes was the inheritor of all the communicable knowledge of the Golden Age of Tuscan sculpture.

He linked his thin arms through those of the new apprentices.

"True, not all skill is communicable," he explained. "Donatello made me his heir, but he could never make me his peer. He poured his experience and craftsmanship into me the way molten bronze is poured into a cast. No man can do more. Without Donato, I would have been a maker of gold jewellery; after more than half a century with him, I remained only a miniaturist. Try as he would he couldn't put his finger on my fist, nor his passion in my bowels. We all are as God made us. I will show you everything Ghiberti taught Donatello, and Donatello taught me; how much you absorb depends on your capacity. A teacher is like a cook; give him a stringy chicken or a tough piece of veal, and not even his most delicious sauce can make it tender."

Michelangelo laughed out loud. Bertoldo, pleased with his own humour, turned them towards the casino.

"And now to work. If you have any talent, it will come out."

Michelangelo thought, "Just let them put a hammer and *subbia* in my hands and they will see the chips fly!"

Bertoldo had no intention of putting these tools into the hands of a beginner. He assigned Michelangelo a drawing desk on the portico between seventeen-year-old Torrigiani and twenty-nine-year-old Andrea Sansovino, who had been apprenticed to Antonio Pollaiuolo and whose commissioned work was to be seen in Santo Spirito.

Supplying him with materials from the inner rooms, Bertoldo said:

"Drawing is a different medium for the sculptor. A man and a block of stone are three-dimensional, which immediately gives them more in common than a man and a wall or a panel of wood to be painted."

Michelangelo found the apprentices in the garden akin to those at Ghirlandaio's. Sansovino was the counterpart of Mainardi: already a professional artist who had earned his living for years at terra-cotta; with Mainardi's sweet disposition, giving generously of his time and patience to the beginners. At the other end of the scale was Soggi, a fourteen-year-old like Cieco, who had stumbled into sculpture and to Michelangelo's rigorous eye was totally without talent.

And there was the inevitable Jacopo, in this case twenty-year-old Baccio da Montelupo, as thoughtless as a wren and, like Jacopo, an amoral, carnal Tuscan who scavenged each night's scandal for the morning's tall tale. On Michelangelo's first morning of work Baccio burst in late with the day's most exciting news: a monster had been born in Venice, with one eye behind each ear; in neighbouring Padua another monster had been born with two heads, and two hands for each arm. The next morning he told of the Florentine who consorted with bad females "so as to save as much as possible his wife's virtue."

He was particularly good with *contadini* humour; he told of the patrician Florentine lady, elaborately gowned in silk and pearls, who asked a peasant coming out of Santo Spirito: "Is the mass for the ill bred over?" "Yes, madam," replied the peasant, "and the mass for the whores is about to begin, so hurry!"

73

Bertoldo clapped his hands in delight.

The counterpart of Granacci was Rustici, fifteen-year-old son of a wealthy Tuscan nobleman, who worked for his own pleasure and the honour of creating art. Lorenzo had wanted Rustici to live in the Medici palace, but the young man preferred to stay by himself in rooms in the Via de' Martelli. Michelangelo had been at the garden only a week when Rustici invited him to dinner.

"Like Bertoldo, I enjoy the homely details of cooking. I'll put a goose in the oven to bake in the morning."

Michelangelo found Rustici, rustic, living up to his name, for the apartment was filled with animals: three dogs, an eagle chained to a perch, a mynah bird trained by the *contadini* of his father's estate who kept screeching: *"Va' all' inferno!"* Even more distracting was the porcupine Rustici had trained to be a pet, who moved restlessly under the dinner table pricking Michelangelo's legs with his quills.

After dinner they entered a quiet room with family paintings on the walls. Against this aristocratic background, the rustic became the cultured young man.

"You can draw, Michelangelo. From this perhaps you will evolve into a sculptor. Then let me warn you: do not go to live in the luxuriousness of the palace."

Michelangelo gave a repudiatory snort.

"Little danger of that."

"Listen, my friend: it's pleasant to get used to the expensive, the soft, the comfortable. Once you're addicted, it's so easy to become a sycophant, to trim the sails of your judgment in order to be kept on. The next step is to change your work to please those in power, and that is death to the sculptor."

"I'm plain, Rustico."

The apprentice to whom he became closest was Torrigiani, who looked to Michelangelo more like a soldier than a sculptor. Torrigiani fascinated Michelangelo; he also terrified him when he knitted his brows and spoke in his deeply resonant voice. Torrigiani came from an ancient family of wine merchants, long since noble, and was the most audacious of the apprentices in handling Bertoldo. He could also be quarrelsome, having alienated several of his fellow apprentices. He gave Michelangelo a quick, warm friendship, talking to him constantly from the adjoining worktable. Michelangelo had never known anyone as handsome as Torrigiani; this kind of physical beauty, almost of human perfection,

74

left him weak in the face of his own lack of fine features and smallness of stature.

Granacci watched the relationship with Torrigiani grow. To Michelangelo's question whether Granacci did not think Torrigiani magnificent, Granacci replied guardedly:

"I have known him all my life. Our families are associated."

"You haven't answered my question, Granacci."

"Before you make a friend, eat a peck of salt with him."

He had been in the garden for a week when Lorenzo de' Medici entered with a young girl. Michelangelo now saw close up for the first time the man who, without office or rank, ruled Florence and had made her a mighty republic, wealthy not only in trade but in art, literature, scholarship. Lorenzo de' Medici, forty years old, had a roughhewn face that appeared to have been carved out of dark mountain rock; it was an irregular countenance, not at all handsome, with muddy skin, a jutting jaw, lower lip which protruded beyond the upper, a turned-up nose, the up-tilting end of which bulked larger than the bony bridge; large dark eyes, cheeks showing dark hollows beyond the corners of the mouth; and a mass of dark hair parted in the centre, then combed down to the middle of each eyebrow. He was dressed in a long sienna-coloured robe, with purple sleeves, the tip of a white collar showing at the neck. He was just over medium height, with a sturdy physique which he kept in condition by days of hard riding, and hawking.

He was also a trained classical student, an omnivorous reader of Greek and Latin manuscripts, a poet whom the Plato Academy likened to Petrarch and Dante, the builder of Europe's first public library for which he had assembled ten thousand manuscripts and books, the largest collection since Alexandria. He was acknowledged to be "the greatest patron of literature and art that any prince has ever been," with a collection of sculptures, paintings, drawings, carved gems, open to all artists and students for study and inspiration. For the scholars who had gathered in Florence to make it the scholastic heart of Europe, he had provided villas on the slope of Fiesole, where Pico della Mirandola, Angelo Poliziano, Marsilio Ficino and Cristoforo Landino translated newly found Greek and Hebraic manuscripts, wrote poetry, philosophic and religious books, helped create what Lorenzo called "the revolution of humanism."

Michelangelo had heard the stories about Lorenzo, the

single favourite topic of conversation in Florence: of how he had weak eyes, and had been born without a sense of smell. Now, as he listened to Lorenzo speaking to Bertoldo, he realized that the voice had a harsh, unpleasing quality.

Yet this would appear to be Lorenzo's only unpleasing quality, just as the weakness of his eyes was his only weakness, and the lack of a sense of smell the only lack with which he had been born. For Lorenzo, single richest man in the world, courted by rulers of the Italian city-states, as well as dynasties as powerful as Turkey and China, had an open, lovable nature and a total lack of arrogance. Ruler of the Republic, in the same sense that the *gonfalonieri di giustizia* and the Signoria were governors of the law and ordinance of the city, he had no army, no guard, walked the streets of Florence unattended, speaking to all citizens as true equals, living a simple family life, romping on the floor with his children and holding open house to the artists, literary men and scholars of the world.

Therein lay his genius. He exercised absolute authority in matters of policy, yet governed. Florence with such good judgment and inherent courtesy and dignity that people who might otherwise be enemies worked together harmoniously. Not even his able father, Piero, or his genius grandfather, Cosimo, called *Pater Patriæ*, by all Tuscany for creating a republic after Florence's several hundred years of bloody civil war between the opposing factions of Guelphs and Ghibellines, had obtained such happy results. Florence could sack Lorenzo, *Il Magnifico*, and his palace, on an hour's notice and drive him out. He knew it, the people knew it, and this knowledge made Lorenzo's untitled governing work. For just as there was no arrogance in him, there was no cowardice: he had saved his father's life in a dashing military coup while only seventeen and had risked his own life by invading the camp of Ferrante in Naples with no more personal protection than he used on the streets of Florence, to save his city from invasion.

This was the man who stood just a few feet from Michelangelo, talking affectionately to Bertoldo about some antique sculptures that had just arrived from Asia Minor that day: for sculpture was as important to Lorenzo as his fleets of ships sailing the world's seas, his chains of banks throughout Europe and the Mediterranean, his millions of golden florins' worth of produce and trade each year in every commodity from Florence's wool, oil, wine to the exotic perfumes, flavourings and silks of the Orient. From some Lorenzo commanded respect because of his wealth, from others because of his power; but by the scholar and artist he was respected and loved for his passion for knowledge; for the freedom of the mind, imprisoned more than a thousand years in dark dank dungeons, which Lorenzo de' Medici had pledged himself to liberate.

Now Lorenzo stopped to chat with the apprentices. Michelangelo turned his gaze to the girl walking beside him. She was a slight thing, younger than himself, dressed in a long-sleeved gown of rose-coloured wool, a *gamurra* with its full skirt falling in soft, loose pleats, and a tight-laced bodice under which she wore a pale yellow blouse with a high rounded neck. Her slippers were of brocaded yellow and on her thick dark hair was a rose satin cap encrusted in pearls. She was so pale that not even the rose-coloured cap and gown could throw colour into her thin cheeks.

As Lorenzo passed his table with an imperceptible nod, suddenly Michelangelo's eyes met those of the girl.

He stopped in his work. She stopped in her walk. He could not take his gaze from this slender, piquant-faced girl. She was startled by the ferocity of expression in his face from the pouring of his energies into the drawing before him. Colour pulsated upward in her ivory cheeks.

Michelangelo felt this awakening between them in quickened breath. For a moment he thought she was going to speak to him, for she moistened her pale lips. Then with a quivering movement she removed her gaze and rejoined her father.

Lorenzo put his arm about the girl's tiny waist. They strolled past the fountain, made their way to the gate and out into the piazza.

Michelangelo turned to Torrigiani.

"Who was that?"

"The Magnificent One, you idiot."

"No, no, the girl."

". . . girl? Oh, Contessina. His daughter. Last one left in the palace."

"Contessina? *Little countess?*"

"Yes. Lorenzo used to call his other daughters 'Contessina' as a nickname. When this puny one was born he had her baptized Contessina. Why do you ask?"

"No reason."

Lodovico had never given his consent to Michelangelo's entering the garden. Although the family knew that he had left the Ghirlandaio studio, they were avoiding the descent into sculpture by declining to acknowledge it. They rarely saw him; he left at dawn when all were asleep, except his stepmother, already out marketing, came home promptly at twelve when Lucrezia brought in the roast or fowl, and worked at the garden until dark, loitering as long as possible on the way home so the family would be in bed and there would be only his brother Buonarroto lying awake to ask the news of the day, or his grandmother waiting in the kitchen to give him a light supper.

" You're outgrowing your shirts, Michelagnolo," Monna Alessandra said, " and your stockings are shabby. Your father feels that since you chose not to earn . . . but no matter. I've had this money put away. Buy yourself what you need."

He pecked at her leathery cheek; their was the abiding love in the family, and they knew only sketchily how to communicate it.

He was austere by nature, and had no desire for things.

" I'll be carving soon and covered from head to foot with stone dust. No one will notice the clothes."

She respected his pride, put the few coins back in a pouch.

" As you will. The money is here for you."

Granacci saw no need to rise so early each morning or to return so late at night; only at midday did the boys come and go together. Granacci was growing more depressed each day, his hunched-over shoulders seemed only an inch or two above Michelangelo's.

" It's that cold clammy clay," he complained. " I hate it. I try to model as badly as possible so Bertoldo won't tell me I'm ready for carving. I've tried *pietra dura* a dozen times and every blow of the hammer goes through me instead of the stone."

" But, Granacci, *carissimo,* marble has resonance," Michelangelo pleaded. " It's receptive. *Pietra dura* is like stale bread. Wait until you work marble, that's like sinking your fingers into fresh dough."

Granacci searched his friends features, puzzled.

"You're so flinty about everything, but put marble in your mouth and you're a poet."

He found himself plunged into a cauldron of drawing. Almost the first sentence Bertoldo uttered to him was: "Here in the garden drawing is the *sine qua non*; when you arrive in the morning draw your left hand, then take off your shoes and draw your feet; it's good practice in foreshortening."

"How about drawing my right hand as well?"

"Another humorist in our midst," groaned Bertoldo with delight.

Even when he had worked the *pietra serena* for the Topolinos Michelangelo had shifted the hammer from right hand to left, feeling no difference in precision or balance. When he had drawn his left hand from a number of positions he shifted the pen and drew his right, first gazing at his palm, then turning it over with the fingers stretched rigidly outward.

Bertoldo came by, picked up the sheet with the half-dozen drawings crowding each other on the paper.

"The hogshead gives the wine it contains," he murmured softly.

"I took no offence. My right and left, they are the same."

Live models were drawn from every quarter of Florence, provided through Lorenzo: scholars in black velvet; soldiers with bullnecks, square heads and thick arching eyebrows; swashbuckling toughs; *contadini* off their carts; bald-headed old men with hooked noses and nutcracker chins; monks in black cloaks, black caps with their flaps turned up over their grey hair; the gay blades of Florence, handsome, with Greek noses running straight from the brow, curly hair worn low on their necks, round empty eyes; the wool dyers with stained arms; the calloused ironmongers; the burly porters; plump house servants; nobles in red and white silk hemmed with pearls; slender boys in violet; chubby children to serve as models for *putti*.

Michelangelo grumbled at Bertoldo's harsh criticism of a torso he had drawn:

"How can we draw only from the outside? All we see is what pushes against the skin. If we could follow the inside of a body: the bone, muscle ... To know a man we must know his guts and blood. Never have I seen the inside of a man."

"*Dio fottuto!*" swore Bertoldo softly. "Doctors are allowed to dissect one body on a special day of the year, in front of the City Council. Other than this it is the worst crime in Florence. Put it out of your mind."

"My mouth, yes; my mind, no. I'll never sculpture accurately until I can see how a human body works."

"Not even the Greeks dissected, and they were a pagan people without a Church to forbid. Nor did Donatello need to cut into a human body for his marvellous knowledge. Do you need to be better than Phidias and Donatello?"

"Better, no. Different, yes."

Michelangelo had never seen Bertoldo so agitated. He reached a hand to the old man's thin arm, patted it quietingly.

In spite of these daily shocks, they became friends. While the others were modelling in clay or carving stone, Bertoldo took the boy into the casino and stood over him for hours while Michelangelo copied Egyptian amulets, Greek medallions, Roman coins, holding each precious work of art in his hand while he explained what the ancient artist had tried to achieve.

To his surprise Michelangelo also acquired the devotion of Torrigiani, who now moved his workbench closer to Michelangelo's. Torrigiani had an overwhelming personality; he swept Michelangelo off his feet with his charm, his attentions, his vivacity. He was a dandy who garbed himself in colourful silk shirts and a broad belt with gold buckles; he stopped at the barber in the straw market every morning before coming to work to be shaved and have his hair combed with a perfumed oil. Michelangelo was a messy worker: he got charcoal on his hands, which he then forgetfully rubbed into his face; he spilled paint on his shirt, ink on his stockings.

Torrigiani turned in a good day's work yet managed to keep immaculate his bright yellow linen *camicia,* a waist-length shirt with puffed sleeves, the green tunic with a " T " embroidered on the shoulder in yellow silk, the dark blue jersey *calzoni.* He had evolved a sculpturing stance which kept the stone dust and chips out of his clothes and hair, unheard of for stonecarvers, who emerge at the end of a day's work looking like monoliths. He was an object of wonder to Michelangelo, who was flattered when Torrigiani put a powerful arm around his shoulders, held his handsome face close to his and exclaimed about his latest design.

"Michelagnolo *mio*, you do the cleanest work and get dirtier doing it than anyone I know."

Torrigiani was always in motion, laughing, posturing, talking good sense and nonsense, but never still, never quiet, waving his hands with their emerald and pearl rings, needing to dominate the air about him. His robust singing voice rang out over the lush spring meadow with its wild flowers, and the *scalpellini* in the far corner of the garden who were building a library to house Lorenzo's manuscripts and books stopped for a moment to listen.

When the apprentices walked in the morning to study the early sun on the Giottos in Santa Croce, or the afternoon rays on Filippino Lippi's Young St. John and Two Saints in Santo Spirito, or to catch the sunset glow on the sculptured figures on the Campanile, designed by Giotto and executed by his pupil, Andrea Pisano, Torrigiani slipped his arm through Michelangelo's, wooed him, kept him a captive though enchanted audience.

"Ah, to be a soldier, Michelangelo. To fight in mortal combat, to kill the enemy with swords and lance, conquer new lands and all their women. That is the life! An artist? Bah! It is work for the sultan's eunuchs. You and I must travel the world together, *amico mio*, find combat and danger anr treasure."

Michelangelo felt a deep affection for Torrigiani, a love almost. He felt himself to be simple; to have won the admiration of so beautiful and desirable a youth as Torrigiani . . . it was heady wine to one who never drank.

4

He now had to unlearn much that he had accumulated at Ghirlandaio's studio because of the differences in drawing for fresco and for sculpture.

"This is drawing for its own sake," Bertoldo cautioned him, in precisely the words Ghirlandaio had used to caution him against it, "to achieve authority of eye and hand."

Bertoldo drummed the differences into him. The sculptor is after three-dimensional figures, not only height and width, but *depth*. The painter draws to *occupy* space, the sculptor to *displace* it. The painter draws still life within a frame; the sculptor draws to surprise movement, to discover the tensions and torsions striving within the human figure.

"The painter draws to reveal the particular, the sculptor draws to unearth the universal. *Comprendi?*" he demanded.

Michelangelo was silent.

"Most important of all the painter draws to externalize, to wrench a shape out of himself and set it down on paper; the sculptor draws to *internalize*, to pull a shape out of the world and solidify it within himself."

Some of this Michelangelo had sensed, but much of it he recognized as the hard wisdom of experience.

"I am a *stufato*," apologized Bertoldo. "Everything that every sculptor in Tuscany has believed for two centuries has been poured into my head. You must forgive me if it leaks *obiter dicta*."

Bertoldo, burdened with the task of rearing a new generation of sculptors, was a dedicated teacher, unlike Ghirlandaio, who simply did not have the time. Sculptors are at best monosyllabic men, the sounds of the hammer and chisel their overlanguage and their true speech, drowning out small voices and smaller worlds. Bertoldo was the exception.

"Michelangelo, you draw well. But it is also important to know why one must draw well. Drawing is a candle that can be lighted so that the sculptor does not have to grope in the dark; a plan for understanding the structure you are gazing at. To try to understand another human being, to grapple for his ultimate depths, that is the most dangerous of human endeavours. And all this the artist essays with no weapon but a pen or charcoal." He shrugged. "That romantic Torrigiani talks about going off to the wars. Child's play! There is no thrill of mortal danger to surpass that of a lone man trying to create something that never existed before."

Michelangelo held his day's work in his hand, searching it as though to understand better what Bertoldo was saying, seeking to find in it some part of what Bertoldo wanted there.

"Drawing is the supreme way of blotting out your ignorance of a subject," the old man exhorted, "establishing wisdom in its place, just as Dante did when he wrote the lines of the *Purgatorio*. Yes, yes, drawing is like reading: like reading Homer so that you will know about Priam and Helen of Troy; Suetonius so that you may learn about the Cæsars."

Michelangelo lowered his head.

"I am ignorant. I do not read Greek or Latin. Urbino

tried for three years to teach me, but I was stubborn, I would not learn. I wanted only to draw."

"*Stupido!* You have missed my point. No wonder Urbino had trouble teaching you. Drawing is learning. It is discipline, a measuring stick with which to see if there is honesty in you. It's a confessional; it will reveal everything about you while you imagine you are revealing someone else. Drawing is the poet's written line, set down to see if there be a story worth telling, a truth worth revealing."

The old man's voice became soft, affectionate.

"Remember this, *figlio mio*: to draw is to be like God when He put breath into Adam; it is the outer breathing of the artist and the inner breathing of the model that creates a new third life on paper. The act of love, Michelagnolo, the act of love: through which everything on earth is born."

Yes, drawing was the breath of life, he had known that; yet for him it was not an end but a means.

He began remaining behind at night, unknown to anyone, picking up tools and working the scraps of stone lying about: yellowish-white travertines from the quarries of Rome, *pietra forte* from Lombrellino, conglomerate *breccia* from Impruneta, dark green marble from Prato, mottled reddish-yellow marble from Siena, pink marble from Gavorrano, transparent *cipollino* marble, blue and white flowered *bardiglio*. But his greatest joy came when someone left behind a fragment of pure white Carrara. As a child he had stood before the marble cutters, hungering to get his hands on this precious stone. It had never been possible; white marble was rare and costly, only enough was brought in from Carrara and Seravezza to fulfil commissions.

Now surreptitiously he began to experiment with the point, the toothed and flat chisels, working surface textures on the marble as he had on the *pietra serena* at the Topolinos'. It was the finest hour of the day for him, alone in the garden, with only the statues for company. Soon, soon, he must have these tools in his hand for good; he must be able to pick them up first thing in the morning because they were his natural appendages, like arms and legs. He always remembered, when dark fell, to chisel off the contours he had worked so no one would know, to clear away his chips, throwing them into the stone pile in the far end of the garden.

Inevitably he was caught; but by the last person he would have expected to surprise him. Contessina de' Medici came to the garden nearly every day now, if not with Lorenzo, then with Poliziano or Ficino or Pico della Mirandola, her father's Platonic scholars. She spoke with Granacci, with Sansovino and Rustici, whom she apparently had known a long time; but no one introduced Michelangelo. She never spoke to him.

He knew instantly, without catching sight of the quick-moving figure or the face that was all eyes, when she entered the gate. He felt a heightened consciousness, as though all movement around him, even of the sun and air, had been speeded up.

It was Contessina who freed Granacci from the drudgery of stone. He spoke to her of his feelings; she told her father. One day Lorenzo came into the garden and said:

"Granacci, I'd like a big panel, a Triumph of Paul Emilius. Would you undertake to paint it?"

"Would I? When need is highest, help is nighest."

When Lorenzo turned aside, Granacci pressed his left hand to his lips and fluttered the fingers to Contessina in gratitude.

She never paused to look at Michelangelo's work. Always she stopped at Torrigiani's table, standing at the far side of the desk so that she was facing Michelangelo, and he could see her every gesture, hear her laughter as Torrigiani amused her. Though he watched, fascinated, their eyes never met.

When at length she left he found himself emotionally exhausted. He could not understand this. He cared nothing for girls. Not even a year of Jacopo's tutelage had led him to discern which were "mattressable." There were no girls in his family, none in their small circle of friends. He could hardly remember having talked to one. He had never even wanted to sketch one! They were alien to him. Then why was it painful when he saw her laughing in comradeship with Torrigiani, only a few feet away? Why did he become furious with Torrigiani, and with her? What could she mean to him, this princess of the noble Medici blood?"

It was a kind of mysterious malady. He wished she would stay away from the garden, leave him in peace. Rustici said she seldom used to come. Why now, every day, staying for an hour or more? The more passionately he threw himself at the blank pages the more conscious he was of her standing shivering at Torrigiani's workbench, flirting with the beautiful muscular athlete while somehow seeing and absorbing his own every stroke of the charcoal like a personal affront.

It was a long time, deep into the heat of summer, with the wild flowers dead and the garden meadows burned brown, before he realized that he was jealous. Jealous of Torrigiani. Jealous of Contessina. Jealous of the two of them together. Jealous of each of them separately, apart.

And he was appalled.

And now she had discovered him in the garden after the others had left. She was with her brother Giovanni, the fat one with the cast in his eye, about his own age, fourteen, Michelangelo would have guessed, already a cardinal-elect; and her cousin, the illegitimate son of Lorenzo's beloved brother Giuliano, stabbed to death in the Duomo by Pazzi conspirators. Michelangelo had been only three at the time, but Florentines still talked of the sight of the conspirators hanging from the windows of the Signoria.

The first words slipped out unannounced.

" *Buona sera.*"

" *Buona sera.*"

" Michelangelo."

" Contessina."

" *Come va?*" This was Contessina.

" *Non c'è male.*" Like a Settignano stonemason.

He had been carving a herringbone pattern on a piece of *pietra serena*. He did not stop working.

" The stone has a smell."

" Of freshly pickled figs."

" And this?" She pointed to a piece of marble on the bench beside him. " Does it smell of freshly pickled plums?"

" No, it has hardly any." He chipped a piece. " Here, smell for yourself."

She crinkled her nose, laughing at him. He set himself before the marble, began raining blows with the chisel that sent the chips flying.

" Why do you work so . . . so furiously? Doesn't it exhaust you? It would me."

He knew of her frailty, the consumption in her family that had taken her mother and sister within the past year. That was why Lorenzo was so devoted to her, Rustici said, because she was not long for this world.

" No, no, cutting stone does not take strength out of you, it puts it back in. Here, try working this white marble. You'll be amazed at how alive it comes under your hands."

" Under your hands, Michelangelo. Will you finish that design on the *pietra serena* for me?"

" But it is nothing, just herringbones, such as we carve for garden walks or cistern covers."

" I like it."

" Then I will finish."

She stood still, just above him, as he crouched over the stone. When he came to a hard spot he looked around for a bucket of water, saw none, spat precisely on the area he wanted to soften, then continued the sweep of the chisel over the stone.

Amused, she asked, " What do you do when you run dry?"

He gazed up at her, his face flushed.

" No good *scalpellino* ever ran out of spit."

5

With the first intense locked-in heat of the garden came the first casualty: Soggi. His enthusiasm had been withering like the grass of the meadow. He had won no prizes or commissions, and although Bertoldo had been paying him a few coins, his earnings were higher only than Michelangelo's, which were non-existent. For this reason Soggi thought that Michelangelo might join with him.

One breathless evening late in August he waited until everyone had left, then flung down his tools and came to the newest apprentice.

" Michelangelo, let's you and I get out of here. All this stuff is so . . . so impractical. Let's save ourselves while there is still time."

" Save ourselves, Soggi? From what?"

" Look, don't be blind. They're never going to give us any commissions or money. Who really needs sculpture in order to live?"

" I do."

The emotions of disgust, renunciation and even fear carved on Soggi's face were more eloquent than anything the lad had been able to work into his wax or clay models.

" Where are we going to find work? If Lorenzo should die . . ."

" But he's a young man, only forty."

". . . then we would have no more patron, no more garden. Are we to wander about Italy like beggars with hats

86

in our hands? Do you need a marble cutter? Could you use a Madonna? A Pietà? I can make you one, if only you'll give me a roof and victuals."

Soggi swept his few personal possessions into a bag.

"*Ma che!* I want to be in a trade where folks come to me. Every day! For *pasta* or pork, for wine or *calzoni*. People can't live without these things, every day they must buy. So every day I must sell. On what I sell, I will live. I have a practical nature, I have to know that each day I will earn so many soldi. Sculpture is the last of the luxuries, on the very bottom of the list. I want to trade in something on top of the list. What do you say, Michelangelo? They haven't paid you a single scudo. Look how ragged your clothes are Do you want to live like a pauper all your life? Quit now, with me. We'll find jobs together . . ."

Soggi's outburst was deeply felt; it had been building up for weeks, perhaps months. Yet at the back of his mind Michelangelo was a little amused.

"Sculpture is at the top of my list, Soggi. In fact, there is no list. I say, 'Sculpture,' and I'm finished."

"Finished is right!" agreed Soggi. "My father knows a butcher on the Ponte Vecchio who is looking for help. The chisel, it's just like a knife. . . ."

The next morning when Bertoldo heard of Soggi's departure he shrugged.

"The casualties of sculpture. Everyone is born with a little talent; but with most people, how quickly the flame flickers out."

He ran a hand resignedly through his thin white hair.

"We always had this in the studios. You start out knowing that a certain amount of teaching will be wasted; but you can't withhold for that reason, or all your apprentices will suffer. These Soggi, their prompting is not love or affinity for sculpture, but the exuberance of youth. As soon as this first flush begins to fade they say to themselves, 'Stop dreaming. Look for a reliable way of life.' When you are the master of a *bottega* you will find this to be true. Sculpture is hard, brutal labour. One should not become an artist because he can, but because he must. It is only for those who would be miserable without it."

The next morning moonfaced Bugiardini, no taller, no plumper, arrived as the new apprentice for the garden. Michelangelo and Granacci embraced him warmly.

Granacci, having completed his painting for Lorenzo, had

shown so much talent at organization that Lorenzo had asked him to become the manager of the garden. He enjoyed being an executive, spending his days making sure that the proper stone, iron or bronze arrived, setting up contests for the apprentices, getting modest commissions from the Guilds.

"Granacci, you mustn't," protested Michelangelo. "You have as much talent as anybody in this garden."

"But I enjoy it," replied Granacci mildly.

"Then stop enjoying it. If we need charcoal, or a model, let us get them for ourselves. Why should you give up your work to help us get ours done?"

Granacci was not insensible to the compliment embedded in Michelangelo's fury.

"There's time for everything, *caro mio,*" he replied. "I have painted. I will paint again."

But when Granacci returned to painting Michelangelo was angrier than ever: for Lorenzo had pressed him into service to design stage settings for a morality play, banners and arches for a pageant.

"Granacci, *idiota,* how can you stand here singing so happily, painting carnival decorations that will be thrown out the day after the pageant?"

"But I like doing what you call trivia. Everything doesn't have to be profound and eternal. A pageant or a party are important because people get pleasure from them, and pleasure is one of the most important things in life, as important as food or drink or art."

"You . . . you . . . Florentine!"

6

As the days of autumn deepened, so did Michelangelo's friendships. On feast days or church holidays, when the garden was locked tight, Rustici invited him for dinner, then took him through the countryside looking for horses, paying farmers, stablemen, grooms for the privilege of drawing in their barns and fields.

"Horses are the most beautiful of God's creatures," exclaimed Rustici. "You must draw them over and over again, every horse you can find."

"But, Rustico, I never intend to sculpture a horse. Only men."

"Once you know a horse, you know the world."

For Your Protection

Details of these attractive **C.I.S. PLANS** to protect You and your Family and your Home are yours for the asking—entirely without obligation. Fill in your name and address and post the card. Postage is paid.

CO-OPERATIVE INSURANCE SOCIETY LTD. MANCHESTER M60 0AL

Tick plan and post card today

CFN

Name _____

Address _____
_____
_____

Mortgage Security Plan

Fire and Domestic Combined

Motor Insurance Plan

Pension Annuity Plan

Savings Plan For Young Men

Savings Plan For Young Women

Special Endowment Plans

Ten Year Savings Plan

Sansovino, the *contadino* from Arezzo, twice Michelangelo's age, had his own philosophy.

"An artist must return frequently to the soil; he must plough it, sow it, weed it, harvest the grain. The contact with the earth renews us. To be only an artist is to feed on oneself, and go barren. That is why I ride my mule home to Arezzo every few weeks. You must come with me, Michelangelo, and feel the tilled earth under your feet."

"I'd like to visit Arezzo with you, Sansovino, if there's any marble I can plough a furrow through."

It was only at home that he was unhappy. Lodovico had managed to keep a rough check on how much each of the apprentices at the garden was receiving of prize money, awards and commissions; he knew that Sansovino, Torrigiani and Granacci were earning good sums.

"But not you?" Lodovico demanded. "Not one single scudo."

"Not yet."

"After a full eight months. Why? Why the others and not you?"

"I don't know."

"I can only come to one conclusion: that you can't compete with the others."

"I have not."

"Wouldn't Lorenzo know if you had any talent as a sculptor?"

"Undoubtedly."

"But he has never noticed you?"

"Never."

"*Allora!* I'll give you another four months to make it a full year. Then if Lorenzo still thinks you're dry fruit, you'll go to work."

But Lodovico's patience lasted only four weeks. He cornered Michelangelo in his bedroom of a Sunday morning.

"Does Bertoldo praise your work?"

"No."

"Does he say you have talent?"

"No."

"He gives no encouragement?"

"He gives me instruction."

"It is not the same thing."

"*Ammesso.* Admitted."

"Does he praise the others?"

"Sometimes."

"Could it be you have the least promise?"

"It could not be."

"Why not?"

"I draw better than they."

"Draw. What does that mean? If they are training you to be a sculptor, why don't you sculpture?"

"Bertoldo won't let me."

"Why not?"

"He says I'm not ready."

"But the others sculpture?"

"Yes."

"Can't you see what that means?"

"No."

"It means that you have less ability than they."

"That will be proved when I get my hands on stone."

"When will that be?"

"I don't know."

"Until you work the stone, you can earn no return?"

"No."

"And they show no sign of letting you start on the stone?"

"None."

"Doesn't it look hopeless to you?"

"No."

"Then how does it look?"

"Puzzling."

"And how long can you remain there puzzled?"

"As long as Bertoldo thinks I should."

"What has happened to your pride?"

"Nothing."

"The same as has happened to you in the garden: nothing."

"One does not lose pride while learning."

"You are almost fifteen now. Are you to earn nothing for ever?"

"I will earn."

"When? How?"

"I don't know."

"Two dozen times you have said 'No,' or 'I don't know.' When will you know?"

"I don't know."

Exhausted, Lodovico cried, "I should beat you with a stick. When will you get some sense in your head?"

"I'm doing what I must. That is sense."

Lodovico slumped into a chair.

90

" Lionardo wants to become a monk. Whoever heard of a Buonarroti a monk? You want to become an artist. Whoever heard of a Buonarroti an artist? Giovansimone wants to become a street rowdy, stoning passers-by. Whoever heard of a Buonarroti as a *malandrino*? Urbino has sent Sigismondo back saying I am wasting my money, he cannot learn his letters. Whoever heard of a Buonarroti as illiterate? I don't know any more what a man has sons for!"

Michelangelo walked over to Lodovico's chair and put a finger lightly on his father's shoulder.

"Trust me, Father. I am not looking for wool on an ass."

Affairs grew no better for him at the garden; they seemed indeed to become worse. Bertoldo was pushing him hard, never pleased with anything he did, jumping from one foot to the other crying: "No, no, you can do it better. Again! Again." Making him redraw models from a ladder above them, the floor beneath, and at the end of a week obliging him to come in on a holiday to create a theme that would embrace all the figures he had sketched during the week.

Walking home with Granacci at night, Michelangelo cried in anguish:

"Why am I discriminated against?"

"You're not," replied Granacci.

"But anyone can see it. I am not permitted to enter any of the competitions for Lorenzo's prize money, or work on any of the commissions. I'm not permitted to visit the palace and see the art works. You're manager of the garden now. Speak to Bertoldo. Help me!"

"When Bertoldo considers you ready to enter contests, he'll say so. Until then . . ."

"*O Dio!*" swore Michelangelo under his breath. "Until then I'll be sleeping in the Loggia della Signoria where my father can't get at me with a stick."

There was something else he was unhappy about but could not mention to Granacci: with the wet weather Lorenzo had forbidden Contessina to leave the palace. To Michelangelo she did not seem frail. He felt a flame in her, a flame strong enough to consume death. Now that she no longer came, the garden seemed strangely empty, the days long and unbroken without the excitement of waiting.

In his loneliness he turned to Torrigiani. They became inseparable. Michelangelo raved about Torrigiani: of his wit, his flair, his physique . . .

Granacci raised an eyebrow.

"Michelangelo, I am in a difficult position: I can't say too much without appearing jealous and hurt. But I must warn you. Torrigiani has done this before."

"Done what?"

"Lavished his affection, won someone over completely, only to fly into a rage and break off the relationship when there is someone new to romance. Torrigiani needs an audience; you are providing him with that audience. Do not confuse this use with loving you."

Bertoldo was not so gentle. When he saw a drawing of Michelangelo's in which he had imitated one that Torrigiani had just completed, he tore it into a hundred shreds.

"Walk with a cripple for a year and at the end you will limp. Move your desk back where it belongs!"

7

Bertoldo knew that Michelangelo had reached a boundary of patience. He put an arm as brittle as an autumnal leaf about the boy's shoulder.

"And so: on to sculpture."

Michelangelo buried his head in his hands; his amber-coloured eyes were intense with feeling, sweat broke out on his forehead. Relief, joy, misery were mixed together, making his heart pound and hands tremble.

"Now what is sculpture?" demanded Bertoldo in a mentor's tone. "It is the art which, by removing all that is superfluous from the material under treatment, reduces it to that form designed in the artist's mind . . ."

"With hammer and chisel," exclaimed Michelangelo, recovering his calm.

". . . or by successive additions," persisted Bertoldo, "as in modelling in clay or wax, which his by the method of putting on."

Michelangelo shook his head vigorously.

"Not for me. I want to work directly on the marble. I want to work as the Greeks did, carving straight from the stone."

Bertoldo smiled wryly.

"A noble ambition. But it takes a long time for an Italian to reach back to the Greeks. First you must learn to model in clay and wax. Not until you have mastered the putting-on method can you dare the method of removing."

" No stone? "

" No stone. Your wax models should be about a foot high. I had Granacci buy a supply of wax for you. To render it supple we use a little of this animal fat. So. If on the other hand you need more tenacity, you add turpentine. *Va bene?*"

While the wax was melting Bertoldo showed him how to make an armature, using sticks of wood or iron wires, and after the wax had cooled, how to make it into rolls. Once the framework was up, Michelangelo started applying the wax to see how close he could come to creating a three-dimensional figure from a two-dimensional drawing.

This then was the miracle he had cried about on the steps of the Duomo. For this he had argued the virtues of sculpture over painting. The real task of the sculptor: depth, the round, the dimension that the painter could only suggest by the illusion of perspective. His was the harsh world of reality; no one could walk around his drawing, but anyone could walk around his sculpture, and judge it from every side.

" And so it must be perfect, not only from the front but from every angle," said Bertoldo. " Which means that every piece has to be sculptured not once but three hundred and sixty times, because at each change of degree it becomes a different piece."

Michelangelo was fascinated; Bertoldo's voice swept through him like a flame.

"*Capisco.*"

He took the wax, felt the warmth against his palms; for hands hungry for stone, the roll of wax could not be pleasant. But Bertoldo's words gave him impetus to see if he could build a head, torso, full figure that in some measure captured the drawing. It was not easy.

" But the sooner begun," he cried, " the sooner ended."

After he had massed his wax on the skeletal frame he followed Bertoldo's orders to work it with tools of iron and bone. After achieving the roughest approximation, he refined it with his strong fingers. The results had a touch of verisimilitude, some raw power.

" But no grace whatever," criticized Bertoldo; " and not the slightest facial resemblance."

" I'm not doing portraiture," growled Michelangelo, who

absorbed instruction like a dehydrated sponge thrown into the Arno, but bridled at criticism.

" You will."

" May I speak plainly?"

" Have you any other way?"

" The devil with portraiture. I never will like it."

" Never is longer at your age than mine. When you're hungry and the Duke of Milan asks you to do his portrait in a bronze medallion . . ."

Michelangelo glowered. " I don't get that hungry."

Bertoldo held his ground. He talked of expression and grace and balance. Of the interrelation of the body to the head: if the figure had the face of an old man, it had to have the arms, body, legs, hands and feet of an old man. If it had the face of a youth, it had in like manner to be round, soft and sweet in expression, the flow of the drapery had to be turned so that it suggested a young nude beneath. The hair and beard had to be worked with delicacy.

Baccio was the leaven. On those days when Torrigiani had the vapours and sulks ; or Sansovino was suddenly homesick for Arezzo ; or Michelangelo cried to move ahead to clay ; when Bertoldo reproved Rustici for drawing horses while sketching from a male model ; when Granacci developed a splitting headache from the constant noise of hammer on chisel ; when Bertoldo, racked with cough, moaned that he could have saved himself a lot of trouble by dying from his last attack ; this was the moment that Baccio rushed to the rescue, bringing with him the humour of the wineshops and brothels.

" Maestro, did you hear about the merchant who complained of his wife's expensive dress: 'Every time I go to bed with you it costs me a golden scudo.' 'If you went to bed with me more often,' replied the young wife tartly, ' it would cost you only a penny each time.' "

" No, I don't keep him on as the garden clown," explained Bertoldo. " He has a promise of talent and is never unperceptive. Baccio as much as anyone in this garden has the will to dedication. He doesn't like to study, he's absorbed by pleasure. But he'll wear these things out. His brother, the Dominican monk, is devoted to purity ; perhaps that's why Baccio is devoted to lasciviousness."

The weeks passed. Bertoldo insisted that Michelangelo perfect himself in the transcription from charcoal to wax. When Michelangelo could stand no more he threw down his bone tools, walked to the far end of the garden, picked up hammer and chisel, and worked out his fury cutting building blocks for Lorenzo's library. The foreman, not sure he should permit this uprising, asked the first time:

" Why do you come to us?"

" I must wear this wax off my fingers."

" Where did you learn to chip stone?"

" In Settignano."

" Ah!"

Each day for an hour or two he worked with the *scalpellini*. The *pietra serena* blocks between his legs and under his hand lent him durity.

Bertoldo capitulated.

" ' *Alla guerra di amor vince chi fugge,*' " he said. " ' In a love fight, he who flees is the winner.' We will go on to clay. . . . Remember that clay worked in a damp state shrinks. Build up your clay bit by bit. Mix in soft cuttings and horsehair to make sure your large models don't split. To clothe your figure, wet a drapery cloth to the consistency of thick mud, then arrange it around your figure in folds. Later you'll learn how to expand the model into the size you intend to carve."

" You've used the word," grinned Michelangelo. " I must be getting closer."

February closed in, with fogs down from the mountains and rain enveloping the walled city until every street became a river. There were few hours of grey light to work by, the churches and palaces were too damp to visit for copying. They were confined to the inner rooms of the casino, with each apprentice sitting on a high stool over a brazier of hot coals. Bertoldo was forced to remain in bed for days at a time. The wet clay seemed clammier and colder than ever. Frequently Michelangelo worked by oil light, frequently alone in the icy casino, not happy, but more content to be here than anywhere else.

April was only a couple of months away. And so was Lodovico's decision to take him out of the garden if he had not reached some paid capacity. Bertoldo, when he came wrapped in heavy robes, was a pale wraith; but Michelangelo knew that he must speak. He showed Bertoldo the clay figures he had been modelling, asked permission to copy them in stone.

" No, *figlio mio,*" croaked Bertoldo hoarsely, " you are not ready."

"The others are; I am not?"

"You have much to learn."

"Admitted."

"*Pazienza,*" exclaimed Granacci. "God shapes the back
to the burden."

8

There were several thorns festering. Bertoldo drove him
the hardest, accompanied by a constant stream of criticism;
try as he might, Michelangelo could earn no word of praise.
Another sore spot was that he still had not been invited to
the palace. Bertoldo would cry:

"No, no, this modelling is overcaressed; when you see
the sculpture in the palace you will understand that marble
wants to express only the most intense and profound of
sentiments."

Michelangelo thought, "Well then, invite me, and I will
see!"

When Lorenzo invited Bugiardini to the palace Michelangelo grew angry. At whom: Bertoldo? Lorenzo? Himself? He could not tell. The exclusion implied rejection. He
felt like the ass who carries gold and eats thistles.

Then, on a cold but sharply bright end-of-March day,
Bertoldo stood over a clay model Michelangelo had just
completed from studies of ancient demigods, half human,
half animal.

"There's a newly discovered Faun at the palace," said
Bertoldo. "We unpacked it last night. Pagan Greek, beyond
doubt. Ficino and Landino think about the fifth century
before Christ. You must see it."

Michelangelo held his breath.

"Right now would be the best time. Come along."

They crossed the Piazza San Marco and turned down the
Via Larga. Bertoldo raised one layer of the heavy wool
scarf wound double around his neck, placed it across the
lower half of his face to protect his mouth from the piercing
cold. On the Via de' Gori side the Medici palace had used
the wall of the second city limit as a foundation. The architect Michelozzo had completed it thirty years before for
Cosimo. It was large enough to house a numerous family of
three generations, the government of a republic, the management of a world-wide business, a centre for artists and

96

scholars who travelled to Florence: a combined home, office, shop, university, *bottega,* art gallery, theatre and library: austere, with a majestic simplicity that characterized the taste of the Medici.

"There is no bad art in the palace," said Bertoldo.

The stonework thrilled Michelangelo as he paused on the Via Larga for a moment to gaze in admiration. Though he had seen the palace a hundred times it always seemed fresh and new. What superb craftsmen these *scalpellini* were. Each rough protruding block of the rustic ground floor was chiselled with the authority of a piece of sculpture: the surface resourcefully textured by the *calcagnuolo,* the edges bevelled with a lyrical "curve-out-of-mass" that made the huge blocks sing; and no two stones any more duplicates than two marble statues by Donatello.

Inserted in the heavy blocks was a row of iron rings to which visitors' horses were fastened; at the corners were large bronze holders in which the night torches were placed. Around the palace on both streets ran a high stone bench on which the convivial Florentines could chat and sun themselves.

"Each stone of the rustic is so good," said Michelangelo, breaking the silence, "it could be set up on a pedestal and placed in the loggia."

"Perhaps," agreed Bertoldo, "but for me, too ponderous. They make a building look too much like a fort. I prefer those flat regular stone panels of the second floor, and even better the miniature stones of the third floor, each carved like a gem. That's what makes the palace grow lighter as it rises in space."

"I have never realized," said Michelangelo, "architecture is almost as great an art as sculpture."

Bertoldo smiled indulgently.

"Giuliano da Sangallo, the finest architect in Tuscany, would tell you that architecture *is* sculpture: the designing of forms to occupy space. If the architect is not a sculptor all he gets is enclosed walls. If you need work, you will design a palace instead of a Pietà."

The corner of the Via Larga and Via de' Gori was an open loggia which the Medici family used for their feasts and festivities, considered as entertainments by the Florentines, who insisted on seeing what was going on. The loggia had magnificent thirty-foot arches carved out of *pietra forte*; it was here that citizens, merchants and politicos came to confer with Lorenzo, artists and students to discuss their projects. For all there was a glass of sweet white Greco wine, "the perfect drink for gentlemen," and a cake of welcome.

They entered through the massive gate and came into the square courtyard with its three complete arches on each side held up by twelve heroic columns with decorated capitals. Bertoldo pointed proudly to a series of eight sculptured classical figures between the tops of the arches and the window-sills.

"They're mine. I copied them from antique gems. You'll see the originals in Lorenzo's collection in his *studiolo*. They're so good people mistake them for Donatellos!"

Michelangelo frowned: how could Bertoldo be content to run so far behind his master? Then his eye moved to two of the great sculptures of the city: the Davids and Donatello and of Verrocchio. He rushed with a cry of joy to touch the pieces.

Bertoldo came to stand by him, running his practised hand over the magnificent bronze surfaces.

"I helped cast this piece for Cosimo. It was intended to stand right here in this courtyard, to be looked at from every side. How excited we were! For centuries we had had only the relief, or figures attached to their background. This was the first isolated bronze to be cast in more than a thousand years. Before Donatello, sculpture was used to ornament architecture: in niches, doors, choir stalls and pulpits. Donatello was the first sculptor in the round since the Romans."

Michelangelo gazed open-mouthed at Donatello's David, so young and soft, with long curls of hair and high-nippled breasts, the slender arm holding a gigantic sword, the left leg curved so gracefully to put the open-sandalled foot on Goliath's decapitated head. It was a double miracle, Michelangelo thought: that the bronze casting had come out with such a satin-smooth perfection; for this he knew Bertoldo shared the credit; and that so delicate a figure, almost as slight as Contessina's, could have killed Goliath.

He had only another moment to study three Roman sarcophagi under the arches, and two restored statues of Marsyas, before Bertoldo started up the great staircase to the chapel above, with its Gozzoli frescoes so brilliant in colour that Michelangelo cried out in astonishment.

Then as Bertoldo led him from room to room his head began to spin: for here was a veritable forest of sculptures and gallery of paintings. He did not have enough eyes in his

98

head or strength in his legs to move from piece to piece, or to carry his emotional excitement. No good Italian artist since Giotto or Nicola Pisano was unrepresented. Marbles by Donatello and Desiderio da Settignano, by Luca della Robbia and Verrochio, bronzes by Bertoldo. Paintings hung in every anteroom, hallway, salon, family room, office, bedroom: Masaccio's St. Paul, Piazza della Signoria; Paolo Uccello's Battle of San Romano, Fight of Dragons and Lions; Giotto's Crucifixion on a wooden table; Fra Angelico's Madonna, Adoration of the Magi; Botticelli's Birth of Venus, Spring, Madonna of the Magnificat. There were Castagnos, Filippo Lippis, Pollaiuolos and a hundred others from Venice and Bruges.

They reached Lorenzo's *studiolo*, the last of a suite of beautiful rooms on what was called " the noble floor of the palace," not Lorenzo's office but his small writing room, its vault sculptured by Luca della Robbia, Lorenzo's desk against the back wall under the shelves that held his treasures: jewels, cameos, small marble bas-reliefs, ancient illuminated manuscripts: a cosy, crowded room intended more for pleasure than work, with small painted tables by Giotto and Van Eyck, antique bronzes and a nude Hercules above the fireplace, small bronze heads on the lintels above the doors, glass vases designed by Ghirlandaio.

" What do you think?" Bertoldo demanded.

" Nothing. Everything. My brain is paralysed."

" I'm not surprised. Here is the Faun that arrived from Asia Minor yesterday. His eyes are telling you how much he has revelled in the carnal joys. Must have been the first Florentine! Now I will leave you for a few minutes while I get something from my room."

Michelangelo went close to the Faun. He found himself looking into gleaming, gloating eyes. The long beard was stained as though red wine had been spilled in merriment. It seemed so intensely alive that Michelangelo felt it was about to speak, yet inside the wicked smile the lips and teeth were no longer visible. He ran his fingertips over the gaping hole, searching for the carving, but it was gone. He threw back his head and laughed, the stone room echoing the sound. The blood had begun to circulate again in his veins.

" Have you lost your mouth by boasting of your droll adventures?" he cried out to the Faun.

Then he took drawing paper and red crayon from inside his shirt, sat at the far side of the room and sketched the

Faun, giving it lips, teeth and an impudent tongue, as he imagined they would have appeared when the Greek sculptor carved them two thousand years before.

He felt someone at his shoulder, then a faint perfume came to his nostrils. He whirled about abruptly.

Many weeks had passed since he had seen her. She was so slight a little body, displacing such a modest amount of space. Her eyes were omnivorous, consuming the rest of her pale sensitive features by dissolving them in the warm brown liquid of her pupils. She was dressed in a blue *gamurra* trimmed in brown fur. White stars were appliquéd on shirt and sleeves. In her hand was a Greek parchment copy of Isocrates' *Orations*.

He sat motionless, consumed like herself in her eyes.

" Michelangelo."

How could there be so much joy from this mere pronouncing of a name which one heard all day without emotion?

" Contessina."

" I was studying in my room. Then I knew someone was here."

" I did not dare hope I would see you. Bertoldo brought me to see the art."

" Father won't let me come with him to the garden until spring. You do not think I will die?"

" You will live to bear many sons."

Colour flooded her cheeks.

" I have not offended you?" he asked apologetically.

She shook her head. " They told me you were blunt." She took a step or two closer to his chair. " When I am near you I feel strong. Why?"

" When I am near you I feel confused. Why?"

She laughed, a gay, light sound.

" I miss the garden."

" The garden misses you."

" I should not have thought it noticed."

" It noticed."

She turned from the intensity in his voice.

" Your work, it goes well?"

" *Non c'è male.*"

" You're not very communicative."

" I do not aspire to be a talker."

" Then you should mask your eyes."

" What do they say?"

" Things that please me."

100

"Then tell me. I carry no mirror."

"What we know of others is our personal secret."

He felt exposed, humiliated for showing any emotion which he could not name. He picked up his sketching paper.

"I must work now."

She stamped her foot. "One does not dismiss a Medici." Anger flared into her eyes, darkening their translucence to opaque, then a tiny smile moved in. "You will not hear such stupid words from me again."

"*Non importa*. I have a variety of my own."

She put out her hand. It was small, the fingers as fragile as birds in his rough, powerful paw. He knew enough not to squeeze. Then after an instant he felt a stirring, a warmth, a robust shaking of his hand in her strong grasp.

"*Addio*, Michelangelo."

"*Addio*, Contessina."

"Work well."

"*Grazie mille*."

She was gone, out of the door of her father's study, leaving behind a faint perfume in his nostrils, a forging of the blood in his hand as though he had been working with a perfectly balanced Swedish iron chisel.

He applied the red crayon to the paper.

9

That night he tossed and turned, sleepless. His first year in the garden was almost up. Suppose that Lodovico should go to Lorenzo, as he had threatened, and demand that his son be released? Would Lorenzo be willing to antagonize a good Florentine family? For an apprentice whom he had never even noticed?

Yet he simply could not go away without once having got his hands on a piece of stone.

He could stand the empty-handed hunger no longer. He leaped out of bed, hurtled into his clothes in the moonlight, bent on reaching Settignano by dawn and spending the day cutting *pietra serena* blocks and columns. But when he had run noiselessly down the circular staircase to the Vie dei Bentaccordi he stopped short. Into his mind there flashed a picture of himself working with the *scalpellini* at the rear of the garden where all stones were stored. He saw one in particular, a modest-sized piece of white marble, lying in the

101

grass a short distance from the building blocks. It came to his mind that this block was exactly the right size for the piece of sculpture he envisioned: a Faun like the one in Lorenzo's *studiolo*, but his own!

Instead of turning to his left and following the street of the ditch towards the open country, he turned to his right, walked the Via dei Benci with its handsome, sleeping Bardi palaces to the high wooden gate in the city wall, identified himself to a guard, crossed the Ponte alle Grazie and climbed up to the ruins of the Belvedere fort, and sat on a parapet with the shimmering Arno at his feet.

Florence, luminous in the full moonlight, so close that he felt he could touch the Signoria or Duomo with his fingers, was a sight of such incredible beauty that he drew in his breath sharply. No wonder the young men of the city sang their romantic ballads to their town, with whom no girl could compete. All true Florentines said, "I will not live out of sight of the Duomo." For him the city was a compact mass of *pietra serena*, the streets cut through with a mason's chisel, looking like dark rivers, the cobbled piazzas gleaming white in the moonlight. The palaces stood sentinel, a couple of ranges higher than the modest houses clustered so tightly about them; and piercing the creamy gold sky the spires of Santa Croce, Santa Maria Novella, the magnificent three-hundred-foot thrust of the Signoria. Making a little group of its own were the great red dome of the cathedral, the glistening small white dome of the Baptistery, the noble flesh pink of the Campanile. Around all was the turreted, tower-studded city wall.

And sitting there, above his beloved city, he knew what he must do.

The moon was beginning to sink beyond the hills; the last of the mist of luminous grey powder settled down on the housetops and was absorbed. Light subtly suggested itself in the east, then flared as though the sun had been hovering jealously below the horizon waiting only a signal to precipitate itself upon the stage of the Arno Valley and rout the magical mystical moonlight with fierce proof of its own greater power to light, to heat, to make everything known. Cocks began to crow in the farms upriver, bordering the marsh lake; the guards at the gate gave the cries to open the heavy barred doors.

He made his way down the hill, walked along the river to the Ponte Vecchio, the bridge with its meat stalls just being opened by sleepy apprentices, and continued down to the Piazza San Marco and the garden. He went directly to the marble block in the grass beyond the new building site, picked it up in his arms and struggled under its weight down the path to the rear. Here he righted a sawed tree trunk, set the marble block securely upon it.

He knew he had no right to touch this marble, that at least by implication he had rebelled against the authority of the garden, overthrown Bertoldo's iron-edged discipline. Well, he was on his way out anyway if his father had his say; and if Bertoldo was going to sack him, let it be done in front of a piece of sculpture for which he had been brought here in the first place.

His hands caressed the stone, searched out its more intimate contours. During the entire year he had never once touched a block of white statuary marble.

"Why," he asked himself, trembling, "do I feel this way?"

For him the milky white marble was a living, breathing substance that felt, sensed, *judged*. He could not permit himself to be found wanting. It was not fear but reverence. In the back of his mind a voice said:

"This is love."

He was not frightened, or even startled. He recognized it for the simple truth. It was his primary need that his love be reciprocated. Marble was the hero of his life; and his fate. Not until this very moment, with his hands tenderly, lovingly on the marble, had he come fully alive.

For this was what he wanted to be all his life: a white-marble sculptor, nothing more, nothing less.

He picked up Torrigiani's tools and set to work: without drawing, without wax or clay model, without even charcoal markings on the tough outer skin of the marble. All he had to go on, beyond impulse and instinct, was the clearly etched image of the Faun in the palace: mischievous, pleasure-sated, wily, wicked and thoroughly enchanting.

He placed his chisel on the block, struck the first blow with his hammer. This was where he belonged. He, the marble, the hammer and chisel, were one.

10

The Faun was completed. For three nights he had worked behind the casino; for three days he had hidden it beneath a wool cloth. Now he carried it to his workbench. Now he was willing for Bertoldo to see it: his own Faun, with full sensual lips, set of saucy white teeth, insouciant tongue barely peeping through. He was polishing the top of the head with *pietra ardita* and water to grind away the tool markings and white dots when the apprentices arrived and Lorenzo came down the walk. He stopped in front of the workbench.

" Ah, the Faun from my *studiolo*," said Lorenzo.

" Yes."

" You left out his beard."

" I did not feel it necessary."

" Isn't the job of the copyist to copy?"

" The sculptor is not a copyist."

" Not even an apprentice?"

" No. The student must create something new from something old."

" And where does the new come from?"

" From where all art comes. Inside himself."

He thought he saw a flicker in Lorenzo's eye. It was quickly suppressed.

" Your Faun is old."

" Shouldn't he be?"

" I wasn't questioning his age. It's just that you left him all his teeth."

Michelangelo gazed at his statue.

" I was making amends for the other mouth that decayed."

" You should have known that there are always some wanting in fellows of his age."

" In a man, yes. But in fauns?" He could not resist an impish grin. " Fauns are supposed to be half goat. Do goats lose teeth?"

Lorenzo laughed good-naturedly.

" I've never looked!"

When he left, Michelangelo took up his chisel and went to work on the Faun's mouth. Lorenzo returned to the garden next day. To-day it was warmer, and Bertoldo was with him. Lorenzo stopped in front of the workbench.

" Your Faun seems to have matured twenty years in a day."

" The sculptor is master of time: he can age his subjects forward or back."

Lorenzo seemed pleased.

" I see you have removed an upper tooth. And two lower ones in the other corner."

" For balance."

" You have also closed his gums where the teeth had been."
Michelangelo's eyes danced.

" It was perceptive of you to rework the entire mouth.
Someone else might have been content just to hammer out
the few teeth."

" It followed logically."

Lorenzo stared at him for a moment in silence, his deep
brown eyes sombre. Then he said, " I'm pleased to see that
we have not been making soup in a basket."

He departed. Michelangelo turned to Bertoldo, who was
pale and trembling a little. Bertoldo said nothing. Then he
too left.

The next morning a page in varicoloured stockings and
scarlet coat appeared in the garden. Bertoldo called out:

" Michelangelo, you are wanted at the palace. Accompany
the page."

" You've got yourself sacked!" exclaimed Baccio. " For
stealing that marble."

Michelangelo looked at Bertoldo, then Granacci. Their
expressions told him nothing. He went with the page, entered
the rear garden through an old battlemented wall, stared
with bulging eyes at the box trees cut into the shape of
elephants, stags, ships under full sail. He stopped short in
front of a fountain with a granite basin on which stood
Donatello's bronze Judith.

" If you please, sir," cried the page, " *Il Magnifico* must
not be kept waiting."

It took an act of violence to tear his eyes and body away
from the powerful yet defeated figure of Holofernes, about
to have his head cut off by Judith's upraised sword. The
page led him down a wooden carriage ramp to the basement,
then up two flights of narrow back stairs.

Lorenzo was seated behind his desk in the library, a large
shelf-lined room housing the books which his grandfather
had begun assembling fifty years before. There were only
two pieces of sculpture in the room, marble busts of Lorenzo's father and uncle by Mino da Fiesole.

Michelangelo walked quickly to the bust of Piero, Lorenzo's father, his face flushed.

" See this high polish: as though a thousand candles were
burning within."

Lorenzo rose, stood by Michelangelo's side to study the
sculpture.

"That was Mino's special gift: he could make white marble appear like warm flesh."

"He used a full-rounded chisel to shape the hair. But see how gently the chisel penetrated the marble."

Michelangelo ran his finger over the flowing waves.

"Yet the lines are sharply incised," said Lorenzo. "That's called *ferrata*; where the tool spontaneously describes a movement of the hair."

"What the stonemasons call 'the long drive,'" added the boy.

"Mino was an exquisite," said Lorenzo. "He substituted sentimentality for technique. Yet this bust of my father is the first full marble portrait ever carved in Florence."

"The first! Then Mino had courage."

In the silence that followed Michelangelo's face suddenly went crimson. He bowed stiffly from the waist.

"I did not present my greetings, *messere*. I became excited about the sculpture and began talking."

Lorenzo waved this aside.

"I forgive you. How old are you, Michelangelo?"

"Fifteen."

"Who is your father?"

"Lodovico di Lionardo Buonarroti-Simoni."

"I have heard the name."

He opened his desk, took out a parchment folio. From it he spread out dozens of drawings. Michelangelo could not believe what he saw.

"But . . . those are mine. . . ."

"Just so."

"Bertoldo told me he destroyed them."

Lorenzo leaned over his desk towards him. "We have put many obstacles in your path, Michelangelo. Bertoldo has borne down hard, with harsh criticism and little praise or promise of reward. We wanted to make sure you had . . . stamina. We knew you had a real talent but did not know your character. If you had left us for lack of praise or money awards . . ."

There was a silence in the beautiful room, permeated with the delicious aromas of parchment pages, leather bindings and freshly printed sheets. Michelangelo's eyes roamed the walls, seeing titles in a dozen different languages of which he could make out not a letter. His back teeth had so locked that his tongue had no room to move or speak.

Lorenzo came around to the boy's side.

"Michelangelo, you have the makings of a sculptor. Bertoldo and I are convinced that you could become heir to Orcagna, Ghiberti, Donatello."

Michelangelo remained tautly silent.

"I should like you to come and live in the palace. As a member of my family. From now on you need concern yourself only with sculpture."

"I like best to work in marble."

Lorenzo chuckled.

"No thanks, no expression of pleasure at coming to live in the palace of a Medici. Only your feeling for marble."

"Isn't that why you invited me?"

"*Senz'altro*. Will you bring your father to me?"

"To-morrow. What must I call you?"

"What you will."

"Not *Magnifico*."

"Why not?"

"What meaning has a compliment if one hears it night and day . . ."

". . . from the lips of sycophants?"

"I did not say that."

"With what name do you think of me?"

"Lorenzo."

"You speak it with affection."

"So I feel."

"Do not in the future ask me what you must do. I have come to expect the unexpected from you."

Once again Granacci offered to plead for him with Lodovico. Lodovico could make no sense out of what Granacci was telling him.

"Granacci, you are leading my son astray."

"The Medici palace is not really astray, Messer Buonarroti; they say it is the finest palace in Europe."

"But what does it mean, a stonecutter in a fine palace? It is the same as a groom."

"Michelangelo is not a stonecutter. He is a sculptor."

"*Non importa*. Under what terms does he go into the palace?"

"You do not understand, *messere*: he is not to be paid."

"Not to be paid! Another year of waste!"

"*Il Magnifico* has asked Michelangelo to come to live in the palace. He will be as a member of the family. He will eat at table with the great of the world . . ."

"Who eats with the powerful will have his eyes squirted out with cherry stones."

"He will learn from the Plato Academy, the finest scholars of Italy," continued Granacci stolidly. "And he will have marble to carve."

"Marble," groaned Lodovico, as though the word were anathema.

"You cannot refuse to speak to *Il Magnifico*."

"I will go," mumbled Lodovico. "What else can I do? But I don't like it, not at all."

In the palace, standing before Lorenzo in the *studiolo*, with Michelangelo at his side, the son found the father humble, almost pathetic. And he felt sorry for him.

"Buonarroti-Simoni, we would like Michelangelo to live with us here, and become a sculptor. Everything will be provided for him. Will you concede the boy?"

"*Magnifico messere*, I know not how to deny you," replied Lodovico, bowing deeply. "Not only Michelangelo, but all of us, with our lives and wits, are at the pleasure of Your Magnificence."

"Good. What do you do?"

"I have never followed any craft or trade. I have lived on my meagre income, attending to the few possessions left to me by my ancestors."

"Then make use of me. See if there is in Florence something I can do for you. I will favour your interest to the utmost of my power."

Lodovico glanced at his son, then looked away.

"I know not how to do anything but read and write. The companion of Marco Pucci in the customhouse has just died, and I should be pleased to have his place."

"The customhouse! It pays only eight scudi a month."

"It seems to me I could fitly discharge that office."

Lorenzo raised both hands to elbow height, shook his fingers as though to rid them of water.

"I had expected you would request something much grander. But if you desire to become the companion of Pucci, you can do so."

He turned back to Michelangelo standing tight-lipped before him. A warm smile lighted the dark homely face.

"It is sixty years since my grandfather Cosimo invited Donatello into his home to execute the bronze statue of David."

108

BOOK THREE

THE PALACE

1

A page escorted him up the grand staircase and along the corridor to an apartment opposite the central courtyard. The page knocked. Bertoldo opened the door.

"Welcome, Michelangelo, to my home. *Il Magnifico* thinks I have so little time left, he wants me to teach you in my sleep."

Michelangelo found himself in an L-shaped interior dividing into separate rooms. There were two wooden beds covered with white blankets and red coverlets, each with a coffer at its foot. Bertoldo had his bed on the inside of the L; covering a wall above his head was a painted tapestry representing the Palazzo della Signoria. There was a big cupboard turned catercorner against the inside angle of the L, filled with Bertoldo's books, including the pigskin-bound manuscript of his cookbook, bronze candlesticks which he had designed for Donatello; and on the various levels the wax or clay models of most of his sculptures.

Michelangelo's bed was in the door half of the L, from which he could see the sculpture on the cupboard but nothing of Bertolo's bed area. On the wall opposite the bed was a wooden tablet with the Baptistery painted on it, and next to a window overlooking the Via de' Gori a hatrack and a table with a vase and pitcher of water.

"This arrangement will give us privacy," said Bertoldo. "Put your things in the coffer at the foot of your bed. If you have any valuables I'll lock them in this antique chest."

Michelangelo glanced at his small bundle of clothes and darned stockings.

"My only valuables are my two hands: I like to keep them by my side."

"They'll take you farther than your feet will."

They retired early, Bertoldo lighting the candles in the bronze holders which sent flickering fingers of light into both wings. They could not see each other, yet their beds were only a few feet apart and they could talk in a quiet tone. The one thing they could both see was the catercornered cupboard, with the models of Bertoldo's work.

"Your sculptures look beautiful in the candlelight."

Bertoldo was silent for a moment. "Poliziano says, 'Bertoldo is not a sculptor of miniatures, he is a miniature sculptor.'"

Michelangelo drew in his breath sharply. Bertoldo heard the sound of protest, said softly:

"There is an element of truth in that cruel witticism. Isn't it a bit pathetic that from your pillow you can take in with one glance my whole lifetime of work?"

"But, Bertoldo, sculpture isn't measured by how many pounds it weighs."

"By any measurement it is a modest contribution. Talent is cheap; dedication is expensive. It will cost you your life."

"What else is life for?"

Bertoldo sighed.

"Alas, I thought it was for many things: falconing, testing recipes, pursuing pretty girls. You know the Florentine adage, 'Life is to be enjoyed.' The sculptor must create a *body of work*. He must produce for fifty to sixty years, as Ghiberti and Donatello did. He must produce enough to permeate the whole world."

The old man was tired. Michelangelo heard him sigh into sleep. He himself lay awake, his hands locked behind his head. He could think of no difference between "Life is to be enjoyed" and "Life is work." Here he was, living in the Medici palace, enjoying the contemplation of unlimited art works to study, and a corner of the sculpture garden full of beautiful marble to carve. He fell asleep with a smile on his lips.

He woke with the first sunlight, quietly dressed and went out into the halls of the palace. He ran his hands over the antique marble of Marsyas, the figures of Faustina and Africanus; studied the richly coloured Venetian paintings in what appeared to be a withdrawing room; contrasted portraits in paint by Pollaiuolo with portraits in marble by Mino da Fiesole; spent an hour in the chapel glorying in the Benozzo Gozzoli frescoes of the Three Wise Men of the East coming down the hill from Fiesole; knocked on doors and entered to find himself gazing in wide-eyed wonder and awe at Donatello's Ascension, Masaccio's St. Paul, Uccello's Battle of San Romano . . . until he became so lightheaded he thought he must be in a dream.

At eleven he returned to his room to find that the palace tailor had left a new outfit on his bed. In a festive mood he slipped on the colourful silks, then stood before the mirror surveying himself with satisfaction. It was amazing how much more attractive the new clothes made him look, the crimson *beretto* sending colour into his cheek, the cowl collar of the violet cloak making his head seem better proportioned, the golden shirt and stockings adding a sheen of gaiety. He remembered the day, two years before, when he had sat on his bed redraughting his features with a crayon while awaiting Granacci's summoning whistle.

As he postured before the mirror he was delighted at the changes in himself. He had not only added a couple of inches of height, now standing five feet four, but he had put on some weight. The high bone ridges of his cheeks no longer seemed skeletal; and with the growth of his mouth and chin it was not so noticeable that his ears were placed too far back on his head. He combed his curly hair forward to cover part of the too broad forehead. His small, heavy-lidded eyes seemed more widely open, their secure expression reflected his having found a place for himself in the world. People need no longer think his face out of plumb.

He worshipped beauty in others; and had so little himself. At thirteen he had reconciled himself to being small, burdened with an insignificant figure. Having the deepest admiration for the magnificent strength and proportion of the male body, his own mediocre limbs and torso had seemed a tattered cloak. Now he no longer cut so dull a figure.

In his absorption, he did not see Bertoldo enter.

" Oh, Bertoldo . . . I was just . . . "

" You fancy yourself in that raiment? "

" I didn't know I could look like this."

" You can't. They're for *fiesta* only."

" Isn't Sunday dinner a holiday? "

" Put on this blouse and tunic. Come the Day of the Virgin, you can show off."

Michelangelo sighed, took off the violet cloak and unlaced the fine yellow linen blouse, then glanced mischievously at his teacher.

" Ah well, put not an embroidered crupper on a plough horse."

They made their way up the broad staircase from the entresol to the long foyer, then turned sharply to their right into the dining-room. He was surprised to find himself in a severe room without a single work of art. The panel frames and lintels were done in gold leaf, the walls in a cool cream colour, quiet and unrestrained. There was a table across the end, seating a dozen, and coming down both sides at right angles to it two more tables formed a U, seating another dozen inside and out, so that no one was more than a few slender gilt chairs from Lorenzo, and sixty could dine in intimacy.

They were early. Michelangelo held back in the doorway. Lorenzo, who had Contessina on his right and a Florentine merchant on his left, saw them.

" Ah, Michelangelo, come sit near us. We have no pre-arranged places ; whoever comes first takes the nearest empty seat."

Contessina put her hand on the chair next to hers, inviting him to join her. As he sat down he noticed the beautiful table settings: square-shaped crystal glasses with gold trim, silver plates with the Florentine *giglio,* lily, inlaid in gold, silver knives, spoons with the Medici crest of six raised balls: three, two and one. As he presented his compliments to Lorenzo, palace pages were removing green plants to reveal the palace orchestra in a shell-shaped niche behind him: a harpsichord with a double keyboard, a harp, three big violas, a large lute.

" Welcome to the palace, Michelangelo," said Contessina. " Father says you are to be one of the family. Am I to call you ' brother '?"

He knew he was being teased, asked himself, " Why was I born with a heavy tongue?" After a moment he replied:

" Perhaps ' cousin ' would be better?"

Contessina chuckled. " It's pleasant for me that your first dinner is on a Sunday. Other days women are not permitted at table. We have our meals in the upper loggia."

" Then I am not to see you during the week?" he blurted out.

Her eyes were as round as Giotto's O.

" The palace is not that large."

He watched the colourful array of diners as they entered

as though into the court of a king, while the musicians played
Un Cavaliere di Spagna: Lorenzo's daughter Lucrezia and
her husband Jacopo Salviati; Lorenzo's second cousins
Giovanni and Lorenzo de' Medici, whom Lorenzo had raised
and educated after they were orphaned; Prior Bichiellini,
brilliant and bespectacled head of the Augustinian Order at
the church of Santo Spirito which housed the libraries of
Petrarch and Boccaccio; Giuliano da Sangallo, who had designed the exquisite villa at Poggio a Caiano; the Duke of
Milan *en route* to Rome with his retinue; the ambassador
from the Sultan of Turkey; two cardinals from Spain;
reigning families from Bologna, Ferrara. Arezzo; scholars
from Paris and Berlin bringing manuscripts, treatises, works
of art; members of the Signoria of Florence; bland, homely
Piero Soderini, whom Lorenzo was training to become chief
magistrate of Florence; an emissary from the Doge of
Venice; visiting professors from the university of Bologna;
prosperous city merchants and their wives; visiting business-
men from Athens, Pekin, Alexandria, London. All came to
pay their respects to their host.

Contessina kept up a running identification. Here were
Demetrius Chalcondyles, head of Lorenzo's public Academy
of Greek and co-publisher of the first printed edition of
Homer; Vespasiano da Bisticci, leading bibliophile and
dealer in rare manuscripts who supplied the libraries of the
late Pope Nicolas V, Alessandro Sforza, the Earl of Wor-
cester, and the Medici; the English scholars Thomas Linacre
and William Gorcyn, who were studying under Poliziano
and Chalcondyles; Johann Reuchlin, the German humanist
and disciple of Pico della Mirandola; the monk Fra Mariano, for whom Lorenzo had built a monastery outside the
Porta San Gallo designed by Giuliano da Sangallo; an
emissary bearing news of the sudden death of Matthias of
Hungary, who had admired " the philosopher-prince Lorenzo."

Piero de' Medici, oldest son of Lorenzo, and his elegantly
gowned wife Alfonsina Orsini, came in late and had to take
places at the foot of one of the long tables. Michelangelo
saw that they were offended.

" Piero and Alfonsina don't approve of all this republicanism," Contessina whispered. " They think we should hold
court, with only Medici allowed at the head table, and the
plebeians seated below us."

Giovanni, Lorenzo's second son, and his cousin Giulio

entered, Giovanni with his tonsure fresh-shaved, the eye with the cast involuntarily blinking. He had his mother's light brown hair and fair complexion, was tall and corpulent, with a heavy face and plump underchin. Giulio, illegitimate son of Lorenzo's dead brother, was dark, handsome, saturnine. His eyes slashed through the assemblage, separating every personage and relationship. He missed nothing that could be useful to him.

The last to enter was Nannina de' Medici on the arm of a handsome, brilliantly dressed man.

"My aunt Nannina," murmured Contessina, "and her husband Bernardo Rucellai. He's a good poet, Father says; he writes plays. Sometimes the Plato Academy meets in his garden."

Michelangelo's eyes studied every aspect of this cousin of his mother. He said nothing to Contessina of the relationship.

The musicians began to play *Corinto,* the music of which had been set to one of Lorenzo's poems. Two servingmen who stood at the lifts began hauling up the food. As the waiters passed among the diners with heavy silver trays of fresh-water fish, Michelangelo was staggered to see a youngish man in a multicoloured shirt pick up a small fish, put it to his ear, then to his mouth as though talking to it, and after a moment burst into tears. All eyes were centred on him. Michelangelo turned his perplexed gaze on Contessina.

"Jacquo, the palace buffoon. 'Laugh. Be a Florentine.'"

"Why are you crying, Jacquo?" asked Lorenzo.

"My father was drowned some years ago. I asked this little fish whether he ever saw him anywhere. He said he was too young to have met him and suggested that I ask those bigger fish who may know more about the matter."

Lorenzo, amused, said, "Give Jacquo some of the big fishes so that he may interrogate them."

The laughter had an annealing quality; strangers at Lorenzo's table who had never met and perhaps came from diametrically opposed ways of life began talking with the people around them. Michelangelo, who knew not the nature of fun and had been shocked to find a buffoon at Lorenzo's table, felt his disapproving scowl soften. Contessina had been watching him.

"Don't you like to laugh?"

"I am unpractised. No one laughs in my house."

114

" You are what my French tutor calls *un homme serieux*. But my father is a serious man too ; it's just that he believes laughter can be useful. You will see when you have lived with us for a time."

The fish dish was removed and he was served with *fritto misto*. Michelangelo was too fascinated watching Lorenzo as he spoke in turn to some thirty or forty guests to more than taste the food.

" *Il Magnifico*, does he work through the entire meal?"

" He enjoys all these people, the noise and talk and fun. Yet at the same time he sits down with a hundred purposes in mind, and rises with them all accomplished."

The servants at the lift took off young suckling pigs roasted on a spit, with rosemary in their mouths. *Il Cardiere*, an improviser upon the lyre, entertained by singing the news and gossip of the week accompanied by satiric comments in rhymed and cadenced verse.

After dessert the guests promenaded in the wide foyer. Contessina slipped her arm through his.

" Do you know what it means to be a friend?" she asked.

" Granacci has tried to teach me."

" Everyone is a friend to the Medici," she said quietly, ". . . and no one."

2

The following morning he and Bertoldo walked through the sentient air of early spring, the sky a cerulean blue, the stones of Florence fire-gold as they absorbed the sun. Above them on the hills of Fiesole each cypress, villa and monastery stood out from the green-grey background of olives and vines. They went to the far end of the garden, to the collection of marble blocks. It was as though they were standing in an ancient cemetery whose tumbled headstones had been bleached by the sun.

Bertoldo turned to his protégé with a shy expression in his pale blue eyes.

" Admittedly, I am not a great marble carver. But with you perhaps I can become a great teacher."

" Here's a beautiful piece of meat," Michelangelo cried impetuously.

Bertoldo smiled at this use of the quarryman's vernacular.

" The figure you want to carve must run with the block.

115

You will know whether you're going with the grain by the way it chips when you hit it. To see how the veins run, pour water on the block. The tiny black marks, even in good marble, are iron stains. Sometimes they can be chipped off. If you hit an iron vein you will feel it because it is much harder than marble, and it will be your metal on the metal of the stone."

" Makes my teeth grind to think of it."

"Every time you hit the marble with a chisel you mash crystals. A mashed crystal is a dead crystal. Dead crystals ruin sculpture. You must learn to carve great blocks without crushing the crystals."

" When?"

" Later."

Bertoldo told him about air bubbles, the spots in the marble that fall out or become hollow after weathering. They cannot be seen from the outside, and one must learn to know when they are inside. It was like selecting an apple ; one could tell it was wholesome because it bulged forth in healthy form into space, while a rotting apple tended to become concave, as if being subdued by space.

" Marble is like man: you have to know everything that is in it before you start. If there are concealed air bubbles in you, I'm wasting my time."

Michelangelo made a childish joke which Bertoldo ignored, going instead for a set of tools from the shed.

"Here is a punch. It is a tool to remove. Here are an *ugnetto* and a *scarpello*. They are the tools to form."

Bertoldo demonstrated that even when he was tearing out marble to get rid of what he did not want he must work with rhythmical strokes so that he achieved circular lines around the block. He was never to complete any one part, but work on all parts, balancing relationships. Did he understand?

" I will, after you turn me loose among these marbles. I learn through my hands, not my ears."

" Then take the wax out! That Faun wasn't too bad, but you arrived at your results through blind intuition. For consistent results you have to know why you are doing what."

The outdoor sculpture workshop was a combination forge, carpenter's and blacksmith's shop. There was on hand a supply of beams, wedges, wooden horses, saws, bevels, hammers, wood chisels to repair the handles of hammers. The floor was cement to allow for solid footing. Standing alongside the forge were newly arrived rods of Swedish iron

116

that Granacci had bought the day before so that Michelangelo could make himself a full set of nine chisels.

Bertoldo told him to start a fire in the forge; chestnut wood made the best charcoal and produced a slow, intense, even heat.

"I already know how to temper tools for *pietra serena*," said Michelangelo. "The Topolinos taught me."

With the fire started, he reached for the blower, an enclosed wheel with metal slabs about its circumference, to feed it a good draught.

"*Basta*," exclaimed Bertoldo. "Tap these iron rods together and see if they ring like bells."

The rods were good grade iron, all except one, which was discarded. When the fire was hot enough he became immersed in making his first set of tools. He knew that "the man who does not make his own tools does not make his own sculpture." The hours passed. They did not stop for dinner. Dusk was falling when the old man became faint, his skin ashen grey. He would have fallen if Michelangelo had not caught him in his arms. He carried him to the casino, marvelling that Bertoldo could weigh so little, less than a rod of Swedish ore. He put his teacher down gently on a chair.

"How could I have let you work so long?" he groaned.

A little colour spread over the brittle bones of Bertoldo's cheeks. "It is not enough to handle marble; you must also have iron in your blood."

The next morning Michelangelo rose in the dark, quietly so that he would not waken Bertoldo, walked through the sleeping streets in order to be in the garden at dawn. He knew that it was the first rays of the sun that revealed the truth about marble. Under these piercing rays marble was almost translucent; all veins, faults, hollows were mercilessly exposed. Quality that could survive the earliest sun would be intact when night fell.

He went from block to block tapping with his hammer. The solid blocks gave out a bell-like sound, the defective ones a dull thud. One small piece that had been exposed to the weather for a long time had developed a tough skin. With hammer and chisel he cut away the membranous coating to get to the pure milky substance below. Wanting to learn the direction of the vein, he held his hammer tightly and fractured off the high corners.

He liked what he saw; took a piece of charcoal and drew

the head and beard of an old man on the marble. Then he pulled up a bench, straddled the block, gripping it with both knees, picked up hammer and chisel. His body settled down with a soughing movement. Tensions within him fell away with each falling chip. Stone filled him out, gave him body; he felt implemented and whole. His arm grew lighter and stronger with the passing of the hours. These metal tools clothed him in their own armour. They made him robust.

He thought, " As Torrigiani loves the feel of a gun in his hand, Sansovino the plough, Rustici the rough coat of a dog, and Baccio a woman, just so am I happiest with a block of marble between my legs and a hammer and chisel in my hands."

White marble was the heart of the universe, the purest substance created by God; not merely a symbol of God but a portrait, God's way of manifesting Himself. Only a divine hand could create such noble beauty. He felt himself a part of the white purity before him, felt its integrity as though it were his own.

He remembered Bertoldo quoting Donatello: " Sculpture is an art which, by removing all that is superfluous from the material under treatment, reduces it to that form designed in the artist's mind."

Was it not equally true that the sculptor could never force any design on the marble which was not indigenous to its own nature? He had the impression that, no matter how honestly a sculptor designed, it would come to nothing if it did not agree with the basic nature of the block. In this sense a sculptor could never be completely master of his fate, as a painter could be. Paint was fluid, it could bend around corners. Marble was solidity itself. The marble sculptor had to accept the rigorous discipline of a partnership. The marble and he were one. They spoke to each other. And for him, the feel of marble was the supreme sensation. No gratification of any other sense, sight, sound, smell, could approach it.

He had removed the outer shell. Now he dug into the mass, entered in the biblical sense. In this act of creation there was needed the thrust, the penetration, the beating and pulsating upward to a mighty climax, the total possession. It was not merely an act of love, it was the act of love: the mating of his own inner patterns to the inherent forms of the marble; an insemination in which he planted seed, created the living work of art.

Bertoldo entered the shop, saw Michelangelo at work, cried out, " No, no, that's wrong. Stop! That's the amateur way to carve."

Michelangelo heard the voice over the pounding of his hammer, turned to flash recognition, but without ceasing the gouging-out movement of his *ugnetto*.

" Michelangelo! You're beginning at the wrong end."

Michelangelo did not hear him. Bertoldo turned away from the sight of his apprentice cutting a furrow through the stone as though it were quince jelly. He shook his head in amused despair.

" As well try to keep Vesuvius from erupting."

3

That evening he bathed in a tub of hot water placed for him in a small room at the end of his hallways, put on a dark blue shirt and hose and accompanied Bertoldo to Lorenzo's *studiolo* for supper. He was nervous. What would he say? The Plato Academy was reported to be the intellectual heart of Europe, a university and a printing press, a fount of literature and a world-exploring expedition which had for its purpose the turning of Florence into a second Athens. If only he had listened to Urbino when his teacher had been reading from the old Greek manuscripts.

There was a fire crackling in the hearth, warm light in the brass lamps on Lorenzo's writing desk, a pleasant air of camaraderie. Seven chairs were drawn up to a low table. The shelves of books, Greek reliefs, cases of cameos and amulets made the room intimate and cosy. The Plato group received him casually, then returned to their discussion of the comparative worth of medicine and astrology as sciences, giving Michelangelo an opportunity to sort out the faces and personalities of the four scholars who were reputed to be the outstanding brains of Italy.

Marsilio Ficino, fifty-seven, had founded the Plato Academy for Cosimo, Lorenzo's grandfather. He was a tiny man, under five feet, and though suffering the continuing ills of the hypochondriac he had translated all of Plato and become a living dictionary of ancient philosophies by translating the body of Egyptian wisdom before devouring the work of the sages from Aristotle through the Alexandrians, Confucianists,

Zoroastrians. Trained by his father to be a doctor, he was well acquainted with the natural sciences as well. He had helped introduce the printing of books in Florence. His own writings attracted scholars from all over Europe who came to listen to his lectures. In his beautiful villa in Careggi, which Cosimo had had Michelozzo design for him, and which was managed by his nieces, he burned an undying lamp in front of a statue of Plato, whom he was trying to have canonized as the " dearest of Christ's disciples," an act of heresy as well as inverted history for which Rome had very nearly excommunicated him. His nieces quipped:

" He can recite the whole of a Plato dialogue but he can never remember where he left his slippers."

Michelangelo next turned his attention to Cristoforo Landino, about sixty-six, tutor of Lorenzo's father, Piero the Gouty, and of Lorenzo himself, brilliant writer and lecturer, training the Florentine mind to free itself from dogma and to apply the findings of science to nature. He had served as confidential secretary to the Signoria, was experienced in politics, and a leader of the Medici circle for three generations. He was the Dante authority, having published his commentary in the first version of *The Divine Comedy* printed in Florence. His lifetime work centred around the Italian language, the *volgare,* which almost singlehanded he was turning from a despised argot into a respected language by translating into it Pliny, Horace, Virgil.

He was known in Florence for his revolutionary credo: " The deepest basis for action is the clear supremacy of contemplation and knowledge." In Lorenzo he had found the hero of Plato's *Republic*: " The ideal ruler of a city is the scholar."

Perched on the edge of a stiff leather chair was Angelo Poliziano, thirty-six years of age, who was said by opponents of the Medici to be kept close at hand because by contrast he made Lorenzo appear attractive. Yet he was acknowledged to be the most fantastic scholar there: publishing in Latin at the age of ten, invited into the Florentine *Compagnia di Dottrina* at twelve to be trained by Ficino, Landino and the Greek scholars brought to Florence by the Medici. He had translated the first books of Homer's *Iliad* by sixteen and been taken into the palace by Lorenzo to become tutor to his sons. One of the ugliest of men, he was possessed of as lucid and limpid a style as any poet since Petrarch; his *Stanze per la Giostra di Giuliano,* a book-length poem celebrating the tournament of Giuliano de' Medici, Lorenzo's younger brother, killed by the Pazzi, had become a model for Italian poetry.

Michelangelo's eyes now went to the youngest and most attractive of the group, twenty-seven-year-old Pico della Mirandola, who read and wrote in twenty-two languages. The other members of the group teased him by saying, " The only reason Pico doesn't know a twenty-third is that he can't find one." Known as the " great lord of Italy," with a sweet and sincere nature, unspoiled by his soft golden hair, deep blue eyes, flawless blond skin, slender figure, Florentines called him " beautiful and beloved." His intellectual concept was the unity of knowledge; his ambition, to reconcile all religions and philosophies since the beginning of time. Like Ficino, he aspired to hold in his mind the totality of human learning. To this end he read Chinese philosophers in Chinese, Arabic in Arabic, Hebrew in Hebrew, believing that all languages were rational divisions of one universal language. Of all Italians the most divinely gifted, he yet made no enemies, even as ugly Poliziano could make no friends.

The door opened. Lorenzo entered, limping from an attack of his recurrent gout. He nodded to the others, turned to Michelangelo.

"This is the *sancta sanctorum*: most of what Florence learns is started in this room. When we are in the palace, and you are free, join us."

Lorenzo moved an ornamented screen and knocked on the dumb-waiter behind, from which Michelangelo assumed that the *studiolo* was directly below the dining-room. He heard the platform moving inside the shaft, and within a few moments the academicians were taking plates of cheese, fruit, bread, honey, nuts and setting them on the low table in the centre of the room. There were no servants about; nor was there anything but milk to drink. Though the talk was light, Michelangelo perceived that the group met for work; and after supper "wine made their hair swell."

The table was cleared, the plates, fruit rinds and nutshells dispatched down the lift. At once the conversation became serious. Sitting on a low stool beside Bertoldo, Michelangelo heard the case against the Church, which the scholars in this room no longer considered synonymous with their religion. Florence in particular was a seat of disaffection because Lorenzo and the majority of his fellow townsmen agreed that Pope Sixtus of Rome had been behind the Pazzi

121

conspiracy which had resulted in the murder of Giuliano and the almost fatal stabbing of Lorenzo. The Pope had excommunicated Florence, forbidding the clergy to fulfil the duties of their office. Florence in turn had excommunicated the Pope, declaring the papal claims to power were based on such eight-century forgeries as the Donation of Constantine. The Pope in an effort to crush Lorenzo had sent troops into Tuscany, which had burned and pillaged as close as the neighbouring towns of Poggibonsi. . . .

With the advent of Innocent VIII in 1484, peace had been re-established between Florence and Rome; but as Michelangelo heard the evidence summarized by the men around the table, it appeared that much of the Tuscan clergy had become increasingly immoral in personal conduct as well as in clerical practice. The outstanding exception was the Augustinian Order at Santo Spirito, living in flawless self-discipline under Prior Bichiellini.

Pico della Mirandola put his elbows on the low table, resting his chin on his clasped hands.

" I think I may have come upon an answer to our dilemma over the Church: in the form of a Dominican monk from Ferrara. I've heard him preach there. He shakes the ribs of the cathedral."

Landino, whose white hair was worn long at the back, with tufts coming over his forehead, leaned across the table, so that Michelangelo could see the fine network of wrinkles circling his eyes.

" This monk, is he all volume?"

" On the contrary, Landino," replied Pico, " he's a brilliant student of the Bible and St. Augustine. He feels even more strongly about the corruption of the clergy than we do."

Angelo Poliziano, of the heavy features and coarse black hair worn string-like down over his ears and covering part of the rough skin, moistened his overly red, projecting underlip.

" It's not only the corruption, it's the ignorance that appals me."

Ficino, light-complected, with a bright, perceptive face and tiny nose and mouth, cried out eagerly:

" It's been a long time since we've had a scholar in a Florentine pulpit. We have only Fra Mariano and Prior Bichiellini."

" Girolamo Savonarola has given himself over to years

of study," Pico assured them. "Plato and Aristotle as well as Church doctrine."

"What are his ambitions?" asked Lorenzo.

"To purify the Church."

"Nothing more? What about power?"

"Only the power within him."

"If this monk would work with us . . ." proffered Lorenzo.

"If Your Excellency will request his transfer of the Lombard Fathers?"

"I'll attend to it."

The subject settled, the oldest, Landino, and the youngest, Pico, now turned their attention to Michelangelo. Landino asked if he had read what Pliny wrote about the famous Greek statue of the Laocoön.

"I know nothing of Pliny."

"Then I shall read it to you."

He took a book down from the shelf, quickly thumbed through it and read the story of the statue in the palace of Emperor Titus, "a work that may be looked upon as preferable to any other production of the art of painting or of statuary. It is sculpted from a single block, both the main figures as well as the children, and the serpents with their marvellous folds."

Poliziano followed with a description of the Venus of Cnidos from Lucian, which represented Venus standing before Paris when he awarded her the prize of beauty. Pico then remembered the Pentelic marble statue at the tomb of Xenophon.

"Michelangelo will want to read Pausanias in the original," said Pico. "I will bring you my manuscript."

"I don't read Greek," said Michelangelo a bit ashamedly.

"I will teach you."

"I do not have the gift for languages."

"No matter," interceded Poliziano, "in a year you will be writing sonnets in Latin as well as Greek."

To himself, Michelangelo murmured, "Permit me to doubt." But it would be bad manners to kill the enthusiasm of these new friends who were now arguing among themselves as to which books he should be taught from.

". . . Homer. For Greek, he is the purest."

"Aristophanes is more fun. To laugh while learning . . ."

He was relieved when the group turned its attention away from him. The most important idea he gleaned from the swift, learned talk was that religion and knowledge could exist side by side, enriching each other. Greece and Rome, before the dawn of Christianity, had built gloriously in the arts, humanities, sciences, philosophy. Then for a thousand years all such wisdom and beauty had been crushed, declared anathema, buried in darkness. Now this little group of men, the sensual Poliziano, the lined Landino, the tiny Ficino, the golden-haired Pico della Mirandola, these few fragile men, led and aided by Lorenzo de' Medici, were attempting to create a new intellect under the banner of a word Michelangelo had never heard before:

Humanism.

What did it mean?

As the hours wore on he found himself caught up in interest. So much so that when Bertoldo signalled that he was leaving, slipping out quietly, Michelangelo remained. And as each of the Platonists poured out his thoughts he slowly gathered the sense of what they meant:

We are giving the world back to man, and man back to himself. Man shall no longer be vile, but noble. We shall not destroy his mind in return for an immortal soul. Without a free, vigorous and creative mind, man is but an animal, and he will die like an animal, without any shred of a soul. We return to man his arts, his literature, his sciences, his independence to think and feel as an individual, not to be bound to dogma like a slave, to rot in his chains.

At the end of the evening when he returned to his room and found Bertoldo still awake, he blurted out:

" They make me feel so stupid."

" They are the best minds in Europe. They can give you heroic themes to ponder on." Then to console the tired youth, he added, " But they cannot carve marble, and that is a language as eloquent as any."

The next morning he reached the garden early. Torrigiani sought him out in the workshed where he had set up his bearded old man to practise on.

" I'm consumed by curiosity," cried Torrigiani. " Tell me about life in the palace."

Michelangelo told his friend of the room he shared with Bertoldo, how he had wandered down the long halls, free to handle the art treasures, of the guests at the Sunday dinner and his exciting supper in Lorenzo's *studiolo* with the Platonists. Torrigiani was interested only in personalities.

" What are Poliziano and Pico della Mirandola like?"

" Well, Poliziano is ugly until he starts to speak, then his words make him beautiful. Pico della Mirandola is the best-looking man I've ever seen, and brilliant."

"You're very impressionable," said Torrigiani tartly. "A new pair of bright blue eyes, long wavy golden hair, and your eyes pop out of their sockets."

"But, Torrigiani, think of being able to read and write in twenty-two languages! When we can barely express ourselves in one."

"Speak for yourself," retorted Torrigiani. "I have a nobleman's education, and I can discuss with the best of them. It is not my fault if you are ignorant."

Michelangelo realized that his friend had become quarrelsome.

"I meant no criticism of you, Torrigiani."

"One night in the Medici palace and already the rest of Florence seems ignorant to you."

"I was merely . . ."

". . . you were merely bragging about your new friends," interrupted Torrigiani, "men who are so much more attractive and intelligent than your old, grubby friends with whom you have been imprisoned in these garden walls."

"I had no such thought. Why do you say such things?"

But Torrigiani had turned away.

Michelangelo sighed, returned to his marble.

4

Palm Sunday was a warm spring day. On his washstand he found three gold florins which Bertoldo said would be left for him each week by Lorenzo's secretary, Ser Piero da Bibbiena. He could not resist the temptation of showing off to his family. On his bed he laid out another new outfit, the white blouse embroidered with grapes and leaves, the short surcoat with cap sleeves belted in front with silver buckles, the wine-coloured stockings. He smiled to himself as he pictured Granacci's expression when he met him in the Piazza San Marco so that they could walk home together.

Rustici stared at him as he came down the path and, when Michelangelo was close enough, mimicked:

"*I'm plain*." Then, more acidly, "Spread your tail."

"My tail?"

"All peacocks have colourful tails."

"Oh, now, Rustici," he wailed, "can't I wear them even once?"

"Can't I wear this jewellery just once? Can't I drink this rare wine just once? Order these servants around just once? Squander some gold coins just once? Sleep with this pretty girl just once? . . ."

"All the temptations of the flesh in one sonnet. Truly, Rustici, I feel as though I were dressed up in a costume for a pageant. But I would like to impress my family."

"*Vai via*," growled Rustico. "Go your way."

Torrigiani came stalking down the path, his flame-coloured cloak and orange plumes on his black velvet hat flying. He hauled up short in front of Michelangelo.

"I want to talk to you, alone."

Torrigiani seized his arm. Michelangelo held back.

"Why alone? We have no secrets."

"We shared confidences. Until you moved into the palace and became so important."

There was no mistaking the emotion behind Torrigiani's outburst. Michelangelo spoke gently, hoping to placate him.

"But you live in your own palace, Torrigiani."

"Yes, and I don't have to play cheap little tricks like knocking out a faun's teeth to ingratiate myself with the Medici."

"You sound jealous."

"Of what! Of an insufferable prig?"

"Why a prig? What's the connection?"

"Because you know nothing about happiness or comradeship."

"I've never been happier."

"Yes, setting down charcoal lines with your grimy hands."

"But good charcoal lines," protested Michelangelo, refusing to take Torrigiani seriously.

Torrigiani went purple in the face.

"Are you implying that mine are not?"

"Why do you always bring a discussion back to yourself? You're not the centre of the universe."

"To myself, I am. And I was to you too, until your head got swollen."

Michelangelo stared at him in amazement.

"You were never the centre of my universe."

"Then you deceived me. You're sucking up for your commissions an awful long time in advance."

The sun went cold on Michelangelo's face. He turned and

126

ran as hard as he could, out of the garden and down the Street of the Cuirass Makers.

The carpenter and grocer sitting in the sun before their shops pulled at their caps respectfully; otherwise his new clothes were no more of a success at home than they had been with Rustici. His father felt hurt, as though the finery were in some way a reproach to him.

Michelangelo took the three gold florins from the purse on his belt and put them on Lodovico's desk. Lodovico gazed at them without comment, but his stepmother Lucrezia bussed him happily on both cheeks, her eyes bright with excitement.

"Now tell me! What sauces do they use on the *pasta?*"

Michelangelo racked his brains, wanting to please.

"I can't remember."

"Then the meats. Do the palace cooks use zedoary? What of their famous sole cooked with banana strips and pine nuts?"

"Forgive me, *madre mia*, I don't know."

She shook her head in despair.

"Don't you remember what you chew? Then make friends with the cooks. Write down the recipes for my sake."

Now the full family had assembled in Lodovico's combination office and sitting-room. His grandmother was happy because he was meeting the great men of Florence. His brother Giovansimone was interested in the parties. His aunt and uncle were pleased because of the gold coins he had brought home. Buonarroto wanted to know about the business arrangement: was he to receive three gold coins every week? Were the stone materials taken out of his salary?

His father called for attention.

"How do the Medici treat you? *Il Magnifico?*"

"Well."

"Piero?"

"He is arrogant; it is his nature."

"Giovanni, the cardinal-to-be?"

"He treats all alike. As though each meeting were the first."

"Giuliano?"

Michelangelo smiled. "The whole palace loves him."

Lodovico cogitated a moment, then announced:

"Piero's attitude will prevail: you are in the palace as a humble workman." He eyed the three gold coins gleaming on the desk. "What are they? A gift? A wage?"

"I am to have three florins each week."

"What did they say when they delivered the money?"

"It was on my wash table. When I asked Bertoldo, he said that it was a weekly allowance."

His uncle Francesco could not contain his delight.

"Splendid. With this steady money we can rent a stall. Michelangelo, you will be a partner, you will share in the profits . . ."

"Imagine," his aunt Cassandra chimed in with a newborn respect, "that Michelangelo should be the one to put us back in commerce."

"No!" It was Lodovico, his face a deep red. "We are not the bashful poor."

"But they were given to Michelangelo as a member of the Medici family," answered his young wife.

"Humpf!" snorted Lodovico. "What makes him a Medici? Three gold coins?"

"It is not charity." Michelangelo was indignant. "I work from light to dark."

"Are you legally apprenticed? Did I sign a Guild agreement?" He turned on his brother Francesco. "A gift is a whim. Next week there may be nothing!"

Michelangelo thought his father was going to throw the money at his head. He had meant only to bring home his earnings like a dutiful son . . . perhaps bragging a little. But the three gold florins were more than Lodovico would earn in months at the customs. Michelangelo realized that he had been indelicate, for now, with his head on his chest, Lodovico commented, "Think how many millions of florins the Medici must have if they can give a fifteen-year-old student three of them each week." Then, with a quick movement of his hand, he swept them into the top drawer of his desk.

Lucrezia seized the moment to summon them to table. After dinner the family reassembled in the sitting-room. Lionardo, silent during the earlier discussion, placed himself in front of Michelangelo to proclaim in a pontifical voice:

"Art is a vice."

"Art, a vice!" Michelangelo was amazed at his brother. "How . . . why?"

"Because it is self-indulgence, concentration on your own lust to create instead of contemplating the glories of what God has created."

"But, Lionardo, our churches are plastered with art."

128

"We have been led astray by the devil. A church is not a fair; people must go to pray on their knees, not to see a play painted on the walls."

"Then there is no place for a sculptor in your world?"

Lionardo clasped his hands, gazing devoutly through the ceiling.

"My world is the next world, where we will sit at the right hand of God."

Lodovico rose from his seat, exclaimed: "Now I have two fanatics on my hands."

He left for his midday nap, followed by the rest of the family. Only Monna Alessandra remained sitting quietly in a corner. Michelangelo too wanted to leave; he was feeling tired. The whole day had been a disappointment.

Lionardo would not let him go. He moved into a frontal attack on Lorenzo and the Plato Academy as pagans, atheists, enemies of the Church, antichrists.

"I promise you, Lionardo," began Michelangelo placatingly, "I have heard no sacrilege, irreverence, at least not to religion itself. Only to the abuses. Lorenzo is a reformer; he wants to cleanse the Church."

"Cleanse! A word that infidels use when they mean destroy. An attack on the Church is an attack on Christianity."

Now in a high rage Lionardo accused Lorenzo de' Medici of carnality, debauchery, of leaving the palace at midnight to ride out with his cronies to nights of revelry and seduction of young women.

"Of these charges, I know nothing," said Michelangelo quietly, "but he is a widower. Should he not love?"

"He was a philanderer before the death of his wife. It is common knowledge. His lust has already enfeebled his body."

He wondered how his brother came into possession of such charges. He did not think of Lorenzo as a saint; he had heard him say laughingly to Landino, "I do not err through wickedness, but rather through some part of my nature that loves pleasure," and he remembered Lorenzo's reply to Ficino, "I cannot regret that I love the pleasures of the flesh; for the love of painting, sculpture, and literature are also sensual in nature." All this seemed to him to be the private affair of a virile, effective man.

"Only a toady like yourself would be unable to see that Lorenzo is a tyrant," continued Lionardo.

Michelangelo thought, "This is the second time to-day I have been called a toady!" He became increasingly miserable, his clothes felt tight and ridiculous.

"He has destroyed the freedom of Florence," cried Lionardo. "He has made things soft and easy for the people. He gives them bread and circuses. . . . The only reason he has failed to take a crown and become king is that he is too devious; he likes to work behind the scenes, controlling every move while the Tuscans are reduced to pawns . . ."

Before Michelangelo could reply, Monna Alessandra said, "Yes, Lionardo, he is softening us. He has kept us from civil war! For years we destroyed each other, family against family, neighbourhood against neighbourhood with blood flowing in the streets. Now we are a unified people. Only the Medici can keep us from each other's throats."

Lionardo refused to answer his grandmother.

"Michelangelo, I wish one last word with you."

Michelangelo faced his brother across a heavy mahogany table. He had never been able to talk to this strange boy, or enjoy any companionship with him.

"This is my farewell to you. I leave the house to-night, to join Girolamo Savonarola in San Marco."

"Then Savonarola has arrived? Lorenzo invited him. I was in the *studiolo* when Pico della Mirandola suggested it, and Lorenzo agreed to write to Lombardy."

"A Medici lie! Why should Lorenzo summon him, when it is Savonarola's intention to destroy the Medici? I leave this house as Fra Savonarola left his family in Ferrara: with only a shirt on my back. For ever. I shall pray for you on the floor of my cell until there is no skin left on my knees and the blood comes. Perhaps in that blood you can be redeemed."

Michelangelo could see from Lionardo's burning eyes that there was no use in answering. He shook his head in mock despair, thought: "Father is right. How did this sane, sensible, money-changing Buonarroti family, who have had nothing but conformists for two hundred years, hatch two fanatics in one generation?"

He murmured to Lionardo, "We shall not be too far apart, only a few hundred feet across the Piazza San Marco. If you lean out of the window of your monastery cell you will hear me cutting stone in the garden."

The following week, when he again found three gold coins on his washstand, he decided not to take them home. He went looking for Contessina, found her in the library.

" I must buy a gift."

" For a lady?"

" For a woman."

" Jewels, perhaps?"

" No." Sullenly. " She is the mother of my friends, the stonecutters."

" How about a linen tablecloth bordered with openwork?"

" They have a tablecloth."

" Has she many dresses?"

" The one she was married in."

" A black dress for mass, then?"

" Excellent."

" How big is she?"

He looked bewildered.

" Draw me her picture."

He grinned. " With a pen I know everything: even a woman's proportions."

" I will ask my nurse to take me to the shop to buy a length of black wool. My *sarta* will cut it to fit your drawing."

" You are kind, Contessina."

She wanted no gratitude. " It is nothing."

He went to the outdoor market in the Piazza Santo Spirito and purchased gifts for the other Topolinos, then arranged with one of the grooms in the basement of the palace to borrow a horse and saddlebag. Sunday morning after attending mass in the palace chapel he packed the bag and set out for Settignano, with the sun burning warmly on his bare head. At first he had thought he would change to his old clothes so that the Topolinos would not think he was putting on airs, but quickly realized that this would be an affectation. Besides he fancied himself in the dark blue shirt and hose which he was already wearing.

The Topolinos were sitting on the terrace overlooking the valley and the Buonarroti house on the ridge opposite, enjoying their weekly hour of idleness after returning from mass in the little village church. They were so surprised to see him come riding up the road on a silver-grey stallion, sitting on a silver saddle, that they forgot to say hello. Michelangelo too was silent. He got down from the horse, tied him to a tree, took off the saddlebag and emptied it on to the rough board table. After a moment of silence the father asked what the packages were. Michelangelo replied: "Gifts."

"Gifts?" The father gazed at his three sons in turn, for except to children, Tuscans do not give presents. "Are you late for the last Befana, or early for the next?"

"Both. For four years I ate your bread and drank your wine."

The father replied roughly, "You cut stone for your soup."

"I took my first money home to the Buonarroti. To-day, for the Topolinos, I bring the second."

"You have a commission!" cried the grandfather.

"No. Each week Lorenzo gives me spending money."

The Topolinos scrutinized one another's faces.

"Spending money?" asked the father. "You mean wages."

"I receive no wages."

"Oh, it is keep money: for your room and food?"

"I do not pay for room and food."

"It is purchase money? For your *calze,* or for marble?"

"Everything is provided."

"Then what is it for?"

"To spend on whatever comes to mind."

"If you have food, bed, marble, what would come to mind?"

"Pleasure."

"Pleasure?" The family rolled this word on their tongues as though it were a new fruit. "What manner of pleasure?"

Michelangelo thought about that.

"Well, gambling at seed cards, for example."

"Do you gamble?"

"No."

"What else?"

After a moment: "To be shaved in the straw market."

"Do you have a beard?"

"Not yet. But I could have oil put in my hair like Torrigiani does."

"Do you want oil in your hair?"

132

" No."

" Then it is not a pleasure. What other? "

In desperation: " Well, the women who wear a cowl with a bell on their heads when they walk on Saturday afternoons."

" Do you want these women? "

" I use it as an illustration. I could buy candles to burn before the Virgin."

" That is a duty."

" A glass of wine of a Sunday afternoon? "

" That is a custom."

He walked to the table.

" It is to bring things to your friends."

Slowly, amidst a deep silence, he began distributing his gifts.

" To *mia madre*, for mass. For Bruno, a leather belt with silver buckle. For Gilberto, a yellow shirt and stockings. For *nonno*, a wool scarf for your throat in winter. For Father Topolino, high boots for when you work in Cave Maiano. Enrico, you said that when you grew up you would own a gold ring. *Eccolo*."

For a long moment they gazed at him, speechless. Then the mother went into the house to put on the dress; the father pulled on the high boots; Bruno clasped the belt about his waist; Gilberto donned the new gold shirt; the grandfather stood wrapping and unwrapping the soft wool scarf around his neck. Enrico mounted the horse, the better to admire his ring in privacy.

Then the father spoke.

" All of these . . . these gifts: they are from spending money? "

" All."

" And Lorenzo, he gives you this money to buy us gifts."

" Yes."

" He is truly The Magnificent One."

Michelangelo noticed another package on the table. Perplexed, he opened it, pulled out a linen tablecloth. He remembered Contessina saying, " How about a linen tablecloth? " Contessina had put this gift in the saddlebag as her contribution. The colour rose to his cheeks. *Dio mio!* How could he explain it? He thrust the cloth into the hands of Mother Topolino.

" This is a gift from Contessina de' Medici. For you."

The Topolinos were stupefied.

"Contessina de' Medici! How would she send us a table-cloth? She does not know we live."

"Yes, she does. I told her about you. Her *sarta* sewed your dress."

The *nonno* crossed himself. "It is a miracle."

Michelangelo thought, "Amen. It is true."

6

Each of the Plato Four had his own villa in the country around Florence. They came in several times a week to lecture and work with Lorenzo in the *studiolo*. Lorenzo seemed eager that Michelangelo take advantage of these opportunities, and so he attended faithfully.

The Platonists tried to interest him in Latin and Greek, working up charts to show him that the calligraphy of the two languages was a drawing similar in nature to his figure drawing. He took their manuscripts and assignments to his room, pored over them for hours . . . and learned little.

"Nothing sticks!" he wailed to Bertoldo.

Stopped, the men taught him to read aloud, poetry in the vulgate: Dante, Petrarch, Horace, Virgil. This he enjoyed, particularly the discussions that followed his reading of *The Divine Comedy*, with the interpretation of its philosophy. The Platonists complimented him on his growing clarity of diction, then brought in Girolamo Benivieni, whom they described as "the most fervent partisan of poetry in the *volgare*," to teach Michelangelo how to write his own verse. When he demurred on the grounds that he wanted to become a sculptor, not a poet, Pico said:

"The structure of a sonnet is as rigorous a discipline as the structure of a marble relief. When Benivieni teaches you to write sonnets he trains your mind in the rules of logic and composition of thought. You simply must take advantage of his talent!"

Landino reassured him, "We will not try to weaken your carving arm by replacing hammer and chisel with pen and ink!"

Poliziano added, "You must not give up studying poetry. You must continue to read aloud. To be a complete artist it is not enough to be a painter, sculptor or architect. One must also be a poet, if one is to attain full expression."

"I do so poorly," Michelangelo complained one night to

134

Benevieni when he had tried to make the lines scan; "how can you bear to read my clumsy attempts?"

Benivieni, also a talented musician, chuckled at Michelangelo's despair, sang a gay song of his own composition, then replied, "My early efforts were no better; worse, if anything. You will think you are a bad poet until the day comes when you have a need to express something; then you'll have the tools of poetry at hand, metre and rhyme, just as you have hammer and chisel on your workbench."

On religious holidays when Lorenzo closed the garden, Michelangelo would ride horseback to Landino's villa on the hill in the Casentino, which had been given to him by the Florentine Republic for his commentaries on Dante; to Ficino's villa at Careggi, a castle with battlements and covered galleries; to Pico's The Oak or Poliziano's Villa Diana, both on the slopes of Fiesole. At the Villa Diana they would settle down in a garden pavilion like the one in which the characters from Boccaccio's *Decameron* spun their tales, and listen to Poliziano read his newest poem:

> Come where green the grass is,
> Green the trees are turning.
> Have no fear, fair lasses,
> Every lad is yearning;
> Beasts and birds are burning
> All with love the May. . . .
>
> Youth's a brittle jewel.
> Grass again is greening,
> Age knows no renewal.
> Fair ones, be not cruel
> To your loves the May.

An idea began to shape in Michelangelo's mind: he too would one day have a house like the Villa Diana, with a sculpture workshop and an annual stipend from Lorenzo which would enable him to buy Carrara marbles from which to carve great statues. Was there any reason why he should not be so treated? He was in no hurry, but when Lorenzo did give him one he would like it to be in Settignano, among stonecarvers.

The days and the weeks passed, drawing from live models, transferring the figures to clay, experimenting with scraps of stone to bring forth a knee joint, a hip movement, the turn of a head on its neck, learning how to avoid a welt when the point of his punch broke, studying Lorenzo's Greek sculptures for techniques.

Lorenzo also pushed his education. One Sunday morning he asked Michelangelo to accompany the Medici family to the church of San Gallo where they would hear Fra Mariano, to whose cloister Lorenzo went when he wanted a serious discussion on theology. "Fra Mariano is my ideal," said Lorenzo, "he has graceful austerity, elegant asceticism, and the liberal religion of enlightened common sense. You will hear."

Fra Mariano preached in a mellow voice, harmonious cadences and apt words. He complimented Christianity on its resemblance to Platonism, quoted from the Greeks, declaimed lines from the Latin poets with polished eloquence. Michelangelo was captivated; he had not heard this manner of priest before. When Fra Mariano modulated his voice he was charmed; when Mariano unfolded his argument he was convinced; when Mariano illustrated with a funny anecdote he smiled; when he pressed with serious truths he yielded to their force.

To Lorenzo he said, "I understand better now what the Academy means by modern religion."

One of Piero's grooms knocked on the door of his apartment and entered.

"His Excellency, Piero de' Medici, commands Michelangelo Buonarroti to present himself in His Excellency's anteroom at the hour before sunset."

Michelangelo thought, "How different from his father, who asks if it would give me pleasure to join him." To the groom he replied courteously, "Inform His Excellency that I shall be present."

There was ample time for a soak in a round wooden tub in the bathing closet at the end of the hall, sitting with his knees clasped under his chin, wondering what the crown prince of the Medici dynasty, who had never favoured him with anything more than a formal bow, could want of him. Some instinct told him that his peacock outfit of embroidered shirt and violet cloak was precisely what Piero would approve.

Piero's suite was on the first floor of the palace, just over the open loggia in the corner of the Via de' Gori and Via Larga. Michelangelo had never been in this wing of the palace, not even to see the art works he had heard discussed, because of Piero's coolness. Now his feet dragged along the corridor leading to Piero's suite, for on the walls there was a brilliant painting by Fra Angelico and a delicate marble relief by Desiderio da Settignano.

The groom was waiting outside Piero's anteroom. He admitted Michelangelo. Madonna Alfonsina, Piero's wife, gowned in grey damask embroidered with jewels, was sitting motionless in a high-backed purple throne chair. Covering the wall behind was a tapestry of leaves and flowers, and on the wall to her left, a large oil portrait of her, the cheeks a pale alabaster. Piero pretended he had not heard Michelangelo enter. He stood on a multi-coloured Persian carpet with his back to his guest, studying a bone tabernacle with glass panels, inside which were painted stories of Christ.

Alfonsina stared at Michelangelo imperiously, giving no sign of recognition but sniffing slightly as she always did, as though Florence and the Florentines smelt bad. She had from the beginning made no attempt to conceal her contempt for the Florentines. To the Tuscans, who had hated Rome and everything Roman for centuries, this was infuriating. And Piero de' Medici, half Orsini by inheritance, was now having the other half of his heritage usurped by this second Orsini.

Piero wheeled around, his long thick hair waving down to his shoulders, the face handsome despite the askew cleft in the chin. Without any formal greeting he announced:

"We instruct you, Michelangelo Buonarroti, that we wish Madonna Alfonsina's portrait sculptured in marble."

"Thank you, Excellency," replied Michelangelo, "but I cannot carve portraits."

"Why not?"

Michelangelo attempted to explain that his purpose was not to create any one person. "I could not capture a likeness, as this painter has, that would satisfy you."

"Twaddle! I order you to carve my wife in marble!"

Michelangelo gazed at Piero's contemptuous expression, heard his father's voice saying, "What is it, to be a stone-cutter in the Medici palace? The same as a groom."

Madonna Alfonsina spoke for the first time.

"Kindly remove this discussion to your own room."

Piero angrily opened a door and stalked through. Michelangelo surmised that he had best follow. He closed the door behind him and was surprised to find that, among

137

Piero's silver prizes of helmets and cups won in tournaments, were many fine works of art: Botticelli's Pallas, Bertoldo's Bellerophon, and in niches, ancient painted wood sculptures against a golden ground. Involuntarily he exclaimed:

"Your Excellency has superb taste in the arts."

Piero was not propitiated.

"When I want your opinion I will ask for it. In the meanwhile you will explain why you think you are better than any other of our hirelings."

Michelangelo clenched his anger with his back teeth, forcing himself to reply politely.

"I am a sculptor. Resident in this palace at your father's request."

"We have a hundred tradesmen living off this palace. What they are told to do, they do. You will commence to-morrow morning. And see that you make Her Excellency into a beautiful statue."

"Not even Mino da Fiesole could do that."

Piero's eyes flashed.

"You ... you ... *contadino!* Pack your rags and get out of our presence."

Michelangelo went to his room, began throwing clothing from the chest on to the bed. There was a knock. Contessina entered with her nurse.

"I hear you have been feuding with my brother."

He leaned down to take something from the bottom of the chest.

"Stand up here and talk to me!" Imperiously.

He rose, went close to her.

"I have nothing to say."

"Is it true that you refused to carve Alfonsina's portrait?"

"I refused."

"Would you refuse if my father asked you to do his portrait?"

Michelangelo was silent. Would he refuse Lorenzo, for whom he felt so deep an affection?

"Would you refuse if I asked?"

Again he was trapped.

"Piero did not ask me," he replied quietly. "He ordered me."

There were hurried footsteps in the corridor. Lorenzo came into the room, his skin unusually dark, his eyes snapping. The nurse stammered:

138

"Excellency . . . I tried to stop her . . ."

Lorenzo waved her away.

"I will not have this happen in my home."

Michelangelo's eyes blazed.

"I asked your father to cede you to me, did I not?"

"Yes."

"Then I am responsible for you."

"I have no apologies to offer."

"I am not asking for apologies. You came in here as one of the family. No one will treat you as . . . as an entertainer . . . or order you out of your own home."

Michelangelo's knees went weak. He sat down on his bed. Lorenzo spoke more gently.

"But you, too, have much to learn . . ."

"Admitted. My manners . . ."

". . . that you do not rush back here every time you are offended, and start packing your possessions. That is poor loyalty to me. Is that understood?"

Michelangelo rose, trying to hold back the tears.

"I owe Piero an apology. I said something unkind about his wife."

"He owes you one. What you wish to say to him in return is your own business."

Contessina lagged behind to whisper over her shoulder:

"Make it up with Piero. He can cause a lot of trouble."

7

The time had arrived to try a theme. What was a theme? And which themes interested him?

"It must be a Greek theme," decreed the Plato Four. "It should come out of the legends: Hercules and Antaeus, the Battle of Amazons, the Trojan War," proffered Poliziano, with particles of cantaloup clinging to his enormous dark lips. "It would be in the mood of the frieze on the Parthenon at Athens."

Michelangelo said, "But I know little of such matters."

Landino, his face grave, replied:

"That, my dear Michelangelo, is what we have been trying to suggest for the past months: that as your *ex officio* tutors we teach you about the Greek world and its culture."

139

Pico della Mirandola laughed, and the *studiolo* was filled with the music of violas and clavichords.

"What I think our friends are trying to say is that they would like to guide you back to the golden age of paganism."

They told him stories of the twelve tasks of Hercules, Niobe suffering for her dying children, of the Athenian Minerva, the Dying Gladiator. Lorenzo moderated the discussion in his slightly unpleasant voice.

"Do not issue edicts to our young friend. He must come to a theme of his own free will."

Michelangelo pulled back into his seat and sat with his head resting on the back of the chair, his eyes gleaming amber in the candlelight that brought whorls of red to his chestnut hair. He listened to his own voices. One thing he knew for certain: his first theme could not come from Athens or Cairo or Rome or even Florence. It had to come from him, something he knew and felt and understood. Otherwise he would be lost. A work of art was not like a work of scholarship; it was personal, subjective. It had to be born within.

Lorenzo had asked, "What do you want to say?" To himself he replied, "Something simple, about which I can feel deeply. But what do I know? Even about myself? That I want to become a sculptor, and that I love marble? I can carve no sculpture out of these sentiments."

Then, against the murmur of voices, he saw himself standing on the steps of the Rucellai chapel the day he had first gone with the Ghirlandaio studio to Santa Maria Novella. He saw the chapel vividly before him, the Cimabue and Nino Pisano Madonnas, and felt again his love for his mother, his sense of loss when she was gone, his aloneness, the hunger for love.

It had grown late. The meeting broke up. Lorenzo remained. Though at times his tongue was said to have a rough edge, he spoke with naturalness and clarity.

"You must forgive our Platonists their enthusiasm," he said. "Ficino burns a lamp before Plato's bust. Landino gives the finest literary banquet of the year on Plato's anniversary. For us, Plato and the Greeks are the key that has let us escape from a dungeon of religious prejudices. We are trying to establish here in Florence another age of Pericles. In the light of our ambition, you must understand the excesses of our zeal."

"If you are not tired, Lorenzo," said Michelangelo, "could we make a little tour of the palace and look at the Madonnas and Child?"

Lorenzo took up the highly polished bronze lamp. They went down the corridor until they came to the anteroom of Lorenzo's office, in which there was a Donatello marble relief, so remote and impersonal, Michelangelo thought, as to prevent identification. From here they went to Giuliano's bedroom. The youngest Medici continued to sleep, the covers pulled up over his face, while Michelangelo and Lorenzo discussed Pesellino's Madonna and Child with Two Little Angels, painted on a wooden table. They trod the corridors examining the Fra Filippi Lippi Virgin Adoring Child on the altar of the chapel, about which Lorenzo explained that the models were the nun, Lucrezia Buti, with whom Fra Filippo had fallen in love, and the child of their mating, Filippino Lippi, now a painter who had been trained by Botticelli, even as Botticelli had been trained by Fra Filippo. They examined the Neri di Bicci Madonna; then went on to Luca della Robbia's Madonna and Child with the Medici crest, all in high glowing colour; and finally to Lorenzo's bedroom to see the Botticelli Madonna of the Magnificat, painted for Lorenzo's father and mother some twenty years before.

"Those two angels kneeling before the Virgin and Child are my brother Giuliano and myself. When the Pazzi murdered him, the brightest light went out of my life. . . . The portrait of me is an idealization, as you can see. I am a homely man, and not ashamed of it; but all painters think I want to be flattered. Benozzo Gozzoli did so in our chapel, as well; they make my dark skin light, my turned-up nose straight, my scraggly hair as beautiful as Pico's."

Lorenzo shot him a piercing look, lips compressed, brow stern.

"You appear to know I don't need flattery."

"Granacci says I'm crusty," said Michelangelo, embarrassed.

"You are armed in adamant," declared Lorenzo. "Stay that way."

Lorenzo told him the legend of Simonetta Vespucci, original of Botticelli's Madonna of the Magnificat, "the purest beauty Europe has known," said Lorenzo. "It is not true that Simonetta was my brother Giuliano's mistress. He was in love with her, as was all Florence, but platonically. He

141

wrote long sentimental poems to her . . . but had my nephew Giulio by his real mistress, Antonia Gorini. It was Sandro Botticello who truly loved Simonetta; though I doubt if he ever spoke to her in person. She is the woman in all his paintings: Primavera, Venus, Pallas. No man has ever painted such exquisite female beauty."

Michelangelo was silent. When he thought of his mother he saw her too as a beautiful young woman; yet it was a different beauty he felt, one coming from within. Not a woman desirable to all men, as was Botticelli's love; but one who would love a son and be loved by him. He turned his face up to Lorenzo, speaking in full confidence.

" I feel close to the Madonna. She is the only image I have of my mother. Since I still have to search for my technique, wouldn't it be best to know what I'm trying to say?"

" It could be best," replied Lorenzo gravely.

" Perhaps what I feel about my mother will be true of what she felt about me."

He haunted the rooms of the palace, drawing after the masters, sometimes with Contessina or Giuliano keeping him company. Then he grew impatient with other men's ideas and went into the poorer parts of town where the women worked on the sidewalks before their houses, weaving cane chair seats or demijohn covers, with their babes on their laps or at the breast. He went into the countryside to the *contadini* around Settignano who had known him since he was a child, and who gave no second thought to his drawing them while they bathed or suckled their young.

He was not looking for portraiture but for the spirit of motherhood. He drew the mother and child in every position he found, seeing the true relation between them through his charcoal and paper; and then, for a few scudi, persuaded the women to move, change, shift themselves and the child to give him more angles of approach, to search for . . . he knew not what.

With Granacci, Torrigiani, Sansovino and Rustici he went out to the art of Florence, drawing concentratedly on the Madonna and Child theme, listening to Bertoldo dissect each piece as they spent their hours trying to learn how their predecessors had achieved their results.

The Bernardo Rossellino in his home church of Stanta Croce, Michelangelo found to be a fat expressionless mother and child; and in the same church a Desiderio da Settignano, a *contadina* and *bambino* wrapped in Tuscan swaddling clothes, ordinary folk in from the country for a *festa*. They went to Orsanmichele to see the Orcagna Virgin of the Nativity, which was tender and loving and had power, but to Michelangelo seemed primitive and wooden. The free-standing Nino Pisano in Santa Maria Novella appeared to be the best carved, but the well-groomed Pisan merchant's wife holding her expensively clothed earthling son was poorly proportioned and without spirituality. A Verrocchio terra-cotta Virgin and Child presented a middle-aged Madonna gazing in perplexity at this son who was already standing up and blessing the world. On they moved to Agostino di Duccio's Virgin and Child, richly garbed young elegants with blank coy faces.

The next morning he went for a walk alone up the Arno towards Pontassieve. The sun was biting hot. He took off his shirt, exposing his chest to its germinal heat. The blue Tuscan hills blurred and faded back in serried ranges. He loved these mountains.

Striking off into the hills, with the feel of the steep slope under him, he realized that he had not yet come to grips with what he wanted to convey about Mary and her child. He knew only that he wanted to attain something fresh and vital. He fell to musing about the character and fate of Mary. The Annunciation was a favourite theme of the Florentine painters: the Archangel Gabriel come down from heaven to announce to Mary that she was to bear the Son of God. In all the paintings he remembered, the news seemed to come to her as a complete surprise, and apparently she had been given no choice.

But could that be? Could so important a task, the most important assigned to any human since Moses, have been forced on Mary without her knowledge or consent? Surely God must have loved Mary above all women on earth to choose her for this divine task? Must He not have told her the plan, related every step of the way from Bethlehem to Calvary? And in His wisdom and mercy have allowed her the opportunity to reject it?

And if Mary did have freedom of choice, when would she be likely to exercise it? At the Annunciation? When she had borne her child? At a moment of suckling, while Jesus was still an infant? Once she accepted, must she not carry her burden from that moment until the day that her child was crucified? Knowing the future, how could she subject her son to such agony? Might she not have said, " No, not my son. I will not consent. I will not let it happen "? But could she go against the wish of God? When He had appealed to her to help Him? Was ever mortal woman cast in so pain-fraught a dilemma?

He decided that he would carve Mary at the moment of decision, while suckling her infant, when, knowing all, she must determine the future: for herself; for her child; for the world.

Now that he understood what he was about, he was able to draw with a purpose. Mary would dominate the marble. She would be the centre of the composition. She would be heroic in stature, a woman not only given the freedom to come to her own decision but with the inner force and intelligence to make it. The child would be secondary; present, vitally alive, but in no way distracting.

He would place the child on his mother's lap, his face buried in his mother's breast, but his back fully turned on his viewers. This would give the child his natural place, caught at the most urgent activity of his day; and by the same symbolism this could be the moment when Mary would feel most urgently that her decision had to be made.

As far as he knew, no one had sculptured or painted Jesus with his back turned. Yet his drama would not be begun for some thirty years. This was the mother's time, and the mother's portrait.

He reviewed the hundreds of sketches of mother and child he had made in the past months, extracting those that would fit his new concept, and with the sketches on a table before him began his search for the background of the theme. Where was Mary at the time? Here was a drawing showing a mother sitting on a bench at the bottom of a flight of stairs. Who besides her child was with her? Here were any number of young children in attitudes of play. The figure of Mary could be a composite of these strong Tuscan mothers. But how did one portray the face of a Madonna? His memory of his own mother's appearance was nearly ten years old now, and had a vague dreamlike quality.

He put the drawings aside. Was it possible to conceive a piece of sculpture without knowing the marble from which it would draw its sustenance?

He sought out Granacci, who had been given one of the largest rooms in the casino as his painting studio, and asked if they could visit the stone shops of the city.

144

"I'll work better if I have the marble at hand so I can see and feel it, and learn about its inner structure."

"Bertoldo says marble shouldn't be bought until the drawings and models are completed; then you can be sure you will choose an adequate block."

"It could work the other way round," he answered thoughtfully. "I think it's a kind of wedding . . ."

"All right, I'll tell Bertoldo some fancy yarn, and we'll go to-morrow."

Florence had dozens of stone stores scattered through the Proconsul section, with all sizes and shapes of granite, travertine, coloured marbles, as well as ready-cut building stones, doorframes, window seats, columns. But they failed to turn up the Carrara block for which Michelangelo was searching.

"Let's walk up to the Settignano yards. We'll have a better chance there," he suggested.

In the old yard where Desiderio had trained Mino da Fiesole, he saw a piece that captivated him at once. It was of modest size, but its crystals were gleaming white. He poured water on it to look for cracks, struck its ends with a hammer to listen for its sounds, tested for flaws, bubbles, stains.

"This is the one, Granacci," he cried with glee. "It will hold the Madonna and Child. But I'll have to see it by the first rays of sunlight. Then I'll know for sure it's perfect."

"If you think I'm going to sit on the ground worshipping your marble until dawn . . ."

"No, no, you settle the price. I'll borrow a horse from the Topolinos for you so you reach home alive."

"You know, *amico,* I don't believe a word of this 'sunrise tells all' nonsense. What can you conceivably see at sunrise that you don't see better right now in a strong light? I think it's a kind of pagan worship: fertility rites you have to perform at dawn to make sure the gods of the mountains are propitiated."

Michelangelo slept on a blanket under the Topolino arches, left before the first morning light and was standing over his marble when the fingers of dawn came over the hills. The block was as though translucent. His eyes could pierce through its width and height and breadth; through the built-up layers of crystals compounded within its structural unity. There was no perceptible flaw: no crack or hollow, no discoloration, the crystals flickering brilliantly on its surface.

"You are a noble block," he said aloud.

145

He paid the owner Granacci's gold coins, loaded the marble on to the Topolino cart and rode off behind the pair of undulating white oxen as he had ridden from the Cave Maiano since he was six. He drove down the hill, turned right at Varlungo, went along the shore of the Affrico River, past the ancient Porta alla Croce marking the fourth limit of the city, along the Borga la Croce, past the hospital of Santa Maria Nuova, turned right at Via Larga in front of the Medici palace, through the Piazza San Marco to the garden gate, as proud as though he were carrying home his bride.

Two of the stonemasons helped take the block to the shed. He then moved his drawing table and working equipment from the casino. Bertoldo came to the back of the garden, puzzled.

" You are ready to begin carving?"

" No. I'm a long way yet."

" Then why move from the casino?"

" Because I would like to work in quiet."

" Quiet? You won't be out of sound of those hammers of the *scalpellini* all day."

" That is a good sound. I was raised with it."

" But I must spend some time at the casino with the others. If you're near me, I can suggest and correct when you need help."

Michelangelo thought for a moment, then said, " Bertoldo, I feel the need to be solitary, to work beyond all eyes ; even yours. I could have instruction when I came to ask."

Bertoldo's lips trembled. " You will make more mistakes that way, *caro*, and continue in them longer."

" Isn't that the best way to learn? To carry one's mistakes to their logical conclusion?"

" A word of advice can save you time."

" I have time."

Bertoldo withdrew behind his tired pale eyes. Then he smiled.

" *Davvero*. You have time. When you want help come to me."

Late that afternoon when the others had left the garden, Michelangelo turned to find Torrigiani glaring at him.

" Now you're too good even to draw next to me."

" Oh, Torrigiani! It's just that I want a little privacy . . ."

" Privacy! From me? Your best friend? You didn't

want privacy all that first year while you needed help and company. Now that *Il Magnifico* has selected you . . ."

"Torrigiani, please believe me, nothing has changed. I've only moved a hundred and fifty feet . . ."

"It's the same as moving fifty miles. I told you that when you were ready I would set up a sculptor's bench next to mine."

"I want to make my mistakes by myself."

"Or is it that you're afraid we'll steal your secrets?"

"Secrets!" Michelangelo was growing angry. "What secrets can a beginning carver have? This is my first theme. You've already done half a dozen."

Torrigiani insisted, "It's me you're rejecting."

Michelangelo fell silent. Was there an element of truth in the accusation? He had admired Torrigiani's physical beauty, stories, songs . . . but he no longer wanted to talk and listen to anecdotes with the block of marble standing challengingly by.

"You spoiled fast!" declared Torrigiani. "I've been patronized before. But the ones who do it always come a cropper."

A few minutes later Granacci arrived, looking dour. He inspected the anvil, rough board table on horses, workbenches and drawing desk on a platform raised off the ground.

"What's wrong, Granacci?"

"It's Torrigiani. He came back to the casino in a black funk. Said some unpleasant things about you."

"I heard them first."

"Look, Michelangelo, I'm now on the other side of the *calcio* field. A year ago I warned you against paying too much attention to Torrigiani. Now I have to warn you that you're not being fair. Don't cut him off. . . . I know of your growing preoccupation with marble, but Torrigiani doesn't see anything so magical about marble, and quite justifiably thinks it results from your life in the palace. If we threw over our friends because we grew fatigued with them, how many of our friendships would last?"

Michelangelo ran his thumb in a silhouetting line over the block.

"I'll try to make it up to him."

8

"Marble" was derived from the Greek word meaning "shining stone." How his block glistened in the early morning sunlight as he set it up vertically on the wooden bench, gazing at the lustre produced by the light penetrating a short way and being reflected at the surface of the deeper-lying crystals. He had lived with this block for several months now, studied it in every light, from every angle, in every degree of heat and cold. He had slowly come to understand its nature, not by cutting into it with a chisel but by force of perception, until he believed he knew every layer, every crystal, and precisely how the marble could be persuaded to yield the forms he needed. Bertoldo said that the forms had first to be released before they could be exalted. Yet a marble contained a myriad of forms; had this not been so, all sculptors would carve identically.

He picked up his hammer and *subbia* and began cutting with the *colpo vivo*, the live blow, his passage handled in one "Go!", the chisel continuing in an uninterrupted direction as he used the point, a finger that dug delicately into the marble and threw out substance; the toothed chisel, a hand that refined the textures left by the point; the flat chisel, which was as a fist, knocking down the grooves of the toothed chisel. He had been right about this marble block. It obeyed every sensitivity he hoped to impart to it as he worked downward towards his figures through the successive layers.

The marble turned light into the dark unexplored corners of his mind, opening him up to the seeds of new conceptions. He was not working from his drawings or clay models: they had all been put away. He was carving from the images in his mind. His eyes and hands knew where every line, curve, mass must emerge, and at what depth in the heart of the stone to create the low relief; for only a quarter of the figure would emerge.

He was at work in his shed when he received a visit from Giovanni, the first time the fifteen-year-old near-cardinal had come to see him since he had been brought to the garden by Contessina a year before. In spite of the fact that he was totally unblessed with looks, Michelangelo found his expression intelligent and alert. Florence said that the easygoing, pleasure-loving second son of Lorenzo had ability but that he would never use it because the obsession of his life was to avoid trouble. He was flanked by his saturnine shadow, his fifteen-year-old cousin Giulio, in whom nature had undertaken the task of creating Giovanni's opposite: tall, spare, with an angular face, straight nose and cleft chin, arched dark eyebrows, large eyes: handsome, graceful, efficient, loving trouble as his natural *métier,* but as cold and hard as a corpse. Recognized as a Medici by Lorenzo, but despised by Piero and Alfonsina because of his illegitimacy, Guilio could make a place for himself only through one of his cousins. He had attached himself to fat, good-natured Giovanni and had craftily insinuated himself into the position where he did all of Giovanni's work, took care of his unpleasantnesses, provided his pleasures and made decisions as Giovanni would have wanted them. When Giovanni became a full cardinal and moved to Rome, Guilio would accompany him.

" Giovanni, how kind of you to visit," said Michelangelo.

" It's not really a visit," replied Giovanni in his plump voice. " I came to invite you to join my big hunt. It is the most exciting day of the year for the whole palace."

Michelangelo had heard about the hunt: how Lorenzo's hunters, horsemen and grooms had been sent to a spot in the mountains which abounded with hares and porcupines, stags and wild boar ; how the entire area had been enclosed by sailcloth and was guarded by the *contadini* of the neighbourhood to keep the stags from jumping the cloth fence or the boars from tearing holes through it, which would let out the sea of game. He had never seen the phlegmatic Giovanni so buoyed with enthusiasm.

" Forgive me, but as you can see I am in the marble, and I cannot leave off."

Giovanni looked crestfallen. " You are not a labourer. You can work when you wish. You are free."

Michelangelo clenched and unclenched his fist around the chisel which he had shaped octagonally so that it would not slip in his fingers.

" That is debatable, Giovanni."

" But who would hold you?"

" Me."

' You would really prefer your work to my hunt?"

149

"Since you give me a choice, yes."

"How very odd. I wouldn't have believed it. You want only to work? You have no room for diversion?"

That word was a stickler to Michelangelo, even as the word "pleasure" had been to the Topolinos. He wiped the matted marble dust off his perspiring upper lip.

"Doesn't everyone have his own definition of diversion? For me, marble has the excitement of the hunt."

Giulio said in an undertone to his cousin, "May we be spared from zealots."

In his first sentence directed to Giulio, Michelangelo asked, "Why am I a zealot?"

Giovanni replied, "Because you are interested in only one thing."

Giulio spoke again in an undertone to Giovanni. Giovanni replied, "You are entirely right," and the two young men moved off without a further word.

Michelangelo returned to his carving, the incident going out of his mind. But not for long. In the cool of dusk Contessina entered the garden. Coming close to Michelangelo's marble and speaking softly, she said, "My brother Giovanni says you frighten him."

". . . frighten him? But I haven't done anything."

"Giovanni says you have a kind of . . . ferociousness."

"Tell your brother not to despair of me. Perhaps I am too young to be broken to pleasure."

Contessina threw him a searching look.

"Giovanni's hunt is his supreme effort of the year. For those few hours he is the head of the Medici family, and even my father takes orders from him. If you reject his hunt it is as though you were rejecting Giovanni, setting yourself up as superior to him. He is kind, he never wants to hurt anyone. Why should you want to hurt him?"

"I don't want to hurt him, Contessina. It's just that I don't want to break the mood. I want to carve all day and every day until I'm finished."

She cried, "You've already made an enemy of Piero! Must you do the same to Giovanni?"

He could think of nothing to answer. Then, the mood broken, he put down his three-toothed chisel, dampened a large white cloth in water at the fountain, covered his piece. The day would come when he would let no one stop him at his work!

" All right, Contessina. I'll go."

For a rhythmical movement he had learned to pick up
hammer and chisel at the same instant, the point held loosely
so that it could move freely without restricting the hammer
force, his thumb curling over the tool and holding it by his
four fingers, automatically shutting his eyes against chips at
the moment of the impact. Working in low relief, he could
cut away but little, and had to chain the physical force
within himself. His point entered the marble at a near-
perpendicular angle, but as he approached the forms with
the highest projections, the Madonna's face and the back of
Jesus, he had to change his position.

There were so many things to think of at one time. His
strokes had to hit towards the main mass, strike the marble
towards the block it came out of, so that it could sustain the
blow. He had designed his figures and stairs in a vertical
position to lessen the possibility of cracking the block, but
found that the marble would not yield to exterior force
without accenting its own essence: stoniness. He had not
realized to what extent marble had to be battled. His respect
for his material grew blow by blow.

Bringing out the live figures involved long hours and
longer days, a slow peeling off, layer by layer. Nor could
the birth of substance be hastened. After each series of
blows he stepped back to inspect his progress.

On the left-hand side of his design there descended the
flight of heavy stone steps. Mary was seated in profile on a
bench to the right, the broad stone balustrade giving the
illusion of ending in her lap, just under her child's
knee. He saw that if Mary's strong left hand, holding the
child's leg securely, were to open more widely, be moved
out a little on a flat plane, it could be holding firmly not
only her son but also the bottom of the balustrade, which
would become an upright beam. Mary would then be supporting on her lap both the weight of Jesus and, if she
made the choice to serve God as He had asked, the cross on
which her son would be crucified.

He would not force the symbolism on the viewer, yet it
would be there for anyone to see who might feel it.

Now he had the upright, but where was the transverse bar?
He studied his drawings to find a way to complete the
imagery. He looked at the boy, John, playing on top of the

steps. If he threw the plump arm across the balustrade at a right angle . . .

He drew a fresh charcoal sketch, then began digging deeper into the crystalline flesh of the marble. Slowly, as he penetrated the block, the boy's body and right arm formed the living, pulsating crossbeam. As it should have, since John was to baptize his cousin Jesus and become an integral part of the passion.

With the carving of images of two other small children playing above the stairs, his Madonna and Child was finished. He began under Bertoldo's rigorous instruction the one task in which he had no training: polishing. Bertoldo hammered into him the evils of " overlicking," which rendered a piece sweetly sentimental. Since he had worked the block on the south wall of his shed he now asked Bugiardini to help him stand the thirteen-by-eighteen-inch plaque against the west wall so that he could polish it in the indirect north light.

First he used a rasp to bring down the rough surfaces, then he washed away the fine marble dust. He found holes which Bertoldo explained had been made at an early stage of his work when the chisel had penetrated too deeply, mashing crystals beneath the surface.

" Use a fine-grain emery stone with water," Bertoldo instructed. " But with a light hand."

This accomplished, he once again washed his block with water. Now his work had a tactile quality similar to that of mat paper. Next he used lightweight pumice stones to refine the surface and expose fresh, sparkling crystals, running his fingers over the surface to feel the new silklike texture. When he found himself needing better lighting to observe the subtle surface changes he took down the planks of the north and east walls. In the new intense light the values changed. He felt obliged to wash down the carving, sponge it, let it dry . . . start all over with emery stone and pumice.

Slowly the highlights emerged: sunlight on the Madonna's face, on the curls, left cheek and shoulder of the child. On the foredrapery covering the Madonna's leg, on the back of John as he straddled the balustrade, on the inside of the balustrade itself to accent its importance in the structure. All the rest, the block-seat, stairs, walls were in quiet shadow. Now, he thought, one saw and felt the crisis, the intense emotional thinking reflected on Mary's face as she felt the tug of Jesus at her breast and the weight of the cross in her hand.

Lorenzo summoned the Plato Four. When Michelangelo entered the room with Bertoldo they found that the block had been mounted on a high flat altar covered with black velvet.

The Plato group was hilarious.

"You have carved a Greek figure, after all!" cried Poliziano exultantly.

Pico said with an intensity unusual for him, "When I look at your carving I am outside Christianity. Your heroic figure has the impenetrable divinity of ancient Greek art."

"I agree," added white-haired Landino; "the carving has a tranquillity, a beauty and superhuman aspect that can only be described as Attic."

"But why should it be?" asked Michelangelo numbly.

"Why? Because you fell right off the Acropolis into Florence," exclaimed Ficino.

"You're a pagan at heart, the same as we are. *Magnifico*, could we have that ancient stele brought from your office, the seated woman on a grave relief?"

Within a matter of moments the palace groom had brought to the studio not only the ancient stele but several of the more portable Madonnas and Child, with which the Platonists attempted to prove that Michelangelo's carving bore no relationship to Christian carvings.

"It was not supposed to," he replied a little heatedly. "I set out to create something original."

Lorenzo had been enjoying the scene.

"Michelangelo has achieved a synthesis: his work is both Greek and Christian, beautifully fused, presenting the best of both philosophies. That should be particularly apparent to you who have spent your lives trying to achieve a unity of Plato and Christ."

Michelangelo thought, "Not one word have they said about Mary and her moment of decision. Is the meaning buried too deep? Or is that the part they find Greek? Because the child is not yet committed?"

Bertoldo, who had remained silent, growled, "*Allora*, let us speak of sculpture. Is it good? Is it bad?"

Michelangelo was ignored as though he were not in the room. He gathered that they liked his first major work be-

153

cause they considered it a child of humanism. They were delighted at the revolutionary idea of the Christ child with his back towards the viewer; of Mary's noble knowledgeability. They were enthusiastic about his achievement in perspective, which was just beginning to be understood in marble; not even Donatello had attempted it in his Madonnas, being content to suggest that angels and cherubs were vaguely behind the main figures. They were impressed with the projecting power of the three main figures, bursting with tension, one of the most vitalic low reliefs they had seen.

There were also things they did not like. They told him without mincing words that they found the Madonna's face to be overstylized, her superabundance of draperies diverting. The figure of the child was too muscular, the position of its arm and hand awkward; the figure of John so oversized as to be brutalized . . .

Lorenzo cried, "Stop, stop, our young friend has worked a half a year on this project . . ."

". . . and thought it through entirely by himself," interjected Bertoldo; "any help I gave was purely academic."

Michelangelo stood up to draw their attention.

"First, I hate draperies, I want to work only in the nude; and I simply failed to control them. As for the Madonna's face, I could never find it. In my own mind, I mean, and that is why I could never draw or carve it with more . . . reality. But I would like to tell you, now that it is finished, what I hoped to accomplish."

"The room is full of ears," quipped Poliziano.

"I wanted the figures to be real and believable so that you would feel that with their very next breath would begin life itself."

Then, shyly, he explained his thinking about Mary and her child, and her moment of decision. Lorenzo and the Plato Four fell silent, studying the marble. He felt them searching, pondering. Then, slowly, one by one, they turned back to him; pride was in their eyes.

When he returned to his apartment he found a leather pouch on his washstand. It was filled with bright gold florins, just how many he could not imagine.

"What is this?" he asked Bertoldo.

"A purse from Lorenzo."

Michelangelo picked up the pouch and walked to the

staircase adjoining the apartment, up to the first floor and down the corridor to Lorenzo's bedroom. Lorenzo was sitting at a small table, before an oil lamp, writing letters. He turned in his chair as his valet announced Michelangelo.

"Lorenzo, I can't understand why . . ."

"Gently, gently. Sit down here. Now, start at the beginning."

Michelangelo gulped, quieted himself.

"It's this purse of money. You should not have to buy the marble. It is yours already. I've lived in the palace while carving it, you've given me everything . . ."

"I was not buying the piece, Michelangelo. It belongs to you. The purse is a kind of completion prize, similar to the one I gave Giovanni when he completed his ecclesiastical studies at Pisa. I thought you might like to travel and see other art works. North through Bologna, Ferrar and Padua to Venice? South through Siena to Rome and Naples? I will give you letters of introduction."

Despite the lateness of the hour Michelangelo rushed home to the Via dei Bentaccordi. Everyone was asleep, but they quickly gathered in the family room, each carrying a candle, their nightcaps askew. Michelangelo spilled out the golden coins in a dramatic sweep across his father's desk.

"But . . . what . . . what . . .?" Lodovico stumbled.

"My prize money. For completing the Madonna and Child."

"It's a lot," exclaimed his uncle. "How much?"

"I haven't stopped to count," replied Michelangelo loftily.

". . . thirty, forty, fifty," counted his father. "Enough to support a family in ease for half a year."

As long as he was showing off Michelangelo decided he should do a thorough job, and so he asked, "Why should not six months of my work support a family for half a year? That is simple justice."

Lodovico was jubilant.

"I haven't had my hands on fifty gold florins for a long time. Michelangelo, you must start on another piece immediately, to-morrow morning, since they are so well paid."

Michelangelo was amused. No word of thanks. Only undisguised joy at running his hands through this pile of gold pieces shimmering in the candlelight. Ironically, he remembered his own cry for marble when Lorenzo first invited him into the palace!

"We're going to look for another farm," cried Lodovico.

"Land is the only safe investment. Then with the extra income . . ."

"I'm not sure I can let you do that, Father. *Il Magnifico* says he is giving me the florins for travel: to Venice or Naples, to see all the sculptures . . ."

"Travel to see sculptures!" Lodovico was aghast, his new acres disappearing before his eyes. "What purpose will it serve to look at sculptures? You look, you leave, the money is gone. But with new farms . . ."

His brother Buonarroto asked, "Are you really going travelling, Michelangelo?"

"No," said Michelangelo laughingly, "I want only to work." He turned to Lodovico. "They're yours, Father."

9

Several times a week Bertoldo insisted that they go to the churches to continue drawing from the masters. They carried wooden stools with them so they could move with the changing light. They were sketching in the Branacci chapel in the Carmine. Torrigiani set his stool so close to Michelangelo's that his shoulder pressed against Michelangelo's arm. Michelangelo moved his stool a little. Torrigiani was offended.

"I can't draw without a free arm," explained Michelangelo.

"What are you so cranky about? All I wanted to do was amuse us while we work. I heard a bawdy new ballad last night . . ."

"I want to concentrate."

"I'm bored. We've drawn these frescoes fifty times. What more is there to learn?"

"How to draw like Masaccio."

"I want to draw like Torrigiani. That's good enough for me."

Without looking up Michelangelo barked impatiently, "But not good enough for me."

"Look who's talking! I won three drawing prizes last year. How many did you win?"

"None. That's why you'd better let me learn."

Torrigiani felt he had been scored against. He said with a

156

crooked smile, " I'm surprised the favourite student still has to submit to these schoolboy exercises."

" Copying Masaccio is not a schoolboy exercise, except to a schoolboy mind."

" Oh, so now your mind is better than mine." Flaring, " I thought it was only your drawing hand?"

" If you could draw, you would know there is no difference."

" And if you could do anything else but draw, you would know how little you are alive. It's as they say: little man, little life, big man, big life."

" Big man, big wind."

Torrigiani was furious. Michelangelo swivelled on his stool to face the painting by Filippino Lippi of the emperor's son whom St. Peter had raised from the dead, the one for which Granacci had posed when he was thirteen. Torrigiani pushed his stool around so that he could stare head on at Michelangelo.

" You meant that as an insult!"

He sprang up from his stool, put his massive hand on Michelangelo's shoulder and yanked him to his feet. Michelangelo had time to see the grim set of Torrigiani's expression, which told him that Torrigiani was striking with all his might; but he had no chance to duck or avoid the blow. Torrigiani's fist exploded on the bridge of his nose with the sound of powder exploding behind a cut of *pietra serena* in the Maiano quarry. He tasted blood and crushed bone in his mouth; and then, as from a distance, heard Bertoldo's anguished cry.

" What have you done?"

While stars burst in a black heaven, Michelangelo heard Torrigiani reply:

" I felt his bone and cartilage crumble like biscuit beneath my knuckles . . ."

Michelangelo slipped angularly to his knees, the blue stars circling the painted chapel. He felt the hard cold cement against his cheek, saw the dead-green Granacci on the fresco, then lost consciousness.

He awakened in his bed in the palace. There were wet cloths over his eyes and nose. His head was a mass of pain. As he stirred, someone removed the cloths. He tried to open his eyes but could achieve only the slightest slit. Bending over him was Pier Leoni, Lorenzo's physician, Lorenzo and

Bertoldo. There was a knock on the door. He heard some-one enter, say:

"Torrigiani has fled the city, Excellency. Through the Porta Romana."

"Send our fastest riders after him. I'll lock him in the stocks with his back against the Signoria wall . . ."

Michelangelo let his lids fall again. The doctor resettled him on the pillow, wiped his mouth, then began exploring his face with his fingers.

"The bridge of his nose is crushed. The bone splinters may take as long as a year to work their way out. The passage is completely closed now. Later, if he's lucky, he'll be able to breathe through it again."

He slipped an arm under Michelangelo's shoulder, raised him slightly and pressed a cup to his lips.

"Drink. It will put you to sleep. When you wake the pain will be less."

It was torture to open his lips, but he gulped down the warm herb tea. The voice above him receded. Once again he slipped off, heard Torrigiani's jeering words in his ears, saw the spinning blue stars and felt the cold paving on his cheek.

When he awakened he was alone in the room. The pain had localized now, and he felt the throbbing behind his eyes and nose. There was light out of the window.

He pushed aside the covers, got out of bed, reeled, caught the side of the wash table to steady himself. Then, summon-ing courage, looked up into the mirror. Once again he had to grip the edge of the table to keep from fainting: for he could barely recognize his own face in the glass. Both of his eyes were swollen the size of blue goose eggs. He struggled to get the lids opened a trifle more, saw a wild palette of discoloration: purples and lavenders, orange and burnt sienna.

He would not be able to know the full consequence of Torrigiani's blow until the swelling went down. It would be weeks, perhaps months before he could see how completely his erstwhile friend had accomplished, in reverse, the re-draughting job on his face for which he had longed. That one powerful blow from Torrigiani's big fist had thrown his face out of focus as surely as though Torrigiani had been shaping soft wax.

Shivering with fever, he crawled on hands and knees back into his bed, pulled the covers over his head as though to

158

wipe out the world and reality. And he was sick at heart. His pride had brought him to this low, beaten state.

He heard the door open. Unwilling to see anyone, he remained motionless. A hand pulled back the cover from his head. He found himself gazing up at Contessina.

" Michelangelo *mio*."

" Contessina."

" I'm sorry it happened."

" Not so sorry as I."

" Torrigiani got away. But Father swears he'll catch him."

Michelangelo moved his head painfully on the pillow.

" It would do no good. I blame myself. I taunted him . . . beyond his powers of endurance."

" He began it. We've heard the story."

He felt hot tears stinging his eyes as he forced himself to say the cruellest words that could escape his lips:

" I'm ugly."

Her face had been close to his as they spoke, almost in whispers to ensure their privacy from her nurse, who lolled uncertainly at the open door. Without moving she placed her lips on the swollen distorted bridge of his nose; and he felt their faint warm moisture like an annealing balm. Then she was gone from the room.

The days passed. He could not bring himself to leave the palace, even though the swelling and pain continued to recede. His father heard the news, came to assess the damage. Lodovico seemed happier to be vindicated in his judgment on art and artists than saddened at what had happened to his son's face. He was also concerned that the three gold florins might not show up while Michelangelo was confined to his room.

" Will Lorenzo stop your wage?"

Michelangelo was furious.

" It isn't a wage. And it won't be stopped because I'm not working. Perhaps nobody will think I have use for the money while I am locked up here."

Lodovico grumbled, " I counted on it," and left.

" He has no right to reproach me," sighed Michelangelo to Buonarroto when he came to visit, bringing a bowl of chicken soup with toasted almonds from Lucrezia. Buonarroto was now apprenticed to the Strozzi in the cloth trade. His expression was serious.

" Michelangelo, men need a little money of their own.

This is a good time for you to put aside some florins. Let me come for a few weeks and mind the money for you."

Michelangelo was touched at his brother's sympathetic concern, and amused at his new-found business acumen.

Lorenzo visited for a few moments each afternoon, bringing a new cameo or ancient coin for them to discuss. *Il Cardiere* wandered by with his lyre to sing a salty version of the goings-on in Florence, including Michelangelo's mishap in rhymed couplets. Landino came to read Dante; Pico to show him some new findings on Egyptian stone carvings which indicated that the Greeks learned their main sculpture principles from the Egyptians. Contessina came with her nurse for the hour before dark, to study and chat. Even Giovanni and Giulio stopped by for a moment. Piero sent condolences.

Jacopo of the implike face and Tedesco the redhead came over from Ghirlandaio's to assure him that if they saw Torrigiani on the streets of Florence they would stone him clear out of the Porta Prato. Granacci spent hours in the apartment, bringing drawing materials and folios. The doctor came to probe his nose with sticks, and finally assure him that he would breathe through one nostril at least. Bertoldo was charming about having his privacy invaded. He tried to comfort Michelangelo.

"Torrigiani thought to flatten your talent with his fist so it would reach his own level."

Michelangelo shook his head. "Granacci warned me."

"Still, it is true: people who are jealous of talent want to destroy it in others. You must come back to work now. We miss you in the garden."

Michelangelo studied himself in the mirror over the washbasin. The bridge of his nose had been caved in permanently. With a massive hump in the middle, the nose careened from the corner of his right eye towards the left corner of his mouth, wiping out whatever symmetry it had had before. He winced.

"What a botched-up piece of sculpture! The stone was soft and filled with holes. It shattered at the first blow of the hammer. Now it is spoiled, without balance or design, scarred like an abandoned quarry in a mountainside. I was never much to look at; but how I loathed this crushed-in view of myself."

He was filled with a bitter despair. Now he would truly be the ugly sculptor trying to create beautiful marbles.

10

The swelling receded, the discoloration faded; but he was
still unable to present himself to the world in this changed,
mutilated form. If he could not face Florence in the light,
he slipped out late at night and walked the silent streets for
hours, working off his caged energies. How different the
city looked with the oil lamps lighted high on the palaces,
how much larger the slumbering stone buildings seemed in
the starlight!

Poliziano came to the apartment one day, ignoring Bertoldo, and asked:

"May I sit down? Michelangelo, I have just completed
my translation of Ovid's *Metamorphoses* into Italian. While
I was translating Nestor's tale of the centaurs I thought of
what a fine carving you could make of the battle between
the centaurs and the Thessalians."

Michelangelo sat on the bed watching Poliziano intently,
comparing their uglinesses as Poliziano crouched forward in
the chair, his beady eyes and oily black hair seeming to
Michelangelo as moist as the purple, repulsively carnal lips.
Yet ugly as Poliziano was, his face was lit by an inner glow
as he spoke of Ovid and his poetic recounting of the Greek
tales.

"The opening lines will set the stage:
Pirithous took as bride young Hippodame;
To celebrate the day, tables were set up
And couches placed for greater luxury
Beside them in a green, well-arboured grotto.
Among the guests were centaurs, rugged creatures
(Half horse, half man, conceived in clouds, they say),
Myself, and noblemen of Thessaly . . ."
In his soft, modulated voice Poliziano went on to tell of the
gaiety of the palace:
". . . Oh the bride was lovely!
Then we began to say how sweet the bride was
But our intentions began to bring ill fortune to the wedding.
Eurytus, craziest of rough-hewn centaurs,
Grew hot with wine, but when he saw the bride
Was that much hotter: tables were rocked,
Turned upside down, then tossed away.

Someone had seized the bride and mounted her.
It was Eurytus, while the other centaurs
Took women as they pleased, first come, first taken,
The scene was like the looting of a city . . ."

Vividly he projected the scenes into the room: Theseus
swinging an ancient urn full of wine across Eurytus' face,
until the creature's brains burst forth from the broken skull;
Gryneus throwing the altar on the heads of two men;
Rhoetus killing his man " by thrusting torch and fire down
his throat."

Michelangelo's eyes went to the cupboard on which stood
the model for Bertoldo's Battle of the Romans and Bar-
barians. Poliziano followed his gaze.

" No, no," he said, " Bertoldo's Battle is a copy of the
sarcophagus at Pisa, a reproduction, actually. Yours would
be original."

Bertoldo was furious.

" You are lying! Michelangelo, I'll take you to Pisa and
show you. To-morrow! You will see that in the centre of
the sarcophagus there are no figures at all. I had to re-
create them. I introduced whole new themes for narrative,
like my riding warrior . . ."

Poliziano put his manuscript into Michelangelo's hands.

" Read it at your leisure. I thought of you carving the
scenes even while I translated them. You could not find a
more powerful theme."

Bertoldo ordered horses that night. At dawn they were
riding down the Arno to the sea, past Empoli, until the
dome and leaning Campanile of Pisa stood against the
powder-blue sky. Bertoldo led Michelangelo directly into
the Camposanto, a rectangular cemetery surrounded by a
wall begun in 1278; its galleries were lined by some six
hundred tombs and ancient sarcophagi. Bertoldo made for
the Roman battle scene and, coveting his pupil's good
opinion, elaborately explained the differences between this
sarcophagus and his own Battle. The more he pointed out
the differences the more Michelangelo saw the similarities.
Placatingly, he murmured:

" You told me that even in art we all have to have a father
and a mother. Nicola Pisano, starting modern sculpture
right on this spot, was able to do so because he saw these
Roman sarcophagi that had been hidden for a thousand
years."

Mollified, Bertoldo took them to an *osteria* behind a

grocery store, where they ate tunny fish and beans, and while the old man slept for a couple of hours Michelangelo returned to the Duomo, and then to the Baptistery, much of it designed by Nicola and Giovanni Pisano, containing Nicola Pisano's masterpiece, a marble pulpit with five high reliefs.

Outside once again, he looked at the Campanile leaning dizzily against the brilliant Pisan sky. He thought, " Bertoldo was only partly right: it is not enough to be an architect and sculptor; one must also be an engineer!"

Riding home in the cool dusk with the soft, modelled hills gliding past, the horses' hoofs rhythmic on the hard-packed dirt road, Michelangelo began to see pictures in his mind; of struggles between men, of the rescue of women, of the wounded, the dying. When they had reached the palace and Bertoldo had fallen into a fast sleep, he lit a lamp and began reading Poliziano's translation.

He had read only a few pages when he asked himself, " But how could one carve this legend? It would require a piece of marble the size of a Ghirlandaio fresco." Nor could a sculptor use all the weapons employed in the mythological battle: altars, torches, spears, antlers, javelins, tree trunks. The marble would turn out to be a jumble.

He recalled an earlier line and leafed back through the pages until he found it:

" Aphareus lifted a sheet of rock ripped from the mountainside . . ."

The image was vivid for him. He became excited. Here could be a unifying theme, and unifying force. His theme! Since one could not portray all weapons he would use only one, the earliest and most universal: stone.

He pulled off his shirt and *brache* and stretched himself under the red coverlet, his hands behind his head. He realized that he had been out all day, among people, and had not once thought of his nose. Equally important, images began crowding through his mind: not of the Camposanto or the Pisano Baptistery; but of the Battle of the Centaurs.

" Glory be to God," he thought, " I'm cured."

Rustici was overjoyed. " Didn't I tell you to sketch horses? A work of art without a horse is nothing."

Amused, Michelangelo replied, " Now if you can show me where to find some centaurs . . ."

The tension was gone from the garden. No one mentioned Torrigiani's name or referred to the quarrel: Torrigiani had not been caught, and probably never would be. Excited by his new project, Michelangelo concentrated on the resolving of his theme. Poliziano, flushed with pleasure, gave a summary of the centaur's role in mythology while Michelangelo sketched rapidly, drawing what he imagined it might be like: the whole of the horse except the shoulders, neck and head; and emerging from the body of the horse, the torso and head of a man.

He cared little for mythological legends, they were foreign to his nature. He was drawn to reality, as much of it as he could grasp; for him, the truest, most significant reality was the male figure, containing within itself the prototype of all other forms and designs.

He began searching within himself for an over-all design into which he could fit some twenty figures. How many separate scenes of action could there be? What would be the central focus, from which the eye would move in orderly, perceptive manner as he, the sculptor, wanted?

In the Roman Battle sarcophagus in Pisa and Bertoldo's Battle relief the warriors and women were clothed. As long as he was going back to Greek legend he felt he had the right to carve nudes, unencumbered by helmets, robes, loincloths which in his opinion cluttered Bertoldo's bronze. Hoping to achieve simplicity and control, he eliminated clothing as he had ruled out horses and the multiplicity of centaurs and weapons.

With this decision he got nowhere. Even Granacci could not help him.

" It was never possible to get nude models."

"Couldn't I rent a small studio somewhere, work alone?"

Granacci shook his head angrily. " You are Lorenzo's protégé; everything you do reflects on him."

" Then there's only one thing left to do. I'll work up at the Cave Maiano."

He walked up to Settignano in the cool of evening. As he came across the dark fields and forded the creek at the bottom of the ravine, he had a moment of apprehension. The Topolinos had heard about the fight with Torrigiani; but they would make no such scene as had occurred in the Buonarroti home the first time he returned, with his stepmother and aunt weeping, his uncle cursing, and his grandmother standing silent, her eyes dry, but suffering for him as he had suffered for himself.

The Topolinos greeted him casually. They were pleased that he was spending the night. If they noted the damage to his face, or even peered through the dark evening to gauge its extent, he could not tell it.

He washed in the creek at dawn, then made his way over the ox roads rutted along the contour of the hills to the quarries, where the stonemasons began work an hour after sunrise. From the top of the mountain he looked down on a castle surrounded by parallel lines of olives and grapevines. In the quarry the *pietra serena* cut the afternoon before was a turquoise blue while the older blocks were taking on a beige tone. Ten columns had been completed, and a huge panther blocked out, surrounded by a sea of chips. The quarrymen and masons were already forging and tempering their tools; each used twenty-five points in a day, so quickly did the *pietra serena* wear them down.

The masons were in good humour, greeting Michelangelo jovially.

" Come back to the quarries to do an honest day's work, eh? Once a stonemason always a stonemason."

" In this weather?" quipped Michelangelo. " I'm going to sit under a cool tree and never pick up anything heavier than a stick of charcoal."

They needed no further explanation.

The *pietra serena* threw off tremendous heat. The masons removed their clothes, everything except breechclout, straw hat and leather sandals. Michelangelo sat watching them. They could not pose, they had their day's stone to cut; and their small bodies, lean, wiry, bumpy, were a long way from the ideal of Greek beauty that he had seen in early statues. But in the warm sun the sweat on their skin caused them to shine and glisten like polished marble. They used every muscle of back and shoulder and leg to cut and lift the stone. They were completely unself-conscious as he sketched them, seeking the strength that lay buried in the indestructible bodies of these skilled craftsmen.

When the morning was half spent the masons gathered in their " hall," a cave cut out of the *pietra serena* as the base of the mountain which remained the same temperature the year round. Here they ate their breakfast of herring and onion, bread and red Chianti wine. Michelangelo told them of his proposed Battle of the Centaurs.

" It's time this ridge of stone under Mount Ceceri produced another sculptor," said a young, hard-bodied quarryman. " We have always had one: Mino da Fiesole, Desiderio da Settignano, Benedetto da Maiano."

In a few minutes they returned to work and Michelangelo to his drawing, working close up now, catching the tensions of the hands, the protrusion about the second phalanges, where the skin was stretched from holding hammer and chisel. How much there was to learn about the human body! How many thousands of intricate parts, each different, each with its fascinating detail. An artist could draw the human figure all his life and still catch only a fraction of its changing forms.

When the sun was high overhead several young boys appeared, carrying on their shoulders long branches with a row of nails in them, and hanging from each nail a basket with a man's dinner. Once again they gathered in the cool " hall." The quarrymen shared their vegetable soup, boiled meat, bread, cheese and wine with Michelangelo, then lay down for an hour's sleep.

While they slept he drew them: sprawled out on the ground, hats over their faces, their bodies quiet, recuperative, the lines tranquil, the forms somnolent. By the time they awakened the children had returned bringing fresh water to drink and for the forge; turning the wheels, sharpening the tools, using their hammers and chisels to help. Michelangelo sketched their supple limbs in action.

The next morning as he left the palace he was surprised to have a monk stop him, ask his name, take a letter from the folds of his black robe, and disappear as soundlessly as he had appeared. Michelangelo unfolded the note, saw his brother's signature, began to read. It was a plea to Michelangelo to abandon the pagan, godless theme which could only put his soul in jeopardy; and if he must persist in carving graven images, to do only those sanctified by the Church.

" The Battle of the Centaurs is an evil story," Lionardo concluded, " told to you by a perverted man. Renounce it and return to the bosom of Christ."

Michelangelo reread the letter, shaking his head with disbelief. How could Lionardo, buried within the monastery walls, know what theme he was carving? And that it had been inspired by Poliziano? He was only an apprentice. How could anyone consider a learning-theme important enough to tattle about? He was a little frightened at how much the monks inside San Marco knew of everyone's business.

He took the letter to the *studiolo,* showed it to Lorenzo.

"If I am doing you harm by carving this theme," he said quietly, "perhaps I ought to change?"

Lorenzo seemed weary. Bringing Savonarola to Florence had been a mistake and a disappointment. "That is precisely what Fra Savonarola is trying to accomplish: to cow us all, to impose his rigid censorship. We are not going to help him convert the Duomo into the Stinche. If we give in on the smallest detail it will be easier for him to win the next one. Continue your work."

Michelangelo threw his brother's letter into a bronze Etruscan pot under Lorenzo's desk.

11

He used pure beeswax which came in cakes, placing a container over his charcoal fire and breaking the wax into small bits. When it had cooled he kneaded it with his fingers into strips. In the morning he poured a little *trementina* on to his fingers to make the wax more pliable. Since this sculpture was to be in high relief, the outer half of the figures would emerge from the marble.

Moonfaced Bugiardini, who was growing to hate stone carving with a ferocity deep as Granacci's, began spending his days at the shed, gradually taking on manual tasks and becoming Michelangelo's assistant. Michelangelo had him chop a wooden block the size of the marble block he intended to use, and drive wires through it for an armature. Then from his exploratory drawings he began modelling the wax figures, attaching them to the armature, balancing the intertwined arms, torsos, legs, heads and stones as they would tumble backward in the final marble.

He found the block he wanted in the palace yard. Bugiardini helped him bring the stone into his shed and set it up on round wooden beams to protect its corners. Just to stand and gaze at it gave Michelangelo a sense of intense power. When he began roughing out he worked with his whole body, planting both feet wide apart for support, throwing all his weight into the arm holding the hammer, achieving the sculptor's equilibrium: the force to remove must be equal to the marble to be taken away. He remembered having scraped a pan with a piece of metal and having felt the metal in his teeth; now he felt the marble in his veins.

167

It was his desire to communicate his existence in space. That was one reason he had known that he must be a sculptor: to fill the void of emptiness with magnificent statues, statues of noble marble, expressing the richest, most profound feelings.

In its formation his four-foot block had a veining like wood, angling off to where the sun rises. He checked for due east and rolled the block into the same position in which it had lain in its mountain bed. He would have to cut across the grain, north and south, otherwise his marble would peel in fragmented layers.

He drew a deep breath, raised his hammer and chisel for the opening assault. Marble dust began to cover his hands and face, penetrating his clothes. It was good to touch his face and feel its dust, it was the same as touching the marble he was working on; he had the sensation of becoming one with his medium.

Saturday nights the palace emptied. Piero and Alfonsina visited with the noble families of Florence, Giovanni and Giulio began a social round, Lorenzo sought pleasure with his group of young bloods, according to rumour, participating in orgies of drinking and love-making. Michelangelo never knew whether these tales were true; but the next day Lorenzo would be wan and listless. His gout, inherited from his father, would keep him in bed or hobbling about the palace with a heavy cane.

On such evenings Michelangelo was free to have supper with Contessina and Giuliano on the open loggia of the top floor, in the soft night air. As they ate cold watermelon and chatted over candlelight, Contessina told him of having read the Boccaccio comments on the centaurs.

"Oh, I've already left the original battle far behind," he laughed.

He took paper from inside his shirt, a piece of charcoal from his purse, and, moving the charcoal rapidly over the paper, he told Contessina what he was after. Man lived and died by stone. To suggest the unity of man and marble, the heads and the blocks being thrown would be indistinguishable. All twenty men, women and centaurs would be but one, each figure a facet of man's many-sided nature, animal as well as human, female as well as male, each attempting to destroy the other parts. He indicated with swift strokes some of the sculptural goals he was trying to achieve: the three receding levels of figures, each level in lower relief but not lower in vitality, the half-released forms appearing to be free-standing, each figure radiating its own force.

"I once heard you say that behind a carving there must be worship. What will there be to worship in your version of man's battle?"

"The supreme work of art: the male body, infinite in its expressiveness and beauty."

Contessina unconsciously looked down at her thin legs, the barely beginning-to-blossom bosom, then met his eyes amusedly.

"I can blackmail you for your pagan worship of the body of man. Plato might agree with you, but Savonarola would have you burned as a heretic."

"No, Contessina. I admire man, but I worship God for being able to create him."

They laughed, their heads close. Seeing Contessina's eyes move to the door and her head come up sharply, a mottled flush come to her cheeks, he turned and could tell from Lorenzo's posture that he had been standing there for a considerable time. Their intimacy had permeated the room, irradiating the atmosphere. Michelangelo had not been conscious of it. But interrupted at its height, it provided an aura that neither he nor Contessina nor Lorenzo could miss. Lorenzo stood silent, his lips compressed.

". . . we were . . . discussing . . . I had made some drawings . . ."

The harshness receded from Lorenzo's brow. He came forward to look at the drawings.

"Giulio reports your meetings to me. Your friendship is good. It can hurt neither of you. It is important that artists have friends. And Medici as well."

A few nights later when the moon was full and the air stirring with wild scents, they sat together in a library window seat overlooking the Via Larga and the enclosing hills.

"Florence is full of magic in the moonlight," sighed Contessina. "I wish I could look down from a height and see it all."

"I know a place," he exclaimed. "Just across the river It's as though you could reach out your arms and embrace the city."

"Could we go? Now, I mean? We could slip out of the back garden, separately. I'll put on a full head cape."

They walked the way he always went, at a sharp angle

towards the Ponte alle Grazie, crossing the Arno and climbing up to the ancient fort. Sitting on the stone parapet, it was as though they were dangling their feet in the grey stone waters of the city. Michelangelo pointed out her father's villa in Fiesole, the Badia just below it; the wall of eight towers guarding the city of the foot of the Fiesole hills; the glistening white cluster of Baptistery, Duomo and Campanile; the golden-stoned, high-towered Signoria; the tight oval city enclosed by its walls and river; and on their side of the river the moonlit Pitti palace built of stone from its own quarry in the Boboli gardens just behind the parapet.

They sat a little apart, touched by the moon, caught up in the beauty of the city and the ranges of hills that embraced them as fondly as was Florence by her walls. Their fingers fumbled slowly towards each other on the rough surface of the stone; touched and interlocked.

The repercussion came quickly. Lorenzo, who had been taking the baths at Vignone for several days, summoned him from the garden. He was seated at the big desk in his office, its walls covered with a map of Italy, a map of the world, the Sforza castle in Milan; the tables and shelves bearing a collection of hard stone vases, ivories, purple leather volumes of Dante and Petrarch, a Bible bound in purple velvet with silver ornaments. Standing beside him was his secretary, Ser Piero da Bibbiena. Michelangelo did not need to be told why he had been sent for.

"She was safe, Excellency. By my side the whole time."

"So I gather. Did you really think you would not be observed? Giulio saw her going out the rear gate."

Miserable now, Michelangelo replied, "It was indiscreet." He lifted his eyes from the richly patterned Persian rug, cried, "It was so beautiful up there; as though Florence were a marble quarry, with its churches and towers cut out of a single stratum of stone."

"I am not questioning your conduct, Michelangelo. But Ser Piero does question its wisdom. You know that Florence is a city of wicked tongues."

"They would not speak evil of a little girl."

Lorenzo studied Michelangelo's face for a moment.

"'Contessina' can no longer be interpreted as 'little girl.' She is growing up. I had not fully realized it before. That is all, Michelangelo, you can return to work now, as I know you are impatient to do."

Michelangelo did not move, even though he had been dismissed.

"Is there not something I can do to make amends?"

"I have already made them." Lorenzo came from behind his desk, put both hands on the boy's trembling shoulders. "Do not be unhappy. You meant no wrong. Change for dinner, there is someone you should meet."

The last thing Michelangelo wanted in his wretched state was to eat with sixty guests; but this was no time to disobey. He washed splashingly out of his bowl, donned a russet silk tunic, and went up to the dining hall where a groom took him to a seat Lorenzo had saved next to Gianfrancesco Aldovrandi, of one of the leading families of Bologna. Lorenzo had named Aldovrandi *podestà* or visiting mayor of Florence for the year 1488. Michelangelo's concentration was not very good, his mind and stomach were in a turmoil. Aldovrandi turned his full attention on him.

"His Excellency was so kind as to show me your drawings and the marble Madonna and Child. I was greatly stimulated."

"Thank you."

"I am not indulging in compliments. I speak because I am a sculpture enthusiast myself, and I have grown up with the magnificent work of Jacopo della Quercia."

Michelangelo numbly asked who he might be.

"Ah, that is why I asked *Il Magnifico* if I could speak to you. Jacopo della Quercia is not known in Florence, yet he is one of the greatest sculptors that Italy has produced. He was the dramatist in stone, as Donatello was the poet. It is my hope that you will come to Bologna and permit me to show you his work. It could have a profound influence on you."

Michelangelo wanted to reply that profound influences were precisely what he wished to avoid; yet Aldovrandi would prove to be a prophet.

During the ensuing days Michelangelo heard that Piero and Alfonsina had several times protested against "a commoner being allowed to associate on such intimate terms with a Medici"; and Ser Piero da Bibbiena had written to Lorenzo at the baths, a veiled but strong note saying, "If some decision is not taken about Contessina, we may regret it."

It was not until several nights later that he learned what Lorenzo meant by amends. Contessina had been sent for a visit to the Ridolfi villa in the country.

12

He received a message from his father. The family was
concerned about Lionardo, who had been reported ill in the
monastery at San Marco.

"Could you use your Medici connections to get in to see
Lionardo?" asked Lodovico, when he went to see them.

"No outsider is allowed in the monks' quarters."

"San Marco is a Medici church and monastery," said his
grandmother, "built by Cosimo and supported by Lorenzo."

After a number of days he found that his requests were
being ignored. Then he learned that Savonarola would
preach in San Marco the following Sunday.

"The monks will all be there," Bertoldo told him. "You
will get a look at your brother. You might even exchange
a few words. Bring us back a report on the friar."

San Marco was delightfully cool in the early morning. His
plan to take up a position at the side door leading in from
the cloister, so that Lionardo would have to pass close to
him, was spoiled by the presence of the tight knot of monks
in their black habits who had been praying and chanting in
the choir since before morning light. Their cowls were pulled
so far forward that their faces were buried. It was impossible
for Michelangelo to see whether Lionardo was in the group.

The church was by no means full. When a murmur announced the entrance of Savonarola, he slipped into a pew
close to the pulpit and sat on the edge of the hard bench.

There was little to mark a difference between Savonarola
and the other fifty-odd monks as he slowly climbed the
pulpit stairs. His head and face were deep in his Dominican
cowl, a slight figure under the robe. Michelangelo could see
little but the tip of his nose and a pair of dark veiled eyes.
His voice had harsh northern accents; at first it was quiet,
but soon it took on a commanding tone as he expounded his
thesis on the corruption of the priesthood. Never, even in
the most heated attacks in the palace, had Michelangelo
heard the slightest part of the charges Savonarola now levied
against the clergy: the priests were political rather than
spiritual, put into the Church by their families for worldly
gain; they were careerists and opportunists seeking only

wealth and power; guilty of simony, nepotism, bribery, selling of relics, accumulation of benefices: "The adulteries of the Church have filled the world."

Warming to his task, Savonarola pushed back the cow' and Michelangelo got his first view of the friar's face. He found it as emotionally disturbing as the words that were coming with accelerating heat and rapidity from the contradictory mouth, the upper lip thin and ascetic as the material of a hair shirt, the lower lip more fleshy and voluptuous than Poliziano's. The black eyes flashing to the farthest corner of the church were sunken under high-boned, hollowed-out cheeks, obviously the victims of fasting; his nose jutted outward in a massive ridge with wide, flaring nostrils. It was a dramatic face that could have been invented by no artist save Savonarola himself. The bone structure fascinated Michelangelo as a sculptor, for the dark marble-like chin was carved from the same flesh as the passionate hanging underlip, polished with pumice and emery stone.

Michelangelo tore his eyes from Savonarola's face so that he might better hear the words that were now pouring like molten bronze, the voice filling the church, reverberating off the hollow chapels, returning to invade the left ear after it had boxed and reddened the right.

"I have beheld your proud ambition to invade Rome and contaminate all things, until she has become a false, proud harlot. O Italy, O Rome, O Florence, your villainies, your impieties, your fornications, your usuries, your cruelties are bringing us tribulations. Give up your pomps and shows. Give up, I tell you, your mistresses and your love boys. The earth is covered with blood, but the clergy cares not a rap. They are far indeed from God, those priests whose worship is to spend the night with harlots, the days gossiping together in the sacristies. The altar itself has been turned into a clerical shop. The sacraments are the counters of your simony. Your lust has made of you a brazen-faced whore. Once you were at least ashamed of your sins; once priests had the grace to call their sons nephews. They no longer bother now. 'I will descend on you in your scurrility and your wickedness,' says the Lord, 'upon your whores and your palaces.'"

He scourged the people of Florence, cried out that Dante had used Florence as his model for the City of Dis:

> *Within the second circle are confined*
> *Hypocrisy and flattery, and those*

Who practise witchcraft, sorcery and theft,
Falsehood and Simony and suchlike filth.

Summoning his will, for Savonarola's voice was a paralyzing agent, Michelangelo looked around and saw that the congregation was sitting as one individual, soldered together.

"The whole of Italy will feel God's wrath. Her cities will fall prey to foes. Blood will run in the streets. Murder will be the order of the day. Unless ye repent! repent! repent!"

The cry of "Repent!" echoed around the church a hundredfold while Savonarola pulled his hood forward, masking his face, prayed long and silently, then came down the pulpit stairs and out of the cloister door, leaving Michelangelo deeply moved, a little exalted, a little sick. When he was again out in the hot glaring sunshine of the piazza he stood blindly blinking, unwilling to go to his home or to the palace, not knowing what to say. Finally he sent word to his father that he had been unable to see Lionardo.

The emotional upheaval had faded when he received a note from Lionardo asking him to come to San Marco at vespers. The cloister was beautiful at dusk, the grass freshly cut, the hedges trimmed, jasmine and sunflowers growing in the shade of the arches, the atmosphere tranquil and secluded from the world.

Lionardo seemed to Michelangelo as cadaverous as Savonarola.

"The family has been worried about your health."

Lionardo's head shrank deeper into the cowl. "My family is the family of God."

"Don't be sanctimonious."

When Lionardo spoke again Michelangelo detected a touch of affection.

"I called for you because I know you are not evil. You have not been corrupted by the palace. Even in the midst of Sodom and Gomorrah, you have not been debauched, you have lived like an anchorite."

Amused, Michelangelo asked, "How do you know these things?"

"We know everything that goes on in Florence." Lionardo took a step forward, held out his bony hands. "Fra Savonarola has had a vision. The Medici, the palace, all the obscene, godless art works within its walls will be destroyed. They cannot save themselves; but you can, for your soul is not yet lost. Repent, and forsake them while there is still time."

"Savonarola attacked the clergy, I heard his sermon, but he did not attack Lorenzo."

"There are to be nineteen sermons, starting on All Saints' Day, through to Epiphany. By the end of them, Florence and the Medici will be in flames."

They stood side by side in the airless corridor along one side of the cloister. Michelangelo was shocked into silence.

"You won't save yourself?" implored Lionardo.

"We have different ideas. All of us can't be the same."

"We can. The world must be a monastery such as this, where all souls are saved."

"If my soul is to be saved, it can only be through sculpture. That is my faith, and my discipline. You said that I live like an anchorite; it's my work that keeps me that way. Then how can that work be bad? Wouldn't God give me a choice, as long as we both serve Him equally?"

Lionardo's eyes burned into Michelangelo's for a moment. Then he was gone, through a door and up a flight of stairs.

"Into a cell decorated by Fra Angelico, I hope," said Michelangelo to himself, a little bitterly.

He felt he owed it to Lorenzo to attend the All Saints' Day sermon. This time the church was full. Again Savonarola began in a quiet, expository manner, explaining the mysteries of mass and the wholeness of the divine word. The new-comers seemed disappointed. But the friar was just working up warmth; soon he had moved into oratory, and then into crescendo, his mighty voice whipping the congregation with its impassioned eloquence.

He attacked the clergy: "Ye hear it said, 'Blessed the house that owns a fat cure.' But a time will come when rather it will be said, 'Woe to that house.' Ye will feel the edge of the sword upon ye. Affliction shall smite ye. This shall no more be called Florence, but a den of thieves, of turpitude and bloodshed."

He attacked the moneylenders: "Ye are guilty of avarice, ye have corrupted the magistrates and their functions. None can persuade ye that it is sinful to lend at usury, but rather ye hold them to be fools that refrain from it."

He attacked the morals of Florence: "Ye have fulfilled the saying of Isaiah: 'They declare their sin as Sodom, for

175

they hide it not,' and that of Jeremiah: 'Thou hadst a whore's forehead, thou refusedst to be ashamed.'"

He declared: "I vowed not to prophesy, but a voice in the night said, 'Fool, dost thou not see that it is God's will that thou shouldst continue?' That is why I cannot stop prophesying. And I say unto ye: know that unheard-of times are at hand!"

There was a deepening murmur in the church. Many of the women were weeping.

Michelangelo rose, made his way up a side aisle, the angry voice following through the door. He crossed the Piazza San Marco, entered the garden and retreated to his shed, shaking as though with ague. He resolved not to return to the church: for what had this recital of lust and avarice to do with him?

13

Contessina found him in the library where he was sketching from the illustrations in an ancient manuscript. She had been away for several weeks. Her face was ashen. He jumped up.

"Contessina, you have been ill? Sit down here."

"I have something to tell you." She sank into the chair, leaned forward to the cold hearth as though to warm her hands. ". . . the contracts have been drawn."

"Contracts?"

"For my marriage . . . to Piero Ridolfi. I did not want you to hear of it from the palace gossip."

After an instant he asked brusquely, "Why should it affect me? Everyone knows that Medici daughters are given in political marriages: Maddaleno to Franceschetto Cibo, the Pope's son; Lucrezia to Jacopo Salviati . . ."

"I don't know why it should affect you, Michelangelo, any more than it should affect me."

He met her eyes squarely, for the first time.

"And does it?"

"How could it? Everyone knows that Medici daughters are given in political marriage."

"Forgive me, Contessina. I was hurt."

"It's all right," she smiled wistfully. "I know you by now."

"And the marriage . . . when?"

176

" Not for a while. I am too young. I asked for another year."

" Yet everything has changed."

" Not for us. We are still friends in the palace."

After a silence, Michelangelo asked, " Piero Ridolfi, he will not make you unhappy? He is fond of you?"

Contessina looked up at him with her head bowed.

" We do not discuss such matters. I will do what I must. But my feelings are my own."

She rose, went close to him. He hung his head like a dumb beast in a storm. When at last he looked up he saw tears sparkling in her eyes. He reached out his hand, tentatively, and slowly she placed her fingers into his until they were locked together quite hard. Then she withdrew, leaving behind only her faint mimosa scent, and a hot dryness in his throat.

There was no way to keep Savonarola's ringing voice out of his ears, for Lionardo's warning became a reality. In the midst of his second sermon against vice in Florence, Savonarola suddenly cried out against the Medici, blamed Lorenzo for the evil of the city, predicted the downfall of the ruling family and, as a climax, the Pope in the Vatican.

The Plato Academy assembled hastily in the *studiolo*. Michelangelo reported the first two sermons, then told of Lionardo's warning. Though Lorenzo had had his monumental battles with the Vatican, at this moment he wanted to keep the peace with Pope Innocent VIII because of Giovanni, who had only a few months to wait before he was invested a full cardinal and would leave for Rome to represent the Medici. The Pope might well imagine that since Lorenzo had summoned Savonarola to Florence, and Savonarola was preaching in a Medici church, he was attacking the papacy with Lorenzo's knowledge and consent.

" It is a good thing he is attacking me at the same time," he murmured ruefully.

" We'll simply have to shut him up," growled Poliziano.

" We need only to put an end to his prophecies," said Lorenzo. " They are no part of our religion or of his office. Pico, that much you will have to undertake."

The first defection came from the sculpture garden. Granacci reported that the fun-loving Baccio fell silent for hours on end, then took to disappearing for a day or two at a time. Soon he began making derogatory remarks about the

177

Medici; then he began extolling the virtues of Savonarola and the spiritual life of the cloister. One day he deserted to the Dominicans.

Savonarola's sermons in San Marco were now attracting such large crowds that late in March, for the second Sunday in Lent, he transferred his activities to the cathedral. Ten thousand Florentines stood packed together, yet dwarfed by the enormousness of space around them. In the few months that had passed since Michelangelo had heard him preach in San Marco, several changes had come over the friar. Because of his rigid fasting, the penance on his knees in the cells of San Marco, he could barely summon the strength to mount the pulpit stairs. He had assumed a complete identification of himself with Christ.

"As ye can see and hear, I do not speak with my own tongue but that of God. I am His voice on earth."

A cold shiver ran through the congregation. Savonarola was no less moved than his admirers.

Michelangelo timed his arrival at the Duomo to meet his father and the rest of the family, deserters from Santa Croce to hear the new prophet, with the end of the service. He stood inside the door and gazed up at the Donatello and Luca della Robbia choir stalls high on either side of the central altar: marble carvings of children at play, singing, dancing, laughing, serenading with musical instruments, pure Greek in their joyous love of life, in their testament to the beauty of their young bodies. For Michelangelo, the marbles cried out, "People are good!" while Savonarola was thundering "Humanity is evil!"

Who was right? Donatello and Della Robbia? Or Savonarola?

The gloom of the church sat heavily around the Buonarroti dinner table. Lucrezia was in tears.

"That wicked man. He has ruined my beautiful white veal. From now on, Lodovico, if you wish to hear Savonarola preach it must be after dinner and not before."

Though the city was shaking in a religious upheaval, Michelangelo kept working calmly. Unlike Savonarola, he could not persuade himself that God was speaking through him, but he did feel that if God saw He would approve the work.

He felt a grudging admiration for Savonarola. Was he not an idealist? As for his fanaticism, had not Rustici said,

"You're like Savonarola, you fast because you can't bring yourself to stop work in the middle of the day"?

Michelangelo grimaced at the accusation. Yet did he not feel a dedication to the task of revolutionizing marble sculpture even as Phidias had taken death-worshipping Egyptian sculpture and rendered it Greek-human? Would he not have been willing to fast and pray until he barely had the strength to drag himself through the garden to his workshop, if that were necessary?

And what was wrong with God speaking to His children? Surely He had the right? The power? He believed in God. If God could create the earth and man, could He not create a prophet . . . or a sculptor?

The Signoria invited Savonarola to address them in the great hall of the Palazzo della Signoria. Lorenzo, the Plato Four, the important Medici hierarchy throughout the city announced its intention of going. Michelangelo took his place on a long bench between Contessina and Giovanni, facing the platform on which Savonarola stood before a wooden lectern, with the city government banked behind.

When Savonarola first mentioned Lorenzo de' Medici as a tyrant, Michelangelo saw Lorenzo's lips lift in a faint smile. He himself barely heard the words, for he was gazing about the great hall with its long side panels of pure white plaster and thinking what magnificent frescoes could be painted there.

Lorenzo's smile vanished as Savonarola mounted his attack: All the evil and all the good of the city depend from its head, and therefore great is his responsibility. If he followed the right path, the whole city would be sanctified. Tyrants are incorrigible because they are proud. They leave all in the hands of bad ministers. They hearken not unto the poor, and neither do they condemn the rich. They corrupt voters and aggravate the burdens of the people.

Now Michelangelo began listening intently, for Savonarola charged that Lorenzo had confiscated the Florentine Dower Fund, monies paid into the city treasury by poorer families as guarantee that they would have the eventual dowry without which no Tuscan girl could hope to marry; that Lorenzo had used the money to buy sacrilegious manuscripts and evil works of art; to stage bacchanals through which he rendered the people of Florence prey to the devil.

Lorenzo's dark skin turned green.

Savonarola was not through: Lorenzo, the corrupt tyrant, must go. The dishonest Signoria sitting behind him must go. The judges, the officials, must go. An entirely new government, ruled by a completely new and rigorous set of laws, must be installed to render Florence a City of God.

Who was to govern Florence? Revise its laws and execute them?

Savonarola.

God had ordered it.

14

When Michelangelo reached the *studiolo* he found Fra Mariano there. The humanist preacher of San Gallo had been losing his congregation to Savonarola. Michelangelo drew his usual chair to the low table, put an apple on his plate, and then sat back.

"We will not attempt to refute Savonarola's personal slanders," Lorenzo was saying. "The facts of such matters as the Dower Fund are clear for all Florentines to see. But his prophesying of doom is causing a mounting hysteria in Florence. Fra Mariano, I have been thinking that you are the one to answer Savonarola. Could I suggest that you preach a sermon on Acts 1:7, 'It is not for you to know the times and seasons which the Father has fixed by his own authority'?"

Fra Mariano's face lighted.

"I could review the history of prophecy, the ways in which God speaks to His people, and show that all Savonarola lacks is a witch's cauldron . . ."

"Gently," said Lorenzo. "Your sermon must be quiet and irrefutable, in fact as well as logic, so that our people will see the difference between revelation and witchcraft."

The discussion centred around what biblical and literary materials Fra Mariano should use. Michelangelo ate a little of the fruit, slipped out unnoticed.

There followed a month of tranquillity and steady work. He locked out all contact with the world, eating and sleeping little, tackling the twenty intertwined entities of his marble block.

The palace spread the word that the faithful should go to San Gallo on Holy Thursday to hear Fra Mariano demolish Fra Savonarola. When Michelangelo walked into the church he found there every important family in Tuscany: nobles, landowners, merchants, scholars, travellers from Europe and England, the Signoria, judges and councillors from the four quarters of Florence.

Fra Mariano mounted the pulpit and began in his cultivated, scholarly voice by quoting from Cosimo de' Medici: "States are not ruled by *paternosters*," which brought a ripple of laughter. He then spoke learnedly on the need for separation of Church and State, and the dangers to human freedom when, as in the past, they had been combined.

It was a good beginning. Lorenzo sat relaxed on his bench. The congregation listened intently with growing satisfaction, as Mariano proceeded by logical steps, quoting from Scripture, to show the true role of the Church and its position in the spiritual life of its people.

Then something went wrong. Fra Mariano's face grew red, his arms were thrown up to the heavens in as violent a gesture as any of Savonarola's. His voice changed as he mentioned for the first time the name of Girolamo Savonarola, spitting it out as something diseased. He threw away his carefully prepared argument, called the friar a "disseminator of scandal and disorder," and a series of evil epithets.

Michelangelo could think of only one answer: Fra Mariano had allowed his jealousy of Savonarola to conquer his judgment. He was still shouting from the pulpit when Lorenzo gathered his family about him and limped down the centre aisle and out of the church.

Now for the first time Michelangelo found the palace soaked in gloom. Lorenzo suffered an acute attack of the gout and could barely hobble about the halls. Poliziano, visibly shaken, clung to Lorenzo like a child, his wit and profundity vanished. Ficino and Landino were apprehensive about their lifetime work, for Savonarola was threatening to burn all the books in Florence except the approved Christian commentaries. Pico was the hardest hit; not only had he recommended bringing the friar to Florence, he was still sympathetic to most of Savonarola's programme, and too honest to conceal it from Lorenzo.

Lorenzo rallied to make another frontal attack by asking Prior Bichiellini of Santo Spirito to join them in the *studiolo*. Michelangelo had become acquainted with the prior at Sunday dinners in the palace, and sometimes returned with him to the church to sketch in the afternoon from such familiar frescoes as the Young St. John. The prior, an

181

energetic man of fifty, was famous in Florence as the only one who wore his spectacles in the street.

"The faces of people as they hurry by," he once explained to Michelangelo, "are like the pages of a book fluttering past. Through these magnifying lenses I study their expressions and character."

Now the prior sat before the low table in the *studiolo* while Lorenzo asked if he would send to Rome for the Augustinians' most brilliant preacher "to spell some sense into the Florentines."

"I think I know our man. I shall write at once."

Florence turned out to hear the visiting Augustinian monk expose, intellectually, the extremities and danger of Savonarola's preaching; came to Santo Spirito, listened politely to his words, and went away unheeding.

Michelangelo again tried to lock himself in his shed, but the walls were too thin to keep out each day's ration of bad news: Pico tried to dissuade Lorenzo from setting spies on Savonarola on the grounds that he was too dedicated to commit the kind of "sin of the flesh" in which Lorenzo hoped to catch him. Savonarola's espionage system caught Lorenzo's spies and exposed them. Fra Mariano had deserted Lorenzo and gone on his knees to Savonarola to implore forgiveness. Only a handful of students had attended the last lectures of the Plato Academy. Florence's printers were refusing to print anything the friar did not approve. Sandro Botticelli had deserted to Savonarola, publicly declaring his female nudes to be lewd, lascivious and immoral.

Michelangelo still approved Savonarola's crusade for reform; he disapproved only of the attacks on the Medici and the arts. When he tried to explain this dilemma, Bertoldo grew querulous and, when Michelangelo next showed him his work, exclaimed that Michelangelo had missed the whole point of the Battle of the Centaurs.

"It's too bare. You haven't learned anything from my Battle or the one in Pisa. You've designed out all the richness. Savonarola's influence, I would guess. You need the horses, the flowing robes, the weapons, else what have you left to carve?"

"People," muttered Michelangelo under his breath.

"Your marble is poverty-stricken. If you want my opinion you'll throw away this block as an exercise that went wrong, and ask Granacci to find you a new one."

Bertoldo did not come to the rear of the garden for several days. Michelangelo had a visitor in his place, his brother Lionardo, in cloak and cowl, sunken-cheeked.

"Welcome to my workshop, Lionardo."

Lionardo gazed with set jaw at the Battle.

"It is your sculpture I have come about. We want you to offer it up to God."

"How can I do that?"

"By destroying it. Along with the drawings Botticelli has brought in, and other art obscenities that the congregation has volunteered. It is to be Savonarola's first fire in the purifying of Florence."

This was the second invitation to destroy his work. "You consider my marble obscene?"

"It is sacrilegious. Bring it to San Marco and fling it on the flames yourself."

Lionardo's voice had an intensity of emotional fervour that set Michelangelo on edge. He took him by the elbow even in his anger able to feel that there was no flesh whatever on his brother's bones, escorted him to the rear gate and put him into the street.

He had planned to do weeks of polishing to bring out the highlights of his figures. Instead he asked Granacci to help him move the block into the palace that night. Granacci borrowed a wheelbarrow which Bugiardini pushed through the Piazza San Marco and down the Via Larga.

With Bugiardini and Granacci helping, he carried the block to Lorenzo's sitting room. Lorenzo had not seen the piece for a month, not since Fra Mariano's sermon. He came into the room, face sallow, eyes lacklustre, hobbling painfully with the aid of a cane, and was taken completely by surprise. "Ah!" he exclaimed, and dropped into a chair. He sat for a long time in silence, his gaze riveted on the sculpture, studying it section by section, figure by figure, the colour rising in his cheeks. Vitality seemed to return to his limbs. Michelangelo remained standing behind him, also studying the marble. Finally Lorenzo turned and looked up at him, his eyes gleaming.

"You were right not to polish. The chisel textures help bring out the anatomy."

"Then you approve the carving, Excellency?"

"What is there to approve? I can feel every body, every stone, every crushed bone, the fingers of the injured youth in

183

the corner, pressed into his hair and skull, his arm sheltering the stones he will never throw. It's unlike any marble I've seen."

" We've already had an offer for the piece."

" A patron? Someone wants to buy?"

" Not exactly. They want it as a contribution. From Savonarola, through my brother Lionardo, to offer it up to God on their bonfire."

There was an almost imperceptible pause before Lorenzo said, " And you answered?"

" That I was not free to give it. The piece belonged to Lorenzo de' Medici."

" The marble is yours."

" Even to give to Savonarola for burning?"

" If that is your wish."

" But suppose, Excellency, that I had already offered the piece to God? The God who created man in His own image of goodness and strength and beauty? Savonarola says that man is vile. Would God have created us in hate?"

Lorenzo rose abruptly, walked about the room with only the barest indication of a limp. A groom came in, set a small table with two places.

" Sit down and eat while I talk to you. I too will eat, though I had no appetite before you came." He reached for a crisp crust of bread. " Michelangelo, the forces of destruction march on the heels of creativity. The arts, finest flowering of each age, are torn down, broken, burned by the next. Sometimes, as you see here in Florence to-day, by erstwhile friends and neighbours in the same city in the same year. Savonarola is not only after what he calls the non-religious works and the ' lascivious ' nudes ; he also means to destroy the painting and sculpture that does not fit into his pattern : the frescoes of Masaccio, Filippo Lippi, the Benozzo Gozzolis here in the palace chapel, the Ghirlandaios, all of the Greek and Roman statuary, most of our Florentine marbles.

" Little will remain but the Fra Angelico angels in the San Marco cells. If he has his way, and his power is growing Florence will be ravished, as was Athens by Sparta. The Florentines are a fickle people ; if they follow Savonarola to the end of his announced road, everything that has been accomplished since my great-grandfather offered his prize for the Baptistery doors will be wiped out. Florence will slip back into darkness."

Shaken by the intensity of Lorenzo's emotion, Michelangelo cried:

"How wrong I was to think that Savonarola would reform only what was evil in Florentine life. He will destroy everything that is good as well. As a sculptor I would be a slave, with both hands cut off."

"Nobody misses the loss of another man's freedom," replied Lorenzo sadly. Then he pushed aside his plate. "I want you to take a walk with me. There is something I must show you."

They went to the rear of the palace and across a small enclosed square to the front of San Lorenzo, the family church of the Medici. Inside was buried Cosimo, Lorenzo's grandfather, near one of the bronze pulpits designed by Donatello and executed by Bertoldo; in the Old Sacristy, designed by Brunelleschi, was a sarcophagus containing Cosimo's parents, Giovanni di Bicci and his wife; and a porphyry sarcophagus of Piero the Gouty, Lorenzo's father, created by Verrocchio. But the principal face of the church remained of rough, unevenly spaced, earth-coloured brick, obviously uncompleted.

"Michelangelo, this is the last great work of art I must complete for my family, a marble façade with some twenty sculptured figures standing in its niches."

"Twenty sculptures! That's as many as stand in the façade of the Duomo."

"But not too many for you. One full-size statue for every figure suggested in your Battle. We must create something over which all Italy will rejoice."

Michelangelo wondered whether the sinking feeling in his diaphragm was joy or dismay. Impetuously he cried, "I will do it, Lorenzo, I promise. But I will need time. I still have so much to learn. . . . I have not yet tried my first free-standing figure."

When he reached his apartment he found Bertoldo wrapped in a blanket, sitting over a live-coal brazier in his half of the L, his eyes red and his face a pasty white. Michelangelo went quickly to his side.

"Are you all right, Bertoldo?"

"No, I'm not all right! I'm a stupid, blind, ridiculous old man who has outworn his time."

"What leads you to this harsh conclusion?" asked Michelangelo lightly, trying to cheer him.

"Looking at your Battle in Lorenzo's room, and remembering the things I said about it. I was wrong, terribly wrong. I was trying to turn it into a cast bronze piece; your marble would have been spoiled. You must forgive me."

"Let me put you to bed."

He settled Bertoldo under the feather-bed quilt, went down to the basement kitchen and ordered a mug of wine heated on the dying embers. He held the silver cup to Bertoldo's lips, feeding consolation with the hot liquid.

"If the Battle is good, it's because you taught me how to make it good. If I couldn't make it like bronze, it was because you made me aware of the differences between solid marble and fluid metal. So be content. To-morrow we will start a new piece, and you will teach me more."

"Yes, to-morrow," sighed Bertoldo. He closed his eyes, opened them again briefly, asked, "Are you sure, Michelangelo, there is a to-morrow?" and dropped off to sleep.

In a few moments there was a change in his breathing. It seemed to become heavy, laboured. Michelangelo went to wake Ser Piero, who sent a groom for Lorenzo's doctor.

Michelangelo spent the night holding Bertoldo so that he could breathe a little more easily. The doctor confessed that he could think of nothing to do. At first light Bertoldo opened his eyes, gazed at Michelangelo, the doctor and Ser Piero, understood his plight, and whispered:

". . . take me to Poggio . . . it's so beautiful . . ."

When a groom came to announce that the carriage was ready, Michelangelo picked Bertoldo up, blankets and all, and held him on his lap for the drive out towards Pistoia to the most exquisite of the Medici villas, formerly owned by Michelangelo's cousins, the Rucellai, and remodelled with magnificent open galleries by Giuliano da Sangallo. Rain lashed at their carriage all the way, but once Bertoldo was installed in the high bed in his favourite room, overlooking the Ombrone River, the sun emerged and lit the lush green Tuscan landscape. Lorenzo rode out to comfort his old friend, bringing Maestro Stefano da Prato to try some new medicines.

Bertoldo died in the late afternoon of the second day. After the priest had given him extreme unction, he uttered his last words with a little smile, as though trying to make his exit as a wit rather than a sculptor.

186

" Michelangelo . . . you are my heir . . . as I was Donatello's."

" Yes, Bertoldo. And I am proud."

" I want you to have my estate . . ."

" If you wish."

" It will make you . . . rich . . . famous. My cookbook."

" I shall always treasure it."

Bertoldo smiled again, as though they shared a secret joke,
and closed his eyes for the last time. Michelangelo said his
good-byes silently, turned away. He had lost his master.
There would never be another.

15

The disorganization of the garden was now complete. All
work stopped. Granacci gave up the painting of a street
festival scene that he had almost completed and spent his
time feverishly supplying models, finding marble blocks,
scaring up small commissions for a sarcophagus, a Madonna.

Michelangelo cornered his friend late one afternoon.

" It's no good, Granacci. School is over."

" Don't say that. We have only to find a new master.
Lorenzo said last night I could go to Siena to seek one . . ."

Sansovino and Rustici drifted into the studio.

" Michelangelo is right," said Sansovino. " I'm going to
accept the invitation from the King of Portugal, and go
there to work."

" I think we've learned all we can as students," agreed
Rustici.

" I was never intended for cutting stone," said Bugiardini.
" My nature is too soft, it's made for mixing oil and pigment. I'm going to ask Ghirlandaio to take me back."

Granacci snapped at Michelangelo, " Don't tell me you're
leaving too!"

" Me? Where would I go?"

The group broke up. Michelangelo walked home with
Granacci to report the death of Bertoldo to the family.
Lucrezia was excited by the cookbook, reading several of
the recipes aloud. Lodovico showed no interest.

" Michelangelo, it is finished, your new sculpture?"

" Sort of."

" Il Magnifico, he has seen it?"

187

" Yes, I took it to him."

" Did he like it?"

" Yes."

" That's all, just yes? Didn't he show pleasure, approval?"

" Yes, Father, he did."

" Then where is the money?"

" What money?"

" The fifty florins."

" I don't know what . . ."

" Come now. *Il Magnifico* gave you fifty florins when you finished the Madonna and Child. Hand over the purse."

" There is no purse."

" No purse? You worked for a whole year. You're entitled to your money."

" I'm not entitled to anything, Father, beyond what I have had."

" *Il Magnifico* paid you for the other and not for this one." Lodovico was emphatic. " That can only mean that he does not like this one."

" It can also mean that he is ill, worried about many things . . ."

" Then there is still a chance that he will pay you?"

" I have no idea."

" You must remind him."

Michelangelo shook his head in despair; returned slowly through the cold wet streets.

An artist without ideas is a mendicant; barren, he goes begging among the hours. For the first time since he had entered Urbino's school seven years before, he had no desire to draw. He avoided the formation of the word " marble " in his mind. His broken nose, which had given him no trouble while he was working, began to pain him; one nostril was closed completely, making it difficult for him to breathe. Again he became conscious of his ugliness.

The garden was lonely. Lorenzo had suspended work on the library. The stonemasons were gone, and with them the rhythmical chipping of building blocks that was the most natural *ambiente* for his work. There was a feeling of transition in the air. The Plato group rarely came in to Florence to lecture. There were no more evenings in the *studiolo*. Lorenzo decided that he must take a complete cure in one of his villas, with six months away from the palace and its duties. There he could not only eradicate his gout but lay his plans to come to grips with Savonarola. This was to be a battle to the death, he said, and he would need his full vitality. Though all the weapons were in his hands: wealth, power, control of the local government, treaties with outside city-states and nations, firm friends in all the neighbouring dynasties; and Savonarola had nothing but the cloak on his back; yet Savonarola, living the life of a saint, dedicated, uncorruptible, a brilliant teacher, an executive who had already effected serious reforms in the personal life of the Tuscan clergy as well as the indulgent life of the rich Florentines who were flocking to his side to renounce the pamperings of the flesh, Fra Savonarola seemed to have the upper hand.

As part of his plan to put his affairs in order, Lorenzo made arrangements for Giovanni to be invested as cardinal, worried lest Pope Innocent VIII, an old man, should die before fulfilling his promise, and the succeeding Pope, perhaps hostile to the Medici as former ones had been, refuse to accept the sixteen-year-old youth into the ruling hierarchy of the Church. Lorenzo also knew that it would be a strategic victory with the people of Florence.

Michelangelo was troubled by Lorenzo's preparations for his departure to Careggi, for he had begun to hand over important business and governmental matters to Pieri. If Piero were to be in command, what would life be like for him here? Piero could order him out of the palace. For that matter, what was his status, now that the sculpture garden had virtually closed down?

Nothing had been said about completion money for the Battle, so he could not go home. The three florins spending money was no longer being deposited on his washstand. He had no need for the money, but its sudden disappearance unnerved him. Who had ordered this? Lorenzo? Ser Piero da Bibbiena, perhaps thinking that it was no longer necessary since the garden was not functioning? Or was it Piero?

In his irresolution, Michelangelo turned to Contessina, seeking out her company, spending hours talking to her; picking up *The Divine Comedy* and reading aloud to her the passages he liked best, such as the one in Canto XI of the *Inferno*:

> *Art, as best it can, doth follow nature,*
> *As pupil follows master; industry*
> *Or Art is, so to speak, grandchild to God.*

From these two sources (if you will call to mind
That passage in the Book of Genesis)
Mankind must take its sustenance and progress.

The Platonists had urged him to write sonnets as the
highest expression of man's literary thought, and had read
from their own poetry in the hope of giving him insight into
the art. While he was expressing himself fully in drawing,
modelling and carving, he had had no need for a supple-
mentary voice. Now in his solitude and confusion he began
putting down his first stumbling lines . . . to Contessina.

Heavenwards I am borne by an enchanting face,
Nought else on earth can yield me such delight.

And later:

A soul none sees but I,
Most exquisite, my spirit sees . . .

He tore up the fragments, knowing them to be high-flown
and adolescent; went back to the deserted garden to wander
along the paths, visit the casino from which Piero had
ordered all the cameos, ivories and folios of the drawings to
be returned to the palace. He was aching to work, but felt
so empty he did not know what to work at. Sitting at his
drawing board in the shed, hearing only the buzzing of
insects in the wild-growing flowers, there welled up in him a
sadness and sense of being alone in the world. .

At last Lorenzo sent for him.

"Would you like to come to Fiesole with us? We are
spending the night in the villa. In the morning Giovanni is
to be invested in the Badia Fiesolana. It would be well for
you to witness the ceremony. Later, in Rome, Giovanni will
remember that you attended."

He rode to Fiesole in a carriage with Contessina, young
Guiliano and the nurse. Contessina asked to get off at San
Domenico, halfway up the hill, for she wanted to see the
Badia to which, as a woman, she would be denied admittance
to her brother's investiture. .

Michelangelo knew the little church intimately, having
stopped off to visit it during his walks to Fiesole and the
Cave Maiano. The Romanesque lower part of the façade
dated back to 1050, but for Michelangelo its great beauty was
in the interior, remodelled in the style of Brunelleschi, every
tiny detail of stonework: the walls, pillars, windows, altars,
flawless works of art of the stonecutters of Fiesole and
Settignano, including his own Topolinos. When he exclaimed
over this perfection, Contessina retorted laughingly:

"You're a heretic, Michelangelo; you think the importance of a church is in its art works."

"Isn't it?"

He was awakened two hours before morning light, dressed himself and joined the procession going down the hill to the Badia, where Giovanni had spent his night in prayer. His heart sank when he saw that Lorenzo was being carried on a litter.

The little church sparkled in the light of a hundred candles. Its walls were covered with the emblems of Giovanni's Medici ancestors. Michelangelo stood by the open door, watching the sun come up over the valley of the Mugnone. With the first streaks of dawn Pico della Mirandola passed him with a solemn nod, followed by the public notary from Florence. Giovanni knelt before the altar to receive the sacrament. High mass was sung, the superior of the abbey blessed the insignia of Giovanni's new rank: his mantle, broad-brimmed hat with the long tassel. The Papal Brief was read, ordering the investment, after which a sapphire ring, emblematic of the Church's celestial foundation, was slipped on to Giovanni's finger by Canon Bosso.

Michelangelo left the Badia and began walking down the road to Florence. In the early spring sunlight the red roofs of the city formed a tightly interwoven pattern beneath him. At the Ponte di Mugnone he met a gaily clad deputation of the most prominent Florentine citizens, some of whom he recognized from Lorenzo's dinner table, followed by a throng of plain citizens and, as a sign that the worst of Lorenzo's troubles might be over, a large portion of Florence's clergymen, some of whom, he knew, had sworn allegiance to Savonarola, coming up to the Badia with songs and cheers to ask for a blessing from the new Cardinal Giovanni de' Medici.

That night at the palace there was music and dancing and pageantry and song. That night, too, the whole of Florence was fed, supplied with wine and lavish entertainment by the Medici.

Two days later Michelangelo stood in a reception line to bid farewell to the cardinal and his cousin Giulio, who was accompanying him. Giovanni blessed Michelangelo and invited him to visit if he should ever come to Rome.

All gaiety left the palace with the cardinal. Lorenzo announced his departure for Careggi. During his absence his son Piero would be in charge.

16

It was two weeks since Lorenzo had left the palace. Michelangelo was sitting alone in his bedroom when he heard voices in the corridor. A thunderbolt had struck the lantern atop the Duomo and it had fallen in the direction of the Medici palace. The city went out into the streets to gaze at the smashed lantern, then turn sorrowfully towards the palace as though in mourning. The following day Savonarola seized the opportunity to preach a sermon presaging such calamities for Florence as destruction from invasion, from earthquake, fire and flood. Michelangelo stood in the dense throng listening, dug his nails into Granacci's arm.

That night a rumour came to him in the palace, brought by the groom of Lorenzo's secretary: instead of getting better, Lorenzo was failing. A new doctor had been sent for, Lazzaro of Pavia, who had administered to Lorenzo a pulverized mixture of diamonds and pearls. This hitherto infallible medicine had failed to help. Lorenzo had sent for Pico and Poliziano to read from his favourite authors to ease his pain.

Michelangelo paced the corridors for the rest of the night in an agony of apprehension. Piero had already left for Careggi, taking Contessina and Giuliano with him. At daylight he rushed down to the basement, threw a saddle over a horse, and rode the four miles into the foothills to Lorenzo's beautiful villa, with its high tower, pigeon house and vegetable gardens running down the slope towards the valley.

He went around the far side of the estate, slipped through the walls and made his way to the courtyard. There was a wailing coming from the kitchen. He climbed the broad staircase silently, for fear someone would hear him. At the head of the stairs he turned to his left, stood for an irresolute moment before Lorenzo's bedchamber, then slowly turned the heavy knob.

The bedchamber was a large high-ceilinged room with heavy draperies covering the walls on either side of the door, the better to keep in the heat from the massive fireplace, now burning a tree trunk. At one end Michelangelo saw Lorenzo in his high-bolstered bed, propped up with many pillows, being bled from the forearm by Dr. Pier Leoni. At the foot of the bed sat Poliziano, the tears streaming down his face, and Pico, reading from his book, *The Being and the One*. He slipped behind the hanging next to the door, even as Lorenzo's confessor, standing nearby, motioned Dr. Leoni to stop the bleeding and banish everyone from the bedside. He took Lorenzo's confession, gave him absolution.

Michelangelo remained motionless as Pico and Poliziano returned to Lorenzo's side. After a moment he heard Lorenzo in a weak voice ask that Piero be summoned from the library. A servant entered, fed Lorenzo a hot broth. Poliziano asked:

"How are you relishing your food, *Magnifico* Lorenzo?"

Michelangelo saw a smile light Lorenzo's tired features.

"As a dying man always does," he replied cheerfully. "I need strength to give Piero his lecture."

Piero came in, his head bowed, humble in the face of death. The servants left the room. Lorenzo began to speak.

"Piero, my son, you will possess the same authority in the state that I have had. But as Florence is a republic, you must realize that it has many heads. It will not be possible for you to conduct yourself on every occasion so as to please everyone. Pursue that course of conduct which strict integrity prescribes. Consult the interest of the whole community rather than the gratification of any one part. If you will do so, you will protect Florence and the Medici."

Piero kissed his father on the forehead. Lorenzo motioned to Pico and Poliziano to come near.

"Pico, I only regret that I was not able to finish our library in the sculpture garden, for I wished you to have charge of it."

There was a hurried movement from the outside hall. To Michelangelo's amazement Savonarola brushed past him, so close that he could have seized his arm. Savonarola went to Lorenzo, dropped his hood so that Lorenzo could see his face. The others fell back.

"You sent for me, Lorenzo de' Medici?"

"I did, Fra Savonarola."

"How can I serve you?"

"I wish to die in charity with all men."

"Then I exhort you to hold the faith."

"I have always held it firmly."

"If you live, I exhort you to amend your life."

"I shall do so, Father."

"Finally I urge you to endure death, if need be, with fortitude."

"Nothing could please me more," replied Lorenzo with a weakening voice.

Savonarola bowed formally, turned and started for the door. Lorenzo leaned up on his pillows, called out hoarsely, "Give me your blessing, Father, before you go."

Savonarola returned, lowered his head, recited the prayers for the dying. Lorenzo, his face grave now, and pious, repeated phrases and snatches as the friar went along. Poliziano and Pico gave way to uncontrollable grief. Savonarola pulled his cowl over his head, blessed Lorenzo, and departed.

Lorenzo lay quietly, recouping his strength, then sent for his servants. When they surrounded his bed he made them farewell, asking their forgiveness if he had ever offended them.

Michelangelo strove with all his might not to push aside the heavy hanging, run to Lorenzo's side, drop to his knees and cry out, "I, too, have loved you! Bid me farewell." He had not been summoned here. He was an intruder, his presence unknown. And so he buried his face in the rough undersurface of the velvet, even as Lorenzo fell back on his pillow.

Dr. Leoni leaned over the bed, closed Lorenzo's eyes and lifted the sheet over Lorenzo's face.

Michelangelo slipped out of the open door, ran down the stairs and into the vegetable garden. His heart felt swollen in his chest. He wondered how the others found it so easy to weep. His own tears were a hot burning blindness behind his eyes as he stumbled from one furrow to another.

Lorenzo was dead! He could not believe it. The truly Magnificent One. How could all that great spirit and brain and talent, so alive and robust only a few months before, be gone for ever? For what reason had he summoned Savonarola, his avowed destroyer, to give him this final satisfaction of seeing his threats and predictions come true? All of Florence would say that Savonarola had defeated Lorenzo, that it must have been God's will for it to have been accomplished so quickly and easily.

He sat at the far end of the garden, his world smashed. With Lorenzo lying up there in his bedroom, dead, he had lost his greatest friend, the one who had taken the place in his loyalty and devotion that should have been occupied by Lodovico Buonarroti.

After a time he lurched to his feet. His throat was locked, dry. He made his way slowly back towards the palace. Coming to a well, he dropped the bucket on its rope, looked down to watch it fill.

There, lying face up, was a man. Almost paralyzed with shock and fear, Michelangelo stared down into the wet darkness. Then he recognized the face. It was Dr. Pier Leoni. He had killed himself.

He stifled the scream in his throat. Wrenching himself away, he ran until he was exhausted and fell. The tears came now, hot and racking, mixing with the Tuscan earth beneath him.

BOOK IV

THE FLIGHT

1

He shared his former bed with Buonarroto. Under it he put his two marble reliefs, wrapped in soft wool cloth. Lorenzo had said that the sculptures were his. Assuredly, he thought with a wry smile, Piero would not want them. After two years of having a comfortable apartment and freedom of movement in the palace, it was not easy for him to live in this small room with his three brothers.

"Why can't you go back and work for Piero de' Medici?" his father asked.

"I would not be wanted."

"But Piero never said in plain words that he didn't want you?"

"Piero has only fancy words."

Lodovico ran both hands through his luxuriant hair.

"You can't afford pride. You haven't the price in your purse."

Michelangelo replied humbly, "Pride is all I have left at the moment, Father."

Out of kindness, Lodovico desisted.

This three months was the longest stretch he could remember having gone without drawing. The idleness made him cranky. Lodovico too was upset, the more so because Giovansimone, now thirteen, was in trouble with the Signoria because of acts of vandalism. When the heat of July came on and Michelangelo was still too distracted to work, Lodovico lost patience.

"The last thing I thought I would say about you, Michelangelo, was that you were lazy. I can't allow you to mope around the house any longer. I've asked your uncle Francesco to get you into the Money Changers Guild. You had two years of education with those professors in the palace . . ."

Michelangelo smiled ruefully as he thought of the Plato Four sitting around the low table in the *studiolo* analysing the Hebraic sources of Christianity.

"Nothing that would help me turn a profit."

". . . and someday you'll form a partnership with Buonarroto. He is going to be a shrewd businessman. You will prosper."

He walked upstream along the Arno to a willow-covered bank where he submerged his hot body in the muddy waters. When his head cooled, he asked himself, "What are my alternatives?" He could go to live and work with the Topolinos. He had walked up the hills several times and sat in silence in the yard, hewing building stone; it was a relief, but not a solution. Should he seek out a sculpture commission by going from palace to palace, church to church, Tuscan village to village like an itinerant knife grinder, singing out, "Any marble to carve to-day?"

Unlike the Plato Four, he had not been given a villa and the resources to continue his work. Lorenzo had asked Lodovico, "Will you cede him?" yet had not made him a member of the family. Lorenzo had in effect commissioned him to do a whole façade for the unfinished front of the Medici church, with twenty marble statues, but had made no provision for the work.

He put his shirt on over his wet body, as tawny now as a Maiano quarryman's from his flights along the river. When he reached home he found Granacci waiting for him. Granacci had returned to Ghirlandaio's *bottega* with Bugiardini a few days after Lorenzo's funeral.

"*Salve*, Granacci. How go things at Ghirlandaio's?"

"*Salve*, Michelangelo. Quite good. Two panels for the abbey of San Giusto at Volterra, the Salutation for the church of Castello. Ghirlandaio wants to see you."

The studio smelled as he remembered it: of fresh ground charcoal, paint pigments in chemists' sacks, bags of fresh plaster. Bugiardini embraced him joyfully. Tedesco pounded him on the shoulder. Cieco and Baldinelli got off their stools to ask the news. Mainardi kissed him affectionately on both cheeks. David and Benedetto shook his hand. Domenico Ghirlandaio sat at his fastidious desk at the rear of the studio observing the scene with a warm smile. Michelangelo gazed up at his first master, thinking how much had happened in the four years since he had first stood here.

"Why not finish out your apprenticeship?" asked Ghirlandaio. "I'll double the contract money. If you need more later, we can discuss it as friends."

Michelangelo stood numb.

"We have much work on hand, as you can see. And don't tell me again that fresco is not for you. If you can't paint the wet wall, you certainly will be valuable in working up the figures and cartoons."

He left the studio, walked into the Piazza della Signoria and stood in the burning sun gazing sightlessly at the statues in the loggia. The offer was timely, it would get him out of the house during the day, the offer of double pay would placate Lodovico. He had been lonely since the garden broke up. The studio would give him companionship. It would also put him under a professional roof again, and at seventeen that was proper. He had no incentive to work, but Ghirlandaio would plunge him into a cauldron of activity and assignments. Perhaps this would shake him out of his lethargy.

Unmindful of the intense heat, he took the road up to Settignano, trudged through the ripe wheat fields, cooled himself in the slow-running creek at the bottom. Refreshed, he continued on to the Topolinos, took a seat under the arches and began chipping stone.

He stayed for several days, working steadily, sleeping in the open with the boys on straw mattresses spread under the arches. The Topolinos knew he was troubled. They asked no questions and proffered no advice. He would have to pound out his answer for himself. His hands groped open and shut for the hammer and chisel; he felt the familiar solidity of them grasped in his clenched palms and fingers; felt the rhythmical movements of his wrist and arm and shoulder as he chipped away, bringing outline and form to the *pietra serena*. Strange how his heart could stand empty because his hands were empty.

In Settignano it was said, "Who works stone must share its nature: rough on the outside, serene within."

As he worked the stone he worked his thoughts: one two three four five six seven for work and no thought; one two three four during the rest to formulate a fragment. Here he could achieve emotional tranquillity and clarity; here his inner strength could resolve itself. As the stones took shape under his hands, so his thoughts matured in his mind; and he knew that he could not go back to Ghirlandaio's. For that was what it would be, a going backward: to an art and a trade that he had never wanted, and had taken only because there was no sculpture studio in Florence. The demands of the frescoes would change his drawing and design and he

198

would lose all that he had learned of sculpture over the past three years. It would be a continuous contest, unfair to Ghirlandaio. It simply would not work. He had to move forward even if he could not see where or how.

He bade the Topolinos good-bye, walked down the hill to the city.

In the Via de' Bardi he met bespectacled Father Nicola Bichiellini, tall, solidly built prior of the Order of Hermits of Santo Spirito. The prior had grown up in Michelangelo's neighbourhood, the best football player on the broad earthen square before Santa Croce. At fifty his close-cropped black hair was shot with grey, but his body under the black woollen tunic and leather belt was still so charged with vitality that he welcomed each twenty-four-hour workday in which he governed his self-sustaining monastery-village of church, hospital, guesthouse, bakehouse, library, school and four hundred silent monks.

He greeted Michelangelo heartily, his sparkling blue eyes enormous behind the magnifying lenses.

"Michelangelo Buonarroti, what pleasure! I have not seen you since Lorenzo's funeral."

"I haven't really seen anybody, Father."

"I can remember you drawing in Santo Spirito before you ever went into the Medici garden. You stayed away from Master Urbino's school to copy those frescoes of Fiorentini's. Did you know that Urbino complained to me?"

Michelangelo began to feel warm inside himself.

"How flattering that you should remember, Father."

Suddenly there came into his mind the picture of the beautifully bound volumes and manuscripts in Lorenzo's *studiolo* and library, books from which he had now locked himself out.

"May I read in your library, Father? I no longer have access to books."

"But of course. Ours is a public library. If you will forgive me the sin of bragging, it is also the oldest library in Florence. Boccaccio willed us his manuscripts and books. And Petrarch as well. Drop into my office."

Michelangelo felt happy for the first time in months.

"Thank you, Father. I'll bring my sketching materials."

Early the next morning he crossed Ponte Santa Trinita to the church of Santo Spirito. He copied for a while before a fresco of Filippino Lippi and a sarcophagus of Bernardo

Rossellino. It was the first work he had done since Lorenzo's death. He felt his vitality rise, his breathing become deep and natural without the obstacle of unhappiness breaking its rhythm.

Then he walked at an angle across the square to the monastery which occupied the entire area behind Piazza Santo Spirito. Here the prior had his office. He had to meet the world, and his door was open to all; but the rest of the monastery maintained complete seclusion. No one was allowed into the monastery itself; the monks were confined to the specific paths of their duties. Prior Bichiellini looked at his drawings, exclaimed, "Good! Good! You know, Michelangelo, we have much older and better works inside the monastery. Frescoes by the Gaddi family in the Cloister of the Masters. Our chapter house walls have fine scenes by Simone Martini . . ."

Michelangelo's amber eyes sparkled with the magnified intensity of the prior's behind his spectacles.

" But no one is allowed inside . . ."

" We can arrange it. I'll draw up a schedule for you when there will be no one in the cloisters or chapter house. I've long felt these art works should be used by other artists. But it was the library you wanted. Come along."

Prior Bichiellini led the way to the library rooms. Here half a dozen Florentine laymen were studying from ancient tomes, while in the alcoves specially trained monks were making copies of valuable volumes that had been loaned to Santo Spirito from all over Europe. The prior led Michelangelo to the full sets of Plato, Aristotle, the Greek poets and dramatists, the Roman historians. He explained in an academic tone, "We are a school. We have no censors here in Santo Spirito. There are no forbidden books. We insist that our students remain free to think, inquire, doubt. We do not fear that Catholicism will suffer from our liberality; our religion is strengthened as the minds of our students grow mature."

" Shades of Fra Savonarola," said Michelangelo ironically.

The prior's hearty, warm-cheeked face went dark at the mention of Savonarola's name.

" You will want to see Boccaccio's manuscripts. They are fascinating. Most people think he was an enemy of the Church. On the contrary, he loved the Church. He hated its abuses, as did St. Augustine. We eat frugally, own nothing but the habits on our backs, and our vows of chastity are as precious to us as our love of God."

"I know that, Father. Santo Spirito is the most respected order in Florence."

"And could we be respected if we were afraid of learning? We believe that the human brain is one of God's most magnificent creations. We also believe that art is religious, because it is one of man's highest aspirations. There is no such thing as pagan art, only good and bad art." He paused for a moment to look about with pride at his library. "Come back to the office when you have finished reading. My secretary will draw a map of the buildings for you, and a schedule of hours when you may work in each cloister."

In the weeks that followed he saw no one whose daily work route did not carry him through the Cloister of the Dead, or through the Second Cloister with its three generations of Gaddi frescoes, or the chapter house where the Sienese painter, Martini, had done the Passion of Christ. The occasional monk or lay brother who passed gave no indication that he was there. The silence he found annealing, as though he were alone in the universe: just he, his drawing materials, the tombs he was copying, or the Cimabue frescoes under the arches. When he was not copying he spent his time in the library reading: Ovid, Homer, Horace, Virgil.

The prior was pleased that he was using all the hours vouchsafed him by the schedule. He would discuss with him the developments of the day. Michelangelo never had had much interest in politics. Under the hand of Lorenzo the domestic government worked so smoothly and the international alliances were so strong that there were few strictly political discussions in the palace, the streets, Ghirlandaio's, on the Duomo steps. Now he desperately needed someone to talk to; the prior, sensing the need, gave freely of his time.

With Lorenzo's death everything had changed. Where Lorenzo had met continually with his Signoria, gaining their agreement through the powers of persuasion, Piero ignored the elected Councils, made arbitrary decisions. Where his father had walked through the street with a friend or two, nodding and speaking to all, Piero never appeared except on horseback, surrounded by hired guards, recognizing no one as he scattered people, carts, donkeys, produce, on his majestic way in and out of the city to his villas.

"Even this might be forgiven," Prior Bichiellini observed,

" if he were good at his job. But he is the poorest ruler Florence has had since our disastrous Guelph and Ghibelline civil wars. Visiting Italian princes from the city-states who come to renew their alliances do not like him, judge him without talent. All he can do is give orders. If only he had the good sense to hold open discussions with the Signoria . . ."

" That is not in his character, Father."

" Then he had better start to learn. The opposition is beginning to join hands: Savonarola and his followers, the Medici cousins, Lorenzo and Giovanni, and their followers; the old families whom he is excluding; the disgruntled members of the City Council; the citizens who accuse him of neglecting the most pressing affairs of state to stage athletic contests, and arranging his tournaments so that he alone can win. We are in for troubled times. . . ."

2

" Buonarroto, how much money are you holding for me?" demanded Michelangelo that evening.

Buonarroto consulted his account book, told his brother how many florins were left from the palace savings.

" Good. It is enough to buy a piece of marble, and leave some over for rent."

" Then you have a project?"

" No, I have only the need. You must back me in my lie to Father. I shall tell him that I have a modest commission, and that they are paying for the marble plus a few scudi a month while I work. We'll pay this money to Lodovico from the savings."

Buonarroto shook his head sadly.

" I shall say that the one commissioning has the right of rejection. In that way I'll protect myself if I can't sell it."

With this Lodovico had to be content.

Michelangelo then moved on to the next problem. What did he want to carve? He felt that the time had arrived to work his first statue in the round. But what figure? What was it to be about? The question was seminal; everything that emerged grew out of the original concept. No concept, no work of art; it was as simple, and as agonizingly complex, as that.

The single desire of his heart rose out of love and sorrow: to do something about Lorenzo, a theme that would express the totality of talent, courage, width and depth of knowledge; the human understanding of this man who had undertaken to lead the world into an intellectual and artistic revolution.

An answer was slow in coming; answers always were. Yet it was only by sticking doggedly to the task that he could arrive at a conception that would swing open the doors of his creative force. His thoughts kept returning to the fact that Lorenzo had often spoken of Hercules, suggesting that the Greek legend did not mean that his twelve labours were to be taken literally: the capture of the Erymanthian boar, the defeating of the Nemean lion, the cleaning of the Augean stables by running a river through. These feats perhaps were meant as symbols for all the varied and near-impossible tasks with which each new generation of man was faced.

Was not Lorenzo the incarnation of Hercules? Had he not gone forth on twelve labours against ignorance, prejudice, bigotry, narrowness, intolerance? Surely he had set a Herculean pattern in founding universities, academies, art and manuscript collections, printing presses, in encouraging artists, scholars, poets, philosophers and scientists to reinterpret the world in vigorous modern terms, and to extend man's reach to all the fruits of the human intellect and spirit.

Lorenzo had said, "Hercules was half man and half god, sprung from Zeus and the mortal Alcmene. He is the everlasting symbol that all of us are half man and half god. If we use that which is half god in us, we can perform the twelve labours every day of our lives."

He must find a way to represent Hercules so that he became Lorenzo as well; not solely the physical giant of Greek legend as depicted on Giotto's Campanile, or in Pollaiuolo's nine-foot painting, but as poet, statesman, world merchant, patron, revolutionist.

In the meanwhile he had to get out of the house, into his own workshop.

Just as he had left bas-relief behind him, so he had outgrown Bertoldo's art of the miniature. Moreover he could not conceive of sculpturing the Hercules, or Lorenzo, in less than life size. By rights it should be half again as large as man, for they were demigods who needed heroic marble from which to be born. But where to find such marble? And how to pay for it? His savings contained but a tithe of such a cost.

He remembered the workshop of the Duomo behind the vast cathedral which had been the headquarters for the workmen and materials while the cathedral was being built, and which was subsequently used by the foreman and his maintenance crew. In passing the gates, while materials were being moved in or out, he recalled having seen several large blocks of marble lying about. He walked to the workshop, made a tour of the yard. The foreman, bald as a slab of pink marble, and with a nose that stuck straight out like a levelled finger from his face, came up to ask if he could be of service. Michelangelo introduced himself.

"I was an apprentice in the Medici garden. Now I must work alone. I need a large marble, but I have little money. I thought the city might be willing to sell something it did not need."

The foreman, a stonemason by trade, closed his eyes to the narrow protective slits against flying chips.

"Call me Beppe. What interests you?"

Michelangelo took a deep breath.

"First, Beppe, this big column. The one that has been worked on."

"That's called the 'Duccio block.' Comes from Carrara. Stands seventeen, eighteen feet high. Board of Works of the Duomo bought it for Duccio to carve a Hercules. To save labour Duccio ordered it blocked out in the quarry. It reached here ruined. I was twelve then, apprenticed." Beppe scratched his behind vigorously with his six-toothed chisel. "Duccio cut for a week. He could find no figure in it, big or small."

Michelangelo walked around the enormous block. He ran his fingers exploringly over it.

"Beppe, was this block really ruined in the quarry? It's awkwardly shaped, yes, but maybe Duccio spoiled it himself by these cuts, like here, where he gouged too deeply around the middle. Would the Board of Works sell it?"

"Not possible. They speak of using it one day."

"Then what about this smaller one? It also has been worked on, though not so badly."

Beppe examined the nine-foot block Michelangelo indicated.

"I could ask. Come back to-morrow."

"And would you plead price for me?"

The foreman opened his mouth in a toothless grin.

"I never yet knew a stonecarver who had to-morrow's *pasta* money in to-day's purse."

The answer was several days in coming, but Beppe had done a job for him.

"She's yours. I told them it was an ugly piece of meat and we'd be glad for the room. They told me to set a fair price. How about five florins?"

"Beppe! I could embrace you. I'll be back to-night with the money. Don't let it get away."

Beppe scratched his bald scalp with the end of an *ugnetto*.

Now that he had his marble he had to find a workshop. Nostalgia drew him to the Medici garden. It was unused since Lorenzo's death, the summer grass high, uncut, turning brown, the little casino in the centre stripped bare, only the piles of stones at the far end, where work on Lorenzo's library had been abandoned, remaining the same. He wondered, "Could I work in my old shed? It wouldn't hurt anything, or cost Piero anything. Perhaps he would let me if I told him what I was carving."

He could not make himself go to Piero.

As he turned to leave through the rear gate, the corner of his eye caught two figures coming through the main door from the Piazza San Marco: Contessina and Giuliano. They had not seen each other since Lorenzo's death. On the porch of the casino they came together. Contessina seemed to have shrunk in size; even in the bright July sun her face was sallow. All that was visible under the wide protective hat were her brown eyes, enormously alive.

Giuliano spoke first.

"Why have you not come to see us? We have missed you."

Contessina's voice was reproachful. "You could have called."

". . . but Piero . . ."

"I too am a Medici. So is Giuliano." She was angry. "The palace is our home. Our friends are welcome."

"I asked Contessina why you did not come," said the boy.

"I have not been invited."

"I invite you," she cried impulsively. "Giovanni must go back to Rome to-morrow, then we will be all alone, except for Piero and Alfonsina, and we never see them."

Contessina continued: "Pope Innocent is dying. Giovanni must be on hand to protect us against a Borgia being elected Pope."

She looked out at the garden.

"Giuliano and I walked over here nearly every day. We thought you would work, and where should you work but here?"

"No, Contessina, I have not worked. But to-day I bought a piece of marble."

"Then we can come and visit you," said Giuliano eagerly.

Michelangelo stood blinking hard at Contessina.

"I have not the permission . . ."

"And if I secure it for you?"

He straightened up.

"It is a nine-foot column, Contessina. Very old. Badly used. But good inside. I'm going to carve a Hercules. He was your father's favourite."

He reached out his hand for hers. Her fingers were surprisingly cold for a hot summer day.

He waited patiently, one day, two, three, four, returning at the sunset hour. But she did not come. Then, on the fifth day, as he sat on the steps of the casino chewing on a handful of hay-brown grass, he saw her walk through the main gate. His heart leaped. Her old nurse was with her. He rushed down the path to meet her.

Her eyes were red.

"Piero has refused!" he cried.

"He has not answered. A hundred times I have asked him. He stands in silence. That is his way. Then it can never be said that he refused."

High bright hope of continuing in the garden crashed.

"I was afraid it would be so, Contessina. That is why I left the palace. And have not come back. Even to see you."

She took a step closer. They now stood with their lips only an inch apart. The nurse turned away.

"Piero says the Ridolfi family will be displeased if we see each other again. . . . Not until after my marriage, at least."

Neither of them moved closer, their lips did not meet, their slight young bodies did not touch; yet he felt himself held and holding in a beloved embrace.

Contessina walked slowly down the centre path, past the little bronze boy taking a thorn out of his foot in the now still fountain. Together she and the nurse disappeared into the piazza.

3

Beppe of the blue-veined, red cheeks, as ugly a man as the original Etruscans had left behind them, Beppe came to his rescue.

"I tell the Board I can use part-time man, that you offer to work for no pay. For free a good Tuscan refuses nothing. Set up your shop along the far wall."

The Florentines, who carried half a dozen family names and believed that a short name meant a short life and fortune, had named this workyard the Opera di Santa Maria del Fiore del Duomo. It was an establishment that could carry its compounded title, for it occupied a full square behind a half-moon fringe of houses, studios and offices that lined the street behind the cathedral. In this front line of buildings Donatello, Della Robbia and Orcagna had carved their marbles, had cast their bronze pieces in the Opera furnaces.

The wooden wall of the yard, semicircular in shape, had an overhang under which the workmen found protection from the beating sun in summer and the rain being driven down the valley of the Arno from the mountains in winter. Here Michelangelo set up a forge, brought sacks of chestnut wood and Swedish iron rods, fashioned himself a set of nine chisels and two hammers, made a drawing desk from pieces of lumber that looked as though they had been lying about the yard since Brunelleschi finished the dome.

Now he had a workshop where he could make his headquarters from first light to dark. Once again he could work within the sound of the hammers of the *scalpellini*. Then, settled in with drawing paper, charcoal, pens and coloured inks, he was ready to begin.

He asked himself questions, for his final result would depend on the ever widening and deepening circles of questions asked and answered. How old was Hercules at the moment of emerging from the marble? Were all twelve of the labours behind him, or was he halfway on his journey? Was he wearing the token of his triumph, the Nemean lion skin, or was he naked to the world? Would he have a sense of grandeur at how much he had been able to accomplish as

a half god, or a sense of fatality that as a half human he
would die poisoned by the blood of the centaur Nessus?

He learned with the passing months that most of the
charges against Lorenzo of debauching the morals and freedom of the Florentines were untrue, that he was perhaps the
greatest human being since Pericles had brought in the golden
age of Greece two thousand years before. How to convey
that Lorenzo's accomplishments were as great as those of
Hercules?

First, Lorenzo was a man. As a man he would have to be
recreated, brought to glowing life out of this weather-stained
block of marble propped up by beams before him. He had
to conceive of the strongest male that ever walked the earth,
overwhelming in all his aspects. Where in Tuscany, land of
small, lean, unheroically designed men, would he find such a
model?

He scoured Florence looking at coopers with their heavy
wooden hammers, the wool dyers with their arms stained blue
and green, the ironmongers, blacksmiths, rustic stone bevel-
lers working the Strozzi palace; the porters running the
streets bent double under their packs, the young athletes
wrestling in the park, the near-naked sand dredgers in their
flat boats pulling up spoons of Arno mud. He spent weeks
in the countryside watching the farmers take in their grain
and grapes, loading heavy sacks and boxes on carts, flailing
the wheat, rolling the granite wheels of the olive crusher,
chopping down old trees, building rock walls. Then he
returned to the Duomo workshop where he doggedly drew
every feature, limb, torso, back under tension, shoulder
muscle lifting, arm pushing, thigh straining, until he had a
folio of hundreds of fragments. He set up an armature,
bought a supply of pure beeswax, began modelling . . . and
was dissatisfied.

"How can I establish a figure, even the crudest outline, if I
don't know what I'm doing? How can I achieve anything but
surface skin sculpture, exterior curves, outlines of bones, a
few muscles brought into play? Effects. What do I know of
the causes? The vital structure of a man that lies beneath
the surface, and that my eye can't see? How can I know
what creates, from within, the shapes I see from without?"

These questions he had already asked Bertoldo. Now he
knew the answer. It had been buried within him for a long
time. He came to grips with its necessity. There was no

escape. He could never become any part of the sculptor he planned to be until he had trained himself through dissection; until he knew the workings of every last component within the human body, precisely what function it served and how it accomplished its end; the interrelation of all the parts, bone, blood, brain, muscle, tendon, skin, guts. Figures in the round had to be complete, seen from every angle. A sculptor could not create movement without perceiving what caused the propulsion; could not portray tension, conflict, drama, strain, force unless he saw every fibre and substance at work within the body that was shaping the power and drive; unless he knew what a movement in front did to the corresponding muscles behind; until he grasped the whole of the human body itself.

Learn anatomy he must! But how? Become a surgeon? That would take years. Even if he could follow that unlikely train, what good would it do to dissect two male corpses a year, in a group effort in the Piazza della Signoria?

There must be some way that he could see a dissection.

He remembered that Marsilio Ficino was the son of Cosimo de' Medici's doctor. He had been trained by his father until Cosimo had suggested that he was " born to doctor men's minds, not their bodies."

He set out on foot for Careggi and Ficino's villa to lay his problem before the near sixty-year-old who was working night and day in his manuscript-strewn library in hopes of completing his commentary on Dionysius the Areopagite. He was admitted to the villa by Ficino's two pretty nieces and escorted into the library. The tiny founder of the Plato Academy sat beneath a bust of Plato, pen in inky fingers, deep furrows in his tight-skinned face.

Michelangelo made it clear at once why he had come. Then added:

" As the son of a doctor, trained to be a doctor yourself, you must know what the insides of a man is like."

" I did not complete my medical studies."

" Do you know if anyone is dissecting now?"

" Assuredly not! Don't you know the penalty for violating a corpse?"

" Banishment for life?"

" Death."

After a silence, Michelangelo asked, " And if one were willing to risk it? How could it be gone about? Watch the poverty fields for burials?"

Aghast, Ficino cried, " My dear young friend, you cannot

conceive of yourself as a grave robber. How many times do you think you would succeed? You would be caught with a mutilated corpse and hanged from the third-floor window of the Palazzo della Signoria. Let's talk of other, more pleasant things. How does your sculpture go?"

"That's what we have been talking about, dear Ficino."

He stuck to his problem. Where to find available corpses? The dead of the rich were buried in the family tombs; those of the middle class were surrounded with religious ritual. Which dead in Florence were unwatched and unwanted? Only the very poor, the familyless, the mendicants who filled the roads of Italy. These people were taken to hospitals when they were sick. Which hospitals? Those attached to churches, with free beds. And the church with the largest charity hospital was the one that had the largest and best known free guesthouse.

Santo Spirito!

He could feel his hair crackle on his forehead. Santo Spirito, of which he knew not only the prior but every corridor, the library, guesthouse, gardens, hospital, cloisters.

Could he ask Prior Bichiellini for his unclaimed corpses? If the prior were caught, something worse would happen to him than death: he would be put out of his order, excommunicated. Yet this was a courageous man who feared no force on earth so long as he did not personally offend God. How proud he was that a former prior of the order had befriended Boccaccio, the most hated and reviled man of his age: taken him in, protected him, used Boccaccio's library for the furthering of human knowledge. These Augustinians, when they thought they were right, knew not fear.

And what was ever accomplished without risk? Had not an Italian from Genoa that very year sailed three little ships over the flat Atlantic Ocean from which he was told he would fall off, seeking for a new route to India?

If the prior were willing to take the awful risk, could he, Michelangelo, be so selfish as to ask it? Would the ends warrant that risk?

He spent agitated days and sleepless nights coming to his decision. He would approach Prior Bichiellini with an honest, straightforward request, telling precisely what he wanted and needed. He would not insult the prior by being subtle; there was nothing subtle about excommunication or a hangman's noose.

But before he was willing to talk to the prior he had to know precisely how the plan could operate. Step by step he groped his way forward. With trepidation he moved in the stonemason's rhythm of no thought for the seven count of the chisel hammering on the stone, and only the few words that could be formulated during the one two three four rest period between chipping. He wandered through Santo Spirito, the cloisters, the outside vegetable gardens, the streets and little alleys that surrounded the section, checking entrances, observation points, approaches to the burial chapel, and within the monastery itself the location of the dead room where the bodies were kept overnight until burial in the morning.

He drew up diagrams, accurate and in scale, of the juxtaposition of the guesthouse to the hospital, the monks' quarters. He traced the route by which he could enter from the back gate on the Via Maffia without being seen, make his way through the gardens and corridors to the dead room. He would come late at night and leave before morning light.

He had to decide when to state his case, the right moment and place, both to increase his chances and to achieve clarity. The place to face up to the prior was in his writing study, amidst his books and manuscripts.

The prior let him recite only a part of his proposal, took a quick look at the diagrams spread out on the desk before him, then stopped him cold.

"Enough! I comprehend fully. Let us never mention this subject again. You have not brought it up. It has vanished like smoke, leaving no trace."

Stunned by the rapidity of the rejection, Michelangelo gathered his maps and found himself standing out in the Piazza Santo Spirito, suddenly cold under an overcast autumnal sky, blind to the market bustling about him in the piazza, aware only that he had put the prior in an intolerable situation. The prior would never want to see him again. The church he could go into; it belonged to everybody, but not the cloisters. He had lost his privileges.

He walked through the blustery streets, sat numbly in front of his Hercules block. What right had he to carve a Hercules, to attempt to interpret Lorenzo's favourite figure? He rubbed his fingers over the bones of his nose as though it were hurting for the first time.

He was desolate.

211

4

He was sitting on a bench before a large fresco. Santo Spirito was quiet after the early morning service. An occasional woman, her head covered with a black handkerchief, knelt before the altars. A man entered, genuflected, and hurried out. A heavy scent of incense was suspended in the sun's rays.

Prior Bichiellini came out from the sacristy, saw Michelangelo and walked towards him. He stood for a moment studying the few hesitant lines of the drawing, then asked:

"Where have you been these past weeks, Michelangelo?"

"I . . . I . . ."

"How is the sculpture going?"

There was no change in his manner, it showed the same interest and affection.

"It's . . . sitting there. . . ."

"I thought of you when we received a new illuminated manuscript. There are some figure drawings from the fourth century that might interest you. Would you like to see them?"

Michelangelo rose timidly and followed the prior through the sacristy, across the cloister and into his study. On the desk was a beautiful parchment manuscript illustrated in blue and gold. The prior reached into his desk and took out a long key which he laid across the binding to keep the leaves spread. They talked for a few moments, then the prior said:

"*Allora*, we both have work to do. Come back again soon."

Michelangelo returned to the church, enveloped in a warm glow. He had not lost the prior's friendship. He had been forgiven, the incident forgotten. If he were no farther along on his search for anatomy, at least he had done no irreparable damage.

But he had no intention of abandoning the search. He sat on the hard bench, unable to work, wondering whether grave robbing was not the most workable solution, since it involved no one else. Yet how was he to dig up a corpse, refill the grave against passers-by, carry the cadaver to a nearby house, return it to the cemetery when he had completed his explorations? It seemed physically impossible.

He returned to the library of Santo Spirito to look among its books for new clues on how the ancients had conceived of Hercules. At the same time he found one illustrated medical manuscript showing how patients were tied to rope mattresses before being operated on; but no illustration of what the surgeon had found after the cutting.

Again the prior offered his assistance, finding him a heavy leather volume on one of the higher shelves, scanning through it, exclaiming, " Ah yes, here is some material," laying the heavy bronze key across the pages.

It was not until the fourth or fifth session that Michelangelo began to notice the key, of and by itself. The prior used it not only to keep books open but as a place marker when he closed a volume, a pointer when he was underscoring lines.

Always the key. Always the same key. But never when he was in the study with others, either monks or lay friends.

Why?

He went back a dozen times in the following weeks. If he set about his drawing for an hour or two the prior would come through the church, greet him cheerily, invite him into the study. And invariably the big bronze key came out of the desk.

At night Michelangelo lay awake, seeing the key before him. During the day he went for long walks in the autumn rain up to the Maiano quarry, holding dialogues with himself.

" It must mean something. But what? What are keys for? Obviously to open doors. How many doors are there in which I am interested? Only one. The dead-room door."

He would have to take a gamble. If the prior meant for him to have it, well and good; if he did not, then he would simply carry it off by accident, forgetfully, and return it the next day. During the night he would let himself in through the rear garden gate of the monastery, make his way to the dead room. If the key fitted the door, then his assumption would be correct. If it did not . . .

It was midnight when he reached the monastery, having slipped out of his house noiselessly so as to waken no one, and taken a circuitous route to the hospital from Santa

213

Croce across the Ponte Vecchio, past the Pitti palace, through a maze of side streets. In this way he missed the night guards who followed a prescribed route with their lanterns and could be seen a piazza away.

He hugged the walls of the infirmary on the Via Sant'-Agostino, turned into the Via Maffia to the little gate in the centre of the block above which the fresco of Our Lady with the Child by Agnolo Gaddi gleamed softly in the darkness. All Santo Spirito keys opened this gate; he admitted himself, slipped past the stables on his left, avoided the main walk because the next building was the dormitory for lay brothers, skirted the walls of the dark kitchen, his breath coming a little faster now, made an angular dart to the inner wall of the infirmary.

He found the open, central arch, slipped into the corridor admitting to the cells for patients, the doors of which were closed, and turned towards the dead room. An oil lamp stood in a niche. He took a candle out of the green canvas bag he carried, lighted the wick, shielded it under his cape.

His only serious danger was from the chief of the infirmary; but since the monk was also encharged with the administration of the properties of the order, working from dawn to dark supplying the needs of the infirmary, guesthouse and monastery, he was not likely to venture out of his cell on nocturnal inspections. Once the five o'clock supper was served, the patients were made ready for sleep and the doors of their cells closed. There was no resident doctor; the patients were not expected to grow sicker or ask for help during the night. They docilely did what was expected of them.

He stood for a moment rigid, before the door of the dead room. He inserted the big key, made a slow movement to the right, then left, felt the lock slip. In an instant he had opened the door, darted into the room, closed and locked the door behind him. And at this moment of commitment he did not know whether he dared face the task ahead.

The dead room was small, about eight feet by ten, windowless. The stone walls were whitewashed, the floor of rough blocks. In the centre of the room, on narrow planks mounted on two wooden horses, and wrapped from head to foot in a burial sheet, was a corpse.

He stood leaning against the door, breathing hard, the candle shaking in his hand like trees in a *tramontana*. It was the first time he had been alone in a room with death,

214

let alone locked in, and on a sacrilegious errand. His flesh felt as though it were creeping along his bones; he was more frightened than he had ever been in his life.

Who lay wrapped in that sheet? What would he find when he unrolled the body and dropped the winding cloth to the floor? What had this unfortunate creature done that he should now, without his knowledge or consent, be mutilated?

"What kind of nonsense is this?" he demanded of himself. "What difference could it make to a man already dead? His body does not get into the kingdom of heaven, only his soul. I have no intention of dissecting this poor fellow's soul, even if I should stumble across it."

Reassured by his own grim humour, he put down his bag and looked for a place to set his candle, of importance to him not only for light but as a clock as well: for he had to be safely out of here before three in the morning when the monks who operated the large bakehouse on the corner of the Via Sant'Agostino and Piazza Santo Spirito rose to make the day's bread for the monastery, the deserving poor and the relatives of all who lived here. It had taken much experimenting to ascertain with accuracy how long each type of candle would burn. This one, for which he was now searching for a resting place, was the three-hour variety; when it began its first spluttering he would have to leave. He must also exercise care that no drippings could be discovered the next morning.

He emptied his bag of its scissors and kitchen knife, flattened it on the floor, held the candle upside down for a moment, then secured it in the soft wax. He took off his cape, for he was already sweating in the cold room, laid it in a corner, uttered a jumbled prayer which sounded like, "Lord forgive me, for I know not what I do," and approached the corpse.

First he would have to unroll it from its winding sheet. The trestle bench was narrow. He had not known that he could be so clumsy. Slowly he wrestled the stiff body, first raising the legs until the sheet pulled out from under the lower half, then lifting it from the waist and holding it in his left arm, against his chest, until he could manœuvre the cloth from around the torso and head. The winding sheet was long, he had to go through the tortuous process five times before he finally divested the cadaver of its protective wrapping.

He picked up his candle from the floor, held it aloft in

215

his left hand to study the body. His first feeling was one of pity for this dead man. His second was one of fear:

"This is how I shall end up!"

Suddenly all the differences between life and death became apparent.

The face was expressionless; the mouth semi-open, the skin green from gangrene. The man had been strongly built and was in mid-life when apparently he had received a stab wound in the chest. The cadaver had been here long enough to sink to the temperature of this freezing room.

His nostrils picked up an odour, something like very old flowers dying in water. It was not strong, it fell away when he backed to the wall to get a moment of relief; but it came to him again as he approached the cadaver, and from that point remained in his nostrils inescapably.

Where to begin? He raised the arm on the side closest to him and felt a cold such as he had never felt before. Not colder than anything else, but different. It was a cold filled with emotional content, a hard cold, not the skin, but the muscle under it. The skin was soft, like velvet. He felt disgust, as though an iron hand were squeezing his stomach. All his memories of warm arms and shoulders recurred to him. He withdrew.

It was a considerable time before he could pick up the knife from the floor, recall what he had read about the human body, the few illustrations he had seen. He poised over the cadaver, frozen himself, swallowing hard. Then he brought the knife down and made his first incision: from the chest-bone down to the groin. But he had not exerted enough pressure. The skin was surprisingly tough.

He started over. Now applying strength behind the knife, he found the substance under the skin quite soft. The skin opened about two inches. He asked himself, "Where is the blood?" for it did not flow. This increased his impression of cold and death. Then he saw the fat, a soft, deep yellow. He knew what it was, for he had seen fat cut from animals in the markets. He made a deeper cut to reach the muscle, which was different in colour from the skin and the fat, and harder to cut. He studied the dark red columns of fibres. He cut again and saw the bowel.

The smell was growing heavier. A nausea started within him. At the first cut he had summoned all his strength to proceed; now all sensations came together: the cold, fear, smell, reaction to death. He was repulsed by the slippery feeling of the tissue, the fat fluidifying on his fingers like oil. He wanted to put his hands in hot water and wash them.

" What do I do now? "

He trembled, hearing his voice echo off the stone walls. He was in little danger of being heard, for he was bound at his back by the solid wall beyond which lay the garden, to his side by the chapel reserved for the death services, on the infirmary side by stone through which no sound could penetrate.

It was dark inside the cavity. He picked up the candle, secured the canvas bag under the foot of the cadaver, placed his candle at body height.

All of his senses were heightened. The intestines that he now began to handle were cold, slippery, moving. A pain ricocheted through his own bowels. He took one side of the flap in one of his hands, the other side in the other, held them apart to have a careful look. He saw a pale grey transparent snake, long, going round and round in coils. It had a superficial aspect of mother-of-pearl, shining because humidified, filled up with something that moved and emptied when he touched it.

His initial emotion of disgust was overcome by excitement. He picked up his knife and started to cut upwards from the bottom of the rib cage. The knife was not strong enough. He tried his scissors but had to angle along the ribs, one at a time. The rib bones were hard; it was like cutting wire.

Suddenly the candle began to splutter. Three hours already! He could not believe it. Yet he did not dare ignore the warning. He set his green bag and candle on the floor, picked up the winding sheet from the corner. The wrapping process was a thousandfold more difficult than the unwrapping because he could no longer turn the corpse on its side or the whole of its guts would spill out on to the floor.

The perspiration ran down into his eyes, his heart pounded so loud he thought it would wake the monastery as he used the last vestige of his strength to lift the corpse from the table with one arm while he pulled the winding sheet under and around the necessary five times. He barely had a moment to make sure that the corpse was stretched out upon the planks as he had found it, to check the floor for possible stains or wax, before the candle gave its last flickering sputter and went out.

He had enough control to take a wandering route home,

stopping a dozen times to retch against the corners of buildings and in the darkness of the open ground. The smell of the corpse was in his nostrils with every breath he took. When he reached home he was afraid to boil water on Lucrezia's glowing embers for fear the noise would wake the family; yet he could not live without getting the feel of that fat off his fingers. He hunted quietly for some harsh lye soap to use in the cold water.

His body, as he got into bed, was icy. He huddled against his brother, but not even Buonarroto's warmth could help him. Several times he had to rise and retch into a pail. He heard Lucrezia get out of bed, dress and make her way through the kitchen and down the circular stairway to the street as the faintest tinge of pearl grey touched his window overlooking the stables on the Via dei Bentaccordi.

He had chills and fever all day. Lucrezia made him a chicken broth, but he could not hold it down. The family came one by one into the bedroom to find out what was the matter with him. He lay there feeling as clammy as the corpse. Nothing was able to remove the smell of death from his nostrils. After he had assured Lucrezia that it was not her supper which had upset him, she returned to the kitchen to boil up a herb bouquet to cure him. Monna Alessandra examined him for spots. By late afternoon he was able to retain a little of the herb tea, for which he thanked Lucrezia most gratefully.

About eleven o'clock he rose, slipped into his shoes, *calze,* warm shirt and cloak, and with his legs rickety beneath him, made his way to Santo Spirito.

There was no corpse in the dead room. Neither was there one on the following night. The two days gave him a chance to recover. On the third night he again found a body in its winding sheet on the planked table.

The second cadaver was older, with white beard patches on a big red face, the skin tight, the fluid under the skin marbleized. This time he used his knife with more authority, opening the abdomen with a clean cut, then using his left hand to pry apart the rib cage, which made a noise like crackling wood. It remained attached at the collarbone.

He picked up his candle, and held the light close to the innards, for this was his first complete view. He saw something pale red, netlike in design, and of solid tissue, which he deduced was the lungs. The network had a black covering, something that he had heard happened to wool workers.

Experimentally, he pressed the lung; a hissing noise came out of the mouth of the corpse. He dropped the candle in fright. Fortunately it did not go out. When he regained his calm and had picked up the candle, he realized that in touching the lung he had forced out the residual air; and for the first time he understood what breathing was, because he could see and feel and hear the communication between the lungs and the mouth, realized what it did to the whole figure.

After he had moved aside the lung he noticed a dark red mass; this must be the heart. It was covered by a shining membrane. Probing, he found that all of the tissue was connected to a form shaped something like an apple, almost free in the chest, attached only at the top of the pyramid.

"Shall I take it out?"

He hesitated a moment, then picked up his scissors, cut across the pyramidal membrane. Substituting his knife, he peeled away the membrane as though he were opening a banana. Now he had the heart in his two hands. Unexpectedly, he was hit by an emotional impact as strong as Hercules' club. If the soul and heart were one, what happened to this unfortunate cadaver's soul now that he had cut out its heart?

As quickly as it had come, the fear departed. In its place came a sense of triumph. He was holding a human heart in his hands! He felt the happiness that arises out of knowledge, for now he knew about the most vital organ of the body, what it looked like, how it felt. He opened the heart with his knife, was shocked to find that there was nothing inside. He replaced it in its cavity, put back the chest's rib structure, which artists had observed so well from the lean Tuscans around them. But now he knew precisely where the heart beat beneath it.

He did not have the faintest idea of how to start work on the snake of the intestine. He picked up a piece, pulled. It came easily for a time, about five feet of it; the bowels were attached loosely to the posterior wall, and came away. Then he began to feel resistance. The upper part was enlarged, a sort of bag was attached, which he deduced was the stomach. He had to use his knife to cut it loose.

He freed some twenty-five feet of bowel, fingered it, feeling the differences of size and content. Some places had fluid in them, some solid; he learned that it was a continuous channel, with no opening from the beginning to the end. To get a concept of its interior aspect he cut into it with his knife at several points. The lower bowel contained stools. The smell was terrible.

To-night he had a four-hour candle, but already it began to splutter. He bundled the viscera back into the abdominal cavity, and with great difficulty got the corpse rewrapped.

He ran to the fountain in the Piazza Santo Spirito and scrubbed his hands, but he could not get the feeling of dirt off his fingers. He stuck his head into the icy water to wash away the sense of guilt, standing for a moment with his hair and face dripping water; then ran all the way home, shaking as though with ague.

He was emotionally exhausted.

He awoke to find his father standing over him, a displeased look on his face.

"Michelangelo, get up. It's noon. Lucrezia is putting food on the table. What kind of new nonsense is this, that you sleep until dinner? Where were you last night?"

Michelangelo lay staring up at Lodovico.

"I'm sorry, Father. I'm not feeling well."

He washed carefully, combed his hair, put on fresh clothing and went to the table. He thought he was going to be all right. When Lucrezia brought in a bowl of beef stew, he rushed back into his bedroom and retched into the chamber pot until his insides were sore.

But that night he was back in the dead room.

Before he had the door locked behind him he was drenched in the smell of putrefaction. He unwound the sheet, saw that the left leg of the corpse was of a brown colour with a green secretion coming out from under the skin, the leg swollen half again its size. The rest of the body was ash grey, the face completely sunken.

He began to work where he had left off the night before, cutting directly to the bowel, and unravelled it piece by piece. He placed it on the floor and raised his candle close to the cavity. There were a number of the organs he had been searching for: the spleen on the left side, the liver on the right. He recognized the liver from the beeves and lambs cut up in the markets; bilaterally, just aside of the bone column, were the kidneys.

He picked them up carefully and perceived that they were connected with the bladder by small tubes, like wires. He went on to where the liver was attached, posteriorly; cut the ligaments with his scissors and removed it from the

220

cavity. He studied the shape in his hands, examining the small bladder attached to its lower side, opened it with his knife. A dark green fluid came out.

He moved his candle closer, saw something that he had missed before: the abdominal cavity was separated from the chest cavity by a dome-shaped muscle. In the centre of this dome were two holes through which passed tubes connecting the stomach with the mouth. The second big channel, alongside the backbone, went up into the chest. He now realized that from the chest to the abdomen there were only two means of communication, one bringing food and liquids The other baffled him. He lifted the bone structure of the chest but could not determine what the second channel was used for. The candle spluttered.

As he crept silently up the stairs of his house he found his father waiting for him.

" Where have you been? What is that horrible odour about you? You smell like death."

Michelangelo mumbled an excuse with eyes cast down, brushed past Lodovico to the security of his bedroom.

He could not sleep.

" Will I never get used to this?" he groaned.

The next night there was no corpse in the dead room. He had an uneasy feeling of impending danger as he noticed that the section of the floor where he had allowed the bowels to rest had been scrubbed, and was brighter than the stones around it. A bit of wax from his candle had been left untouched at the foot of the plank table. Yet even if his activities had been noticed, he was protected by the vow of silence in the monastery.

The following night he found a boy of about fifteen who showed no external evidence of disease. The pale skin, almost completely white, was soft to the touch. The eyes were blue when he raised the lids, deep in colour, contrasting with the pale white of the eyelids. Even in death he was attractive.

" Surely he will wake up," he murmured.

He saw that the boy was still without hair on his chest, and felt a pity deeper than he had known since he had viewed his first corpse.

He turned away; he'd wait until another night. Then, facing the corner of the whitewashed walls, he stopped. By the next morning this lad would be buried under four feet of earth in the Santo Spirito cemetery. He touched the boy, found him as cold as winter; beautiful, but as dead as all the others.

He made his incisions expertly now, put his hand under the chestbone. It came away easily. Up towards the neck he felt a tubelike appendage, about an inch in diameter, that gave the impression of a series of hard rings; among these rings he found a soft membranous tube that came down from the neck. He could not find where this tube ended and the lung began, but when he pulled on it the boy's neck and mouth moved. He took his hand out swiftly and shuddered away from the table.

A moment later he cut the tube blindly, not being able to see it, then lifted the lungs out separately. They were light in weight and when he squeezed them he found that the sensation was rather like squeezing snow. He tried to cut the lung open with his knife, put it on the table and, with a hard surface under him, found that it was like cutting through dry sponge. In one of the lungs he found a pale yellow-white mucus which kept the lung moist, in the other a pink-red mucus. He wanted to get his hand down the boy's mouth in order to search out the throat and neck, but the feel of the teeth and tongue repelled him.

Suddenly he felt as though someone were in the room with him, though he knew it was impossible because he had locked the door from the inside. To-night was just too difficult.

He wrapped up the corpse easily, for it weighed so little, put it back on the table, and let himself out.

5

He could not risk his father's again detecting the odour of death, so he walked the streets until he found a wineshop in the workmen's quarter that was open. He drank a little of the Chianti. When the proprietor turned his back, he sprinkled the rest of the wine over his shirt.

Lodovico was outraged when he smelled the strong wine.

"It is not enough that you wander the streets all night doing God alone knows what, associating with what manner of loose women, but now you come home smelling like a cheap tavern. I can't understand you. What is driving you to these evil ways?"

The only protection he could give his family was to keep them in ignorance. It was best for his father to believe that he was carousing, about which Lodovico was learning a great deal from Giovansimone, who frequently came in with his face bloodied and clothes torn. But as the days passed, and Michelangelo stumbled into the house every morning towards dawn, the family rose in arms. Each was outraged for his own special reason. Lucrezia because he was not eating, his uncle Francesco because he was afraid Michelangelo would run into debt, his aunt Cassandra on moral grounds. Only Buonarroto brought a smile to his brother's lips.

"I know you are not carousing," he said.

"How could you know that?"

"Simple: you haven't asked me for a scudo since you bought those candles. Without money you do not buy women in Florence."

He realized that he would have to find somewhere else for his daily rest. The Topolinos would never ask questions, he could stay there, but Settignano was so far away; he would lose valuable hours coming and going. In the morning he went to the Duomo workshop and mounted the stool before his drawing table. Beppe came over to greet him, a puzzled expression on his homely old face.

"My young friend, you look like a cadaver. What have you been making with yourself?"

Michelangelo looked up sharply.

"I've been . . . working, Beppe."

Beppe cackled toothlessly.

"Ah, that I were young enough for that kind of work! Well, do not try to raise Hercules' club every night. Remember, what you put into the ladies at night you don't have left to spend on marble in the morning."

That night he came across his first ugly corpse, one that made him shiver as he observed what could happen to God's handiwork. The man was about forty, with a big dark red face, swollen near the neck. The mouth was open, the lips blue, the whites of the eyes full of red spots. Through the yellow teeth he could see the dark red tongue, swollen, filling almost the whole mouth.

He put his hand on the man's face. The cheeks felt like uncooked dough. Now seemed a good time to get at the structure of the human face. He picked up the smaller of his knives and cut from the hairline to the bridge of the nose. He tried to peel the skin off the forehead but he could not, it was too closely attached to the bone. He cut on top of each eyebrow to the edge of the eye, stripped the skin from the corner of the eye outward, continued from the eye to the ear, then down along the cheekbone.

The effect of the mutilation was so ghastly that he could not work on it. He picked up the winding sheet from the corner, covered the man's head, and turned his attention to the hipbone, to the fibred muscles of the heavy thigh.

A couple of nights later when there was a new corpse, he cut lightly into the skin of the face, peeling it off with scissors. Under the thin yellow tissue of fat he discovered a large membrane of red muscular tissue which went continuously from the ear around the lips to the other ear. Now he had his first understanding of how these muscles could move the face to laughter, smiles, tears, grief.

Under it was a thicker tissue extending from the corner of the jaw to the base of the skull. Putting his finger under this second layer, he pushed the tissue a little and saw the jaw move. He worked it up and down to simulate the chewing movement, then searched for the muscle that would move the eyelid. He had to see inside the cavity of the eye to know what made it move. Trying to push his finger inside, he exerted too much pressure. The eye globe broke. A white mucus poured out over his fingers, leaving the cavity empty.

He turned away terror-stricken, walked to a corner of the whitewashed wall and crushed his forehead against its coldness, fighting desperately the desire to retch. When he had regained control of himself he went back to the corpse, cut the tissue from around the second eye, found where it was attached at the bottom of the cavity. Then putting his finger in above the eye and moving it slowly inside, he plucked it out. He turned it around and around in his hand, trying to find out how it moved. He held his candle close, peered into the empty cavity. On the bottom he could perceive a hole through which grey soft tissuelike wires went up into the skull. Until he could remove the top of the skull and expose the brain, he could learn nothing about how an eye sees.

His candle had only a bit of tallow. He cut the flesh

away from the bridge of the nose, saw clearly what had happened to his own under Torrigiani's fist.

The candle spluttered.

Where to go? He dragged himself away from Santo Spirito. His body ached with tiredness, his eyes smarted, his stomach and spirits were in a state of revulsion. He could not face Lodovico, who would surely be waiting for him at the top of the stairs, screaming that he was going straight to the Stinche.

He made his way to the workshop of the Duomo. It was easy to throw his bag over the gate, then hoist himself over. In the moonlight the blocks of white marble glistened with white luminosity, the chips around the semi-finished columns were like snow, clean and refreshing. The cold air settled his stomach. He went towards his workbench, cleared a place under it, stretched out, covered himself with a heavy piece of canvas and fell asleep.

He woke a few hours later; the sun had risen. In the piazza he could hear the noise of the *contadini* setting up their stalls. He walked to the fountain, washed, bought himself a slice of *parmigiano,* two thick-crusted *panini,* and returned to the workyard.

He tried to cut marble around the edges of the Hercules block, thinking that the feel of the iron instruments would bring him enjoyment. He soon set them down, climbed up on his stool and began to draw: the arm, muscles and joints, the jaw, the heart, the head. When Beppe arrived, came close to give him a *buon giorno,* he spread a concealing hand over the sheet before him. Beppe stopped short; but not before he got a look at an empty eye socket and exposed viscera. He shook his head grimly, turned and walked away.

At noon Michelangelo went home to dinner, to allay Lodovico's fears about his absence.

It took him several days to work up the courage to return to the dead room and crack a man's skull. Once there he began working rapidly with hammer and chisel, cutting backward from the bridge of the nose. It was a nerve-racking experience, for the head moved each time he made a stroke. Nor did he know how much force to exert to break the bone. He could not get the skull open. He covered the head, turned the man over, spent the rest of the night studying the structure of the spinal column.

With the next cadaver he did not make the mistake of

cutting backward on the skull, but instead cut around the head, from the tip of the left ear along the hairline, taking three or four hard blows of the hammer to penetrate the half inch of bone. There was now room enough to keep his scalpel under the skull and cut all the way around. A white-yellow cream escaped; the fissure opened wider. When he had cut the bone more than halfway, he used his scalpel as a lever and ripped. The skull lifted off in his hands.

It was like dry wood. He was so shaken he barely prevented its dropping on to the floor. He shifted his eyes from the skull to the corpse. He was horrified, for with the top of the head off, the face was absolutely destroyed.

Again he was overcome by a sense of guilt; but with the skull lifted off he had his first look at a human brain. As an artist he had been fascinated by what created expression; what was it in the brain that enabled the face to convey emotion? Holding his candle close to the brainpan, he saw that the mass inside was yellow-white, with red-blue lines on the surface, the arteries and veins going in all directions. He could see that the mass of the brain was divided in the middle, exactly corresponding to the divided line of the skull. He could detect no odour, but to his first touch it was wet, very soft and even, like the skin of a soft fish.

He put the skull back on top of the head, wrapping the sheet tightly at the top to hold it in place. He was neither ill nor distressed as he had been on most other nights, but could hardly wait to get back to his next corpse and open the brain itself.

When he took off his next skull he was astonished to think that men could be so different when their brains looked and felt so much alike. From this he deduced that there must be a physical substance inside the brain which differed with each man. Using his index finger, he moved around the base of the skull, learned that the brain was completely detached and free from the bone. Putting his fingers in on both sides, he tried to take it out whole. It would not lift.

Where his fingers came together the mass was attached by something like a series of wires to the bottom of the skull basin. He cut the wires, pulled out the mass. It was so soft, and at the same time so slippery, he had to concentrate tremendously just to hold it together. He looked at it in wonderment and admiration: from this relatively small substance, which could weigh no more than a couple of pounds, emerged all the greatness of the human race: art, science, philosophy, government, all that men had become for good as well as evil.

When he cut the brain down the line of division it was similar to cutting very soft cheese; there was no noise, no spoilage, no odour. The two halves were exactly alike. No matter where he cut, it was all the same, grey in colour, a little yellowish. He pushed the corpse over on the table to make enough space to lay the brain out on the wooden plank and was amazed to see that in and by itself it had no structure, that it slowly collapsed over the wooden boards.

The holes in the skull he found filled with the same wire-like substance he had had to break in order to detach the brain. Following these strands down through the neck, he surmised that this substance was the sole connection between the brain and the body. The front holes he discerned were between the brain and the eyes; the other two holes corresponded to the ears. He pushed through the inch-and-a-half hole at the back base of the skull, connecting to the vertebræ; this was the connection between the brain and the back.

He was exhausted now, for he had worked for five hours and was glad when his candle burned out.

He sat on the edge of the fountain in the Piazza Santo Spirito throwing cold water at his face and asking himself:

"Am I obsessed to be doing these things? Have I the right to do this just because I say it is for sculpture? What price might I have to pay for this precious knowledge?"

Spring arrived, the air warmed. Beppe told him of some sculpture that needed doing for the new vault of the vestibule of Santo Spirito: carved capitals and a number of worked stones to decorate the vault and the doors. It never occurred to him to ask Prior Bichiellini to intervene. He went directly to the foreman in charge of constructing the square stone vault and asked for the job. The foreman did not want a student. Michelangelo offered to bring his Madonna and Child and Centaurs to prove that he could do the work. The foreman reluctantly agreed to look. Bugiardini borrowed one of Ghirlandaio's carts, came to the Buonarroti house, helped him wrap and carry the marbles down the stairs. They stowed them safely on a bed of straw, then wheeled the cart through the streets, across the Ponte Santa Trinita to Santo Spirito.

The foreman was unimpressed. The pieces were not suited to what he had to do.

"Besides, I already hired my two men."

"Sculptors?" Michelangelo was surprised.

"What then?"

"What are their names?"

"Giovanni di Betto and Simone del Caprina."

"Never heard of them. Where were they trained?"

"In a silversmith's shop."

"Are they ornamenting the stones with silver?"

"They worked at Prato on a similar job. They are experienced."

"And I am not? After three years in Lorenzo's sculpture garden, under Bertoldo?"

"Don't take it so hard, son. These are older men with families to support. You know how little marble work there is. But of course if you brought an order from Piero de' Medici, since you are a Medici protégé, and Piero is paying for the work . . ."

Michelangelo and Bugiardini wheeled the reliefs through the cobbled streets, put them back under the bed.

Lodovico waited resignedly for his son to reform. Michelangelo continued to come in at dawn, after having dissected the knee and ankle bone, the corresponding elbow and wrist bone, the hip and pelvis, the private parts. He studied the muscular structure again and again, the shoulders and forearms, the thighs and calves. Lodovico cornered him.

"I order you to give up this dissolute life at once, to go back to work during the day and to bed after supper at night."

"Give me a little more time, Father."

Giovansimone was delighted that Michelangelo had taken off on the wild life. Florence was agog over its latest scandal: Piero had interceded with the Dominican authorities and had Savonarola banished to Bologna as "too great a partisan of the people." But for Giovansimone there had been no change in activity.

"How about coming with me to-night? I'm going where there's good gambling and whoring."

"No, thank you."

"Why not? Are you too good to go out with me?"

"Everyone to his own evil, Giovansimone."

6

An unexpected death put an end to his dissecting.

Working in robust good health, Domenica Ghirlandaio contracted a pestilence and in two days was dead. Michelangelo went to the *bottega* to take his place with Granacci, Bugiardini, Cieco, Baldinelli, Tedesco and Jacopo on one side of the coffin, while the son, brothers and brother-in-law stood on the other, and the friends came to say good-bye. Together they all walked behind the funeral procession, over the route on which Michelangelo had driven the cart for his first day of frescoing in Santa Maria Novella, to attend the mass, and then the burial.

That afternoon he went to visit Prior Bichiellini, casually laid the long bronze key over the pages of the book the prior was reading, and said, " I should like to carve something for the church."

The prior showed pleasure but not surprise.

" I have long felt the need of a crucifix for the central altar. I've always envisioned it in wood."

" Wood? I wonder if I can?"

For once he had the good sense not to say, " Wood is not my trade." If the prior wanted a Crucifixion in wood, then wood it must be, though he had never even whittled. There was no material of sculpture that Bertoldo had not obliged him to handle: wax, clay, the varying stones. But never wood; probably because Donatello had not touched wood for the last thirty-five years of his life, after he had completed his Crucifixion for Brunelleschi.

He accompanied the prior through the sacristy. The prior stopped and pointed out the arch behind the main altar, which formed one of the two entries to the chancel, then asked:

" Could it carry a life-size figure?"

" I will have to draw the arches and the altar to scale to be sure; but I should think it could be almost life size. May I work in the monastery carpenter shop?"

" The brothers would be pleased to have you."

The lay brothers in the carpenter shop worked with sunlight streaming on their shoulders from overhead windows. In the relaxed atmosphere of the workbenches he was treated

229

as another carpenter come to make still one more useful article among the hundreds needed for Santo Spirito. Though there was no order of silence in the busy shop, no one who liked to gab ever came close to an Augustinian monastery.

This suited Michelangelo; he felt at home working in the comfortable silence framed by the pleasant sounds of saw, plane and hammer. The smell of sawdust was salutary. He worked on the various woods the monastery had to offer to get the knack of carving in this material which he found so unlike marble. The wood did not seem to fight back.

He took to reading the New Testament, the story of Christ as related by Matthew and Mark. The more he read, the more the terror-laden, agony-infused Crucifixion of previous centuries to be seen in the chapels of Florence, receded from his mind, and into it came the image of Prior Bichiellini: cheerful, hearty, dedicated, serving all humanity in God's name, with a great mind and noble spirit that gloried in living.

It was a need of his nature to be original. But what could one say about Christ on the cross that had not been carved and painted before? Though the theme of the Crucifixion would not have occurred to him, he was eager to do something particularly fine to justify the prior's faith in him. The finished work would have to be intensely spiritual, lest the prior wonder if he had made a mistake in letting him dissect.

He started drawing in front of the earliest Crucifixions, those of the thirteenth century, carved with the head and knees of Christ turned in the same direction, perhaps because this was the simplest form for the sculptor and because the design evoked, in terms of emotion, the simplicity of unquestioning acceptance. By the fourteenth century the sculptors were showing Christ in full face, with all parts of the body symmetrically disposed on either side of a central, structural line.

He spent time in front of Donatello's Santa Croce Crucifixion, marvelling at the magnificence of its conception. Whatever emotion Donatello had set out to achieve, strength combined with idyllic fulfilment, power to forgive as well as subdue, the ability to be destroyed as well as resurrected, all these emotions he had succeeded in conveying. Yet Michelangelo did not feel within himself any of the things that Donatello felt. He had never been altogether clear in his own mind why God could not accomplish by Himself all the things He sent His son down on earth to do. Why did God need a son? The exquisitely balanced Donatello Christ said to him:

"This is how God wanted it to be, exactly the way it was planned. It is not hard to accept one's fate when it has been preordained. I have anticipated this pain."

This was not acceptable to Michelangelo's temperament.

What had the violent end to do with God's message of love? Why did He permit violence to take place, when its very form would create hatred, fear, retribution and continuing violence? If He were omnipotent, why had He not devised a more peaceable way to bring His message to the world? His impotence to stop this barbarism was a terrifying thought to Michelangelo . . . and perhaps to Christ as well.

As he stood in the bright sunlight on the steps of Santa Croce, watching the boys play football on the hard earth of the square, then walked slowly past the palaces of the Via de' Bardi, patting affectionately the carved stones of the buildings as he went by, he thought:

"What went through the mind of Christ between the sunset hour when the Roman soldier drove the first nail through his flesh, and the hour when he died? For these thoughts would determine not only how he accepted his fate, but also the position of his body on the cross. Donatello's Christ accepted in serenity, and thought nothing. Brunelleschi's Christ was so ethereal that he died at the first touch of the nail, and had no time to think."

He returned to his workbench, began exploring his mind with charcoal and ink. On Christ's face appeared the expression, "I am in agony, not from the iron nails, but from the rust of doubt." He could not bring himself to convey Christ's divinity by anything so obvious as a halo; it had to be portrayed through an inner force, strong enough to conquer his misgivings at this hour of severest trial.

It was inevitable that his Christ would be closer to man than to God. He did not know that he was to be crucified. He neither wanted it nor liked it. And as a result his body was twisted in conflict, torn, like all men, by inner questioning.

When he was ready to begin carving he had before him a new concept: he turned Christ's head and knees in opposite

231

directions, establishing through this contrapuntal design a graphic tension, the intense physical and spiritual inner conflict of a man who is being pulled two ways.

He carved his figure in the hardest wood available in Tuscany, walnut, and when he had finished with hammer and chisel, sandpapered it down, and rubbed the surface with stainless oil and wax. His fellow carpenters made no comment, but they stopped by his bench to observe progress. Nor, for that matter, did the prior enter into a discussion of its message. He said simply:

"Every artist's Crucifixion is a self-portrait. It is what I envisioned for the altar. Thank you."

On Sunday morning Michelangelo brought his family to Santo Spirito. He led them to a bench close to the altar. His Christ loomed above them. His grandmother whispered:

"You make me feel compassion for him. Always before I thought Christ was feeling compassion for me."

Lodovico was not feeling compassion for anybody. He asked, "How large was the commission?"

"It wasn't a commission. I volunteered."

"You mean you're not getting paid?"

"The prior has been good to me. I wanted to repay my debt."

"Good to you in what way?"

". . . well . . . he let me copy the works of art . . ."

"The church is open to everybody."

"In the monastery. And to use his library."

"It is a public library. Are you *pazzo* that a penniless lad should work free for a rich monastery?"

A heavy snowstorm that lasted for two days and nights left Florence a white city. Sunday dawned clear, crisp and cold. He was alone in the enclosed Duomo workshop, huddled over a brazier while trying to make the first of the Hercules drawings, when Piero's groom came looking for him.

"His Excellency, Piero de' Medici, asks if you could come to the palace."

He made his way to the barber in the straw market, where he had his hair cut, the patches of beard down the sides of his cheek and chin shaved, then returned home, boiled himself in a tub of hot water, bathed, put on his blue wool tunic and set out for the first time in over a year and a half for the palace. The statues in the courtyard, as he came through, were piled high with snow. He found the Medici children and grandchildren assembled in Lorenzo's *studiolo*, a bright fire burning.

It was Giuliano's birthday. Cardinal Giovanni, who had settled in a small but exquisite palace in the quarter of Sant'Antonio when a hostile Borgia had been elected Pope, looked plumper than ever sitting in Lorenzo's chair, hovered over by his cousin Giulio. Their sister Maddalena, married to the former Pope Innocent VIII's son, Francheschetto Cibo, was back with their two children; so was Lucrezia, married to Jacopo Salviati of the Florentine banking family, who owned the home of Dante's Beatrice; their aunt Nannina and her husband, Bernardo Rucellai; Piero and Alfonsina with their oldest son. They were dressed in their gayest brocades, jewelled satins and cut velvets.

And Contessina was there, elegantly gowned in aquamarine silk interwoven with silver threads. Michelangelo noted with surprise that she was taller, that her arms and shoulders had filled out a little, and her bosom, propped by stays under the embroidery, was approaching maturity. Her eyes, when they met his, sparkled as brightly as the silver jewels with which her dress was ornamented.

A servant handed him a glass of hot mulled wine. The drink combined with the warmth of the reception, the sharp nostalgia the room evoked, and Contessina's bemused smile, all went to his head.

Piero stood with his back to the fire. He smiled, and seemed to have forgotten their quarrel. "Michelangelo, it is our pleasure to welcome you back to the palace. To-day we must do everything that pleases Giuliano."

"I should like to help make Giuliano happy to-day."

"Good. The first thing he said this morning was, ' I should like to have the greatest snowman ever made.' And since you were our father's favourite sculptor, what would be more natural than that we should think of you?"

Something within him sank like a stone. While the Medici children turned their faces towards him, he remembered the two tubes in the cadaver that extended downward from the mouth, one to carry air, the other food. Should there not be a third, to swallow crushed hopes?

"Please do it for me, Michelangelo," cried Giuliano. "It would be the most wonderful snowman ever made."

His acrid impression of having been summoned as an entertainer passed with Giuliano's plea. Was he to reply, " Snow is not my trade "?

" Do help us, Michelangelo." It was Contessina, who had come close to him. "We'll all serve as your assistants."

And he knew it was all right.

Late that afternoon, when the last of the Florentine crowds had thronged through the palace grounds to see the hilariously grotesque, giant snowman, Piero sat at his father's desk in the big office, under the maps of Italy.

"Why not move back into the palace, Michelangelo? We would like to bring together again my father's circle."

"Could I ask under what conditions I would return?"

"You would have the same privileges as when my father was alive."

Michelangelo gulped; he was fifteen when he had come to live in this palace. He was almost eighteen now. Hardly an age to receive spending money left on his washstand. Yet it was a chance to get out of the dread Buonarroti house, the nagging domination of Lodovico, to earn some money, perhaps to carve something good for the Medici.

7

A groom moved him back into his old apartment, with Bertoldo's sculptures still untouched on the catercornered shelves. A palace tailor came with fabrics and measuring tapes; and on the following Sunday Piero's secretary, Ser Bernardo da Bibbiena, deposited three gold florins on the washstand.

Everything was the same; yet everything was different. The scholars of Italy and Europe no longer came to the palace. The Plato Academy preferred to hold its meetings in the Rucellai gardens. At Sunday dinner only those noble families with pleasure-loving sons were at table. The great families from the Italian city-states were not present on the pleasant duties of treaty making, nor were the merchant princes who had prospered with the Medici, nor yet the *gonfalonieri, buonuomini* or councilmen from the Florentine districts whom Lorenzo had kept close to him in bonds of intimacy. All these were replaced by entertainers and Piero's young sporting friends.

The Topolinos rode into the city behind their white oxen on Sunday after mass and hoisted the Hercules block on to their cart. The grandfather drove, while the father, three sons and Michelangelo walked through the quiet streets that had been hosed and swept immaculately clean at sunrise, each holding an end of the lashing ropes. They drove in through the back entrance of the garden, unloaded and propped the marble next to his old sculpture shed.

Comfortably settled, he returned to his drawings, made one in red chalk of the youth pulling apart the jaws of the Nemean lion with his bare hands; the man in his middle years wrestling Antaeus to death; the old man fighting the hundred-headed hydra; all of which he found too pictorial. Finally rejecting the outspread figure of earlier Florence Herculeses, the legs wide apart, arm on the hip, he designed a closed, compact figure closer to the Greek concept, in which all of Hercules' bursting power was held in a unifying force between torso and limbs.

What concession must he make to the conventional? First, the huge club: this he designed as a tree trunk upon which Hercules leaned. The inevitable lion's pelt, which had always formed a frame for the figure, he knotted far out on one shoulder, letting the barest suggestion fall across the chest, concealing nothing of the heroic torso. He extended one arm only a little, patently enclosing the round firm apples of the Hesperides. The club, the long lion skin, the apples had been used by former sculptors to depict fortitude; his Hercules, naked before the world, would carry within its own structure everything that mankind needed of fortitude and resolution.

He was not daunted by the fact that his would be the largest Hercules ever carved in Florence. As he marked out the proportions of the great figure, seven feet seven inches in height, with a foot-and-a-half base and five inches of safety marble above the head from which he would carve downward, he recalled that Hercules had been the national hero of Greece, as Lorenzo had been of Florence. Why then portray him in small, exquisite bronzes? Both Hercules and Lorenzo had failed, but oh! how much they had accomplished in the trying! How richly they deserved to be carved bigger than life.

He built a rough clay model, working out the shifts of weight and stance, the movements of the back muscles because of the extended arm, the muscle distribution because the figure was leaning, the straining of tendon and ligament, the swivel of hip and shoulder, all of which he now knew and could project with conviction. Yet some instinct kept him from using measuring cords and iron pegs to enlarge the model to scale. For his first life-size figure in the round, which was also the first work he was creating in absolute independence, he wanted to see how far and faithfully his hand could follow his eye.

He forged his tools for the initial massing, pounded the rods to increase their length, giving them a stubbier end to withstand the greater hammer blows, and once more, with the handling of the metal, achieved in himself a feeling of hardness, durability. He squatted on his haunches before the marble. Looking at the huge block gave him a sense of power. He removed the edges with heavy point and heavy hammer, thought with satisfaction that by this very act he was already adding to the stature of the block before him. He had no wish to conquer the nine-foot slab, only to persuade it to express his creative ideas.

This was Seravezza marble, quarried high in the Apuan Alps. After he had penetrated its weathered outer skin it behaved like a lump of sugar under his dog's-tooth chisel, its pure milky-white slivers crumbling between his fingers. He used a flat stick to gauge approximately how deep he had to cut to get down to neck depth, armpit depth, torso depth, the bended knee. Then he went back to the forge, made a *calcagnuolo,* and attacked the marble with fury, the chisel hugging close to the surface like a plough through the earth. And now the Seravezza marble suddenly became hard as iron, and he had to struggle with all his strength to achieve his forms.

Ignoring the instructions of Bertoldo, he did not attempt to work his block all around, develop it as a whole, but went after the head, shoulders, arms, hips, using his flat stick and naked eye to measure his high points as he dug deeper. Then he almost ruined his block. He had cut too deeply to free the neck and head, and now his strong chisel strokes on the emerging shoulder muscles caused intense vibrations to run up through the neck into the head. The shivering marble looked for an instant as though it would crack at the narrow point; his Hercules would lose his head, and he would have to begin again on a reduced scale. Then the trembling ceased.

He sat down on a nearby box to wipe the perspiration from his face.

He forged new fine-edged tools, making sure every point was symmetrical. Now each blow of his hammer was transferred directly to the carving end of the tool, as though it were his fingers rather than the chisels that were cutting through the crystals. Every few moments he stepped back and circled the block because, no matter how deep he cut, a fog of texture obscured the contour of knee socket, rib cage. He used a brush to clear away the dust.

He made a second series of mistakes; his eye failed to measure accurately the receding planes, and he delivered some hard blows which spoiled the frontal harmony. But he had left himself spare marble at the back, and so he was able to push the entire figure deeper into the block than he had intended.

His progress became swifter as he stepped inside the marble, so passionately tearing out deepening layers that he felt as though he were standing in the midst of a snowstorm, breathing its flurries, closing his eyes at the moment of the hammer impact.

The anatomy of the marble began matching the anatomy of his clay model: the powerful chest, magnificently rounded forearms, the thighs like the white meat under the bark of giant trees, the head focusing enormous power within its limited area. Hammer and chisel in hand, he stood back from the galvanic male figure before him, still faceless, standing on a rough-gouged base to show the material from which it had emerged, thinking that from the very beginning the marble had yielded to love: pliable, vulvar. With marble he was the dominant male; his was the choice, his the conquest. Yet coming together with the object of his love, he had been all tenderness. The block had been virginal but not frigid; it had been set on fire by his own white heat. Statues came out of the marble, but not until the tool had penetrated and seeded its female form. From love came all of life.

He finished the surface with a good pumicing, but gave it no polish, afraid that to do so would diminish its virility. He left the hair and beard in a crude state, with just a suggestion of curls, angling the small three-toothed chisel so that he could dig in with the last tooth for accent.

Monna Alessandra went to bed feeling tired one night, and never awoke. Lodovico took the loss hard; like most Tuscans, he was deeply attached to his mother, and had for her a gentleness he showed no one else in the family. For Michelangelo the loss was poignant; since the death of his own mother thirteen years before, Monna Alessandra had been the only woman to whom he could turn for love or understanding. Without his grandmother the Buonarroti house seemed gloomier to him than ever.

The palace, by contrast, was in an uproar over Contessina's marriage, which was to take place late in May. Since Contessina was the last of the Medici daughters, Piero was ignoring all of the sumptuary laws and preparing to spend fifty thousand florins to give Florence the greatest celebration in its history. Contessina went her busy way, whirling from *sarto* to *sarta* for her gowns, commissioning dowry chests to be painted, interviewing merchants from all over the world to select her linens, brocades, jewellery, silver and goldware, dishes, blankets, furnishings that were her rightful and imperative dowry as a Medici.

Then one evening they met by accident in the *studiolo*. It was so like old times, with Lorenzo's books and art works about them, that they forgot for the moment the impending ceremonies and linked arms affectionately.

"I hardly see you any more, Michelangelo. You are not to be unhappy at my wedding."

"Am I to be invited?"

"The wedding takes place here. How could you not attend?"

"The invitation must come from Piero."

"Stop being difficult!" Her eyes flashed with the anger he remembered flaring up at his other obstinacies. "You will celebrate for three days, just as I will."

"Not quite," he replied; and they both blushed.

Granacci was commissioned by Piero to take charge of the scenery for the wedding pageant, ball, banquet, theatricals. The palace was full of singing, dancing, drinking, revelry. Yet Michelangelo was lonely. He spent most of his time in the garden.

Piero was polite but distant, as though having his father's sculptor under his roof was all he had been after. The feeling of being an exhibit was strengthened when he heard Piero boast that he had two extraordinary persons in the palace: Michelangelo, who made great snowmen, and a Spanish footman who ran so fast that Piero, riding his best horse at a gallop, could not outrun him.

"Excellency, could we speak seriously about my carving marbles? I wish to earn my keep."

There was incredulity in Piero's expression.

"A couple of years ago you were offended because I treated you as a tradesman. Now you are offended because I do not. How is one to keep you artists happy?"

"I need a goal such as your father outlined to me."

"What was that?"

"To build a façade for San Lorenzo, with niches for twenty life-size marble figures."

"He never mentioned it to me."

"It was before he went out to Careggi the last time."

"Ah well, the fleeting dreams of a dying man. Not very practical, are they? You just keep yourself busy as best you can, Buonarroti, and someday I'll think of something for you to do."

He watched the wedding gifts roll in from all over Italy, Europe and the Near East, from Lorenzo's friends, from business associates of the Medici: rare jewels, carved ivories, perfumes, costly satins from Asia; goblets and bowls of gold from the Orient, carved furniture. He too wanted to give Contessina a gift. But what?

The Hercules! Why not? He had bought the marble with his own money. He was a sculptor, he should give her sculpture for her wedding. The Hercules for the garden of the Ridolfi palace! He would not tell her about it, he would simply ask the Topolinos to help him move it there.

Now for the first time he came to grips with Hercules' face. It would be a portrait of *Il Magnifico*: not of his upturned nose, muddy skin, scraggly hair; but of the inner man and mind of Lorenzo de' Medici. The expression would convey intense pride, coupled with humility. It would have not only the power but the desire to communicate. Matching the devastating strength of the body would be a gentleness that would yet convey the fighter who would do battle for mankind, be concerned with remoulding man's treacherous world.

His drawings finished, he started carving excitedly, using the hand drill to bring out the nostrils and ears, the profusion of hair falling about the face, the finest edged chisel to round the cheekbones, the hand-twirling bore to touch ever so lightly the eyes to achieve the clear, piercing communication with every soul who looked upon him. He worked from dawn to dark, not bothering to eat at midday, and falling into bed at night like a dead man.

Granacci praised him for his completion of so complex a task, then added quietly:

" *Amico mio,* you can't give it to Contessina. It wouldn't be right."

" Why not?"

" It's too . . . too big."

" The Hercules is too big?"

" No, the gift. The Ridolfi might not think it proper."

" For me to give Contessina a gift?"

" So large a gift."

" Are you speaking of size? Or value?"

" Both. You are not a Medici, nor a member of a ruling house of Tuscany. It might be considered in bad taste."

" But it has no value. I couldn't sell it."

" It has value. You can sell it."

" To whom?"

" The Strozzi. For the courtyard of their new palace. I brought them here last Sunday. They authorized me to offer you a hundred large gold florins. It will enjoy a place of honour in the courtyard. It is your first sale!"

Tears of frustration smarted behind his lids, but he was older now, he could blink them back.

" Piero and my father are right; no matter how an artist may strive, he ends up as a hireling, with something to market."

There was no way to escape the excitement of the three thousand wedding guests pouring into the city and filling Florence's palaces to capacity. On the morning of May 24 he donned his green silk tunic with velvet sleeves, the violet cloak. In front of the palace was a fountain garlanded with fruits, in its centre two figures designed by Granacci from which red and white wine flowed so abundantly that it ran down the Via de' Gori.

He walked with Granacci behind the wedding party as Contessina and Ridolfi paraded through streets decorated with flags, preceded by trumpeters. At the entrance to the Piazza del Duomo was a replica of a Roman triumphal arch festooned with garlands. On the steps of the cathedral a notary read aloud the marriage contract to the thousands who jammed the piazza. When Michelangelo heard the extent of Contessina's dowry, he blanched.

At the family church of San Lorenzo, Piero formally presented Contessina to Ridolfi, who placed the betrothal ring on her finger. Michelangelo remained at the back of the church and slipped out a side door in the middle of the nuptial mass. A wooden stand filled one side of the square, to accommodate the crowds, while in the centre there was a fifty-foot tree supporting a white pavilion in which musicians played. The surrounding houses were hung with tapestries.

The wedding party emerged from the church, Ridolfi tall in his white satin coat, jet-black hair framing his thin, pale face. Michelangelo stood on the steps watching Contessina in her crimson samite gown with its long train and collar of white ermine, on her head an elaborate headdress mounted on a crimson support and adorned with carved gilt beads. As soon as she was seated in the bedecked stands the entertainment began: a play depicting " A Fight Between Chastity and Marriage," a tournament in which Piero jousted ; and as the climax, a contest of the " Knights of the She-Cat " in which a man, naked to the waist and with shaven head, entered a cage on a wooden platform where he had to kill a cat with his teeth, without using his hands.

A seat had been reserved for him in the dining salon. The finest produce of Tuscany had been brought to the palace for the feast: eight hundred barrels of wine, a thousand pounds of flour, of meat, of game, of marzipan. He watched the ceremonial acts of a child being placed in Contessina's arms and a gold florin in her shoe to bring fertility and riches. Then, after the nuptial feast, when the guests went into the ballroom which Granacci had converted into ancient Bagdad, he left the palace and walked from piazza to piazza, where Piero had set up prodigal tables of food and wine for all of Florence to participate. But the people seemed glum.

He did not return to the palace where there were to be two more days of feasting and celebration before Contessina would be escorted to the Ridolfi palace. Instead, in the dark of night, he walked slowly up to Settignano, spread an old blanket under the Topolino arches and, his hands locked behind his head, watched the sun emerge over the hills to light the roof of the Buonarroti house across the ravine.

8

Contessina's marriage proved to be a turning point: for himself; for Florence. He had witnessed the resentment of the people on the first night of the feasts, heard the general murmurings against Piero. There was little need for the fiery sermons preached against him by Savonarola, returned to the city with more power than ever in his Dominican Order, demanding that Piero be prosecuted by the Signoria for violation of the city's sumptuary laws.

Puzzled at the intensity of the reaction, Michelangelo went to visit Prior Bichiellini.

"Were the marriages of the other Medici daughters less sumptuous?" he asked.

"Not particularly. But with Lorenzo, the people of Florence felt he was sharing; with Piero, they felt he was giving. It made the wedding wine turn sour in their mouths."

The completion of Contessina's wedding celebration was a signal to the Medici cousins to begin their political campaign against Piero. Within a few days the city was awash with scandal: at a party the night before Piero and his cousin Lorenzo had fought over a young woman. Piero struck Lorenzo a blow on the ear; the first time one Medici had ever struck another. They had both pulled their knives and there would have been a killing if friends had not stepped in. When Michelangelo went in to midday dinner he found a few more of the older friends missing. The laughter of Piero and his comrades sounded a trifle hysterical.

Granacci came into the garden at dusk to tell him that someone had seen his Hercules in the Strozzi courtyard, was waiting for him there, and would like to speak to him about a commission. Michelangelo hid his surprise when he found the new patrons to be the Medici cousins, Lorenzo and Giovanni. He had met them many times in the palace while Lorenzo was alive, for they had loved him as a father, and the Magnificent One had given them the highest of diplomatic posts, even sending them to Versailles eleven years before to congratulate Charles VIII on ascending the French throne. Piero had always condescended to them as coming down through the lesser branch of the family.

The Medici cousins were standing on either side of his Hercules. Lorenzo, who was twelve years older than Michelangelo, had regular features full of expression, though his skin was pockmarked; he was a powerfully built man with a strong neck, shoulders and chest. He lived like a great lord in the family palace on Piazza San Marco, with villas on the declivity of the hill below Fiesole and at Castello. Even now Botticelli was living on his commission to illustrate Dante's *Divine Comedy*. He himself was a respected poet and dramatist. Giovanni, the younger brother, twenty-seven, was called "The Handsome" by Florentines.

They greeted him heartily, spoke highly of the Hercules, then got to the point. Lorenzo was the spokesman.

"Michelangelo, we saw the two marble pieces you sculptured for our uncle Lorenzo, and we have often said, my brother and I, that one day we should like you to carve a piece for us."

Michelangelo remained silent. The younger brother continued.

"We've always yearned for a young St. John. In white marble. As the patron saint of our home. Would the theme interest you?"

Michelangelo shifted awkwardly from foot to foot, gazing out of the main gate of the Strozzi palace to the intense pool of sunlight lying in the Via Tornabuoni. He needed work, not merely because of the money involved but because he was growing restless. It would put marble in his hands.

"We are prepared to pay a good price," said Lorenzo, while his brother added, "And there is a place at the back of our garden for a workshop. What do you say?"

"To be wanted is always good. May I think it over?"

"Of course," replied Lorenzo heartily. "We have no desire to rush you. Give us the pleasure of your company at Sunday dinner."

He walked home in silence, his head down. Granacci proffered no word or suggestion until they parted at the corner of the Via dei Bentaccordi and Via dell'Anguillara.

"I was asked to bring you. I brought you. That does not mean that I necessarily think you should accept."

"Thank you, Granacci. I understand."

His family had no such tolerance.

"Of course you'll take the commission!" boomed Lodovico, pushing masses of his grey-black hair back out of his eyes. "Only this time you can dictate the fee because they came to you."

"Why did they come to me?" persisted Michelangelo.

"Because they want a St. John," replied his aunt Cassandra.

"But why at this moment, when they are setting up an opposition party to Piero? Why didn't they ask me at any time during the past two years?"

"What business is that of yours?" demanded his uncle

Francesco. "Who is crazy enough to look a sculpture commission in the mouth?"

"But something more is true, Uncle Francesco. Prior Bichiellini says the aim of the cousins is to drive Piero out of Florence. I think they want to strike another blow at Piero."

"And are you a blow?" Lucrezia's face was puzzled.

"A modest one, *madre mia*." Michelangelo's whimsical smile offset the ugliness of his flattened nose.

"Let's get out of politics," commanded Lodovico, "and back into business. Are times so good for the Buonarroti that you can afford to turn down a commission?"

"No, Father, but I can't be disloyal to Lorenzo."

"The dead don't need loyalty."

"They do. As much as the living. I just gave you the hundred florins from the Hercules."

The cousins reserved him a place of honour at their festive Sunday dinner, spoke of everything but Piero and the St. John. When, after dinner, Michelangelo stammered that he appreciated their offer but could not at the moment accept, Lorenzo replied easily:

"We are in no hurry. The offer stands."

There was no real place for him in the palace. He served no purpose and was valuable to no one except Giuliano, who needed the affection. He went looking for jobs to justify his presence: sorting Lorenzo's collection of drawings, adding Piero's occasional acquisition of an ancient medallion or carved gem to its proper place in the cabinets. Lodovico had told him that he did not have the price of pride; but sometimes a man's nature did not give him the choice of deciding whether he could afford a trait of character with which he had been born.

Piero too was unhappy, sitting at table pale, cold, as he asked his few remaining friends:

"Why can't I get the Signoria to see things my way? Why do I have trouble with everything, when my father had life so smooth?"

Michelangelo posed the question to Prior Bichiellini, who sat back in his black tunic with the white shirt showing crisp and clean at that throat. His eyes snapped with anger.

"His four Medici ancestors considered the *act* of governing as the *art* of governing. They loved Florence first, themselves second. Piero . . ."

244

Michelangelo was surprised at the denunciatory edge to the prior's voice.

"I have not heard you bitter before, Father."

". . . Piero won't listen to counsel. A weak man at the helm, and a power-hungry priest working to replace him . . . These are sad days for Florence, my son."

"I have heard some of Savonarola's 'plank by plank' sermons on the coming Flood. Half the people of the city believe Judgment Day is the next rain away. What is his purpose in terrorizing Florence?'"

The prior took off his spectacles.

"He wants to become Pope. But his ambition doesn't end there: he has plans to conquer the Near East, then the Orient."

Michelangelo asked banteringly, "You have no passion for converting the heathen?"

The prior was quiet for a moment. "Would I like to see an all-Catholic world? Only if the world wished to be converted. And certainly not by a tyrant who would burn down the humanities and destroy the world's mind to save its soul. No true Christian would want that."

At the palace he found an urgent message from his father. Lodovico led him into the boys' bedroom, lifted a pile of clothing from the top of Giovansimone's locker, and scooped out a pile of jewellery, gold and silver buckles, medallions.

"What does this mean?" he asked Michelangelo. "Has Giovansimone been burglarizing people's homes at night?"

"Nothing quite so illegal, Father. Giovansimone is a captain in Savonarola's Army of Boys. They strip women in the streets who violate the padre's orders against wearing jewellery in public; they knock on doors, twenty or thirty of them, if they bear of a family violating the sumptuary laws and strip it bare. If they meet opposition, they stone people half to death."

"But is Giovansimone allowed to keep these things? They must be worth hundreds of florins."

"He is supposed to bring them all to San Marco. Most of the children do. But Giovansimone has converted his old gang of hoodlums into what Savonarola calls his 'white-shirted angels.' The Council is powerless to stop them."

Lionardo chose this time to summon Michelangelo to San Marco to show him the school for painters, sculptors and illuminators Fra Savonarola had set up in the cells off the cloister garden.

"You see, Michelangelo. Savonarola is not against art, only obscene art. Now is your chance to join us and become the sculptor for our order. You'll never want for marble or commissions."

"What will I sculpture?"

"What does it matter to you what you sculpture, as long as you are working?"

"Who will tell me what to carve?"

"Fra Savonarola."

"And if I don't want to carve what he wants?"

"As a monk you will not question. You will have no personal desires. . . ."

He went back to his workbench in the abandoned casino. Here at least he was free to draw from memory anatomical pictures of the things he had learned during his months of dissection. He burned the crowded, overscrawled papers, yet it was hardly necessary since no one came to the garden any more except the fifteen-year-old Giuliano, who sometimes walked over, books under his arm, to study in companionable silence at Torrigiani's old worktable on the casino porch. They would walk back to the palace through the summer dusk that sifted downward like grey powder on the city, quenching the serene blue and golden-tan light of the building stones.

9

With autumn, Florence became embroiled in an international dispute that could lead to the city-state's destruction. It was all happening, Michelangelo gathered, because Charles VIII, King of France, had built the first permanent army since Cæsar's legions, consisting of some twenty thousand trained and heavily armed men. He was now bringing that army across the Alps and into Italy to claim the Kingdom of Naples through inheritance. During Lorenzo's lifetime Charles VIII would have been too friendly to the Medici to threaten a march across Tuscany; if he had, Lorenzo's allies, the city-states of Milan, Venice, Genoa, Padua, Ferrara, would have closed ranks to keep him out. But Piero had lost these allies. The Duke of Milan had sent emissaries to Charles, inviting him to Italy. The Medici cousins, who had been at Versailles for his coronation, assured the king that Florence awaited his triumphal entry.

246

Because of the alliance of the Orsini, his mother's and wife's family, with Naples, Piero refused Charles safe passage. Yet during the months from spring to autumn he did nothing to assemble soldiers or arms to stop the French king if he did invade. The citizens of Florence who would have fought for Lorenzo were ready to welcome the French because they would help drive out Piero. Savonarola too invited Charles to enter Florence.

By the middle of September Charles VIII had brought his army across the Alps, been welcomed by the Duke of Milan, and sacked the town of Rapallo. The news threw Florence into a fever. All normal business was suspended, yet when Charles again sent his emissaries to ask for safe passage, Piero turned them away without a definite answer. The French king vowed to storm through Tuscany and conquer the city.

Michelangelo now had a new neighbour in the palace. Piero imported Alfonsina's brother, Paolo Orsini, to lead one hundred mercenaries . . . to stop Charles's army of twenty thousand. A dozen times Michelangelo vowed he would flee the palace, travel to Venice as Lorenzo had suggested. Loyal to Lorenzo, to Contessina, Giuliano, and even to Cardinal Giovanni, he had no feeling whatever for Piero, who had given him a home, a place to work and a salary. But he could not bring himself to join the deserters.

His three years under Lorenzo in the garden and palace had been years of excitement, growth, learning, mastery of his tools and trade, every day a precious jewel to be valued, cherished; every day like a year of maturing. And now, for the better part of these last two and a half years since Lorenzo's death, he had been stopped in his tracks. He was a better draughtsman, yes, thanks to Prior Bichiellini and his months of dissection, but he felt less alive, less knowledgeable, less creative than he had in the flush of his training by Bertoldo, *Il Magnifico,* Pico, Poliziano, Landino, Ficino, Benivieni. For a long time he had been traversing the bottom half of a circle. How did he get into an upward swing again? How did he rise above the tumult, fears, paralysis of Florence, start his mind and hands working again as a sculptor?

How indeed, with even Poliziano going to Savonarola for absolution, begging in his last words to be taken into the Dominican Order so that he could be buried in a monk's habit inside the walls of San Marco?

Granacci would give him no counsel. Bugiardini said

simply, "If you go to Venice, I go along." When Jacopo heard that Michelangelo was thinking of the journey he sought him out and cried:

"I always wanted to see Venice. On somebody else's florins. Take me along. I will protect you on the road from assassins. . . ."

"By telling them jokes?"

Jacopo screwed up his face, said, "Laughter is a lance. What do you say?"

"Agreed, Jacopo. When I leave for Venice, I'll take you with me."

On September 21, Fra Savonarola, in a final effort to drive Piero out, preached a climactic sermon in the Duomo. Florentines jammed the cathedral. Never before had the friar had such power, and never had his voice rung out with such a clap of doom. The hair of the Florentines stood on end as they cried and lamented while Savonarola portrayed the destruction of Florence and every living creature in it.

"Now the earth was corrupt in God's sight, and the earth was filled with violence. And God saw the earth, and behold, it was corrupt; for all flesh had corrupted their way upon the earth.

"'For behold, I will bring a flood of waters upon the earth, to destroy all flesh in which is the breath of life from under heaven; everything that is on the earth shall die . . .'"

The friar's faintest whisper pierced the remotest corners of the vast cathedral. Each stone served as a rebounding wall. Michelangelo, standing just inside the doors, felt closed in on every side by a sea of sound, drowning him like rising waters. He returned to the street surrounded by a mass of people half dead with fright, speechless, their eyes glassy.

Only Prior Bichiellini was calm.

"But, Michelangelo, this is necromancy. From the darkest ages of man. God himself promised Noah and his sons, in Genesis 9:9-11, that there would never be a second Deluge: 'Here is a covenant I will observe with you and with your children after you. . . . Never more will the living creation be destroyed by the waters of a flood; never again a flood to devastate the world.' Now tell me, by what right does Savonarola rewrite the Bible? One day Florence is going to find out it has been made a fool of. . . ."

The prior's soft voice dispelled Savonarola's spell.

"At that time you can open the gates of Santo Spirito to him, to save him from the mob," suggested Michelangelo.

The prior smiled wryly.

"Can't you imagine Savonarola taking the vow of silence? He'd sooner burn at the stake."

The web closed tighter each day: Venice declared herself neutral, Rome declined to provide troops. Charles attacked the frontier fortresses of Tuscany, a few of them fell, Pietrasanta's marble quarrymen put up a good fight; but it could be only a few days before the French army entered Florence.

He had little opportunity for rational thought. Alternating hysterias of fear and relief swept the populace, with all of the city in the streets, summoned to the Piazza della Signoria by the ringing of the great bell in the tower, to hear the news. Was the city to be sacked? The Republic overthrown? Was the wealth, art, trade, security, prosperity to be gobbled up by an invading monarch with a powerful army, after Florence had lived at peace with the world for so long that it had no more army, weapons, no will to fight? Had the Second Deluge begun?

One morning Michelangelo rose to find the palace abandoned. Piero, Orsini and their staffs had rushed out to treat with Charles. Alfonsina had left with her children and Giuliano for refuge in a hillside villa. Aside from a few old servants, Michelangelo seemed alone. The magnificent palace was frightening in its hollow silence. Lorenzo's body had died in Careggi, and now the great spirit of the man, represented by his magnificent library and art works, seemed to be dying as well. As he walked the echoing corridors and looked into the big empty rooms, something of the dread odour of death pervaded them. He ought to know, he who had become an expert in the Santo Spirito dead room.

Chaos continued. Piero prostrated himself before Charles, offered the conqueror the coast fortress, Pisa and Leghorn and two hundred thousand florins if he "would continue down the coast and avoid Florence." Outraged at this humiliating capitulation, the City Council rang the bell on top of the Signoria, summoned the people, and castigated Piero for his "cowardice, foolishness, ineptitude, surrender."

A delegation, including Fra Savonarola, was sent to Charles. It ignored Piero. Piero dashed back to Florence to reassert his rights. The city was wild in its rage against him. He demanded to be heard. The crowd yelled, "Go away! Do not disturb the Signoria!" Piero turned away in contempt. The crowd in the piazza wagged their hoods in denunciation, small gangs of boys hissed and threw stones. Piero drew his sword. The crowds chased him through the streets. He disappeared into the palace and diverted the throngs momentarily by having the remaining servants bring out wine and cake.

Then couriers came down the street crying, "The Signoria has banished the Medici! For life! There is a price of four thousand florins on Piero's head. Down with Piero!"

Entering the palace, Michelangelo found that Piero had escaped through the rear garden, joined Orsini's band of mercenaries at the Porta San Gallo and fled. Cardinal Giovanni, his fat face red with perspiration from the armload of manuscripts he was carrying, behind him two of his house servants also loaded down with fine bindings, was cutting through the garden and out by the rear gate to safety. His apprehensive face lit up when he saw Michelangelo.

"Buonarroti! I've saved some of Father's rarest manuscripts, the ones he loved best."

Florence was only a moment behind.

Into the courtyard surged the mob. Cries of "The Medici are banished!" were followed with "Everything in the palace is ours!" Rioters poured down into the wine cellars, broke open bins, and when they could not edge out the corks, smashed the bottles against the walls. Hundreds of bottles and demijohns passed from hand to hand and mouth to mouth, were drunk from blindly in long untasting gurgles, the wine spilling so freely it flooded the cellar. Now, brutally, this first contingent mounted the stairs, passing those pressing their way down, to sack the palace.

Michelangelo stood defensively before the Donatello David. The crowd still poured through the main gate, jamming the courtyard, individual faces that he had seen all his life on the streets and in the piazzas, quiet, good-natured people, suddenly inflamed, bent on destruction, with the faceless irresponsibility of the mob. What had caused the change? Was it the sense of being within the Medici palace for the first time as masters rather than outsiders?

He was knocked very hard against the David and a lump was raised on his head. The Donatello Judith and Holofernes standing nearby was picked up base and all, and with a roar of approval carried out through the rear garden. What was too big to move, Roman portraits and marble busts, was shattered with smashes of pikes and poles.

He edged along the wall, raced up the main staircase, ran at top speed down the corridor to the *studiolo*, slammed the door behind him, searched for the bolt. There was none. He looked about at the priceless manuscripts, cases of rare cameos, amulets, carved jewels, old coins, the Greek bas-reliefs above the door, the marble and bronze reliefs by Donatello, the painted wooden tables with Giotto's Deposition of Christ. Van Eyck's St. Jerome. What could be done to protect them?

His eyes fell upon the dumbwaiter. He opened the door, pulled on the ropes and, when the lift was level, began piling in the small paintings, enamelled and mosaic tablets, cups of jasper, sardonyx and amethyst, a small statue of Plato, a crystal clock mounted on gilt silver, glass vases by Ghirlandaio, manuscripts, rings and brooches. The old toothless Faun that he had copied for his own first piece of sculpture he stuffed inside his shirt. Then he pulled the opposite rope, sent the box down a way and closed the door. A mass of humanity reached the *studiolo* at that moment and began looting the room like locusts. He fought his way to his own apartment, where he threw Bertoldo's models and a few of the bronzes under the beds.

It was the end of his usefulness. Hundreds of rioters were sweeping through the palace and into the great rooms, pilfering the family plate in the dining-room, smashing the dishes and glassware, fighting and screaming with joy over the Medici collections of medals of gold and silver, taking from Piero's rooms his cups and trophies, throwing half-full bottles of wine at Pollaiuolo's Hercules and the Lion. In Lorenzo's room he watched helplessly as they grabbed up the four jasper vases with *Il Magnifico's* name inscribed, carried out the painted tables of Masaccio, Veneziano, cut paintings out of their frames, ripped sculptures off their bases, smashing the chairs and tables, what was too large to be moved, destroying chests. In the library, rare books and manuscripts had been pulled down from the shelves, the volumes trampled on.

Were these Florentines revenging themselves on Piero? But these magnificent collections were not Piero's. Watching the men brutally rip velvet hangings and slash silk upholsteries, he shook his head in despair. "Who can look into the mind of a mob?"

He recognized only one of the Medici faithful, his cousin Bernardo Rucellai, Nannina de' Medici's husband, standing before Botticelli's Pallas Subduing the Centaur in the anteroom adjoining a parlour. He was crying out:

"You are Florentine citizens! Why are you ravaging your own treasures? Stop, I implore you."

To Michelangelo he appeared a heroic figure, his eyes blazing and arms outstretched to protect the canvas. Then Rucellai was knocked down. Michelangelo struggled to the prostrate form, picked the man up in his arms, and carried him, bleeding, into a small storage room next door. He thought, ironically:

"This is the most intimate contact I have had with my mother's side of the family."

The palace was a shambles. Then, in Lorenzo's office, after tearing the maps and tapestries from the walls, some burly porters succeeded in smashing open the safe. Out came a rain of twenty thousand florins which sent the mob into a final paroxysm of joy as they fought each other for the gold coins.

He made his way down the rear staircase and out through the garden, then through back alleys to the Ridolfi palace. He asked a groom for pen and ink, wrote Contessina a brief note: *When it is safe . . . send someone to your father's studiolo. . . . I loaded the food lift as full as I could.* He signed it *M.B.*

He made two stops on his way home: at Bugiardini's and Jacopo's, leaving word for them to meet him at the Porta San Gallo at midnight. When the city at last slept he slipped past the quiet houses to the Medici stables. Two of the grooms had stayed with the horses, keeping them quiet during the pandemonium around them. They knew that he had the right to take out horses whenever he desired. They helped him saddle up three. He rode one, led the other two.

There was no guard at the gate. Bugiardini was waiting, complacently standing in the dark cutting his long fingernails with a knife. Jacopo arrived shortly after. They started out for Venice.

10

By afternoon of the second day they had crossed the Apennines and dropped down out of the Futa Pass into Bologna, enclosed by orange brick walls, its turrets and almost two hundred towers, several of them leaning more crazily than the one at Pisa, puncturing the pellucid Emilian skies. They entered the city towards the river side, through the littered remains of a produce market which a bevy of old women in black were sweeping with brooms made of twigs tied to small branches. They asked one of the crones for a direction, and made for the Piazza Communale.

The narrow tortuous streets, covered over by the protruding second floor of the houses, were suffocatingly airless. Each Bolognese family had built a tower for protection against its neighbours, a Florentine custom that had been abolished by Cosimo, who had obliged the Florentines to saw off their towers at roof height. The wider streets and the piazzas were lined with arches of orange brick to protect the people from snow, rain and the intense summer heat, so that the Bolognese could traverse his town from any direction and never be exposed.

They reached the main square with its majestic church of San Petronio at one end, and the Communal Palace covering an entire side; dismounted, and were promptly surrounded by Bolognese police.

"You are strangers in Bologna?"

"Florentines," Michelangelo replied.

"Your thumbs, if you please."

"Thumbs? What do you want with thumbs?"

"To see the mark of the red wax."

"We don't carry red wax."

"Then you will have to come with us. You are under arrest."

They were led to the customs office, a series of rooms buried behind porticoes, where the officer in charge explained that every stranger coming into Bologna had to register and be thumbprinted as he came through one of the city's sixteen gates.

"How could we know?" demanded Michelangelo. "We've never been here before."

"Ignorance of the law excuses no one. You are fined fifty Bolognese pounds."

"Fifty Bolognese . . . We don't have that much money."

"Too bad. Fifty days in jail."

Michelangelo stared with open-mouthed speechlessness at Bugiardini and Jacopo. Before they could recover their wits a man stepped forward.

"May I speak with the young men, Officer?"

"Certainly, Excellency."

To Michelangelo the man said, "Is not your name Buonarroti?"

"It is."

"Is not your father an officer of the Florentine customs?"

"Yes, sir."

The Bolognese turned to the customs official.

"Our young man here comes of a fine Florentine family; his father has charge of a branch of their customs office, as you have. Do you not think our two sister cities might exchange hospitality with its important families?"

Flattered, the officer replied, "Assuredly, Excellency."

"I will guarantee their conduct."

Back in the brittle winter sun of the piazza, Michelangelo studied his benefactor. He had a broad pleasant face, without a vestige of strain. Though a touch of grey indicated that he might be in his mid-forties, he had the smooth skin, high colouring and beardless face of a younger man, with small, perfect white teeth and small mouth held almost prisoner between a strong nose and chin. His brows came only halfway across his eyes from the bridge of his nose, then pointed upward quizzically. He was wearing a soft black wool robe with a white ruffled collar.

"You are most kind, and I am stupid: you remembered my unmemorable face, while I, though I knew we had met . . .?"

"We sat next to each other at one of Lorenzo de' Medici's dinners," explained the man.

"Of course! You are Signor Aldovrandi. You were *podestà* of Florence. You told me about the work of a great sculptor which is here in Bologna."

"Jacopo della Quercia. Now I will have an opportunity to show it to you. Won't you and your friends give me the pleasure of your company at supper?"

"The pleasure will be ours," grinned Jacopo. "We haven't delighted our stomachs since we lost sight of the Duomo."

"Then you have come to the right city," replied Aldo-vrandi. "Bologna is known as *La Grassa,* The Fat. Here we eat better than anywhere in Europe."

They left the piazza, walked to the north, with the church of San Pietro on their right, the connecting seminary on the left, then turned on to the Via Galliera. The Aldovrandi palace was number 8 on the left side of the street, a grace-fully proportioned building of brick, three stories high. There was an ogive door framed by a coloured terra-cotta frieze with the family coat of arms; the windows were arched and divided by marble columns.

Bugiardini and Jacopo arranged the care of the horses while Aldovrandi took Michelangelo to see his wood-panelled library, of which he was enormously proud.

"Lorenzo de' Medici helped me assemble the volumes."

He had a copy of Poliziano's *Stanze per la Giostra* in-scribed by Poliziano. Michelangelo picked up the leather-bound manuscript.

"You know, Messer Aldovrandi, that Poliziano died a few weeks ago."

"I was heartbroken. For such a great mind not to exist any longer. And Pico too: on his deathbed. How bleak the world will be without them."

"Pico?" Michelangelo swallowed brine. "I did not know. But Pico is young. . . ."

"Thirty-one. When Lorenzo died it was the end of an era. Nothing will be the same again."

Michelangelo held the poem in his hand, began reading aloud, hearing the voices of the Plato Four instructing him. Aldovrandi said with respect:

"You read well, my young friend. Your diction is clear and you have a way of phrasing a line . . ."

"I had good teachers."

"You like to read aloud? I have all of the great poets: Dante, Petrarch, Pliny, Ovid."

"I had not thought I liked it."

"Tell me, Michelangelo, what brings you to Bologna?"

Aldovrandi already knew about Piero's fate, for the Medici party had passed through Bologna the day before. Michelangelo explained that he was on his way to Venice.

"How does it happen that you do not have fifty Bolognese pounds between the three of you if you are travelling so far?"

"Bugiardini and Jacopo haven't a soldo. I'm paying the expenses."

Aldovrandi smiled. "I too should like to travel the world if you will pay my costs."

"We hope to find work in Venice."

"Then why not remain in Bologna? There is Della Quercia to study from; we may even discover a sculpture commission for you."

Michelangelo's eyes gleamed.

"After supper I will speak to my two companions."

The brush with the Bolognese police had been enough to take the wanderlust out of Jacopo and Bugiardini. Neither were they interested in the sculpture of Della Quercia. They decided they would prefer to return to Florence. Michelangelo gave them the money for the journey and asked them to lead back his Medici horse. He then told Aldovrandi he would remain in Bologna and find lodgings.

"Unthinkable!" replied Aldovrandi. "No friend and protégé of Lorenzo de' Medici may live in a Bolognese inn. A Florentine trained by the Plato Four is a rare treat for us. You will be our guest."

He awakened to the orange Bolognese sun streaming into his room, lighting the tapestry behind him and the bright-coloured boxed ceiling. In a painted coffer at the foot of the bed he found a linen towel, then washed himself in a silver bowl on a chest under the window, his naked feet warm on the Persian rug. He had been invited into a joyful house. He heard voices and laughter ringing through this wing of the palace which housed Aldovrandi's six sons. Signora Aldovrandi, an attractive young second wife who had contributed her quota of sons, was a pleasant woman who enjoyed all six of the boys equally, and welcomed Michelangelo as warmly as though he were a seventh son. His host, Gianfrancesco, belonged to the branch of the Aldovrandi family which had split off from the ancient parental palace, applied itself to trade and money changing, and prospered so greatly that Gianfrancesco, graduated from the university as a notary, and an able banker in his younger years, was now free to spend his time in the arts. An enthusiast of poetry, he was able an able versifier in the vulgate. He had risen rapidly in the political life of the city-state; senator, *gonfaloniere* of justice, member of the ruling

Sixteen Reformers of the Free State which governed Bologna, an intimate of the ruling Bentivoglio family.

"It is the one regret of my life that I cannot write in Greek and Latin," he told Michelangelo over a sweet bun and hot water flavoured with spice as they sat at the end of the forty-place walnut dining table with its coat of arms inlaid in the centre. "I read them, of course, but in my youth I spent too much time changing money instead of metres."

He was an avid collector. He escorted Michelangelo through the palace to show him painted diptychs, carved wooden tablets, silver and gold bowls, coins, terra-cotta heads, ivories, bronzes and small carved marbles.

"But no important local art, as you can see," he explained ruefully. "It is a mystery to me: why Florence and not Bologna? We are as rich a city as you, our people are as vigorous and courageous. We have a fine history in music, scholarship; but we have never been able to create great painting or sculpture. Why?"

"With all respect, why are you called 'Bologna, the Fat'?"

"Because we are gourmets, and have been famous since Petrarch's time for the pleasures of the flesh. We are a self-avowed carnal city."

"Could that be the answer?"

"That when all wants are satisfied there is no need for art? Yet Florence is rich, it lives well . . ."

"The Medici, the Strozzi, a few families. Tuscans are lean by nature. And frugal. We don't derive pleasure from spending. I don't ever remember another family eating in our house; or our family eating with friends. I don't remember the Buonarroti giving or receiving a gift. We like to earn money, but not to spend it."

"And we Bolognese think money is made only to be spent. Our whole genius has gone into the refinement of our pleasures. Did you know that we have created an *amore bolognese*? That our women will not wear Italian patterns, but only French? That they must use several different materials in a single dress? That our sausages are so special, we guard the recipe as though it were a state secret?"

At the midday dinner there was the full component of forty at the table: Aldovrandi's brothers and nephews, professors from the University of Bologna, reigning families from Ferrara and Ravenna passing through, princes of the Church, members of Bologna's ruling Sixteen. Aldovrandi was a charming host but, unlike Lorenzo, he made no effort to hold his guests together, to transact business or accomplish any purpose other than enjoyment of the superb fishes, sausages, meats, wines, storytelling and camaraderie.

After the *riposo* Aldovrandi invited Michelangelo for a tour of the city.

They walked under the arches where the shops displayed the most delicious foods of Italy: exquisite cheeses, the whitest of breads, rarest of wines, the rows of butcher shops in the Borgo Galliera displaying more meat than Michelangelo had seen in a year in Florence; then the Old Fish Market, with the sweet produce of the marshy valleys around Ferrara: sturgeon, craw-fish, mullet. The hundreds of game sheds were selling the fruit of yesterday's hunt: roe deer, quail, hare, pheasant; and in every block of the city their world-famous *salame*. Everywhere Michelangelo passed students from the university, who did their studying at the little cafés under the orange-coloured porticoes, playing dice and cards between pages of their assignments.

"There is one thing I miss, Messer Aldovrandi. I have seen no stone sculpture."

"Because we have no stone quarries. A simple equation, eh? But we have always brought in the best marble carvers who would come: Nicola Pisano, Andrea from Fiesole near you, Della Quercia from Siena, Dell'Arca from Bari. Our own sculpture is of terra-cotta."

It was not until they reached Santa Maria della Vita, where Aldovrandi showed him Dell'Acra's Lamentation over the Dead Christ, that Michelangelo found himself excited. This large terra-cotta group was melodramatic and profoundly disquieting, for Dell'Arca had caught his people in fully expressed agony and lamentation.

A few moments later they came upon a young man making terra-cotta busts to be placed above the capitals of the Palazzo Amorini in the Via Santo Stefano. He was powerfully built, with enormous shoulders and biceps, but with an egg-shaped head that was narrower at the top than at its base; his skin was burnt the precise orange of Bologna's brick. Aldovrandi called him Vincenzo.

"This is my friend Buonarroti," he said, "the best young sculptor in Florence."

"Ah, then it is proper that we meet," replied Vincenzo,

258

"for I am Bologna's best young sculptor. I am Dell'Arca's successor. I am to finish the great Pisano tomb in San Domenico."

"You have received the commission?" asked Aldovrandi sharply.

"Not yet, Excellency, but it must come to me. After all, I am Bolognese, I am sculptor. What could be more natural?" He turned to Michelangelo. "If you need help in Bologna, I show you everything."

As they walked on Aldovrandi said:

"Successor to Dell'Arca indeed! He is the successor to his grandfather and father, who are the finest brickmakers in Bologna. Let him stick to his trade."

They made their way to the church of San Domenico, built in 1218 by the Dominican brothers. The interior had three naves, more ornate than most Florentine churches, with a sarcophagus of St. Dominic by Nicola Pisano to which Aldovrandi led him. He pointed out the marble carvings that had been done in 1267, and then the work that had been continued by Niccolò dell'Arca.

"Dell'Arca died eight months ago. There are three figures left to be sculptured: an angel here on the right, St. Petronius holding the model of the city of Bologna; and a St. Proculus. These are the marbles that Vincenzo said he was going to carve."

Michelangelo looked hard at Aldovrandi. The man added nothing more, merely led him out of the church and to the Piazza Maggiore to see the work of Jacopo della Quercia over the main portal of San Petronio. He held back, letting Michelangelo go forward alone.

Michelangelo stood transfixed, gasping in astonishment and delight. Aldovrandi came forward.

"Did you know that Della Quercia competed for the bronze doors of the Baptistery in Florence? Back in 1400? Ghiberti beat him out. These five scenes on either side of the lateral supports, and the five above, are his answer to the rejection. Here in Bologna we think they are as good as Ghiberti's."

Michelangelo stood before the stone panels shaking his head in disbelief. This could be the single greatest sculpture he had ever laid eyes on.

"Perhaps as good, perhaps better, certainly different," he replied. "Della Quercia was as much an innovator as Ghiberti. Look at how alive he makes his human figures,

259

how they pulsate with inner vitality." Raising and lowering his arms, he indicated first one then another of the panels, exclaiming, " That carving of God. Of Adam and Eve. Of Cain and Abel. Of Noah drunk. Of the Expulsion from the Garden. See the strength and depth in the design. I'm stunned."

He turned to his friend, added hoarsely:

" Signor Aldovrandi, this is the kind of human figure I've dreamed of carving."

11

He found another excitement in Bologna, one he had not dreamed of.

He went everywhere with Aldovrandi: to the palaces of the brothers for family dinner, to friends' for intimate suppers. The Bolognese were a naturally hospitable people who loved to entertain. It was at a supper given by Marco Aldovrandi, his host's nephew, that he met Clarissa Saffi, in Marco's villa in the hills where she was serving as his hostess. There were no other women present, just Marco's men friends.

She was slender, golden-haired, the hair plucked back from the natural hairline of the brow in the fashion of the day. A lithe, willowy figure that moved with a delicate sensuousness ; every slight rhythm of the arm and shoulder and leg as smooth as music, and as pleasurable. She appeared to be one of those rare creatures whose every breath was made for love. Sketching her figure in his mind, he found a wholeness here, an undulant softness of manner, voice, gesture, motion.

From the beauty of neck and shoulder and bosom he thought of Botticelli's passion for the perfect female nude : not to love, but to paint. Clarissa had much of the golden loveliness of Simonetta, without the sad innocence Botticelli had given her.

She was unlike any woman he had ever seen. He was aware of her not merely through his eye but through every pore and part of his body. Her very presence in Marco's drawing room, before she moved or said a word, sent the blood pounding through his veins, shot his back and shoulders involuntarily upward, thrust his pelvic structure forward alive with new life. Jacopo would have cried as she passed

260

the Duomo steps, "How mattressable!" but Clarissa, he perceived, was more than that. She was love in its ultimate female form.

Clarissa's welcoming smile for him was embracing; she liked all men, had a natural affinity for them. Her movements had a captivating grace that was a delight to his senses. The long braids of burnished golden hair seemed to have the hot Italian sun on them, even in this cool room, and warmed him as thoroughly. Though an inner drum was pounding in his ears, he heard the soft, sibilant music of her voice that shocked him to intense awareness.

She had been Marco's mistress for three years, since he had stumbled across her cleaning her father's cobbler shop. The first to recognize her beauty, he had set her up in a secluded villa, taught her how to wear rich gowns and jewels, had brought in a tutor to teach her to read and write.

After supper, while the old friends were involved in a discussion of politics, Michelangelo and Clarissa found themselves alone in a little French music room. In spite of his protestations that he had no interest in the female form, that he found no excitement worthy of sculpturing, he could not tear his eyes away from Clarissa's bodice, clothed in a net of fine woven gold which accomplished the harrowing miracle of seeming to expose her breasts while at the same time keeping them under cover. The harder he looked, the less he could actually see: for he was confronted by a masterpiece of the dressmaker's art, designed to excite and intrigue, yet reveal nothing beyond a suspicion of white doves nestling.

Clarissa was amused at his gaucherie.

"You are an artist, Buonarroti?"

It was an effort to meet her gaze, for her eyes too were soft and rounded, now concealing, now revealing their intimacies.

"I am a sculptor."

"Could you carve me in marble?"

"You're already carved," he blurted out. "Flawlessly!"

A touch of colour rode the high cheekbones of her slender, creamy cheeks.

They laughed together, leaning a little towards each other. Marco had trained her well, and she spoke with a good inflexion. Michelangelo was also aware of a quick and intuitive perception.

"Will I see you again?" he asked.

"If Signor Aldovrandi brings you."

" Not otherwise?"

Her lips parted in a smile.

" Is it that you wish me to pose for you?"

" No. Yes. I don't know. I don't even know what I am saying, let alone what I mean."

She laughed heartily. Her movements tightened the net over her bosom, and once again he found himself watching the lovely forms take discernible shape beneath the gold bodice. To himself he said:

" This is crazy! What has happened to me?"

It was his friend Aldovrandi who saw the naked longing in his eyes. He slapped him smartly on the shoulder and cried:

" Well, Michelangelo, you have too much sense to get involved in our local political talk. We will have some music now. You knew that we are one of the great music centres of Europe?"

On the way home, as they rode their horses side by side down the sleeping orange streets, Aldovrandi asked:

" You were taken with Clarissa?"

Michelangelo saw that he could be honest, replied, " She makes my flesh crawl; I mean the flesh inside my flesh."

" Our Bolognese beauties can do that. To cool you down a trifle, can you guess how expensive she is?"

" I see that her gowns and jewels are costly."

" Only the beginning: she also has an exquisite box of a palace, with servants, a stable of carriages . . ."

" Enough!" cried Michelangelo, with a wry grin. " But I have never seen a woman like her. If ever I was to carve a Venus . . ."

" Don't! My nephew has the quickest temper and rapier in Bologna."

That night he writhed in fever. When he found himself turning and twisting in an effort to bury his face between her breasts he realized what had happened to him, but he was as incapable of stopping the burrowing in the soft warm pillows as he had been of stopping his search for them under the gold net.

The next day he passed her in the Via Drapperie, the street of cloths and drapes, accompanied by an older woman. She was wearing a wreath of flowers through her hair and moved through the street with the same effortless magic under her silken gown with its gold belt encrusted with precious stones, woollen cape over her shoulders. She bowed, smiled slightly, and walked on, leaving him standing there rooted to the brick pavement.

That night, when again he could not sleep, he went down to Aldovrandi's library, lit a lamp, took up his host's pen, and after many false starts, wrote:

THE GARLAND AND THE GIRDLE

What joy hath yon glad wreath of flowers that is
Around her golden hair so deftly twined,
Each blossom pressing forward from behind,
As though to be the first her brows to kiss!

The livelong day her dress hath perfect bliss,
That now reveals her breast, now seems to bind:
And that fair woven net of gold refined
Rests on her cheek and throat in happiness!

Yet still more blissful seems to me the band,
Gilt at the tips, so sweetly doth it ring,
And clasp the bosom that it serves to lace:

Yea, and the belt, to such as understand,
Bound round her waist, saith: Here I'd ever cling!
What would my arms do in that girdle's place?

He suspected that this was not exactly the kind of sonnet for which Benivieni had spent the hours training him. Yet the writing had, in Aldovrandi's expression, "cooled him down." He returned to his bedroom and slept.

A few Sundays later Aldovrandi invited him for the evening to Clarissa's villa, where a group of Marco's intimates were gathering for their favourite game, *tarocchino di Bologna*, played with sixty oversized cards. Michelangelo knew nothing of such games, nor had he any money with which to gamble. After Clarissa had seen to it that Marco's friends were supplied with food and drink, she sat with Michelangelo before a crackling log fire in a side parlour with a handsome terra-cotta frieze. He watched her face in the firelight, the features so fragile, yet with such implicit passion.

"It's pleasant to have someone my own age to talk to," Clarissa confided. "All of Marco's friends are older."

"You do not have young friends?"

"Not any more. But I am happy. Is it not odd, Buonarroti, that a girl can grow up in utter poverty yet fit so naturally into all this elegance?"

"I don't know, Madonna, you are out of my quarter."

"Just what is your quarter? Beside sculpture, that is."

"Poetry." He tendered a wan smile. "You cost me two nights' sleep before I could get the sonnet down on paper."

"You wrote a sonnet to me?" She was amazed. "It is the first. Could I hear it?"

He flushed.

"I think not. But I will bring you a copy sometime. You can read it in privacy."

"Why are you embarrassed? It is good to be desired. I accept it as a compliment."

He cast his eyes down. How could he confess that he was as new at this game as he would have been at *tarocchino*? How could he acknowledge the fire burning in his loins?

He looked up suddenly, found her eyes on him. She had read his feelings. She put her hand in his, studied his bashed-in face. These minutes of perception changed the relationship.

"What fell on your nose, Michelangelo?"

"A ham."

"From a butcher's rack? Did you forget to duck?"

"The way the people on Vesuvius forgot to run from the lava: it had covered them before they knew it was coming."

"Have you ever been in love?"

". . . in a way."

"It's always 'in a way.'"

"Is love never whole?"

"Not that I know of. It's political, like the marriage of Violante Bentivoglio to Pandolfo Malatesta in Rimini, in which your friend Aldovrandi headed the wedding party; or to get the children born and scrubbing done, as with the *contadini*; or for the pleasure of pearls and palace . . . as with myself. . . ."

"Also what we feel for each other?"

Her body stirred in its gown, causing a sibilance of the silk. Her fashionably shod foot rested lightly against his calf. His insides somersaulted.

"We are young people together. Why should we not want each other?"

Again he thrashed the night through, his feverish body no longer content to nestle its face between her breasts; now he was pulsating to enter whole. He kept hearing her words over and over again in the darkness of his room while he throbbed with an unbearable urgency.

"Why should we not want each other?"

He rose, went down to Aldovrandi's library, began writing scraps, phrases, lines, as they came tumbling into his head:

> *Kind to the world, but to itself unkind,*
> *A worm is born, that, dying noiselessly,*
> *Despoils itself to clothe fair limbs, and be*
> *In its true worth by death alone divined.*

> *Oh, would that I might die, for her to find*
> *Raiment in my outworn mortality!*
> *That, changing like the snake, I might be free*
> *To cast the slough wherein I dwell confined!*

> *Nay, were it mine, that shaggy fleece that stays,*
> *Woven and wrought into a vestment fair,*
> *Around her beauteous bosom in such bliss!*

> *All through the day she'd clasp me; would I were*
> *The shoes that bear her burden! When the ways*
> *Were wet with rain, her feet I then should kiss!*

It was during the Christmas festivities, with the symbolic "good wish" log burning in the drawing-room fireplace, and the poor children of the town singing carols outside for their gifts, with Signora Aldovrandi presiding over the annual appearance of the servants for the game of "fortune extracting" from a sack, that Michelangelo was rescued from his turmoil.

When the servants had drunk their toasts and departed, and the Aldovrandi family, some thirty strong, had "extracted" their gifts, Aldovrandi turned to Michelangelo:

"Now you must try your fortune."

He put his hand into the hemp bag. There was one package left. From the broad smiles all about him it was apparent that everyone was in on the joke. He pulled, and out came a terra-cotta replica of the Dell'Arca San Domenico tomb. In the three empty places, where the angel, St. Petronius and St. Proculus were missing, were oversized caricatures of himself, broken nose and all.

265

" I . . . I have the commission?"

Aldovrandi smiled at him happily. " The Council awarded it to you last week."

When the guests had departed Aldovrandi and Michelangelo went into the library. Aldovrandi explained that he would send to Carrara for the marble when the drawings were ready and the dimensions established. Michelangelo was sure that his host had not only secured him this commission, which would pay him thirty gold ducats, but would be paying for the marble as well, and the haul over the Apennines by oxcart. His heart was too full to know how to thank him. Impulsively he opened a copy of Dante, leafed through. He picked up a pen and at the top of the page, in the margin and below, quickly sketched scenes from Florence: the Duomo and Baptistery, the Palazzo della Signoria and the Ponte Vecchio over the Arno, stone Florence lying in the womb of its walls.

" By your leave, each day I shall illustrate another page of Dante."

Aldovrandi stood over him, studying the rough-hatched pen sketches, his eyes shining.

He went with Aldovrandi to Dell'Arca's workshop at the rear of San Petronio, part of an enclosed courtyard admitting to the vestment room of the church, partly covered by a portico, with workstalls for the maintenance crew similar to those in the Duomo, though smaller than the one in which he had worked his Hercules. The shop had been left untouched since Dell'Arca's sudden death some ten months before. On his workbench were his chisels, hammers, dried wax and clay improvisations, miniatures, folios of sketches for the remaining figures of the tomb, stubs of charcoal: a portrait of a man interrupted in the midst of life and work.

It was cold in the raw January manner of Emilia, but two capacious braziers kept the open-faced shed warm. After two months of copying in the churches of Bologna, and drawing from the Della Quercias, he was desperately eager to get back to work: to the early modelling in clay, the firing of the forge and making of tools, the setting up of the marble on its wooden blocks and the first fastidious knocking off of the corners to begin searching for the figures in the round. It was half a year since he had finished the Hercules.

He had been working only a few days, crouched over his drawing table, heavy wool hat covering his head and ears, when a massive shape loomed before him. He looked up, saw that it was Vincenzo, the terra-cotta sculptor. His face was a raw umber from the cold, his eyes were intense.

"Buonarroti, you got the work I been after."

Michelangelo remained silent for a moment, then murmured: "I'm sorry."

"No, you're not. You're a stranger. I'm Bolognese. You take bread out of the mouths of us native sculptors."

Placatingly, Michelangelo replied, "I understand. I lost some carving at Santo Spirito last year to silver workers."

"It's good you understand. Go to the Council, tell them you decide against it. Then the commission comes to me."

"But, Vincenzo, if it hasn't come to you since Dell'Arca died . . .?"

Vincenzo brushed this aside with a sweep of his powerful brickmaker's arms.

"You stole the commission with Aldovrandi influence. No one even knows you sculpt."

Michelangelo sympathized with the big fellow standing before him, sick with frustration.

"I'll speak to Messer Aldovrandi."

"You better. Or I make you sorry you came to Bologna."

When Michelangelo told Aldovrandi of the encounter, he replied:

"It is true he is Bolognese. He watched Dell'Arca work. He knows what our people like. He has only one shortcoming: he can't carve marble. He should be making our fine Bolognese brick if he wishes to immortalize himself."

"Shall I offer him a job as my assistant?"

"Do you need one?"

"I'm being a diplomat."

"Be a sculptor instead. Forget him."

"I'll never let you forget me," said Vincenzo the following day when Michelangelo reported that there was nothing he could do to help him.

Michelangelo looked at the enormous bony hands of Vincenzo, twice the size of his own. Vincenzo was his own age, about nineteen, but probably weighed twice as much as his own one hundred and twenty pounds, and loomed a head taller than his own five feet four inches. He thought of Torrigiani, could see Torrigiani's powerful fist coming through the air, hitting him, could taste the blood and feel the crushed bone. He became a little faint.

267

"What's the matter, Buonarroti? You don't look good. Afraid I make life miserable for you?"

"You already have."

But no more miserable than he would be to have to relinquish the opportunity to carve three beautiful blocks of white Carrara marble. If this were the price . . .

12

He did not write to his family, nor did he receive letters from home, but once a week business associates of Aldovrandi made the trip over the Futa Pass to Florence. They took news of Michelangelo to the Buonarroti, and brought it back in turn.

A week after Michelangelo had fled, Charles VIII had entered the city with his lance levelled to indicate that he was a conqueror, though no shots had been fired. He was welcomed through streets draped with tapestries and awnings and oil lamps. The Ponte Vecchio had been festively decorated; he was graciously received by the Signoria for prayers in the Duomo. He was given the Medici palace as his headquarters. But when it came to the peace treaty, Charles had acted haughtily, threatened to recall Piero, demanded an emperor's ransom. Fighting had broken out in the streets, French soldiers and Florentines had attacked each other, the Florentines had shut down their city and prepared to evict the French. Charles grew more reasonable, settled for a hundred and twenty thousand florins, the right to maintain two fortresses in Florence until his war with Naples was over, and took his army out of Florence. The city was proud of having faced up to the leader of twenty thousand armed soldiers, of having replied, when he threatened, "We shall sound our trumpets!" with "And we will ring our bells!"

Yet the wheels of the city-state had creaked to a painful halt. Ruled for so long by the Medici, the governmental structure did not work without an executive. Former councillors had been Medici adherents who had developed a modus vivendi for working together. Now the city was torn by factions. One group wished to instal the Venevian form of government; another wanted one Council of the People to pass the laws and elect magistrates, a second Council, smaller, of experienced men to establish domestic and international policy. Guidantonio Vespucci, spokesman for the wealthy nobles, called these measures dangerously democratic, fought to keep all power in a few hands.

By mid-December news reached Bologna that Savonarola had stepped into the crisis with a series of Haggai sermons in which he backed the proposed democratic structure. Visitors to the Aldovrandi palace outlined the priest's concept of elected councils: only real property was to be taxed; every Florentine was to have a vote; all over twenty-nine years of age, who had paid their taxes, were to be eligible to the Grand Council. By the end of the sermons, Vespucci and his nobles had been defeated, Savonarola's plan had been adopted. From Bologna it appeared that Savonarola had become political as well as religious leader of Florence. His victory over *Il Magnifico* was complete.

With the coming of the New Year, Piero de' Medici returned to Bologna to set up headquarters. Coming home from his workshop, Michelangelo found a group of Piero's professional soldiers in the street before the Aldovrandi palace. Piero was inside with Giuliano. Though Charles, when he made the peace with Florence, had insisted that the price on Piero's head and on Giuliano's be revoked, all Medici estates had been confiscated, and Piero himself banished to two hundred miles from the Tuscan border.

When they met at the entrance to the dining room, Michelangelo exclaimed, "Excellency, how good to see you again. Though I could wish it were at the Medici palace."

"We'll be back there soon enough," growled Piero. "The Signoria drove me out by force. I am assembling an army and shall drive them out by force."

Giuliano, now grown as tall as Michelangelo, had bowed formally to Michelangelo, but when Piero took Signora Aldovrandi in to dinner, the two young men hugged each other.

There was little pleasure at the usually gay Aldovrandi table, for Piero immediately outlined his plan for the reconquest of Florence. All he required was sufficient money, hired mercenaries, weapons, horses. Piero expected Aldovrandi to contribute two thousand florins to his campaign.

"Excellency, are you sure this is the best way?" asked Aldovrandi respectfully. "When your great-grandfather Cosimo was exiled he waited until the city found it needed him and called him back. Wait for that hour, Excellency."

"I am not as forgiving as my grandfather. Florence wants

me back right now. It is just Savonarola and my cousins who have schemed against me."

He turned to Michelangelo.

"You shall enter my army as an engineer, help design the wall fortifications after we have conquered the city."

Michelangelo sat with his head bowed. "Would you wage war on Florence, Excellency?" he murmured after a moment.

"I would, and I shall. As soon as I have a force strong enough to batter down the walls."

"But if the city were bombarded it could be destroyed . . ."

"What then? Florence is a pile of stones. If we knock them down, we will put them together again."

"But the art . . ."

"What is art? We can replace the paint and marble in a year. And it will be a Florence that I will command!"

No one touched a bite of food. Aldovrandi turned to Piero.

"In the name of my friend, *Il Magnifico,* I must decline. The money you ask for is yours, but not for purposes of war. Lorenzo would have been the first to stop you, were he alive."

Piero turned to Michelangelo.

"And you, Buonarroti?"

"I too, Excellency, must decline. I will serve you in any way you ask, but not to wage war against Florence."

Piero pushed his chair back, rose to his feet.

"The kind of people I inherited from my father! Poliziano and Pico, who preferred dying to fighting. You, Aldovrandi, who were my father's *podestà* of Florence. And you, Michelangelo, who have lived under our roof for four years. What kind of men are you that will not fight back?"

He swept out of the room. Michelangelo said with tears in his eyes: "Forgive me, Giuliano."

Giuliano had also risen, turned to leave the room.

"I too shall refuse to wage war. That would only make Florence hate us the more. *A rivederci,* Michelangelo, I shall write Contessina that I have seen you."

He was still skittish about angels. He remembered the first one he had done for the Ghirlandaio fresco, using the son of the carpenter downstairs of the Buonarroti house. The other apprentices had called him a fraud because he had cheated on the halo, making it fade into the background. What was an angel: male or female, human or divine? Prior

Bichiellini had once called it " a spiritual being attendant on God."

His embarrassment as he drew hundreds of angels was the more acute after his months of dissection. Now that he knew the tissue and function of human anatomy he could hardly refrain from using that knowledge. But did an angel have a twenty-five-foot snake of bowel? He must also carve his angel fully clothed to match the one on the other end of the Ark. With the angel and the two saints he was right back where Ghirlandaio had told him he would stay all his life: able to portray hands, feet, perhaps a little of the neck and throat. For the rest, all his hard-earned knowledge would be hidden under flowing robes.

For his " spiritual being attendant on God," he chose a *contadino* boy, in from the farm with his family to attend church, looking a little like Bugiardini, with a wide, fleshy face but the features cut square in the Greek tradition. He had well-developed arms and shoulders, built by guiding a plough behind oxen. This powerful young male held high a candelabrum that would have required a giant to lift. Instead of compensating with delicate, diaphanous wings, as he knew he ought, he rubbed salt into the wound of his own befuddlement by designing the two wings of an eagle, about to take off, coming all the way down the boy's back. These he carved out of wood to attach to his clay model, wings so heavy they would have floored the delicate Dell'Arca angel on the opposite side.

He invited Aldovrandi to visit the workshed. Aldovrandi was not at all upset by the vigour of the model.

" We Bolognese are not spiritual beings. Carve a lusty angel."

And so he did, setting up the thickest of Aldovrandi's three Carrara blocks. He felt complete again with the hammer and chisel in his hands, the dry caking marble dust in his nostrils, the white chips and powder covering his hair and clothes. When he worked stone he was a man of substance. Now he did not need the braziers, for he created his own warmth, moving the workbench out into the open courtyard when there was any winter sun, to feel the space around him.

In the evenings, after he had read aloud to Aldovrandi and illustrated a page of Dante, he would do his exploratory drawing for the St. Petronius, patron saint of Bologna, convert to Christianity from a noble Roman family, and builder

271

of San Petronio. He used as his models the older guests in the Aldovrandi palace: members of the Sixteen, professors from the university, justices, sketching their faces and figures in his mind while he sat with them at table, then retiring to his room to hammer down on paper the lines, forms, inter-relation of feature and expression that makes every human being different from another.

There was little he could do with St. Petronius that could be original. The Dominicans of San Domenico and the Bolognese government officials were set on what they wanted: St. Petronius must be no less than sixty. He must be fully gowned in luxuriant robes, an archbishop's crown on his head. He must hold in his arms a model of the city of Bologna with its towers and palaces piled high above its protecting walls.

He acquired a neighbour in the stall opposite. It was Vin-cenzo, whose father had secured a contract for making new brick and tile for a cathedral repair job. A crew of mechanics came in to fill the stalls for the repairs, and the enclosed courtyard rang with the noise of materials being unloaded. Vincenzo afforded the workyard running entertainment by taunting Michelangelo throughout the workday.

" Our brick lasts for a thousand years. It's harder than your Florentine stone."

" It's true you make durable brick, Vincenzo."

" Don't patronize me," said Vincenzo. " You Florentines think you are the only artists in Italy."

Michelangelo blushed. Vincenzo cried to the workmen, " Look at his face. I caught him out."

When Vincenzo arrived with a wagonload of fresh tiles, he badgered Michelangelo with: " I made a hundred durable stones yesterday. What did you make? Charcoal scratches on a paper?" Encouraged by the laughter of his townsmen, the brickmaker continued, " That makes you a sculptor? Why don't you go home and leave Bologna to its natives?"

" I intend to, when I have finished my three pieces."

" Nothing can hurt my brick. Think how easy it's going to be for an accident to happen to one of your statues."

The workmen stopped in their tasks. Silence filled the yard. Vincenzo, who made words much as he did brick, with shaping movements of his hands, continued with a crafty smile:

" Somebody brushes too close to the Ark. Smasho! Your angel is in a dozen pieces."

Michelangelo felt anger rise in his throat.

" You wouldn't dare!"

" No, no, Buonarroti, not I. I am too graceful. But someone clumsy might stumble."

The laughter of the workmen as they picked up their tools made him a little ill: the forces of destruction always one short step behind creation! He suffered through the days and weeks.

St. Petronius emerged with a sad and deeply furrowed face ; but there was inherent power in the body. The set of the head on the shoulders, the gripping strength of the feet in the thin-soled sandals, the puissant stance of the knees, hips, shoulders under the rich robe, the arms in which he firmly held Bologna, this vigour he could convey. As a craftsman he knew he had done a good job. It was as a creative artist that he felt he had contributed little.

" It is very fine," said Aldovrandi when he saw the polished piece. " Dell' Arca could not have surpassed it."

" But I am determined to give you something more," said Michelangelo doggedly. " I must not leave Bologna without carving something exciting and original."

" Very well, you disciplined yourself to give us the St. Petronius we wanted. I will discipline Bologna to accept the St. Proculus that you want."

Bologna the Fat became Bologna the Lean for him. He did not return home for the big midday dinner. When an Aldovrandi groom brought him hot food he let it grow cold if it was not a moment when he wanted to stop. Now that spring was approaching he was able to work longer each day, and frequently did not reach the Aldovrandi palace until after dark, dirty, sweaty, charcoal- or chip-covered, ready to fall into bed of exhaustion. But the Aldovrandi servants brought him a big wooden tub filled with hot water, and laid out his clean clothes. He knew he was expected to join his patron in the library for a few hours of companionable talk.

Clarissa he saw rarely, since he was attending few parties. But when he did see her the delight and the torment racked him for nights, obliterating his sleep and permeating his mind for days while he tried to create the figure of St. Proculus, and drew instead Clarissa nude under her silks.

He preferred not to see her. It was too painful.

On the first of May, Aldovrandi told him he might not work. This was the happiest day in the year for Bologna, when the Countess of Love reigned, people gathered wild flowers in the country for their relatives and friends, romantic young courtiers planted leafy trees with coloured silk ribbons under the windows of their beloved while their friends serenaded her.

Michelangelo accompanied the Aldovrandi outside the main gate of town where a platform had been erected, covered with damask and festoons of flowers. Here the Countess of Love was crowned, with all Bologna gathered to pay homage.

Michelangelo too wanted to pay homage to love, or whatever it was that had been started boiling in his blood by the intoxicating air of the wild spring morning, the fragrance of the thousands of blossoms, the perfumes of the Bolognese women, beautiful on this ritual day, gowned in silks and jewels.

But he did not see Clarissa. He saw Marco in the midst of his family with two young maidens, apparently the family choices for marriage, hanging on either arm. He saw the older woman who had accompanied her on her shopping trips to the city, saw her maid and several other of the servants picnicking in the fields beyond the platform where the ceremonies took place. But no Clarissa. Search as he might.

And then he found he was no longer before the May platform, or in the celebrating Bolognese crowds. His feet were carrying him swiftly up the road to Clarissa's villa. He did not know what he would do when he got there. What he would say, how he would explain when someone opened the gate to him. Trembling all over, he half walked, half ran up the foothill road.

The front gate was unbolted. He went to the front door, pushed on the clapper, knocked again and again. Just as he was beginning to think that no one was at home, and that he had acted stupidly, the door was opened a crack. There stood Clarissa, in a peignoir, her golden hair hanging loosely down her back, almost to her knees, without cosmetics or jewels, smelling aseptically of soap; and her face, to Michelangelo, more beautiful, her whole body more desirable because it was unornamented.

He stepped inside the door. There was no sound in the house. She threw the bolt. Then they were in a passionate embrace, their bodies merging, knee and crotch, breasts and chest, their mouths moist and sweet and glued and drinking deep, their arms with all the power of an unquenchable life force crushing each to the other in a total pulsating time- and place- and sense-annihilating embrace.

She led him to her bedroom. She had nothing on beneath the robe. The slender body, the red-pointed breasts, the golden Mount of Venus were as his draughtsman's eye had known them all along: a female beauty, made for love.

It was like penetrating deep into white marble with the pounding live thrust of his chisel beating upward through the warm living marble with one "Go!", his whole body behind the heavy hammer, penetrating through ever deeper and deeper furrows of soft yielding living substance until he had reached the explosive climax, and all of his fluid strength, love, passion, desire had been poured into the nascent form, and the marble block, made to love the hand of the true sculptor, had responded, giving of its inner heat and substance and fluid form, until at last the sculptor and the marble had totally coalesced, so deeply penetrating and infusing each other that they had become one, marble and man an organic unity, each fulfilling the other in the greatest act of art and of love known to the human species.

After May Day he completed the drawing of his virile St. Proculus, who had been martyred before the gates of Bologna in 303, while in the full flower of his youth and strength. He clothed him in a belted tunic which did nothing to conceal the vigorous torso and hips and bare legs. It was anatomically true and convincing. As he made his clay model his experience with the Hercules bore fruit, for he was able to achieve the corded, driving thighs, the bulging stamina-packed calves: truly the torso and legs of a heroic warrior and deliverer, powerful, indestructible.

Then, quite unabashedly, he modelled his own portrait from a mirror of his bedroom: the punched-in bridge of the nose, the flat spread of the cheekbones and wide spread of the eyes, the thatch of hair worn halfway down his forehead, the steadfast gaze, resolved to triumph: against the enemies of Bologna? The enemies of art? Of life? Was it not all the same?"

Carving in marble, feeling the blow of his chisel, Vincenzo was blotted out, the orange-earth figure and the heavy sound of his voice. With his eyes slitted against the flying chips, with the emergence of form from the block, he again felt himself to be fifteen feet tall. Vincenzo began to shrink in size, then fade; until finally he stopped coming to the courtyard.

When the early afternoon sun made it too hot to work in the enclosed courtyard, he took crayon and paper to the front of the church, sat on the cool stone before Della Quercia's carvings and each day refreshed himself by copying a different figure: God, Noah, Adam, Eve, trying to capture some part of Della Quercia's power of imparting emotion, drama, conflict and reality through his half-released Istrian stone figures.

The hot summer months passed in fulfilment: up before first light, working the marble by dawn, carving for six hours before he ate from his basket of cold sliced *salame* and bread. At night when the light had begun to hide the planes and surfaces of the figure, he would drape it in moist cloth, put it back in his shed, lock the doors securely behind him; walk to the wide, shallow Reno River for a cool soak and swim, then to the Aldovrandis', watching the stars be born in the deep blue canopy of the Emilian plain.

Vincenzo had disappeared, and so had Clarissa. He learned from a passing remark of Aldovrandi's that Marco had taken her to his hunting lodge in the Apennines for the hot summer months. The Aldovrandi family too departed for their summer villa in the mountains. For most of July and all of August, Bologna was shut down as though decimated by the plague, its shops locked behind iron, roll-down shutters. He stayed alone in the palace with a pair of servants who considered themselves too old to travel, and saw his host only when Aldovrandi rode in for a day to take care of his affairs, his face tanned by the mountain sun. Once he brought startling news from Florence. His short, quizzical eyebrows pointed almost vertically as he exclaimed:

"Your Fra Savanarola has come out into the open. He has declared war on the Pope!"

"You mean the way Lorenzo did when Rome excommunicated Florence?"

"Ah, no. This is personal and punitive."

Aldovrandi read from a report of Savanarola's latest Duomo sermon: "When you see a head which is healthy, you can say that the body is healthy also; but when the head is bad, look out for the body. And so when the head of the administration happens to be ambitious, lustful, and in other ways vicious, be sure that the scourge is near.... When you see therefore that God allows the head of the Church to wallow in crime and simony, then I say that the scourge of the people approaches. . . ."

Michelangelo was not as shocked as Aldovrandi expected, for Prior Bichiellini had predicted long ago that the Pope was Savonarola's ultimate target.

" How has the Pope replied?"

" He summoned Savonarola to Rome to explain his divine revelations. But Savonarola has declined, declaring, ' All good and wise citizens judge that my departure from this place would be to the great detriment of the people, yet of little use to you in Rome. . . . Because of the furtherance of this work I am quite sure these difficulties in the way of my going spring from God's will. Therefore it is not the will of God that I should leave this place at present.' " Aldovrandi chuckled. " An infallible system, don't you think?"

Michelangelo too declined to leave " this place " when Aldovrandi suggested he spend a cool holiday in the mountains with him.

" Thank you, but I'm moving along rapidly with the St. Proculus. At this rate I shall finish by autumn."

The summer was over, Bologna rolled up its shutters and became a living city. Autumn set in, and the St. Proculus was finished. Michelangelo and Aldovrandi stood before the figure. Michelangelo ran his hand caressingly over the high polish. He was exhausted, but happy with it. So was Aldovrandi.

" I will ask the fathers to set an unveiling date. Perhaps during the Christmas holidays?"

Michelangelo was silent; it was the sculptor's job to carve and the patron's to unveil.

" We could honour you in San Domenico."

" My work is done, and I have grown homesick for Florence," said Michelangelo quietly. " You have been a good friend."

Aldovrandi smiled. " For a year of bed and board I have extracted from you countless hours of reading poetry, and an illustrated copy of The Divine Comedy! What Aldovrandi ever drove a shrewder bargain?"

He could not go without saying good-bye to Clarissa. That took a little waiting. Finally Aldovrandi invited him to a party at a secluded villa in the hills where the wealthy young Bolognese felt free to bring their mistresses for feast-

277

ing and dancing. Michelangelo saw that there would be no chance for even a moment of privacy in a quiet library or music-room. They would have to say good-bye in the middle of a drawing-room surrounded by twenty couples; and on their faces they would have to wear the bantering Bolognese smile which meant that charming pleasantries were being exchanged.

"I have waited to say good-bye, Clarissa. I am going back to Florence."

Her eyebrows came together for a moment, but the fixed smile never wavered.

"I'm sorry. It has been pleasant to know you were here."

"Pleasant? A torture, pleasant?"

"In a way. When will you return?"

"I don't know. Perhaps never."

"Everyone returns to Bologna. It's on the road to everywhere."

"Then I'll be back."

13

The family was genuinely glad to have him home, kissing him on both cheeks and exclaiming at his stubble of beard. Lodovico was delighted with the twenty-five ducats Michelangelo brought him. Buonarroto seemed to have grown a full foot; Sigismondo, no longer a child, was apprenticed to the Wine Guild; and Giovansimone had left the house entirely, maintaining himself regally in a flat across the Arno as one of the leaders in Savonarola's Army of Boys.

"He does not come home any more," sighed Lodovico; "we ask too many embarrassing questions."

Granacci was working in deadly earnest from first light to dark at Ghirlandaio's in an effort to keep the *bottega* afloat. When Michelangelo visited the studio he saw the cartoons being drawn for the new frescoes for the chapel of San Zanobi by David and Benedetto Ghirlandaio, by Mainardi, Bugiardini, Tedesco. They seemed well done.

"Yes," agreed David, "but always we face the same criticism: 'With Domenico dead, the studio is finished.'"

"We work twice as hard as before," sighed Mainardi, "but none of us has Domenico's genius. Except his son Ridolfo here; but he's only twelve, it will be ten years before he can take his father's place."

278

On the walk home Granacci reported, "The Popolano family wants you to sculpture something for them."

"Popolano? I don't know any Popolanos."

"Yes, you do." Granacci's usually bland voice had an edge to it. "It's the Medici cousins, Lorenzo and Giovanni. They have changed their names to coincide with the People's party, and are now helping to rule Florence. They asked me to bring you around when you returned."

The brothers Lorenzo and Giovanni Popolano received him in a drawing-room filled with precious art works from Lorenzo's palace. Michelangelo glanced from a Botticelli to a Gozzoli to a Donatello stupefied.

"We did not steal them," said Giovanni easily; "the city auctioned them off in public sale. We bought them."

Michelangelo sat down, uninvited. Granacci came to the defence of the cousins.

"This way the paintings and sculptures are safe. Some of the best pieces are being sold outside Florence."

Michelangelo rose to his feet. "I was taken by surprise . . . so many memories flooded over me."

Giovanni Popolano ordered sweet wine and cake. Lorenzo then said they were still interested in having a young St. John. If he cared to move into the palace, for convenience' sake, he would be welcome.

That evening when all the bells of the city were ringing loud enough to remind him of the Tuscan adage, "Bells ring to summon others, but never go to church themselves," he crisscrossed the narrow streets of the city to the Ridolfi palace. He had been shaved and had his hair cut by Torrigiani's barber in the Straw Market; had bathed and donned his best blue woollen shirt and stockings for the visit.

The Ridolfi had been members of the *Bigi,* or Grey party, which had been pardoned by the Council for being followers of the Medici, and were now ostensibly members of the *Frateschi,* or Republicans. Contessina received him in the drawing-room, still attended by her old nurse. She was heavy with child.

"Michelangelo."

"Contessina. *Come va?"*

"You said I would bear many sons."

He gazed at her pale cheeks, burning eyes, the upturned nose of her father. And he remembered Clarissa, felt her standing in this room beside Contessina. "All love is ' in a way.' "

279

"I have come to tell you that your cousins have offered me a commission. I could not join Piero's army, but I want no other disloyalty on my conscience."

"I heard of their interest. You proved your loyalty, Michelangelo, when they first made the offer. There is no need for you to continue demonstrations. If you wish to accept, do so."

"I shall."

"As for Piero . . . at the moment my sister and I live under the protection of our husbands' families. If Piero ever attacks with a strong force, and the city is in real danger, who knows what will happen to us?"

The major change had taken place in the city itself. As he walked the familiar streets he felt an air of hostility and suspicion. Florentines who had lived at peace with each other since Cosimo de' Medici had ordered their defence towers cut down to roof level had now split into three antagonistic party factions, shouting imprecations at each other. He learned to recognize them by their symbols. The *Arrabbiati,* or Maddened, were the men of wealth and experience who now hated Piero and Savonarola both, calling the friar's followers Snivellers and Prayer-mumblers. Next he distinguished the Whites, or *Frateschi,* which included the Popolanos, who liked Savonarola no better than the Maddened, but had to support him because he was on the side of popular government. Lastly there was Piero de' Medici's group, the Greys, who were intriguing for Piero's return.

When he met Granacci in the Piazza della Signoria, Michelangelo was shocked to see Donatello's bronze Judith, which had been stolen out of the Medici courtyard, standing in front of the Signoria, and the David from the Medici courtyards installed in the Signoria courtyards.

"What is the Judith doing here?" he asked.

"She's now the reigning goddess of Florence."

"Stolen by the city. And the David too?"

"Harsh words, my friend. Confiscated."

"What does that plaque say?"

"That citizens placed this statue here *as a warning to all who should think to tyrannize over Florence.* Judith with that sword in her hand is us, the valiant citizens of Florence. Holofernes, about to have his head cut off, represents the party one doesn't belong to."

"So that a lot of heads will be rolling in the piazza? Are we at war with ourselves?"

Granacci did not answer; but Prior Bichiellini said:
"I am afraid so."

Michelangelo sat in his study surrounded by the shelves of leather-bound manuscripts and the desk piled high with records and sheets of an essay the prior was writing. The prior folded his hands into his black Augustinian sleeves to warm them.

"We have achieved some reform in taxes and morals. We have a more democratic government, more people can participate. But the government is paralyzed unless Fra Savonarola approves its acts."

With the exception of the dedicated group at Ghirlandaio's studio, art and artists had vanished in Florence. Rosselli had fallen ill, and his studio was not working. Two of the Della Robbia family, who had inherited Luca's sculpture processes, had become priests. Botticelli would paint only subjects which his mind could shape from Savonarola's sermons. Lorenzo di Credi, trained by Verrocchio, was reduced to restoring Fra Angelico and Uccello, and had entered a monastery.

"I thought of you," observed the prior, "when the friar announced a sermon for artists. I have some notes jotted down . . . accurately, I assure you: 'In what does beauty consist? In colour? No. In form? No! God is beauty itself. Young artists go about saying of this woman or man, Here is a Magdalene, here a Virgin, there a St. John; and then ye paint their faces in the churches, a great profanation of divine things. Ye artists do very ill, ye fill the churches with vain things. . . .'"

"I've heard it all from my brother. But if Savonarola prevails . . ."

"He prevails."

". . . then perhaps I should not have returned. What place is there for me here?"

"Where would you go, my son?"

Michelangelo was silent. Where indeed?

On New Year's Day of 1496 a large group of men converged on the monastery in Piazza San Marco carrying lighted torches and chanting:

"Burn down his house! Burn down San Marco! Burn down this dirty fellow of a friar!"

Michelangelo stood quietly in the shadow of the Popolano palace. The San Marco monks came out in their habits and cowls, stood shoulder to shoulder in a line across the front of the church and monastery, arms linked in a solid phalanx. The crowd continued to shout imprecations against Savonarola, but the monks stolidly held their ground; and after a time the torch carriers began to drift out of the piazza, their fires vanishing down the half dozen streets facing into the square.

Leaning against the cold stone wall, Michelangelo felt a chill sweep through him. Into his mind came Donatello's Judith, standing with sword raised, ready to cut off . . . whose head? Savonarola's? Prior Bichiellini's? Piero's? Florence's?

His own?

14

He went to see Beppe in the Duomo workyard and heard of a small, quite good piece of marble in a neighbouring yard which he could buy at a reasonable price. The rest of the money advanced to him for the St. John he turned over to Lodovico.

He could not bring himself to live in the renamed "Popolano palace," but he did set up his workbench in the garden. The cousins treated him as a friend, frequently inviting him inside, work clothes and all, to see a new piece of art or illuminated manuscript. At home there were only three in the boys' bedroom now, but since Buonarroto had volunteered to share with Sigismondo, Michelangelo was able to continue in the luxury to which he had grown accustomed: a bed to himself. The weather was cold and he ate and drank nothing until midday, so he brought home a substantial appetite which kept Lucrezia happy. Even Lodovico seemed pleased with him.

The Popolano garden was formal, enclosed by a high protecting wall, with a covered three-sided porch under which he worked for warmth. Yet he could find little joy, and no creative surge. He kept asking himself, "Why?"

It was a sympathetic subject: young St. John setting out for the desert to preach in the wilderness, "a garment of camel's hair and a leather girdle about his loins, and locusts and wild honey were his food." Florence had many St. Johns: Andrea Pisano's St. John Baptizing on the Baptistery door, Ghiberti's bronze statue at Orsanmichele, Donatello's marble on the Campanile, Ghirlandaio's fresco in Santa

Maria Novella, Verrocchio's Baptism of Christ painted for San Salvi with the assistance of Leonardo da Vinci.

As he read his Bible, Michelangelo gathered that John would have been fifteen years old when he set out for the desert, Palestine, to preach to the Samaritans. Most of the representations showed him as a small boy, slight in figure, with a childlike face. But that did not need to be. At fifteen many Italian youths were already men. Why could not the young St. John be a robust, healthy, hearty creature, well equipped to endure the rigours to which he was about to expose himself? The kind of figure he found it exciting to carve?

Was it the anxious confusion of the city that depleted his enthusiasm, that caused him concern about his place in his own home? The stories going the rounds included all manner of fantastic rumours and fears: Savonarola would rule the city completely. Florence, having refused to join an Italian City-State League, frightened that the League would put Piero back in power, was again in danger of being conquered. Venice, the Duke of Sforza in Milan, the Borgia Pope in Rome, finding Piero a convenient ally against Savonarola, had helped Piero accumulate ten thousand ducats for the hiring of troops.

But art had been threatened before. Artists had worked in a troubled world. In truth would there ever again be any other kind?

Or was the difficulty of his approach to the St. John the old disturbing question, the elusiveness of John's meaning? Why should God have had to send someone to prepare the world for Jesus? Since he had God's capacity to set aside the laws of nature and perform miracles with which to convince the sceptical, why would the ground have to be ploughed in advance for him?

Michelangelo's mind was an inquiring one. He needed to know the reasons behind things; the motivating philosophic principles. He read the story of John in Matthew:

"In those days John the Baptist appeared, preaching in the wilderness of Judaea; Report, he said, the kingdom of heaven is at hand. It was of him that the prophet Isaiah spoke, when he said, There is a voice of one crying in the wilderness, Prepare the way of the Lord, straighten out his paths."

But the boy of fifteen first going out to preach was not the older man who later baptized Jesus. What was he like then?

What was his importance to Christianity? Was his story imperative, or was it merely a fulfilment of the Old Testament prophecy, because the first Christians felt that the more strongly they based their religion on the Old Testament the better chance it would have to survive?

If he was not a trained theologian, he was a good craftsman. He spent weeks sketching throughout the city, every youth he could detain for a few moments. Though he was not intending to create a massive John, neither would he have anything to do with the fragile, elegant St. John with which Florence was adorned. And so he designed, and then carved into the block, the suppleness of limb of a fifteen-year-old, using only the loincloth as a cover. He refused to carve a halo for the boy or give him the traditional tall cross to carry, as Donatello had, since he did not think that the young John carried a cross that many years before the cross came into Christ's life. It turned out to be a vital portrait of a youth; but when he finished polishing the piece, he still did not know what he meant by it.

The Medici cousins needed less meaning. They were well pleased, placing the statue in a protective niche in the far garden wall where it could be seen from the rear windows of the palace. They paid him the balance of the florins and told him he was welcome to continue using their garden as his workshop.

But not a word about another commission.

"Nor can I blame them," Michelangelo commented to Granacci with a melancholy air. "It is nothing very special."

A despair enveloped him. "I've learned to carve in the round; but when do I carve something extraordinary in the round? I feel that I know less now, with my twenty-first birthday coming, than I did at seventeen. How can that be possible?"

"It isn't."

"Bertoldo told me, 'Create a body of work.' I have carved six pieces in these four years: the Hercules, the wood Crucifixion, the Angel, St. Petronius and St. Proculus in Bologna, and now this St. John. But only the St. Proculus has something original in it."

On his birthday he walked disconsolately into the workshop in the Popolano garden. He found a block of white marble sitting on his workbench. Across it, scrawled in Granacci's handwriting, was the greeting:

"Try again!"

284

He did, immediately, without sketching or going into wax or clay, an infant that had half formulated itself in his mind while he was slogging away at the St. John: robust, lusty, pagan, carved in the Roman tradition. He never imagined he was doing a serious piece, it was an exercise really, something he got fun out of, an antidote to the confusions and tensions of the St. John. And so the marble flowed freely, and out of the block emerged a delightful child of six, sleeping with his right arm under his head, his legs spread comfortably apart.

The piece took him only a few weeks to carve and polish; he was neither attempting perfection nor hopeful of selling it. The whole project was a lark, designed to cheer him up; and now that it was finished he intended to return the marble to Granacci with a note which would read:

"Only a little the worse for wear."

It was Lorenzo Popolano who changed his mind. When he saw the completed piece his face flushed with pleasure.

"If you were to treat it so that it seemed to have been buried in the earth, I would send it to Rome, and it would pass for an antique Cupid. Would you know how to do that?"

"I think so. I antiqued a whole folio of drawings once."

"You would sell it for a far better price. I have a shrewd dealer there, Baldassare del Milanese. He will handle it."

He had seen enough Greek and Roman statues to know how his marble should look. He worked first with the scraps left from the Bambino, rubbing the dirt of the garden into the crystals with his fingers, then sandpapering lightly before applying another layer, staining the outside edges heavily with earth tans and rust, using a hard bristle brush to bury the discoloration.

When he was satisfied that he had a good process, he began on the Bambino, working carefully, as amused at the idea of the impending fraud as he had been at the carving itself.

Lorenzo liked the result.

"It is convincing. Baldassare will get you a good price. I have packets going to Rome in a few days, and I'll include your little statue."

Lorenzo had guessed rightly: the Bambino was sold to the first customer to whom Baldassere offered it: Cardinal Riario di San Giorgio, grand-nephew of Pope Sixtus IV. Lorenzo poured a pouch of gold florins into Michelangelo's hands, thirty of them. Michelangelo had thought an antique Cupid in Rome would bring at least a hundred florins. Even so, it was twice what it would have brought in Florence; if indeed anyone would have wanted it, with Savonarola's Army of Boys forcibly sequestering all such pagan images from private homes.

Just before Lent Michelangelo saw his brother Giovansimone hurrying down the Via Larga at the head of a group of white-robed boys, their arms laden with mirrors, gowns of silk and satin, oil paintings, statuary, jewel boxes. Michelangelo grabbed his brother, almost toppling his load of loot.

"Giovansimone! I have been home for four months and haven't laid eyes on you."

Giovansimone shook his arm loose with a broad grin, exclaimed:

"Haven't time to talk to you now. Be sure to be in the Piazza della Signoria to-morrow at dusk."

It would not have been possible for Michelangelo or anyone else in Florence to miss the giant spectacle the following evening. In the four main quarters of Florence the Army of Boys in their white robes were shaped into military formations and, preceded by drummers, pipers and mace bearers carrying olive branches in their hands and chanting, "Long live Christ, the King of Florence! Long live Mary, the Queen!" they marched on the Piazza della Signoria. Here, in front of the tower, a huge tree had been erected. Built around it was a pyramidal scaffold. The citizens of Florence and the outlying villages poured into the square. The section for the burning was roped off by the monks of San Marco standing arm in arm, with Savonarola in commanding position.

The boys built their pyre. At the base they threw bundles of false hair, rouge pots, perfumes, mirrors, bolts of silk from France, boxes of beads, earrings, bracelets, fancy buttons. Then came all the paraphernalia of gambling, a shower of playing cards dancing for a moment in the air, dice and checkered boards with their pawns and characters.

On the next layer of the pyramid were piled books, leatherbound manuscripts, hundreds of drawings, oil paintings, every piece of ancient sculpture the boys had been able to lay their hands on. Thrown on to the highest tier were violas, lutes and barrel organs, their beautiful shapes and glistening woods converting the mad heap to a scene of bacchanalia; then came masks, costumes from pageants, carved ivories and

286

oriental art works; rings, brooches, necklaces sparkled as they landed. Michelangelo recognized Botticelli as he ran up to the pyre and threw on to it sketches of Simonetta. Fra Bartolommeo followed with his studies, the Della Robbia monks, with frenzied motion, added their vari-coloured terra-cotta sculptures. It was difficult to tell from the alternating outbursts of the crowd whether they greeted the sacrifices with fear or ecstasy.

On the balcony of the tower stood the members of the Signoria watching the spectacle. The Army of Boys had gone from house to house asking for " all art works inappropriate to the faith," all ornaments, fineries and decorations not permitted by the sumptuary laws; if they had not been given what they considered a sufficient contribution, they had brushed past the owners of the house and looted it. The Signoria had done nothing to protect the city against these " white-robed angels."

Savonarola raised his arms for silence. The guarding line of monks unlocked their arms and raised them to the heavens. A monk appeared with a lighted torch and handed it to Savonarola. Savonarola held the torch high while he gazed around the square. Then he walked around the pyre, touching it in one place after another until the entire scaffolding was one huge mass of flames.

The Army of Boys marched about the burning pyre chanting, " Long live Christ! Long live the Virgin!" Great answering shouts went up from the packed mass. " Long live Christ! Long live the Virgin!"

Tears came to Michelangelo's eyes. He wiped them away as a child would, first with the back of his left hand and then with his right. But they continued to well up, as the flames mounted higher and higher and the wild singing and crying reached an ever greater crescendo, until they rolled down his cheeks and he felt their saltiness on his lips.

He wished with all his heart that he could go away, as far from the sight of the Duomo as he could get.

15

In June a groom came with a message from Giovanni Popolano asking Michelangelo if he would come to the palace to meet a Roman nobleman interested in sculpture. Leo Baglioni, the Popolanos' guest, was a man of about thirty, blond, well spoken. He walked with Michelangelo out to the workshop.

"My hosts tell me you are an excellent sculptor. Could I see something of your work?"

"I have nothing here, only the St. John in the garden."

"And drawings? I am particularly interested in drawings."

"Then you are a rarity among connoisseurs, sir. I should welcome your seeing my folio."

Leo Baglioni pored over the hundreds of sketches.

"Would you be so kind as to make a simple drawing for me? A child's hand, for example."

Michelangelo drew rapidly, a number of memories of children in various poses. After a time Baglioni said:

"There can be no question about it. You are the one."

"The one?"

"Yes. Who carved the Cupid."

"Ah!"

"Forgive me for dissembling, but I was sent to Florence by my principal, Cardinal Riario di San Giorgio, to see if I could find the sculptor of the Cupid."

"It was I. Baldassare del Milanese sent me thirty florins for the piece."

"Thirty! But the cardinal paid two hundred . . ."

"Two hundred! Why, that . . . that thief . . ."

"Precisely what the cardinal said," declared Leo Baglioni with a mischievous gleam in his eye. "He suspected it was a fraud. Why not return to Rome with me? You can settle your account with Baldassare. I believe the cardinal would be pleased to offer you hospitality. He said that anyone who could make such an excellent fake should be able to make even better authentic carvings."

Michelangelo shook his head in perplexity over the series of events; but there was no faltering in his decision.

"A few articles of clothing from my home, sir, and I shall be ready for the journey."

BOOK FIVE

THE CITY

1

He stood on a rise just north of the city. Rome lay below in its bed of hills, destroyed, as though sacked by vandals. Leo Baglioni traced the outlines of the Leonine Wall, the fortress of Sant'Angelo.

They got back on their horses and descended to the Porta del Popolo, passing the tomb of Nero's mother to enter the small piazza. It stank from piled garbage. Above them to the left was the Pincio hill covered with vineyards. The streets they followed were narrow lanes with broken cobbles underfoot. The noise of carts passing over the stones was so deafening that Michelangelo could barely hear Baglioni identifying the dilapidated tomb of the Roman emperor Augustus, now a grazing field for cows; the Campo Marzio, a plain near the Tiber inhabited by the poorer artisans whose shops were huddled between ancient palaces that looked as though they would topple at any moment.

More than half of the buildings he passed were gutted. Goats wandered among the fallen stones. Baglioni explained that the previous December the Tiber had flooded and the people had had to flee for three days to the surrounding hills, returning to a dank, decaying city in which the plague struck and one hundred and fifty corpses were buried each morning on the island in the river.

Michelangelo felt sick to his stomach: the Mother City of Christendom was a waste heap and a dunghill. Dead animals lay under the feet or their horses. Wrecking crews were breaking out walls of building stone for use elsewhere, burning marble slabs and columns for their lime content. He guided his horse around a piece of ancient statuary sticking up through the dirt of the road, passed rows of abandoned houses, salt and vines growing in their crumbling mortar. Skirting a Grecian temple, he saw pigs penned between its columns. In a block-square subterranean vault with broken columns half emerging from an ancient forum there was a horrendous odour, rising from hundreds of years of dumped refuse, and generations of men whose descendants even now were squatting over its void, defecating into its depth.

His host led him through a series of dark, winding streets where two horses could barely pass each other, past the theatre of Pompey with hundreds of families living in its yawning vault; and then at last into the Campo dei Fiori where he saw his first signs of recognizable life: a vegetable, flower, cheese, fish and meat market, crowded with row upon row of clean colourful stalls, the cooks and housewives of Rome shopping for their dinner. For the first time since they had decended into Rome he was able to look at his host and tender him a wisp of a smile.

" Frightened?" Leo Baglioni asked. " Or revulsed?"

" Both. Several times I almost turned my horse and made a run for Florence."

" Rome is pitiful. You should see the pilgrims who come from all over Europe. They are robbed, beaten, ridden down by our princely processions, bitten half to death by vermin in the inns, then separated from their last denaro in the churches. Bracciolini wrote some sixty years ago, 'The public and private buildings lie prostrate, nude and broken like the limbs of a giant. Rome is a decaying corpse.' Pope Sixtus IV made a real effort to widen the streets and repair some of the buildings; but under the Borgias the city has fallen into a worse condition than that of which Bracciolini wrote. Here's my home."

Standing on a corner overlooking the market was a well-designed house of three floors. Inside, the rooms were small and sparsely furnished with walnut tables and chairs, but richly carpeted, with tapestries and precious cloths on the walls, and decorated with painted wooden cupboards, gold mirrors and red leather ornaments.

Michelangelo's sailcloth bag was carried up to the third floor. He was given a corner room overlooking the market and a staggeringly huge, new stone palace which his host told him was just being completed by Cardinal Riario, who had bought his Bambino.

They had an excellent dinner in a dining-room that was protected from the noises of the street. Late in the afternoon they strolled to the cardinal's old villa, through the Piazza Navona, former site of the long stadium of Domitian, where Michelangelo was fascinated by a half-buried, half-excavated marble torso, brilliantly carved, standing before the house of one of the Orsini, a relative of Piero's wife Alfonsina, and which Leo thought might be Menelaus Carrying Patroclus.

They continued on to the Piazza Fiammetta, named after the mistress of Cæsar Borgia, son of the Pope, and then to the Riario palace facing the Via Sistina and the city's cleanest inn, the Hostaria dell'Orso, Inn of the Bear. Baglioni filled in his background on Raffaelle Riario di San Giorgio, a grandnephew of Pope Sixtus IV who had been made a cardinal when an eighteen-year-old student at the University of Pisa. The young cardinal had gone for a visit to the Medici palace in Florence, and had been worshipping at the altar in the Duomo when assassins killed Giuliano de' Medici and stabbed Lorenzo. Though Lorenzo and the Florentines had been convinced that it was Pope Sixtus and his nephews who had connived with the Pazzi to murder both Medici, Lorenzo had absolved the cardinal of knowledge of the plot.

Cardinal Riario received Michelangelo amidst piles of boxes and half-packed trunks that were being readied for moving. He read Lorenzo Popolano's letter of introduction, bade Michelangelo welcome to Rome.

"Your Bambino was well sculptured, Buonarroti, even though it was not an antique. I have the impression that you can carve something quite fine for us."

"Thank you, Excellency."

"I should like you to go out this afternoon and see our best marble statues. Start with the arch of Domitian on the Corso, then go to the column of Trajan, after that see the Capitoline collection of bronzes that my grand-uncle, Sixtus IV, started . . ."

By the time the cardinal finished he had named some twenty pieces of sculpture in a dozen different collections and parts of the city. Leo Baglioni guided him first to see the river god Marforio, a monstrous-sized statue lying in the street between the Roman forum and the forum of Augustus, which was supposed to have been in the temple of Mars. From here they moved on to the column of Trajan, where Michelangelo exclaimed over the carving of the Lion Devouring the Horse. They walked up the winding Quirinal hill where he was stunned by the size and brute force of the eighteen-foot-high marble Horse Tamers and the gods of the Nile and the Tiber, the Nile resting an arm on a sphinx, the Tiber leaning on a tiger, which Leo thought came out of the baths of Constantine. Near them was a nude goddess of breath-taking beauty, "probably a Venus," proffered Leo.

They continued on to the garden of Cardinal Rovere at San Pietro in Vincoli, Leo explaining that this nephew of Sixtus IV was the founder of the first public library and museum of bronzes in Rome, had accumulated the finest collection of antique marbles in Italy, and had been Sixtus' inspiring force in the project to fresco the walls of the Sistine Chapel.

Michelangelo stood breathless when he entered the little iron gate of Cardinal Rovere's garden, for here was an Apollo, just the torso remaining, that was the most staggering piece of human projection he had ever seen. As he had in the Medici palace on his first visit with Bertoldo, he moved half stunned in a forest of sculpture, from a Venus to an Antaeus to a Mercury, his mind captivated, only dimly hearing Leo's voice telling him which pieces had been stolen from Greece, which had been bought by Emperor Hadrian and sent to Rome by the shipload. If Florence were the richest centre in the world for the creation of art, surely this miserably dirty, decaying city must hold the greatest collection of antique art? And here was the proof of what he had tried to tell his fellow Ghirlandaio apprentices on the steps of the Duomo: here were marble carvings as alive and beautiful as the day they were carved, two thousand years ago.

" Now we shall go to see the bronze Marcus Aurelius before the Lateran," continued Leo. " Then perhaps . . ."

" Please, no more. I'm quivering inside. I must lock myself in my room and try to digest what I've already seen."

He could eat no supper that night. The next morning, Sunday, Leo took him to mass in the little church of San Lorenzo in Damaso, next to Cardinal Riario's new palace, and attached to it by a break-through in one of its walls. Michelangelo was staggered to find himself surrounded by a hundred marble and granite columns, no two alike, carved by expert stonemasons, each with a differently sculptured capital, " eclectically borrowed from all over Rome," Leo explained, " but mainly from the front of the portico of the theatre of Pompey. . . ."

The cardinal wished Michelangelo to come to the new palace. The vast stone edifice, twice the size of the Medici palace, was finished except for the central courtyard. Michelangelo climbed a broad flight of stairs, went through the audience chamber with rich tapestry curtains and mirrors framed in jasper, the drawing-room with oriental carpets and carved walnut chairs, the music-room with a beautiful harpsichord, until he came upon the cardinal in his red hat and vestments, sitting in his antique sculpture room, with a dozen pieces lying in open boxes filled with sawdust.

"Tell me, Buonarroti, what do you think of the marbles you have seen? Can you do something equally beautiful?"

"I may not carve anything as beautiful. But we will see what I can do."

"I like that answer, Buonarroti, it shows humility."

He did not feel humble, all he had meant was that his pieces would be different from anything he had seen.

"We had best start at once," continued Riario. "My carriage is outside. It can take us to the stoneyard."

As the cardinal's groom drove them across the Sisto bridge and through the Settimiana gate to the Trastevere stoneyards, Michelanglo studied the face of his new patron. It was said that Riario had been so shocked at the Medici stabbings that his face had turned purple; in fact it remained so to this day. He had a long, hooked nose that clamped down on a tight-lipped mouth.

Once in the stoneyard Cardinal Riario seemed impatient. Michelangelo wandered among the blocks wondering how large a piece he dared select. Finally he stopped before a white Carrara column over seven feet tall and four feet thick. His eyes lighted with excitement. He assured the cardinal that there could be a fine statue contained in it. Cardinal Riario quickly paid out thirty-seven ducats from the purse on his belt.

The next morning Michelangelo rose at first light, made his way downstream to the Florentine bridge and crossed the Tiber to Trastevere, densely inhabited section of Rome, home of the potters, tanners, millers, ropemakers, metalworkers, fishermen, boatmen, gardeners, a brawling, sprawling population descended from the original Romans, self-contained within high walls and the Tiber, their crowded quarters unchanged for hundreds of years. He wound through a labyrinth of narrow streets, watched workmen handling raw materials in dark shops, all light cut off by projecting upper stories, the narrow houses jammed together, while above them the roofs pitched angularly, surmounted by bristling square towers. Pedlars were calling their wares, women and children brawling, open fish, cheese and meat marketeers crying out bargains, the whole of the tumultuous noise and smell locked in to overwhelm one's ears and eyes and nose.

He walked along the Via della Lungara to the stoneyard just outside the Vatican wall and Santo Spirito hospital. Not a soul was stirring. He listened through a cacophony of cockcrows before the owner showed up.

"What are you doing here?" he demanded, still half asleep and sullen. "We say we deliver to-day. What we say, we do."

"I wasn't worried about your failure to deliver. I just thought I'd help load . . ."

"You telling me we don't know how to load?" Now the owner was insulted. "We been carting marble in Rome for five generations, and we need a Florentine statue maker to teach us our business?"

"My family trained me in the Maiano quarries. I'm a pretty good hand with a crowbar."

Mollified, the owner replied, "Quarryman, eh? That's different. We quarry travertine in our family. Guffatti is our name."

Michelangelo made sure there was a sufficient bed of saw-dust and that the block was securely lashed before the open-end wagon started on its journey through streets rutted to the hubs of the wheels. He walked behind, patting the end of the column while praying that the rickety farm wagon, in the family for five generations, would not collapse in a pile of splinters and leave the marble block in the roadbed.

Arriving at the palace, Guffatti asked, "Where do we unload?"

Michelangelo suddenly realized that he had not been told where he would work. He cried, "Wait right here!" ran through the courtyard and up the broad staircase to the reception room . . . to come head on against one of the palace secretaries, who glanced disapprovingly at this bundle of work clothes dashing into the main foyer of the newest palace in Rome.

"I have to see the cardinal immediately. It's urgent."

"Urgent for the cardinal, or you?"

The cool tone slowed Michelangelo down.

"It's the marble block . . . we bought it yesterday . . . it's arrived and I have no place . . ."

He stopped, watching the secretary thumb through an appointment calendar.

"His Excellency has no time available until next week."

Michelangelo stood with his mouth open.

"But . . . we can't wait."

" I'll take the matter up with His Eminence. If you would care to return to-morrow."

He ran back down the central staircase at full speed, out the palace, to the corner and across the street to Leo Baglioni's house. Leo was being barbered, a towel over his shoulders to catch the clipped locks. His eyes danced while he listened to Michelangelo's outburst. He told the barber to wait, removed the towel, rose from the only cushioned chair in the house.

" Come, we'll find a space for you."

Leo located a shed behind the cupola of San Lorenzo in Damaso, in which the workmen who built the palace had left their tools at night. Michelangelo removed the doors from their hinges. Leo returned to his barber. The Guffatti unloaded the marble.

Michelangelo sat on the earthen floor before the block, holding his knees under his chin. " You are a beautiful piece of meat," he said fondly ; and fell to musing about the kind of theme a prince of the Church might choose for a life-size figure. Would it not have to be a religious subject? Yet the cardinal had a liking for ancient Greek and Roman carvings.

That afternoon the cardinal sent for him. He was received in an austere room bare of all furniture. There was a small altar at one end, and a doorway beside it. Riario was wearing a severely tailored red cassock and skullcap.

" Now that you are about to undertake a prolonged piece of work, you had better move into the palace. Signor Baglioni's guestroom has a long list of lovely ladies waiting to share it."

" On what terms am I to live in the palace, Excellency?"

" Let us just say that your address is the palace of the Cardinal Riario. And now we must leave you."

No word about what the cardinal wanted sculptured. Or what the price would be. Or whether he was to have regular payments during his year of work. The palace would be his address ; he knew nothing more.

But he learned. He was not to live here as a son, as he had in the Medici palace, nor as a close friend as in the Aldovrandi home in Bologna. A chamberlain directed him to a narrow cell at the rear of the ground floor, one of perhaps twenty such rooms, where he unpacked his few possessions. When he went looking for his first meal he found himself relegated to what was known as the " third category " dining-room, in which he found his companions to be the cardinal's scriveners, the head bookkeeper, the purchasing agent for the palace, the managers of his far-flung farm lands, timber stands, ships, benefices all over Italy.

The Cardinal Riario had made himself clear; Michelangelo Buonarroti was to live in the palace as one of the crew of skilled workmen. Nothing more, and nothing less.

2

Early the next morning he went to see Baldassere the art dealer, who had just been obliged to return Cardinal Riario's two hundred ducats for the Bambino. Baldassere was a swarthy fat man with three jowls and an enormous stomach which he pushed ahead of him as he came from the back of his sculpture yard, just off the forum of Julius Cæsar. Michelangelo's progress was slow in coming down the yard, for the dealer had a number of antiques mounted on bases.

"I am Michelangelo Buonarroti, sculptor of Florence."

Baldassere made an obscene noise with his lips.

"I want you to return my Bambino. I will repay the thirty florins you sent me."

"Certainly not!" the dealer cried.

"You defrauded me. All you were entitled to was your commission. You sold the marble for two hundred ducats and kept one hundred and seventy."

"On the contrary, it is you and your friend Popolano who are the frauds. You sent me a false antique. I could have lost the cardinal's patronage."

Michelangelo walked fuming out of the yard, half ran down the Via Santa. He crossed the street, stood gazing at Trajan's column until his head cleared. Then he burst into laughter.

"Baldassere is right. It is I who was the cheat. I falsified the Bambino."

He heard someone behind him exclaim:

"Michelangelo Buonarroti! Do you always talk to yourself?"

He turned, recognized a fellow of his own age who had been apprenticed to the Money Changers Guild and worked briefly for his Uncle Francesco in an early period of prosperity. They might have known each other for a hundred years in Florence and never become friends, but here they fell on each other's necks.

"Balducci. What are you doing in Rome?"

"Working for Jacopo Galli's bank. Head bookkeeper. The dumbest Florentine is smarter than the smartest Roman. That's why I'm moving up so fast. How about having dinner together? I'll take you to a Tuscan restaurant in the Florentine section. I can't stand this Roman food. Wait till you taste the *tortellini* and beefsteak, you'll think you're back in sight of the Duomo."

"There is time before noon. Come with me to the Sistine Chapel, I want to see the Florentine frescoes."

The Sistine Chapel, built between 1473 and 1481, was a mammoth barrel-roofed structure with high windows towards the ceiling and a railed balcony-walk beneath them. The rectangular dome was painted blue with gold stars scattered about. At the far end was the altar and, dividing the sanctuary and the nave, a marble screen by Mino da Fiesole. What would have appeared a clumsily proportioned and graceless building was saved by a magnificent frieze of frescoed panels on both sides of the chapel, running full length to the altar.

Michelangelo went excitedly to the Ghirlandaio frescoes which he remembered from the cartoons in the studio: the Resurrection and the Calling of Peter and Andrew. His admiration for Ghirlandaio's pictorial skill was renewed. Next he went to Rosselli's Last Supper, which he did not find as garish as Ghirlandaio had charged; then turned his gaze raptly to the Botticelli Moses Before the Burning Bush, and to the Umbrian masters, Perugino, Pinturicchio and Signorelli. As he moved about the chapel he sensed that under this awkward, unbalanced roof there had been assembled the greatest combination of masters to be found in Italy. He decided that Perugino's Christ Giving the Keys to St. Peter stood up with the finest of the Florentine tradition, the highest compliment he could pay any artist. He remarked to Balducci how strange it was that this topheavy, cavernous chapel, as inept and arid a piece of architecture as he had yet seen, could have called forth the painters' richest creative efforts.

Balducci had not even glanced as the frescoes.

"Let's get to the *trattoria*. I'm famished."

While eating, Michelangelo learned that Torrigiani was in Rome.

"But you won't see much of him," said Balducci. "He consorts with the Borgias so the Florentines don't receive him. He's doing stuccos for the tower of the Borgia palace, also a bust of the Pope. He has all the sculpture work he wants. He also say he is going to join Cæsar Borgia's army to conquer Italy."

That evening Balducci took him to the home of Paolo Rucellai, a cousin of the Rucellai in Florence and hence a distant cousin of his own. Rucellai lived in the district of Ponte, known as "a little Florence, walled within itself." Here, centred around the Florentine consul's house and the Tuscan banks, the Florentines in Rome lived close together, with their own markets, which imported their *pasta*, meats, vegetables, fruits and sweets from Tuscany. They had acquired land on which to build a Florentine church, and had bought the few remaining houses on the Via Canale so that no Romans could move in. The hatred was mutual. The Romans said:

"Better a corpse in the house than a Florentine at the door."

The Florentines reinterpreted the S.P.Q.R. of the Romans' *Senatus Populus Que Romanus* to read, "*Seno Porci, Questi Romani*. They are pigs, these Romans."

The Florentine section of Ponte was the area held within a wide bend of the river, in the centre of which was the Florentine bridge leading to Trastevere. In the area were fine palaces, two streets of solidly built houses, with flower and vegetable gardens interspersed. The Florentine banks were on the Via Canale, adjoining the Camera Apostolica, the official bank of the Vatican. At the extreme end of the colony, near the bridge of Sant' Angelo, were the Pazzi and Altoviti palaces. Near the riverbank was an open space filled with flowers and vegetables which became a lake when the Tiber overflowed, as it had the year before.

In the midst of the chaos and filth of Rome the prosperous Florentines swept and washed down their streets every day at dawn, replaced the cobblestones to make a smooth and quiet roadbed, put their houses in a good state of repair, sold or leased only to Florentines. There were prohibitive fines against dumping refuse in the streets or hanging laundry from the front windows instead of the back. Armed guards policed the quarter at night; it was the only section where one was sure not to stumble over a corpse on one's stoop at daybreak.

At the Rucellai house he was presented to the leading families of the community: the Tornabuoni, Strozzi, Pazzi, Altoviti, Bracci, Olivieri, Ranfredini and Cavalcanti, to whom he was carrying a letter of introduction.

Some of the Florentines were bankers, others were silk and wool merchants, jewellers, importers of wheat, gold- and silversmiths, shipowners and shipbuilders who had thriving ports at Ripa Grande and Ripetta, where boats came up the Tiber from the sea carrying luxuries from the Near East, wines and oil from Tuscany, marble from Carrara, timber from across the Adriatic.

A number of the men asked, " Who is your father?" When he replied, " Lodovico Buonarroti-Simoni," they nodded their heads, said, " I know the name," accepting him forthwith.

The Rucellai had converted their Roman house into pure Florentine, with a recessed fireplace surrounded by *pietra serena,* the floor of the dining-room tiled in the tradition of Lucca della Robbia, and the familiar inlaid furniture so beloved of his countrymen. He did not tell handsome affable Paolo that he too was a Rucellai. The Rucellai had terminated the family relationship with the Buonarroti. His pride would never let him be the first to speak.

He set up his seven-foot block on beams braced from behind so that he could move around it. His disappointment that the cardinal did not immediately present him with a specific subject gave way to the realization that it would be better if he himself knew what he wanted to carve. Then he would not have to ask humbly, " What would Your Excellency like me to make out of this marble?"

" Exercise extreme care," Leo warned him, " not to touch that column until Cardinal Riario gives you permission to do so. He is adamant about his properties."

" I could not hurt the marble, Leo, by rounding the edges and exploring a little. . . ."

He was humiliated at being cautioned like a labourer not to manhandle the property of his *padrone.* Yet he had to promise not to chip a single crystal off the block.

" You can use your time profitably," said Leo placatingly. " There are wonderful things in Rome to study."

" Yes, I know," said Michelangelo. Why try to explain his marble fever? He changed the subject. " Can one secure nude models in Rome? It is not allowed in Florence."

Leo replied mischievously, " That's because we Romans

are a clean and moral people. But you Florentines . . .!"
He laughed as Michelangelo flushed. "I suppose it's because
we have never suffered from the Greek sickness, and Florence
has been famous, or should I say infamous, for it. Here our
men have been making business deals, arranging political
alignments and marriages while they take their leisure and
exercise in the nude."

"Could you arrange for me to have models?"

"Tell me what kind you want."

"All kinds: short, tall, skinny, fat, young and old, dark
and light, labourers and idlers, traders."

He set up a low screen to give him a modicum of privacy.
The next morning Leo's first nominee arrived, a burly
middle-aged cooper who shed his stinking shirt and sandals
and moved about unconcernedly as Michelangelo directed
him to a variety of poses. Each morning at sunrise he
went out to his workshop to prepare his paper, chalk, ink,
charcoal, coloured crayons, not knowing what new task the
day's model would bring: Corsicans who formed the papal
bodyguard, German typographers, French perfumers and
glovemakers, Teutonic bakers, Spanish booksellers, Lombard
carpenters from the Campo Marzio, Dalmation boatbuilders,
Greek coypists, Portuguese trunkmakers from the Via dei
Baullari, goldsmiths from beside San Giorgio. Sometimes
they were superb figures whom he drew in full frontal or
rear positions, posed straining, turning, lifting, pushing,
twisting, battling with an array of work tools, clubs, stones.
More often the whole figure would not be interesting, only
a specially knotted shoulder, the shape of a skull, an iron-
corded calf, a barrel chest, and then he would spend the
entire day drawing only that one segment, seen from a dozen
angles and in differing postures.

His years of training were coming into focus. The months
of dissection had given his drawing an authority, an inner
truth that had changed the projection of his work. Even the
urbane and sophisticated Leo commented on the propulsive
force of these figures.

"Each morning you come out to a different model as
though you were going on an exciting adventure. Don't you
get tired drawing the same thing over and over again: head,
arms, torso, legs . . .?"

"But, Leo, they are never the same! Every arm and leg
and neck and hip in the world is different, with a true
character of its own. Listen, my friend, all forms that exist in

God's universe can be found in the human figure. A man's body and face can tell everything he represents. So how could I ever exhaust my interest in it?"

Baglioni was entertained by Michelangelo's intensity. He glanced at the batch of sketches under Michelangelo's arm, shook his head unbelievingly.

"What about the inner qualities? In Rome we conceal rather than reveal what we are."

"That is a measure of the sculptor: how deeply can he penetrate the shell? With every subject I say to myself, 'What are you, truly, as you stand naked before the world?'"

Leo pondered on this for a moment. "Then, for you, sculpture is a search."

Michelangelo smiled shyly.

"Isn't it, for all artists? Every man sees truth through his own funnel. I feel about each new figure the way an astronomer does each time he discovers a new star: one more fragment of the universe has been filled in. Perhaps if I could draw every male on earth I could accumulate the whole truth about man."

"Well then," said Leo, "I would recommend that you come with me to the baths. There you can do a hundred in a sitting."

He took Michelangelo on a tour of the staggeringly vast and ornate ruins of the ancient baths of Caracalla, Trajan, Constantine, Diocletian, telling him of how the early Romans had used the baths as clubs, meeting halls, spending every afternoon of their lives in them.

"You have heard the line attributed to Cæsar, 'Give the populace bread and circuses.' Several of the emperors felt it equally important to give them water, believing their popularity depended on how beautiful they made their public baths."

Now that the baths were run for profit they were far less lavish, but they had several pools for swimming, steam and massage rooms, courts where the clients entertained each other with the day's gossip while musicians and jugglers made the rounds, food vendors came through hawking their wares, the younger men played a variety of ball-games.

Leo was well known in the bath on the Piazza Scossacavalli which belonged to the Cardinal Riario. After they had had their warm bath and a swim in a cold pool, they sat on a bench at the far end of the area where knots of men were sitting and standing, arguing, laughing, telling anecdotes, while Michelangelo composed scene after scene in a fever of composition, so superb were the modelled planes, curves and masses of the figures against each other.

"I've never seen anything like it. In Florence public baths are for the poor," he exclaimed.

"I will spread the word that you are in Rome on the cardinal's invitation. Then you'll be able to sketch here to your heart's content."

In the weeks that followed he took Michelangelo to the baths connected with the hostels, monasteries, old palaces, to the one in the Via dei Pastini, to Sant'Angelo in the Pescheria. Everywhere Leo introduced Michelangelo so that he could come back alone; and in each new setting of light, wall colour, reflection of sun and water on the bodies, he found fresh truths and ways of expressing them in simple bold lines.

But he never quite got used to sketching while he himself was naked. "Once a Florentine . . .!" he muttered to himself.

One afternoon Leo asked, "Wouldn't you like to sketch some women? There are several baths for both sexes within the city walls, run by prostitutes, but with quite respectable clienteles."

"I have no interest in the female form."

"You're summarily dismissing half the figures in the world."

"Roughly, yes." They laughed together. "But I find all beauty and structural power in the male. Take a man in any action, jumping, wrestling, throwing a spear, ploughing, bend him into any position and the muscles, the distribution of weight and tension, have their symmetry. For me, a woman to be beautiful or exciting must be absolutely still."

"Perhaps you just haven't put them into the proper positions."

Michelangelo smiled. "Yes, I have. I find it a sight for love, but not for sculpture."

3

He disliked Rome as a city; but then it was not one city but many, the Germans, French, Portuguese, Greeks, Corsicans, Sicilians, Arabs, Levantines, Jews all compacted within their own areas, welcoming outsiders no more than did the Florentines. Balducci had said to him, "These Romans are an ugly race. Or, should I say, a hundred ugly races." He had found it a heterogeneous gathering of peoples who wore different clothes, spoke different languages, ate different foods, cherished different values. Everybody appeared to have come from somewhere else, habitually calling down a pox on the city for its decay, floods, pestilences, lawnessness, filth and corruption. Since there was no government, no laws or police courts or councils for protection, each section governed itself as best it could. The convenient cemetery of crimes was the Tiber, where floating corpses regularly greeted the early morning risers. There was no equitable distribution of wealth, justice, learning, art.

As he walked for hours about Rome he found it a shambles, its widespread walls, which had protected half a million people in the days of the Empire, now enclosing less than seventy thousand. Whole areas that had been populated were neglected ruins. There was hardly a block, even in the heavily populated sections, without black gaping holes between buildings, like missing teeth in an old crone's mouth. Its architecture was a hodgepodge of crude dungcoloured brick, black tufa stone, tan travertine, blocks of grey granite, pink and green marble stolen from other eras. The manners of the people were execrable: they ate in the streets, even the well-dressed wives emerging from bakery shops to walk along munching on fresh sugar rolls, chewing pieces of hot tripe and other specialities from the vendors' carts and street cookstoves, consuming dinner piecemeal in public.

The residents had no pride in their city, no desire to improve it or provide rudimentary care. They told him, "Rome is not a city, it's a church. We have no power to control or change it." When he asked, "Then why do people stay?" he was answered, "Because there is money to be made." Rome had the most unsavoury reputation in Europe.

The contrasts with homogeneous Florence, compact within its walls, immaculately clean, a self-governing Republic, inspired of art and architecture, growing rapidly without poverty, proud of its tradition, revered throughout Europe for its learning and justice, were for him sharp and painful. Most personally painful was the atrocious stonework of the buildings as he passed each day. In Florence he had rarely been able to resist running his fingers over the beautifully carved and fitted *pietra serena* of the edifices ; here he winced as his practised eye picked out the crude strokes of the chisel, the gouged and blemished surfaces, the unmatched bevelling. Florence would not have paved its streets with these botched building stones!

He stopped in front of a construction in the Piazza del Pantheon, with its wood and iron-pipe scaffolding held together at the joints by leather thongs. Masons putting up a wall of a house were pounding large blocks of travertine, bruising the substance because they did not know how to split it. He picked up a sledge, turned to the foreman and cried:

" *Permettete?*"

" Permit you what?"

He tapped the end of a block, found its point of stratification, with a swift authoritative blow split it longways. Taking a hammer and chisel from a workman's hands, he shaped and bevelled blocks out of the two layers, tooling the surfaces with long rhythmic strokes until the stone changed colour as well as form, and glowed beneath his hand.

He looked up to find himself surrounded by resentful eyes. One of the masons growled, " Stonework is for beasts. Do you think we would be here if we didn't have to eat?"

Michelangelo apologized for intruding. He walked down the Via Pellicciaria feeling a fool ; yet for a Florentine stonemason the surfacing of a block constituted his self-expression. He was respected by his friends according to his skill and resourcefulness in modelling the stones to bring out their individual character. Working the stone was considered the most venerable of crafts, an inherent part of the elemental faith that man and stone had natural affinities.

When he returned to the palace he found an invitation from Paolo Rucellai to attend a reception for Piero de' Medici, who was in Rome attempting to gather an army, and Cardinal Giovanni de' Medici, who had taken a small house near the Via Florida. Michelangelo was touched to have been included, happy to leave his own dull room and board, to see Medici again.

Saturday morning at eleven, as he finished shaving and combing his hair, forming deep curls on his forehead, he heard the sound of trumpets and ran out to see the spectacle, excited to lay eyes at last on this Borgia Pope whom the Medici had feared and Savonarola had picked as his special target. Preceded by red-robed cardinals and the cross, and followed by purple-cloaked princes, Pope Alexander VI, born Rodrigo Borgia in Spain, dressed all in white, white stole and precious pearls, white robe on a white horse, was leading a procession through the Campo dei Fiori on his way to the Franciscan convent in Trastevere.

Sixty-four-year-old Alexander VI appeared to be a man of enormous virility, built big of bone and flesh, with a widely arched nose, swarthy complexion and fleshy cheeks. Though he was called a theatre actor in Rome, he possessed many attributes besides the " brilliant insolence " for which he was known. As Cardinal Rodrigo Borgia he had won the reputation of amassing more beautiful women and vaster sums of wealth than anyone preceding him. As early as 1460 he had been reproved by Pope Pius II for " unseemly gallantry," a euphemism that covered his six known children of varying mothers, of whom his three favourites were Juan, playboy, exhibitionist, prodigious spender of the vast fortunes his father had absorbed from the Roman clergy and barons ; Cæsar, handsome sensualist, sadist and warrior, accused of clogging the Tiber with corpses ; and the beautiful Lucrezia, accused by Rome of having informal love affairs between her growing list of official marriages.

The high walls around the Vatican were guarded by three thousand armed guards, but Rome had developed a communications system that spread news of the happenings therein to the seven hills. If good things occurred, little of it leaked out.

The full panoplied procession having passed, Michelangelo walked up the Via Florida to the Ponte. Because he had arrived too early, Paolo Rucellai received him in his study, a room with dark wood panelling, containing bound manuscripts, marble bas-reliefs, oil paintings on wood, a Florentine carved desk and leather chairs. Paolo's handsome face resembled Bernardo Rucellai's, with its strong regular features, large expressive eyes and light skin, none of which, Michelangelo mourned, had he inherited from his mother's family.

"We Florentines are a tightly knit colony here," Paolo was saying. "As you know by now we have our own government, treasury, laws . . . and means of enforcing them. Otherwise we could not exist in this morass. If you need help, come to us. Never go to a Roman. Their idea of a square deal is one in which they are protected on five sides."

In the drawing-room he met the rest of the Florentine colony. He bowed to Piero, who was cool and formal after their quarrel in Bologna. Cardinal Giovanni, despised by the Pope and frozen out of all church activity, seemed genuinely happy to see him, though Giulio was frigid. Michelangelo learned that Contessina had been brought to bed with a son, Luigi, and was again *incinta*. To his eager question about whether Giuliano was also in Rome, Giovanni replied:

"Giuliano is at the court of Elisabetta Gonzaga and Guidobaldo Montefeltro in Urbino. He will complete his education there." The court of Urbino, high in the Apennines, was one of the most cultured in Italy, Giuliano would thrive.

Thirty Florentines sat down to dinner, eating *cannelloni* stuffed with fine chopped beef and mushrooms, veal in milk, tender green beans, drinking Broglio wines and talking animatedly. They never referred to their adversary as the Pope, or Alexander VI, but only as "the Borgia," striving to preserve their reverence for the papacy while expressing their utter contempt for the Spanish adventurer who through a series of calamitous mishaps had seized the Vatican and was ruling on the premise, according to Cavalcanti, that:

"All the wealth of Christendom belongs to the papacy. And we shall have it!"

The Florentines in turn were not popular with the Pope. He knew them to be adversaries, but he needed their banks, world trade, the high import duties they paid on products brought into Rome, their stability. Unlike the Roman barons, they did not wage was against him, they just prayed fervently for his demise. For this reason they favoured Savonarola in his struggle against the Pope, and found Piero's mission embarrassing.

Over their port the guests grew nostalgic, spoke of Florence as though they were only a few minutes from the Piazza della Signoria. It was a moment for which Michelangelo had been waiting.

"What about art commissions in Rome?" he asked. "The Popes have always called in painters and sculptors."

"The Borgia summoned Pinturicchio from Perugia to decorate his apartments in the Vatican," said Cavalcanti, "and several rooms in Sant'Angelo. Pinturicchio finished last year and left Rome. Perugino has frescoed the Borgia's sitting room, as well as the tower in the papal palace. Perugino is gone now too."

"What of marble?"

"My friend Andrea Bregno is the most respected sculptor in Rome; he seems to have a monopoly on tomb carving. Runs a big shop with a number of apprentices."

"I should like to meet him."

"You'll find him an able man, a lightninglike worker who has decorated most of the churches. I'll tell him that you are coming in to see him."

Balducci shared his countrymen's detestation of Rome, yet there was one phase of Roman life that he relished: the seven thousand public women, assembled from all parts of the world. The next Sunday, following their midday dinner at the Trattoria Toscana, Balducci took Michelangelo for a tour. He knew Rome's piazzas, fountains, forums, triumphal arches, temples, not for their historical background but for the nationality of the women who made these areas their headquarters. They walked the streets for hours peering into the faces, adjudging the figures beneath the *gamurre,* while Balducci kept up a running fire of commentary on the virtues, drawbacks, pleasurable qualities of each. The Roman women, carrying parrots or monkeys on their shoulders, covered with jewellery and perfume and followed by their shiny black servants, arrogantly lorded it over the foreigners: the Spanish girls, with their jet-black hair and eyes of great clarity; the tall Greek girls dressed in their native white robes buckled at slender waists; the dark-skinned Egyptian women in cloaks hanging straight down from the shoulders; the blue-eyed blondes from the north of Europe, with flowers twined through their braids; the straight-haired Turkish women, peering from behind veils; the sloe-eyed Orientals swathed in yards of brightly coloured silks . . .

"I never take the same one twice," Balducci explained. "I like variety, contrast, different colours, shapes, personalities.

That's the interesting part for me, like travelling around the world."

"How can you tell, Balducci, that the first one you pass won't be the most attractive of the day?"

"My innocent friend: it's the hunt that counts. That's why I prolong the search, until late at night sometimes. The externals are different: size, shape, mannerism? But the act? The same, largely the same: routine. It's the hunt that counts. . . ."

Michelangelo was amused. His experience with Clarissa had given him no desire for a simulation of love with some strange hired woman, only a desire for Clarissa.

"I'll wait for something better than routine."

"For love?"

"In a way."

"*Che rigorista!* I'm surprised to find an artist so conventional."

"I save all my unconventionality for my carving."

He could go without carving so long as he was drawing with a sculpture in mind. But the weeks passed and no word came from Cardinal Riario. He applied to the appointment secretaries several times, only to be put off. He understood that the cardinal was busy, for next to the Pope he was said to be the richest man in Europe, running a bank and commercial empire comparable to Lorenzo de' Medici's. Michelangelo never saw the man perform a religious service, but Leo volunteered that he said his offices in the palace chapel early in the morning.

Finally Leo arranged an appointment. Michelangelo carried a folio of sketches. Cardinal Riario appeared pleased to see him, though mildly surprised that he was still in Rome. He was in his office, surrounded by ledgers, the bookkeepers and scriveners with whom Michelangelo had been eating several times a week, but with whom he had not become friends. They stood at tall desks and did not look up from their work. When Michelangelo asked if the cardinal had decided what he might like to see sculptured from the seven-foot block, Riario replied:

"We will think about it. All in good time. In the meanwhile, Rome is a wonderful place for a young man. There are few pleasures of the world that we have not developed here. And now we must be excused."

Michelangelo walked slowly down the broad staircase to the unfinished courtyard, his chin burrowing into his chest.

Apparently he was in the same position as he had been with Piero de' Medici: once one was under the roof of these gentlemen they were content: nothing further needed to be done.

Waiting for him in his room was a gaunt figure in black mantle over a white habit, eyes sunken, looking hungry and exhausted.

"Lionardo! What are you doing in Rome? How did you leave our family?"

"I have seen no one," said Lionardo coldly. "I was sent on a mission by Savonarola to Arezzo and Perugia. Now I go back to Viterbo to discipline a monastery there."

"When did you eat last?"

"You may give me a florin to take me to Viterbo."

Michelangelo dug into his money pouch, handed Lionardo a gold coin. He took it without change of expression.

"Don't you say thank you?" Michelangelo asked, nettled.

"For money you give to God? You are helping in His work. In return you will have a chance for salvation."

He had barely recovered from his surprise at seeing Lionardo when a letter arrived from his father, brought in by the weekly mail courier from Florence. Lodovico was writing in a high state of perturbation, for he had fallen into debt over a supply of textiles and the mercer was threatening to take him into court. Michelangelo turned the sheet over several times, searching amidst the news of his stepmother, brothers, aunt and uncle for some clue as to how much the mercer was demanding, and how Lodovico had fallen into debt to him in the first place. There was no clue. Only the entreaty, "Send me some money."

He had been anxious to settle down to a steady project because of his need for a consuming work. Now the time had come to face his money situation. He still did not know how much Cardinal Riario was going to pay him for his sculpture.

"How could His Eminence decide," Leo replied tartly to his question, "when he doesn't know what you are going to carve or how good it will be?"

He had been provided with drawing material and models, and it had cost him nothing to live in the palace; yet the few florins he had saved out from the Popolanos' payment for the St. John were gone. He had been eating with Balducci several times a week at the Florentine restaurant, and had had to buy an occasional shirt or pair of stockings for his visits to the Florentine homes, as well as a warm robe for the coming winter. The thirty florins he had brought to Rome to buy back his Bambino were lightening in his pouch. It appeared that he would have no cash payment from the cardinal until his sculpture was completed; and that would be many months away.

He counted his florins. There were twenty-six. He took thirteen of them to Jacopo Galli's bank, asked Balducci to send a credit draft to Galli's correspondent in Florence. He then returned to his workshop and sat down in deadly earnest to conceive a theme that would compel Cardinal Riario to order. Not knowing whether the man would prefer a religious or antique subject, he planned to prepare one of each.

It took a month to evolve, in rough wax, a full-bodied Apollo, inspired by the magnificent torso in the Cardinal Rovere's garden; and a Pietà which was a projection of his earlier Madonna and Child, at the end of a journey rather than the beginning.

He wrote the cardinal a note, telling him that he had two models ready for His Eminence to choose from. There was no reply. He wrote again, this time asking for an appointment. No answer came. He walked to Leo's house, interrupted his friend at supper with a beautiful woman, and was unceremoniously thrown out.

Leo came by the next morning, urbane as usual, promised to speak to Riario.

The days passed, and the weeks, while Michelangelo sat by, staring at the marble block, aching to get his hands on it.

"What reason does he give?" he stormed at Leo. "I need only one minute to let him choose between the themes."

"Cardinals don't have to give reasons," replied Leo. "Patience."

"The days of my life are going by," groaned Michelangelo, "and all I get to carve out of time is a block of 'Patience.'"

4

He could get no appointment with the cardinal. Leo explained that Riario was worried about a fleet of ships long overdue from the Orient and "had no stomach for art." All he could do, according to Leo, was pray that the cardinal's ships would come up the Tiber. . . .

From the sheer hunger to carve he went to see Andrea Bregno. Bregno was from Como, in northern Italy, a vitalic man of seventy-five. He stood in the middle of a large stable belonging to an ancient palace which he had converted into the most active sculpture studio in Rome by ripping out two of every three stalls, erecting workbenches, and putting a northern Italian apprentice into each of the expanded stalls.

Before going to the studio Michelangelo had stopped to see Bregno's altars and sarcophagi in Santa Maria del Popolo and Santa Maria sopra Minerva. Bregno was prolific, had taste, proficiency in the classical style, and was good at carving decorative reliefs. But he had no more inventiveness than a cat; no idea of creating illusion in carving, perspective, the dimension of depth. He could do anything he thought of with hammer and chisel; but he never carved anything that he had not already seen carved. When he needed new themes he searched for old Roman tombs and copied the patterns.

Bregno welcomed him cordially when Michelangelo told him that he was from Settignano. The old man's speech and manner were staccato, the only evidence of age the maze of wrinkles on his parchmentlike face.

" I did the earliest Riario tomb with Mino da Fiesole. He was an exquisite carver, made the loveliest cherubs. Since you come from his neighbourhood, you are as good as Mino?"

" Perhaps."

" I can always use helpers. You see here, I have just finished this tabernacle for Santa Maria della Quercia in Viterbo. Now we are working on this Savelli monument for Santa Maria in Aracoeli. I did my apprenticeship for a silversmith, so we are never rushed and never late because I know within a matter of minutes how long each panel of fruit or spray of leaves will take to carve. I run my *bottega* like a silversmith's shop."

" But suppose you run into something new, Messer Bregno, an idea not carved before?"

Bregno stopped short, wagged his left hand back and forth in front of him.

" Sculpture is not an inventing art, it is reproductive. If I tried to make up designs, this studio would be in chaos. We carve here what others have carved before us."

" You carve it well," said Michelangelo, glancing about at the many projects in work.

311

"Superbly! I have never had a rejection in half a century. Very early in my career I learned to accept the convention, ' What is, must continue to be.' This wisdom of mine, Buonarroti, has paid me a fortune. If you want to be successful in Rome you must give the people exactly what they have grown up with."

"What would happen to a sculptor who said to himself, ' What is, must be changed '?"

"Changed? For the sake of change?"

"No, because he felt that each new piece he carved had to break through the existing conventions, achieve something fresh and different."

Bregno moved his jaws in a chewing movement, as though trying to pulverize this concept with his teeth. After a moment he spat into the sawdust underfoot, put a paternal hand on Michelongelo's shoulder.

"That is your youth speaking, my boy. A few months under my tutelage and you would lose such foolish notions. I might be willing to apprentice you for two years: five ducats the first, ten the second."

"Messer Bregno, I have already served a three-year apprenticeship under Bertoldo, in the Medici sculpture garden of Florence . . ."

"Bertoldo, who worked for Donatello?"

"The same."

"Too bad. Donatello has ruined sculpture for all you Florentines. However . . . We have quantities of angels to be carved on the tombs. . . ."

The wind-swept rains of November brought with them the departure of Piero de' Medici with troops to reconquer his empire; and Buonarroto's arrival. The rain had driven Michelangelo indoors to his bedroom, where he was drawing by lamplight on an ash-grey afternoon, when his brother appeared, drenched but with a happy smile lighting his small dark features. He embraced Michelangelo.

"I finished my apprenticeship and just couldn't bear Florence without you. I have come to look for work at the Wool Guild here."

Michelangelo was warmed by Buonarroto's affection.

"Come, get into dry clothes. When the rain stops I'll take you over to the Bear Hotel."

"I can't stay here?" asked Buonarroto wistfully.

Michelangelo glanced at the narrow monklike cot, the

single chair. "I'm only a . . . guest. The Bear Inn is comfortable. Tell me quickly about Father and the mercer's suit."

"Quiet for the moment, thanks to your thirteen florins. But Consiglio claims that Father owes him much more money. Father ordered the textiles, all right, but what he intended to do with them, not even Lucrezia can find out."

While Buonarroto changed into Michelangelo's dry shirt, drawers and warm wool stockings he related the happenings of the last five months: Uncle Francesco had been ill; Lucrezia too had been bedded, apparently with a miscarriage. With nothing coming in except the rent from the Settignano farm, Lodovico could not meet his bills. He worried about finances night and day. Giovansimone had refused Lodovico's entreaties to contribute to the family coffers.

Buonarroto rented a bed at the Bear Inn; the brothers ate their suppers together at the *trattoria*. By the end of a week it was plain that there was no work for Buonarroto in Rome; the Florentines had no Wool Guild here, and the Romans would not hire a Florentine.

"I think you must return home," said Michelangelo regretfully. "If his four oldest sons are away, contributing nothing, how will Father manage?"

Buonarroto departed amidst a downpour; Piero de' Medici arrived back in Rome equally rain-soaked. The last remnants of his army were scattered, he was without funds, deserted even by the Orsini. He carried on his person a list of the families in Florence he was going to crush once he had regained power. Alfonsina had settled with her children in one of her ancestral homes; from here Piero scandalized Rome by his heavy gambling losses and violent quarrels in public with his brother Giovanni. He spent his mornings at the San Severino palace, then passed the hours until dark with his favourite courtesan of the moment. At night he went into the streets of Rome to take part in every evil the city offered, crawling back at daybreak to Alfonsina's palace. Equally bad, from the viewpoint of the Florentine colony, was his arrogance and tyranny. He announced that he would govern Florence by himself, without the help of any Council, because "I prefer to manage badly on my own account than well by others' help."

Michelangelo was surprised to have delivered to him an invitation written by Piero to attend Christmas dinner at Cardinal Giovanni's. The party was a lavish one. Giovanni's house was beautiful with the objects he had brought from Florence on his first trip: Medici paintings, bronzes, tapestries and silverplate . . . all pledged, at twenty per cent interest, to cover Piero's debts; so that now, as the Florentine bankers commented, " every florin the Medici spend costs them eight lire." Michelangelo was shocked to see the ravages of Piero's life: his left eyelid was almost closed, white patches of scalp showed through where clumps of hair had fallen out. The once handsome face was bloated and red-veined.

" Buonarroti," cried Piero, " I felt in Bologna that you were disloyal to the Medici. But I have learned from my sister Contessina that you saved many valuable gems and works of art at the palace."

" I was fortunate to have the opportunity, Excellency."

Piero imperiously raised his right arm. His voice was loud enough for everyone in the drawing-room to hear.

" In return for your loyalty, Buonarroti, I commission you to do me a marble."

" That would make me happy, Excellency," replied Michelangelo quietly.

" A large statue," continued Piero loftily.

" Better make it small," contributed Giovanni, his plump face twisted in a deprecatory smile. " My brother seems to be moving around a lot, and he couldn't carry a life-size Hercules under his arm."

Piero waved his brother's words aside.

" I will send for you shortly. At that time, I shall give you my orders."

" I will await word."

On the way home from the tension-filled evening he caught his first glimpse of Torrigiani. He was with a group of young Romans, richly dressed in camlet with gold braid, his handsome face wreathed in laughter as he walked down the street, arms thrown affectionately about the shoulders of his companions, all of them full of wine and good cheer, roaring with laughter at Torrigiani's performance.

Michelangelo felt ill. He asked himself if what he was feeling was fear. Yet he knew it was something more, something in his experience akin to the sacking of the Medici palace, the deterioriation of Piero, an awareness of the senseless destructiveness that lay inherent in time and space, ready to lash out and destroy.

Cardinal Riario's ships at last reached the Ripetta docks.

Leo wangled an invitation for Michelangelo to a New Year's reception.

"I'll get a couple of collapsible black boxes lined with velvet," he explained, "the kind the jewellery people use to display tiaras and crowns. We will put in your two clay models. When the cardinal is surrounded by people he likes to impress, I'll give you the signal."

And so he did. Cardinal Riario was surrounded by the princes of the Church, the Pope, his sons Juan and Cæsar, Lucrezia and her husband, cardinals, bishops, the noble families of Rome, the women in gowns of silk and velvet with lavish jewellery.

Leo turned to Riario and said, "Buonarroti has been making sculpture models for you to choose between, Your Grace."

Michelangelo set the black boxes on a table, released the springs and let the sides fall away. He took one of his models in the palm of each hand, extending them for the cardinal to see. There was a murmur of pleasure from the men, while the women clapped their gloved hands discreetly.

"Excellent! Excellent!" cried the cardinal, looking at the models. "Keep working, my dear boy, and soon we'll have the one we want."

Michelangelo asked hoarsely, "Then Your Grace would not have me carve either of these in marble?"

Cardinal Riario turned to Leo. "Bring your friend to me as soon as he has new models. I'm sure they will be exquisite."

Outside the reception room, Michelangelo's anger stormed in torrential words.

"What kind of man is that? He's the one who asked me to carve something, who bought the marble for me. . . . I have a living to make. I could be here for months, for years, and not be allowed to touch that block."

Leo was despondent. "I thought he might like to flatter his guests by letting them choose. . . ."

"That's a fine way to decide what is to be carved out of a seven-foot column of Carrara marble!"

"But better than no decision at all! I'm sorry."

Michelangelo became contrite.

"Forgive my bitterness. I've spoiled your day. Go back to the reception."

Alone, he walked the streets, crowded now with families and children out to celebrate the holiday. From the Pincio hill fireworks of radiating rockets and revolving wheels burst into the air. Soggi was right! Sculpture was on the bottom of everybody's list. He would wander like a pedlar singing, "Who wants an Apollo? A Pietà?"

"Time," he muttered to himself. "Everybody wants me to give them time. But time is as empty as space unless I can fill it with figures."

He went into a black funk, unable to speak civilly to anyone. Balducci found a golden-haired Florentine girl to help bring him out of his melancholy. Michelangelo smiled for the first time since he had left Cardinal Riario's reception.

"Ah, Balducci, if life were as simple as you conceive it."

In the Trattoria Toscana they came upon Giuliano da Sangallo, the Florentine architect, friend of Lorenzo, and the first man to instruct Michelangelo in the art of architecture. The luxuriant long golden moustaches still rolled down the sides of his mouth, but he looked lonely. He had had to leave his wife and son behind in Florence while he lived in rented rooms in Rome, waiting for better commissions than his present job of building a wooden ceiling for Santa Maria Maggiore, overlaying it with the first gold brought from America by Columbus. He invited Michelangelo and Balducci to join him, asked Michelangelo how things were going for him here in Rome, listening intently while the younger man spilled out his frustration.

"You are in the service of the wrong cardinal," Sangallo concluded. "It was Cardinal Rovere who came to Florence in 1481 to commission Ghirlandaio, Botticelli and Rosselli to paint murals for his uncle Sixtus IV's chapel. It was he who persuaded Sixtus to start the first public library in Rome, and to assemble the Capitoline Museum of bronzes. When Cardinal Rovere returns to Rome, I shall introduce you."

Heartened, Michelangelo asked, "When does he return?"

"He is in Paris now. He is bitter about the Borgia, and has stayed away for several years. But there is every indication that he will be the next Pope. To-morrow I will come for you and show you the Rome I like best; not this stinking shambles of to-day, but the Rome of grandeur, when the world's greatest architects built here; the Rome I shall re-create stone upon stone once Cardinal Rovere becomes Pope. By to-morrow night you'll forget you wanted to sculpture, and give yourself over to architecture."

It was a needed diversion.

Sangallo wanted them to start first with the Pantheon because it was to the top of this magnificent Roman vaulted structure that Brunelleschi had climbed to learn an architectural secret forgotten for fifteen hundred years: that this was not one dome, but two, built one inside the other, the two domes interlaced structurally. With this revelation of Roman genius from 27 B.C., Brunelleschi had been able to return to Florence and apply the idea to closing the dome of the cathedral, which had stood open for more than a hundred years.

Sangallo handed Michelangelo a block of architectural paper, exclaimed, " Very well, now we re-create the Pantheon as the Romans of the time of Augustus saw it."

First they sketched inside, re-establishing the marble-faced interior, with the opening to the sky at the centre of the dome. They moved outside, drew the sixteen red and grey granite columns holding up the portico, the giant bronze doors, the dome covered with bronze tiles, the vast brick circular structure as the historians had described it.

Then with paper pads under their arms they made their way to the Via delle Botteghe Oscure, and climbed up the Capitoline hill. Here, overlooking the great Roman forum, they were at the heart of the early Roman capital. Now it was a rubble heap with rough earthen mounds on which goats and swine were grazing, yet here on the two summits had been the temple of Jupiter and the temple of Juno Moneta, from the sixth century B.C.

While Sangallo talked about the roof of the temple of Jupiter, bronze overlaid thickly with gold, as described by Dionysius of Halicarnassus, then about the three rows of columns on the front, the single row on each side, the inside consisting of three parallel shrines to Jupiter, Juno and Minerva, they brought the structure to life on their paper. Plutarch had described the fourth temple of Domitian: slender pillars of Pentelic marble, the buildings of tremendous rustic stone, on the portico enthroned statues before which the emperors and magistrates had made their sacrifices to the gods; all this they sketched.

They scrambled down the side of the hill to the Roman forum, spent the remainder of their hours here, drawing the buildings as they had been in the days of their greatness: the temples of Saturn and Vespasian, the senate house of Julius Cæsar, built of severely plain yellow brick; the great columned Castor's temple with its rich Corinthian capitals;

then on through the arch of Titus to the colosseum . . . Michelangelo's hands flying faster than they ever had in his life, trying to keep up with Sangallo, who was pouring out a stream of sketches and verbal descriptions.

Night fell. Michelangelo was exhausted, Sangallo triumphant.

" Now you have uncovered the glory that was Rome. Work in it every day. Go up to the Palatine and reconstruct the baths of Severus, Flavian's palace. Go to the Circus Maximus, the basilica of Constantine, the golden house of Nero at the bottom of the Esquiline. The Romans were the greatest architects the world has known."

Michelangelo glanced at Sangallo's mobile, attractive face, the excitement glowing in his eyes.

" Sangallo has old Roman architecture to make his days important, Balducci his girls. And I could use a sculpture commission," he murmured to himself.

5

Deep in his bosom was the growing doubt that he would ever get Cardinal Riario's approval to carve the seven-foot block. In desperation he sought out Pierio at the Orsini palace. He would suggest only a small, attractive piece to increase his chance of acceptance. Piero was in the midst of an uproarious quarrel with the servants over the way they had cooked his dinner. Alfonsina sat opposite him at the huge oak table. Her tired eyes gave him a brief flash of recognition.

" Excellency, I have the time now to make you a beautiful sculpture, if you would give me the order to commence."

Piero was half awake.

" Do you not recall? At your Christmas reception you ordered . . ."

" What about it?"

" I have a design for a Cupid, if you think that would please you."

" A Cupid? Well, why not?"

" I only needed your approval."

Piero had started shouting again. Michelangelo knew that he had been dismissed ; but he had also been told to go ahead. He walked along the riverbank to the stoneyards by the docks on the Tiber, saw a small block, paid five florins from his dwindling supply, and trudged behind the barrow as a boy wheeled it home for him.

It took him two days to find out that the marble was bad. He had acted stupidly, walked into a yard and bought the first block that looked good to him. He never would have done such a thing in Florence. But here in Rome he had behaved like a novice. His five florins were thrown away.

The next morning at dawn he was in the yard of the Guffatti, from whom Cardinal Riario had bought the seven-foot column. Now he tested the blocks, at length found a white marble that looked translucent in the early rays of the sun, that showed no gullies or fissures when under water. This time he had invested his five florins well; but his purse was reduced to a last three florins.

He sketched for a morning in the workingmen's quarter in Trastevere, children playing in the streets, lying on pallets in front of the clanging metal shops. It was only a matter of days before he had his hammer and chisel raised for the first blows. Balducci asked:

"Hadn't you better get a signed commitment from Piero? He's pouring every florin he can commandeer into mercenaries to mount another attack on Florence."

Piero was not having any contracts.

"My dear Buonarroti, I'll be leaving Rome before you can finish this Cupid. In all likelihood I'll never be back. . . ."

"Are you telling me, Excellency, that you have changed your mind?" His need had put a sharp edge to his tongue.

"A Medici never changes his mind," said Piero coldly. "It's just that I'm preoccupied. Postpone the matter for a year . . ."

Out in the freezing Piazza Sant' Apollinare, Michelangelo cried, "It serves me right!" He had said it out loud, his voice bitter, his face contorted with disgust. Only his eagerness to begin a piece for someone could have considered Piero's flimsy agreement a commitment.

He carved the Cupid anyway, for the joy of working in the white marble and breathing its dust.

Two frustrating months passed before he could get another appointment with Cardinal Riario.

"What have you got for me to-day?" he asked in good humour. "Something vigorously pagan, to match those fine antiques in the Cardinal Rovere's garden?"

Michelangelo lied quickly. "Yes, Your Grace."

He sat on the bed in his narrow room with the sweat pouring off him as though he had a fever, searching his mind for the most totally joyous, pleasure-giving Greek god he could find. In the Florentine quarter one night, Altoviti had asked:

"Have you ever thought of doing a Bacchus?"

"No, I rarely drink wine."

"Bacchus is also Dionysius, a nature god, symbolizing fruitfulness. He is the god who brought strange and wondrous gifts to man, enabling him to forget his misery, drudgery, the brute tragedy of life. If it is good for man to have pleasure, to laugh, sing, be happy, then we owe much to Bacchus."

Into his memory came a youth he had seen at the baths, with the proportioned body of an athlete: slim legs and waist, powerfully muscled chest and arms, pantherlike.

His work was his only reward: on Good Friday violence broke out in Rome, the cobblestones of the city running with blood. It started with a riot incited by the Pope's Spanish mercenaries, who were so bitterly hated by the Romans that they fought the armed soldiers with clubs and stones; moved on to Lucrezia Borgia's husband, as Sforza, fleeing Rome after announcing that the Borgias were about to murder him because they wanted a Spanish alliance for Lucrezia; moved on to another departure of Piero de' Medici at the head of an army of thirteen hundred mercenaries to storm Florence; moved on to revolt in the Florentine quarter when the Pope excommunicated Savonarola; and ended in the grisly murder of Juan Borgia. Fishermen angling in the Tiber found Juan Borgia's body and brought it ashore, still dressed in velvet coat and mantle, boots and spurs, slashed with nine knife wounds, the hands tied. The Romans did little to conceal their joy.

A reign of terror settled over Rome. The Vatican and the city were paralyzed. The Pope's police forced their way into every house Juan had ever visited, tortured servants in their search for clues, ransacked the home of the Florentines to prove a conspiracy, accused Lucrezia's rejected husband of the murder, then every noble Roman family that had ever fought the papacy . . . until word got around that the Pope, along with the rest of Rome, was convinced that Cæsar had killed his older brother to get him out of the way of his own career.

Cardinal Riario went into mourning with his Pope. The palace was closed to all but the most compelling business. Sculpture was far from compelling business. It was a luxury to be abandoned the moment anything went wrong.

"The cardinal won't talk sculpture for a long time," said Leo Baglioni. "I would advise you to look for another patron."

"In Rome? Won't Cardinal Riario's attitude be reflected all over the city?"

"Unfortunately, yes. But is Florence any better under Savonarola?"

"No. But it's home. Could you arrange one last appointment? So that I can get paid."

"Paid? You haven't made a sculpture."

"I've worked. I've made drawings, models. But you wouldn't let me begin carving. The cardinals' a rich man, and I'm down to my last denari."

He tossed on his bed through the night, was cranky when Balducci insisted that he come with him to hunt ducks in the marshes:

"The air will be good for you. Make a man of you. I spend every spare hour tramping and shooting to keep up my manhood."

Michelangelo knew what Balducci meant by his manhood. He said satirically, "Building up your coin of the realm to spend on the women."

"But of course!" cried Balducci. "Every man builds up his fortune to spend somewhere."

Troubles all come ripe at the same time, like tomatoes. Lionardo showed up again, his habit torn, blood on his face. From his incoherent story, Michelangelo gathered that the monks at Viterbo had turned on him, beaten him and ejected him from the monastery for his championing of the excommunicated Savonarola.

"I want to get home to San Marco," he said hoarsely, licking his cracked lips. "Give me money for the journey."

Michelangelo took his last coins out of the leather pouch.

"I, too, feel badly beaten. My hope is also to get home. But stay here with me for a few days, until you feel better."

"Thank you, no, Michelangelo. And thank you for the money."

It was the first softness Michelangelo had heard in his brother's voice in years.

The second blow was the news of his stepmother Lucrezia's

death, written in a few broken sentences by his father. "*Il Migliore*," he thought with affection, "The Best." She had bought only the best, and given of her best to all of them, the nine Buonarroti she had undertaken to feed. Had Lodovico loved her? It was hard to say. Had she loved them? This big family into which she had moved as a second wife? Yes, she had. It was not her fault if her only talent or excitement was for cooking. She had given unstintingly of what she had ; and her stepsons shed a tear for her passing.

A few days later a hotel groom brought a note from the Bear Inn announcing that Buonarroto was back. He hurried over, past the city market in Piazza Navona, the factories and shops between the ruined theatre of Pompey and the stadium of Dominian, the vegetable gardens leading to Piazza Sant'Apollinare.

"What of Father?" demanded Michelangelo. "How has he taken Lucrezia's death?"

"Badly. Locks himself in his bedroom."

"We must find him another wife."

"He says he would rather live alone than go through another death." He paused, then added, "The mercer is about to have him arrested for the bad debt. Consiglio can prove that Father took the goods, and since we have only a few florins left it could mean prison."

"Prison! *Dio mio!* He must sell the Settignano villa and farm."

"He can't. It's under long-term lease. Besides, he says he would rather go to the Stinche than deprive us of our last inheritance."

Michelangelo was furious.

"Our last inheritance? a house? Our last inheritance is the Buonarroti name. We've got to protect it."

"But what to do? I earn only a few scudi a month . . ."

"And I earn nothing. But I will! I'll make Cardinal Riario see the justice of my position."

The cardinal listened, playing quietly with the long gold chain around his neck.

"I would not expect you to have given this time for nothing."

"Thank you, Excellency ; I knew you would be generous."

"Indeed I shall. I relinquish all right and title to the marble block and the thirty-seven ducats it cost me. The marble is yours, in return for patient waiting."

He had only one recourse: the Florentine bankers, Rucellai

and Cavalcanti. He would go into debt. He sat down and wrote his father a letter telling him, " I shall send you whatever you ask me, even if I should have to sell myself as a slave," then went to Paolo Rucellai to explain his plight.

" A loan from the bank? No; it is too expensive for you at twenty per cent interest. From me, yes, as a personal loan without interest. Will twenty-five florins help?"

" I will pay it back; you will see."

" You are to forget about it until you have money in your belt."

He ran through the labyrinth of unpaved streets crowded with heavy traffic and clogged with sand from the river, gave Buonarroto the credit slip signed by Rucellai, added to it a note to Consiglio stating that he would take responsibility for the balance of the debt, guaranteeing to pay it within the year.

" That's what Father wanted, of course," Buonarroto said thoughtfully, fingering the two notes. " He's not going to earn anything more; nor is Uncle Francesco. You and me, we are the Buonarroti now. We can expect no help from Lionardo or Giovansimone. And the little one, Sigismondo . . . the Wine Guild has released him. Once Father sees these papers you will have the support of the Buonarroti family on your hands."

Good fortune comes in bunches, as do peaches when the trees turn ripe. Michelangelo finished polishing his Cupid, a lovely child just awakened from sleep and holding up its arms to be taken by his mother. Balducci was enchanted with its lighthearted warmth, the beautiful satiny texture. He asked if they could carry it to the Galli house to show his master, Jacopo Galli.

There was no Bugiardini to wheel the marble through the streets. Balducci rented a mule with a large saddlebag. Michelangelo wrapped his Cupid in a blanket, led the animal past San Lorenzo in Damaso, through the lane of Lentari in Parione. The Casa Galli had been built by one of Jacopo Galli's ancestors. Galli was grateful to this predecessor because he had begun, at the same time, a collection of ancient sculptures that was second only to Cardinal Rovere's.

Balducci tied the mule while Michelangelo unwrapped the Cupid. After descending a broad flight of stone stairs, Michelangelo found himself in an atrium, closed on three sides by the house, and on the fourth by the flight of steps, giving the area the illusion of being a sunken garden; or,

Michelangelo thought as he glanced hastily about him, a sunken wilderness of statues, marble friezes, crouching animals.

Jacopo Galli, who had been educated at the university in Rome, and had been reading every day of his life since, put down a copy of Aristophanes' *Frogs,* began pulling himself out of a low-lying chaise. He seemed never to stop getting up as he unfolded: six feet, six and a half, surely not seven? The tallest man Michelangelo had ever seen, hunched over at the shoulders from a lifetime of stooping to the short-statured Romans. Michelangelo was as a child before him.

" Ah you come with a marble in your arms. That is the sight I like best in my garden."

Michelangelo set the Cupid down on the table next to Galli's book, turned to look up into the man's blue eyes.

" I'm afraid I've brought my Cupid into a rough arena."

" I think not," murmured Galli in a voice that he made an effort to keep reasonable-sized. " Balducci, take your friend Buonarroti into the house for a slice of cold water-melon."

When they returned to the garden a few minutes later they found that Galli had removed a torso from a pedestal on the low wall next to the steps and replaced it with the Cupid. He had settled back into the chaise. Standing behind his host, Michelongelo had an opportunity to study the three Greek torso, Roman sarcophagus, temple frieze, wall slab with huge seated griffin, Egyptian lion with near-human head.

Galli's eyes were twinkling. " I feel as though your Cupid has been sitting there since the day I was born, a lineal descendant of any of these carvings. Would you sell it to me? What price shall we set?"

Humbly, Michelangelo murmured, " That is up to you."

" First, tell me your circumstances."

Michelangelo related the story of his year with Riario.

" So you end up without a scudo of pay, and a seven-foot marble block? Shall we say the Cupid is worth fifty ducats? Because I know you need money I will allow my cupidity to knock the price down to twenty-five ducats. Then, because I detest shrewdness in dealing with the arts, I will take the twenty-five ducats I was going to underpay you, and add them to my original estimate. Do you approve my formula?"

Michelangelo's amber eyes shone.

"Signor Galli, for a year I have been thinking bad things about the Romans. In your name, I apologize to the whole city."

Galli bowed while sitting down. "Now tell me about this seven-foot marble block. What do you think might be carved from that?"

Michelangelo told him about his drawings for an Apollo, for a Pietà, for a Bacchus. Galli was intrigued.

"I've never heard of a Bacchus unearthed hereabouts, though there are one or two that were brought from Greece, figures of old men with beards, rather dull."

"No, no, my Bacchus would be young, as befits a god of joy and fertility."

"Bring me the drawings to-morrow at nine."

Galli brought a purse from the house and handed Michelangelo seventy-five ducats. Michelangelo led the mule through the darkening streets to the stable where he paid for his hire, then walked to Rucellai's to return the twenty-five florins he had borrowed.

The next evening he presented himself in the Galli garden at the appointed time. No one was present. It seemed as though hours passed. He saw himself abandoning his marble, or reselling it to Guffatti for a fraction of its cost and returning to Florence with the next pack train. Then Galli came into the garden, welcomed him, poured them an apéritif, and settled down to study the drawings. Soon Signora Galli, a tall, lithe woman, no longer young but preserving a patrician beauty, joined them for supper over candlelight. A cool breeze stirred the summer heat. When supper was over, Galli asked:

"Would you be willing to move your block here, and carve this Bacchus for me? You could have a room to live in. I would pay you three hundred ducats for the completed statue."

Michelangelo bowed his head so that the candle gleam would not betray him. He had been saved from an ignominious return to Florence, from defeat.

Yet the next morning when he walked alongside the Guffatti wagon carrying his marble column from the Riario palace to Galli's, with his small bag of clothes under his arm, he felt like a mendicant. Was he to spend his years moving from one charitable bedroom to another? He knew that many artists travelled from court to court, from patron to patron, for the most part well housed, fed and entertained; but he also knew he would not be content to do so. He promised himself that one day soon he must become his own man, inside his own walls.

6

He was shown into a bedroom on the wing of the U opposite from the one occupied by the Galli, a pleasant room warm with sunlight. A door on the far side admitted to a fig orchard. At the edge of the orchard was a storage shed with a hard earthen floor. Michelangelo took off the plank roof, letting the fig trees close it over in shade. The building backed on to a rear lane, through which friends could come and visit him and materials be delivered. He could not see the house through the trees, and he was far enough away so that they could not hear his hammering. On the outside he rigged up a barrel so that he could bring water from the well and shower at night before putting on clean clothes and joining the Galli for supper in the garden. Jacopo Galli did not leave his bank at midday; no dinner was served except on Sundays and religious holidays. A servant brought Michelangelo a light meal on a tray, which he ate off his draughting board. He was grateful not to have to change clothes at midday, or be sociable.

He had a letter from his father, acknowledging the twenty-five florins. The mercer had accepted Michelangelo's assurance of payment, but he wanted half of the fifty florins still owed him. Could he possibly send another twenty-five florins by the Saturday post?

Michelangelo sighed, donned a lightweight blouse, took twenty-five ducats to Jacopo Galli's bank in the Piazza San Celso next to the bank of the Chigi family. Balducci was not in, so he went to Jacopo Galli's desk. Galli looked up, gave no sign of recognition. Nor did Michelangelo recognize Jacopo Galli; the face was stern, cold, expressionless. He asked in an impersonal tone what Michelangelo desired.

" A credit . . . for twenty-five florins. To send to Florence."

He put his coins on the desk. Galli spoke to a clerk nearby. The transaction was swiftly made. Galli returned his masked eyes and hard-set mouth to his papers.

326

Michelangelo was staggered. "What have I done to offend?" he demanded of himself.

It was dark before he could bring himself to return to the house. From his room he saw lights in the garden. He opened the door gingerly.

"Ah, there you are!" cried Galli. "Come have a glass of this fine Madeira."

Jacopo was sprawled relaxedly in his chaise. He asked whether Michelangelo had set up his shop, what more he would need. His change of manner was simply explained. Jacopo Galli apparently could not, or would not, establish a bridge between the halves of his life. At his bank he held himself rigid, brusque. His business associates admired the way in which he dispatched their affairs and brought them the most profitable result, but did not like him as a person. They said he was not human. When he reached home Galli shed this skin as though he were a lizard, was gay, indulgent, humorous. No word of business ever passed his lips. Here in the garden he talked art, literature, history, philosophy. The friends who dropped in each evening loved him, considered him overgenerous with his family and household.

For the first time since he reached Rome, Michelangelo began to meet interesting Romans: Peter Savinus, professor of Eloquence at the university, who cared little for Galli's sculptures but who had what Galli described as "an incredible number of early Christian inscriptions"; the collector Giovanni Capocci, one of the first Romans to attempt disciplined excavating at the catacombs; Pomponius Laetus, one of Galli's old professors, an illegitimate son of the powerful Sanseverino family, who could have dawdled in idle elegance but lived only for learning, ill clad in buckskins and housed in a shack.

"I used to go to his lecture hall at midnight to get a seat," Galli told Michelangelo. "Then we'd wait for dawn, until we saw him coming down the hill, lantern in one hand, old manuscript in the other. He was tortured by the Inquisition because our Academy, like your Plato Academy in Florence, was suspected of heresy, paganism, republicanism." Galli chuckled. "All perfectly true charges. Pomponius is so steeped in paganism that the sight of an antique monument can move him to tears."

Michelangelo suspected that Galli too was "steeped in paganism," for he never saw a man of the Church at Galli's, with the exception of the blind brothers, Aurelius and

327

Raffaelle Lippus, Augustinians from Santo Spirito in Florence, who improvised Latin songs and poetic hymns on their lyres; and the French Jean Villiers de la Groslaye, Cardinal of San Dionigi, a wisp of a man in an elegantly trimmed white beard and scarlet cassock who had begun his religious life as a Benedictine monk and, beloved by Charles VIII for his devoutness and learning, had been made a cardinal through the king's intervention. He had nothing to do with the corruption of the Borgias, living the same devout life in Rome that he had in the Benedictine monasteries, continuing his studies of the Church Fathers, on whom he was an authority.

Not all the scholars were aged. He made friends with Jacopo Sadoleto from Ferrara, twenty years old, a fine poet and Latinist; Serafino, an idolized poet in the court of Lucrezia Borgia, who never mentioned the Borgias or the Vatican when he visited at Galli's, but read his historical poems while he accompanied himself on the lute; Sannazaro, forty, but seeming thirty, who mingled pagan and Christian images in his verse.

The Galli made the minimum numbers of gestures of conformity; they went to mass most Sundays and on the important holy days. Jacopo Galli confided that his anticlericalism was the only gesture he could make against the corruption of the Borgias and their followers.

"From my reading, Michelangelo, I have been able to follow the rise, fulfilment, decay and disappearance of many religions. That is what is happening to our religion to-day. Christianity has had fifteen hundred years to prove itself, and has ended in . . . what? Borgia murders, greed, incest, perversion of every tenet of our faith. Rome is more evil to-day than Sodom and Gomorrah when they were destroyed by fire."

"Even as Savonarola has said?"

"As Savonarola has said. A hundred years of Borgias and there will be nothing left here but a historic pile of stones."

"The Borgias can't rule for a hundred years, can they?"

Galli's big, open face was creased by furrows.

"Cæsar Borgia has just crowned Federigo as King of Naples, returned to Rome in triumph, and been consigned his brother Juan's estate by the Pope. An archbishop has been caught forging dispensations. A bishop was caught with ten thousand ducats from the sale of offices in the Curia. And so it goes."

Now all the drawings he had made for the Bacchus, the Greek god of joy, seemed superficial and cynical. He had tried to project himself backward into an Elysian age; but he was playing with a myth as a child plays with toys. His present reality was Rome: the Pope, Vatican, cardinals, bishops, the city plunged deep into corruption and decadence because the hierarchy battened off it. He felt a total revulsion for this Rome. But could he sculpture from hate? Could he use his pure white marble, which he loved, to depict the evil and smell of death that were destroying what had once been the capital of the world? Was there not the danger that his marble too would become hateful? He could not bring himself to abandon the Greek ideal of beauty-out-of-marble.

He slept fitfully. Often he went to Galli's library, lit a lamp and took up writing materials, as he had at Aldovrandi's after he had met Clarissa. It had been love that churned him then, made him pour out lines to "cool himself off." Now it was hate, as searing an emotion as love, that caused him to pour out hundreds of lines until, at dawn, he had had his say.

> *Here helms and swords are made of chalices:*
> *The blood of Christ is sold so much the quart:*
> *His cross and thorns are spears and shields, and short*
> *Must be the time ere even his patience cease.*

> *Nay, let him come no more to raise the fees*
> *Of this foul sacrilege beyond report!*
> *For Rome still flays and sells him at the court*
> *Where paths are closed to virtue's fair increase. . . .*

> *God welcomes poverty perchance with pleasure:*
> *But of that better life what hope have we,*
> *When the blessed banner leads to nought but ill?*

He went searching through the collections in Rome for ancient carvings. The only young Bacchus he could find was about fifteen years old, dead sober. From the way he held a bunch of grapes, negligently, he seemed bored with the fact that he had conceived this strangest of fruits.

His sculpture would have joy in it, try to capture the sense of fertility of Dionysius, the nature god, the power of the intoxicating drink that enabled a man to laugh and sing and forget for a while the sorrow of his earthly miseries. And then, perhaps, at the same time he could portray the decay that came with too much forgetfulness, that he saw all around him, when man surrendered his moral and spiritual values for the pleasures of the flesh. The Bacchus would be the central figure of his theme, a human being rather than a demigod; then there would be a child of about seven, sweet-faced, lovable, nibbling from a bunch of grapes. His composition would have death in it too: the tiger, who liked wine and was loved by Bacchus, with the deadest, dead skin and head conceivable.

He went to the baths to look for models, thinking he might put together a composite Bacchus as he had his Hercules from hundreds of Tuscans: a throat here, a forearm there, a belly in the next place. But when after a few weeks he welded his features together with hard silver pen, his composite portrait was not convincing. He took himself to Leo Baglioni.

"I need a model. Young. Under thirty. Of a high family."

"And a beautiful body?"

"That once was, but is no longer. A figure that has been corrupted."

"By what?"

"Wine. Sensuousness. Self-indulgence."

Leo thought for a moment, flicking over in his mind the figures and features of the Roman youths he knew.

"I may know your man. The Count Ghinazzo. But he's wealthy, of a noble family. What can we offer him by way of inducement?"

"Flattery. That he is to be immortalized as the great Greek god Bacchus. Or Dionysius, if he prefers."

"That might work. He's idle, and can give you his days . . . or what's left of them after he awakens from his bacchanals of the night before."

The count was delighted with his new role. When he had walked through the orchard with Michelangelo, stripped off his clothes and taken the pose Michelangelo requested, he said:

"You know, it's a coincidence my being selected for this. I've always thought of myself as a kind of god."

Michelangelo went to his drawing-board, sucked in his breath with pleasure. If he had searched all of Italy he could not have found a more fitting subject than Leo had selected for him: the head a bit too small for the body, the belly soft and fleshy, the buttocks too large for the torso, the upper arm a touch flaccid, the legs as straight and firmly moulded as a Greek wrestler's. It was a figure desexed, the eyes unfocused from too much wine at dinner, the mouth dazedly half open; yet the arm that held the wine cup aloft flexed with muscular power, and over all a flawless satin-smooth skin glistened in the strong frontal sunlight that made him appear illumined from within.

"You're perfect!" Michelangelo cried impulsively. "Bacchus to the very life."

"Delighted you think so," said Count Ghinazzo without turning his head. "When Leo first proposed serving as a model I told him not to be a bore. But this may prove to be interesting."

"What time can I expect you to-morrow? And don't hesitate to bring your wine with you."

"That makes everything splendid. I can remain the entire afternoon. Without wine, the day is so dull."

"You will never appear dull to me, *messere*. I will see you in a new light every minute."

He cast the man in a hundred poses, his right leg bent sharply at the knee, toes barely touching the rough wooden base; the body slumped over on one leg, striving to stand up, the torso leaning backward; the small head thrust forward, turned one way and another, moving slightly, satiated with pleasure. And in the late afternoons, when Ghinazzo had drunk much wine, Michelangelo wound bunches of grapes through his hair, sketching him as though the grapes were growing there . . . which amused the Roman inordinately. Until one afternoon he drank too much of the wine, began to sway dizzily, fell off the wood block and hit his chin on the hard earth, knocking himself out. Michelangelo revived him by throwing a bucket of water over him. Count Ghinazzo shivered into his clothes, disappeared through the orchard and from Michelangelo's life.

Jacopo Galli found him a lively boy of seven, with curling golden hair and large tender eyes, a delightful lad with whom Michelangelo made friends as he sketched. His only problem was to get the boy to maintain the difficult pose of holding his left arm in a *contrapposto* position against his chest, so that he could crush the bunch of grapes in his mouth. Next he went into the countryside, spending a whole day drawing the legs, hoofs and curling fur of the goats cropping the hillsides.

That was how his pen finally designed his sculpture: in the centre the weak, confused, arrogant, soon to be destroyed young man holding cup aloft, behind him the idyllic child, clear-eyed, munching his grapes, symbol of joy; between them the tiger skin. The Bacchus, hollow within himself, flabby, reeling, already old; the Satyr, eternally young and gay, symbol of man's childhood and naughty innocence.

Sunday morning he invited Galli to the workshop to show him his drawing: the bowl held high in Bacchus' hand, the intertwined grapes and leaves that made up his hair, the long, curving bunch of grapes that formed a structural bond between the Bacchus and the Satyr, the tree trunk on which the Bacchus leaned and the Satyr would be sitting, and lastly the tiger skin held in the Bacchus' falling hand, winding down through the Satyr's arm, its head hanging between the Satyr's open-stanced goat's hoofs, the hollow tiger head a picturization of what would happen to the Bacchus' head, ere long.

Galli asked countless questions. Michelangelo explained that he would do some wax or clay modelling, some carving on scrap marble to test the component parts, " the way the Satyr's head rests against the Bacchus' arm, for instance."

" And the way the boy's thigh melts into the furry leg of the Satyr."

" Exactly."

Galli was fascinated. "I don't know how to thank you."

Michelangelo laughed a little embarrassedly.

" There is one way. Could you send some florins to Florence?"

Galli hunched his huge shoulders over Michelangelo protectively.

" Would you like our correspondent in Florence to deliver a few florins each month to your father, I mean regularly? Then you won't be distressed each time a packet of mail arrives. It will cost you no more that way; and we'll keep a record for you against the commmission price."

". . . it isn't his fault, really," Michelangelo proffered, his pride hurt. " My uncle is ill, there are some debts . . ."

7

He lowered his column to a horizontal position on the ground, secured it on tightly wedged beams, then, using a point, bit into the corner where the wine cup would emerge. He concentrated on the frontal view, then started to join up the two sides to establish the visual flow. After heading for the high points of the fingers of the hand holding the cup, and the extended right kneecap, he struck in between to find the stomach, to establish the relationship between the highest projections and the deepest penetration. The intermediary forms would follow in natural sequence, as the forms of the side and back would take their cue from the front. He massed about the upper torso to indicate the reeling position of the upright figure, then turned the block over clockwise so that he could work on the width-plane, roughing out the cup-arm which was in the key position.

He summoned one of the Guffatti to help him set the column vertical again. Now the marble presented its personality: its size, proportion, weight. He sat in front of the block, studied it concentratedly, allowed it to speak, to establish its own demands. Now he felt fear, as though he were meeting an unknown person. To sculpture is to remove marble; it is also to probe, dig, sweat, think, feel and live with it until it is completed. Half the original weight of this block would remain in the finished statue; the rest would lie out in the orchard in chips and dust. His one regret was that he would sometimes have to eat and sleep, painful breaks when his work must stop.

The weeks and months of uninterrupted carving flowed by in a continuous stream. The winter was mild, he did not have to put back the roof of the shed; when the weather was sharp he wore his wool hat with its ear-muffs, and a warm tunic. Thoughts, feelings, perceptions often came in a flash as the Bacchus and Satyr began to emerge, but to express these ideas in marble took days and weeks. Inside himself he had to grow as his sculpture grew and matured. The unfinished block haunted him at every hour of the night and day. It would be dangerous to release the bowl and the flexed knee in space; he would have to keep a webbing of marble between the oustretched bowl and forearm, between the knee and elbow, between the base and knee to give them support while he dug deeper. Now he was chiselling the side plane, the face and head, part of the neck and curls of grapes, now the depth of the left shoulder, thigh and calf. At the rear he evolved the Satyr, the stump he was sitting on, the grapes he was eating, the tiger cloth tying the two figures together. It was the most complicated piece he had yet attempted. He turned the Satyr's head, arms and grapes adroitly to the Bacchus' arm, yet ran out of marble.

His real battle began the moment a muscle became defined or a structural element began to emerge. Standing out from the rough blocking, he felt a thumping in his heart to shed away quickly the rest of the marble skin to reveal the human form below. The marble was tenacious; he was equally tenacious to achieve the delicate play of muscle under the fleshy stomach, the soft, claylike trunk of the tree, the spiral torsion of the Satyr, the grapes on the Bacchus' head which seemed to be part of the vine of his hair. Each completed detail brought peacefulness to all of the faculties he had used in its creation; not only to his eyes and mind and bosom, but to his shoulders, hips and groin.

When unable to formulate a detail he dropped his tools, walked outside and gazed up through the trees to the skies. When he returned he approached the marble from a distance, saw its contours and masses, felt its continuity. The detail became part of the whole. He grabbed his tools again and worked furiously: one two three four five six seven strokes; then one two three four of rest, every few cycles stepping back to see what he had accomplished. His feelings were always ahead of his physical capacity to carve. If only he could work the four sides of the block at once!

When he was releasing a rounded kneecap, the hairy leg and hoof of the Satyr, the tiger skin, he strove to pull out as much wholeness as possible in one " Go." Each day had to be fruitful, he had to find a handful of form for each session of carving before he could put aside his hammer and chisel. Upon awakening he was heavily charged with nervous energy and his hours were one long drive. He could not leave one finger of a hand in a more advanced state than the others for he worked in units. Each day's work was a full unit. It was these small bundles of intense entities throughout his sculpture that characterized his potency as a sculptor.

Just before retiring he looked over his work, spotted what
334

had to be done the next day. During the evening, when he wrote to his family, he proudly signed the letters:

Michelangelo, Sculptor in Rome.

Because he would take no time off for friends or rest or social life, Balducci accused him of trying to escape the world by fleeing into marble. He admitted to his friend that he was half right: the sculptor carries into the marble the vision of a more luminous world than the one that surrounds him. But the artist was not in flight; he was in pursuit. He was trying with all his might to overtake a vision. Did God really rest on the seventh day? In the cool of that long afternoon, when He was refreshed, might He not have asked Himself, "Whom have I on earth to speak for Me? I had best create another species, one apart. I will call him 'artist.' His will be the task to bring meaning and beauty to the world."

Nevertheless Balducci arrived faithfully every Sunday afternoon in the hope of seducing him out of the shed. He found for Michelangelo a girl so like Clarissa that Michelangelo was tempted. But the marble was exhausting. Between the two there could be no choice.

"When I have completed the Bacchus, I'll go out with you," he promised Balducci.

Balducci shook his head in despair.

"Just think of putting off the good things of life for so long. It's throwing time into the Tiber!"

Keyed up with his own fulfilment, Michelangelo threw back his head and laughed heartily with his friend.

His deepest emotional reaction came when breaking through a supporting web, noting the translucent quality of the marble where the breakthrough was to take place, aware that space would shortly be pouring through, the space that gave the limbs their freedom of movement, their independence, that permitted his forms to breathe air the moment his point felt no resistance.

His most delicate task was carving away the marble between the arm that held the lovely, ornamented wine cup and the side of the tilted head. He worked with infinite gentleness until he reached the sloping shoulder line. He did not yet feel secure enough to hammer away the web supporting the upheld arm and outstretched knee.

Balducci ragged him mercilessly.

"This is sheer prejudice. How come you didn't keep a column to hold up the poor fellow's privates? Suppose they

335

fell off? That would be worse than his dropping that bowl you're so frightened of losing."

Michelangelo reached for a handful of marble dust and threw it at him.

"Have you never had a thought that didn't originate in the erogenous zone?"

"Does anyone?"

He finally acceded to Balducci's importuning that he watch some of the Roman spectacles, and went with him to Mount Testaccio to see Rome celebrate carnival before Lent. They stood on a hillside while four young pigs, combed and tied with ribbons by special barbers, were bound into beflagged carts. At a signal from the trumpeters the carts were rolled down the hill towards the Aventine, with the populace rushing after them, armed with knives, yelling, *" Al porco! Al porco!"* At the bottom of the hill the carts smashed, the people fell upon the animals, fighting each other to see who could slice off the best pieces of meat.

When Michelangelo returned to the house he found the French Cardinal Groslaye of San Dionigi there. Galli broke a self-imposed rule by asking if they might take the cardinal out to the workshop to see the Bacchus. Michelangelo could not refuse.

In the lamplighted shed Michelangelo explained that he was working all around the figure simultaneously, to keep the forms advancing in the same stage of development. He showed how, in order to open the space between the two legs, and between the left arm and torso, he worked the front and then the back of the clock, continuously making the marble web thinner and thinner. As the Cardinal of San Dionigi watched, he picked up a point and demonstrated the extremely light tapping required for the breakthrough, then used an *ugnetto* to remove the rest of the web, freeing the limbs.

"But how do you achieve in a half-finished figure this sense of throbbing vitality? I can feel the blood and muscle under your marble skin. It is good to see new marble masters arising."

A few days later a servant brought a note to the workshed from Galli. *" Won't you join Groslaye and myself for supper to-night?"*

Michelangelo quit work at sundown, went to the baths close by, steamed the marble dust out of his pores, put on a fresh shirt and hose, brushed his hair forward over his brow.

Signora Galli served a light supper, for the cardinal still followed the disciplines of his early years, ate no meat, and touched all foods sparingly. His fading eyes gleamed in the candlelight as he turned to Michelangelo.

"You know, my son, I am growing old. I must leave something behind me, something of singular beauty to add to the beauties of Rome. A tribute from France, from Charles VIII and my humble self. I have secured permission from the Pope to dedicate a sculpture in the Chapel of the Kings of France in St. Peter's. There is a niche that will take a life-size sculpture."

Michelangelo had not touched any of Galli's excellent Trebbiano wine, but he felt as though he had drunk more than Count Ghinazzo on a warm afternoon. A sculpture for St. Peter's, the oldest and most sacred basilica in Christendom, built over the tomb of St. Peter! Could it be possible that the French cardinal would choose him? But from what? The little Cupid? The still nascent Bacchus in his workshed?

By the time he brought his senses back to the table, the conversation had changed. The cardinal was telling Jacopo Galli of the writings of two unorthodox post-Nicene Fathers. Then the cardinal's carriage came for him. He bade Michelangelo a pleasant good night.

That Sunday Michelangelo went to mass in St. Peter's to see the Chapel of the Kings of France and the niche about which the Cardinal of San Dionigi had talked. He climbed the thirty-five stairs of marble and porphyry leading up to the basilica, crossed the atrium, passed the centre fountain surrounded by porphyry columns and stood at the base of the Carlovingian bell tower, aghast at the dilapidated condition of St. Peter's, which was leaning sharply to the left. Inside he found the Chapel of the Kings of France to be of modest size, dark, the main light coming from small windows up near the roof, the only ornamentation some sarcophagi borrowed from pagan and early Christian tombs, and a wooden crucifix in a niche on the side. He measured with his eye the vacant niche on the opposite wall, disappointed to find it so deep that a statue would be seen only from the front.

It was seven days before Galli brought up the subject again.

"You know, Michelangelo, this commission of the Cardinal of San Dionigi's could be the most important since Pollaiuolo was assigned to do a tomb for Sixtus IV."

Michelangelo's heart began to pound. "What are my chances?"

Galli counted on his long supple fingers as on an abacus that reckoned artistic probability.

"First, I must convince the cardinal that you are the best sculptor in Rome. Second, you must conceive a theme that will inspire him. Third, we must secure a signed contract."

"It would have to be a spiritual theme?"

"Not because Groslaye is a member of the Church, but because he is a deeply spiritual man. He has lived in Rome for three years in such a state of grace that he literally has not seen and does not know that Rome is rotten at its core."

"Is it innocence? Or blindness?"

"Could we say that it is faith? If a man is as pure in heart as the Cardinal of San Dionigi, he walks with God's hand on his shoulder; he sees beyond present evil to the Church Eternal."

"Can I create a marble that would have the hand of God on it?"

Galli shook his leonine head.

"That is a problem you must wrestle with yourself."

To carve decay all day, and at the same time conceive a devout theme, seemed an impossible undertaking. Yet he knew very soon that his theme would be a Pietà: Pity, Sorrow. He had wanted to do a Pietà ever since he had completed his Madonna and Child: for just as the Madonna and Child was the beginning, the Pietà was the end, the preordained conclusion of everything that Mary had decided in that fateful hour God had allotted her. Now, thirty-three years later, her son was again on her lap, having completed his journey.

Galli was intrigued with his thinking, took him to the Cardinal of San Dionigi's palace, where they waited for the cardinal to complete the five daily hours of prayer and offices required of every Benedictine. The three men sat in the open loggia, facing the Via Recta, with a painted Annunciation behind them. The cardinal was ashen after his long devotions. Michelangelo's practised eye could perceive almost no body lines beneath his robe. But when the cardinal heard about the Pietà his eyes sparkled.

"What about the marble, Michelangelo? Could you find such a perfect piece as you speak of, here in Rome?"

"I think not, Your Grace. A column, yes; but an oblong

block that is wider than it is tall, and cut deep, that I have not seen."

"Then we must turn to Carrara. I shall write to the brothers in Lucca, asking for aid. If they cannot find what we need you must go yourself to the quarries and find our marble."

Michelangelo bounded out of his chair.

"Did you know, Father, that the higher one quarries the purer white the marble becomes? No earth stains, no pressure to make holes or hollows. If we could quarry at the peak of Monte Sagro, there we would find the supreme block."

On the way home Galli said, "You must go to Carrara at once. I will advance the expenses for your trip."

"I can't."

"Why not?"

"I must finish the Bacchus," he replied.

"The Bacchus can wait. The cardinal can't. One day soon God will rest His hand just a trifle more heavily on his shoulder, and Groslaye will go to heaven. From heaven he cannot comission a Pietà."

"That is true. But I cannot stop work now," Michelangelo insisted stubbornly.

"I release you from our agreement. When you have finished the Pietà you will come back to the Bacchus."

"For me there is no coming back. The sculpture is growing complete in my mind. I must finish it now to get it perfect."

"I'm always amazed to find a romantic in affairs of practical business." Galli sighed. "I shan't burden the cardinal with the details of your orthodoxy."

"Until the Bacchus is completed the Pietà cannot begin. I behave virtuously because I must."

8

He removed the short column between the base and the heel of the Bacchus, and the right foot which was half suspended in the air, poised on its toes. Then he raised his drill to release the web between the elbow and the cup, drilling a series of holes close to the arm, delicately filing away the remaining marble. Finally he cut away the right-hand corner under the cup, to free the hand and cup now extending high into space. The Satyr in the lower left-hand corner and the cup at the upper right completed each other. His whole figure in the round was balanced superbly. He walked about it, satisfaction in his face and shoulders as his eye reviewed the line from the thrust of the right knee to the tip of the opposite shoulder; the tension from the edge of the bowl through the crotch to the corner of the Satyr's hoof.

The emphasis of his figure was in its weight masses. In the head projecting forward, the hard torso projecting outward, then flowing into the stomach, which pulled the whole body downward towards the loins. In the rear the too heavy buttocks served as a steadying weight, the balance held by the beautiful legs, though not too securely because the body was reeling; the left foot planted solidly, the right on tiptoe increased the sense of vertigo.

" You're like an engineer," said Galli when he saw it, his expression rapt as he traced Michelangelo's design.

" That's what I told Bertoldo a sculptor had to be."

" In the days of the emperors you would have been designing colosseums, baths and reservoirs. Instead, you've created a soul."

Michelangelo's eyes glowed yellow at the compliment.

" No soul, no sculpture."

" Many of my ancient pieces were found broken in several places, yet when we put them together their spirit persisted."

" That was the sculptor still alive in the marble."

The following Sunday he went to dine with the Rucellai, eager to hear news of Florence. Savonarola was at the heart of most of the happenings. The Florentine colony had been delighted with him for defying the Pope, for advising the Borgia that unjust excommunications were invalid, and for celebrating three forbidden masses in San Marco at Christmas. Savonarola had then written to kings, statesmen and churchmen all over Europe urging that a council be called to purge the Borgia, and to institute sweeping reforms that would rid the Church of simony, the purchase not only of cardinalates but of the papacy itself. On February 11, 1498, he had again preached in the Duomo against the Pope, and two weeks later had walked outside the cathedral with the host in his hand, before thousands of Florentines packed into the piazza, and beseeched God to strike him dead if he deserved excommunication. When God refrained, Savonarola celebrated his vindication by ordering another Burning of the Vanities. Florence was once again looted by the Army of Boys.

Savonarola's letters calling for a reformation were circulated secretly by the Florentines in Rome, to whom he had become an idol. When Michelangelo described to them the Burning of the Vanities that he had witnessed, the hundreds of irreplaceable manuscripts, books, paintings, sculptures that had been destroyed, they were not distressed.

"Any price is cheap in a famine," cried Cavalcanti. "We must destroy the Borgia at any cost."

Michelangelo was thoughtful.

"What will you think of this price in a few years when the Pope and Botticelli are both dead? There will be another Pope, but there can never be another Botticelli. All the works he threw on that fire are gone for ever. It seems to me you are approving lawlessness in Florence to rid yourselves of lawlessness here in Rome."

If he could not touch them with his reasoning, the Pope touched them where it hurt: he promised to confiscate all business properties of the Florentines and to turn them out of the city penniless unless the Signoria of Florence sent Savonarola to Rome to stand trial. From what Michelangelo could gather, the colony made a complete capitulation: Savonarola had to be silenced; he had to honour his excommunication, to seek absolution from the Pope. They petitioned the Signoria to act in their behalf and to send Savonarola under guard to Rome. All the Pope asked, they explained, was that Savonarola come to Rome and receive absolution. Then he could return to Florence to save souls.

Before the end of March a rumour spread through Rome that sent Michelangelo racing to the Ponte: Savonarola's second in command, Fra Domenico, had committed himself to an ordeal by fire. The colony assembled at the home of the patriarch, Cavalcanti. When Michelangelo entered the house he was plunged into a hubbub that tumbled down the stairs from the drawing-room.

"What does it mean, ordeal by fire?" he asked. "Is it what Savonarola tried before carnival, asking to be struck dead if his words were not inspired by God?"

"Similar. Except that fire burns."

This last development had been originated either by Fra Domenico himself or by the Dominicans' enemy in the struggle for power, the Franciscans, led by Francesco di Puglia. In a fiery sermon in defence of their leader, Fra

Domenico had declared that he would enter fire to prove that everything Savonarola taught was inspired by God; and he challenged a Franciscan to enter with him. The next day Fra Francesco di Puglia accepted the challenge, but insisted that Savonarola himself must enter the fire, saying that only if Savonarola came through the fire alive could Florence believe him to be a true prophet. Meeting for supper at the Pitti palace, a young group of *Arrabbiati* assured Fra Francesco and the Franciscans that Savonarola would never accept; that by his refusal he would prove to Florence that he had no true faith in God's saving him.

At this point the voters of Florence turned against Savonarola politically. They had already endured seven years of wrangling, the Pope's theat to put an interdict on the entire population, which amounted to an excommunication that could paralyze trade and cause bitter turmoil. The city needed a three per cent tax on church property which the Pope now agreed to allow, once Savonarola was quieted They defeated the Signoria pledged to Savonarola and elected a new Council which was against him. Florence was threatened with another Guelph and Ghibelline-like civil war.

On April 7 a platform was erected in the Piazza della Signoria, the logs smeared with pitch. A vast crowd assembled to watch the show. The Franciscans refused to enter the piazza until Fra Domenico agreed not to take the host into the fire. After a number of hours of waiting, a fierce winter rainstorm drenched the platform, scattering the crowd and putting an end to any burning.

The following night the *Arrabbiati* mobbed the monastery of San Marco, killing a number of Savonarola's followers. The Signoria moved in, arrested Savonarola, Fra Domenico and Fra Silvestro, the third in command, and jailed them in the bell tower of the Palazzo della Signoria. The Pope sent a courier to Florence demanding that Savonarola be delivered to him in Rome. The Signoria refused, but appointed a Commission of Seventeen to examine Savonarola and secure a confession that his words were not divinely inspired.

Savonarola refused to recant. The commission tortured him; first using the rack and the screw, then roping him to a pulley, raising him in the air, dropping him with a sudden jerk of the rope. Savonarola became delirious, agreed to write a confession. He was released to his cell. What he wrote was not satisfactory to the Signoria. He was tortured again. Weak from fasting and all-night prayers, Savonarola again succumbed, signed a confession written by a notary; but not before he rejected the paper and had to be tortured a third time.

The commission declared Savonarola guilty of heresy. The special advisory council called by the Signoria sentenced him to death. At the same time the Pope granted the city its long-desired three percent tax on all church property in Tuscany.

Three platforms were built from the steps of the Palazzo della Signoria into the square. The throng began filling the piazza during the night, pushing up against the gibbet. By dawn the square and all the streets leading into it were a seething mass.

Savonarola, Fra Domenico and Fra Silvestro were led out on to the Signoria steps, stripped of their vestments, their tonsures scraped. They mounted the scaffold, praying silently. They climbed a steep ladder to the top of the gibbet. Ropes and chains were put about their necks. Within an instant, all three were dangling, their necks broken.

The pyre under the gibbet was lighted. The flames rose. The three bodies were held aloft by the chains after the ropes had burned. The *Arrabbiati* stoned the half-consumed corpses. The ashes were collected, carried in carts to the Old Bridge, and dumped into the Arno.

The martyrdom of Savonarola shook Michelangelo profoundly. He had sat as a boy and listened to Pico della Mirandola recommend to Lorenzo that the friar be invited to Florence. Savonarola had contributed to the deaths of Lorenzo, Pico, Poliziano, and now he too was dead. He hardly knew what to think or feel: except pity.

He turned to his work. Marble was dependable in a chaotic world. It had its own will and intelligence and stability. With marble in his hands, the world was good.

He became impatient to be finished with the Bacchus. He had only indicated the position of the forehead, nose, mouth, wanting to let the rest of the figure suggest the expression on the face. Now he completed the features, the expression dazed as the Bacchus stared at the cup of wine; the eyes bulging, the mouth opened greedily. For the grapes he used a drill, making each one round and juice-laden. To achieve the hair on the Satyr's goat legs he sliced the rough-edged marble with a fully rounded chisel which brought out the rhythmic play of curls, each tuft designed separately.

There was left two months of polishing to get the glowing

flesh effects he wanted. Though this work involved infinite care and precision, it was technical in nature and used only that part of him which was the craftsman. It left his mind free during the warm spring hours to reflect on the Pietà and its meaning. In the cool of the evenings he began searching for this last moment that mother and son would spend together.

He asked Jacopo Galli if he could not complete a contract with the Cardinal of San Dionigi. Galli explained that the cardinal's monastery in Lucca had already ordered a block to Michelangelo's dimensions. The block had been cut, but the quarry at Carrara had refused to ship it to Rome before being paid. The monastery at Lucca had in turn refused to pay until the cardinal approved the block. The quarry had grown tired of holding it and had sold it to a buying agent.

That night Michelangelo wrote an agreement which he thought would be fair to himself and to the Cardinal of San Dionigi. Galli read it without expression, said he would take it to his bank and put it in a safe place.

By the end of summer the Bacchus was finished. Galli was overjoyed with his statue.

" I feel as though Bacchus is fully alive, and will drop his cup at any moment. The Satyr is innocent and naughty at the same time. You have made for me the finest sculpture in all Italy. We must place it in the garden and give it a party."

The blind Augustinians, Aurelius and Raffaele Lippus, studied the Bacchus with their sensitive fingers, running them over every detail and saying they had never " seen " a male figure so powerful in projecting its inner life force. Professor Pomponius Laetus, who had been tortured by the Inquisition for paganism, was moved to tears, avowing that the statue was pure Greek in its structure and its gleaming white satiny finish. Serafino, the poet from Lucrezia Borgia's court, hated it on sight, declaring it " ugly, wanton, without any sense of loveliness." Sannazaro, the poet who mixed Christian and pagan images in his verses, declared it " a complete synthesis, Greek in carving, Christian in emotion, combining the best of both," even as the Plato Four had commented on his Madonna and Child. Peter Sabinus, professor of Eloquence at the university, collector of Christian inscriptions, and his friend Giovanni Capocci, who was excavating the catacombs, came back three times to debate the statue's virtues between themselves, finally concluding that, although they did not care for antique themes, this Bacchus was something new in the art of sculpture.

It was Giuliano da Sangallo's opinion Michelangelo valued most. Sangallo gleefully traced the intricate structural design. "You've built this Bacchus the way we build a temple or a palace. It was a dangerous, and courageous, experiment in construction. You could easily have suffered a collapse of material. This fellow will stand erect as long as there is space for him to displace."

The following night Galli brought home a contract he himself had written between Michelangelo and the Cardinal of San Dionigi, and which the cardinal had signed. In it Michelangelo found himself called *maestro* for the first time; but he was also described as *statuario*, statue maker, which was deflating. For the sum of four hundred and fifty ducats in papal gold he agreed to make a Pietà of marble, one hundred and fifty ducats to be paid as he began, and a hundred ducats every fourth month. By the end of a year the statue was to be completed. In addition to guaranteeing the cardinal's payments to Michelangelo, Galli had written:

I, Jacopo Galli, do promise that the work will be more beautiful than any work in marble to be seen in Rome to-day, and such that no master of our own time will be able to produce a better.

Michelangelo gazed at Galli with affection.

"You must have written this contract at home, rather than the bank."

"Why?"

"Because you have taken quite a gamble. Suppose when I finish the cardinal says, ' I have seen better marbles in Rome.' What happens then?"

"I give His Grace back his papal ducats."

"And you are stuck with the carving!"

Galli's eyes twinkled. "I could endure it."

He went searching the stoneyards of Trastevere and the ports for the kind of block he needed; but a seven-foot-wide, six-foot-tall, three-foot-deep cut of marble was rarely quarried on the chance of sale. It took him only two days to complete the rounds; there was nothing even faintly resembling the massive block he needed. The next day, when he had decided that he would have to go to Carrara at his own expense, Guffatti came running up the rear alley to his workshed, crying out:

". . . just unloaded a barge . . . the very size you're looking
345

for. It was cut for some order in Lucca. The quarry never got paid, so they sold it."

He dog-trotted down to the Ripetta dock. There it stood, gleaming pure and white in the summer sun, beautifully cut by the quarrymen high in the mountains of Carrara. It tested out perfect against the hammer, against water, its crystals soft and compacted with fine graining. He came back before dawn the next morning, watched the rays of the rising sun strike the block and make it as transparent as pink alabaster, with not a hole or hollow or crack or knot to be seen in all its massive white weight.

His Pietà block had come home.

9

He removed the last reminders of the Bacchus, settled down to the Pietà. But the Bacchus had become a controversial figure. Many people came to see it. Galli brought the visitors to the workshop or sent a servant to the shed to ask if Michelangelo would mind coming to the garden. He found himself plunged into explanations and defences, particularly from the Bregno enthusiasts, who attacked it as " a perversion of the Dionysius legend." When there were admirers he found himself involved in describing his concept and technique. Galli wanted him for supper every night now, and Sundays, so that he could make as many friends as possible, open the way to more commission.

The Rucellai, Cavalcanti, Altoviti were proud of him. They gave parties in his honour, from which he awoke the next morning feeling tired. He yearned to put the Bacchus behind him, to wipe the slate of his mind clean of the pagan carving and make the transition to the spirituality he needed to think about the Pietà. After a month of festivities it became clear that he was not going to be able to conceive or carve a Pietà under these diverting conditions ; that with his emergence as a professional sculptor had come the time to establish his own quarters and workshop where he could live quietly, secluded, work night and day if he wished, dedicate himself to abstemiousness. He had grown up, he was on his own. He could see no other way.

Perceptive Jacopo Galli asked, "Something is troubling you, Michelangelo?"

"Yes."

"It sounds serious."

"Just ungrateful."

"You owe me nothing."

"The men to whom I owe the most have all said that: Lorenzo de' Medici, Bertold, Aldovrandi, and now you."

"Tell me what you want to do."

"To move out!" he blurted. "Life with the Galli family is too pleasant. . . ." He paused. "I feel the need to work in my own household. As a man, rather than a boy, and perennial guest. Does this sound foolish?"

Galli gazed at him wistfully. "I want only that you be happy, and that you carve the most beautiful marbles in Italy."

"For me they are one and the same."

He was directed to several houses in which the ground floor was available, one recommended by Altoviti in the Florentine quarter, another near the Piazza del Quirinale, with a fine view of Rome. They were too elaborate and expensive. On the third day, on the Via Sistina, across from the Bear Inn and on the edge of the Campo Marzio lying below the embankment of the Tiber, he found a big corner room with two windows, one facing north for steady light, the other east for the sharp sunlight he sometimes needed. At the rear was a smaller room with a fireplace. He paid a few scudi for two months' rent, drew up the oiled linen on wooden frames that served as window covering, and studied the shabby space: the wooden floor, thin in spots, broken in others, cement crumbling between the stones of the walls, the ceiling plaster falling in patches, exposing variegated colours of decay where the rain had leaked through. He put the key in his pocket and returned to the Gallis'.

He found Buonarroto waiting for him. His brother was jubilant. He had come as a guard on a mule train, and so the trip had cost him nothing. He was going back the same way. Michelangelo gazed with pleasure at the stubby features, the hair combed over Buonarroto's brow in imitation of his own. It had been a year since they had seen each other.

"You couldn't have come at a better time," he cried. "I need help in setting up my new home."

"You have taken a place? Good, then I can stay with you."

"Wait till you see my palatial quarters before you settle

in," said Michelangelo, smiling. "Come with me to Trastevere, I need a supply of plaster, whitewash and lye. But
first I will show you my Bacchus."

Buonarroto stood gazing at the statue a long time. Then
he asked:

"Did people like it?"

"Most did."

"I'm glad."

That was all. Michelangelo observed to himself, "He
doesn't have the faintest notion of what sculpture is about.
His only interest is that people approve what I've done, so
that I can be happy, and get more work . . . none of which
he will ever understand. He's a true Buonarroti, blind to
the meaning of art. But he loves me."

They bought the supplies, had dinner at the Trattoria
Toscana, then Michelangelo took his brother to the Via
Sistina. When Buonarroto entered the room he whistled
sharply.

"Michelangelo, surely you're not thinking of living in
this . . . this hole? The place is falling apart."

"You and I are going to put it back together," replied
Michelangelo grimly. "It is adequate work space."

"Father would be distressed."

Michelangelo smiled. "Don't tell him." He set a tall
ladder in the centre of the room. "Let's scrape this ceiling."

When they had scraped and given the ceiling a coat of
plaster, they began on the walls, then set to work patching
the broken floor with odd-sized pieces of wood. Next they
turned their attention to the private courtyard. The only door
to it was from the side of his room, but the other tenants
had access from their windows, as a result of which it was
covered with a thick compost of garbage and debris. The
odour was as thick as the enclosing walls. It took two days
to shovel the refuse into sacks and carry it through his own
room to a vacant lot below the Tiber.

Balducci, who held all physical labour in abhorrence,
showed up after Michelangelo and Buonarroto had finished
their repairs. He knew a secondhand furniture dealer in
Trastevere, where he bargained shrilly for the best prices on
a bed, rope mattress, kitchen table, two cane chairs, chest of
drawers, a few pots, dishes and knives. When the donkey
cart arrived a few hours later, the brothers set up the bed
under the window to the east, where Michelangelo would be
waked at first light. The chest of drawers went on the back

wall, next to the opening to the kitchen. Under the front north window he placed a table of four planks on horses, for his drawing, wax and clay modelling. The centre of the big room he kept clear for his marble. In the rear cubicle they installed the kitchen table, two chairs, pots and dishes.

Balducci returned, having explored the neighbourhood.

"There's a plump little partridge lives just behind your rooms: blonde, about fifteen, beautifully made, French, I think. I could persuade her to become your servant. Think how pleasant it would be to finish work at noon and find her in your kitchen over a pot of hot soup." Balducci did a little dance. ". . . and at night, to find her in your bed. It's part of their job; and you're going to need a little natural warmth in this cave."

Michelangelo and Buonarroto chuckled at Balducci's ebullience. In another minutes he would be out of the front door and down the street after the girl.

"Look, Balducci," cried Michelangelo. "I want no entanglements, and have no money for a servant. If I need anyone, I'll stick to the artist's custom of taking in a young apprentice and training him in return for services."

Buonarroto agreed. "I'll keep my eyes open in Florence for a bright young lad."

Buonarroto settled Michelangelo in, shopped and cooked the food, cleaned the rooms. The housekeeping went downhill the moment he left. Immersed in his work, Michelangelo took no time off to cook, to go out to a restaurant or eat in the streets. He lost weight, even as his rooms lost their tidy appearance. He saw nothing about him but his workbench and the huge white block sitting on beams in the centre of the floor. He never bothered to make his bed or to wash the dishes he left on the kitchen table. The rooms became covered with dust from the street, ash from the kitchen fire where he boiled water for an occasional hot drink. He knew by the end of a month that this system was not going to work. He even began to eye Balducci's little French girl, who passed his door more frequently than he thought strictly necessary.

Buonarroto solved his problem. Michelangelo answered to a knock late one afternoon to see standing in the street a plain-faced, olive-complected lad of about thirteen, travel-stained, holding out a letter on which Michelangelo recognized his brother's handwriting. The note introduced Piero Argiento, who had come to Florence looking for a sculptor to whom he could be apprenticed. He had been sent by someone to the Buonarroti house, then made the long trip on foot to Rome.

Michelangelo invited him in, studied the boy while he told of his family and their farm near Ferrara. His manner was quiet, his voice plain.

"Can you read and write, Argiento?"

"The Gesuati fathers in Ferrara taught me to write. Now I need to learn a trade."

"And you think sculpture might be a good one?"

"I want a three-year apprenticeship. With a Guild contract."

Michelangelo was impressed by the forthrightness. He gazed into the muddy brown eyes of the stringy lad before him, at the soiled shirt, worn-out sandals, the thin, hungry cheeks.

"You have no friends in Rome? No place to go?"

"I came to see you." Stubbornly.

"I live simply, Argiento. You can expect no luxury."

"I am of *contadini*. What is to eat, we eat."

"Since you need a home, and I need a helper, suppose we try it for a few days? If it doesn't work out, we part as friends. I'll pay your way back to Florence."

"Agreed. *Grazie.*"

"Take this coin, and go to the baths near Santa Maria dell' Anima. On the way back, stop at the market for food to cook."

"I make a good soup-of-the-country. My mother taught me before she died."

The fathers had taught Argiento not only to count but also to be doggedly honest. He left the house before dawn for the markets, carrying with him a scrap of crayon and paper. Michelangelo was touched by the way he painfully kept his accounts written down: so many denari for vegetables, so many for meat, for fruit, for bread and *pasta,* with every coin accounted for. Michelangelo put a modest amount in a cooking pot as their weekly allowance. Argiento was a relentless pursuer of bargains. Within a week he knew every stall selling produce. His shopping took him the better part of the morning, which suited Michelangelo because it gave him the solitariness he sought.

They established a simple routine. After their one-dish midday dinner, Argiento cleaned the rooms while Michelangelo took an hour's walk along the Tiber to the docks to listen to the Sicilians sing as they unloaded the boats. By the time he returned home Argiento was taking his *riposo* on the truckle bed in the kitchen under the wooden sink. Michelangelo had two more hours of quiet at his workbench before Argiento woke, washed his face noisily in a basin, and came to the worktable for his daily instruction. These few hours in the afternoon appeared to be all the teaching Argiento wanted. At dusk he was back in the kitchen, boiling water. By the time dark settled in he was asleep on his truckle bed, a blanket drawn securely over his head. Michelangelo then lit his oil lamps and returned to his workbench. He was grateful to Buonarroto for sending Argiento to him; the arrangement looked as though it would be satisfactory, despite the fact that Argiento showed not a shred of talent for drawing. Later, when he began working the marble, he would teach the boy how to use a hammer and chisel.

In the Bible he read from John 19:38-40:

After this Joseph of Arimathea, who was a disciple of Jesus . . . asked Pilate to let him take away the body of Jesus . . . so he came and took Jesus' body away; and with him was Nicodemus . . . he brought with him a mixture of myrrh and aloes, of about a hundred pounds' weight. They took Jesus's body, then, and wrapped it in winding-clothes with the spices; that is how the Jews prepare a body for burial.

Listed as present at the Descent were Mary, Mary's sister, Mary Magdalene, John, Joseph of Arimathea, Nicodemus. Search as he might, he could find no place where the Bible spoke of a moment when Mary could have been alone with Jesus. Mostly the scene was crowded with mourners, such as the dramatic Dell'Arca Lamentation in Bologna, where the grief-stricken spectators had usurped Mary's last poignant moment.

In his concept there could be no one else present.

His first desire was to create a mother and son alone in the universe. When might Mary have had that moment to hold her child on her lap? Perhaps after the soldiers had laid him on the ground, while Joseph of Arimathea was at Pontius Pilate's asking for Christ's body, Nicodemus was gathering his mixture of myrrh and aloes, and the others had gone home to mourn. Those who saw his finished Pietà would take the place of the biblical witnesses. They would feel what Mary was undergoing. There would be no haloes, no angels. These would be two human beings, whom God had chosen.

He felt close to Mary, having spent so long concentrating on the beginning of her journey. Now she was intensely alive, anguished; her son was dead. Even though he would later be resurrected, he was at this moment dead indeed, the expression on his face reflecting what he had gone through on the cross. In his sculpture therefore it would not be possible for him to project anything of what Jesus felt for his mother; only what Mary felt for her son. Jesus' inert body would be passive, his eyes closed. Mary would have to carry the human communication. This seemed right to him.

It was a relief to shift in his mind to technical problems. Since his Christ was to be life size, how was Mary to hold him on her lap without the relationship seeming ungainly? His Mary would be slender of limb and delicate of proportion, yet she must hold this full-grown man as securely and convincingly as she would a child.

There was only one way to accomplish this: by design, by drawing diagrams and sketches in which he probed the remotest corner of his mind for creative ideas to carry his concept.

He started by making free sketches to loosen up his thinking so that images would appear on paper. Visually, these approximated what he was feeling within himself. At the same time he started walking the streets, peering at the people passing or shopping at the stalls, storing up fresh impressions of what they looked like, how they moved. In particular he sought the gentle, sweet-faced nuns, with head coverings and veils coming to the middle of their foreheads, remembering their expressions until he reached home and set them down on paper.

Discovering that draperies could be designed to serve structural purposes, he began a study of the anatomy of folds. He improvised as he went along, completing a life-size clay figure, then bought yards of an inexpensive material from a draper, wet the lightweight cloth in a basin and covered it over with clay that Argiento brought from the bank of the Tibe., to the consistency of thick mud. No fold could be accidental, each turn of the drapery had to serve organically, to cover the Madonna's slender legs and feet so that they would give substantive support to Christ's body, to intensify her inner turmoil. When the cloth dried and stiffened, he saw what adjustments had to be made.

352

" So that's sculpture," commented Argiento wryly, when he had sluiced down the floor for a week, " making mud pies."

Michelangelo grinned. " See, Argiento, if you control the way these folds are bunched, like this, or made to flow, you can enrich the body attitudes. They can have as much tactile appeal as flesh and bone."

He went into the Jewish quarter, wanting to draw Hebraic faces so that he could reach a visual understanding of how Christ might have looked. The Jewish section was in Trastevere, near the Tiber at the church of San Francesco a Ripa. The colony had been small until the Spanish Inquisition of 1492 drove many Jews into Rome. Here, for the most part, they were well treated, as a " reminder of the Old Testament heritage of Christianity "; many of their gifted members were prominent in the Vatican as physicians, musicians, bankers.

The men did not object to his sketching them while they went about their work, but no one could be persuaded to come to his studio to pose. He was told to ask for Rabbi Melzi at the synagogue on Saturday afternoon. Michelangelo found the rabbi in the room of study, a gentle old man with a white beard and luminous grey eyes, robed in black gaberdine with a skullcap on his head. He was reading from the Talmud with a group of men from his congregation.. When Michelangelo explained why he had come, Rabbi Melzi replied gravely:

" The Bible forbids us to bow down to or to make graven images. That is why our creative people give their time to literature, not to painting or sculpture."

" But, Rabbi Melzi, you don't object to others creating works of art?"

" Not at all. Each religion has its own tenets."

" I am carving a Pietà from white Carrara marble. I wish to make Jesus an authentic Jew. I cannot accomplish this if you will not help me."

The rabbit said thoughtfully, " I would not want my people to get in trouble with the Church."

" I am working for the Cardinal of San Dionigi. I'm sure he would approve."

" What kind of models would you prefer?"

" Workmen. In their mid-thirties. Not bulky labourers, but sinewy men. With intelligence. And sensitivity."

Rabbi Melzi smiled at him with infinitely old but merry eyes.

"Leave me your address. I will send you the best the quarter has to offer."

Michelangelo hurried to Sangallo's solitary bachelor room with his sketches, asked the architect to design a stand which would simulate the seated Madonna. Sangallo studied the drawings and improvised a trestle couch. Michelangelo bought some scrap lumber. Together he and Argiento built the stand, covering it with blankets.

His first model arrived at dusk. He hesitated for a moment when Michelangelo asked him to disrobe, so Michelangelo gave him a piece of towelling to wrap around his loins, led him to the kitchen to take off his clothes. He then draped him over the rough stand, explained that he was supposed to be recently dead, and was being held on his mother's lap. The model quite plainly thought Michelangelo crazy; only the instructions from his rabbi kept him from bolting. But at the end of the sitting, when Michelangelo showed him the quick, free drawings, with the mother roughed in, holding her son, the model grasped what Michelangelo was after, and promised to speak to his friends. . . . He worked for two hours a day with each model sent by the rabbi.

Mary presented quite a different problem. Though this sculpture must take place thirty-three years after her moment of decision, he could not conceive of her as a woman in her mid-fifties, old, wrinkled, broken in body and face by labour or worry. His image of the Virgin had always been that of a young woman, even as had his memory of his mother.

Jacopo Galli introduced him into several Roman homes. Here he sketched, sitting in their flowing gowns of linen and silk, young girls not yet twenty, some about to be married, some married a year or two. Since the Santo Spirito hospital had taken only men, he had had no experience in the study of female anatomy; but he had sketched the women of Tuscany in their fields and homes. He was able to discern the body lines of the Roman women under their robes.

He spent concentrated weeks putting his two figures together: a Mary who would be young and sensitive, yet strong enough to hold her son on her lap; and a Jesus who, though lean, was strong even in death . . . a look he remembered well from his experience in the dead room of Santo Spirito.

He drew towards the composite design from his meticulously accurate memory, without need to consult his sketches.

Soon he was ready to go into a three-dimensional figure in clay. Here he would have free expression because the material could be moved to distort forms. When he wanted to emphasize, or get greater intensity, he added or subtracted clay. Next he turned to wax because there was a similarity of wax to marble in tactile quality and translucence. He respected each of these approach techniques, and kept them in character: his quill drawings had a scratchiness, suggesting skin texture; the clay he used plastically to suggest soft moving flesh, as in an abdomen, in a reclining torso; the wax he smoothed over to give the body surface an elastic pull. Yet he never allowed these models to become fixed in his mind; they remained rough starting points. When carving he was charged with spontaneous energy; too careful or detailed studies in clay and wax would have glued him down to a mere enlarging of his model.

The true surge had to be inside the marble itself. Drawing and models were his thinking. Carving was action.

10

The arrangement with Argiento was working well, except that sometimes Michelangelo could not figure who was master and who apprentice. Argiento had been trained so rigorously by the Jesuits that Michelangelo was unable to change his habits: up before dawn to scrub the floors, whether they were dirty or not; water boiling on the fire for washing laundry every day, the pots scoured with river sand after each meal.

"Argiento, this is senseless," he complained, not liking to work on the wet floors, particularly in cold weather. "You're too clean. Scrub the studio once a week. That's enough."

"No," said Argiento stolidly. "Every day. Before dawn. I was taught."

"And God help anyone who tries to unteach you!" grumbled Michelangelo; yet he knew that he had nothing to grumble about, for Argiento made few demands on him. The boy was becoming acquainted with the *contadini* families that brought produce into Rome. On Sundays he would walk miles into the *campagna* to visit with them, and in

355

particular to see their horses. The one thing he missed from his farm in the Po Valley was the animals: frequently he would take his leave of Michelangelo by announcing:

"To-day I go see the horses."

It took a piece of bad luck to show Michelangelo that the boy was devoted to him. He was crouched over his anvil in the courtyard getting his chisels into trim, when a splinter of steel flew into his eye and embedded itself in his pupil. He stumbled into the house, eyes burning like fire. Argiento made him lie down on the bed, brought a pan of hot water, dipped some clean white linen cloth and applied it to extract the splinter. Though the pain was considerable Michelangelo was not too concerned. He assumed he could blink the splinter out. But it would not come. Argiento never left his side, keeping the water boiled, applying hot compresses throughout the night.

By the second day Michelangelo began to worry; and by the second night he was in a state of panic: he could see nothing out of the afflicted eye. At dawn Argiento went to Jacopo Galli. Galli arrived with his family surgeon, Maestro Lippi. The surgeon carried a cage of live pigeons. He told Argiento to take a bird out of the cage, cut a large vein under its wing, let the blood gush into Michelangelo's injured eye.

The surgeon came back at dusk, cut the vein of a second pigeon, again washed out the eye. All the next day Michelangelo could feel the splinter moving, pushing. By nightfall it was out.

Argiento had not slept for some seventy hours.

"You're tired," said Michelangelo. "Why don't you take a few days off?"

Argiento's stubborn features lit up with pleasure. "I go visit the horses."

At first Michelangelo had been bothered by the people going in and out of the Bear Hotel across the street, the noise of their horses and carts on the cobbles, the cries of the grooms and babble of a dozen dialects. By now he had grown to enjoy the interesting characters who came from all over Europe for their pilgrimage, some wearing long gowns, others short tunics of brilliant greens and purples, others stiff hats. They served as an unending source of models for him to sketch at his worktable as he saw them through the open window. Soon he came to know the clients; as a guest
356

reappeared he quickly pulled out his drawing, made corrections or additions, caught the bodies in a variety of movements: unloading carriages, carrying valises, unshouldering packs, getting on and off mules.

The noise in the street, the voices, the welcomes, the departures gave him company without intruding upon his privacy. Living in isolation as he was, this sense of other people in the world was companionable. It was all he needed, for with marble in his hands he would never stand on the periphery looking in; he would stand at the focal core looking out.

In his pen and ink sketches for the Pietà he had cross-hatched the negative spaces, those parts of the block that had to be thrown away, indicating the tool strokes that should be used. Now, with hammer and chisel in hand, he found this roughing out unpleasing, impatient for that first moment when a flicker of a buried image shone through, when the block became a source of life that communicated with him. Then, from the space outside the block, he entered into his composition. After he had completed the sculpture, life would vibrate outward from the figures. But at this beginning moment the action was in reverse: the point of entry must be a force that sucked in space, pulling inward his gaze and attention. He had envisaged so big a block because he wanted to sculpture with an abundance of marble. He did not want to have to compress any portion of his forms, as he had had to compact the Satyr close to the Bacchus.

He broke into his marble block at the left side of the Madonna's head, worked to the left of the block, the north light behind him. By getting Argiento to help him turn the block on its beams he was able to have the shadows fall exactly where the cavities were to be carved, a play of light and shadow to show him where he must cast out stone; for the marble he took away was also sculpture, creating its own effects.

Now he had to plunge in boldly to find his principal features. The weight of the material of the Madonna's head covering, forcing her head downward to the inner hand of Christ that crossed her heart, compelled attention to the body stretched across her lap. The tight band which ran between the Virgin's breasts was like a tight hand constricting and crushing a palpitating heart. The lines of the drapery led to the Madonna's hand, with which she held her son, securely, under his arm, then to the human aspects of Christ's body, to his face, the eyes closed serenely in deep sleep, the nose straight but full, the skin clear and firm, the soft moustache and delicate curling chin whiskers, the mouth filled with anguish.

Because the Madonna was gazing down on her son, all who looked must turn to her face, to see the sadness, the compassion for all men's sons, asking with tender despair: " What could I have done to save him?" And from the depth of her love, "What purpose has all this served, if man cannot be saved?"

All who saw would feel how insupportably heavy was her son's dead body on her lap, how much heavier was the burden in her heart.

It was unusual to combine two life-size figures in the same sculpture, revolutionary to put a full-grown man on to the lap of a woman. From this point of departure he left behind all conventional concepts of the Pietà. Once again, even as Ficino had believed that Plato could have been Christ's most loving disciple, it was Michelangelo's desire to blend the classical Greek concept of the beauty of the human body with the Christian ideal of the immortality of the human soul. He banished the lugubrious death throes of the earlier Pietàs, bathed his two figures in tranquillity. Human beauty could reveal sacredness as clearly as could pain. At the same time, it could exalt.

All of this, and much more, the marble must be persuaded to say. If the end result were tragic, then doubly must they walk in beauty; beauty that his own love and dedication could match in this flawless white block. He would make mistakes, but the mistakes would be made with loving hands.

Winter came down like a clap of thunder: cold, wet, raw. As Buonarroto had predicted, there were leaks. Michelangelo and Argiento moved his workbench and bed to dry sections of the room, brought the forge in from the courtyard. He wore his Bologna cap over his head and ears. His nostrils swelled, giving him constant pain, making breathing difficult.

He bought a black iron brazier to put under his work stool, which warmed him posteriorly; but the moment he moved to another section of the room his blood froze. He had to send Argiento out for two more braziers, and baskets of coal, which they could hardly afford. When his fingers were blue he tried to carve while wearing woollen mittens. Within the hour he had an accident, some marble fell away and he felt his heart go down to his feet as the chunk hit the floor.

One Sunday Argiento returned from an outing feeling hot and strange. By midnight he had a high fever. Michelangelo picked him up off his truckle bed and put him into his own. By morning Argiento was in a delirium, sweating profusely, crying out names of relatives, fragments of stories, of beatings, accidents. Michelangelo wiped him dry, and a number of times had to restrain him from jumping out of bed.

At dawn he summoned a passer-by and sent him for a doctor. The doctor stood in the doorway, cried, "It's the plague! Burn everything he has touched since he came in here!" and fled.

Michelangelo sent a message to Galli. Maestro Lippi took one look, said scoffingly:

"Nonsense, it is not the plague. Quartan fever. Has he been around the Vatican lately?"

"He walked there on Sunday."

"And probably drank some stagnant water in the ditch beneath the walls. Go to the French monks on the Esquiline, they make a glutinous pill of sagepen, salt, coloquint . . ."

Michelangelo begged a neighbour to sit with Argiento. It took him almost an hour in the pelting rain to cross the city, go down the long street from Trajan's forum, past Augustus' forum and the basilica of Constantine, the colosseum, then up the Esquiline hill to the monastery. The pills lessened Argiento's headache, and Michelangelo thought he was making good progress during two quiet days; then the delirium returned.

At the end of the week Michelangelo was exhausted. He had brought Argiento's bed into the big room, and was catching a few moments of sleep while Argiento dozed, but worse than the lack of sleep was the problem of food, for he was unwilling to leave the boy alone.

Balducci knocked on the door.

"I told you to take that French girl at the rear. Then when she got sick, her family would have nursed her."

"Let's not go backward," said Michelangelo wearily. "Forward is hard enough."

"You can't keep him here. You look like a skeleton. Take him to the Santo Spirito hospital."

"And let him die?"

"Why should he die any faster at a hospital?"

"Because they don't get any care."

"What kind of care are you giving him, Dr. Buonarroti?"

"I keep him clean, watch over him. . . . He took care of me when I hurt my eye. How can I abandon him to a ward? That's not Christian."

"If you insist on committing suicide, I'll bring you food each morning before I go to the bank."

Michelangelo's eyes filled with gratitude. "Balducci, you just play at being cynical. Here's some money, buy me towels, and a sheet or two."

Michelangelo turned to find Argiento watching him.

"I'm going to die."

"No, you're not, Argiento. Nothing kills a countryman but a falling cliff."

The illness took three weeks to pass. What hurt most was the loss of almost a month of work; he began to worry that he could not finish his statue within the stipulated year's time.

Winter was mercifully short in Rome. By March the *campagna* was flooded with a bright, brittle sunlight. The stones of the workshop began to thaw. And with the warmer weather came the Cardinal of San Dionigi to see how his Pietà was faring. Each time Michelangelo saw him there appeared to be more material and less body in his robes. He asked Michelangelo if he had been receiving his payments regularly. Michelangelo assured him that he had. They stood in front of the massive white block in the middle of the room. The figures were still rough, with much webbing left for support; but he had done considerable carving on the two faces, and that was what interested the cardinal most.

"Tell me, my son," he said softly, "how does the Madonna's face remain so young, younger than her son's?"

"Your Grace, it seemed to me that the Virgin Mary would not age. She was pure; and so she would have kept her freshness of youth."

The answer was satisfactory to the cardinal.

"I hope you will finish in August. It is my dearest wish to hold services in St. Peter's for the installation."

11

He carved in a fury from first light to dark, then threw himself across his bed, without supper and fully clothed, like a dead man. He awoke around midnight, refreshed, his mind seething with sculptural ideas, craving to get at the marble. He got up, nibbled at a heel of bread, lit the brass lamp in which he burned the dregs of the olive oil, and tried to set it at an angle that would throw light on the area he was carving. The light was too diffused. It was not safe to use a chisel.

He bought some heavy paper, made a hat with a peak, tied a wire around the outside and in the centre fashioned a loop big enough to hold a candle. The light, as he held his face a few inches from the marble, was bright and steady. Nor did his pounding waken Argiento under the kitchen sink, blanket over his head. The candles burned quickly, the soft wax running over the peak of his paper cap and on to his forehead, but he was delighted with his invention.

Late one night there was a sharp rap at the door. He opened it to find Leo Baglioni, dressed in an indigo velvet cloak, surrounded by a group of his young friends who were holding horn lanterns or wax torches on long poles.

" I saw the light and came to see what you were doing at this ungodly hour. You're working! What's that stuff all over your eyebrows?"

Michelangelo proudly showed them his cap and candle. Leo and his friends burst into a paroxysm of laughter.

"Why don't you use goat's tallow, it's harder, you won't be eating it all night," exclaimed Leo, when he caught his breath.

Argiento disappeared the next day after supper, came back at the second hour of evening weighed down with four heavy bundles which he dumped on the bed.

" Signor Baglioni sent for me. These are a present."

Michelangelo extracted a hard yellow taper.

" I don't need his assistance!" he cried. " Take them back."

" They have broken my arm from the Campo dei Fiori. I won't carry them back. I'll set them in front of the door and burn them all at once."

" Very well, let me see if they are better than wax. But first I'll have to widen this wire loop."

Leo had known what he was talking about: the goat's tallow melted more slowly and remained in a pool where it fell.

He divided the night into two halves, one for sleep, the other for work, and made rapid progress carving the voluminous outer folds of Mary's robe, Christ's lower torso, his legs, the inner one raised so that it would be visible from the

361

front, leaving a webbing connecting it with Mary's outstretched hand to protect it.

He refused all invitations, saw few of his friends though Balducci kept bringing the news: Cardinal Giovanni, unwanted and unnoticed by the Borgia, had left to travel in Europe; Piero, trying to raise an army for a third attack on Florence, had been ostracized by the colony; Florence's intermittent war with Pisa had flared again; Torrigiani had joined Cæsar Borgia's troops as an officer to help conquer the Romagna for the Vatican. The Borgia was excommunicating lords and churchmen, appropriating their lands; no Florentine knew when his turn would be next.

It was on a glorious summer morning with the air so translucent that the Alban hills seemed only a piazza away, that Paolo Rucellai sent for him to come as soon as possible. Michelangelo wondered what news it could be that Paolo considered urgent.

"Michelangelo, you look so thin."

"The sculpture grows fat, I grow thin. That is the natural order of things."

Rucellai regarded him in wonderment. "I had to tell you that on yesterday's post I received a letter from my cousin Bernardo. Florence is planning a sculpture competition."

Michelangelo's right hand began to tremble; he put his left hand over it to quiet it.

"To compete for what . . .?"

"Bernardo's letters says: *'To bring to perfection the marble column already blocked out by Agostino di Duccio, and now stored in the workshop of the cathedral.'*"

"The Duccio block!"

"You know it?"

"I tried to buy it from the Signoria for my Hercules."

"That could be an advantage, if you remember it well."

"I can see it before my eyes as though it were lying at our feet in this room."

"Can you make something good of it?"

Michelangelo's eyes shone. "*Dio mio.*"

"My letter says the Council described the marble as 'badly blocked.'"

"No, no, it is a noble block. The original massing in the quarry was badly done, and Duccio dug in too deeply at the centre . . ."

"Then you want to try for the competition?"

"More than anything in my whole life! Tell me, what

must the theme be: political, religious? Is it for Florentine sculptors only? Must I be there to compete? Will they . . .?"

"Whoa, whoa," cried Rucellai. "I have no further information. But I will ask Bernardo to send me full particulars."

"I'll come next Sunday to hear the news."

Rucellai laughed. "There won't be time for a reply, but come to dinner and we'll fatten you up for the competition."

"May I wait until you receive an answer?"

It took three weeks for Rucellai to summon him. Michelangelo sprinted up the steps to the library.

"Some news, not much. The date of the competition has not been set. It won't be until next year at the earliest. Themes can be submitted only by sculptors in Florence. . . ."

"I shall have to be back there."

"But the nature of the work has not yet been determined by the Council of the Wool Guild and the overseers of the cathedral."

"The cathedral? Then it will have to be a religious marble. After the Pietà, I was hoping to carve something different."

"The Wool Guild is paying, so I imagine the choice will be theirs. If I know these gentry, it will be a Florentine sculpture."

"Florentine? Like Marzocco?"

Rucellai chuckled at Michelangelo's dismay.

"No, not another lion. A symbol representing the new Republic, perhaps. . . ."

Michelangelo scratched his scalp in perplexity, using his fingers like a toothed chisel.

"What kind of statue would represent the Republic?"

"Perhaps that will be part of the competition? For the artist to tell them."

Paolo kept feeding him the news as it arrived over the Sabatini mountains from Florence: the competition would take place in 1500, to celebrate the hundredth anniversary of the competition for the Baptistery doors. The Wool Guild hoped that, like the Ghiberti, Brunelleschi and Della Quercia competition a century before, the Duccio block would attract sculptors from all over Italy.

"But this is already summer of '99. I have so much work left on the Pietà." His face was anguished. "I cannot rush, it is too important, too dear to me. Suppose I don't finish in time . . ."

Paolo put an arm about his trembling shoulders.

"I will bring you information steadily. The Wool Guild will debate through many meetings and many months before they set the terms."

It was the Cardinal of San Dionigi who lost the race with time. His Grace never did get to see his sculpture completed, though he sent the last hundred ducats to Galli's bank at the beginning of August, when the sculpture was to have been installed. The cardinal died quietly in the midst of his offices. Jacopo Galli attended the funeral with Michelangelo, standing below a catafalque sixteen feet long between the columns of the church, and nine feet wide, with singers behind the main altar. Returning to the Galli home, Michelangelo asked:

"Who decides whether or not the Pietà is 'more beautiful than any work in marble to be seen in Rome to-day'?"

"The cardinal already decided that. After his visit with you in May. He said you were fulfilling the contract. That's good enough for me. When do you think it will be finished?"

"I have still six to eight months of work."

"In time for the Centennial Year, then. That will give you an audience from all over Europe."

Michelangelo shifted uneasily in his seat.

"Would you send that last hundred ducats to my family? They are in some kind of trouble again."

Galli looked at him sharply. "That was your last payment. You say you have six to eight months of work left, and I have sent almost all of the cardinal's ducats to Florence. It begins to look like a bottomless well."

"This money I want to invest in buying a shop for my brothers, Buonarroto and Giovansimone. Buonarroto cannot seem to find a place for himself. Giovansimone, since Savonarola's death, takes jobs, then disappears for days. If they could find a good shop, and I shared in the profits . . ."

"Michelangelo, if neither of them is a good businessman, how are they going to make a profit?" Galli was exasperated; but when he spoke again his voice was solicitous. "I can't let you pour your last money down a hole. You must be practical and protect yourself against the future. Eighty per cent of your money from the Bacchus and the Pietà has gone to your family. I ought to know, I'm your banker."

Michelangelo hung his head, whispered, "Buonarroto won't work for anyone else, so I must set him up in business.

364

And if I don't get Giovansimone in a straight path now, I may never have another chance."

The money was transferred to Florence, Michelangelo keeping a few ducats for himself. At once, he began to need things: equipment for his carving, utensils for the house, clothes for himself and Argiento. He went on short rations, gave Argiento money for nothing but the simplest foods. Their clothing became ragged. It took a letter from Lodovico to bring him to his senses.

Dearest Son:
Buonarroto tells me that you live there in great misery. Misery is bad, since it is a vice displeasing to God and to one's fellow man, and also will hurt the soul and the body. . . . Live moderately and mind not to be in need, and abstain from discomfort. . . . Above all, take care of your head, keep it moderately warm and never wash yourself. Allow yourself to be rubbed, but do not wash yourself.

He went to Paolo Rucellai, borrowed the twenty-five florins he had returned two years before, took Argiento to the Trattoria Toscana for *bistecca alla fiorentina*. On the way home he bought himself and Argiento each a new shirt, a pair of long hose and sandals.

The next morning Sangallo arrived at the studio in a state of agitation, his golden moustaches bristling.

"Your favourite church, San Lorenzo in Damaso, is being destroyed. The hundred carved pillars are being pulled out."

Michelangelo was unable to follow his friend.

"Here, sit down. Now start over. What is happening to San Lorenzo?"

"Bramante, the new architect from Urbino. He has ingratiated himself with Cardinal Riario . . . sold him the idea of removing the pillars from the church and using them to complete his palace courtyard." Sangallo wrung his hands, as though wailing manually. "Do you think you could stop Bramante?"

"Me? But how? I have no influence with the cardinal, I have not seen him for almost two years . . ."

"Leo Baglioni. He has the cardinal's ear."

"I will go at once."

As he made his way to the Campo dei Fiori he tried to recall what he had been told about Bramante: fifty-five years old, from Urbino, he had worked as an architect for the

Duke of Milan, and had come to Rome early in the year, intent upon living on his Lombard savings until he had studied and mastered the architectural genius of the ancient Romans; somewhat, thought Michelangelo, as Sangallo had.

He had to wait for several hours for Baglioni. Leo listened with his features still, as he always did to other people's outbursts, then said quietly:

"Come, we'll go to see Bramante. It's his first commission in Rome. Since's he's ambitious, I doubt if you'll be able to get him to relinquish it."

On the short walk to the palace courtyard Leo described Bramante as "a quite amiable man, really, delightful to be with, always gay and cheerful, and a magnificent teller of jokes and riddles. I've never seen him lose his good nature. Bramante is making a lot of friends in Rome." He glanced sidewise at Michelangelo. "I can't say as much for you!"

They approached the palace. Leo said, "There he is now, measuring off the bases for the columns."

Michelangelo stood at the opening to the court, gazing at Bramante, disliking intensely at first sight the big-skulled head, bald, a few remaining curls at the nape, the big-boned forehead and eyebrows, the pale green eyes; a snubbed nose and rosebud-like mouth lost in the hugeness of the head. As Michelangelo watched, Bramante moved some stones aside, his bull-neck and muscled shoulders showing the power of an athlete.

Leo introduced them. Bramante greeted Michelangelo jovially, told them a humorous anecdote. Leo laughed heartily. Michelangelo was not amused.

"You do not like to laugh, Buonarroti?" asked Bramante.

"Reducing San Lorenzo to a shambles doesn't strike me as funny."

Bramante hunched his shoulders up around his jowl, as though he were a boxer protecting himself. Both men looked to Leo. Baglioni was remaining neutral.

"What business of yours are those columns?" asked Bramante, still courteous. "Are you Cardinal Riario's architect?"

"No, I'm not even his sculptor. But I happen to think this church one of the most beautiful in Italy. To destroy it is pure vandalism."

"On the contrary, those columns are coin of the realm. You know they were taken from the theatre of Pompey in 384 to put in the church? All of Rome is quarry for those who know how to use its stone. There is nothing I would not tear down if I had the opportunity to build something more beautiful in its place."

"Stone belongs in the place for which it was designed and carved."

"That's an old-fashioned idea, Buonarroti; stone belongs wherever an architect has need for it. What is old, dies."

"And a lot of new things are born dead!"

Bramante's good temper was exhausted.

"You do not know me. You cannot have come here of your own accord. Someone has put you up to it. Tell me, who is my adversary?"

"Your critic is the finest architect in all Italy, builder of Lorenzo de' Medici's Poggio a Caiano villa, designer of the palace of the Duke of Milan: Giuliano da Sangallo."

Bramante burst into sneering laughter.

"Giuliano da Sangallo! What has he been doing in Rome? Restoring the ceiling of a church! That's what the old fossil is good for. Within a year I shall chase him out of Rome for ever. Now if you will take yourself out of my way, I'll continue with the work of creating the most beautiful courtyard in all the world. Come back sometime and see how Bramante builds."

Walking to Baglioni's house, Leo said, "If I know Rome, he will make his way to the top. A bad man to have as an enemy."

"Something tells me I've got him," said Michelangelo grimly.

12

It was his task to impregnate the marble with manifest spirit; yet even in a religious theme he felt deeply for the whole man, alive to every nerve, muscle, vein, bone, to the skin and hair, fingers, eyes and mouth. All must come alive if he were to create power and monumentality by incorporating into the marble the strength of man. He carved upward, using his knowledge of the forms already released below, and an intuition as old and deep as the long-buried marble, to achieve the expression for Mary that emerged not only from her emotion but from the feeling of the whole sculpture. He stood with his head lower than Mary's, his hands opposite his forehead, the tools angled upward, carving as close as he could get to the drama of the Pietà. The block saw him face to face, the sculptor and the sculptured involved in the tender restrained sadness. He left far behind him the dark, unforgiving Pietàs, their message of love blotted out by blood. He would not sculpture agony. The nail holes in Christ's hands and feet were tiny dots. There was no sign of violence. Jesus slept peacefully in his mother's arms. Over the two figures there was a suffusion, a luminosity. His Christ awakened the deepest sympathy, not abhorrence for those who stood outside the sculpture and had been responsible.

His religious faith he projected in terms of the sublimity of the figures; the harmony between them was his way of portraying the harmony of God's universe. He did not attempt to make Christ divine, since he would not have known how, but exquisitely human. The Virgin's head emerged delicate, the features Florentine, the face of a maiden with silent pale composure. In her expression he made a distinction between divine and sublime; sublime, for him, meant supreme and perfect. He reflected, "The meaning of the figures lies in their human qualities; the beauty of face and form portrays the grandeur of their spirit."

He found that he was achieving a tactile richness, with the forms mirroring the loving days he had devoted to them.

Balducci brought him the news that Sansovino, his fellow apprentice in the Medici garden, had returned to Florence after working for a number of years in Portugal, and been commissioned to do a marble group of St. John Baptizing Christ for the Baptistery. He was looked upon as the logical choice to win the Duccio block commission.

"Sansovino is a good sculptor," said Michelangelo loyally.

"Better than you?"

He swallowed hard before he replied. "He finishes well everything he starts."

"Do you think he can win over you?"

Again Michelangelo struggled with his answer. "We both will do our best."

"I've never seen you modest before."

Michelangelo blushed. He was grimly determined to out-design Sansovino and win the contest; but he would not talk Sansovino down.

"Leo Baglioni tells me I have few friends. Sansovino is a friend. I intend to keep him."

"Torrigiani is also entering the competition, and is telling everyone that he will get the Duccio marble because he was an anti-Medici man; and that, since you backed Piero, you won't be allowed to compete. Paolo Rucellai says you must return to Florence in time to make your peace with the Signoria."

This intelligence cost him several nights of sleep. He had occasion to bless Baglioni for his generous supply of goat tallow candles.

In mid-January snow began to fall, and fell heavily for two days, accompanied by wind from the north. The piercing cold lasted for several weeks. Michelangelo's enclosed courtyard was piled high with snow. Inside the rooms were frigid. There was no way to keep the icy boreal wind from coming in through the wood and linen shutters. The three braziers made no impression. Michelangelo worked with his hat and earmuffs on, and a blanket pinned around his shoulders. Again in February the snow and ice came. The city was still, the markets abandoned, the shops closed because the ice, sleet and frozen mud made the streets impassable.

Michelangelo and Argiento suffered. Michelangelo took the boy into bed with him to combine their warmth. Damp oozed through the whitewash on the walls. The leaks were slower under the compacted snow, but lasted longer. Coal was in short supply, the price went up so heavily that Michelangelo could buy only a minimum amount. Argiento spent hours scratching in the snow of the surrounding fields looking for wood for his fire.

Michelangelo caught cold, went down with fever. Argiento found two bricks at an interrupted building job, heated them in his fire, wrapped them in towels and alternated them on Michelangelo's feet to keep down the chill. He fed him hot beef broth. No work was done; for how many days Michelangelo lost count. Fortunately there remained only the polishing. He did not have the strength for the heavy manual labour involved in the cutting.

For his Pietà he hoped to achieve the highest polish of which marble was capable, a faultless velvety loftiness. On the first warm day he walked to Trastevere and bought several large lumps of pumice, divided them with a blow of the hammer, searching for flatter surfaces. Now he could grip the pieces in the palm of his hand, using the long, silky parallel strands to polish the broad planes of the Madonna's robe, of Christ's chest and legs: slowly, with infinite patience, over long days and weeks.

Now he needed sharper edges, split the pumice with his chisel, cut the appropriate shapes to reach into the recessions, cavities and undulations of hair, cloth, fingernails. Finally, he made sharp-edged slivers that looked like primitive arrow-heads to polish the curves around Christ's nostrils. He did not finish the back of Mary since the statue was to sit in a niche, but left the marble lined and blocked, as were the rough rocks on which she was sitting. The white marble, polished and gleaming, lighted up the dinghy room as though it were a stained-glass chapel. The homely artist had indeed created a work of beauty.

Sangallo was the first to see the finished sculpture. He made no comment on the religious aspect of the marble, but congratulated Michelangelo on the architecture of the tri-angular composition, the balance of lines and masses.

Jacopo Galli came to the studio and studied the Pietà in silence. After a time he said softly, " I have fulfilled my con-tract with the Cardinal of San Dionigi: this is the most beautiful work in marble to be seen in Rome to-day."

" I'm nervous about the installation," said Michelangelo. " Our contract doesn't say that we have the right to put the Pietà in St. Peter's. With the cardinal dead . . ."

" We wont' ask any questions. We'll install it without a sound. What no one knows, no one can object to."

Michelangelo was aghast. " You mean, sneak my sculp-ture in?"

" Nothing furtive. Just discreet. Once the Pietà is sitting in its niche, no one will bother to have it removed."

" But the Pope was fond of the cardinal. He gave him a three-day funeral. He granted him permission to put a sculpture in the Chapel of the Kings. Why should anyone want to have it removed?"

" I'm sure they won't," said Galli reassuringly. " Suppose you hire those stoneyard friends of yours to help you. To-morrow, after dinner, while the city is resting."

There were so many obtruding parts: hands, feet, folds, that he did not dare to entrust the moving of the marble to beams or crowbars, no matter how securely he wrapped it. He asked Guffatti to come to the workshop, showed him the Pietà and discussed the problem with him. Guffatti stood in front of the sculpture in silence, then said:

" I bring the family."

The family turned out to include not merely three husky sons but a variety of cousins. They would not allow Michelangelo to touch the piece, wrapping it in a half dozen mangy blankets and then, accompanied by a medley of cries, arguments and commands, lifting it on its base. They carried the Pietà, eight strong, to the ancient wagon with its bed of straw, and roped it in. With Michelangelo guarding the tailgate, they made their way cautiously along the cobbled Via Posterula, across the Sant'Angelo bridge, then down the newly opened, smooth Via Alessandrina, which the Pope had rebuilt to celebrate the Centennial Year. For the first time since he had come to Rome, Michelangelo had occasion to bless the Borgia.

The Guffatti stopped their wagon at the foot of the thirty-five steps. Only the fact that they were under a sacred burden kept them from cursing as they carried the heavy marble up the first three sections of seven steps, set it down to rest and wipe the perspiration from their brows, then picked it up again to carry to the atrium, past the splashing fountain and to the church door.

Here, while the Guffatti stopped once more to rest, Michelangelo had a chance to observe that the basilica was leaning even more sharply than when he had begun work. It was now so dilapidated it seemed beyond repair. He swallowed hard at the thought of putting his lovely Pietà in a basilica which had not long to remain upright. Surely the first wind to roar down off the Alban hills would flatten it? He had an image of himself crawling over the rubble to find the fragments of his shattered statue, was reassured only when he remembered Sangallo's architectural drawings which showed how St. Peter's could be counterpropped.

The Guffatti once again picked up the load. Michelangelo led them into the basilica, with its five corresponding naves and hundreds of columns assembled from all over Rome; then into the Chapel of the Kings of France, to the left of a huge figure of Christ enthroned. The Guffatti lowered their bundle carefully before the empty niche, unwrapped the blankets, wiped their hands clean of sweat, raised the Pietà reverentially to its place. Michelangelo straightened it to the position he wanted. The Guffatti family bought candles from an old woman in black, lit them before the statue.

They refused to take one scudo for their hours of back-breaking labour.

"We take our pay in heaven," said the father.

371

It was the best tribute Michelangelo could receive. It was also the only tribute he received.

Jacopo Galli came into the chapel, accompanied by Balducci. His head bobbed with pleasure. Guffatti, standing amidst his relatives, asked: "Is this all? No services? No blessing by the priest?"

Galli answered, "It was blessed in the carving."

The Guffatti and Argiento knelt before the Virgin, crossed themselves, murmured a prayer. Michelangelo gazed up at the Pietà, feeling sad and depleted. As he reached the door of the chapel and turned back for a last look, he saw that the Virgin too was sad and lonely; the most alone human being God ever put on earth.

He returned to St. Peter's day after day. Few of the city's pilgrims bothered to visit the Chapel of the Kings of France. Those who did hastily genuflected before the Pietà, crossed themselves and moved on.

Because Galli had advised discretion, few in Rome knew the statue had been installed. Michelangelo could get no reaction, even of the mixed kind he had received in Galli's garden from the poets and academicians. Paolo Rucellai, Sangallo, Cavalcanti visited St. Peter's; the rest of the Florentine colony, grieved over the execution of Savonarola, refused to go inside the Vatican walls.

After nearly two years of dedicated work, Michelangelo sat in his cheerless room, now empty, despondent. No one came to speak of sculpture. He was so exhausted that he could not even think of the Duccio block. Nor did Galli believe this the appropriate time to cry up a new job for him.

One afternoon he wandered into St. Peter's, saw a family with several grown children, from Lombardy, he guessed by their clothes and dialect, standing in front of his Pietà, making elaborate gestures of the hands. He went to their side to eavesdrop.

"I tell you I recognize the work," cried the mother of the family. "It is by that fellow from Osteno, who makes all the tombstones."

Her husband waved the fingers of both his hands loosely, shaking off this idea as a dog shakes off water.

"No, no, it is one of our countrymen, Cristoforo Solari, called 'The Hunchback,' from Milan. He has done many of them."

That night Michelangelo made his way through the streets,

green sailcloth bag in hand. He entered St. Peter's, took a candle from the bag, put it in the wire loop of his hat, reached into the bag again for hammer and chisel. He raised his tools, leaned forward across the Christ so that the candle cast a steady glow on the Virgin's bosom. On to the band going tightly between the breasts he cut in swift, decorative letters:

MICHAEL·AGLVS·BONAROVS·FLOENT FACEBAT

Michelangelo Buonarroti of Florence made this.

He returned to his rooms, packed his things. The hundreds of drawings he had done for the Bacchus and Pietà he burned in Argiento's fire, while Argiento summoned Balducci. Balducci arrived, his shirt askew and hair tousled, promised to resell the furniture to the dealer in Trastevere.

Just before dawn, each carrying a sailcloth bag, Michelangelo and Argiento made their way to the Porta del Popolo. Michelangelo rented two mules, joined the pack train, and at first light set out for Florence.

BOOK SIX

THE GIANT

1

The warm June Florentine sun flooded his face as he gazed out of the window at the tawny stone towerhouse of the superintendent of the Florentine Guilds. Returning from Rome with no commissions, and no funds, he had been obliged to send Argiento back to his family's farm outside Ferrara, and himself return to his father's board. However, he occupied the front and best room of the commodious apartment in which the Buonarroti now lived, for Lodovico had invested some part of the Rome earnings to good advantage. He had bought a small house in San Pietro Maggiore, used the income from it to clear the title to the disputed Buonarroti property near Santa Croce, then raised the family's social position by renting this floor in this house in the more fashionable Street of St. Proculus, a block from the superb stone pile of the Pazzi palace.

The death of Lucrezia had aged Lodovico; his face was thinner, the cheeks sunken; in compensation he had allowed his hair to grow in a thick mass down to his shoulders. As Jacopo Galli had predicted, nothing had come of the business Michelangelo had hoped to set up for Buonarroto and Giovansimone. Buonarroto had at last settled down in the Strozzi wool shop near the Porta Rossa; Giovansimone was a crushed youth, apathetically taking jobs, then disappearing after a few weeks. Sigismondo, barely able to read and write, was earning a few scudi as a hired soldier for Florence in its present hostilities against Pisa. Lionardo had disappeared, no one knew into what monastery. His aunt Cassandra and uncle Francesco were beset with minor ills.

He and Granacci had clasped each other in a hilarious embrace, happy to be together. During the past years Granacci had come into the first half of his fortune and, as the gossip Jacopo of the Ghirlandaio *bottega* reported gleefully, was keeping a mistress in a villa in the hills of Bellosguardo, above the Porta Romana. Granacci still maintained his headquarters at Ghirlandaio's, helping out David Ghirlandaio after his brother Benedetto's death, in return for using the studio for his own work. He riffled through the sketches on Michelangelo's worktable.

"Open for business, I see."

"Best-stocked shop in Florence."

"Any customers?"

"None. I'm joining Soggi."

Granacci chuckled. "He's been quite a success. Just bought space for a butcher shop in the New Market."

"The Bertoldo method of carving calves."

They set out for an *osteria* under the trees, turned left on the Via del Proconsolo, past the gracious Badia church, into the Borgo dei Greci with its Serristori palace designed by Baccio d'Agnolo and into the Via dei Benci. Here were the ancient Ghibelline Bardelli palace and the first of the Alberti palaces, with its columned courtyard and capitals by Giuliano da Sangallo.

Florence spoke to him. The stones spoke to him. He felt their character, the variety of structures, the strength of their impacted layers. How wonderful to be back where *pietra serena* was the material of architecture. To some people stone was dead; "hard as stone," "stone cold," they said. To him, as he once again ran his fingers along its contours, it was the most alive substance in the world, rhythmic, responsive, tractable: warm, resilient, colourful, vibrant. He was in love with stone.

The restaurant was on the Lungarno, located in a garden shaded by fig trees. The owner, who was also the cook, went down to the river, raised a basket on ropes, wiped off a bottle of Trebbiano on his apron and opened it at the table. They drank to Michelangelo's return.

He climbed the familiar Settignano hills to see the Topolinos, found that Bruno and Enrico had married. Each had added a stone room to his new family on the far side of the house. Already there were five grandchildren, and both wives were again pregnant. He commented:

"The Topolinos are going to control all the *pietra serena* carving of Florence, if you keep up this pace."

"We'll keep up," said Bruno. The mother added, "Your friend, Contessina de' Medici, she too had another son, after her daughter died."

He had already learned that Contessina had been banished from Florence and lived in exile with her husband and son in a peasant's house on the north slope of Fiesole, their home and possessions having been confiscated when her father-in-law, Niccolò Ridolfi, was hanged for participating in a conspiracy to overthrow the Republic and bring Piero back as King of Florence. His affection for Contessina had not changed, though the years had passed without his seeing her. He had never felt wanted at the Ridolfi palace, and so he had not gone to visit; how then could he go to her after his return from Rome, when she was living in poverty and disgrace? Might not any visit, now that they were plagued by misfortune, be construed as pity?

The city itself had undergone many perceivable changes in the almost five years he had been gone. Walking through the Piazza della Signoria, the people bowed their heads in shame when they passed the spot where Savonarola's body had been burned; at the same time they were smothering their consciences under a tornado of activity, trying to replace what Savonarola had destroyed, spending large sums with the gold and silversmiths, the gem cutters, the costume makers, the embroiderers, designers of terra-cotta and wood mosaics, the makers of musical instruments, the manuscript illuminators. Piero Soderini, whom Lorenzo de' Medici had trained as the brightest of the young men in politics, and whom Michelangelo had often seen at the palace, was now at the head of the Florentine Republic as *Gonfaloniere,* or mayor-governor of Florence and the city-state. He had achieved a measure of harmony among the Florentine factions for the first time since the mortal battle between Lorenzo and Savonarola had begun.

Florentine artists who had fled the city had sensed the upsurge of activity and returned from Milan, Venice, Portugal, Paris: Piero di Cosimo, Filippino Lippi, Andrea Sansovino, Benedetto da Rovezzano, Leonardo da Vinci, Benedetto Buglioni. Those whose work has been stopped by Savonarola's influence and power were now producing again: Botticelli, Pollaiuolo, the architect, known as *Il Cronaca,* the storyteller, Rosselli, Lorenzo di Credi, Baccio da Montelupo, jester and scandal bearer of the Medici sculpture garden. They had organized a Company of the Cauldron, and while it was restricted to only twelve members, each was allowed to bring four guests to the monthly dinner meeting in Rustici's enormous sculpture studio. Granacci was a member. He had immediately invited Michelangelo to accompany him.

Michelangelo had refused, preferring to wait until he had a commission.

The months since his return had contained little real pleasure. He had left for Rome a boy, returned a man, ready to carve mountains of marble; but as he turned to gaze sightlessly at his Madonna and Child and Centaurs, which he had affixed on nails to the side wall of his combination workroom and bedroom, he thought unhappily that as far as Florence knew he might never have carved the Bacchus or Pietà.

Jacopo Galli was still working for him in Rome: the Mouscron brothers from Bruges, who imported cloth from England into Rome, had seen the Pietà and were interested in a Madonna and Child. Galli thought he could secure an excellent contrast on the Mouscrons' next visit to Rome. He had also interested Cardinal Piccolomini in employing Michelangelo to carve the figures needed to complete the family altar honouring his uncle Pope Pius II, in the cathedral in Siena.

" Without Galli," he muttered, " I'm out of business. While the grass is growing, the horse starves."

Immediately on his return he had gone to the Duomo workshop to study the seventeen-foot Duccio column called by some a " thin piece," by others " emaciated," to search its innerness for ideas, testing it again and reiterating to Beppe:

" *Il marmo è sano*. The marble is sound."

At night he read by candlelight in Dante and in the Old Testament, looking for a mood and a heroic theme.

Then he learned that the members of the Wool Guild and the Board of Works of the cathedral had been unable to make up their minds about the carving of the giant block. It was just as well, thought Michelangelo, for he also had heard that many favoured giving the commission to Leonardo da Vinci, recently returned to Florence, because of the magnificent reputation of his huge equestrian statue of Count Sforza, and his painting of the Last Supper in the refectory of Santa Maria delle Grazie in Milan.

Michelangelo had never met Leonardo, who had abandoned Florence for Milan some eighteen years before, after being acquitted on a morals charge; but Florentine artists were saying that he was the greatest draughtsman in Italy. Nettled, curious, Michelangelo had gone to Santissima Annunziata when the cartoon for Leonardo's Virgin and Child and St. Anne was on exhibition. He had stood before the cartoon with his heart beating like a hammer. Never had he seen such power or authenticity of drawing, such forceful truth about the figure, except, of course, in his own work. In a folio on a bench he had found the sketch of a male nude seen from the rear, with arms and legs outstretched. No one had rendered the male figure in this fashion, so galvanically alive and convincing. Leonardo, he was certain, had dissected! He had pulled the bench up in front of the three figures and plunged into copying, had left the church chastened. If the Boards granted the commission to Leonardo, who could contest their decision? Could he, with only a few reports of his Bacchus and Pietà beginning to filter northward to indicate his stature?

Then Leonardo had rejected the commission. On the grounds that he despised marble sculpture as an inferior art, good only for artisans. Michelangelo heard the news in a state of turmoil. He was glad to have the Duccio block free, and Leonardo da Vinci out of the running; but he felt a resentment against the man for his belittling statement, which all Florence took up and was repeating.

One darkness before dawn he rose, dressed hurriedly, ran through the empty Via del Proconsolo to the Duomo workshop, and stood at the corner of the column. The diagonal beams of first sunlight streamed across the marble, projecting his shadow upward the full seventeen-foot length of the column, magnifying his silhouette and turning him into a giant. He caught his breath, thought of David as he knew his story from the Bible. "This is how David must have felt," he told himself, "on that morning when he stepped forth to face Goliath." A giant for the symbol of Florence!

He returned home, reread the David chapter with heightened perception. For days he drew from memory virile male figures, seeking a David worthy of the biblical legend. He submitted design after design to his former Medici palace acquaintance, Gonfaloniere Soderini; to the Wool Guild; to the Board of Works of the cathedral. But nothing happened. He was stalemated; and he was burning up with marble fever.

2

His father was waiting for him in a black leather chair in the family room at the rear of the apartment. On his lap was an envelope which had just arrived on the Rome post. Michelangelo opened it with a knife. Inside were several closely written sheets in Jacopo Galli's handwriting informing Michelangelo that he was about to get Cardinal Piccolomini's signature on a contract. "However I must warn you," Galli wrote, "that it is by no means the kind of commission you want or deserve."

"Read it to me," cried Lodovico, his dark amber eyes alight with pleasure.

Michelangelo's face dropped as he learned that he would have to carve fifteen small figures, all of them fully clothed, to fit into the narrow niches of an Andrea Bregno traditional altar. The drawings would have to be approved by the cardinal, and the marbles recarved if the final pieces did not please His Grace. The pay was five hundred ducats; Michelangelo could take no other contract for three years, by the end of which time the final figure had to be completed and approved.

Lodovico warmed his hands in front of his chest as though it were a brazier.

"Five hundred gold ducats for three years' work. Not as good as you did in Rome, but added to our rents, a modest living."

"Not really, Father. I must pay for the marble. And if the cardinal doesn't approve I must rework the figures or carve altogether new ones."

"Since when can't you please a cardinal? If Galli, a shrewd banker, is willing to guarantee you make the best statues in Italy, why should we be foolish enough to worry? How much are they paying in advance? 'He that gives quickly, gives twice.'"

"There is no advance."

"How do they imagine you are going to buy supplies? Do they think the money is coming from me?"

"No, Father, I'm sure they know better than that."

"Thanks to God! Galli must make it part of the contract that they advance you one hundred gold ducats before you begin work. Then we're safe."

Michelangelo slumped into a chair.

"Three years of carving draperies. And never once a figure of my own choosing."

He jumped up out of the chair, ran through the apartment and slammed out of the door. He took the short cut past the Bargello and the Piazza San Firenze, through a narrow side street into the blazing light of the Piazza della Signoria. He turned aside from a pile of fine grey ash, put there in the deep of night by the faithful to commemorate the spot where Savonarola had been burned, went to the broad steps leading up into the Signoria courtyard. On the left was a stone staircase which he took three steps at a time, then was in the majestic high-ceilinged Council Hall where the meetings of the Florentine Council were held, with space for a thousand citizens to take their stand. The vast hall was empty and bare except for a table and a dozen chairs on a podium at the far side.

He turned to a door on his left admitting to the chambers which had always been occupied by the *podestà,* such as his friend Gianfrancesco Aldovrandi had been, but was now occupied by Piero Soderini, latest in the tradition of sixteen Soderini ancestors who had been Gonfalonieri before him.

Michelangelo was readily admitted to Soderini's office. It was a magnificent corner room overlooking the piazza and rooftops of much of Florence; elegant, panelled in dark wood, with a broad ceiling painted with the lilies of Florence. Behind a massive oak desk sat the chief magistrate of the Republic. On his last trip to Rome, Soderini had been told by the Florentine colony about the Bacchus, and been taken to St. Peter's to see the Pietà.

"*Ben venuto,*" Soderini murmured, "what brings you to the seat of your government on this warm afternoon?"

"Troubles, Gonfaloniere," replied Michelangelo, "but I suppose no one comes up here to unburden his pleasures?"

"That's why I sit behind such a capacious desk: so that it can hold all the problems of Florence."

"It is your shoulders that are broad."

Soderini ducked his head deprecatingly: by no means a handsome head. At fifty-one his blond hair, covered by a strangely shaped cap, was bleaching white, his chin was long and pointed, his nose hooked, his skin yellowish, the eyebrows irregularly arched over mild hazel eyes that were devoid of audacity or cunning. Florence said that Soderini had three virtues not combined in any other Tuscan of the day; he was honest, he was plain, and he could induce opposing factions to work together.

Michelangelo told Piero Soderini about the proposed Piccolomini contract.

"I don't want this commission, Gonfaloniere. I'm on fire to carve the Giant! Can't you force the Boards of the Duomo and the Wool Guild to decide about the competition? If I don't get it, at least it will be out of my range of possibility. I could go on to this Piccolomini contract as something I can't escape."

He was breathing hard. Soderini gazed at him blandly across the broad desk.

"This is not a good time to force things. We're exhausted from our war with Pisa. Cæsar Borgia is threatening to conquer Florence. Last night the Signoria bought him off. Thirty-six thousand gold florins a year for three years, his salary for serving as captain general of the Florentine forces."

"Blackmail," said Michelangelo.

Soderini's face turned red. "Many do kiss the hand they wish to see cut off. The city has no way of knowing how much more it will have to pay Cæsar Borgia. The Guilds have to provide this money for the Signoria. So you can understand why the Wool Guild is not in the mood to discuss a sculpture competition."

An emotional silence filled the space between them.

"Hadn't you better be more receptive to the Piccolomini offer?" suggested Soderini.

Michelangelo groaned. "Cardinal Piccolomini wants to choose all fifteen subjects. I cannot carve until he approves the designs. And what wages: thirty-three and a third ducats for each figure, enough to pay rent, but supplies . . ."

"How long since you've carved marble?"

"More than a year."

"Or been paid?"

"More than two."

Michelangelo's lips trembled. "You don't understand. This altar was made by Bregno. All the marbles have to be fully clothed; they must go into dark niches where they will be seen only as rigid still lifes. How can I tie up three whole years of my life filling Bregno's highly decorated altar with more decorations?"

His agonized cry hung heavily in the room.

"Do to-day what you must do to-day," said Soderini in an

annealing voice. "To-morrow you will be free to do what you must do to-morrow. We bought off Cæsar Borgia. For you as an artist it is the same as with us as a city-state; only one law prevails: survival."

At Santo Spirito, Prior Bichiellini, sitting behind the desk in his manuscript-lined office, pushed his papers aside, his eyes blazing behind the spectacles.

"Survival on what plane? To stay alive as an animal stays alive? For shame! The Michelangelo I knew six years ago could never think, 'Better mediocre work than no work at all.' This is opportunism, fit for mediocre talent."

"I agree, Father."

"Then don't take the commission. Do the best that is in you, or nothing at all."

"In the long run, you are right; in the short run I suppose Soderini and my father are right."

"There are no long and short runs," the prior cried, his voice heavy with indignation. "There is only a God-given number of years in which to work and fulfil yourself. Don't squander them."

Michelangelo hung his head in shame.

"If I sound like a moralist," said the prior quietly, "please remember that it is my job to be concerned with your character."

Michelangelo went out into the bright sunlight, sat on the edge of the fountain in the Piazza Santo Spirito and splashed cold water on his face, even as he had on those nights when he had emerged from the dead room. He groaned aloud, "Three years! *Dio mio!*"

Back in his studio, Granacci barely listened to him.

"Without work, Michelangelo, you are the most wretched creature alive. What does it matter if you have to carve dull statues? Your worst will be better than anybody else's best."

"You're maddening: you insult and flatter me in the same breath."

Granacci grinned. "Do as many figures as you have time for. Everybody in Florence will help you outwit Siena."

"Outwit a cardinal?"

Granacci grew serious. "I'm trying to face reality. You want to carve, ergo, take the Piccolomini contract and do the best you can. When something better comes along, you'll sculpture better. Come and have dinner with me and the Company."

Michelangelo shook his head. "No."

3

He returned to the drawing board, to sketches of the Madonna for the Mouscrons, attempts to capture saints for the Piccolomini contract. But he could think of nothing but the Duccio column and the Giant-David. In 1 Kings 16: 17, he found himself reading:

Meanwhile the Lord's spirit passed away from Saul . . . an evil mood came upon him that gave him no rest. When Saul said, "Find one who can play the harp well, and bring him to me," one of his servants replied, "I myself have met such a man, a skilful player indeed, a son of Jesse the Bethlehemite. He is sturdy besides and a tried warrior, well spoken and personable, and the Lord is with him . . .

Some time later, when Saul questioned the wisdom of David's meeting Goliath in battle, David replied:

My Lord, I used to feed my father's flock; and if lion or bear came and carried off one of my rams, I would go in pursuit, and get the mastery and snatch the prey from their jaws. Did they threaten me, I would catch them by the throat and strangle them. Lion or bear, my Lord, I would slay them.

He sat staring at the lines: "lion or bear . . . I would catch them by the throat and strangle them." Was there any greater feat of strength or courage in the Bible? A young man, without weapons or armour, had pursued the most powerful of beasts, caught them and strangled them with his bare hands.

Could any of the Davids he had seen in Florence have conceived such an act, let alone executed it? In the morning he stopped before the Castagno painting, gazing at the youthful David, with slender arms and legs, small hands and feet, a mass of hair blowing about the delicate-featured, pretty face, somehow seeming halfway between man and woman. He next went to see Antonio Pollaiuolo's David Victor, somewhat older than Castagno's, with feet solidly on the ground, but with tiny, ladylike fingers crooked as though he were about to eat a custard. There was a well-developed torso and a determination about the stance, but he was dressed in the lace-trimmed coat with matching lace under-

shirt of a Florentine nobleman, the most expensively, aristocratically dressed shepherd boy on earth, mused Michelangelo.

He ran to the Palazzo della Signoria, mounted the steps to
the Sala dei Gigli. Outside the door stood Verrocchio's
bronze David, a wistful adolescent. Inside the Sala was
Donatello's first David, carved in marble. Michelangelo
never saw it but he gasped at the sensitivity and finish of
the flesh. The hands were strong, the one visible leg under
the long, luxuriant robe was heavier than in the paintings of
Castagno and Pollaiuolo, the neck thicker. But the eyes were
blank, there was a flaccid underchin, a weak mouth, a wreath
of leaves and berries crowning the expressionless face.

He descended the stone steps to the courtyard and stood
before Donatello's bronze David, with which he had lived
for two years in the courtyard of the Medici, and which
had been appropriated by the city after the sack of the
palace. It was a sculpture he admired passionately, the
legs and feet sturdy enough to carry the body, with strong
arms and neck. Yet now that he looked at it critically he
saw that, like the other Florentine Davids, this one had
pretty features, an almost feminine face under the decorated
hat, and long curls hanging down over the shoulders.
Though it had the genitals of a young boy, it also had the
budding breasts of a young girl.

He returned home, fragments of ideas racing through his
mind. These Davids, particularly the two beloved Donatellos,
were boys. They could no more have strangled lions and
bears than they could have killed Goliath whose head
rested between their feet. Why had the best artists of
Florence depicted David as either an adolescent or an elegantly
garbed and groomed young dandy? Had no other artist
read beyond the description of David as " red-cheeked, fair of
face, pleasant of mien "; had they not gone on to, " Did they
threaten me, I would catch them by the throat and strangle
them. Lion or bear . . . I would slay them."

David was a man! He had accomplished these feats before
the Lord chose him. What he did he did alone, with his
great heart and great hands. Such a man would not
hesitate to face a Goliath so gigantic that he could carry
a breastplate of mail weighing a thousand pounds. What
was Goliath to a young man who had mixed with lions
and bears and beaten them in fair battle?

At dawn he walked streets still wet from their scrubbing,
carrying his measuring equipment to the Duomo workyard.

He computed his figures on the column, calculated to a hairsbreadth the distance between the deepest point of gouging to the point on the opposite side to see if it were possible to design a David whose thighs, the shortest distance across the body, could be fitted into the marble that was left.

"No good," commented Beppe. "For fifty years I watch sculptors measure across here. Always they say, 'Too bad. No figure will fit.'"

"It's a matter of invention, Beppe. Look, I'll draw the silhouette of the block, for you. This dot indicates the deepest point of gouging, halway down the column. Now suppose we were to swivel the hips away from this narrow area, and opposite use a strongly out-pushing wrist or hand to compensate . . .?"

Beppe raked his behind.

"Ah," cried Michelangelo, "you think it might work! I can tell how pleased you are by what part of your anatomy you scratch."

The weeks passed. He learned that Rustici had decided that the project was too big for him. Sansovino required an added block of marble to get anything out of the Duccio column. The half dozen other sculptors in town, including Baccio, Buglioni andd Benedetto da Rovezzano, had walked away from the column, saying that since the deep gouging had been done midway down its length it must certainly break in two at that narrow point.

A courier brought a packet from Rome containing the Piccolomini contract:

. . . The most Reverend Cardinal of Siena commits to Michelangelo, son of Lodovico Buonarroti-Simoni, sculptor from Florence, to make fifteen statues of Carrara marble, which is to be new, clean, and white and not veined, but as perfect as it is necessary to make first-quality statues, each one of which should be two *braccia* high, and which should be completed in three years for the amount of five hundred large gold ducats . . .

Jacopo Galli had secured an advance of a hundred ducats by guaranteeing to return the money to Cardinal Piccolomini if Michelangelo died before he finished the last three statues. Cardinal Piccolomini approved Michelangelo's first sketches. But there was a line in the contract which carried the crowning indignity. "As a figure of St. Francis has already been sculptured by Pietro Torrigiani, who left the draperies and head unfinished, Michelangelo will complete the statue out of honour and courtesy, in Siena, so that the statue can stand among the others made by him, and anybody who sees it would say that it is the work of Michelangelo's hand."

" I never knew that Torrigiani started this contract," Michelangelo cried to Granacci. " Think of the ignominy of my scavenging after him."

" Harsh words," said Granacci. " Let's just say that Torrigiani was incapable of finishing even one figure adequately, and so Cardinal Piccolomini had to turn to you to make it right."

Galli urged that Michelangelo sign the contract and commence work at once. " Next spring, when the Mouscron brothers come from Bruges, I will get you that free-standing Madonna and Child to carve. There will be better things for the future."

He gathered up an armful of new sketches for the David and went again to plead with Piero Soderini. The commission must come to him if only the Gonfaloniere could force the Wool Guild to act.

" Yes, I might force it through," agreed Soderini. " But then the Boards would have acted against their will. They would resent you. They must want this piece carved and must choose you as their sculptor. You perceive the difference?"

" Yes," said Michelangelo sadly, " it makes sense. Only I can't wait any longer."

Off the Via del Proconsolo, a few steps down from the Badia, was an archway that looked as though it led into the courtyard of a palace. Michelangelo had passed it innumerable times on his way from his house to the sculpture garden, and knew that it provided the opening to an artisans' piazza, a private world surrounded by the backs of palaces, truncated towers and two-story houses. It sheltered some twenty workshops of leather tanners, coppersmiths, carpenters, wool dyers, flax weavers, scissors makers preparing their products for the shops in the open markets and on the popular streets of the Corso and Pellicceria. Here he found a workshop for rent, one that had been occupied by a shoemaker, on the south side of the oval shaped piazza, getting most of the day's sun. He paid three months' rent in advance, sent a letter in care of the Gesuati of

Ferrara to Argiento telling him to come back to work, bought a truckle bed for the shop for him to sleep on.

In the June heat the craftsmen worked at benches in front of their narrow slots, the dyers' arms stained blue, green and red, the metal-workers in their leather aprons, bare to their burly waists, the carpenters sawing, planing, filling the air with clean-smelling shavings; all making the indigenous noises of their trade, blended together compactly in the closed-in area, creating the kind of companionable background music in which Michelangelo felt at home. Surrounded by simple workmen, the workshop afforded him the same busy privacy he had enjoyed from his worktable in Rome, overlooking the bustle of the Bear Hotel.

Argiento arrived, dust-covered and footsore, chattering straight through a morning as he scrubbed out the vestiges of the shoemaker's tenancy, unable to contain his relief at being off his brother's farm.

" Argiento, I don't understand. In Rome you walked into the *campagna* every Sunday to see the horses . . ."

Argiento raised his perspiration-streaked face from his bucket of suds. " Farms I like to visit, not to work."

The carpenter across the way helped them build a draughting table just inside the door. Argiento scoured the Street of the Ironmongers to find a secondhand forge. Michelangelo bought iron rods, baskets of chestnut wood to make his chisels. He found two blocks of marble in Florence, sent specifications for three more to Carrara. Then, without clay or wax models, without looking at the designs approved by Cardinal Piccolomini, he set up the four-foot blocks and in the sheer joy of having his hands back in marble carved first the St. Paul, bearded, with fine features bespeaking the first Christian missionary's Roman citizenship and contact with Greek culture, the body, though covered by voluminous robes, muscular and tense. Without pause he went on to the St. Peter, closest of Christ's disciples, witness of Christ's resurrection, a rock on which the new Church was founded. This statue was quieter physically and mentally, reflective in spirit, with an interesting arrangement of vertical draperies accented by a softly flowing horizontal scarf over the chest and arms.

The workmen of the piazza accepted him as another skilled artisan who arrived in labourer's clothes at dawn, just after an apprentice had washed down the communal square, and who quit at dark, his hair, face, nostrils, shirt, bare legs and feet covered with white marble dust, even as they were covered with wood shavings or dye or tiny strands of leather or flax. Sometimes one of them would call out in a full voice above the saws, hammers and scraping knives, while Michelangelo's chisels were singing through the white marble like ploughs through the spring earth:

"It's a miracle! All Florence swelters in the heat, and in our piazza we have a snowstorm."

He kept the whereabouts of his workshop a secret from everyone except Granacci, whose visit on the way home to his midday dinner brought Michelangelo news of the city.

"I can't believe it! You signed the contract on June 19; here it is only the middle of July, and you have two of the statues completed. They're quite good, in spite of all your moaning that you could carve nothing worth while. At this rate you'll be finished with the fifteen statues in seven months."

Michelangelo gazed at his St. Peter and St. Paul, replied soberly: "These first two figures are not bad, they contain my hunger to carve. But once they're shoved into those narrow niches, they'll die a quick death. The next two statues are of Pope Pius II and Gregory the Great, in their full papal crowns and long stiff robes . . ."

"Why don't you go to Siena," Granacci interrupted, "and get rid of Torrigiani? You'll feel better."

He left that day.

4

Tuscany is a state of grace. The countryside is so lovingly designed that the eye sweeps the mountains and valleys without stumbling over a single stone. The lilt of the rolling green hills, the upsurging cypresses, the terraces sculptured by generations that have handled the rocks with skilful tenderness, the fields geometrically juxtaposed as though drawn by a draughtsman for beauty as well as productivity; the battlements of castles on the hills, their tall towers standing grey-blue and golden tan among the forest of trees, the air of such clarity that every sod of earth stands out in dazzling detail. Below him the fields were ripening with July barley and oats, beans and beets; on both sides of the road the grape-heavy vines were espaliered between the horizontal branches of silver-green olive trees, composing orchards of webbed design, rich in intimation of wine, olive oil and lacy-leaf poetry.

He had a sense of physical delight as his horse moved along the contours of a ridge, rising ever higher into the flawless Italian sky, the air he breathed so pure that his whole being felt ennobled, meanness and pettiness falling away from him: a rapture he experienced only when he carved white marble. Tuscany untied the knots in a man's intestines, wiped out the ills of his world. God and man had combined to create this supreme work of art. Pictorially, Michelangelo thought, this might be the Garden of Eden. Adam and Eve had departed, but to his sculptor's eye, scanning the undulating ranges which flowed backward in space with the lyricism of the green river winding through the valley below him, dotted with stone houses, sun-mellowed tile roofs, hayricks, Tuscany was paradise. He recited a verse from his childhood:

> Italy is the garden of Europe,
> Tuscany is the garden of Italy,
> Florence is the flower of Tuscany.

Towards sundown he reached the heights above Poggibonsi, the Apennines covered with virgin forest, rivers and lakes shining like rolled silver under the oblique sunset rays. He descended the long hill to Poggibonsi, a wine centre, dropped his saddlebag in a scrubbed, bare-floored inn, then climbed the hill beyond the town to explore Giuliano da Sangallo's towering Poggio Imperiale, a fortress palace that Lorenzo had ordered built to keep invading armies from passing beyond this heavily fortified point which controlled the valley leading to Florence. But Lorenzo had died; the Poggio Imperiale had been abandoned. . . .

He scrambled down the rocky footpath. He was served supper in the yard of the inn, slept soundly, rose at cockcrow and set out on the second half of his journey.

Siena was a warm reddish-brown city, made of brick from its reddish-brown earth, even as Bologna was a burnt-orange city from its native earth. He entered the gate of the encompassing city wall, made his way to the Piazza del Campo, shell-shaped, running rapidly downhill from its top line of private palaces to the Palazzo Pubblico at the other end, and piercing the skies above it the beautiful and daring Tower of Mangia, a breath-taking stone sculpture.

He walked to the centre of the piazza around which Siena ran its mad horse race each summer, to Della Quercia's lovely fountain, then mounted a steep flight of stone steps and came to the Baptistery, with its baptismal font sculptured by Della Quercia, Donatello and Ghiberti.

After circling the font to study the work of Italy's best sculptors, he left the Baptistery and climbed the mountain-steep hill to the cathedral. He stood gaping in awe at the black and white marble façade with its magnificent carved figures by Giovanni Pisano, its rose windows, black and white marble Campanile. Inside, the floor was a mine of marble slabs, inlaid with black and white marquetry depicting scenes from the Old and New Testaments.

Then his heart sank. Before him stood the Bregno altar, the niches shallower than he had imagined, each of them topped by a heavily incised shell-like dome, against which the heads and faces of his figures would have to be seen, draining their expression. Some of the niches stood so high in the air that no one on the floor would know what kind of sculpture they contained.

He measured the niches, revised in his mind the height of the bases on which his figures would stand, sought out the caretaker, a pleasant red-faced man of middle years who greeted him loquaciously.

" Ah, you're the Michelangelo Buonarroti we've been waiting for. The St. Francis arrived from Rome weeks ago. I set it up in a cool room off the Baptistery, forge and all. The Cardinal Piccolomini instructed me to take good care of you. Got a room all ready in our house across the square. My wife prepares the best Sienese *pappardelle alla lepre,* wide noodles with a hare sauce . . ."

Michelangelo swam into the river of words.

" Would you take me to the St. Francis? I must see how much work there is."

" Of course! Remember, you're Cardinal Piccolomini's guest here, and the cardinal is our great man . . ."

Michelangelo swallowed hard at the sight of Torrigiani's sculpture: wooden, lifeless, a plethora of flowing robes under which no part of a living, breathing human could be discerned; hands without veins, skin or bone; a rigid, stylized expressionless face . . . all these points he ticked off to himself as his eyes mercilessly tore through the unfinished block.

He vowed to give this poor marred St. Francis, whom even

the birds would not recognize, all of the love and skill at his command. He would have to re-enter the block, shed its artificial trappings, throw out the committed marble and redesign the whole figure, recast the concept so that St. Francis might emerge as Michelangelo thought of him, the most gentle of the saints. But he would sleep on it first, then bring drawing materials and sit in this cool room carved out of the cathedral mountain, with diffused light from an overhead window, and search his mind until St. Francis emerged in his love of the poor, the stricken, the abandoned.

The next day he made his drawings. By nightfall he was putting new edges on old chisels, balancing them for his hand, getting accustomed to the heft of the hammer. The following dawn he began carving in white heat; and out of the now skinny block there emerged a travel-weary body beneath a slight robe, the emaciated shoulders down to bone, the hands touchingly expressive, the legs thin, knock-kneed, the feet that had trod the roads to give sustenance and to adore everything in nature, tired.

He felt an identity with St. Francis, and with this maimed block from which he was emerging. When he came to the head and face he carved his own hair, brushed in a straight line down the forehead, his own caved-in face as he had seen it in the Medici mirror the morning after Torrigiani stove it in: the nose squashed between the eyes, snaking downward in an S, a lump over the eye, the swollen cheek-bone below; a St. Francis saddened by what he saw when he looked out at God's world, yet over the pained features a forgiveness, a sweetness and acceptance.

A mood of sadness pervaded him as he rode home through the Chianti hills. Wearily he dropped off his horse, made his way to his workshop, saddlebag over his shoulder. He found Argiento wiggling excitedly from one foot to the other, waiting for Michelangelo to look at him.

" Well, Argiento, what are you bursting with?"

" Gonfaloniere Soderini, he wants to see you, he sends a page every hour!"

The Piazza della Signoria was aglow with orange light from the burning oil pots that hung from every window and from the top of the crenallated tower. Soderini detached himself from his Council associates in the raised loggia and met Michelangelo at the base of Donatello's Judith. He was dressed in a plain silk shirt against the locked-in heat of

391

the evening, but his expression was one of being coolly pleased with himself.

"Why the oil pots? What are we celebrating?"

"You."

"Me?"

"In part." Soderini's eyes twinkled wickedly in the orange light. "The Council agreed this afternoon on a new constitution. That's the official explanation. The unofficial explanation is that the directors of the Wool Guild and the Duomo voted you the Giant . . ."

Michelangelo went rigid. It was incredible. The Duccio column was his!

Soderini's voice continued gaily. "When we realized that our best Florentine carver was bound by a Sienese cardinal, we asked, 'Does Siena suppose that Florence does not appreciate its own artists? Or that we can't afford to employ them?' After all, we've spent years at war with the Sienese . . .!"

"But the Piccolomini contract . . ."

"Out of patriotic duty you must postpone the Piccolomini contract, and on September first take over the Duccio block."

Michelangelo felt the familiar stinging behind his eyelids. "How do I thank you?"

Soderini slowly shook his elongated head with its yellow-streaked hair, murmured, "We are sons of *Il Magnifico*; we must observe that bond."

5

His feet carried him down the Borgo Pinti into the Via degli Artisti, then out a gate of the wall, along the Affrico River, and up the hills to Settignano. The Topolino family was in the yard enjoying the evening breeze from the hills.

"Listen," he called out, "I just heard. The Duccio column. It's mine!"

"We should be able to trust you now with a few window frames," teased the father.

Michelangelo spread his hands in front of him. "Thank you for the honour, *padre mio,* but a good *scalpellino* likes to shape building block."

He remained the night, sleeping on an old straw pad under the arches between the grandfather and youngest son. At dawn he rose to join the men chipping *pietra serena.* He worked for a few hours, while the sun climbed high in the valley, then went into the house. The mother handed him a jug of cold water.

" *Madre mia,* how goes it with Contessina?" he asked.

" She is frail. . . . But it is more. The Signoria has forbidden anyone to help them." She made the eloquent Tuscan gesture of hopelessness, her hands circling outward and down. " The hatred of Piero still poisons."

Michelangelo drank deeply of the water, went back to the workyard and asked Bruno:

" Can you spare a few pieces of iron?"

" There is always to spare."

Michelangelo put wood in the forge, lit it, fashioned a set of small chisels and hammers, the kind the Topolino father had made for him when he was six. Then he cut out an oblong of *serena,* carved the *scalpellino's* alphabet on it, from the herringbone to the lines of the dog's-tooth chisel.

He made the Topolinos " Addio." The family knew, by some mystical system of communication, that he had come to them first after learning of his good fortune. His visit here overnight, the companionable work hours on the blocks, told them of his continued love for them.

The horse he had borrowed was old and tired. Halfway up the steep trail Michelangelo dismounted and led the animal. At the top of the ridge he turned west as the sun flooded the sky over the Mugnone Valley with rose and purple. It was a short haul into Fiesole, northern anchor of the Etruscan league of cities that began at Veii, just outside Rome, and that Cæsar's legions had had a difficult time conquering. Cæsar thought he had levelled Fiesole, but as Michelangelo started down the north slope, seeing Poliziano's Villa Diana in the distance, he passed Etruscan walls still cemented and intact, and new houses rebuilt of the original stones of the city.

Contessina's house was at the bottom of a steep, narrow track, halfway down the slope to the Mugnone River. It had formerly been the peasant's house for the castle on top of the hill. Michelangelo tied his horse to an olive tree, made his way through a vegetable garden and looked down at the Ridolfi family on the small stone-paved terrace in front of their cottage. Contessina was sitting on a cane-backed chair, the baby at her breast, a six-year-old playing at her feet. He called softly from the bank above:

"It is I, Michelangelo Buonarroti, come to visit."

Contessina lifted her head sharply, covered her breast.

"Michelangelo! What a surprise. Come down, come down. The path is over to the right."

There was a constrained silence as Ridolfi lifted his proud, hurt face. Michelangelo took the *serena* slab and tools from the saddle bag and made his way down the path. Ridolfi was still looking upward to him, standing stiffly. He set the toy chisels, hammer and slab at Contessina's feet.

"Yesterday I received the Duccio column. I had to come to tell you. *Il Magnifico* would have wanted it. Then I realized that your oldest son must now be six. It is time he started learning; I shall be his teacher. Just as the Topolinos taught me when I was six."

Contessina's peals of laughter rang out over the fields of olives, Ridolfi's stern mouth twitched with amusement. He said in a low voice, "You are kind to come to us this way. You know that we are pariahs."

It was the first time Ridolfi had ever addressed him; and it was the first time Michelangelo had been close to him since the day of Contessina's wedding. Ridolfi was short of thirty, but ostracism and bitterness were already ravaging his face. Though he had not been involved in the conspiracy to bring back Piero de' Medici, he was known to despise the Republic and to be ready to work for the return of an oligarchic control of Florence. His family fortune, based on world trade in wool, was now being used to help finance the city-state.

"Which makes it a doubly noxious brew for me to imbibe," said Ridolfi; "but one day we shall be returned to power. Then we shall see!"

He felt Contessina's eyes burning into his back. He turned to gaze at her, head on. Her attitude was one of calm acceptance of what was, even though they had just finished a plain dinner, were wearing threadbare clothes, and were housed in a peasant's cottage after having lived in the richest palaces of Florence.

"Tell us the news of yourself. Of the years in Rome. What have you sculptured? I heard about the Bacchus."

Michelangelo reached into his shirt for a sheet of drawing

paper, took charcoal from his belt and sketched the Pietà, explaining what he had tried to accomplish. It was good to be with Contessina again, to gaze into those dark eyes. Had they not loved each other, if only with the love of children? Once you have loved, should not that love last? Love was so rare, so difficult to come upon.

Contessina divined his thoughts; she always had. She turned to her son.

"Luigi, would you like to learn Michelangelo's alphabet?"

"Can I help carve the new statue, Michelangelo?"

"I will come and teach you, the way Bertoldo taught me in your grandfather's garden. Now, take this hammer in one hand, the chisel in the other. On the opposite side of the stone I will show you how to spell. With a hammer and chisel we can write sculptures as beautiful as Dante's poetry. Is it not so, Contessina?"

"It is so," she replied. "Each of us has his own alphabet with which to make poetry."

It was midnight by the time he had returned the Topolino horse and walked down the hill. His father was awake, waiting in the black leather chair. This was apparently his second night of sitting up, and he was thoroughly exasperated.

"So! It takes you two nights to come home to your father with the news. Where have you been all this time? Where is the contract? What price are they paying?"

"Six florins a month."

"How long will it take you to carve?"

"Two years."

Lodovico figured rapidly, then turned a ravaged face upward to his son.

"But that adds up to only a hundred and forty-four florins."

"The Board agrees to pay more, when I'm finished, if they think I deserve a larger compensation."

"Who shall that decision be left to?"

"Their conscience."

"Conscience! Don't you know that a Tuscan's conscience stops short of his belt?"

"The David will be so beautiful they will want to pay me more."

"Even the Piccolomini contract is better: you earn three hundred and thirty two florins in the same two years of work, more than double!"

Michelangelo lowered his head in despair. Lodovico did not consult his son's expression. He said in a tone of finality:

"The Buonarroti are not rich enough to make a charitable contribution of one hundred and eighty-eight florins to the Wool Guild and the Duomo. Tell them that the David will have to be postponed until you have earned the five hundred ducats from Siena."

Michelangelo knew better than to get angry. He replied quietly, "Father, I am going to carve the David. Why do you always bring up these futile arguments?"

Several hours later his brother Buonarroto commented:

"Not so futile. Before the argument, how many florins a month were you planning to pay Father?"

"Three. Half for him, half for me."

"And now you have agreed to give him five."

"I had to quiet him down."

"So, for a few hours' argument, he has earned himself two extra florins a month for twenty-four months."

Michelangelo sighed wearily.

"What can I do? He looks so old and white. Since the Board is paying my costs, what do I need the other two florins for?"

Buonarroto groaned. "You were better off as an apprentice in the Medici palace. Then, at least, I was able to put away some savings for you."

Michelangelo gazed out of the window at the figure of the night guard strolling down the Via San Proculo.

"You're right about Father: I'm his quarry."

6

Granacci launched a celebration party built around the meeting of the Company of the Cauldron. To salute Michelangelo's good fortune, eleven members of the Company showed up, Botticelli limping painfully on crutches, and Rosselli, of the rival studio to Ghirlandaio, so ill that he had to be carried in on a litter. Rustici received him heartily, Sansovino pounded him on the back, the others offered congratulations: David Ghirlandaio, Bugiardini, Albertinelli, Filippino Lippi, *Il Cronaca,* Baccio d'Agnolo, Leonardo da

Vinci. The twelfth member, Giuliano da Sangallo, was away.

Granaccio had been provisioning Rustici's studio all afternoon with chains of sausages, cold beef and suckling pig, figures carved out of pastry, demijohns of Chianti. When Granacci approached Soggi with the news, he contributed an enormous basin of pickled pigs' feet.

The food and drink was all needed, for Granacci had invited the town: the entire Ghirlandaio studio, including Domenico's talented son, Ridolfo, now eighteen; all of the Medici garden apprentices; a dozen of the better-known sculptors and painters including Donato Benti, Benedetto da Rovezzano, Piero di Cosimo, Lorenzo di Credi, Franciabigio, the young Andrea del Sarto, Andrea della Robbia, the maker of glazed terra-cottas, the leading Florentine craftsmen, goldsmiths, clockmakers, gem cutters, bronze casters; the mosaicist Monte di Giovanni di Miniato; the illuminator Attavanti; wood carvers; the architect Francesco Filarete who was chief herald of Florence.

Wise in the ways of the Republic, Granacci had also sent invitations to Gonfaloniere Soderini, the members of the Signoria, the Boards of the Wool Guild and the Duomo, to the Strozzi family to whom he had sold the Hercules. Most of them came, happy to join in the fun, for the huge assemblage now spilled out of Rustici's jammed, noisy studio into the square, where Granacci's hired band of acrobats and wrestlers were entertaining, and musicians and minstrels were chanting songs for the young men and girls dancing in the square. Everyone wrung Michelangelo's hand, pounded him on the back and insisted upon drinking a toast with him, friend, casual acquaintance and stranger alike.

Soderini shook Michelangelo's hand, said, " This is the first major commission agreed upon by all of the city Boards since the coming of Savonarola. Perhaps a new era will start for us, and we can wipe out our deep-lying sense of guilt."

" Which guilt are you referring to, Gonfaloniere?"

" The mass guilt, the individual guilt. We have suffered bad times since the death of *Il Magnifico*; we have destroyed much that made Florence the first city of the world. The bribing of Cæsar Borgia was only the latest in nine years of indignities. But to-night we like ourselves. Later, perhaps, we will be proud of you, when the marble is finished. But now it is ourselves we are proud of. We believe that great commissions for frescoes, for mosaics, for bronzes and marbles will be forthcoming for all our artists. We are seeing a rebirth." He laid a hand on Michelangelo's shoulder. "You happen to be the midwife. Handle the baby well!"

The party lasted until dawn; but before that, two incidents occurred which would affect the pattern of his days.

The first filled him with joy. The ill and aged Rosselli gathered the ten members of the Company about him, announced:

"It is not meat and drink, if you will forgive a pun, for a member of this Company of the Cauldron to be carried to these orgies on a litter. Therefore, much as I dislike promoting anyone from the Ghirlandaio studio, I herewith resign from the Company and nominate Michelangelo Buonarroti to succeed me."

He was accepted. He had been no part of any group since the Medici sculpture garden. He remembered again his lonely childhood, how difficult it had been for him to make friends, to be gay. He had been skinny, unsociable, unwanted. Now all these artists of Florence, even those who had long waited to be invited into the Company, were applauding his election.

The second incident was to cause him considerable anguish. It was begun, though unwittingly, by Leonardo da Vinci.

Michelangelo was already angry at Leonardo by the first time he had seen him crossing the Piazzo della Signoria, accompanied by his inseparable and beloved apprentice-companion, Salai, a boy with features straight off a Greek statue, a mass of curly hair waving around his head, with a small round mouth and soft round chin, dressed by Leonardo in an expensive linen shirt, a cloak rich in silver brocade. Yet compared to Leonardo, Salai was dull in appearance; for Leonardo's was the most perfect face to appear in Florence since the golden beauty of Pico della Mirandola. He carried his big sculptural head thrown back aristocratically the magnificently broad forehead topped by a haze of reddish hair, softly curled and worn down to his shoulders; a chin carved out of the heroic Carrara statuary marble he despised; a flawlessly designed broad nose, rounded, full-blooded lips, the face dominated by cool blue eyes of a piercing penetration and intelligence; and the fair complexion of a country girl.

Leonardo's figure, as Michelangelo watched him cross the square followed by his usual retinue of servants and hangers-on, matched the flawless face: tall, graceful, with the broad shoulders, and narrow hips of a wrestler, with the agility and strength as well, dressed in regal splendour and a disdain for convention: a rose-coloured cloak barely covering his shoulders, and falling short at the knees, wearing his shirt and *calze* tight to the point of bursting.

He had made Michelangelo feel ugly and malformed, conscious that his clothes were inexpensive, ill fitting and worn. Leonardo's coiffured golden hair and scent of perfume, the lace about his neck and wrists, the jewels, the ineffable exquisiteness of the man's presence made him feel tattered and dirty by comparison.

When he had spoken of this to Rustici, who was Leonardo's friend, Rustici had reproved him.

" Don't be fooled by an elegant exterior. Leonardo has a magnificent brain. His studies of geometry are extending the work of Euclid. He has been dissecting animals for years, and keeping meticulous notebooks of his anatomical drawings. In his pursuit of geology he has discovered fish-shell fossils on top of the mountains of the upper Arno, proving that they were once under water. He is also an engineer and inventor of unbelievable machines: a multiple barrel gun, cranes for lifting heavy loads, suction pumps, wind and water gauges. Even now he is completing experiments for a machine that will fly through the air as the birds do. The dazzling performance of imitating a rich nobleman is his effort to persuade the world to forget that he is the illegitimate son of a Vinci innkeeper's daughter. Actually he is the only man in Florence who works as hard and long as you do: twenty hours a day. Look for the real Leonardo beneath that defensive elegance."

In the face of this brilliant recital, Michelangelo could not bring himself to mention his anger at the man's outspoken deprecation of sculpture. Leonardo's hearty welcoming of him into the Company of the Cauldron this evening had also assuaged his uneasiness. Then he heard Leonardo's high-pitched voice behind him, declaring:

" I refused to compete for the Duccio block because sculpture is a mechanical art."

" Surely you would not call Donatello a mechanic?" asked a deeper voice.

" In some ways, yes," answered Leonardo. " Sculpture is so
399

much less intellectual than painting; it lacks so many of its natural aspects. I spent years at it, and I tell you from experience that painting is far more difficult, and reaches the greater perfection."

"Still, for a commission as important as that . . .?"

"No, no, I would never carve marble. It causes a man to sweat and wearies his body all over. The marble carver comes out of a day's work as filthy as a plasterer or baker, his nostrils clogged with dust, his hair and face and legs covered with powder and chips, his clothes stinking. When I paint I work in my finest clothes. I emerge at the end of a day immaculately clean and refreshed. Friends come in to read poetry to me, and play music while I draw. I am a fastidious man. Sculpture is for labourers."

Michelangelo felt his spine stiffen. He glanced over his shoulder. Leonardo's back was to him. Again a rage rose in his bowels. He yearned to spin Leonardo around, smash him in his beautiful face with the sculptor's fist he held in such contempt. Then quickly he moved to the other end of the room, hurt not only for himself but for all marble carvers. One day he would make Leonardo eat those words.

The following morning he awoke late. The Arno was down to a trickle. He had to go miles upstream to find a deep pool. Here he bathed and swam, then walked back, stopping at Santo Spirito. He found Prior Bichiellini in the library. The prior heard his news without expression.

"And the Cardinal Piccolomini contract?"

"When the two Boards sign this commission, I will be free of the other."

"By what right? What you have begun, finish!"

"But the Giant is my great opportunity. I can create something glorious . . ."

"After you fulfil your obligation," interrupted Bichiellini. "This is a worse variety of opportunism than led you to sign a contract you detested." His voice became more friendly. "I understand that you do not want to give your energies to figures which are unsatisfying to you. But you knew that to begin with. You may also be surrendering your integrity for no gain. Cardinal Piccolomini may be our next Pope, and then the Signoria will order you back to the Siena pieces just as they obeyed Alexander VI and put Savonarola on the rack."

"Everyone has the next Pope!" said Michelangelo caustically. "Giuliano da Sangallo says it will be his Cardinal

Rovere. Leo Baglioni says it will be his Cardinal Riario.
Now you say it will be Cardinal Piccolomini . . ."

The prior rose, abruptly left Michelangelo's side, made his
way to the open archway overlooking the piazza. Michelangelo hurried after him.

"Forgive me, Father, but I've got to carve my David now."

The prior made his way across the corner of the piazza,
leaving Michelangelo standing flat-footed in the merciless
glare of the August sun.

7

Beppe gave him a raucous welcome. "So you own the
Duccio block for free!" He grinned, scratching his bald
scalp.

"Beppe, like it or not, you've got me under your wing for
two full years."

The foreman groaned. "As though I don't have troubles
enough keeping the cathedral from falling down. But the
Board of Works say give him everything he wants: marble,
chisels, pretty girls . . ."

Michelangelo laughed aloud, bringing the artisans running.
They welcomed him to the yard.

The Duomo workyard ran the full width of the block
behind the Duomo Works buildings from the Via dei Servi
on the north side to the Street of the Clock on the south,
bound in by an eight-foot brick wall. The front half, where
the Duccio column had lain, was the quarters for the artisans
maintaining the cathedral; the rear half was used for storage
of lumber, brick, paving stone. Michelangelo wanted to be
close to the workmen so that he could hear the sound of
their tools and voices, yet not be involved. In the centre
of the rear yard there was an oak tree, and behind it, in
the wall admitting to a nameless passage, an iron gate,
locked, rusted. The gate was exactly two blocks from his
house. He could work nights when he wished, and holidays
when the main yard would be locked.

"Beppe, is it permitted to use this gate?"

"Nobody forbids. I locked it myself, ten, twelve years ago,
when tools and material were missing."

"Would it be all right if I used it?"

"What's wrong with the front entrance?"

401

" Nothing. But if we could build my workshop around this gate, I could come and go without bothering anybody."

Beppe chewed toothlessly on this idea to make sure Michelangelo was not repudiating him or his crew. Then he said: " I do it. Draw me plans."

He needed thirty feet along the back wall to be paved for his forge and tools, and for keeping his wood dry; the brick wall would have to be raised another nine feet so that no one could see the column or watch him working on it when he mounted his scaffold. On each side, for a distance of about twenty feet, he wanted low plank walls, but the work area would be open to the sky for the nin· dry months of the year, and at the front as well. The Giant would be bathed in the full sunlight of the sou:hern arc as the brilliant Tuscan sun made its daily transit across the city.

He decided to keep the workshop in the piazza; it would be a place to go to when he wanted to get away from the large marble. Argiento would sleep there, and work with him here during the day.

The Duccio block was so seriously gouged in the centre of its seventeen-foot length that any attempt to move it in its present state could prove fatal; a jarring motion or lurching impact would split the column in two. He bought several of the largest pieces of paper he could find, pasted them over the face of the horizontal column and cut out a *sagoma,* a silhouette, taking care to measure the deep cut accurately. He then took the sheets to the workshop in the piazza and had Argiento nail them up on the wall. He moved his workbench around to face the paper silhouette, began fitting together a second series of sheets on which to draw a design of the David, indicating which parts of the existing block would be discarded, which parts used. Back at the yard, he chipped out marble from the top and bottom corners, balancing the weight so that the column would no longer be in danger of cracking.

Beppe's workmen established a smooth path to the new work area. They used a block and tackle to raise the two-thousand-pound column and get rollers under it. The column was moved slowly; as each rounded beam fell out the back end, a workman ran ahead to reinsert it under the front end. By nightfall the column, though still in a horizontal position, was inside Michelangelo's enclosure. He and his Giant-David block were alone.

Now, for the first time, he realized that the drawings that had satisfied the Boards were no longer of any use to him. He had outgrown these elementary stages of his thinking. All he knew for sure was that his was to be the David he had rediscovered, that he would use the opportunity to create all of the poetry, the beauty, the mystery and the inherent drama of the male body, the archetype and essence of correlated forms.

He burned his earlier drawings, settled down to the simplest beginning, probing within himself.

The Greeks had carved bodies from their white marble of such perfect proportion and strength that they could never be surpassed; but the figures had been without mind or spirit. His David would be the incarnation of everything Lorenzo de' Medici had been fighting for, that the Plato Academy had believed was the rightful heritage of man: not a sinful little creature living only for salvation in the next life, but a glorious creation capable of beauty, strength, courage, wisdom, faith in his own kind, with a brain and will and inner power to fashion a world filled with the fruit of man's creative intellect. His David would be Apollo, but considerably more; Hercules, but considerably more; Adam, but considerably more; the most fully realized man the world had yet seen, functioning in a rational and humane world.

How to draw these convictions on paper?

During the early weeks of autumn he achieved only fragmentary answers. The more he was frustrated the more complicated he made his drawings. The marble lay silent and inert.

" Maybe nobody can bring it to life?" suggested Beppe, when Michelangelo seemed depressed.

" Fine time to tell me! Like asking a girl does she want to be a mother after she's in the family way. Beppe, I'm going to have to model in marble instead of clay. Could you buy me a piece, about a third as large as this one?"

" I dunno. They said give workmen, material. But a five-foot block, that's money."

He delivered, as always, a fair enough block. Michelangelo plunged into the marble, trying to rough his way through his problem with hammer and chisel. What emerged was a strongly built, primitive young man, the face idealized and indeterminate. Granacci, seeing the marble, said with a puzzled expression:

403

"I don't understand. He stands with his foot resting on Goliath's head; but at the same time he's got a rock in one hand and is reaching over his shoulder for his slingshot. You're of two minds: the upper half is about to use the slingshot, the bottom is already resting triumphantly on its victim."

"You flatter me. I have no mind at all."

"Then why not spend a couple of days with me at the villa?"

Michelangelo looked up sharply; it was the first time Granacci had acknowledged that he had a villa.

"You will be diverted; you'll forget your David for a couple of days."

"Agreed. I can't remember smiling for weeks."

"I have something at the villa that will bring a smile."

He did indeed: a girl by the name of Vermiglia, blonde in the Florentine tradition, with her hair plucked back to give her a higher brow, her breasts propped up in a gown of green taffeta. She proved a charming mistress of the villa, presiding over their late candlelit supper on a porch overlooking the Arno as it wound its way to the sea. When she had gone inside, Granacci said:

"Vermiglia has a wide variety of cousins. Would you like her to choose one for you? I think she's lonely here. You could have a suite overlooking the city. It would be a pleasant way of life for us."

"Thank you, *caro*. I have a way of life. As for casual encounters, Beppe says, 'What you put into the ladies at night, you can't put into the marble in the morning.'"

He sat by his window, sleepless, watching the towers and domes of Florence under a scimitar of moon, rising to pace through the series of three small rooms, then going back to his vigil by the window. Why had he carved two Davids into his five-foot block, one already triumphant over Goliath, the other just preparing to hurl the stone? No piece of sculpture could stand at two different moments in the realm of time, any more than it could occupy two different areas in the realm of space. He would have to take a stand, decide which of the two warriors he was going to sculpture.

By dawn he had worked his way back, step by step. Sharp light flooded his mind. Goliath had to go. His head, black, dead, blood-spotted, ugly, had no place in the realm of art. It should never have been included in the first place. The full meaning of David was obscured by having that horrendous head for ever chained to his ankles. What David had done became a mere physical act ending in the slaying of an opponent. Yet to him this was only a small part of the meaning of David, who could represent the daring of man in every phase of life: thinker, scholar, poet, artist, scientist, statesman, explorer: a giant of the mind, the intellect, the spirit as well as the body. Without the reminder of Goliath's head, he might stand as the symbol of man's courage and his victory over far more important enemies.

David had to stand alone. Even as he had stood on the plains of the Valley of the Terebinth.

This decision left him exalted . . . and exhausted. He climbed between Granacci's fine linen sheets, fell into a deep sleep.

He sat in his shed before the column, drawing David's head, face and eyes, asking himself:

"What is David feeling at this moment of conquest? Glory? Gratification? Would he feel himself to be the biggest and strongest man in the world? Would there be a touch of contempt for Goliath, of arrogance as he watched the fleeing Philistines, and then turned to accept the plaudits of the Israelites?"

All unworthy emotions, none of which he could bring himself to draw. What could he find in David triumphant, he asked himself, worthy of sculpturing? Tradition portrayed him after the fact. Yet David after the battle was certainly an anticlimax, his great moment already gone.

Which then was the important David? When did David become a giant? After killing Goliath? Or at the moment he decided that he must try? David as he was releasing, with brilliant and deadly accuracy, the shot from the sling? Or David before he entered the battle, when he decided that the Israelites must be freed from their vassalage to the Philistines? Was not the decision more important than the act itself, since character was more critical than action? For him, then, it was David's decision that made him a giant, not his killing of Goliath. He had been floundering because he had imprisoned himself and David at the wrong moment in time.

How could he have been so stupid, so blind? David pictured after Goliath could be no one but the biblical David, a special individual. He was not content to portray one man; he was seeking universal man, Everyman, all of whom, from

405

the beginning of time, had faced a decision to strike for freedom.

This was the David he had been seeking, caught at the exultant height of resolution, still reflecting the emotions of fear, hesitation, repugnance, doubt; the man who wished to follow his own ways among the hills of Jerusalem, who cared little for the clash of arms and material reward. The man who killed Goliath would be committed all his life to warfare and its consequence, power. The reluctance would still be fading from his face, this giving up of the pastoral life in which he had been happy for a life of courts and kings, of jealousy and intrigue, of control and disposition of other men's destinies. This was the dichotomy in all men: the reflective life and the active. David would know that the man who gave himself to action would have sold himself to an inexorable master who would command him all the days and years of his life; he would know intuitively that nothing gained as reward for action, no kingdom or power or wealth, could compensate a man for the loss of his privacy.

To act was to join. David would not be sure he wanted to join. He had been a man alone. Once he tackled Goliath there would be no turning back, far more true if he vanquished Goliath than if he were vanquished. It was what he sensed that he would do to himself, as well as what the world would do to him, that made him doubtful and averse to changing the pattern of his days. His had been a hard choice, indeed.

This concept opened wide vistas to Michelangelo. He soared, he drew with authority and power; he modelled in clay, eighteen inches high, his fingers unable to keep pace with his thoughts and emotions; and with astonishing facility he knew where the David lay. The limitations of the block began to appear as assets, forcing his mind into a simplicity of design that might never have occurred to him had it been whole and perfect. The marble came alive now.

When he tired of drawing or modelling he would join his fellow members of the Cauldron for an evening of talk. Sansovino moved into the Duomo workyard to begin carving a marble St. John Baptizing Christ for over the east door of the Baptistery, setting up his workshed between Michelangelo and Beppe's stonemasons. When Rustici became bored with working alone on his drawings for a Boccaccio head and an Annunciation in marble, he would come to the yard and sketch with Michelangelo or Sansovino. Next Baccio joined them in the Duomo workyard, to design a crucifix which he hoped the church of San Lorenzo was going to commission. Bugiardini would bring in a hot dinner in pots from a nearby *osteria,* and the former apprentices would spend a companionable hour, Argiento serving the food on Michelangelo's plank worktable against the rear wall. Soggi, proud of his former associates, visited once in a while, wheeling in a cart of cooked sausages for the communal dinner.

Every now and then he would climb the hill to Fiesole to give Luigi a lesson on *pietra serena,* which the six-year-old seemed to enjoy. He was a bright-eyed, handsome child, resembling his uncle Giuliano, with Contessina's alert mind.

" You are wonderful with Luigi, Michelangelo," remarked Contessina. " Giuliano loved you too. Sometime you must have your own son."

He shook his head.

" Like most artists, I am a mendicant. When I finish one commission I must go in search of the next, work in whatever city it takes me to: Rome, Naples, Milan, or even Portugal, as Sansovino did. That is no life for a family."

" It goes deeper than that," said Contessina in her small, sure voice. " Marble is your marriage. The Bacchus, Pietà, David are your children." They stood close, as close as they sometimes had in the Medici palace. " While you are in Florence, Luigi will be as your son. The Medici need friends. And so do artists."

Cardinal Piccolomini sent a representative to Florence who demanded to see the statues for the Bregno altar. Michelangelo showed the agent the completed St. Peter and St. Paul, and the roughed-out figures of the Popes, promising to finish them soon. The next day Baccio came into the shed, his once again mischievous face wreathed in smiles. He had received the commission for the crucifix. Since San Lorenzo had no work space for him, he asked Michelangelo if he might share the shop in the piazza.

" Instead of paying rent, I could finish the two Popes from your drawings," he exclaimed. " What do you say?"

He did the pieces credibly. With four figures and the St. Francis completed, Michelangelo felt he would have a respite from Cardinal Piccolomini. When Baccio began carving his crucifix, Michelangelo was glad he had taken him in; the work was honest and full of feeling.

Argiento swept out the shop each evening when he returned from the Duomo. He too was content in Florence, working in the Duomo workshed all day, at night having the company of the other young apprentices of the piazza who also slept in their shops, each providing food for a common cookpot.

Best of all, Giuliano da Sangallo returned from Savona where he had completed a palace for Cardinal Rovere at the family estate. Leaving Savona, Sangallo had been intercepted and kept a prisoner for six months by the Pisans and had to be ransomed for three hundred ducats. Michelangelo stayed with him at the family home in the Quarter of the Sun, near Santa Maria Novella. He still insisted that Cardinal Rovere would be the next Pope.

" Tell me about your design for the Giant," he demanded. " And what have you heard of interesting architectural jobs in Florence?"

" There are several of great urgency," said Michelangelo. " A revolving table strong enough to turn a two-thousand-pound column of marble, so I can control the light and sun. A fifteen-foot scaffold, one in which I can change the height and work all around the block."

Sangallo was amused. " You are my best client. Let's get pen and paper. What you need is a series of four towers, with open shelves that take planks from either direction, like this. . . . As for your turntable, that's an engineering task. . . ."

8

There were heavy rain clouds overhead. Beppe and his crew built a wooden roof that arched upward at a sharp angle from the back wall, leaving space for the seventeen-foot column, then tiled it securely to keep out the rain.

His marble was still lying flat on the ground. He made a wooden lid to fit its length, with lead-weighted strings hanging over the sides to show at what level in the block he would be seeking for the back of David's head, the arm raised to take the slingshot, the hips swivelled away from the gouge, the rock inside the huge right hand, the tree trunk

408

dous he could work is without fear of the head breaking off. He left considerable marble about the heroic head so that later he could carve a shock of short wavy hair.

Soderini came into the yard to observe progress. He knew that Michelangelo would have no peace at home until a price was set on the finished David. Towards the middle of February, after Michelangelo had been working for five months, he asked:

"Do you feel you have moved far enough along now for the Boards to see the work? I can have them meet here, and arrange a final contract . . ."

Michelangelo looked up at the David. His study of anatomy had strongly influenced his carving; in this early stage his chisel had roughed out the muscle movements of the calves, the thighs, the chest, pulling the inner action to the surface of the skin. He pointed out to Soderini how a muscle structure consists of fibres that run in a parallel direction; all action that took place in the David ran along these parallel fibrous lines. Then, reluctantly, he turned back to Soderini's question.

"No artist likes to have his work seen in this crude state."

"The Boards might pay considerably more if you could wait until it is finished. . . ."

"I can't," sighed Michelangelo. "No extra amount of money could compensate me for two more years of my father's misery."

"Two more years? Even with the figure emerging as well as it is?"

"This is the work that goes fastest."

"I'll bring the members as soon as we meet on a sunny day."

The rains vanished. The sun came out, clear and warm, to dry the stones of the city. Michelangelo and Argiento took the tiles off the roof and stacked them against the next winter, then removed the planks and let the full light bathe the shed. The David pulsated with life in every fibre of its body, beautiful bluish-grey veinings running up the legs like human veins, the considerable weight already firmly carried on the right leg.

Word arrived from Soderini that he would bring the members of the Boards at noon the following day. Michelangelo exclaimed, "Argiento, start cleaning! This must be two months of marble chips I'm walking on."

"Don't blame me," cried Argiento, "you won't keep out of

411

here long enough to let me sweep. I think you like to wade through them, ankle deep."

"You're right, I do. But there'll be enough distraction for the Board members."

How much should he tell the men who were coming to pass judgment? If this concept of the David had taken him months of painful intellectual search, he could not expect to justify his departures from Florentine tradition in one short hour. Might not the men think of what his tongue was saying instead of what his hand had carved?

Argiento had everything scrubbed and orderly in the workshed. Soderini, with sixteen men, arrived just as Giotto's Campanile bells began to chime. Michelangelo greeted them warmly, remembering the names of Michelozzo, chancellor of the Wool Art Guild, Consuls Pandolfini and Giovanni di Pagno degli Albizi, Paolo de' Carnesecchi of the Board of Works, the notary of the Board, Bambelli, a number of others. The older men were still guarding against the cold by wearing full dark clothes fastened at the neck and reaching their square-toed, thonged shoes, but the younger and more venturesome were saluting spring in particoloured stockings patterned with the family blazon, and shirts with slashed sleeves.

They crowded around the half-born David, gazing up ten feet in the air with awe. Chancellor Michelozzo asked if Michelangelo would demonstrate to them how he worked the marble. He picked up his hammer and chisel, showed them how the back of his chisel sank into the hammer just as it sank into the marble, creating no explosion, but rather a gentle insinuative force. He indicated that the abrupt termination of each chisel passage caused a slight chipping as the tool was lifted, therefore the longer the "Go!" the fewer chippings.

He had them circle the David, pointed out its vertical structural strength, how the arms would be released from the protective webbing which ran at an angle into the torso, the tree trunk which would be the only object to support the giant nude. The figure was still tilted twenty per cent in the upright block, but he demonstrated how, as he discarded the negative marble now surrounding it, the David would stand head on.

The next afternoon Soderini came into the Duomo yard with an official-looking document in his hand, clapped Michelangelo on the back.

"The Boards were pleased. Shall I read? 'The Honourable Lord Consuls of the Wool Art Guild decided that the Board of Works of the Duomo can give the sculptor Michelangelo Buonarroti four hundred large golden florins in payment of the Giant called David existing in the Opera and that Michelangelo shall complete the work to perfection within two years from to-day.'"

"Now I can forget about money until I have finished. That is paradise for an artist."

He waited until Lodovico brought up the subject the next time. "The reward has been fixed, Father: four hundred large gold florins."

Lodovico's eyes sparkled, lighting his hollow cheeks.

"Four hundred florins! Excellent! Plus six florins a month for as long as you work . . ."

"No."

"Surely they're adding the florins you've earned each month? They're not so niggardly as to take those back?"

"I continue to receive six florins a month for two more years. . . ."

"Ah, good." Lodovico picked up his pen. "Let's see, twenty-four times six equals one hundred and forty-four, added to four hundred, equals five hundred and forty-four florins, a much better price."

Bleakly, Michelangelo replied, "No. Just four hundred florins. *In toto*. All the florins paid by the month are in advance. They will be deducted at the end."

The pleasure went out of Lodovico's expression as he saw himself losing one hundred and forty-four florins.

"It's not right," he muttered, "first they give you money, then they take it away."

And Michelangelo knew how it would be: Lodovico would go around with a wounded expression, as though someone had taken advantage of him. He had not earned his peace, after all. Perhaps there was no such thing as peace.

9

To mark the frontal projections, David's left foot, left knee, right wrist, the left elbow and hand at the shoulder, he affixed nailheads in the marble. With these fixed points established he was able to carve the upsurging line from the knee through the thigh and chest, delineating David's hard physical stamina; the flesh of the belly in which David was feeling quiverings of anxiety; the left hand holding the slingshot, the great right hand standing cocked, rock at the ready. To protect himself he had left half again as much marble at the rear as he would ultimately need, keeping in mind the fact that there were forty views of a statue as one walked around it.

He had designed David as an independent man, standing clear of all space around him. The statue must never be fitted into a niche, stood against a wall, used to decorate a façade or soften the harsh corner of a building. David must always be free. The world was a battlefield, man for ever under strain, precarious on his perch. David was a fighter; not a brutal, senseless ravager, but capable of achieving freedom.

Now the figure became aggressive, began to push out of its mass, striving to define itself in space. His own pace matched the drive of the material, so that Sangallo and Sansovino, visiting him of a Sunday afternoon, were staggered by his passion.

" I've never seen anything like it," cried Sangallo. " He's knocked off more chips from this hard marble in the last quarter of an hour than any three of his stonecutter friends in the quarry could cut in four."

" It's not the quantity that frightens me," added Sansovino, " it's the impetuosity. I've been watching fragments get hurled four feet in the air, until I thought the whole marble would fly to pieces."

" Michelangelo," cried Sangallo. " You've been shaving the line so closely that if you had overpassed it by a hairs-breadth, you risked losing all!"

Michelangelo stopped work, turned and faced his friends.

" Once marble is out of its quarry, it is no longer a mountain, it is a river. It can flow, change its course. That's what I'm doing, helping this marble river change its bed."

When the others had returned to their homes, Michelangelo sat at the David's feet and gazed up at him. He thought, " It takes as long for a marble column to bear, as it does a fruit tree." Yet each separate form within the sculpture was beginning to mirror the time and love he had lavished on it. Nor was he frightened by Sansovino's warning, for he identified himself with the centre of gravity of the block, fitting himself into the core, feeling the balancing weight of the arms, legs, torso, head, as though they were his own. When he sliced off marble he did so with the precise knowledge of how much flesh he could safely spare.

The one thorn in this flesh, his own and the David's, was Leonardo da Vinci's belittling of the sculptor's art. To Michelangelo it appeared a serious threat. Leonardo's influence in Florence was spreading; if it should convince enough people that marble carving was a second-rate craft, when his David was completed it would be received with indifference. Growing within him was a need to counter-attack.

The following Sunday when the Company of the Cauldron was meeting at Rustici's, and Leonardo made light of stone carving, Michelangelo said:

"True, sculpture shares nothing with painting. It exists on its own premises. But primitive man carved in stone for thousands of years before he began to paint on cave walls. Sculpture is the first and original art."

"By that very claim it is condemned," answered Leonardo in his high-pitched voice. "It satisfied only until the fine art of painting was developed. It is now becoming extinct."

Infuriated, Michelangelo struck back with a personal attack.

"Isn't it true, Leonardo," he demanded, "that your equestrian statue in Milan is so colossal that it can never be cast? And hence will never come into existence as bronze sculpture? And that your huge clay model is disintegrating so fast that it's becoming the joke of Milan? No wonder you talk against sculpture, you're not capable of bringing a piece to completion!"

There was an uncomfortable silence in the room.

A few days later Florence learned that, despite its payments to Cæsar Borgia, he was marching on Urbino and helping to incite a rebellion in Arezzo against Florentine rule. Leonardo da Vinci joined Cæsar Borgia's army as an engineer, to work alongside Torrigiani and Piero de' Medici. Michelangelo was outraged.

"He's a traitor," he cried angrily to Rustici, who was taking care of Leonardo's possessions while he was gone. "Cæsar Borgia offers him a big salary, and so he will help conquer Florence. After we gave him hospitality, commissions to paint important pictures . . ."

"It really isn't that bad," said Rustici placatingly. "Leonardo is at loose ends, he can't seem to finish his painting of Monna Lisa del Giocondo. He's more interested in his new war machines than in art. He saw in Cæsar Borgia's offer a chance to test out a lot of his inventions. He doesn't understand politics, you know."

" Tell that to the Florentines," replied Michelangelo acidly, " if his new machines batter down the walls."

" You're justified in feeling as you do, Michelangelo, but try to remember that he is amoral. He is not interested in right and wrong as it applies to people; only in the true and false in science and knowledge."

" I suppose I ought to be glad to be rid of him. He fled once before, for eighteen years. I hope we can count on as long this time."

Rustici shook his head wistfully.

" You two stand like the Apennines above the rest of us, yet you hate each other. It doesn't make sense. Or does it?"

The cycle of the seasons brought gloriously hot weather. Occasional showers did nothing to the David but wash the marble dust off him. Michelangelo worked stripped to his drawers and sandals, letting the sun beat down on his body and pour its strength into him. He scampered up and down the ladder as lightly as a cat, working the stout neck, heroic head and mass of curls from the top of the scaffold, carving the spine with great care to indicate that it carried and directed the whole body and was the mainspring of all movement. There could be no part of the David that was not palpable, and perfect. He had never understood why the erogenous zone had been represented as unbeautiful. If God made man as the Bible said he had made Adam, would he have made the area of procreation something to hide, something vile? Perhaps man had perverted the uses thereof, as he had managed to pervert so much else on earth; but what did that have to do with his statue? That which had been despised, he would make godlike.

He kept no track of time. He carved all day. Late of a stifling evening he might sit on the cool marble steps of the Duomo, where the young artists of Florence still gathered, to listen to improvised songs on guitars, exchange news of coming commissions throughout Tuscany, and listen to Jacopo discuss which of the passing girls were mattressable . . . even as he had fourteen years before. In June, Piero Soderini was elected to another two months as Gonfaloniere. People were beginning to ask why, since he was the best man in Tuscany for the job, he could not be allowed to govern longer.

When Michelangelo learned that Contessina was going to have another baby, he went to Soderini's office overlooking the Piazza della Signoria, to plead her cause.

"Why can she not return to her home for the birth of her child? She has committed no crime against the Republic. She was *Il magnifico's* daughter before she was Ridolfi's wife. Her life is being endangered by this isolation in a cottage where there are no facilities . . ."

"The country people have managed to have their babies in those houses for a thousand years."

"Contessina is not country people. She's frail. She wasn't raised this way. Couldn't you plead to the Council of Seventy for justice?"

"It is impossible." Soderini's voice was flat, expressionless. "The kindest thing you can do is not bring up the Ridolfi name."

It was in the middle of Soderini's two-month term, with Arezzo and Pisa again in revolt, Piero de' Medici welcomed in Arezzo and promised help in conquering Florence, Cæsar Borgia kept from attacking only through fear of French retaliation, and the city's gates kept locked during the day, with "all who lived along the river forbidden to lower ladders, to prevent anyone entering the town," that Michelangelo received a message to have supper with the Gonfaloniere at the Palazzo della Signoria. There was good work light until seven, after which he returned home to put on a linen shirt.

Soderini was sitting before a low table, his long yellow-white hair still wet from washing. They exchanged news on the state of the David, Soderini told that the Council of Seventy was about to change the constitution. The next man elected Gonfaloniere would have a lifetime position. Then he leaned across the table in a relaxed, confiding manner.

"Michelangelo, you have heard of Pierre de Rohan, the Maréchal de Gié? He was here in the 1494 invasion with Charles VIII, as one of his closest advisers. You may also recall that in the Medici courtyard Donatello's bronze David had the place of honour."

"The day the palace was sacked I was knocked into it so hard I had a lump on the back of my head."

"Then you know it well. Now, our ambassador to the French court has written that the Maréchal fell in love with the David while staying at the Medici palace, and would like to have one. For years we have been buying France's protection with money. Isn't it gratifying that for once we can pay for it with a work of art?"

Michelangelo looked at this man who had become such a good friend to him. It would be impossible to deny him. Instead he asked, " I am not to copy the Donatello?"

" Let's say that it would be safe to create minor variations, but not enough to disappoint the Maréchal's memory."

Michelangelo put a slice of cheese on a quartered pear.

" I've never had a chance to do anything for Florence. It gives me a good feeling. If only I had not been an idiot, and refused to learn casting from Bertoldo."

" We have good casters in Florence: Bonaccorso Ghiberti, the cannon maker, and Lodovico Lotti, the bell caster."

The sensation of being a patriot faded when he again stood in front of Donatello's David in the courtyard of the Signoria. He had come so far from this conception in his own figure! If he could not bring himself to copy it, and at the same time could not change it . . .?

He returned to the courtyard in the morning, carrying a box to sit on, and sheets of old drawing paper. His David emerged several years older than Donatello's, more male and muscular, drawn with the inner tensions that can be transplanted to marble, few of which were present in the smooth-surfaced bronze youth before him. He set up an armature on the back bench in the workshed, used his occasional rest hours to transpose his drawings into a rough clay structure, slowly building up a nude with a turban binding up the hair. He was amused to think that, in the interests of Florence, he had to model a head of Goliath, on which David rested his foot in triumph. The Maréchal would never be happy without that head.

The perfect weather lasted through November first, when Soderini was installed as Gonfaloniere for life in a colourful pageant on the Signoria steps, with all of Florence in the piazza, and Michelangelo up front, feeling proud and secure. Then freezing winter clamped down. Michelangelo and Argieto put up the roof, reset the tiles. The four braziers could not cut the intense cold. He wore his cap with the earmuffs. Beppe hung a canvas over the side opening, but there was little light from the overcast skies and the canvas cut out that little. Now he suffered from darkness as well as cold. He worked by candlelight and lamp. Nor was spring much help; heavy rains began in early March and lasted for months.

Towards the end of April he received an invitation to dinner in the new apartment of the Signoria, presided over by Monna Argentina Soderini, the first woman ever permitted to live in the palace. The suite had been decorated by Giuliano da Sangallo and young Baccio d'Agnolo, the living, dining and bedrooms converted from first- and second-floor offices formerly used by the city notary and chancellor. The dining-room was frescoed, the ceiling done in gilt, the cupboards and buffet of inlaid woods. The dinner table was laid before a fire, warm and cheerful. Michelangelo took off his green cloak, pleased with his appearance in his smocked woollen shirt. Soderini showed off his wife's flower pots in the windows.

" I know some people are complaining about the expense of the window boxes," he said shyly; " but actually I think it's their way of saying that women shouldn't live in the Palazzo della Signoria."

After dinner Soderini asked Michelangelo to accompany him to the Duomo.

" For years Florence has been talking of having the Twelve Apostles in marble for the cathedral. Larger than life size. Of perfect Seravezza marble. That would fill the cavernous space, would it not?"

" With the light of a thousand candles."

Soderini stopped at the back of the central altar, facing the Donatello and Della Robbia marble choirs.

" I've been speaking to the members of the Boards. They think it a magnificent idea."

Numbly, Michelangelo murmured, " It's a lifetime of work."

" So were Ghiberti's doors."

" That's what Bertoldo wanted for me: a body of work."

Soderini linked his arm through Michelangelo's, walked him down the long nave towards the open door.

" It would make you the official sculptor of Florence. The contract I have been discussing with the Boards includes a house we will build for you, and a studio of your own design."

" A home of my own! And a studio."

" I thought that would please you. You could do one Apostle a year. As each was delivered, you would own another twelfth of your house and studio."

Michelangelo stopped in the doorway. He turned about to look at the enormous and empty cathedral. Assuredly it could use the Twelve Apostles.

"To-morrow is the monthly meeting of the Joint Boards. They have asked you to appear."

Michelangelo's smile was sickly. He made his way, cold and shivering, through the streets towards the hills, glad that he had worn a warm cloak. When he began to climb to Settignano he perspired as heavily as though he had a fever. He could not concentrate his thoughts on any one aspect of Soderini's proposed commission. Then, as he reached the Settignano farmhouse, pride took precedence: he was only twenty-eight, and he was going to have a home of his own, and a sculpture studio adequate to carve heroic pieces. He stood on the terrace in the midst of the five Topolino men, began slicing *pietra serena* blocks into long slabs.

"Better tell us," said the father, "before you burst."

"I am now a man of substance."

"What kind of substance?" asked Bruno.

"I shall have a house."

He told them about the Twelve Apostles. The father brought out a bottle of old wine, reserved for marriages and births of sons. They drank a glass to his good fortune.

His anxieties rushed upward to drown out the pride. He descended the hill, jumped stones to cross the creek, climbed the opposite side to stand for a moment gazing at the house and rooms in which he remembered his mother. How proud she would be, how happy for him.

Then why was he not happy for himself? Was it because he did not want to carve the Twelve Apostles ? Because he hesitated to lock himself into a commission that would consume the next twelve years of his life? Once again be obliged to handle fully clothed and draped figures? He did not know whether he could endure it, after the glorious freedom of the David. Even Donatello had done only one or two apostles in marble. How was he going to create something fresh and different for each of the twelve?

His feet carried him to Giuliano da Sangallo, where he found his friend at his draughting table. Sangallo already knew about the proposal; Soderini had asked him and *Il Cronaca* to appear at the meeting the following afternoon to witness the signing of the contract. *Il Cronaca* was to design the house.

"Sangallo, this project isn't anything I conceived for myself. Should a sculptor undertake a twelve-year task unless he's passionately eager to do it?"

Sangallo replied noncommittally, " It's a lot of years."

" As long as a sculptor lives from one commission to another he remains someone who is hired."

" Painting and sculpture have always been commissioned. Is there an alternative?"

" To create art works independently, sell them to whoever will buy."

" Unheard of."

" But not impossible?"

" . . . perhaps not. But can you turn down the Gonfaloniere and the Boards? They are offering you the biggest commission since Ghiberti's doors. The members would be offended. That would put you in a difficult position."

Michelangelo sat with his head in his hands, glum.

" I know. I can't take it, and I can't turn it down."

Sangallo brought a hand down sharply on Michelangelo's shoulder.

" Take the contract, build your house and studio, carve as many Apostles as you can do well. When you're through, you're through; you'll pay off the rest of the house in cash."

" Another Piccolomini contract," said Michelangelo mournfully.

He signed the contract. The news spread through the city with the speed of a fresh scandal. Strangers bowed to him respectfully in the Via de' Gori. He nodded back, wondering what they would think if they could know how miserable he was. He reached home to find the Buonarroti in the family room, excitedly planning their new house. Uncle Francesco and Aunt Cassandra decided they wanted a third floor to themselves.

" Get it built quickly," said his father. " The faster we move in, the sooner we stop paying rent here."

Michelangelo turned away to gaze sightlessly into the street. He spoke without emotion.

" This is to be my home. And my workshop. It is not to be the family residence."

There was a stunned silence. Then his father, uncle and aunt all began talking at once, so that he could not disentangle the voices.

" How can you say such a thing? Your home is our home. We can save rent. Who will cook and clean . . ."

He knew better than to say, " I am now twenty-eight, and it is time I had my own house. I have earned it." Instead he replied, " The land is provided, but I am allowed only six hundred florins for building purposes. I need a huge studio to handle these marbles, with a thirty-foot roof, and a large outdoor paved court. There will be enough left for a small house, one bedroom, two at the most . . ."

The storm lasted the rest of the day, until everyone was worn out. Michelangelo was adamant; the least he could get out of the contract was private work quarters, a secluded island to live in. But he had to agree to pay the rent for this apartment out of his monthly advances.

When he had a clay model of the Maréchal's David he sent Argiento to Lodovico Lotti, the bell caster, and Bonaccorso Ghiberti, the cannon caster. The two artisans came from their foundries in clothes streaked with grime. The Gonfaloniere had requested them to help Michelangelo get the bronze ready. When they saw Micheangelo's model they looked at each other, Lotti wiping black soot from the back of his hand across his eyes.

" It won't cast," he declared.

" Why not?"

" Because you got to make a plaster mould," said Ghiberto.

" I know nothing of this confounded art."

"We can only cast what another man makes," replied Lotti.

Michelangelo sought help from Rustici, Sansovino, Bugiardini, to see if they had listened more closely to Bertoldo about bronze. From them he learned that he would have to make his clay statue full size and exact, then build over it with plaster, piece by piece, marking on every piece a numerical key for identification, oil the pieces where the edges had to be connected, set the plaster cast aside . . .

" *Basta!*" groaned Michelangelo. " No wonder I never learned."

The casters brought him back his David. He gazed dully at the ugly red bronze figure, streaked, bumpy, ridged, with protuberances of metal where it was not wanted. He was going to need punches, files, chasing tools to make it look human; then burnishers, metal chisels, polishers, pumice and oil to make it presentable. Even then, would the Maréchal's memory so fail him as to imagine this David resembled Donatello's? He doubted it.

10

The first fruit of his contract for the Twelve Apostles was a visit from a neighbour he had known in the Piazza Santa Croce, Agnolo Doni, his own age, whose father had made a beginning competence in the wool trade and bought a neglected palace near the Albertini palace in the Santa Croce quarter. Agnolo Doni had taken over his father's business and palace, earned the reputation of being the sharpest bargainer in Tuscany, made a fortune and remodelled the palace. He had come so high in the financial and social worlds of Florence that he was now engaged to Maddalena Strozzi.

Beppe brought Doni into the workshed with an apologetic expression. Michelangelo was high on the scaffold carving on the sling over David's left shoulder. He laid down his tools, climbed down the ladder. Doni was wearing an expensive doublet, from which a shirt puffed out at the shoulders, fastened at the breast and waist with golden clasps.

"I'll come straight to the point, Buonarroti," he said as Michelangelo reached the ground. "I want you to do a Holy Family as a wedding present for my bride-to-be, Maddalena Strozzi."

Michelangelo flushed with pleasure; Maddalena had been brought up with his Hercules.

"The Strozzi have good taste in the arts," he murmured. "A Holy Family in white marble . . ."

Doni's small mouth, framed between the vertical creases on either side, fell visibly.

"No, no, it is I who have the good taste! I thought of commissioning you, not Maddalena. And who said anything about marble? That would cost a lot of money. All I want is a painting, to be used as an inset in a round table."

Michelangelo picked up his hammer and chisel.

"Why should you come to me for a painting? I haven't put colour on a brush for fifteen years."

"Pure loyalty. We are of the same quarter. Remember how we used to play football in the Piazza Santa Croce?"

Michelangelo smiled ironically. Doni pressed.

"What do you say? A Holy Family. Thirty florins. Ten

for each figure. That's a generous sum, isn't it? Shall we call it a bargain?"

"I don't know how much the painters will charge you, Doni, but you can have your choice of half a dozen of the best in Italy: Granacci, Filipino Lippi. What about Ghirlandaio's son, Ridolfo? He's going to be a fine craftsman, and he'll do it cheap."

"Look Buonarroti. I want you to paint a Holy Family. I don't want one by Lippi or young Ghirlandaio. I already have Gonfaloniere Soderini's permission."

"But, Doni, it makes no sense. You don't take your wool to a scissors maker to be woven . . ."

"It is well known that to carve marble is to be only a fraction of an artist."

"Enough," growled Michelangelo, furious at this repetition of Leonardo's denunciation. "I'll paint your Holy Family. For one hundred gold florins."

"One hundred!" screamed Doni, so that he could be heard the length of the Duomo workyard. "How can you cheat one of your oldest friends? The playmate of your youth. It's like stealing the purse off your brother's belt."

They compromised on seventy florins; but not until Michelangelo's eardrums felt broken. By the crafty smile in Doni's shrewd eyes, Michelangelo perceived that Doni had outwitted, or at least outshouted, him and would have paid the hundred florins. From the door Doni said not unkindly, "You were the worst *calcio* player in the neighbourhood. That puzzles me: how could you be so bad at football and so good at sculpture? But you certainly are the artist of the moment."

"That's why you want me, because I'm fashionable?"

"What better reason could there be? When will I see the sketches?"

"The sketches are my business. The finished product is yours."

"You agreed to let Cardinal Piccolomini see your drawings."

"Get yourself appointed a cardinal."

When Doni had left, Michelangelo realized that he had been an idiot to let the man goad him into taking the commission. What did he know about painting? Or care? He could design a Holy Family, the drawing would be fun. But paint and colour! Young Ridolfo could handle these better than he.

Yet his interest was piqued. He had dozens of drawings for a Madonna and Child that he had made for the merchants from Bruges, should the Mouscrons sign Jacopo Galli's contract. They were intensely spiritual, removed from the mundane world. For a Holy Family the concept should be the opposite in spirit: earthy, a family of simple people.

As always during the hot summer days when he permitted himself a rest, he tramped the roads of Tuscany, sketching the farmers in the fields, eating before their door in the cool of evening, the young country mothers nursing their young before putting them to sleep in cribs under the outdoor arches. Over the days he drew for the Doni portrait a strong-limbed, healthy young girl from one household, a plump, red-cheeked curly-haired child from another, a bald-headed bearded grandfather from a third, put them together in an affectionate grouping on the grass. The flesh tones of the arms, faces, feet, the naked *bambino* he had no trouble with, but the robes of the mother and Joseph, the blanket of the child, eluded him.

Granacci dropped by, amused at Michelangelo's bafflement.

"Would you like me to fill in the colours? You're making such an awful mess."

"Why didn't Doni honour you with the commission in the first place? You are of the Santa Croce quarter. You played football with him too!"

In the end he did a series of monotones, as though they were coloured marble. The mother's dress he painted pale rose and blue, the child's blanket light to burnt orange, Joseph showing only a shoulder and arm of faded blue. In the foreground he painted a few simple bunches of flowers growing in the grass. The background was bare, except for the impish face of John looking upward. To amuse himself he painted a sea on one side of the family, mountains on the other; before the sea and the mountains he drew in five nude youths, sitting on a wall, glorious bronze figures with the sun on them, creating the effect of a Greek frieze.

Doni's face went the colour of his red tunic when he answered Michelangelo's summons to see the finished picture.

"Show me one thing that is holy about this picture of peasants! One sentiment that is religious! You're mocking me!"

"Would I be such a fool as to throw away my work on a

mockery? These are fine people, tender in their love of the child."

"I want a Holy Family in a palace."

"Holiness has nothing to do with surroundings. It's an inner spiritual quality."

"I cannot give this picnic on the grass to my delicate bride. I would lose caste with the Strozzi family. You have put me in the worst imaginable light."

"Might I remind you that you did not reserve the right of rejection?"

Doni's eyes narrowed to slits, then flew open at the same time as his mouth as he cried in horror:

"What are those five naked boys doing in my Holy Family?"

"Why, they've just come out from a swim in the sea," replied Michelangelo calmly, "and are drying themselves in the sun."

"You've been touched by the moon," screamed Doni. "Whoever heard of five naked youths forming a background for a Christian picture?"

"Think of them as figures on a frieze. This gives you both a Christian painting and a Greek sculpture, at no extra charge. Remember your original offer was thirty florins, ten for each figure. If I wanted to be greedy I could charge you fifty florins extra for the five youths. But I won't, because we are of the same quarter."

"I'll take the picture to Leonardo da Vinci," growled Doni, "and have those five obscene idlers painted out!"

Until now Michelangelo had been amused. Now he cried, "I'll sue you for defacing a work of art!"

"I'm paying for it, and I can deface it all I want."

"Remember Savonarola! I'll haul you before the Council."

Doni groaned, stormed out. The next day his servant arrived with a pouch of thirty-five florins, half the price agreed upon, and a release for Michelangelo to sign. Michelangelo sent Argiento back with the pouch. On a scrap of paper he scrawled:

The Holy Family will now cost you one hundred and forty florins.

Florence enjoyed the contest, with bets on who would win. Michelangelo found himself on the short end of the odds because no one had ever bested Doni in a deal. However the time was growing short to Doni's wedding day, and he had bragged all over town that he was having Florence's official artist paint a wedding gift for his bride. Doni arrived at the Duomo workshed with a leather purse containing seventy florins, crying:

"Here's your money, give me my painting."

"Doni, that wouldn't be fair. You hate the picture, and I release you from your agreement."

"Don't try to outwit me. I'll go to Gonfaloniere Soderini and have him force you to fulfil your contract."

"I didn't know you loved the painting that much. Now I believe that you're a great art collector. Just hand over the hundred and forty florins . . ."

"You're a swindler! You agreed to paint the picture for seventy . . ."

". . . an agreement you threw open to renegotiation by offering me thirty-five florins. My price is now one hundred and forty."

"Never," screamed Doni, "for that mediocre peasant picture. I'll see you hanged from the Bargello first."

Michelangelo decided he had had his fun, was about to send the painting to Doni when a barefooted *contadino* boy brought him a note which read:

I hear that Maddalena wants your painting. She has said no wedding present will please her more. *C*.

He had immediately recognized the handwriting. He knew that Maddalena Strozzi had been Contessina's friend; he was happy to realize that some of her old friends had remained in touch with her. He chuckled, sat down at his workbench, and wrote a note which he sent to Doni:

I fully appreciate how expensive my painting must seem to you. As an old and dear friend, I will release you from any financial embarrassment by giving the Holy Family to another friend.

Doni came running on Argiento's heels; flung down a pouch with a clang loud enough to be heard above all the stone chipping in the yard.

"I demand the painting! It is now mine by legal right."

He picked up the leather bag, untied the thong and poured the hundred and forty gold pieces on to the worktable. "Count them! One hundred and forty pieces of gold! For a miserable peasant family sitting on the grass. Why I let you exploit me this way is beyond my comprehension!"

Michelangelo picked up the painting, handed it to Doni.

"My compliments to your wife-to-be."

Doni made his way to the door, grumbling, "Artists!

Supposed to be impractical. Ha! You'd bankrupt the shrewdest merchant in Tuscany!"

Michelangelo gathered up the coins. He had enjoyed the whole affair. It was as refreshing as a vacation.

11

There was considerable rejoicing in August when the Borgia Pope, Alexander VI, died. When Cardinal Piccolomini of Siena was elected to the papacy, Giuliano da Sangallo was crushed, Michelangelo was apprehensive. He had done no further work on the Piccolomini statues, not even a line of drawing. One word from the new Pope, and Gonfaloniere Soderini would be obliged to take him off the David until the remaining eleven figures were completed and delivered.

He refused to allow anyone into the workshed for a month as he worked frenziedly, before the Vatican axe could fall. Most of David's body was realized, only the face and head remained. For the first time he realized the weight of the contract for the Twelve Apostles, which would also hang over his head for years. He wanted to throw himself into the Arno.

Cardinal Piccolomini lasted as Pope Pius III for one month, dying suddenly in Rome. This time Giuliano da Sangallo proved to be the prognosticator: Cardinal Rovere was elected Pope Julius II. There was an uproarious celebration at the Sangallos', where Giuliano told everyone he was taking Michelangelo to Rome with him to create great marble sculptures.

Leonardo da Vinci returned from Cæsar Borgia's army, was given the keys to the Great Hall of the Signoria in anticipation of being awarded a commission to create a fresco for the wall just behind the platform on which Gonfaloniere Soderini and the Signoria sat. The payment was to be ten thousand florins!

Michelangelo was livid. This was the largest and most important painting commission given by Florence in decades. Ten thousand florins to Leonardo for a fresco which was to be completed in two years. Four hundred florins to him for the Giant-David! For the same amount of work! Given to a man who would have helped Cæsar Borgia conquer Florence! Leonardo was to be paid twenty-five times as much as the city was paying him. By that very fact, he had again struck a mortal blow against sculpture.

He ran in his rage to Soderini's office. Soderini heard him out; it was part of his talent to let his people have their say. He also allowed a few moments of silence for Michelangelo to hear his angry words echoing off the walls before answering in the quietest possible voice.

"Leonardo da Vinci is a great painter. I have seen the Last Supper in Milan. It is tremendous. No one in all Italy can equal him. I am frankly covetous of Milan's fresco, and I am anxious that he paint one for Florence. If it is as fine, it will enrich us enormously."

Michelangelo had been reproved and dismissed, all in the same breath.

There began the final months of work, so highly pleasurable to him now that the two years of labour were coming into focus. He went to David's face, carved it tenderly, with all the love and sympathy in his being; the strong, noble face of the youth who would, in one more moment, make the leap into manhood; but at this instant was still sad and uncertain over what he must do; the brows deeply knit, the eyes questioning, the full lips expectant. The set of the features had to be of a whole with the body. The expression on David's face must communicate that evil was vulnerable, even though it wore armour weighing a thousand pounds. There would always be some spot in it which was undefended; and if the good in man were dominant it would find that exposed area and evolve a way to penetrate it. The emotion must convey the idea that his conflict with Goliath was a parable of good and evil.

The head was to have a feeling of illumination about it coming not only from within but from the area around it. To achieve this, he left volume about David's lips, jaws, nostrils. For the eyes and nostrils he used an auger; for the eyebrows a small chisel. For the deep penetration in the ear-holes and between the teeth he drilled with a small-size bit, then larger bits as the openings grew larger. Between the strands of hair he made a series of penetrations, the holes following one another, orderly, controlled, using a long thin needle, holding it between both palms, rotating it, exerting only the slightest pressure of the hands. He took the most exquisite pains with the skin creases on the forehead, the tense slightly drawn-in nostrils, the slightly parted lips.

With the last of the webbing slowly cut away, he began to

polish. He did not want as high a sheen as he had achieved for the Pietà. What he wanted was the outward expression of blood, muscle, brain, vein, bone, tissue; true, convincing, lifelike, in beautiful proportion: David in the warm palpitant human flesh, with a mind and a spirit and a soul shining through; a David quivering with emotion, the cords in his neck pulled taut by the head turned hard to Goliath, yet withal knowing that to live is to act.

In early January of 1504 Florence learned that Piero de' Medici had acted for the last time. Fighting with the French army, because he hoped to secure help from Louis XII against Florence, Piero had drowned in the Garigliano River when a boat in which he was saving four pieces of artillery from the Spanish army overturned. A member of the Signoria exclaimed publicly, "We Florentines are much rejoiced to hear that news!" Michelangelo had a moment of sadness, then pity for Alfonsina and her children; he remembered Lorenzo on his deathbed, telling Piero how to rule Florence. Then he was conscious that Piero's death meant that Contessina was nearer to being released from her exile.

At the end of January, Soderini called a meeting of artists and artisans of Florence to decide where the Giant-David should be placed. Michelangelo was summoned to the Signoria and shown the list of people invited to the discussion. He saw that the painters included Botticelli, Rosselli, David Ghirlandaio, Leonardo da Vinci, Filippino Lippi, Piero di Cosimo, Granacci, Perugino, Lorenzo di Credi. The sculptors were Rustici, Sansovino and Betto Buglioni, the architects Giuliano and his brother Antonio da Sangallo, *Il Cronaca,* Baccio d'Agnolo. There were four goldsmiths, two jewellers, an embroiderer, a terra-cotta designer, an illuminator; two carpenters on their way to becoming architects; the cannon caster Ghiberti; the clockmaker Lorenzo della Golpaia.

"Can you think of anyone left out?" asked Soderini.

"Me."

"I don't think you should be included. The others might be constrained in speaking."

"I'd like to express my opinion."

"You already have," replied Soderini dryly.

The meeting was called for the following day in the upstairs library of the Duomo headquarters, before the supper hour. Michelangelo had not meant to hover, but there were windows in the library facing the workyard, and he heard the hubbub of many voices above him as the artists collected. He walked through the yard, climbed a back stair to a small adjoining vestibule. Someone rapped for order, silence fell, Michelangelo recognized the voice of Francesco Filarete, herald of the Signoria.

"I have turned over in my mind those suggestions which my judgment could afford me. You have two places where the statue might be set up: the first, where the Donatello Judith stands; the second, in the middle of the courtyard where the bronze David is. The first might be selected because the Judith is an omen of evil and no fit object where it stands; besides, it is not proper that the woman should kill the male; and above all, this statue was erected under an evil constellation, since we have gone continually from bad to worse since then. The David is imperfect in the right leg; and so I should counsel you to put the Giant in one of these places, but I give the preference myself to that of the Judith."

That suited Michelangelo fine. Another voice started speaking, one he did not recognize. He peeked into the library, saw that the speaker was Monciatto, the wood carver.

"I say that the Giant was meant to be put on the pillars outside the Duomo, or spurs around the church. I do not know why it should not be put there, and it seems to me that it would look fine and as a suitable ornament to the church of Santa Maria del Fiore."

Michelangelo watched Rosselli rise feebly.

"Both Messer Francesco Filarete and Messer Francesco Monciatto spoke all right. However I had originally thought that the Giant should be placed on the stairs of the Duomo, to the right side, and, according to my opinion, this would be the best place."

Other opinions came fast. Gallieno, the embroiderer, thought it should be placed where the Marzocco, the Lion, stood, in the piazza, with which David Ghirlandaio agreed; several, including Leonardo da Vinci, chose the loggia because the marble would be protected. Il Cronaca suggested the Great Hall, where Leonardo's fresco was to be painted.

Michelangelo muttered, "Isn't there one artist here who will say I should have the right to select the spot myself?"

Then Filippino Lippi said, "I think that everyone said wise things, but I am sure that the sculptor will propose the best place, as he certainly has considered longer and with more authority the spot where the Giant should be placed."

There was a murmur of agreement. Angelo Manfidi concluded:

"Before your magnificent lords decide where the statue ought to be placed, I suggest that you ask the advice of the Signori among whom there are some high intellects."

Michelangelo closed the door noiselessly and went down the back stairs to the yard. Gonfaloniere Soderini would now be able to guide the Giant-David to the spot Michelangelo wanted: in front of the Palazzo Signoria where the Judith now stood.

Crusty Pollaiuolo, *Il Cronaca,* as supervising architect of the Duomo, was in charge of moving the David; but he appeared grateful for the offer of Antonio da Sangallo, as well as Giuliano, to design a carrier. Baccio d'Agnolo, the architect, volunteered his services, as did Chimente del Tasso and Bernando della Cecca, the two young carpenter-architects, since they were interested in the problem of moving the largest marble sculpture ever to be carried through the streets of Florence. The statue must be anchored securely so that it would not topple, yet not so rigidly that a jolt, jar or sudden movement could damage it.

"The David will have to be carried upright," said Giuliano. "The framework in which it is being transported must be moved so that the marble feels no motion."

"The solution?" replied Antonio. "A carrier within a carrier. We won't fasten him down; we'll put him in a sling, inside a big wooden frame; then he'll sway gently back and forth with the movement."

The two carpenter-architects built a twenty-foot cage of wood to the Sangallos' specifications, open at the top. Antonio devised a series of slip knots which ran easily on the ropes, becoming tighter under weight, loosening as the pressure slackened. The David was encased in a net of enormous ropes, lifted by grapples, moved inside the open cage, suspended and held in its web. The wall behind the workshed was ripped out, the cage raised on to round rollers, the roadbed made smooth. The statue was ready for its mile-long journey through the Florentine streets.

Il Cronaca hired forty men to drag the huge crate on its round logs, using windlasses turned by a bar. As the heavy frame inched its way forward the rear log was released, picked up by a workman who ran forward to put it under the front of the framework. David, secured at the crotch

432

and upward along Michelangelo's columnar structure over the strong chest, swayed only along the distance of the slip knots.

In spite of the forty workmen, the statue was moved but a few feet an hour. By nightfall they had got it out of the wall, down the Street of the Clock to the corner, manœuvred the sharp turn into the Via del Proconsolo, with hundreds of people watching the procession, and then only half a block down the street before darkness settled.

Everyone cried their "Good night. Until to-morrow." Michelangelo went home. He paced the bedroom, trying to pass the hours. At midnight, uneasy, he left the house to return to the David. There it stood, gleaming white in the moonlight, unfettered in its roped-in security, still facing towards Goliath, the hand reaching for the sling, the profile chiselled and polished to flawless beauty.

He threw a blanket inside the cage, in the space behind the David where the right calf joined the tree trunk. There was room for him to lie on the wooden floor. He had fallen into a state halfway from wakefulness when he heard running feet, the sound of voices, then stones hitting the side wall of the frame. He sprang up, cried:

"Guards!"

He heard the running feet go down the Proconsolo, gave chase, calling at the top of his lungs:

"Stop! Night guards! Stop them!"

The half dozen fleeing forms seemed to be young boys. His heart pounding wildly, he returned to the David, found two guards standing there with lanterns.

"What's all the noise?"

"The statue was being stoned."

"Stoned? By whom?"

"I don't know."

"Did they hit it?"

"I don't think so. I heard only the sound on wood."

"You're sure you weren't having a bad dream?"

"I tell you I saw them. And heard them. If I hadn't been here . . ."

He circled the David, peering through the darkness, wondering who would want to injure it.

"Vandals," said Soderini, arriving early to watch the moving process resume. "But I'll put a guard out to-night."

The vandals came back, a dozen strong, after midnight.

He heard them while they were still sneaking up the Street of St. Proculus, shouted a warning which made them unload their barrage of stones too soon. The next morning all of Florence knew that there was a movement to damage the David. Soderini summoned him to a meeting of the Signoria to ask who the attackers might be.

" Do you have enemies?"

" None that I know of."

" We should rather ask, ' Does Florence have enemies?' " said Herald Filarete. " Just let them try it to-night."

They did, at the bottom corner of the Piazza della Signoria, where Piazza San Firenze joined the big square. But Soderini had concealed armed guards in doorways and yards surrounding the David. Eight of the gang were captured and taken to the Bargello. Michelangelo, half dead from lack of sleep, scanned the list of names. There was not one he recognized.

In the morning the upper hall of the Bargello was jammed with Florentines. Michelangelo gazed at the culprits. Five were young, perhaps fifteen years old ; they testified that they had merely joined in the adventure proposed by their older friends, and did not know what they were stoning. Their families were fined, the boys released.

The other three were older, resentful and vindictive in mood. The first said he had stoned the David because it was obscenely naked, that Savonarola would have wanted it destroyed. The second said that it was bad art, and he wanted to show that some people knew better. The third claimed that he was acting for a friend who wanted the David broken ; but he would not mention the friend's name.

All three were sentenced to the Stinche by the judge, who quoted a Tuscan adage, " Art has an enemy called ignorance."

That evening, the fourth day of its journey, the David arrived at its destination. D'Agnolo and the young carpenter knocked down the cage. The Sangallos unslipped the knots, removed the rope mantle. The Judith was carried away, David installed in her place at the foot of the palace steps facing the open piazza.

Michelangelo drew in his breath sharply as he came into the piazza. He had not seen the David at such a distance. There it stood in all its majestic grace, lighting up the Signoria with pure white light. He stood below the figure, feeling insignificant, weak and homely, powerless now that the statue was out of his hands, asking himself, "How much of what I wanted to say have I managed to convey?"

He had stood guard for four nights, was only half conscious from exhaustion. Should he keep guard again to-night? Now that the David was completely exposed, at anyone's mercy? A few large stones, well directed, could tear off its arm, even the head. Granacci said firmly:

"Things happen while something is in transit that stop when it takes its permanent place."

He guided Michelangelo home, took off his boots, helped him into bed and put a blanket over him. To Lodovico who was watching from the door, he said:

"Let him sleep. Even if the sun goes twice around."

He woke feeling refreshed, and ravishingly hungry. Though it was not time for dinner he ate his way through pots of soup, *lasagne* and boiled fish that were supposed to feed the family. His stomach was so full he could hardly crowd himself into the wooden tub for a bath. He enjoyed the fresh white linen shirt, stockings and sandals, the first he could remember in weeks.

He turned off the Piazza San Firenze into the lower end of the Signoria. A crowd was standing below the David in silence. Fluttering from the statue were pieces of paper stuck to the marble during the night. He had seen this sight in Rome, when people had pasted up verses derogatory to the Borgia on the library door of the Vatican, or affixed their smouldering complaints to the marble torso of the Pasquino statue near the Piazza Navona.

He walked across the square, through the crowd. It fell back to let him pass. He tried to read their expressions, to see what was in the wind. They seemed big-eyed.

He came to the David, climbed up on the base, began taking off the papers, reading them one by one. By the end of the third, his eyes began to mist: for they were messages of love and acceptance:

You have given us back our self-respect.

We are proud to be Florentines.

How magnificent is man!

Never can they tell me man is vile; he is the proudest creature on earth.

435

You have made a thing of beauty.

Bravo!

His eye caught a familiar paper, of a kind he had held in
his hands before. He reached for it, read:

Everything my father hoped to accomplish
for Florence is expressed in your David.
                    Contessina Ridolfi de' Medici

She had made her way into the city at night, past the
guards. She had taken the risk to come and see his David, had
joined her voice to that of Florence's.

He turned, stood above the crowd gazing up at him. There
was silence in the square. And yet he had never felt such
complete communication. It was as though they read each
other's thoughts, as though they were one and the same:
they were a part of him, every Florentine standing below,
eyes turned up to him, and he was a part of them.

12

A letter arrived from Jacopo Galli enclosing a contract signed
by the Mouscron brothers, who agreed to pay him four
thousand guldens, and saying, "You are free to do any
Madonna and Child you can conceive. Now, after sweet
meat, comes sour sauce. The Piccolimini heirs insist that
you carve the balance of their statues. I prevailed upon them
to extend the contract for another two years; that was the
best I could do."

A two-year extension! He quickly dispatched the pieces to
the back of his mind.

An immediate repercussion of the David was a call at
the Buonarroti apartment by Bartolommeo Pitti, from the
secondary branch of the wealthy Pitti who lived in a stone
palace on the opposite side of the Arno. Bartolommeo was
a shy and retiring man whose modest house on the Piazza
Santo Spirito had a draper's shop on the ground floor.

"I am just beginning an art collection. So far I have
three small painting on wood, lovely, but not important.

My wife and I would give anything if we could help a work of art to be born."

Michelangelo was taken by the man's simple manner, the mild brown eyes shining beneath the bald crown.

" In what way would you like to participate, *messere*?"

" We wondered if there were some small piece of marble you might have had in mind, or would take pleasure in thinking about, for us. . . ."

He took his very first sculpture off the wall, the Madonna and Child relief he had carved under Bertoldo's guidance. " For a long time, Messer Pitti, I have perceived how much I failed in this first bas-relief, and why. I should like to try again, but in the circular, tondo shape. I think I could bring whole figures out of bas-relief, create the impression of sculpture in the round. Would you like me to try this for you?"

Pitti wet his dry, ridged lips with his tongue. " I cannot convey how much happiness that would bring us."

Michelangelo escorted Bartolommeo Pitti down the stairs to the street.

" Something good will emerge for you, I feel it in my bones."

The Signoria passed a resolution urging *Il Cronaca* to get Michelangelo's house and studio built. Pollaiuolo had allowed the drawings to become lost under a pile of bric-à-brac on his cluttered desk that always contained a couple of dozen hard-boiled eggs, the only food he ate.

" Suppose I set up the structure and the room space?" he asked Michelangelo. " I imagine you will want to design the stone blocks?"

" I should like that. Could I make a few stipulations?"

" What client doesn't?" growled *Il Cronaca*.

" I'd like the kitchen upstairs, between the family room and my bedroom. A fireplace with the chimney built into the wall. A pillared loggia outside my bedroom, overlooking the back yard. Brick floors, good windows, a second-story latrine. A front door with a cornice over it of thin hewn stone. All interior walls plastered. I'll paint them myself."

" I can't see what you need me for," grumbled *Il Cronaca*. " Let's go over to the land and place the studio for light and sun."

Michelangelo asked if the Topolinos could do the stone-work.

" Providing you guarantee the work."

" You will get the most beautifully carved blocks ever hewed in Settignano."

The open lot was on the corner of the Borgo Pinti and the Via della Colonna, forty-six feet on the Borgo adjoining the Cestello monastery, the Via della Colonna side considerably longer, ending at the shop of a blacksmith and carpenter. They bought some pegs from him, paced off the land and drove in the boundary stakes.

Il Clonaca returned in a couple of weeks with the plans for the house and adjoining studio, uncompromisingly square on the outside but designed for comfort within. There was an open loggia off the second-story bedroom where Michelangelo would eat and rest in warm weather.

The Topolinos were soon cutting *pietra serena* according to his specifications, the stones emerging a luminous blue-grey, with marvellous grainings. They cut the blocks for his fireplace, using the strongs he brought them for length, the thin hewn stones for the cornice ; and when the building blocks were ready the entire family built the house. *Il Cronaca* brought in the plasterers for the interior walls, the tilemakers to put on the roof, but at night Michelangelo could not resist going to the house to quench the lime with water from the well that had been dug in the yard, to temper the loggia, and to paint the interior walls the warm blues, rose and orange colours he had evolved for the clothes of the Doni Holy Family. The entire south wall of the studio admitted to the courtyard.

The furniture money had to come out of his own purse. He could buy only modestly : a wide bed, chest, single chair for his bedroom, for the loggia chairs and table which could be moved inside in wet or cold weather ; a leather chair and bench for the family room, pots, bowls, frying pans, boxes for salt and sugar and flour for the kitchen. Argiento moved his bed from the workshop in the piazza, putting it in the small downstairs bedroom near the front door.

" You should put pictures of sacred objects in your house," his aunt Cassandra told him ; " to look at them will be good for your soul."

Michelangelo hung his earliest Madonna and Child opposite his bed, put the Centaurs in the family room.

" Pure narcissism," commented Granacci ; " your aunt tells you to put up sacred objects, so you hang your own work."

" They're sacred to me, Granacci."

He worked joyfully in the late summer sun flooding the open studio, his head and hands rich with ideas that came tumbling over each other in profusion: the wax figure of the Bruges Madonna, the sketches for the Pitti tondo, exploratory figures for the Apostle St. Matthew for the Duomo; filing the bronze David for the French Maréchal. When the five-foot block arrived from Carrara for the Madonna, Argiento helped him set it up on a turntable in the middle of the studio. Within the hour he was massing around the edges, feeling the figures stir inside the marble, baptizing the brick floor of the studio with its first snow-storm.

His personal fulfilment did not lead him to evolve a cheerful Madonna; on the contrary this Madonna was sad; she had already, through his sculptures, known the Descent. The tranquillity of his early bas-relief, when Mary still had her decision to make, could never be recaptured. This young mother was committed; she knew the end of her boy's life. That was why she was reluctant to let him go, this beautiful, husky, healthy boy, his hand clasped for protection in hers. That was why she sheltered him with the side of her cloak.

The child, sensitive to his mother's mood, had a touch of melancholy about the eyes. He was strong, he had courage, he would step forth from the safe harbour of his mother's lap; but just now he gripped her hand with the fingers of one hand, and with the other held securely to her side. Or was it his own mother he was thinking about, sad because she must leave her son alone in the world? Himself, who clung to her?

He worked as though he were on a holiday, the chips of marble flying, these smaller, compact figures coming almost without effort after the overpowering male massiveness of the David. His hammer and chisels had the weight of feathers as he evolved the Madonna's simple draperies, her long fingers, the rich braids over the long-nosed face, the heavy-lidded eyes, the boy's head of curls, powerfully shaped body, the plump cheeks and chin: an aura of compassion permeating the marble. He did not idealize the Madonna's face as he had before; he hoped to make her noble through her sentiment.

Granacci commented, " They will be the most alive beings in any chapel they may be put into."

Prior Bichiellini, who had made no comment on the David, came to give Michelangelo's new house the traditional blessing. He bent on his knee, spoke a prayer to the Madonna. Then he rose, put both hands on Michelangelo's shoulder.

"This Madonna and Child could not have evolved in such tender purity if you did not feel tenderly and were not pure in heart. Bless you and this workshop."

He celebrated the completion of the Bruges Madonna and Child by setting up a square block, rounding off its corners to give him the roughly circular tondo form, beginning work on the piece for the Pitti. The wax model on the armature took shape quickly, for it was an idyllic period for him, working in his own studio, wanted. This was the first circular sculpture he had attempted; by tilting the marble saucer-like, he was able to achieve planes-in-depth in which the Madonna, seated on a solid block, as the most important figure, emerged full-bodied; the child, though leaning on an open book in his mother's lap, receded to a secondary plane, John, peeking over Mary's shoulder, was buried deep in the saucer.

He used half a dozen different textures in his finish, almost the whole alphabet of the chisel; only Mary's face was polished in the flesh tones of the Pietà, enriching the emotional tactility. He felt this Mary to be the strongest of his Madonnas, mature; the child embodied the sweetness and charm of a happy youngster; the figures moved freely within their circle.

Argiento wrapped the tondo carefully in blankets and, borrowing a barrow from the carpenter next door, wheeled the marble through the streets to the Pitti house. Michelangelo walked beside him. They carried it up the stairs above the draper's, set it on a high narrow buffet. The Pitti were speechless, then the parents and children began to talk and laugh all at once, to run about the room to see the piece from different angles.

The months that followed were the happiest he had known. The David, still called the Giant by most Florentines, was accepted by the city as its new symbol, mentor and protector. Things took a sharp turn for the better: Cæsar Borgia, seriously ill, ceased to be a menace; Arezzo and Pisa seemed subdued; Pope Julius II, friendly to Florence, made Cardinal Giovanni de Medici important at the Vatican. There was a spirit of confidence and energy in the air. Trade was booming; there was work for all, a market for every man's product. The government, with Soderini as its permanent head, was stable and secure, the last of the internecine Florentine feuds forgotten.

Much of this the city-state attributed to the Giant-David. The date of its installation marked a new era in the minds of the Florentines. Contracts and agreements were dated, "One month after the unveiling of the Giant." In conversation, time was divided by saying: "This was before the Giant," or, "I remember it well because it happened in the second week following the Giant."

From Soderini Michelangelo extracted the promise that Contessina, her husband and children would be permitted to go to the protection of Cardinal Giovanni in Rome, just as quickly as he could persuade the members of the Council of Seventy. He was friendly and companionable at the dinners of the Company, stopped attacking Leonardo, helped other sculptors with their designs when they were seeking commissions. He obliged Argiento to spend more time in training with him. He climbed the hills to Settignano to watch the pile of thin decorative strips for his front cornice grow, each carved as though it were a gem. From there he walked to Contessina's to give Luigi a lesson and play with the growing Niccolò. He was patient with his own family, listened quietly as Lodovico told of searching for more houses and farms to buy in order to build an estate for his sons.

The Pitti family sent him Taddeo Taddei, a Florentine intellectual who loved the arts. Taddei wondered if Maestro Buonarroti might be willing to carve him a tondo. Michelangelo already had a point of departure, born while working the Pitti piece. He sketched the fresh idea for Taddei, who was enchanted. Now he had still another delightful commission from a sensitive man who appreciated what he was going to sculpture for him.

A few months short of thirty, he seemed to have reached the full expression and acceptance for which he had yearned.

His period of grace was short-lived.

Every few weeks since Sangallo had been summoned to Rome by Julius II, he had sent encouraging word to Michelangelo: he had told the Pope about the David; he had urged His Holiness to look at the Pietà in St. Peter's; he had persuaded the pontiff that there was no equal master in all Europe. The Pope had begun to think about marble sculptures; soon he would decide what he wanted carved, then he would summon Michelangelo to Rome. . . .

Michelangelo passed several of these notes around at the Company of the Cauldron meetings, so that when Julius II summoned Sansovino to Rome to erect two tombs, one for the Cardinal of Recanati, the other for Cardinal Sforza in Santa Maria del Popolo, it stunned him. The Company gave Sansovino a noisy farewell party, in which Michelangelo joined, pleased over his old comrade's good fortune, hiding his own humiliation. He had suffered a severe blow to his prestige. Many in Florence asked:

"If it is true that Michelangelo is the first sculptor of Florence, why did the Pope not send for him instead of Sansovino?"

During the early months of 1504 Leonardo da Vinci had spent his time in a series of mechanical inventions, suction pumps, turbines, conduits for the rerouting of the Arno away from Pisa, an observatory under his skylight with a magnifying glass for studying the moon. Rebuked by the Signoria for neglecting his fresco, he had started in May to work on it in earnest. The cartoon became the talk of Florence: artists flocked to Leonardo's workroom in Santa Maria Novella to study, admire, copy, change their styles. Word went around the city that something startling and wondrous was in the making.

With the passing months the city became caught up in admiration of Leonardo and his cartoon, crying out about its marvels. It became the chief topic of conversation. The David was taken for granted now, as were the good times it had brought. Michelangelo began to perceive that he was being superseded. Admiring acquaintances and strangers who had stopped him on the street to pay their respects now nodded casually. He had had his day; it had passed.

Leonardo da Vinci was the figure of the moment. Florence proudly proclaimed him "the first artist of Tuscany."

This was bitter medicine to Michelangelo. How fickle were his Florentines! Relegating him to second place so quickly! Knowing Santa Maria Novella from the months he had spent there with Ghirlandaio, he managed to see the Leonardo cartoon without anyone knowing he was there. The Battle of Anghiari was tremendous! Leonardo, who loved horses as dearly as did Rustici, had created a masterpiece of the horse at war, in violent combat, ridden by men in ancient Roman armour, savagely trying to destroy each other, striking, biting, slaying as though they were the furies, men and horses alike caught up in violent, bloodthirsty conflict, many individual groups designed to fit into the brilliantly integrated pattern.

Leonardo was a great painter, he could not dispute that; perhaps the greatest the world had yet seen. Instead of reconciling him, this inflamed him the more. At sunset, as he was passing Santa Trinita, he saw a group of men talking on the benches in front of the Spina banking house. They were discussing a passage from Dante, of which Michelangelo recognized the lines as coming from Canto XI of the *Inferno*.

"Philosophy," my master answered me,
"To him who understands it, demonstrates
How nature takes her course, not only from
Wisdom divine, but from its art as well.
And if you read with care your books of physics,
After the first few pages, you will find
That art, as best it can, doth follow nature,
As pupil follows master."

The man in the centre of the group looked up.

"Here is Michelangelo," said Leonardo da Vinci; "he will interpret the verses."

Michelangelo looked so much like a labourer returning home from his day-long tasks that some of the younger admirers around Leonardo laughed.

"Explain them yourself," cried Michelangelo, blaming Leonardo for the laughter. "You who made a model of a horse to be cast in bronze, and to your shame had to leave it unfinished!"

Leonardo's face turned a flaming red.

"I was not mocking you, I asked in earnest. It is not my fault if these others laughed."

Michelangelo's ears were plugged with the bubbling hot wax of anger. He turned away without hearing, struck out for the hills. He walked all night, trying to put down his anger, humiliation, sense of frustration and shame. He could not reconcile himself to having been passed by, treated cavalierly by the city that now turned its eyes elsewhere.

He had walked a long way in the night, up the river to Pontassieve. At dawn he stood at the confluence of the Sieve and the Arno, on the road that led to Arezzo and Rome. He knew that there was only one answer to his problem: he could never surpass Leonardo in handsomeness, in regality of figure, in superiority of manner. But he was the best draughtsman in all Italy. No one would believe him, merely saying so; he would have to prove it. And no proof would serve except a fresco, of the same proportions as Leonardo's.

Leonardo's fresco was going to occupy the right half of the long eastern wall of the Great Hall. He would ask Soderini for the left half. He would put his work up side by side with Leonardo's, prove that he could outpaint him, figure for figure! All the world could see and judge. Then Florence could say who was the first artist of the time!

Granacci tried to cool him down.

"This is a sickness, a fever. We must find some way to physic you."

"You're not funny."

"*Dio mio,* I wasn't trying to be. What you can't stand is Leonardo's proximity."

"The smell of his perfume, you mean."

"Don't be nasty. Leonardo doesn't use perfume, only scent."

Granacci looked at his friend's sweat-caked arms and legs, the shirt dirty from the smoke of his forge.

"There are times when a bath wouldn't kill you."

Michelangelo picked up a heavy beam, brandished it at Granacci and screamed, "Get out of my studio, you . . . you traitor!"

"I didn't bring up the subject of scents, you did. Why disturb yourself over his painting, when you have years of sculpture at hand? Forget him."

"He's a thorn in my foot."

"Suppose you come out second best, with a wall full of bandaged toes?"

Michelangelo grinned. "Trust me, Granacci, I'll come out first. I've got to."

Late that afternoon he presented himself at Gonfaloniere Soderini's office, bathed, barbered, wearing his clean blue shirt.

"Phew," said the Gonfaloniere, leaning as far away as he could, "what did the barber put on your hair?"

Michelangelo flushed. ". . . a scented oil . . ."

Soderini sent a groom for a towel. When it arrived he handed it to Michelangelo, saying, "Rub that stuff out. Stick to your own smells. At least they're indigenous."

Michelangelo told Soderini why he had come. Soderini was flabbergasted; it was the first time Michelangelo had ever seen him lose his presence.

"But that is unreasonable!" he cried, walking around his broad desk and staring at Michelangelo. "You've told me yourself that you never liked the fresco work at Ghirlandaio's."

"I was wrong." His head was down, his voice dogged. "I can paint fresco. Better than Leonardo da Vinci."

"Are you sure?"

"I'll put my hand in fire."

"Even supposing you can, why would you want to take the years away from marble? Your Madonna for the Bruges merchants is divine. So is the Pitti tondo. Your talent is a gift from God. Why should you throw it away for an art of which you want no part?"

"You were so thrilled, Gonfaloniere, to have Leonardo paint one-half your wall. You said the world would come to see it. Why would not twice as many visitors come to two panels, one by Leonardo the other by me? It would be a great *palio,* a race that would excite people."

"And you think you can surpass him?"

"I'll put my hand in fire."

Soderini walked back to the gold-emblazoned chair, dropped into it hard, shaking his head in disbelief.

"The Signoria would never approve. You already have a contract with the Wool Guild and Duomo to carve the Twelve Apostles."

"I'll carve them. But the other half of the wall must be mine. I don't need two years, the way Leonardo does, I'll do it in one year, ten months, eight . . ."

"No, *caro.* You are wrong. I won't let you get yourself into bad trouble."

"Because you don't believe I can do it. You're right not to believe since I come here with only words in my hands. Next time I come back it will be with drawings, and then you will see what I can do."

"Please," said Soderini wearily, "come back with a marble Apostle instead. That's why we built you that house and studio, so you would carve Apostles."

Soderini looked up at the lilies on the ceiling.

"Why wasn't I content with two months as Gonfaloniere? Why did I have to take this job for life?"

"Because you are a wise and persuasive Gonfaloniere who is going to get the city to appropriate another ten thousand florins for the painting of the other half of the wall."

To excite the Signoria sufficiently to spend an additional sum, to delight the Wool and Duomo Boards enough to release him from his contract for a year, he would have to paint a scene of glory and pride for the Florentines. He did not want to paint horses covered with protective trappings, soldiers in their breastplate armour and helmets, sword and spear in hand, with the confusion of rearing animals, wounded and dying men. This was not for him.

But what was?

He went to the Santo Spirito library, asked the Augustinian monk in charge to recommend a history of Florence. The librarian gave him Filippo Villani's *Cronaca*. He read about the wars between the Guelphs and Ghibellines, the wars with Pisa and other city-states. His fresco did not necessarily have to be a battle, but it did have to be a triumph of some sort to puff the national honour. Where in Florentine history was he to find such a scene, of the kind that he could paint; and which would stand in dramatic contrast to Leonardo's battle spectacle? One from which he could emerge the victor?

It was not until he had read for several days that he came upon a story that quickened his pulse. The scene was laid at Cascina, near Pisa, where the Florentine forces had made camp on the bank of the Arno on a hot summer day. Feeling themselves safe from attack, a number of the soldiers had gone bathing in the river, others were coming out to dry themselves, while still a third group, having shed their heavy armour, was sun-bathing on the grass. Suddenly a guard burst into the group, crying, "We are lost! The Pisans are about to attack!" The Florentines scrambled out of the

446

river, those on the bank hastily buckled on their armour, others went rushing for weapons . . . in time to beat back three Pisan attacks and to rout the enemy.

Here was a chance to paint a large group of men, young and old, with the water and the sun on them, galvanized into action, all of them at a moment of danger, of tension, of pressure, recorded not only on their faces but in the bending, reaching, straining to prepare for the attack and save their lives. Here was a chance to create something exciting. They would all be Davids; a complete portrait of mankind, startled out of its momentary Garden of Eden.

He went to the Street of the Stationers, bought the largest squares of paper he could find, coloured inks, chalks, black, white, red and brown crayons, took them back to his work-bench. Drawing swiftly, he organized the scene on the Arno at Cascina, in the centre Donati crying to Captain Malatesta, "We are lost!", some of the soldiers still in the water, others trying to climb the steep bank, others throwing on a garment while reaching for a weapon.

Three days later he stood in Soderini's office. The two men stared at each other, wide-eyed. Michelangelo fitted together on the floor beside the desk the dozen large sheets with twenty male figures, some crosshatched with the pen, others outlined in charcoal or drawn with long bold slashing lines heightened with white lead, still others glowing with flesh colours.

He dropped into one of a row of tall leather chairs against the side wall, feeling tired and let down. Soderini studied the drawings in silence. When he looked up, Michelangelo recognized the affectionate regard in which Soderini held him.

"I was wrong to discourage you. To be an artist one must sculpture and paint and create architecture with equal authority. This fresco can be as revolutionary as the David, and bring us the same joy. I'm going to get you this commission, even if I have to fight every member of the Council."

And so he did, for a sum of three thousand florins, less than a third of Leonardo da Vinci's pay. It was Michelangelo's largest commission, though he felt disgruntled that the Signoria thought his work worth so much less than Leonardo's. They would change their minds when they saw the finished fresco.

Now people stopped to tell him they heard he was going to paint a forest of Davids.

"And so you have been repatriated," said Granacci, a touch caustically. "You are once again our first artist, providing the fresco comes out brilliantly. I only hope you're not paying too high a price."

"A man pays what he must."

14

He was given a long narrow room at the Hospital of the Dyers, a charitable hospital that had been founded by the Art Guild of the Dyers in 1359. It fronted on the Street of the Dyers, just a couple of blocks from his early home near Santa Croce; he remembered it because as a boy he used to walk in the gutters which ran blue, green, red and crimson. His room faced the Arno, south, so that he had sun all day; the back wall was larger than his half of the Hall of the Great Council. He would be able to mount his cartoon sheet by sheet, and see it whole before painting the fresco. He ordered Argiento to keep the street door locked.

He worked in an absolute fury, determined to show the city that he was a sure and swift master who did not need to be rebuked by the Signoria for dawdling over drawings of canal pumps and other mechanical engines. When the weather turned cold he sent Argiento out for wax and turpentine in which to steep the paper the Dyers used for windows. He drew his overall design on an oblong strip of paper, cut to scale, then divided it into the number of squares he would need to assemble to fill the twenty-two by fifty-eight-foot wall. In contrast to his early Battle of the Centaurs, the key figures would stand ten feet high; yet this scene would have a similar sense of a group of nude warriors crowded into a limited area, all the arms, legs, torsos, heads intertwined organically, as though integral parts of a whole, engaged in a melodramatic mêlée to get out of the water, into their clothes, their armour and ranks before the enemy fell upon them.

He drew one young warrior, his back turned, wearing a cuirass and shield, a sword under his feet; naked youths who had picked up their spears and swords, ignoring their clothes; hardened warriors with powerful legs and shoulders, ready to spring at the oncoming enemy barehanded; three young soldiers just scrambling out of the river; a

448

central group around Donati caught between consternation
and the beginnings of preparation; a warrior shoving an
arm powerfully through a shirt; an old soldier wearing an
ivy wreath on his head, trying to draw his hose over wet
legs, " so that all the muscles and sinews of his body are
seen in strain," Michelangelo explained to Granacci, " the
contortions of his mouth show his agony of haste, and how
his whole frame labours to his toetips."

Worked carefully, the Cascina cartoon which he called
the Bathers, would have taken a full year; done at the height
of a young man's power and talent, it might conceivably have
been done in six months. By New Year's Day of 1505,
three months after he had started, driven by a force he
could not contain, Michelangelo's cartoon was completed.
Salvadore, the bookbinder, had spent the two previous days
gluing the separate sheets together; now Argiento, Granacci,
Antonio da Sangallo and Michelangelo stretched and tacked
the cartoon to a light frame against the rear wall. It filled
the room with fifty to sixty desperately challenged men. In
the panel were contained fear, terror, hopelessness; and
at the same time all the manly emotions surging upward
to overcome surprise and disaster by swift purposeful action.

Granacci stood gazing at the overpowering force of this
body of men caught between life and death, each reacting
according to his individual character and resolution. He
was stunned by the authority of the draughtsmanship.

" How strange," he murmured, " that poor motivation can
create rich art." When Michelangelo did not answer, he continued. " You must open these doors and let everyone see
what you have accomplished."

" There has been grumbling over your closed doors,"
added Antonio; " even members of the Company have asked
me why you should lock everybody out. Now that they can
see the miracle you have wrought in three short months,
they will understand."

" I'd like to wait another three months," grumbled Michelangelo. " Until I have the fresco completed in the Great
Hall. But if you both say I must, then I must."

Rustici arrived first. Being Leonardo's close friend, what
Rustici said would carry weight. He weighed his words
carefully.

" Leonardo painted his panel for the horses, you for the
men. Nothing as superb as Leonardo's has ever been done of
a battle scene. Nothing as magnificently shocking as yours

has ever been painted of human beings. The Signoria is going to have one hell of a wall!"

Twenty-two-year-old Ridolfo Ghirlandaio, who was studying at Rosselli's studio, asked if he might sketch. Andrea del Sarto, nineteen-year-old Florentine who had transferred from a goldsmith's shop to the painters' *bottega* of Piero di Cosimo, also arrived with drawing materials. Antonio Sangallo brought his twenty-four-year-old nephew, who was apprenticed to Perugino. Twenty-one-year-old Raphael Sanzio, a former apprentice of Perugino's, was brought by Taddeo Taddei, who had commissioned Michelangelo's second tondo.

Michelangelo liked Raphael Sanzio immediately. He had a sensitive, patrician face, with wide, gentle, perceptive eyes, a full-lipped but disciplined mouth; long, luxuriant hair, fastidiously kept: as exquisite a face as Leonardo da Vinci's, yet in spite of a creamy skin, altogether manly. He carried himself with an expression of gracious warmth. His strong face was imbued with confidence, but there was not the slightest trace of haughtiness. His clothes, too, were as fine as Leonardo's, with a white shirt and lace collar, richly coloured cloak with tight-fitting cap to match; but he wore no jewels or scent. The beauty of the soft-spoken young man's face, figure and clothes did not make Michelangelo feel ugly, awkward or shabby, as Leonardo's inevitably did.

Raphael turned to the cartoon, spoke no word for the rest of the afternoon. When dark fell, he came to Michelangelo and said in a voice which lacked the slightest shred of flattery.

"This makes painting a wholly different art. I shall have to start back at the beginning. Even what I have learned from Leonardo is no longer sufficient."

The eyes he turned on Michelangelo were not so much admiring as incredulous; his expression conveyed the thought that it was not really Michelangelo who had done all this, but some outside force.

Raphael asked if he might move his materials from Perugino's studio and work before the cartoon. Sebastiano da Sangallo terminated his apprenticeship to Perugino to study the shape and movement of the muscles in the figures in the cartoon, while at the same time painstakingly writing down his theories of what had impelled Michelangelo to draw the figures in such difficult positions. Without willing it, or even wanting it, Michelangelo found himself at the head of a school of talented young apprentices.

A surprise visitor was Agnolo Doni, who had been spreading

the word that it was he who was responsible for having started Michelangelo on his career as a painter. Had not Michelangelo protested that he was not a painter? Had not he, Doni, perceived that all he had needed to start him on this glorious career was Doni's confidence in him? The story was plausible. Because some people believed it, Doni was becoming one of the more important art connoisseurs in Florence.

Now he arrived at the Dyers' to commission Michelangelo to paint portraits of himself and his wife. He said loftily, " This commission could be the making of you as a portrait painter."

Michelangelo was amused. In his basic tenet, Doni was right. He had badgered him into painting the Holy Family. And if he had not got the feel of brush and paint, he might still have thought himself a world removed, unwilling and unable to touch the medium. But he was still beyond portraits!

At that moment Raphael entered the hall. Michelangelo turned to Doni.

" Raphael will paint your pictures, with charm and likeness. Since he's just beginning, you can get him cheap."

" You are sure he can measure up to the high level of my art collection?"

" I guarantee it."

Towards the end of January, Perugino came to the Dyers' Hall, having been moved to do so by Raphael's enthusiasm. He was twenty-five years older than Michelangelo, with the lurching gait of a countryman, a face scarred with gullies from years of privation when he had had to go without food for lack of the meanest coin. Perugino had been trained in Verrochio's studio and had carried forward the immeasurably difficult technique of perspective begun by Paolo Uccello. Michelangelo welcomed him warmly.

Perugino stood near the windows of the oblong hall in silence. After a time Michelangelo felt him advancing slowly towards the large cartoon. His face had turned charcoal, his eyes seemed glazed, his lips were fluttering as though in an effort to force out words. Michelangelo picked up a stool, put it behind Perugino.

" Please . . . sit down . . . I'll get some water."

Perugino knocked the stool out from behind him with a savage backward kick.

" . . . beastly . . ."

Dumbfounded, Michelangelo stared. Perugino thrust his left hand across his chest, fingers stiff as he swept away the cartoon before him.

"Give a wild animal a brush, and he would do the same. You will destroy us . . . all we have spent a lifetime to create!"

Sick at heart, Michelangelo could only murmur, "Perugino, why do you attack me? I admire your work . . ."

"My work! How dare you speak of my work in the presence of this . . . this filthiness! In my work I have manners, taste, respectability! If my work is painting, then yours is not. It is a debauchery, every square inch of it."

Ice-cold now, Michelangelo asked, "You mean the technique is bad, the drawing, the design . . .?"

"You know nothing of such matters," cried Perugino. "You should be thrown into the Stinche and kept from destroying the art that decent men have created."

"Why am I not a decent man? Is it that I have painted nudes? That this is . . . new?"

"Don't talk to me of originality! I have done as much as any one man in Italy to revolutionize painting."

"You have done much. But painting does not come to an end with you. Every true artist re-creates the art."

"You go backward, before civilization, before God."

"You sound like Savonarola."

"You will never get one figure of this immorality up on the Signoria wall. I shall organize the artists of Florence . . ."

He stormed out of the Dyers' Hall, walking stiff-legged, his head held stiffly on his neck. Michelangelo righted the stool and sat down, trembling. Argiento, who had been hiding in a far corner, came forward with a cup of water. Michelangelo dipped his fingers, touched them to his feverish face.

He could not understand what had happened. That Perugino might not have liked his cartoon was understandable. But to launch so bitter a personal attack, to talk of putting him in the Stinche . . . of having his cartoon destroyed . . . Surely he would not be so foolish as to go to the Signoria?

He rose, turned his back on the cartoon, shut the door of the room, walked quietly with eyes on the cobblestones, through the streets of Florence to his house. He let himself into the studio. Slowly he became normal, the nausea passed. He picked up a hammer and chisel, worked the gleaming marble of the Taddei tondo. He turned his thinking upside down from the Pitti concept, creating everything in reverse: this would be a playful, joyous mother and child. He carved Mary on a secondary plane of depth in order that the son might dominate the scene, sprawled diagonally across her lap to avoid the goldfinch that John was mischievously thrusting towards him.

He had chosen a deep, resourceful block. With a heavy point he gouged out a background to give a sense of the deserts of Jerusalem, the white chips flying about his head as he happily stripped out marble with a clawtool *gradina* to achieve the saucer-like effect, the bodies of Mary and John forming the circular rim, Jesus cutting across but connecting them, none affixed to the background, moving freely with every change of light. The smoky-smelling marble dust tasted as sweet in his nostrils as sugar on the tongue.

He had been a fool. He should never have left sculpturing.

The door opened. Raphael came in, quietly stood by his side. This was Perugino's countryman. Why had he come?

" I came to apologise for my friend and teacher. He's had a shock, and is now ill . . ."

Michelangelo gazed into Raphael's eloquent eyes.

" Why did he attack me?"

" Perhaps it is because for a number of years now Perugino has been . . . imitating himself. Why should he think he should change, when he is one of Italy's most famous painters, beloved for his work here in Florence, at home in Perugia, and even in Rome?"

" I admired his work in the Sistine Chapel."

" Then can't you see? When he saw the Bathers he felt exactly as I had: that this was a different world of painting, that one had to start over. For me, this was a challenge; it opened my eyes to how much more exciting an art I had entered than I had suspected. But I am not yet twenty-two. I have life before me. Perugino is fifty-five; he can never start over. This work of yours will make his art old-fashioned." He paused, thought hard. " It can make one ill . . ."

" I appreciate your coming here, Raphael."

" Then be generous. Have the goodness to ignore him. It won't be easy. He has already gone to the Signoria to protest, and he has called a special meeting of the Company for to-night, leaving you out . . ."

Michelangelo was aghast.

"But if he is organizing a campaign against me, I must defend myself."

"Surely you need no defence? Here in Florence, where the young painters look to you? Let him talk himself out; in a few days he will tire, it will blow away . . ."

"All right, Raphael, I'll hold my tongue."

It grew increasingly difficult to keep his promise. Perugino had begun what amounted to a crusade. His fury and energy were rising with the passing of time rather than abating. He had lodged complaints not only with the Signoria but with the Boards of the Duomo and Wool Guild.

By February, Michelangelo discovered that Perugino had not been ineffective; he had gained a small group of adherents, the most vociferous of them seventeen-year-old Baccio Bandinelli, son of Florence's most important goldsmith, an aspiring sculptor; and several friends of Leonardo.

He sought out Granacci. Granacci tried to preserve his usual calm.

"They are joining Perugino for various reasons. There was some murmuring when you, a sculptor, got a painter's commission. But for others, the cartoon is a point of departure. If it were conventional, or mediocre, I think they would not care. . . ."

"Then it is . . . jealousy?"

"Envy, perhaps. Of the kind you feel for Leonardo. Surely you should be able to understand that."

Michelangelo flinched. No one but Granacci would have dared say such a thing to him; or have known how true it was.

"I promised Raphael I would say nothing against Perugino. But now I'm going to strike back."

"You must. He's talking to people everywhere he goes: in the streets, the churches . . ."

As a start in his own campaign, Michelangelo went to see the Perugino paintings around town, a Pietà which he remembered from his home church of Santa Croce, a triptych in the convent of the Gesuati, a panel in San Domenico in Fiesole. He saved for last the Servite altarpiece in Santissima Annunziata for which Perugino had painted the Assumption. There was no question that his earlier work had line, brilliance in the use of clear, light colour, that his landscapes were attractive; his later work seemed to Michelangelo to be flat, decorative, lacking vigour or perception.

That Sunday he went to the dinner meeting of the Company. The moment he entered Rustici's studio the laughing banter fell away; a feeling of restraint came over the room.

"You don't have to turn your eyes away and fall silent," he cried with a tinge of bitterness. "I didn't start this; I didn't want it."

"*È vero,*" several voices answered.

"Nor did I invite Perugino to the Dyers'. He came by himself, then launched into the worst attack I ever heard. You are my judges that I have not answered back."

"We are not blaming you, Michelangelo."

At that moment Perugino entered the studio. Michelangelo gazed at him for a moment, then said, "When one's work is in danger, one must protect himself. I have just studied Perugino's paintings here in Florence. Now I understand why he wishes to destroy me. It is to protect himself." There was a deadly silence in the room. "This I can prove to you," he continued, "canvas by canvas, figure by figure . . ."

"Not in my home," broke in Rustici. "A truce is herewith declared. Either party breaking it will be forcibly ejected."

The truce lasted until the following morning, when Michelangelo learned that Perugino had been so incensed by his statement before the Company that he was going before the Signoria to demand a public hearing on the decency of the Bathers. An adverse vote could mean the cancellation of the contract. His counter-attack was harsh, but he could see no alternative. Perugino, he told Florence, had exhausted his talent. His present works were antiquated, still-life figures without anatomy, feeble rearrangements of earlier pictures.

A messenger summoned him to the Signoria: Perugino had accused him of slander. He was suing for damage done to his reputation and earning power. Michelangelo presented himself at Soderini's office at the appointed hour. Perugino was already there, seeming old and tired.

Soderini, pale and constrained behind his broad desk, with his fellow members of the Signoria ranged on either side of him, did not look at Michelangelo when he entered the room. He spoke to Perugino first, determined that Perugino had opened the attack, without provocation other than the sight of the cartoon. He asked Michelangelo if he had made certain charges against Perugino. Michelangelo admitted that he had, but claimed they were made to defend himself. The other members asked questions, then nodded to Soderini. Soderini spoke with considerable sadness.

"Perugino, you did wrong. You attacked Michelangelo without provocation. You attempted to do him and his work personal damage. Michelangelo, you did wrong to belittle Perugino's talent in public, even though you acted in defence of your interests. You have hurt each other. But your Signoria is less concerned with this than it is with the harm you have done Florence. We are famous all over the world as the capital of the arts. So long as I am Gonfaloniere we shall continue to deserve that reputation. We cannot allow our artists to indulge in quarrels that hurt us.

"The Signoria therefore orders that you both apologise; that you shall desist from attacking each other; and that you shall both return to the work from which Florence draws its fame. The case of slander against Michelangelo Buonarroti is dismissed."

Michelangelo walked back to the Dyers' Hall alone, sick with revulsion. He had been vindicated, but he felt hollow inside.

15

It was at this moment that the summons arrived from Giuliano da Sangallo: Pope Julius II wanted Michelangelo to come to Rome at once, and was providing him with a hundred florins travel allowance.

It was a bad time for him to leave, for it was important that he transfer the cartoon to the Signoria wall while the painting was fresh and glowing in his mind, before there could be other outside threats to the project. After that, he had to carve the Apostle Matthew, for he had been living in his home for a considerable time and must start to pay for it.

Yet he wanted desperately to go, to learn what Julius II had in mind, to receive one of those magnificent commissions that only Popes could grant. The aura of good will in which he had lived and worked these past five years had been broken by the Perugino quarrel.

He reported the summons to Gonfaloniere Soderini. Soderini studied Michelangelo's face carefully for what seemed a long time before he spoke.

"One cannot refuse the Pope. If Julius says 'Come!' you must go. His friendship is important to us in Florence."

" And my house . . . the two contracts . . .?"

" We will hold these things in abeyance until you learn what the Holy Father wants. But remember that the contracts must be honoured!"

" I understand, Gonfaloniere."

He walked up to Fiesole to see Contessina, whose baby had died in childbirth, and to ask permission to speak to Cardinal Giovanni in her behalf.

" But I am not a Medici any longer, I am a Ridolfi."

" He is still your brother . . ."

Her eyes, as they rested affectionately on him, still seemed larger than her face.

" You are kind, *caro.*"

" Have you a message to send to Giovanni?"

Her expression altered only a trifle.

" Tell His Grace that I trust he is enjoying Rome."

Michelangelo had only to enter the Porta del Popolo to see and smell the startling changes. The streets had been washed. Several of the stinking forums had been covered with crushed rock. Gaping walls and abandoned houses had been torn down so that the streets could be widened. The Via Ripetta had been repaved ; the swine market cleaned out of the Roman forum. A number of new buildings were under construction.

He found the Sangallos living off the Piazza Scossacavalli, in one of many such palaces belonging to Pope Julius II, rather severely designed on the outside but with a spacious inner court surrounded by octagonal columns. When he was admitted by a liveried footman he found the interior richly hung with Flemish tapestries, the rooms decorated with costly vessels of gold and silver, paintings and antique sculptures.

The palace was teeming with people. A big music room overlooking the courtyard had been converted to a draughtsmen's workshop. Here half a dozen young architects who had apprenticed themselves to Sangallo were working on plans for broadening the piazzas, building bridges over the Tiber, constructing new academies, hospitals, churches : the plans originally conceived by Sixtus IV, who had built the Sistine Chapel, neglected by Alexander VI, now revived and expanded by Julius, nephew of Sixtus.

Sangallo appeared twenty years younger than when Michelangelo had last seen him. His oriental moustaches had been trimmed to European length, his hair was immaculately dressed, his clothes of expensive cloth; he exuded the air of a man who was fulfilling himself. Sangallo led him up a broad marble staircase to the family apartment, where he was embraced by Signora Sangallo and their son Francesco.

"I have waited these many months to welcome you to Rome. Now that we have the commission formulated, the Holy Father is eager to see you. I shall go to the Papal palace at once and ask for an appointment for to-morrow morning."

Michelangelo sat down on a fragile antique chair that creaked beneath him.

"Not so fast," he cried. "I still don't know what it is the Pope wants me to carve!"

Sangallo drew up a second fragile chair, sat facing Michelangelo, their knees touching, overcome with excitement.

". . . a tomb. Not a tomb, the Tomb. The Tomb of the World."

". . . a tomb," groaned Michelangelo. "Oh no!"

"You don't understand. This tomb will be more important than the tomb of Mausolus or Asinius Pollio's Memorial, or the mausoleums of Augustus or Hadrian . . ."

"Augustus . . . Hadrian . . . Those are gigantic!"

"So will yours be. Not in architectural size but in sculpture. The Holy Father wants you to carve as many heroic marbles as you can conceive: ten, twenty, thirty! You'll be the first sculptor to have that many sculptured marbles in one place since Phidias did the frieze on the Parthenon. Think of it, Michelangelo, thirty Davids on one tomb! Never has there been such an opportunity for a marble master. This commission make you the first *statuario* of the world."

Unable to assimilate the words, he said stupidly, "Thirty Davids! What would the Pope want with thirty Davids?"

Sangallo laughed. "I don't blame you for being dumbfounded. So was I, as I watched the project grow in the Holy Father's mind. Statues as great as the David, I meant."

"Whose idea was this tomb?"

Sangallo hesitated for a moment before answering. "Whose inception? We evolved it together. The Pope was speaking of ancient tombs, and so I seized the opportunity to suggest that his should be the greatest the world had ever known. He thought that tombs ought to be built after a Pope's death, but I convinced him that such crucial affairs should not be left to the negligent hands of posterity; that only by utilizing his own fine judgment could be sure to have the monument he deserved. The Holy Father grasped my reasoning at once. . . . And now I must run to the Vatican."

Michelangelo made his way down the Borgo Vecchio to the Sant' Angelo bridge, crossed and went along the familiar Via Canale to the Via Florida. Every step brought memories of his earlier stay, some of them pleasant, some painful. He pulled up short in front of the Jacopo Galli home; the house seemed strangely shut up. As he knocked on the door he felt uneasy, realizing suddenly that he had not heard from Galli for many months.

He waited a long time in the drawing-room, airless, unused, without any of the disarray of books and manuscripts that Galli always left strewn behind him. When Signora Galli entered he saw that she looked unwell, with a sallow paleness draining the last of her beauty.

" What has happened, Signora?"

" Jacopo is desperately ill. He has been confined to his bed."

" But what . . .?"

" This past winter he caught cold. Now his lungs are affected. Dr. Lippi has brought his colleagues, but they do nothing for him."

Michelangelo turned away, gulped. " Could I see him? I bring good news . . ."

" That will help. But I must warn you: do not show sympathy or mention his sickness. Talk only about sculpture."

Jacopo Galli lay beneath warm blankets, his body making only the slightest bulge. The flesh of his face was wasted away, the eyes sunken. They lit with joy when Michelangelo entered.

" Ah, Michelangelo," he cried, " how good to see you. I have heard wonderful things of your David."

Michelangelo ducked his head deprecatingly, flushed.

" Plenty brings pride," said Galli. " I am happy to see you are still humble, as humble as you can ever be."

" Put not an embroidered crupper on an ass," Michelangelo quoted with a crooked grin.

" If you are in Rome, it can only mean that you have a commission. From the Pope?"

" Yes. Giuliano da Sangallo arranged it."

" What will you carve for His Holiness?"

" A monumental tomb, rich with marbles."

Galli's eyes were amused.

459

"After the concept of the David, which created a whole new world for sculpture! A tomb! From the greatest tomb hater in Italy."

"But this is to be different: a tomb to hold all the sculptures I can conceive."

"That should be quite a few!"

Was there a touch of twitting in Galli's voice? Michelangelo could not be sure. He asked, "Is His Holiness good to work for? It was he who commissioned the murals in the Sistine . . ."

"Yes, good to work for, providing you don't overemphasize the spiritual, or get him angry. He has an uncontrollable temper. He is a militant Pope, honest, decent: he issued a new constitution a few months ago which will do away with simony. There will be none of the scandals of the Borgias. But there will be more wars. Julius wants an army, which he will command himself, to recapture all of Italy that once belonged to the Church . . ."

"You must conserve your strength, *caro*," said the *signora*. "Michelangelo will learn these things soon enough."

Jacopo Galli fell back on his pillow.

"So he will. But remember, Michelangelo, I am still your manager in Rome. You must let me draw your contract with the Pope, so it will be right. . . ."

"I would not move without you."

That night there was a gathering at Sangallo's: high churchmen, wealthy bankers and traders, some of whom Michelangelo knew from Galli's garden, many of the Florentine colony. Balducci embraced Michelangelo with a shout of joy, arranged for them to meet for dinner at the Trattoria Toscana. The palace was aglow with hundreds of candles in high candelabra. Uniformed servants circulated among the guests with food and wine and sweets. The Sangallos were surrounded by admirers; it was the success for which Guiliano had waited for fifteen years. Even Bramante was there. He had not aged in the five years that had passed; he had the same curls at the base of his bald head, the pale green eyes still danced with laughter, the bull-like neck, muscular shoulders and chest had lost none of their wrestler's power. He seemed to have forgotten their argument in the courtyard of Cardinal Riario's palace. If Bramante were disappointed at the turn of fate that had made Sangallo the architect of Rome, he showed none of it in his manner.

As the last guest left, Sangallo explained, "It wasn't

a party. Just our friends coming in. This happens every night. Times have changed, eh?"

Though Julius II hated the very mention of the Borgia name, he was obliged to occupy Alexander VI's rooms because his own quarters were not yet ready. As Sangallo led Michelangelo through the great hall of the Appartamento Borgia, he had time to take in the gold ceilings, silken hangings and oriental carpets, Pinturicchio's colourful murals of landscaped gardens, the enormous throne surrounded by stools and velvet cushions. Beyond was the smaller of the two reception halls, with its large windows framing green gardens and stretches of orange and pine trees as far as Monte Mario.

Sitting on a high, purple-backed throne was Pope Julius II, about him his private secretary, Sigismondo de' Conti, two masters of ceremonies, Paris de Grassis and Johannes Burchard, several cardinals and bishops in full regalia, several men who appeared to be ambassadors, all waiting their turn for a private word with the Pope, who was pouring out an uninterrupted flow of observations, condemnations and detailed instructions.

Michelangelo studied the sixty-two-year-old former Cardinal Giuliano della Rovere who, when deprived of the papacy twelve years before by the Borgia's purchase of the office, had had the courage to issue a proclamation for a council to depose " this false pontiff, betrayer of the Church." The act had forced him into exile in France for ten years ; and had set Sangallo to mending church ceilings.

Michelangelo saw before him the first pontiff to wear a beard, a spare figure, lean from abstemious living, once handsome in a strong-featured fashion, but now with deep lines in his face, his beard showing streaks of white. What Michelangelo felt most was the enormous energy, what Sangallo had described on their walk to the Papal palace as Julius' " fiery impetuosity," echoing off the walls and ceiling. " Here is a man," Michelangelo thought, " who has been planning to be Pope for so many years, he will try to accomplish as much in a day as his predecessors have been content to do in a month."

Pope Julius II looked up, saw them standing in the doorway, waved them in. Sangallo knelt, kissed the Pope's ring, introduced Michelangelo, who also knelt and kissed the ring.

" Who is your father?"

" Lodovico Buonarroti-Simoni."

461

"It is an old Florentine family," Sangallo proffered.

"I have seen your Pietà in St. Peter's. That is where I wish my tomb to be erected."

"Could Your Holiness stipulate where in St. Peter's?"

"In the centre," replied Julius coldly.

Michelangelo guessed that he had asked something wrong. The Pope was obviously a blunt man. Michelangelo liked his manner.

"I shall study the basilica. Would you speak, Holy Father, about your wishes for the tomb?"

"That is your task, to give me what I wish."

"And, so I shall. But I must build on the foundation of Your Holiness' desires."

This answer pleased Julius. He began speaking in his rough-timbered voice, pouring out plans, ideas, bits of historical data, ambitions for the Church. Michelangelo listened as concentratedly as he could. Then Julius struck terror into him.

"I desire you to design a frieze of bronzes to go around all four sides of the tomb. Bronze is the best medium for storytelling; through it you can relate the most important episodes of my life."

Michelangelo locked his back teeth, bowing low to conceal the expression on his face, wanting to exclaim, "To tell stories is for those who sing ballads."

16

When the last of the apprentices had left, Michelangelo sat on a stool before a draughting table in Sangallo's converted music room. The house was quiet. Sangallo set before him tablets of the size they had used to sketch Rome, seven years before.

"Tell me if I am correct," said Michelangelo. "First the Pope wants a walk-in tomb. Second, he wants the tomb to suggest that he will have glorified and solidified the Church . . ."

". . . brought art, poetry, scholarship back to Rome. Here are my notebooks on ancient and classical tombs. Here is one of the first, for Mausolus, in 360 B.C., in Asia Minor; here are my drawings of Augustus' and Hadrian's tombs, as described by the historians."

Michelangelo studied the drawings closely:

" Sangallo, in these drawings sculpture is used to decorate the architecture, to ornament a façade. My tombs will use the architectural structure to hold my sculptures."

Sangallo stroked his moustaches, seemed surprised to find them so short.

" Design a solid structure first, or your marbles will fall off."

He excused himself. Michelangelo was left alone to pore over the drawings of gods and goddesses, allegorical figures, all overwhelmed by the structural mass. He would keep his tomb smaller, design the sculptures larger, so that they would dwarf the architecture.

It was dawn by the time he put aside his pencils and charcoal. The sunless March morning sifted colour into the room as though it were thin grey smoke. He made his way to the bed in the room next to Sangallo's son Francesco, climbed between the icy sheets.

He slept a couple of hours, awoke refreshed and walked to St. Peter's, overjoyed to see that it had been securely counterpropped. He went into the Chapel of the Kings of France to see his Pietà. Strong morning light was coming in from the high windows in the opposite wall, suffusing the faces of Mary and Jesus. The marble was alive with poignancy. Fragments of memory stabbed through him as he ran his fingertips over the two figures, the exquisitely polished marble warm and alive to his touch. How he had worked to achieve this!

He entered the main basilica, gazed at the altar in the centre of the transept, under which was the tomb of St. Peter. This was where the Pope wanted his tomb to be. He then walked about the ancient brick building, with its hundred columns of marble and granite forming the five naves, wondering where in this central nave, which was three times as broad as the others and rose to a timbered ceiling, there could be a place for Julius' tomb to join the other ninety-two Popes buried there.

He stopped in to visit with Leo Baglioni and learned that, although Cardinal Riario had missed the papacy, he was as powerful as ever because Julius was his cousin; then he went on to the palace of Cardinal Giovanni de' Medici, near the Pantheon.

Cardinal Giovanni, plumper than ever, the cast in his eye more pronounced, had had good times with Cardinal Rovere while they were both in exile. Now Rovere was Pope Julius II and Giovanni enjoyed his friendship. He was genuinely glad to see Michelangelo, to hear about the David. Giuliano entered the room, a full-grown man now, as handsome as the portraits Michelangelo had seen of Lorenzo's brother, after whom he had been named. And, for the first time that Michelangelo could remember, Cousin Giulio greeted him without hostility. He too was changed; with Piero dead, and Cardinal Giovanni head of the house of Medici, Giulio no longer feared that he would be repudiated.

" Do I have Your Grace's permission to speak of a delicate matter?" Michelangelo asked.

Cardinal Giovanni still did not like delicate matters; they were usually painful. But he granted Michelangelo permission to speak.

" It is about Contessina. She suffers from the poorness of that little house. And almost no one dares visit or help her."

" We are getting money to her."

" If it would be possible, Excellency, to bring her to Rome . . . to her proper place."

A flush rose slowly on Giovanni's cheeks.

" I am touched by your loyalty to our house. You may be sure I have thought of this."

" The Florentine Council must not be offended," added Cousin Giulio. " We are only now becoming friends with Florence again. If we hope to regain the palace, all the Medici holdings . . ."

Cardinal Giovanni waved a hand at him, lightly.

" All these things will be effected in good time. Thank you for calling, Michelangelo. Come as often as you can."

Giuliano took him to the door. Out of eyeshot of his brother and cousin, he seized his arm affectionately.

" It is good to see you, Michelangelo. And good to hear you plead for my sister. I hope we can all be together again."

He stopped at the Bear Inn, opposite his old rooms, rented an apartment at the rear overlooking the Tiber and the Castel Sant'-Angelo, where he could have quiet and privacy, neither being available in the Sangallo palace.

Then he went on to meet Balducci at the Trattoria Toscana. Almost automatically he had slipped into his old routine. He had had a magnificent fulfilment in the David, a public acceptance. He had a house and studio of his own. Yet somehow as he walked the streets, their rough cobblestones not yet reset, he had the strange feeling that nothing had happened. Nothing had changed.

What kind of memorial could he design for Pope Julius II? With nothing to disturb his gaze but the muddy waters of the Tiber, he asked himself, "What do I want to carve? How many large figures can I use? How many smaller? What about the allegories?" The tomb itself did not take him long: thirty-six feet long, twenty-three feet wide, thirty feet high, the ground floor thirteen feet, the first story, which would carry his giant figures, nine feet, the recessed third story, seven feet.

Reading in the Bible he had borrowed from Sangallo, he found a figure vastly different from the David, but a figure that also emerged as a summit of human achievement and represented a model for man to seek in his own life: Moses, symbolizing the maturity of man, even as David represented man's youth. Moses, the leader of his people, the law giver, the bringer of order out of chaos, of discipline out of anarchy; yet himself imperfect, capable of anger, of weakness. Here was Lorenzo's half-man, half-god, who had triumphed for humanity, codified for the ages the concept of a single God, helped to create a civilization. He was a loving kind of figure, not a saint, but a loving kind of figure.

Moses would occupy one corner of the first story. For the opposite corner he thought of the Apostle Paul, about whom he had read when carving the saint for the Piccolomini altar. Paul, born a Jew, a well-educated, well-bred Roman citizen and student of the Greek culture, was also a lover of the law. He had heard a voice that said, " I am Jesus, whom thou persecutest," and had devoted his life to carrying the message of Christianity to Greece and Asia Minor, laying the foundation of a Church as widespread as the Roman Empire. These two would dominate the tomb. For the other corners he would find equally interesting figures to carve; eight in all, massive in volume, eight feet high though seated.

Since these would be draped figures, he now gave himself the freedom to carve many nudes on the main level: four male Captives on each side of the tomb, with shoulders and heads towering over the columns to which they were bound: sixteen figures of all ages, build, spirit, caught in the anguish of the captured, the enslaved, the crushed, the dying. His excitement rose. There would be figures of Victors too, the uncrushables, the struggling, hoping, fighting, conquering. The tomb would have the scope of the Bathers in the three-dimensional, heroic character of marble.

Julius had asked for a bronze frieze, and Michelangelo would give it to him, but it would be a narrow band, the least part of the structure. The true frieze would be this band of magnificent nudes extending around the four sides of the tomb.

He worked in a fever of exultation for several weeks, nourished by the unending flow of sketches that were born in his brain and brought to life in India ink. He took his portfolio to Sangallo.

"His Holiness won't want a totally naked male tomb," said Sangallo, his smile somewhat forced.

"I was planning to make four allegories. They will be feminine, figures from the Bible, such as Rachel, Ruth, Leah . . ."

Sangalo was studying the architectural plan.

"You're going to have to have a few niches, you know . . ."

"Oh, Sangallo, not niches!"

"Yes. The Holy Father keeps asking what you are going to put in the niches. If, when you submit the design, he doesn't find a single niche on the entire tomb . . . His Holiness is a stubborn man; he gets what he wants, or you get nothing."

"Very well, I'll design niches . . . between each group of bound captives. But I'll make them high, eight or nine feet, and keep the figures well out in front of them: Victories, for example, and female figures. Then we can put angels up on this third level . . ."

"Good, now you're beginning to think the way the Pope does."

But if Sangallo grew more excited with the mounting pile of sketches, Jacopo Galli grew increasingly quiet.

"How many figures will there be in all? Do you intend to set up a studio, with helpers? Who is to carve these cherubs at the feet of the Victories? I remember you told me you couldn't design convincing *putti,* yet I see a good many of them indicated. . . ." He searched Michelangelo's face with sunken, burning eyes. " . . . these angels holding up the Pope's sarcophagus? Do you recall your lamentations about carving angels?"

"These are only rough sketches, to please the Pope, to gain his consent."

466

He brought Sangallo his latest drawing. The Captives and Victories on the ground level rested on a platform of marble blocks, each richly decorated. Starting from the second story, between the Moses and Paul, was a short pyramid form, an arched temple containing the sarcophagus, and hovering over it, two angels. He had designed the front in detail, indicating that the other three sides would carry out the Pope's concept of having the captured provinces represented as well as his homage to the arts.

By now he had between thirty and forty large sculptures indicated for the tomb, which left relatively little architecture to intrude upon his carvings.

Sangallo was enthralled by the magnitude of his concept.

" It's a colossal mausoleum! Exactly what the Pope envisaged for himself. I'll go immediately to make our appointment with the Holy Father."

Jacopo Galli was furious. Over Signora Galli's protests he called for a servant to get him up, wrap him in warm blankets and help him into the library to study Michelangelo's drawings on the same antique desk where Michelangelo had written his sonnet to Alexander VI. His ill-suppressed anger lent him strength, he again seemed seven feet tall. His voice, grown hoarse during his sickness, was burned clear.

" Even Bregno wouldn't have been this obvious!"

" Why is it obvious?" Michelangelo demanded hotly. " It will give me the chance to carve magnificent nudes, the like of which you've never seen."

Galli cried, " I would be the last to dispute that. But the good figures will be surrounded by so much mediocrity they will be lost. These endless chains of decorative sausages, for instance . . ."

" They're rows of garlands."

" You are going to carve them yourself?"

" . . . well, no, I'll be too busy . . ."

" Are you going to sculpture these angels?"

" I could make the clay models."

" And this figure of the Pope on top? You're going to carve that monstrosity?"

Michelangelo cried, " You're being disloyal."

" The best mirror is an old friend. Why are you intruding a bronze frieze on an all-marble tomb?"

" The Pope wanted it."

" And if the Pope wants you to stand on your head in the Piazza Navona on Shrove Thursday with your buttocks painted purple, you'll do that too?" Galli's manner softened. He said quietly, " *Caro mio,* you will carve a glorious tomb, but not this one! How many actual statues do you have indicated here?"

" About forty."

" Then you are dedicating the rest of your life to this tomb?"

" Why must I?"

" How long did you carve on the Bacchus?"

" One year."

" The Pietà?"

" Two."

" The David?"

" Three."

" Then by the simplest arithmetic, these forty figures on the tombs will take you between forty and a hundred years."

" No." Stubbornly. " I've learned my craft now. I can work fast. Like lightning."

" Fast, or good?"

" Both. Please don't exhaust yourself, my dear friend, I'll be all right."

Jacopo Galli shot him a piercing look.

" Will you? Let's make sure."

He opened a cabinet of the desk, took out a batch of papers tied with a thin leather cord, the name Michelangelo Buonarroti scrawled across the top.

" Here are the three contracts I drew for the Pietà, Piccolomini altar, and the Bruges Madonna. Pick up that pen, we'll write the best clauses from each."

Signoria Galli came to his side. " The doctor ordered you not to get out of bed. You must conserve your strength."

Jacopo looked up at his wife with a shy smile, asked, " For what? This may be the last service I can render our young friend, and I cannot in all conscience let him go without it." He turned back to the contracts. " Now, if I know the Pope, he will want the tomb completed immediately. Hold out for ten years, more if you can. As for price, he drives a hard bargain because he wants his money to finance an army. Don't take a scudo less than twenty thousand ducats. . . ."

Michelangelo wrote as Galli dictated from the three earlier contracts. Suddenly Jacopo went deathly pale, began to cough, put the blanket to his mouth. Two servants half carried him back to his bed. He gave Michelangelo a fleeting "Farewell," tried to hide the bloodstained towel, turned his face to the wall.

When he again entered the Appartamento Borgia, Michelangelo was taken aback to find Bramante engaged in animated conversation with the Pope. He felt uneasy; why was Bramante present at this hour appointed for the examination of the tomb drawings? Was he to have a voice in the decision?

He and Sangallo knelt, were graciously received. A chamberlain set a table before Julius, who took the folio of sketches from Michelangelo's hand, spread them eagerly before him.

" Holy Father, if I may presume to explain . . ."

The Pope listened attentively, then brought his hand down sharply on the table.

" It is even more impossible than I had dreamed. You have caught my spirit exactly. Bramante, what do you say? Will it not be the most beautiful mausoleum in Rome?"

" In all Christendom, Holy Father," replied Bramante, his green eyes boring into Michelangelo's.

" Buonarroti, Sangallo informs me that you wish to choose the marbles yourself in Carrara."

" Only in the quarries can I be certain of getting perfect blocks, Holy Father."

" Then set out immediately. One thousand ducats will be provided to you by Alamanno Salviati for the purchase of the stones."

There was a moment of silence. Michelangelo asked respectfully, " And for the sculpturing, Your Holiness?"

Bramante raised his eyebrows, threw a glance at Julius which to Michelangelo insinuated, " This stone carver does not consider it a sufficient honour to work in the service of Pope Julius II. He is grasping at this work for profit." The Pope thought for an instant, decreed:

" The Papal Treasurer shall be instructed to pay you ten thousand ducats when the tomb is satisfactorily completed."

Michelangelo gulped, heard Galli's voice crying, " Do not take a scudo less than twenty thousand ducats. Even that will be short pay for a task that will take ten to twenty years."

But how could he bargain with the Holy Father? Demand double what the Pope had offered? Particularly with Bramante standing by, a mocking expression on his face. The thousand ducats the Pope was advancing would barely pay for the major marble blocks and get them transported to Rome. But he wanted to carve these marbles! His need to sculpture had to come first. He shot a swift look at Bramante.

" You are generous, Holy Father. And now may I speak of the time for completion? If I could have a minimum of ten years . . ."

" Impossible!" thundered Julius. " It is my dearest wish to see the tomb completed. I will grant you five years."

Michelangelo felt his heart plummet, the way it did when he had accidentally knocked off a piece of marble. Forty marble carvings in five years! Eight a year! His Moses could not be less than a year's work all by itself. Each of the Captives and Victors should have half a year to a year for full realization, the Apostle Paul . . .

His jaw stiffened with the same obstinacy he had shown to Galli. One could no more bargain with the pontiff over time than over money. He would manage. . . . It was not humanly possible to create the entire tomb with its forty marble figures in five years, Jacopo Galli had been right about that. Then he would simply have to achieve the super-human. He had inside himself the power of ten ordinary sculptors, of a hundred, if necessary. He would complete the tomb in five years, even if it killed him.

He bowed his head in resignation. " All will be done, Holy Father, as you say. And now that it is arranged, could I presume to ask that the contract be drawn?"

What he heard in response was a peculiar silence. Bramante lowered his head into his bull-like shoulders. Sangallo was stony-faced. The Pope glared. After what seemed to Michelangelo a tortured time, Julius replied:

" Now that everything is arranged, I should like you and Sangallo to visit St. Peter's to determine the proper place for the tomb."

Not a word about the contract. Michelangelo put his left hand across his chest, feeling in his shirt the paper Jacopo Galli had dictated to him.

He kissed the Pope's ring, started for the door. The Pope called, " One moment." He turned, his hopes flaring. " I wish Bramante to accompany you, to give you the benefit of his advice."

There simply was no room in the basilica, and no proper

place for so imposing a marble tomb. It was obvious that his sculptures would be crowded in by pillars, without space around them in which to move or breathe. There would be no proper light from the small windows. At best it would be a bulking obstacle, a hindrance to all movement in the basilica.

He went outside, circled towards the rear where he remembered a half-completed structure outside the west apse. Sangallo and Bramante joined him before the six-foot-high brick wall.

" What is this, Sangallo?"

" According to my studies there was an ancient Templum Probi here. Pope Nicholas V had it torn down, and started a Tribune to house a platform for the bishop's throne. He died when the building had reached this height, and it has been left this way ever since."

Michelangelo jumped the wall, paced off the width and length.

" This could be a solution," he exclaimed. " There would be space around the tomb on all sides. We could build the roof at the height we needed, plaster the interior walls to set off the white marble, put in windows for light, break through the walls of the basilica for a square arch . . ."

" It has the prerequisites," Bramante commented.

" No," decreed Sangallo. " It would never be better than a makeshift. The roof would be too high for the width, and the walls would slant inward as they do in the Sistine."

Disappointed, Michelangelo cried, " But, Sangallo, we can't use the basilica!"

" Come with me."

In the surrounding area were a number of ill-assorted buildings, built over the centuries since St. Peter's had first been erected by Constantine in 319; chapels, choirs, altars, a miscellany thrown up in total confusion of whatever material happened to be available: black tufa, cream-coloured travertine, dull red brick, *peperino* speckled with dark lava and white limestone.

" For a tomb as original as the one you are going to create," said Sangallo, " we must have a completely new building. The architecture of the building must be born of the tomb itself."

Hope revived in Michelangelo's bosom.

" I will design it," Sangallo continued. " I can convince His Holiness. Here on this eminence, for example, there is sufficient space if we clear out these wooden structures and a couple of those decaying shrines. It would be visible from the city below."

Michelangelo felt Bramante's eyes boring holes in his back. He spun around. To his surprise, Bramante's eyes were sparkling with approval.

"Then you like the idea, Bramante?" Michelangelo asked.

"Sangallo is completely right. What is needed here is a beautiful new chapel, with all these surrounding impairments swept away."

Sangallo beamed with pleasure. But when Michelangelo turned to Bramante to thank him, he found that the architect's eyes had gone opaque, there was a twitching at one corner of his mouth.

BOOK SEVEN

THE POPE

1

He had no way of knowing, during his stay in the mountains of Carrara, that his years of grace were over. He returned to Rome in time for Julius' New Year's reception of 1506, and to unload the boats as they arrived at the Ripa Grande, only to find that the war between himself and the Pope had begun. Bramante had persuaded Julius to abandon Sangallo's idea for a separate chapel to house his tomb; instead, a new St. Peter's was to rise on the hill where the chapel was to have gone, the best design to be chosen through public competition. Michelangelo heard of no provision for his tomb. He had spent the Pope's entire thousand ducats for marbles and shipping, but Julius refused to give him more money until he had seen one of the statues carved. When Julius provided him with a house behind the Piazza San Pietro, a papal secretary informed him that he would have to pay several ducats a month for its use.

"Could I wait until I am paid something by the Holy Father before I return his rent money?" he asked caustically.

He went to the docks in a grey January overcast, accompanied by Piero Rosselli, a Livorno muralist who was known as the best preparer of walls for fresco. A peppery, freckle-faced chap who had gone to sea as a youth, Rosselli walked along the quays with a swaying movement as though to accommodate a rolling deck.

"I've fought this current many times in winter," said Rosselli, looking downstream at the swollen Tiber: "It'll be days before a boat can make its way up here."

Back at Sangallo's house, Michelangelo warmed his hands before the library fire while his old friend showed him his finished designs for the new St. Peter's, incorporating the Old Basilica. Sangallo believed that he had overcome the objections of the Sacred College and the public to replacing the original church.

"Then you don't think Bramante has a chance to win the competition?"

" He has talent," replied Sangallo; "his Tempietto in San Pietro in Montorio is a gem. But he has had no experience in building churches."

Francesco Sangallo broke into the room, crying, "Father! They've unearthed a big marble statue in the old palace of Emperor Titus. His Holiness wants you to go at once and supervise excavating it."

A crowd had already gathered in the vineyard behind Santa Maria Maggiore. In a hollow, the bottom half still submerged, gleamed a magnificent bearded head and a torso of tremendous power. Through one arm, and turning around the opposite shoulder, was a serpent; on either side emerged the heads, arms and shoulders of two youths, encircled by the same serpent. Michelangelo's mind flashed back to his first night in Lorenzo's *studiolo*.

" It is the Laocoön," Sangallo cried.

" Of which Pliny wrote!" added Michelangelo.

The carving was over eight feet in height and equally long, an awesome sight. When the news spread through Rome the vineyard and streets and steps of Santa Maria Maggiore became jammed with high church officials, merchants, noblemen, all hoping to acquire the prize. The farmer who owned the land announced that he had sold the statue to a cardinal for four hundred ducats. The Vatican's Master of Ceremonies, Paris de Grassis, offered five hundred. The farmer yielded. Paris de Grassis turned to Sangallo. " His Holiness asks that you bring it to the Papal palace immediately." Then, to Michelangelo, he added, " He requests your attendance this afternoon to examine the block."

The Pope had ordered the Laocoön set up on the closed terrace of the Belvedere pavilion, across a valley and on the hill above the Papal palace.

" I wish you to examine the figures minutely," said Julius, " and tell me if they are truly carved from one block."

Michelangelo began working the statue, front and back, with sharp eyes and sensitive finger tips, finding four vertical junctures where separate pieces of marble had been joined together by the sculptors of Rhodes.

He left the Belvedere, walked to the bank that had been Jacopo Galli's. How different Rome felt without Galli in it; how desperately he needed his friend's counsel now. Baldassare Balducci was the new manager-owner of the bank. His family in Florence had invested in Rome, as had many

474

members of the Florentine colony; Balducci had seized the opportunity to marry the plain-faced daughter of a wealthy Roman family, with a considerable dowry.

"What do you do with your Sundays now, Balducci?"

Balducci flushed. "I spend them with my wife's family."

"Don't you miss the exercise?"

"I still go hunting . . . with a gun. The owner of a bank has to be respectable."

"*Che rigorista!* I never expected to find you conventional."

Balducci sighed. "You can't grow rich and amuse yourself at the same time. One's youth should be spent on women, his middle years on money, his old age on bowling."

"You've become quite a philosopher. Could you lend me a hundred ducats?"

He stood in the wind-driven rain watching the boat with his marbles struggle to make its way to the docks. Twice the prow went under the white-caps. It seemed that the boat and its precious cargo would sink to the bottom of the swollen Tiber, carrying with it thirty-four wagonloads of his best quarried marbles. While he stood drenched on the river bank, the sailors made a last frenzied effort; ropes were thrown from the docks, the boat tied up. The job of unloading in the torrential downpour was nearly impossible. He helped carry ten of the smaller blocks off the bobbing boat which the current whipped away from its lashing several times, but he was unable to move the six-, ten-, and twelve-foot columns until Sangallo came to direct the use of a loading crane.

Dark fell before the job was completed. He lay awake listening to the storm increase in fury. When he reached the docks in the morning he found that the Tiber had overflowed. The Ripa Grande was a marsh. His beautiful marbles were covered with mud and yellow silt. He waded through water up to his knees to clean off the loose debris, remembering the months he has spent in the quarries searching for the purest bed, supervising the cutting of the big blocks from the mountainside, lowering them down the precipitous slopes on cables and rollers, loading them on wagons which took them to the beach, rolling them gently over the sand on to the boats at low tide, all without a chip or crack or stain. And look at them now, after the barest few hours in Rome!

It took three days for the rain to stop and the Tiber to

recede from the quay. The Guffatti sons came with the family wagon to carry the marbles to the rear portico of the house. Michelangelo paid them out of the loan from Balducci, then bought a large tarpaulin to cover the blocks, and some used furniture. On the last day of January, surrounded by his wet and stained marbles, he sat down at the plank table and wrote his father a letter, enclosing a note to Argiento, which he asked Lodovico to send on to the farm at Ferrara, where Argiento had gone when the Signoria reclaimed Michelangelo's house until he could resume work for them.

Pending Argiento's arrival, Sangallo recommended an elderly carpenter by the name of Cosimo, with a thin thatch of silver hair and rheumy eyes, who needed lodgings. His cooking tasted of resin and shavings, but Cosimo in a methodical fashion helped Michelangelo build a wooden model of the first two floors of the tomb. Twice a week young Rosselli would go to the fish markets at the Portico of Octavia to buy fresh clams, mussels, shrimp, squid and sea bass, cooking a Livornese *cacciucco,* or fish stew, over Michelangelo's fire. The three men mopped up the spicy orégano sauce with crusts of bread.

To buy a forge, Swedish iron and chestnut wood, it was necessary for him to visit Balducci's bank to borrow another hundred ducats.

" I don't mind making a second loan," said Balducci. " But I do mind your getting deeper into the hole. When do you expect to put this tomb on a businesslike basis?"

" As soon as I have some carving to show Julius. First I must decorate several of the base blocks, to establish models for Argiento and a stone-carver I'm planning to bring from the Duomo workshop. Then I can start massing the Moses . . ."

" But that could take months! What do you intend to live on until then? Be sensible, go to the Pope. From a bad paymaster, get what you can."

He returned home, measured Cosimo's wooden model for the size of the block at the corner of the tomb, then cut a marble to shape, carving a series of three masks, two in profile, a full face below, surrounded by flowing calligraphic lines. That was as far as he got: three structural support blocks. Argiento sent no word in response to his letter. The stonemason from the Duomo workyard could not come. Sangallo did not think it a good time to ask the Pope for money.

"The Holy Father is judging the plans for St. Peter's. The winner is to be announced on March first. At that time I will take you to His Holiness."

But on the first of March the Sangallo palace fell silent. When Michelangelo arrived at the house he found it deserted, not even the draughtsman having come to work. Sangallo, his wife and son were huddled together in an upstairs bedroom as though someone in the family had died.

"How could this have happened?" cried Michelangelo. "You are the Pope's official architect. You are one of his oldest and most loyal friends."

"All I hear is rumour: the Romans around the Pope hate all Florentines, but they are friendly to Urbino, and hence to Bramante. Others say he makes the Holy Father laugh, hunts with him, entertains him . . ."

"Clowns! Do they build great churches?"

"They ingratiate themselves . . ."

"I will get the truth from Leo Baglioni."

Baglioni gazed at him in genuine astonishment. "The truth? Don't you know the truth? Come with me."

Bramante had bought an old palace in the Borgo, close to the Vatican, torn it down and rebuilt it with simple elegance. The house was jammed with important personages of Rome: courtiers from the Vatican, princes of the Church, nobles, professors, artists, merchants, bankers. Bramante held court, the centre of all eyes and admiration, his red face beaming, the green eyes crackling with excitement and triumph.

Leo Baglioni steered Michelangelo upstairs to a large workroom. Pinned to the walls and scattered about the worktables were Bramante's drawings for the new St. Peter's. Michelangelo gasped: it was an edifice to dwarf the cathedral of Florence, yet of an elegant, lyrical design, noble in its conception. By comparison Sangallo's Byzantine conception, a dome over a square, seemed ponderous and fortress-like.

Now Michelangelo knew the truth: it had nothing to do with the Romans hating Florentines or Bramante being an entertainer. It had to do with talent. Bramante's St. Peter's was the more beautiful and modern in every aspect.

"I'm sorry for Sangallo's sake," said Baglioni matter-of-factly, "but this was a competition, and there's no doubt in anyone's mind who won it. What would you do, if you
477

were the Pope? Award the commission to a friend and build a church that was outmoded before it began? Or give it to a newcomer, and create the most beautiful church in Christendom?"

Michelangelo did not trust himself to answer. He fled down the steps, out into the Borgo, circled the Leonine Wall until he was drugged with exhaustion. If he, Michelangelo Buonarroti, had been Pope Julius II, he too would have been obliged to choose Bramante's plan. This church, far more than the paved streets and enlarged piazzas, could be the beginning of a new and glorious Rome.

That night, as he lay cold and sleeplesss in his bed, listening to Casimo snore as though each breath were his last, it became obvious to him that Bramante, from the moment the Pope had sent him with them to find a proper spot for the tomb, had laid his plans to see that the special chapel would never be built. He had used Sangallo's idea for a separate building, and Michelangelo's grandiose plan for the mausoleum, for his own purpose: the securing of a commission to build a new cathedral.

There was no question but that Bramante's St. Peter's would be a glorious abode for the tomb. But would Bramante allow it in his church? Would he be willing to share credit and attention with Michelangelo Buonarroti?

2

By the middle of March the sun came out. Michelangelo had the Guffatti family set three giant columns upright. Soon he would be ready to remove the negative marble and probe for the Moses and the Captives. On April first it was announced that the Pope and Bramante would lay the cornerstone of the new cathedral on April 18. Paris de Grassis was busy establishing protocol. When the workmen began digging the wide hole which the Pope was to descend to bless the laying of the first stone, Michelangelo saw that the sacred old basilica was not to be included in the new structure, but would be demolished piecemeal to make room for the new church.

He was outspoken in his disapproval. He loved the columns and ancient carvings; he also felt that it was sacrilege to destroy the earliest temple of Christendom in Rome. He spoke of it with whomever he met, until Leo Baglioni warned him that some of Bramante's less savoury hangers-on were saying that unless he stopped attacking their friend his tomb might be built before that of the Pope.

"I wouldn't want you turning up in the Tiber, my unpolitic young friend," laughed Leo.

He received a letter from the man who owned the boats in Carrara, advising him that another shipment of marbles would reach the Ripa Grande early in May. Michelangelo would have to make payment at the docks before the marbles could be released. The bill was for more ducats than he had. He washed, went to the Papal palace. Pope Julius, his bristling beard protruding from a high ermine collar, was in his small throne room surrounded by courtiers. Beside him was his favourite jeweller. Julius turned on the man, cried:

"I do not mean to spend a *baiocco* more for stones, small or great."

Michelangelo waited until the gem cutter had retired and the Pope seemed calmer, then pressed forward.

"Holy Father, the next shipment of your marbles for the tomb are on the way. The boat charges must be paid before I can have them carried home. I am without funds to meet the bill. Could you give me expense money to secure the blocks?"

"Return Monday," said the Pope curtly, and turned away.

Rome was beautiful in the butter-yellow spring sunlight; but Michelangelo walked the streets blindly, a torrent raging in his head. He had been dismissed like the tradesman! Why? Because that was all an artist was, a skilled tradesman? But the Pope had called him the best marble master in all Italy.

He took his story to Baglioni, asking if his friend knew what had caused the change in the Holy Father. Leo had trouble keeping his voice matter-of-fact.

"Bramante has convinced the Pope that it is bad luck to build one's own tomb. That it could hasten the day when it has to be pressed into service."

Michelangelo sank on to a wooden bench, breathing hard. "What shall I do?"

"Go back on Monday. As though nothing had happened."

He went back on Monday. Then on Tuesday, Wednesday, Thursday. Each time he was admitted, received coolly, told to return. On Friday the guard at the Papal palace refused him entrance. It was hot in the midday sun, but Michelangelo felt cold all over. Thinking there might be some misunderstanding, he again tried to enter the palace. His way was barred. At that moment the Pope's cousin, the Bishop of Lucca, arrived.

"What is the matter with you?" cried the bishop to the guard. "Do you not know, Maestro Buonarroti?"

"I know him, Your Grace."

"Then why are you sending him away?"

"Excuse me, Excellency, but I have my orders."

Michelangelo walked home, his shoulders jerking as though in spasms. His brain on fire. He quickened his pace, without actually running, bolted the door of his house, sat down and scrawled:

Most Blessed Father, I have been turned out of the palace to-day by your orders; therefore, if you want me, you must look for me elsewhere than in Rome.

He addressed the letter to Messer Agostino, the Pope's steward, sent a neighbouring boy to find Cosimo. The old man came hurrying.

"Cosimo, I must leave Rome to-night. To-morrow send for a dealer and sell this furniture."

At the second hour of the night he rented a horse at the Porta del Popolo and left with the post for Florence. At the rise north of town, where he had caught his first glimpse of Rome, he turned in the saddle to gaze back at the sleeping city. Into his mind came a favourite Tuscan adage, born of centuries of feuding:

> How much the fool who goes to Rome
> Excels the fool who stays at home.

Early the second day he dropped off his horse at Poggibonsi at the inn where he had stopped on his way to Siena to recarve Torrigiani's St. Francis. He was washing in a bowl near the wall when he heard thunderous hoofs storming up the road. It turned out to be Baglioni at the head of a party of five couriers, their horses lathering at the bit from hard riding. He stood gazing at his fastidious friend's face, covered with dried perspiration, his clothes discoloured by the dust of the road.

"Leo! What brings you to Poggibonsi?"

"You! The Holy Father knew we were friends. He ordered me to head the party."

Michelangelo blinked at the five armed men of the Pope's guard sitting their horses and glaring at him.

" What . . . party? I'm on my way home to Florence. . . ."

" No you're not! " Baglioni dismounted, brushed the hair out of his eyes. He took a parchment from his saddlebag. " This is a letter from Pope Julius. He commands you to return forthwith to Rome under penalty of disgrace. . . ."

" I did not deserve to be driven from his presence."

" All will be set to rights."

" Permit me to doubt."

" I have the Holy Father's word for it."

" The Holy Father has lapses of memory."

A burly horseman asked, " Shall we truss him up, Messer Baglioni? We could sling him over his own saddle."

" I was not instructed to use force. Michelangelo, you're not the first to be kept waiting by a Pope. If Julius says, ' Wait!' you wait, if it takes a week, a month or a year."

" I'm going back to Florence for good."

" Not for good. Nobody leaves the Pope dangling! Upon my oath, the Holy Father is sorry about what happened. He wants you to return and resume work."

" I will not allow any man to treat me as dirt."

" The Pope is not ' any man.' " Leo came close, so that the guards could not hear, said, " Bravo! You sound like the Florentine Marzocco. But now that you have asserted your independence, come back. Do not put me in a difficult position."

Michelangelo was silent; Baglioni had always been a good friend. But what about his own self-respect? No one should ask another man to surrender his pride. He told Leo so. Baglioni's face became stern.

" It is not possible to defy the pontiff. You will see. Now or later. And later could be worse. As your friend I urge you not to match your will against his. How could you win?"

Michelangelo lowered his head, crinkled his eyes and studied the pattern of the earth beneath his feet.

" I don't know, Leo. . . . But if I return now I lose everything. I'm going on to Florence to get my house and my contract back. If he wishes it, I'll sculpture the Pope's tomb . . . under the shadow of the Signoria tower."

3

His father was not pleased to see him; he had imagined Michelangelo to be earning large sums from the Pope in Rome. He took over his front room again, set Taddei's Our Lady on a workstand, checked his marble for the Apostle Matthew where it was stored in a Duomo workshed, carried home from the foundry the still unfinished bronze David. His cartoon for the Bathers had been moved from the Dyers' Hall, mounted on a fir-tree frame and attached to the wall of the gallery beyond the Great Hall of the Palazzo della Signoria.

The news of the exchange in the yard of the Poggibonsi inn took only a few hours to make its way over the mountain. When he and Granacci reached Rustici's studio for supper with the Company, he found himself a hero.

"What a tremendous compliment Pope Julius has paid you!" cried Botticelli, who had painted frescoes in the Sistine Chapel for Julius' uncle, Pope Sixtus IV, "to send an armed recovery party after you. When has this ever happened to an artist?"

"Never," growled *Il Cronaca*. "One artist is like another; if he vanishes, there are a dozen to take his place."

"But here is the Pope acknowledging that an artist is an individual," added Rustici excitedly. "With special talents and gifts, not to be found in exactly the same combination in anyone else in the world."

Michelangelo felt more put upon than a hero.

"What else could I have done?" he cried, as Granacci shoved a glass of wine into his hand. "I was barred from the Vatican . . ."

The following morning Michelangelo was awakened to the fact that the Florentine government did not agree with the Company of the Cauldron on the beneficent effects of his revolt. Gonfaloniere Soderini's face was grave when he received Michelangelo in his office.

"I'm apprehensive about what you did. At Rome, as the Pope's sculptor, you could be of considerable help to Florence. Defying him, you become a source of potential danger to us. You're the first Florentine to defy a Pope since Savonarola. I'm afraid your fate will be about the same."

" You mean I'll be hanged from a gibbet in the piazza, and then burned?" He shivered involuntarily.

Soderini smiled for the first time, wobbling the end of his nose.

" You are not guilty of heresy, only of disobedience. But in the end the Pope will have his way."

" Gonfaloniere, all I want to do is settle down in Florence. I'll start carving the St. Matthew to-morrow so that I can have my house back."

Soderini's skin went as yellow-white as his hair.

" Florence cannot renew your sculpture contract now. His Holiness would consider it a personal affront. No one can employ you, not Doni, or Pitti or Taddei, without incurring the Pope's enmity. Not until you complete Julius II's tomb, or the Holy Father releases you."

" Would it embarrass you if I were to complete existing contracts?"

" Finish the David. Our ambassador in Paris keeps writing that the king is irritated with us because we do not send the statue."

" And the Bathers; can I do the fresco?"

Soderini looked up at him. " You have not been in the Great Hall?"

" The groom brought me through your apartment."

" I suggest you go out that way."

He went directly to the east side of the Council platform where Leonardo da Vinci had painted the Battle of Anghiari. The back of his hand swung up to his mouth.

" *Dio mio,* no!"

The entire lower half of Leonardo's fresco was in ruin, the colours having run as sharply downward as though pulled by powerful magnets: horses, men, spears, trees, rocks, having flowed into each other in an indistinguishable chaos of colour.

All the antagonism, the quarrels, the feuds washed away in whatever solvent had destroyed Leonardo's magnificent mural. Michelangelo felt only the deepest regret for a fellow artist who had created mightily for a whole year of his life, only to have the results wiped out. What could have gone wrong? Tuscans had been the masters of fresco for over three hundred years. He felt Soderini at his shoulder.

" Gonfaloniere, how did it happen?"

" Leonardo was determined to revive ancient encaustic painting. He took the recipe for the plaster from Pliny, used wax with a solvent, and then gum to harden the mixture. When he finished, he applied heat by lighting fires on the floor. He said he had tried it on a small mural in Santa Maria Novella, and it had worked well. But this mural is twenty-two feet high, and in order for the heat to reach the upper portion, he had to heap on the fuel. The intense heat on the lower half caused the wax to run . . . and pulled all the colours down with it."

Leonardo lived in the San Giovanni quarter. Michelangelo knocked on the clapper. A servant answered. He was ushered into a large, beam-ceilinged room filled with art works, musical instruments, tapestries, oriental rugs. Leonardo, in a Chinese-red robe, was writing in a notebook at a high ledgerlike desk. He looked up, saw Michelangelo, put the notebook into a drawer and locked it with a key. He came forward, limping markedly from a fall he had sustained in his flying machine on a hill near Fiesole. An edge of his shining beauty had faded from his face, his eyes held a touch of melancholy.

" Leonardo, I've just come from the Signoria. I want you to know how sorry I am about the fresco. I, too, have just wasted a year of my life so I know what it must mean to you."

" You are kind." Leonardo's voice was cool.

" But that was not my main purpose in coming. I wanted to apologize to you . . . for my crustiness . . . for the wretched things I have said about you, about the statue in Milan . . ."

" You were provoked. I said slighting things about marble carvers "

Leonardo was beginning to thaw. Colour had returned to the alabaster skin.

" I saw your cartoon for the Bathers while you were away. It is truly magnificent. I sketched from it, even as I did from your David. It will become a glory of Florence."

" I don't know. I've lost all appetite now that your Battle of Anghiari will not be fought beside mine."

If he had straightened out an enmity, he was endangering his most valuable friendship. Gonfaloniere Soderini sent for him two days later to read to him from a letter from the Pope, demanding that the Signoria return Michelangelo Buonarroti to Rome at once, under pain of pontifical displeasure.

" Looks as if I had better keep going north," replied

Michelangelo mournfully; "maybe to France. Then I will no longer be your responsibility."

"You can't run from the Pope. His arm reaches over all Europe."

"Why am I so precious to the Holy Father in Florence? He locked me out in Rome."

"Because in Rome you were an employee who could be ignored. Having repudiated his service, you become the most desirable artist in the world. Don't push him too far."

"I'm not pushing anybody," Michelangelo cried in anguish; "I just want to be let alone."

"Too late. The time for that was before you entered Julius' service."

On the next post he received a letter from Piero Rosselli which made him feel as though the curls over his forehead were dancing on his head like snakes. The Pope did not want him back in Rome to continue work on the marbles; Bramante definitely had the Holy Father convinced that the tomb would hasten his death. His Holiness now wanted Michelangelo to paint the vault of the Sistine Chapel, the ugliest, most clumsy, ill-conceived and Godforsaken piece of architecture in all Italy. He read and re-read Rosselli's lines:

Last Saturday evening, when the Pope was at supper, he called for Bramante and said: "Sangallo is going to Florence to-morrow, and will bring Michelangelo back with him." Bramante answered: "Holy Father, he will not be able to do anything of the kind. I have conversed with Michelangelo, and he has often told me that he would not undertake the chapel, which you wanted to put upon him; and that, you notwithstanding, he meant only to apply himself to sculpture, and would have nothing to do with painting. Holy Father, I do not think he has the courage to attempt the work, because he has small experience in painting figures, and these will be raised high above the line of vision. That is something different from painting on the ground."

The Pope replied: "If he does not come, he will do me wrong; and so I think that he is sure to return." Upon this, I up and gave Bramante a sound rating in the Pope's presence, and spoke as I believe you would have spoken for me; and for the time he was struck dumb, as though he felt that he had made a mistake in talking as he did. I proceeded as follows: "Holy Father, Bramante never exchanged a word with Michelangelo, and if what he has just said is the truth, I beg you to cut my head off. . . ."

Michelangelo cried aloud, "Me talk with Bramante? It's a fantastic lie! Why would he want to tell the Pope such a story?"

The letter threw Michelangelo into deeper turmoil. He could do no work at all. He set off for Settignano to sit silently and cut building blocks with the Topolinos, then visited Contessina and Ridolfi. The baby, Niccolò, now five, insisted that he too be taught how to "make the marble fly." He put in an occasional hour filing and burnishing the Maréchal bronze, went several times to the Great Hall in a futile effort to whip up enthusiasm for his fresco. He knew even before Gonfaloniere Soderini summoned him at the beginning of July that the coming months would be torn by strong winds from the south.

Soderini began reading at once from the Pope's *breve*:

"Michelangelo the sculptor, who left us without reason, and in mere caprice, is afraid, as we are informed, of returning, though we for our part are not angry with him, knowing the humours of such men of genius. In order then that he may lay aside all anxiety, we rely on your loyalty to convince him in our name, that if he returns to us, he shall be uninjured and unhurt, retaining our apostolic favour in the same measure as he formerly enjoyed it."

Soderini put the letter down. "I'm going to have the Cardinal of Pavia write a letter by his own hand, in which he will promise you safety. Will that satisfy you?"

"No. Last night at the Salviati I met a Florentine merchant by the name of Tommaso di Tolfo who lives in Turkey. There is a chance for me to go out there and work for the Sultan."

His brother Lionardo asked to see him by the brook at the foot of their field in Settignano. Lionardo sat on the Buonarroti bank, Michelangelo on the Topolino side, cooling their feet in the narrow creek.

"Michelangelo, I want to help you."

"In what way?"

"Let me first admit that I made mistakes in the early years. You were right in following your course. I have seen your Madonna and Child in Bruges. Our brothers in

486

Rome speak reverently of your Pietà. You have been worshipping God too. Forgive my trespasses against you."

" You are forgiven, Lionardo."

" I must explain to you that the Pope is the viceroy of God on earth. When you disobey His Holiness you disobey God."

" Was that true," Michelangelo asked, " when Savonarola fought Alexander VI?"

Lionardo let the black cowl slip forward to mask his eyes. " Savonarola disobeyed. No matter what we think of any one Pope, he is the descendant of St. Peter. If each of us were to judge him, the Church would fall into chaos."

" Popes are men, Lionardo, elected to high office. I have to do what I feel is right."

" You're not afraid that God will punish you?"

Michelangelo looked across the brook at his brother. " Every man's courage is important. I believe God loves independence more than He does servility."

" You must be right," said Lionardo, his head lowered again, " or He would not help you carve such divine marbles."

Lionardo rose, walked up the hill towards the Buonarroti house. Michelangelo climbed the opposite bank to the Topolino's. From the top of the ridges they turned, waved to each other. They were never to meet again.

The only one who was not frightened for him was Contessina, who was irreverent about Pope Julius. A daughter of one of the ruling dynasties of the world, she had seen her family driven out of the city it had helped make the greatest in Europe, had seen her home sacked by fellow townsmen who had loved and benefited from her family's efforts, had seen her father-in-law hanged from the Signoria, had been exiled for eight years in a peasant's cottage. Her respect for authority was fading.

Her husband did not share these feelings. Ridolfi wanted to get to Rome. Therefore he did not wish to offend the Pope.

" It is with reluctance, Buonarroti, that I must ask you not to come here again. It will be reported to the Pope. The Holy Father, through Cardinal Giovanni, is our last hope. We must not endanger it."

Contessina asked in a constrained voice, " Michelangelo could come here to visit during the years when he risked his position in Florence, but not now, when he is risking your position in Rome?"

" Not my position, Contessina, ours. If the Pope turns

487

against us . . . After all, Buonarroti has a trade; if Florence banishes him he can ply his craft elsewhere. Rome is the only place we have left to go. Our future depends on it, and that of our sons. It is too dangerous."

"Being born into this world is the primary danger," observed Contessina, gazing head on at Michelangelo. "Everything after that is a game of seed cards."

"I will not come again, Messer Ridolfi," said Michelangelo quietly. "You must protect your family. It was thoughtless of me "

4

In late August Julius left Rome with an army of five hundred knights and nobles. He was joined by his nephew, the Duke of Urbino, at Orvieto, and made a bloodless conquest of Perugia. Cardinal Giovanni de' Medici was left in command of the city. The Pope was joined by the Marquis Gonzaga of Mantua with a trained army, crossed the Apennines to avoid Rimini, which was held by hostile Venice; bribed the Cardinal of Rouen out of the eight thousand French troops sent to protect Bologna by offering cardinalate hats to his three nephews; and publicly excommunicated Giovanni Bentivoglio, the ruler of Bologna. The Bolognese drove out Bentivoglio. Julius marched into Bologna.

Yet nothing sufficiently diverting had happened to Pope Julius II to make him forget his errant sculptor. At the Palazzo della Signoria, Soderini, flanked by the other eight members of the Signoria, shouted at Michelangelo as he entered:

"You have tried a bout with the Pope on which the King of France would not have ventured. We do not wish to go to war with the pontiff on your account! The Holy Father wants you to do some works in Bologna. Make up your mind to go!"

Michelangelo knew he was beaten. He had known for weeks, actually, for as the Pope advanced through Umbria, reconquering it for the Papal State, then Emilia, the people on the streets of Florence began turning their heads when he passed. Florence, which had no defence, so desperately needed the Pope's friendship that it had sent hired mercenaries, including Michelangelo's brother Sigismondo, to help him with his conquests. No one wanted the Pope's now swollen and confident army crossing the Apennines to attack. The Signoria, the townspeople, all were determined that he be sent back to the Pope, regardless of the consequences to him.

They were right. Florence came first. He would go to Bologna, make his peace with the Holy Father as best he could. Soderini did not abandon him. He gave Michelangelo a letter to his brother, the Cardinal of Volterra, who was with the Pope:

The bearer of this letter will be Michelangelo, sculptor, who is sent to you in compliance with the request of His Holiness. We assure Your Lordship that he is a good young man, and unique of his art in Italy, perhaps in the world. He is such that, using good words and kind manners, one can obtain everything from him; one must be tender and kind to him, and he will do such things that anyone who sees them will be amazed. Said Michelangelo comes upon my honour.

By now it was November. The streets of Bologna were crowded with courtiers, soldiers, foreigners in colourful costumes who had thronged to the court of the Pope. In the Piazza Maggiore a monk was suspended in a wire cage from the Palazzo del Podestà, having been caught coming out of a house on the Street of the Bordellos.

Michelangelo found a messenger to take his letter of protection to the Cardinal of Volterra, then mounted the steps of San Petronio, gazing in veneration at the Della Quercia Istrian stone sculptures of the Creation of Adam, the Expulsion from Paradise and the Sacrifices of Cain and Abel. How far he was from fulfilling his hope of carving these scenes in free-standing marble! He entered the church, where mass was being said, and was recognized by one of the Pope's body servants from Rome.

" Messer Buonarroti, His Holiness has been waiting impatiently."

The Pope was at dinner in a palace, surrounded by his court of twenty-four cardinals, the generals of his army, the noblemen, knights, princes, perhaps a hundred at dinner in the banner-strewn hall. Michelangelo was escorted the length of the room by a bishop sent by the Cardinal of Volterra, who was ill. Pope Julius looked up, saw him, fell silent. So did the rest of the hall. Michelangelo stood by the side of the Pope's big chair, at the head of the table. The two men glared at each other, their eyes flashing fire. Michelangelo threw his shoulders back, refusing to kneel. The Pope was the first to speak.

"You have delayed long! We have been obliged to come to meet you!"

Michelangelo thought grimly that this was true: the Pope had travelled a good many more miles than he had. He said stubbornly, "Holy Father, I did not deserve the treatment I received in Rome in Easter week."

The silence deepened in the big hall. The bishop, attempting to intervene in Michelangelo's behalf, stepped forward.

"Holiness, one must be indulgent towards this race of artists. They understand nothing, outside their trade, and often lack good manners."

Julius rose from his chair, thundered:

"How dare you say to this man things that I myself would not say? It is you who lack manners!"

The bishop stood dumbfounded, unable to move. The Pope gave a signal. Several courtiers seized the terror-stricken prelate and ushered him from the hall with a rain of blows. Having received as close to a public apology as a Pope could proffer, Michelangelo knelt, kissed the Pope's ring, murmured his own regrets. The Pope bestowed his benediction, said, "Come to my camp to-morrow. We will arrange our affairs."

At dusk he sat before a fire in Aldovrandi's library. Aldovrandi, who had been sent as ambassador to Julius on two earlier occasions, and had been appointed by the Pope as a ruling member of the Council of Forty, could not stop chuckling at the happenings in the dining-hall. His fair skin and jovial eyes looked as young as Michelangelo remembered them from ten years before.

"You're so much alike," he commented, "you and Julius. You both have a *terribilità*, a terrifying awesomeness. I'm sure you are the only one in Christendom who would have thought of reproaching the pontiff after having openly defied him for seven months. No wonder he respects you."

Michelangelo pulled on the steaming mug of hot water flavoured with brown sugar that Signora Aldovrandi had brought against the end-of-November cold.

"What do you suppose the Holy Father intends to do with me?"

"Put you to work."

" At what?"

" He'll think of something. You'll stay with us, of course?"

Michelangelo accepted with pleasure. Later as they sat over supper, he asked:

" How is your nephew Marco?"

" Quite well. He has a new girl, one he found in Rimini two summers ago during *ferragosto,* the mid-August holiday."

" And Clarissa?"

" One of the Bentivoglio uncles . . . adopted her. When he had to flee with Giovanni Bentivoglio, she leased her villa to one of the Pope's courtiers for a handsome rental."

" Would you know where I can find her?"

" I believe in the Via di Mezzo di San Martino. She has an apartment there."

" Would you excuse me?"

Aldovrandi rose, murmured, " Love and a cough cannot be hid."

She stood in the open doorway of the roof penthouse over-looking the Piazza di San Martino, silhouetted against the orange glow of the oil lamps behind her, her face framed in the fur cowl of a woollen robe. They stared at each other in silence, as he and the Pope had, though with a rather different emotion. His mind went back to the first time he had seen her, when she was nineteen, slender, golden-haired, with an undulant softness of manner, her lithe, willowy figure moving with delicate sensuousness, the beauty of her neck and shoulders and bosom recalling Botticelli's Simonetta. Now she was thirty-one, at a lush peak of ripe-ness, only a little heavier, a little less scintillating. Again he was aware of her magnificent body through every pore of his own. She spoke with the same sibilance of voice that seemed to enter his every orifice, making it difficult for him to separate the words because of the pounding in his ears.

" The last thing I told you was, ' Bologna is on the road to everywhere.' Come in."

She led him into a small sitting-room, warmed by two braziers, then turned to him. He slipped his arms inside her fur-lined robe. Her body was warm from the soft fur. He held her to him, kissed her yielding mouth. She mur-mured:

"When I first said, 'It is natural for us to want each other,' you blushed like a boy."

"Artists know nothing of love. My friend Granacci describes it as a diversion."

"How would you describe it?"

"What I feel for you?"

"Yes."

"As a torrent . . . that hurtles a man's body down through rocky canyons, sweeps him along at flood tide . . ."

"And then?"

". . . I can talk no more. . . ."

The robe came undone, slipped off her shoulders. She raised her arms, released a few pins and the long braids of golden hair fell to her waist. There was no voluptuousness in her movement, but rather the quality he remembered of sweetness, as though love were her natural medium.

Later, they lay in each other's arms under a double cover lined with azure cloth and filled with fine wool.

"The torrent . . .?" she teased.

". . . and then, washes him out to sea."

"You have found love?"

"Not since you."

"There are available women in Rome."

"Seven thousand. My friend Balducci used to count them every Sunday."

"You did not want them?"

"It is not my kind of love."

"You never showed me my sonnets."

"One was about the silkworm:

> *Were it mine, that shaggy fleece that stays,*
> *Woven and wrought into a vestment fair,*
> *Around her beauteous bosom in such bliss!*

> *All through the day she'd clasp me! Would I were*
> *The shoes that bear her burden! When the ways*
> *Were wet with rain, her feet I then should kiss!*

She savoured the lines.

"How did you know I had a beauteous bosom? You had only seen me clothed."

"You forget my craft."

"And the second sonnet?"

He quoted a few lines from his first agony-wrought stanzas:

What joy hath yon glad wreath of flowers that is
Around her golden hair so deftly twined,
Each blossom pressing forward from behind,
As though to be the first her brows to kiss!

"I have heard that you are a marvellous sculptor; travellers have spoken of your Pietà and David. You are a poet, as well."

"My master, Messer Benivieni, would be pleased to hear you say so."

They ceased talking, were together again. Clarissa murmured in his ear, holding his face down hard against her shoulder and neck, running her hand over the well-developed shoulders, the hard muscled arms like those that he had gone to sketch among the Maiano quarrymen, "To love for love . . . How wonderful. I had affection for Marco. Bentivoglio wanted only to be entertained. To-morrow I will go to church to confess my sin, but I do not believe this love to be a sin."

"God invented love. This is beautiful."

"Could the devil be tempting us?"

"The devil is an invention of man."

"There is no evil?"

"Ugliness is evil."

5

He reached Julius' military encampment on the bank of the Reno River, through heavy snows. Julius was reviewing his troops, wrapped in an enormous furred and wadded overcoat up to his chin, on his head a grey woollen hood which covered his ears, forehead and mouth. Apparently Julius did not like the condition of the soldiers, for he was abusing his officers in coarse language, calling them "thieves and villains."

Aldovrandi had told him stories about the Pope: how he had won acclaim from his admirers as "well fitted for the military life" because he spent long hours with his troops in wretched weather, equalling them in enduring hardships, outswearing them, looking like an Old Testament prophet as he stormed up and down his lines, shouting orders, causing the troops to cry, "Holy Father, we look upon you as our commanding officer!" and his detractors to murmur behind their hands, "Holy Father, indeed! Nothing is left of the priest but the frock and the name."

Julius led the way to his tent, hung with warm furs. Courtiers and cardinals gathered about the throne.

"Buonarroti, I have been thinking what I would like you to sculpture for me. A tremendous bronze statue. A portrait in my ceremonial robes and triple crown . . ."

"Bronze!" It was an agonized cry, wrung from his vitals. Had he thought it even remotely possible that the Pope would condemn him to bronze, he would never have returned to Bologna. He protested:

"It is not my trade!"

The peculiarly hushed silence he had heard in the palace dining-hall the day before fell among the soldiers and prelates in the tent. The Pope's face flushed with anger.

"We are informed that you created a bronze David for the Maréchal de Gié of France. Is it your trade for him but not for your pontiff?"

"Holiness, I did that piece because I was urged to do it as a service to Florence."

"*Ecco!* You will do this statue as a service to your Pope."

"Holy Father, it is a bad sculpture! It is not completed. I know nothing of casting, finishing . . ."

"*Basta!*" The Pope's face was livid as he roared into a violent temper. "It is not enough that you defy me for seven months, refusing to return to my service! Even now you continue to pit your will against mine. You are incorrigible!"

"Not as a marble carver, Holy Father. Let me return to the blocks, and you will find me the most tractable worker in your service."

"I command you, Buonarroti, to stop issuing ultimatums. You will create a bronze statue of me for San Petronio which Bologna will worship when I return to Rome. Go now, and study the space above the main portal. We will build a niche for you, as large as the space between the portal and the window will allow. You will create as stupendous a bronze as the niche will hold."

Michelangelo knew he was going to have to do this miserable bronze in order to get back to his marbles. Yet perhaps it was no worse a penance than the seven months he had already thrown away in rebellion.

By midafternoon he was back at the Pope's camp.

"How large a statue can you fit there?" Julius demanded.

"For a seated figure, thirteen to fourteen feet."

"How much will it cost?"

"I think I can cast it for one thousand ducats, but it is not my profession, and I do not wish to take the responsibility."

"You shall cast it over and over until it succeeds, and I will give you enough money to make you happy."

"Holy Father, you can only make me happy by promising that if my bronze statue pleases you, you will permit me to resume carving the marble columns. If Your Holiness would make that promise, I would have twenty fingers with which to model the bronze."

"The pontiff does not make bargains!" cried Julius. "Bring me your drawings in one week from this hour. Dismissed!"

Humiliated, he made his way back to the Via di Mezzo di San Martino, climbed the stairs to Clarissa's apartment. Clarissa was dressed in a deep pink silk, with low neckline and bucket sleeves, a ████████████ her waist, her hair caught up in a ████████████ threads. She took one look at his pale, ████ face, kissed him on the sunken bridge of the nose. Feeling returned to his numbed mind and body.

"Have you eaten to-day?" she asked.

"Only crow."

"There is hot water on the fire. Would you like a bath to relax you?"

"Thank you."

"You can take it in the kitchen, while I find some food for you. I will wash your back."

"I've never had my back washed."

"Apparently there are a lot of things you have never had."

"And may never again."

"You are depressed. What is the bad news from the Pope?"

He told her that the Pope had demanded a bronze almost as large as Leonardo's enormous equestrian statue in Milan, which could not be cast.

"How long will it take you to make the drawings?"

"To please Julius? An hour . . ."

"Then you have a full week free."

She poured hot water into a long oval tub, handed him a scented cake of soap. He dropped his clothes on the kitchen floor, stepped gingerly into the hot water, then stretched his legs with a sigh of relief.

495

"Why don't you spend it here, the week," said Clarissa, "just the two of us? No one will know where you are, you will be undisturbed."

"A whole week to think only of love! Is that possible! Not one thought of clay or bronze?"

"I am not clay or bronze."

He reached wet soapy arms up to her. She leaned down.

"All these years I have said the female form was not beautiful to sculpture. I was wrong. You have the most beautiful body in the world."

"You once told me that I was flawlessly carved."

"In pink Crestola marble. I am a good sculptor, but I could never capture you."

"You have captured me."

She laughed, a soft musical tone that dissipated the last of the day's humiliation.

"Here, dry yourself before the fire."

He rubbed his sk̶i̶n̶ ̶▒▒▒▒▒▒▒▒▒ Clarissa wrapped him in a second c̶h̶▒▒▒▒▒▒▒▒▒▒▒ at a table before a steaming dish of thin sl̶i̶c̶e̶s̶ ▒▒▒▒▒ piselli.

"I must send word to Gianfrancesco Aldovrandi. He invited me to stay with him."

She stiffened for a moment, as though confronted with a past that was far gone from her mind.

"Non importa, cara. He knew I wanted you, ten years ago."

Her body relaxed, resumed its feline grace. She sat across the table from him, her face cupped in her hands, her eyes wide as she gazed at him. He ate ravenously. Content, he pushed his chair back from the table, turned towards the fire to let the flames lick his hands and face. Clarissa came to sit at his feet, her back against his shins. The feel of her flesh through her gown burned him more fiercely than the heat from the logs.

"No other woman has made me want her," he exclaimed. "How can it be explained?"

"Love is not to be explained." She turned, got on her knees, wrapped her long slender arms about his neck. "It is to be enjoyed."

"And to be marvelled at," he murmured. He burst into peals of laughter. "I'm sure the Pope didn't mean to do me a kindness, but he has . . . the first."

On the last afternoon of the week, filled with a delicious

lassitude, unable to feel any part of his body without a determined effort, oblivious to the cares of the world, he picked up drawing-paper, a piece of charcoal, was amused to find he barely had the will to move it across the paper. He remembered the lines from Dante:

Neither upon down
Nor under coverlets, men come to fame;
Without which, he who runs his course of life
Leaves of himself on earth the selfsame trace
That smoke leaves in the air, or foam on water.

With an effort he called to mind Julius sitting in the big throne room in the Appartamento Borgia in his long white robes. His fingers started to move. For several hours he drew Julius in a dozen tentative positions before catching a formal pose with the Pope's left leg extended, the right leg bent inward, resting on a raised base for support, one arm reaching out, perhaps in benediction, the other holding some solid material object. The robes would cover the Pope's feet, so Michelangelo would be casting almost thirteen feet of solid bronze draperies. Two sets of fingers would be exposed, and whatever could be seen of Julius' features under the triple crown.

"What about the Pope's face?" Clarissa asked. "The Holy Father is not going to be happy unless he recognizes himself."

"The only thing I hate worse than making robes is making portraits. As my friend Jacopo Galli used to say, 'After sweet meat comes sour sauce.'"

At the appointed hour he appeared before Julius, sketches in hand. The Pope was delighted.

"You see, Buonarroti, I was right: you can make bronze statues."

"Begging your pardon, Holy Father, this is not bronze, it is charcoal. But I will do my best so that I may return to the marbles in Rome. And now, if you will direct your treasurer to pay out some money to me, I shall buy supplies and begin work."

Julius turned to Messer Carlino, his papal treasurer, and said, "You are to give Buonarroti whatever he needs."

The treasurer, a sallow, thin-lipped man, gave him a hundred ducats from a chest. Michelangelo sent a messenger for Argiento, only a few miles away in Ferrara, and wrote to Manfidi, the new Herald of the Signoria, asking if the two bronze casters Lapo and Lotti, who were employed by the Duomo, could be sent to him in Bologna to help cast the Pope's statue. He offered a liberal wage.

He rented a former carriage house on the Via de' Toschi, Street of the Tuscans, with a high ceiling, stone walls and an uneven orange-coloured brick floor. There was a garden with a door at the back, and a walk-in fireplace for cooking. The walls had not felt a drop of paint in a hundred years, but unlike his rooms in Rome they were dry and unstained by watermarks. His next stop was at a used-furniture shop, where he found a Prato marriage bed, ten feet wide. On both sides and at the end was a low footboard which served as bench and chest. The bed came with a canopy, curtains and a striped mattress, old and lumpy, but clean. He also bought a kitchen table, some unpainted wood chairs.

Argiento arrived from Ferrara, explained that he had been unable to leave his brother's farm when Michelangelo called him to Rome in the spring, and set up his kitchen in the fireplace.

" I like to learn about bronze," he told Michelangelo while scrubbing down the walls and then the floor.

Lapo and Lotti arrived two days later, attracted by the offer of a higher wage than they were earning in Florence. Lapo, forty-one years old, considerably smaller than Michelangelo in stature, had such an honest face that Michelangelo put him in charge of all buying of supplies: wax, clay, cloth, brick for the casting ovens. Lotti, who had been trained as a goldsmith in the workshop of Antonio Pollaiuolo, was lean, purple-cheeked, a conscientious craftsman of forty-eight who served as master caster of the Florentine artillery.

The Prato marriage bed proved to be a godsend; after Lapo had bought supplies and Argiento had shopped for food and a few cooking utensils for his kitchen, the hundred ducats were exhausted. The four men slept together in the bed, which at ten feet was wide enough for them to be comfortable. Only Argiento was unhappy, protesting to Michelangelo:

" Everything costs too much! The shops are so crowded with courtiers and priests that a poor man like me isn't waited on."

" Patience, Argiento, I'm going to ask Messer Carlino for more money, then I'll buy you a haircut and a new shirt."

" Not worth it," replied Argiento, who looked like an unsheared sheep; " barbers are charging the double."

Messer Carlino listened to Michelangelo's request with darkly brooding eyes.

"Like most commoners, Buonarroti, you have a mistaken conception of the role of a papal treasurer. My job is not to give money, it is to be resourceful in ways of refusing it."

Michelangelo said doggedly, "I did not ask to make this statue. You heard me say that the bare cost would be a thousand ducats. The Holy Father said to pay me the costs. I cannot set up a bronze caster's workshop without funds."

"What did you do with the first hundred ducats?"

"None of your business. The Pope said he would give me enough money to keep me happy."

"There isn't enough money in the world for that," said Carlino coldly.

Michelangelo lost his temper, called the treasurer an incisive Tuscan name. Carlino winced, bit his underlip.

"Unless you hand over another hundred ducats," continued Michelangelo, "I shall go to the Pope and inform him that you are forcing me to abandon the statue."

"Bring me receipted bills for the first hundred, and written estimates of what you want to spend the second hundred for. I must keep the Pope's books accurately."

"You're like the gardener's dog, that neither eats cabbage himself nor lets anyone else."

A ghostlike smile was transferred quickly from the ledgers of the treasurer's eyes to the till of his lips. "It is my job to make people hate me. Then they return as seldom as possible."

"I'll be back."

Lapo quieted him. "I remember what I spent. I'll write up the bills."

Michelangelo walked through the Piazza Maggiore, then along the side of San Petronio to the open-sided gallery, flanked by the houses of bankers and the University of Bologna, crossed the Borgo Salamo and headed south-east to the Piazza of San Domenico. Inside the church, heavy with incense from a morning service, he went straight to the Dell'Arca marble sarcophagus, smiling to himself as he gazed at his own husky *contadino* boy with the wings of an eagle, ran his hands lovingly over the aged St. Petronius holding the model of Bologna in his hands, the face intelligent, saintly. He leaned down to sniff the clean white crystals of young St. Proculus, with his belted shirt, magnificently corded legs. Suddenly he straightened. The St. Proculus had been broken in two places, awkwardly repaired.

He felt someone staring at him, whirled, saw a man with an egg-shaped head, narrower at the top than at the base, a ragged shirt covering his chest, his bulging arms and shoulders orange-coloured with the dust of the Bolognese earth.

" Vincenzo!"

" Welcome back to Bologna."

" You wretch, you made good your promise to break one of the marbles."

" The day it fell I was in the country, making brick. I can prove it."

" You saw to that."

" It could happen again. There are wicked folk who say your statue of the Pope will be melted down the day his soldiers leave Emilia."

Michelangelo blanched. " If I report that to the Holy Father, he will have you drawn and quartered in the public square."

" Me? I am a most devout man! I plan to kneel and cross myself before it. It's other sculptors who make threats."

6

He started work at white heat, driven by a fury to get finished almost before he began. Lapo and Lotti knew what could be cast, advised him on the technical structure of his armature under the wax model, the composition of the enlarged clay. They worked together in the cold carriage room, which Argiento's fire heated only for a radius of a few feet. Come warm weather, he would return to the enclosed courtyard at the rear of San Petronio where he had carved his earlier marble figures. He would need this kind of outdoor space when Lapo and Lotti began building the giant baking oven for the fourteen-foot bronze.

Aldovrandi sent him models, spread the word that those men most closely resembling Pope Julius would be paid a special wage. Michelangelo sketched from light to dark, Argiento cooked and cleaned, Lotti built a small brick oven to test the local metals for fusing, Lapo did the buying, paid off the models.

Tuscans say that the appetite comes while eating; Michelangelo found that craftsmanship comes with working. Though he did not consider clay modelling authentic sculpturing, since it was the art of adding on, he was also learning that there was nothing in his nature which would permit him to do a sleazy job. Much as he detested bronze, he was going to have to make the best bronze statue of the Pope that he could conceivably dig out of himself, even if it took twice as long. The Pope had not done right by him, either in Rome or here in Bolognia, but that did not free him from doing right by himself. He would finish this giant bronze so that it brought honour on himself and the Buonarroti name; if it earned him neither the happiness the Pope had promised nor the creative ecstasy that came from carving marble, that was of secondary importance. He was a victim of his own integrity, which forced him to do his best, even when he would have preferred to do nothing at all.

His only joy was Clarissa. Though he often worked after dark, drawing and modelling by candlelight, he managed to steal off a couple of nights a week to spend with her. No matter what hour he arrived there was food by the side of the fire, ready to be heated, pots of hot water for the oval-shaped tub.

"You're not eating very much," she commented when she saw his ribs beginning to arc through the skin. "Is it because Argiento is a bad cook?"

"More because I have been turned away three times by the papal treasurer when I went for money. He says my costs are falsified, yet Lapo puts down every cent he spends . . ."

"Couldn't you come here each night for your supper? Then at least you would have one good meal a day."

She laughed as her words echoed in her ears.

"I have been talking like a wife. In Bologna we have a saying 'Wives and wind are necessary evils.' "

He put his arms about her, kissed her warm, stirring lips.

"But artists do not marry?" she added.

"An artist lives everywhere. This is the closest I will come."

She returned his kiss. "We will have no more serious talk. In my house I want you to have only happiness."

"You are better at keeping your promises than the Pope."

"I love you. That makes it easier."

"I hope that when he sees himself in fourteen feet of
501

bronze he will be so pleased he too will love me. Only in that way can I get back to my columns."

" Are they so exquisite?"

" ' How fair thou art, my true love, how fair! Eyes soft as doves' eyes, half-seen behind thy veil; the neck rising proudly, nobly adorned; graceful thy breasts as two fauns that feed among the lilies . . . Fair in every part, no fault in all thy fashioning.' So, too, my marble columns. . . ."

Mail from home came irregularly over the Futa Pass. Michelangelo looked forward to news of the family, but mostly he received requests for money. Lodovico had found a farm at Pozzolatico; it was good income property, but a deposit had to be paid right away. If Michelangelo could send five hundred florins, or even three hundred . . . From Buonarroto and Giovansimone, both working at the Strozzi wool shop near the Porta Rossa, there was rarely a letter without the lines, " You promised us a shop. We are tired of working for someone else. We want to make lots of money. . . ."

Muttering to himself, " Me too," Michelangelo wrapped himself in a blanket in the freezing carriage house while his three assistants slept in the Prato bed, and answered the family:

" As soon as I come to Florence, I will set you up in business by yourselves, or with a company, as you wish. I shall try to get money for your deposit on the farm. I think I shall be ready to cast my statue around the middle of Lent; so pray God that it turns out well; for if it does, I think I will be in luck with the Pope. . . ."

He spent hours following Julius about, sketching him in a variety of poses: saying mass, walking in procession, holding court, shouting in anger, laughing uproariously at a courtier's joke, fidgeting in his chair while he received deputations from all over Europe; until at length he knew through his drawing hand every muscle, bone and sinew of the Pope's body beneath his robes. Then he returned to the carriage house to model in wax or clay each characteristic turn and twist.

" Buonarroti, when do I see some work?" the pontiff demanded on Christmas Day, after saying mass in the cathedral. " I do not know how much longer I will keep the court here, I needs must return to Rome. Inform me when you are ready, and I will come to your workshop."

Spurred by this promise, Michelangelo, Lapo, Lotti and Argiento worked day and night, building the thirteen-foot-high armature of wood, then slowly adding on the clay, touch by touch, spatula by spatula, to create the model from which the bronze would be cast. He created the naked figure of the Pope, seated on his big throne, one arm raised, the left leg extended as he had envisaged him in his drawings. He derived keen pleasure from seeing the true figure of Julius emerge before him, vast in size, true in composition, line, mass, movement. He worked huge rolls of linen cloth over a duplicate model that Lotti and Argiento built for him, practising with mud from the yard as he had with Tiber mud in Rome, to see how best to model the Pope's regal robes without concealing the fiery figure beneath.

Caught up in the heat of his own creation, he worked absorbedly for twenty hours a day, then threw himself on the bed between Argiento and Lotti. In the third week of January he waited on the Pope.

"If Your Holiness would come to my workshop, the model is ready to be approved."

"Excellent! I shall come this afternoon."

"Thank you. And could you bring your treasurer? He seems to think I am building the statue out of Bolognese sausages."

Julius arrived at midafternoon, accompanied by Messer Carlino. Michelangelo had draped a quilt over his one comfortable chair. Here the Pope sat in silence, studying his portrait.

Julius was pleased. He rose, walked around the model several times, commenting on its accuracy and lifelike qualities. Then he stopped in front of the statue, looking perplexedly at his right hand, which was raised in a haughty, almost violent gesture.

"Buonarroti, does this hand intend to bless or curse?"

Michelangelo had to improvise, for this was the Pope's favourite gesture while sitting on his throne ruling the Christian world.

"The right hand lifted, Holy Father, bids the Bolognese be obedient though you are in Rome."

"And the left hand. What shall it hold?"

"A book?" asked Michelangelo.

"A book?" cried the Pope scornfully. "A sword! I am no scholar. A sword!"

Michelangelo winced.

" Could the Holy Father perhaps be holding in his left hand the keys to the new St. Peter's?"

" *Bravissimo!* We must extract large sums from every church for the building, and the symbol of keys will help us."

Glancing at Carlino, Michelangelo added, " I must buy seven to eight hundred pounds of wax to create the model for the oven. . . ."

The Pope authorized the expenditure and swept out to join his train waiting in the street. Michelangelo sent Lapo to shop for the wax. Lapo returned shortly.

" I cannot get it for less than nine florins and forty soldi a hundred. Better buy it at once, it is a good bargain."

" Go back and tell them that if they will knock off the forty soldi I'll take it."

" No, the Bolognese people would be the last in the world to take a lira off what they ask."

Michelangelo was disturbed by a strange note in Lapo's voice. " It can wait until to-morrow."

When Lapo was occupied Michelangelo said quietly to Argiento, " Go to the same shop and ask the price."

Argiento returned, whispered, " They are asking only eight and a half florins, and I can get off the brokerage charge."

" That's what I thought. Lapo's honest face has made a fool of me! Carlino was right. Here, take the money, get a receipt, and wait for their wagon to deliver."

It was dark by the time the donkey pulled up in front of the carriage house and the men brought in the wrapped bales of wax. When they had gone Michelangelo showed Lapo the bill.

" Lapo, you've been taking a profit from me. On everything you bought."

" Why shouldn't I?" the man demanded without change in expression. " When you pay so little."

" Little? I've given you twenty-seven florins in the last six weeks, far more than you earn at the Duomo."

" But we live so miserably! There isn't enough to eat!"

" You eat what we eat," growled Argiento, his heavy-knuckled fists clenched. " Food's expensive in the markets, the court and the visitors buy it up. If you had stolen less there would have been more for all of us."

" There's food in the restaurants. And wine in the wineshops. And women in the Street of the Bordellos. I would not live the way you live."

"Then return to Florence," said Michelangelo bitterly, "where you live better."

"You're firing me? You can't do that. I've told everybody that I am the artist on the job, and am in favour with the Pope."

"Then you go right back and tell them that you're a liar and a petty thief."

"I'll complain against you to the Signoria. I'll tell Florence what a miser you are. . . ."

"Kindly leave behind the seven florins I advanced you against future work."

"Never! It will be my travel money home."

He began packing his possessions. Lotti came to Michelangelo, said apologetically, "I'm afraid I must go with him."

"But why, Lotti? You have done nothing wrong. We have been friends."

"I admire you, Messer Buonarroti, and I hope I can work for you again sometime. But I came with Lapo, and I must go with him."

That night, alone in their empty, echoing carriage house, Michelangelo and Argiento were unable to eat the *stufato* that Argiento had thrown together. Michelangelo waited until Argiento was asleep in the enormous bed, then went to Aldovrandi's, wrote a full account to the Herald of the Signoria, and one as well to his father. He then walked the deserted streets to Clarissa's, found her asleep. Cold, nervous, shaking inwardly with frustration and rage, he got under the quilts, warmed his body by clasping her to him. But that was all. He was worried and upset, lay wide-eyed. Unhappiness is not the climate for love-making.

7

He lost not only Lapo and Lotti but Clarissa as well.

The Pope announced that he would return to Rome for Lent. This gave Michelangelo only a few weeks in which to perfect the wax model and get the Pope's approval. Without experienced helpers, without a bronze caster to be found in Emilia, it meant that he had to work through the days and weeks with no thought of food, sleep, relaxation.

On those rare hours when he could tear himself away he had no time to sit companionably with her, to talk to her, tell her what he was doing. He went only when he could no longer contain his own passion, when hunger for her drove him blindly through the streets, to seize her, possess her, and then to leave at once. This vestigial shred was all that the demands of his job left for love. Clarissa was sad, she gave less of herself each time he came, until she was giving nothing at all, in an act that bore no resemblance to the full sweetness of their early love.

Leaving the apartment one night, he studied his fingers, discoloured from the wax.

"Clarissa, I'm sorry for the way things are."

She raised, then lowered her hands hopelessly.

"Artists live everywhere . . . and nowhere. You are inside that bronze statue. Bentivoglio has sent a groom from Milan. With a carriage to take me there. . . ."

A few days later the Pope visited the workyard for the last time, approved the model, the hand holding the keys of St. Peter's, the face at once fierce and benign. Julius liked this image of himself, gave Michelangelo his benediction, as well as an order on Antonmaria da Lignano, a Bolognese banker, to continue paying his costs.

"Farewell, Buonarroti, I shall see you in Rome."

Hope flared in Michelangelo. "Then we will continue on the tomb . . . I mean the marbles?"

"Only God can predict the future," replied the pontiff loftily.

Desperately needing a bronze caster, he wrote to the Herald in Florence, asking him to send Master Bernardino, the best in Tuscany. The Herald wrote that Master Bernardino was not available. Michelangelo scoured the countryside until he found a French cannon maker who agreed to come, build the big oven and cast his statue. He returned to Bologna to wait. The Frenchman never arrived. He wrote again to the Herald in Florence. This time Master Bernardino agreed to come, but it would be weeks before he could finish his tasks in Florence.

Unseasonal heat struck early in March, killing the spring crops. Bologna the Fat became Bologna the Lean. The plague followed, invading forty families within a few days. Those who dropped in the streets were left exposed, no one daring to touch the bodies. Michelangelo and Argiento moved their workshop out of the carriage house and into the yard at the side of San Petronio, where there was an occasional breath of air.

Master Bernardino arrived in a blaze of May heat. He approved the wax model, built a tremendous brick oven in the centre of the courtyard. There folowed weeks of experimenting with the fires, testing the way the metals fused, making an enclosing envelope of ash, earth, horse manure and hair, applying them layer by layer, and enclosing the wax to the width of half a span. Michelangelo was filled with impatience to cast, and go home.

"We must not hurry," Bernardino warned him. "One untested step, and all our work will be for nothing."

He must not hurry; but it was already more than two years since he had entered the employ of Pope Juilius. He had lost his house, his years, and he had not been able to save a single scudo. As far as he could gather he was the only one who did not profit from his contact with a Pope. He read again the letter that had arrived from his father that morning, crying for money for another wonderful opportunity to invest. The details Lodovico dared not write, they had to be kept secret for fear someone might steal them; but he had to have two hundred florins immediately or he would lose the great bargain, and he would never forgive Michelangelo for his stinginess.

Feeling put upon by both his Holy Father and his earthly father, Michelangelo went to the bank of Antonmaria da Lignano. He set down the figures and details of his two barren years in Julius' service, his urgent need. The banker was sympathetic.

"The Pope has only authorized me to pay out money as you need supplies. But tranquillity is an important supply too, for an artist. Suppose we compromise: I'll advance you one hundred florins against future needs, and you can send the money home to-day."

Aldovrandi came frequently to watch the preparations. "This bronze of yours is going to make me a rich man," he commented, wiping his brow as the testing of the oven turned the workyard into an inferno.

"How so?"

"Bologna is betting that your statue is too large to cast. Giving good odds. I'm taking all bets."

"It will cast," replied Michelangelo grimly. "I have watched Master Bernardino step by step. He could make bronze without fire."

But when they finally poured in June, something went wrong. The statue came out well as far as the waist; the rest of the material, nearly half of the metal, remained in the furnace. It did not fuse. In order to take it out it was necessary to dismantle the furnace. Aghast, Michelangelo cried:

"What could have gone wrong?"

"I don't know. This has never happened to me before." Bernardino was as wretched as Michelangelo. "There must have been something wrong with the second half of the copper and brass. I'm so ashamed."

Hoarsely, Michelangelo replied, "You are a good artisan, and you put your heart into your work. But he who works, at times fails."

"I feel ill. I'll start again to-morrow morning."

Bolognia, like Florence and Rome, had its system of instantaneous communication. In a flash it was all over town that Michelangelo had failed to cast the pontiff's statue. Crowds started to pour into the courtyard to see for themselves Among them was Vincenzo, who slapped the still warm bricks of the furnace triumphantly and cried:

"Only a Bolognese knows how to use Bologna brick. Or make Bolognese statues. Back to Florence, puny one."

Michelangelo whirled around to pick up an iron bar. Aldovrandi arrived in time to intervene, curtly ordered Vincenzo from the yard, then cleared the others out.

"How serious is the failure, Michelangelo?"

"Only half. As soon as we can rebuild the furnace we'll be able to pour into the mould from the top again. If the metal fuses we'll be all right."

"You'll make it next time."

When Bernardino entered the courtyard in the morning his face was green.

"What a cruel city this is! They think they have gained a victory because of our failure."

"They don't like Florentines, and I guess they don't like the Pope either. If we fail we kill two birds with one bronze."

"I can't raise my eyes in the streets."

"Let us live here in the courtyard until we can pour again."

Bernardino worked heroically, night and day, rebuilt the

furnace, tested the channels to the mould, experimented with the metals that had not fused. Finally, under the blinding heat of the mid-July sun, he poured again. Slowly, as they nervously waited, the heated metal began to run from the furnace to the mould. With that, Bernardino said:

"There's nothing more you need me for. I leave for Florence at dawn."

"But don't you want to see how the statue comes out? Whether the two halves join well? Then you can laugh in the faces of the Bolognese."

Bernardino wearily pushed the thought aside. "I don't want revenge. Only escape. If you'll pay me what you owe me I'll be gone."

Michelangelo was left to discover the results himself. He had to sit on his hands for three weeks, while the country burned up in a drought and Argiento could find fewer fruits and vegetables in the market, until the mould cooled sufficiently for him to tear it down.

Bernardino had done his job. The two halves of the statue were joined without a serious mark. The bronze was red and rough, but there were no imperfections. "A few weeks of filing and polishing," Michelangelo thought, "and I, too, will be on my way."

He had misgauged the task. August, September, October went by, water became almost unavailable at any price, while he and Argiento went through the hateful manual labour, neither of them understanding the nature of bronze, their nostrils filled with the filings and scrapings, seemingly condemned to an eternity of cleaning up the tremendous statue.

Finally in November the bronze was finished, rubbed down to a shiny dark tone. It was a full year since he had come to Bologna. Michelangelo went to Antonmaria to ask him for a final inspection and dismissal. The banker was delighted with the result.

"You have surpassed the Holy Father's greatest hopes."

"I leave it in your care."

"You can't do that."

"Why not?"

"I have received an order from the Pope saying that you must install it properly on the façade of San Petronio."

"But my agreement says that I may leave it where I finish it."

"The Pope's latest order is the one to be obeyed."

"Does the Holy Father say that I am to be paid?"

"No. Only that you are to install."

No one quite knew why there were delays: the ledge was not yet finished; it had to be painted; the Christmas holidays were approaching; then the Epiphany. . . . Argiento decided to return to his brother's farm. As he bade Michelangelo good-bye there was a puzzled expression on his face.

"An artist is like a *contadino*; his chief harvest is trouble." He was not killing time, time was killing him. He rolled the full width of the Prato bed burning with marble fever, aching to have hammer and chisel in his hands, to be tearing through the white crystalline stone with the sweet acrid dust caking in his nostrils; his loins swollen and throbbing for Clarissa, longing to possess her; the two acts mystically cojoining in a continuous "Go."

At last a crew came, after the middle of February, to move the statue under its protective cloth to the front of San Petronio. Bells rang all over the city. The statue was hoisted into the niche, over the Della Quercia portal. The whole city assembled in the Piazza Maggiore, listening to the fifes, trumpets and drums. At the hour which the astrologers had told Julius was propitious, three in the afternoon, the covering was removed from the statue. The crowd cheered, then fell to its knees and crossed itself. That evening there were fireworks in the square.

Michelangelo, standing in his worn workman's shirt at the far end of the piazza, went unnoticed. Looking up at Julius in his niche, illuminated by shooting rockets, he felt nothing. Not even relief. He was dry, barren, used up, too exhausted from the long, senseless wait and waste to wonder if at long last he had bought his freedom.

He walked the streets of Bologna all night, hardly knowing where he was. There was a cold drizzle. He had exactly four and a half florins left. At dawn he knocked at Aldovrandi's door to bid his friend god-bye. Aldovrandi loaned him a horse, as he had eleven years before.

Only a little way into the foothills the rain began to fall in torrents. It rained all the way into Florence, the horse's hoofs slopping through the wet earth. The road seemed endless. His hands loosened on the reins, his head began to spin, exhaustion overtook him . . . until he lost consciousness, fell off the horse and struck his head on the roadbed.

8

"My dear Michelangelo," said Gonfaloniere Soderini, "it seems to me that you are more often covered with mud than with capon broth."

He sat back, let the brittle early March sunlight stream over his face. Michelangelo had learned in the several days since his return to Florence that Soderini had good reason to be satisfied with himself: through his brilliant roving ambassador, Nicolò Machiavelli, whom he had been training in the same manner that Lorenzo de' Medici had trained him, Florence had concluded a series of amiable treaties which should enable the city-state to live in peace and prosperity.

"All reports from Bologna and the Vatican tell us that Julius is delighted. . . ."

"Gonfaloniere, the five years I spent carving the David, the Bruges Madonna and the tondos were the happiest of my life. I hunger for only one thing: to carve marble."

Soderini leaned across the desk, his eyes sparkling.

"The Signoria knows how to express its gratitude. I am empowered to offer you a fine commission: a gigantic Hercules, to match your David. With one of your figures on either side of the main gate to the Palazzo della Signoria, ours will be the noblest entrance to a city-state government in the world."

Michelangelo drew in his breath. A giant Hercules! Representing all that was the strongest and finest of the classical culture of Greece. Il Magnifico had made Florence the Athens of the West; here was an opportunity to establish the connecting link between Pericles and Lorenzo, to follow through his early experiments with a Hercules. He shook with excitement.

"Can I have my house back? And my studio to carve the Hercules in?"

"It's rented now, but the lease expires soon. I will charge you eight florins a month rental. When you begin carving the Apostles the house will become yours again."

Michelangelo sat down, suddenly weak.

"This is where I will live and carve all the rest of my life. May God hear my words."

Soderini asked anxiously, "What about Rome, and the tomb marbles?"

"I've written to Sangallo. He has made it clear to the Pope that I will go back to Rome only to revise my agreement and bring the marble columns back to Florence. I will work them all together: Moses, Hercules, St. Matthew, the Captives . . ."

His voice was full of the joy he felt inside himself. Soderini gazed over his wife's red geraniums to the roofs of Florence.

"It is not part of my job to interfere in family life, but the time has come for you to secure your freedom from your father. I want him to go with you to a notary and sign a legal emancipation. Up to now the money you have earned has been legally his. After your emancipation it will belong to you, and you can control it. What you give to your father then will be a gift, not an obligation."

Michelangelo was silent. He knew all of his father's failings yet he loved him, shared Lodovico's pride in the family name, the desire to rebuild its place in Tuscan society. He shook his head, slowly.

"It would do no good, Gonfaloniere. I would have to turn over the money to him anyway, even if it were mine."

Soderini persisted. "I shall make an appointment with the notary. Now, about the marble for the Hercules . . ."

"Could I select at Carrara?"

"I will write to Cuccarello, the quarry owner, telling him that you are to have the biggest and purest block ever quarried in the Apuan Alps."

Lodovico was heartbroken at being obliged to appear before the notary, Ser Giovanni da Romena, for under Tuscan law an unmarried son became free only at the death of his father. There were tears in Lodovico's eyes as they walked home, past the ancient church of San Firenze, and up the Via del Proconsolo.

"Michelangelo, you won't abandon us now? You promised Buonarroto and Giovansimone that you would set them up in a shop. We need to buy several more farms, to build our income . . ."

Because of a few lines on paper Michelangelo's relationship with his father had been reversed. Now he was the one in authority; he could no longer be badgered or driven. Yet, glancing out of the corner of his eyes, he saw that sixty-four-year-old Lodovico had aged ten years in the ten-minute legal ceremony; his head was bowed, his shoulders hunched.

"I will always do everything in my power for the family, Father. What else have I? My work and my family."

He renewed his friendships at the Company of the Cauldron. Rosselli had died, Botticelli was too ill to attend, and so younger members had been elected, including Ridolfo Ghirlandaio, Sebastiano da Sangallo. Franciabigio, Jacopo Sansovino, Andrea del Sarto, a talented painter. He was delighted with Granacci, who had completed two works that had absorbed him for several years: a Madonna with Infant St. John, and St. John the Evangelist at Patmos.

"Granacci, you acknowledged scoundrel! These are glorious. The colour is beautiful, the figures fine. I always told you that you would become a great painter, if you worked at it."

Granacci flushed. "What do you say we have a party at the villa to-night? I'll invite the Company."

"How is Vermiglia?"

"Vermiglia? Married. To a clerk in Pistoria. She wanted to start a family. I gave her a dowry. I have a new girl: hair redder than Tedesco's, plump as a partridge . . ."

He learned that Contessina's lot was considerably better now; with the growing popularity and importance of Cardinal Giovanni in Rome, the Signoria had permitted the Ridolfi family to move up the hill to the main villa, far more commodious and comfortable. Cardinal Giovanni sent the supplies and money they needed. Contessina was permitted to come into Florence whenever she wished, but not Ridolfi. She would have been permitted to join her brother in Rome, but since Ridolfi was still an avowed enemy of the Republic the Signoria was not willing to let him out of its earshot.

She caught him flat-footedly gazing at his David.

"It is still good? You have not worn out your pleasure in it?"

He whirled at the sound of her voice, found himself gazing into the piercing brown eyes that had always been able to stab through his thoughts. She had high colour in her cheeks from the walk in the brisk March air; her figure had filled out; she was growing a little matronly.

"Contessina! How well you look. It is good to see you."

"How was Bologna?"

"Dante's Inferno."

"All of it?"

Though her question was innocently asked, he flushed to the curls brushed down over his square brow.

"What was her name?"

"Clarissa."

"Why did you leave her?"

"She left me."

"Why didn't you follow?"

"I had no carriage."

"Then you have known love, some portion of it?" she asked seriously.

"In full measure."

Tears flooded her eyes.

"Permit me to envy you," she whispered, and was gone, walking quickly out of the piazza before he could follow her.

Gonfaloniere Soderini advanced him two thousand florins against future work. He went to see young Lorenzo Strozzi, whom he had known since his family bought the Hercules. Lorenzo Strozzi had married Lucrezia Rucellai, daughter of *Il Magnifico's* sister Nannina, and of Michelangelo's cousin, Bernardo Rucellai. Michelangelo asked Strozzi if he could invest a modest sum in his brothers' names, so that they might begin to share in the profits of the shop.

"If the arrangement works well, Messer Strozzi, I could keep building the fund as I accumulate money, so that my brothers will earn more."

"That will be agreeable to my family, Buonarroti. And if at any time you wish your brothers to open an independent shop, we will provide them with the wool from our looms in Prato."

He walked to the Duomo workyard, was raucously welcomed by Beppe and his stonehewers. Only Lapo turned away.

"You want me to build another shop for you?" Beppe cackled toothlessly.

"Not yet, Beppe, not until I go to Carrara and find a block for the Hercules. But if you would help me move the St. Matthew so I won't be in your way . . ."

He had chosen St. Matthew because his was the first gospel in the New Testament, and because Matthew had not met a violent end. His early sketches of Matthew had envisaged him as a tranquil scholar, book in one hand, chin held reflectively in the other. Though he had broken into the front wall of the block, uncertainty had kept him from probing further. Now he understood why; he could find no historical Matthew. His was not the first gospel written, for he had absorbed much of Mark; he was said to have been close to

514

Jesus, yet he had not written his gospel until fifty to seventy years after Christ's death. . . .

He took his problem to Prior Bichiellini. The prior's deep blue eyes had grown larger behind his magnifying lenses as his face shrank with age.

"Everything about St. Matthew is disputed," he murmured in the quiet library. "Was he Levi, a tax collector in the service of Herod Antipas? Perhaps, perhaps not. The sole reference to him outside the New Testament is in Greek, and in error; it says that Matthew composed the Oracles in the Hebrew language. But they were written in Greek, for Greek-speaking Jews, to prove to them that Jesus was several times predicted in the Old Testament."

"What am I to do, Father?"

"You must create your own Matthew, even as you created your own David and Pietà. Walk away from the books; the wisdom lies in you. Whatever you carve about Matthew will be the truth."

Michelangelo smiled as he shook his head up and down. "Father, your words are kind; no one has ever had so much faith in me."

He started over again, searching for a Matthew who would symbolize man in his tortuous quest for God. Could he carve Matthew in an upward spiralling movement, trying to break his way out of the marble block, even as man had struggled to release himself from the stone mountain of polytheism in which he had lain enchained? He designed Matthew's left knee to push forcibly against the stone, as though striving to release the torso from its imprisoning cowl, arms held close, head twisted agonizingly away from the body, searching for a way of escape.

At last he was back in the column, feeling whole again, and a master, the fierceness of his joy sending the chisel through the block like lightning through cumulus clouds. He carved in a heat as great as that of the forge in which his tools were tempered; the marble and the flesh of Matthew became one, with Matthew projecting out of the block by the sheer force of his will, to achieve a soul with which to rise to God. Did not every man strive to emerge from the womb to achieve immortality?

Thirsting for a more lyrical mood, he returned to Taddei's Our Lady, carving the round frame, the serene, lovely face of Mary, the textured skin of the infant Jesus across his mother's lap. Then came word from Pope Julius that

Florence was to celebrate a Jubilee of Guilt and Punishment in order to raise funds with which to build the new St. Peter's.

" I have been put in charge of the decorations," announced Granacci gleefully.

" Granacci, you're not going back to theatre scenery again, after those fine paintings? It's a waste of your talent. I protest."

" My talent has plenty of time," said Granacci. " A man should have some fun."

A Jubilee to pay for Bramante's church would be no fun for Michelangelo. It was scheduled for April. He vowed to flee the city and spend the days with the Topolinos. Again the Pope interfered with his plans.

" We have just received a *breve* from Pope Julius," said Soderini. " You see, it was sealed with the Fisherman's ring. He asks you to come to Rome. He has good news for you."

" That can only mean he is going to let me carve again."

" You will go?"

" To-morrow. Sangallo wrote that my second shipload of marbles has been lying exposed in the Piazza San Pietro. I want to rescue them."

9

His eyes bulged when he saw the marbles dumped like a cord of firewood, discoloured by rain and dust. Giuliano da Sangallo gripped his arm.

" The Holy Father is waiting for you."

They passed through the smaller of the throne rooms of the Papal palace, filled with a variety of supplicants hoping for an audience. Once in the large throne room, he advanced towards the throne, bowing to Cardinal Giovanni de' Medici, nodding formally to Cardinal Riaro. Pope Julius caught sight of him, suspended a conversation with his nephew Francesco, Prefect of Rome, and Paris de Grassis. Julius was dressed in a white linen cassock, his pleated knee-length tunic had tight sleeves, while the elbow-length scarlet velvet cape was trimmed in ermine, as was the scarlet velvet skull-cap.

" Ah, Buonarroti, you have returned to us. You are pleased with the statue in Bologna, are you not?"

" It will bring honour on us."

" You see," cried Julius triumphantly, throwing out his
516

arms energetically to include the entire room. "You had no confidence in yourself. When I made this splendid opportunity available to you, you cried out, ' It is not my trade!' " The Pope's mimicking of Michelangelo's slightly hoarse voice brought appreciative laughter from the court. " Now you see how you have made it your trade, by creating a fine bronze."

" You are generous, Holy Father," murmured Michelangelo with a twinge of impatience, his mind occupied with the pile of stained marbles lying just a few hundred yards away.

" I intend to continue being generous," cried the Pope heartily. " I am going to favour you above all the painting masters of Italy."

" . . . ' painting ' masters?"

" Yes. I have decided that you are the best artist to complete the work begun by your countrymen Botticelli, Ghirlandaio, Rosselli, whom I myself hired to paint the frieze in the Sistine Chapel. I am commissioning you to complete my uncle Sixtus' chapel by painting the ceiling."

There was a light patter of applause. Michelangelo was stunned. Nausea gripped him. He had asked Sangallo to make it clear to the Pope that he would return to Rome only to begin carving on the sculptures for the tomb. He cried passionately:

" I am a sculptor, not a painter!"

Julius shook his head in despair.

" I had less trouble conquering Perugia and Bologna that I have in subduing you!"

" I am not a Papal State, Holy Father. Why should you waste your precious time subduing me?"

The room went silent. The Pope glared at him, thrust out his bearded chin, demanded icily, " Where did you have your religious training, that you dare to question your pontiff's judgment?"

" As your prelate said in Bologna, Holiness, I am but an ignorant artist, without good manners."

" Then you can carve your masterpiece in a cell of Sant'-Angelo."

All Julius had to do was wave a hand at a guard, and he could rot in a dungeon for years. He gritted his teeth.

" That would bring you little honour. Marble is my profession. Let me carve the Moses, Victors, Captives. Many would come to see the statues, offering thanks to Your Holiness for making them possible."

"In short," snapped Julius, " I need your sculpture to assure my place in history."

"They could help, Holy Father."

There was an audible gasp from those around the throne. The Pope turned to his cardinals and courtiers.

" Do you hear that, gentlemen? I, Julius II, who recovered the long-lost Papal States for the Church and brought stability to Italy, who have cleared out the scandals of the Borgias, published a constitution abolishing simony and elevated the decorum of the Sacred College, achieved a modern architecture for Rome . . . I need Michelangelo Buonarroti to establish my historical position."

Sangallo had gone deathly pale. Cardinal Giovanni stared out of a window as though he were not there. The Pope loosened the collar of his cape against his own warmth, took a deep breath and started again.

" Buonarroti, my informants in Florence describe your panel for the Signoria as ' the school of the world ' . . ."

" Holiness," interrupted Michelangelo, cursing himself for his envy of Leonardo that had led him into this trap, " it was an accident, something that could never be repeated. The Great Hall needed an accompanying fresco for the other half of the wall. . . . It was a diversion."

"*Bene.* Make such a diversion for the Sistine. Are we to understand that you will paint a wall for a Florentine hall, but not a ceiling for a papal chapel?"

The silence in the room was crushing. An armed courtier, standing by the Pope's side, said, " Your Holiness, give me the word and we will hang this presumptuous Florentine from the Torre di Nona."

The Pope glowered at Michelangelo, who stood before him defiant but speechless. Their eyes met, held in an exchange of immovability. Then a wisp of a smile drifted across the pontiff's face, was reflected in the tiny amber sparkle of Michelangelo's eyes, the barest twitching of his lips.

" This presumptuous Florentine, as you call him," said the Pope, " was described ten years ago by Jacopo Galli as the best sculpture master in Italy. So he is. If I had wanted him fed to the ravens I would have done so long ago."

He turned back to Michelangelo, said in the tone of an exasperated but fond father:

" Buonarroti, you will paint the Twelve Apostles on the ceiling of the Sistine, and decorate the vault with customary designs. For this we will pay you three thousand large gold ducats. We shall also be pleased to pay the expenses and wages of any five assistants you may choose. When the Sistine vault is completed, you have your pontiff's promise that you shall return to the carving of the marbles. My son, you are dismissed."

What further word could he say? He had been proclaimed supreme among his country's artists, made a promise that he would resume work on the tomb. Where could he flee? To Florence? To have Gonfaloniere Soderini cry out, "We cannot go to war with the Vatican because of you." To Spain, Portugal, Germany, England . . .? The Pope's power reached everywhere. The Pope demanded much, but a lesser pontiff might well have excommunicated him. And if he had refused to come back to Rome? He had tried that too, for a barren seven months in Florence. There was nothing to do but submit.

He kneeled, kissed the Pope's ring.

"It shall be as the Holy Father desires."

Later, he stood by the front entrance of the Sistine Chapel, his mind aswirl with revulsion and self-incrimination. Sangallo was just behind him, his face haggard, looking as though he had been whipped.

"I did this to you. I persuaded the Pope to build himself a triumphal tomb, and to call you here to sculpture it. All you have had is grief. . . ."

"You tried to help me."

"I could not have controlled the Pope. No. But I could have been more realistic about Bramante. Come to grips with his . . . charm . . . his talent . . . Because of him I am no longer an architect and you are no longer a sculptor."

Sangallo wept. Michelangelo shepherded him inside the protective doorway of the chapel, put an arm about the trembling shoulders.

"*Pazienza, caro,* patience. We will work our way out of this predicament."

"You are young, Michelangelo, you have time. I am old. Nor have you heard the crowning indignity. I volunteered to erect the scaffolding for you, since I renovated the chapel and know it well. But even this I was denied. Julius had already arranged with Bramante to build it. . . . All I want now is to return to my home in Florence, enjoy a little peace before I die."

"Do not speak of dying. Let us speak instead of how we

can tackle this architectural monstrosity." He threw both arms up in a despairing gesture that embraced the Sistine. " Explain this . . . edifice . . . to me. Why was it built this way?"

Sangallo explained that when it was first completed the building had looked more like a fortress than a chapel. Since Pope Sixtus had intended to use it for the defence of the Vatican in the event of war, the top had been crowned by an open battlement from which soldiers could fire cannons and drop stones on attackers. When the neighbouring Sant'Angelo had been strengthened as a fortress that could be reached by a high-walled passageway from the Papal palace, Julius had ordered Sangallo to extend the Sistine roof to cover the crenellated parapet. Quarters for the soldiers, above the vault that Michelangelo had been ordered to paint, were now unused.

Strong sunlight was streaming in from three tall windows, lighting the glorious frescoes of Botticelli and Rosselli opposite, shooting strong beams of light across the variegated marble floor. The side walls, one hundred and thirty-three feet long, were divided into three zones on their way up to the barrel vault, sixty-eight feet above: the lowest area was covered by tapestries, the frieze of frescoes filled the second and middle area. Above these frescoes was a cornice or horizontal moulding, projecting a couple of feet out from the wall. In the topmost third wall area were spaced the windows, on either side of them portraits of the Popes.

Taking a deep breath, he craned his neck and looked up the more than sixty feet into the air at the ceiling itself, painted a light blue and studded with golden stars, the enormous area he was to fill with decorations. Arising out of the third level of the wall and going up into the curved vault were pendentives, which in turn were based on pilasters, column-like piers buried in the third tier. These pendentives, five on each wall and one at either end, constituted the open areas on which he was to paint the Twelve Apostles. Above each window was a semicircular lunette, outlined in sepia ; the outer borders of the pendentives formed triangular spandrels, also coloured in sepia.

The motive for the commission now became crushingly clear to him. It was not to put magnificent paintings on the ceiling that would complement the earlier frescoes, but rather to mask the structural supports which made the harsh transition from the top third of the wall into the barrel vault. His Apostles were not to be created for themselves but rather to capture the gaze of people on the floor so that their attention would be diverted from the ungainly architectural divisions. As an artist he had become not merely a decorator but an obliterator of other men's clumsiness.

10

He returned to Sangallo's, spent the rest of the day writing letters: to Argiento, urging him to hurry to Rome; to Granacci, pleading with him to come to Rome and organize a *bottega* for him; to the Topolinos, asking if they knew of a stonehewer who might like to come and help him mass the marble columns. In the morning a groom arrived from the Pope, informing him that the house where his earlier marbles had lain these two years was still available to him. He went to the Guffatti stoneyard, hired the family to haul the marbles from the Piazza San Pietro to the house. Several of the smaller blocks had been stolen.

He could not find Cosimo, the carpenter; the neighbours thought he had died in Santo Spirito hospital; but that afternoon freckle-faced Piero Rosselli lurched in, laden with bundles, to cook his Livorno fish stew. While the *cacciucco* simmered in its orégano, Michelangelo and Rosselli examined the house, which had been unoccupied since Michelangelo abandoned it in haste two years before. The kitchen was of unpainted brick, small, but comfortable enough for cooking and eating. What had formerly been the family room could be converted into a tolerable workshop. The covered porch would hold all the marbles if they were carefully stacked; and the two unpainted brick bedrooms would sleep the *bottega*.

In May he signed his contract for the Sistine Chapel, was given five hundred large gold ducats from the papal purse. He paid his long-overdue debt to Balducci, returned to the furniture dealer in Trastevere to buy pieces that looked startlingly like the ones Balducci had sold back to the dealer eight years before. He hired a young Roman boy to take care of the house. The lad cheated on the market bills, so he let him go. The second boy stole several ducats out of Michelangelo's purse before he was caught.

521

Granacci arrived at the end of the week. He had stopped by a barber to have his blond hair cut. He had already found the elegant men's shops on the Piazza Navona and brought to Michelangelo's house a new outfit of black trunk hose, a shirt, gold-embroidered hip-length cloak and a small ribbed cap, worn on the side of the head.

"I never was so glad to see anybody in my life!" cried Michelangelo. "You must help me draw up a list of assistants."

"Not so fast," said Granacci, his light blue eyes dancing; "this is my first trip to Rome. I want to see the sights."

"To-morrow I'll take you to the colosseum, baths of Caracalla, the Capitoline hill . . ."

"All in good time. But to-night I want to visit the fashionable taverns I've heard about."

"What would I know of such things? I'm a working man. But if you're serious, I'll ask Balducci."

"I'm always serious about my pleasures."

Michelangelo drew two chairs up to the kitchen table.

"I'd like to assemble the painters we worked with at Ghirlandaio's: Bugiardini, Tedesco, Cieco, Baldinelli, Jacopo."

"Bugiardini will come. Tedesco, too, though I don't think he knows much more about painting now than he did at Ghirlandaio's. Jacopo will go anywhere on somebody else's money. But Cieco and Baldinelli, I don't know whether they're still in the art."

"Who can we get?"

"Sebastiano da Sangallo, first of all. He considers himself a follower of yours copies before your Bathers every day, gives lectures on it to new painters. I'll have to search for a fifth. It's not easy to get five painters all free at the same time."

"Let me give you a list of colours to send for. These Roman colours are no good at all."

Granacci glanced shrewdly at his friend. "It appears to me that you don't find anything good in Rome."

"Does any Florentine?"

"I'm going to. I've heard about the sophisticated and beautiful courtesans who have the charming villas. As long as I must stay here to help you get that vault plastered, I'm going to find an exciting mistress."

A letter brought him news that his uncle Francesco had died. Aunt Cassandra, after living with the family for forty years, had moved back to her parental home, starting suit against the Buonarroti to oblige them to return her dowry and to pay Francesco's debts. Though there had never been any real friendship between Michelangelo and his uncle, he had a strong blood-loyalty. He was grieved to see the next to last of the elder Buonarroti go. He was also worried. His father obviously intended him to fight Cassandra's lawsuit, hire a notary, see it through the courts. . . .

The next day he summoned up the courage to return to the Sistine. He found Bramante there, directing carpetners who were hanging a scaffolding from the ceiling by means of forty pipe-poles that had been driven through the cement vault and lashed together with ropes interlocked through the soldiers' quarters above.

" There's a scaffolding that will hold you securely for the rest of your life."

" You'd like to think so, Bramante, but actually it will only be a matter of months." Bramante stuck in his throat like a half-swallowed fly. The Pope by himself would hardly have thought of inflicting this ceiling on him. He inspected the scaffolding, knit his brows. " Just what do you intend to do with the holes in the ceiling after the poles come out?"

" Fill them."

" How do we get up to the holes to fill them after the scaffolding is down? Ride on an eagle's back?"

" . . . I hadn't thought of that."

" Nor of what we are to do with forty ugly cement fills in the middle of my painting after I have finished the job? Let's discuss it with the pontiff."

The Pope was dictating *breves* simultaneously to several secretaries. Michelangelo laid out the situation in a few clear words.

" I understand," said Julius. He turned a puzzled expression to Bramante. " What *did* you intend to do with those holes in the ceiling, Bramante?"

" Just leave them, the way we leave holes in the sides of buildings when we pull out the poles that hold up the scaffolding. It can't be helped."

" Is that true, Buonarroti?"

" Assuredly not, Holy Father. I will design a scaffold which will never touch the ceiling. Then the painting will remain perfect."

"I believe you. Take down Bramante's scaffold and build your own. Chamberlain, you will pay the expenses for Buonarroti's new scaffold."

As Michelangelo turned away he saw Bramante biting the corner of his lip.

He ordered the carpenters to take down the scaffold. When all of the timber and rope had been lowered to the floor of the chapel, Mottino, the hunchbacked foreman of the carpenters, said:

"You will be using these materials for your own scaffolding?"

"Not the rope. You may have it."

"But it is valuable. You could sell it for a considerable sum."

"It is yours."

Mottino was ecstatic. "This means I will have a dowry for my daughter. Now she can be married! They say in Rome that you are a difficult man, Messer Buonarroti. Now I see it is a lie. May God bless you."

"That's precisely what I need, Mottino. God's blessing. Come back to-morrow."

That night he tackled the problem inside his own head, which he found to be his best workshop. Since he had never seen such a scaffolding as he had promised the Pope, he would have to invent one. The chapel itself was divided into two parts, separated by Mino da Fiesole's carved screen: the half for laymen, which he was going to paint first, the larger division, or presbyterium, for cardinals. Then came the altar and the Pope's throne. On the rear wall was the fresco of the Assumption of the Virgin by his erstwhile enemy Perugino. The walls were thick and strong; they could stand any amount of pressure. If he built with planks that were solidly wedged against them, then the more weight put on his scaffold the more pressure it would apply and the more secure his framework would be. The problem was how to anchor the ends of his planks, since he could not cut niches into the walls. Then he remembered the projecting cornice; this ledge would not be strong enough to carry the weight of the scaffolding and men, but it could give his planks anchorage.

"It might work," said Piero Rosselli, who frequently had to build his own scaffolding. He directed Mottino in the bolting of the planks and construction of the bridge. Michelangelo and Rosselli tested it, summoned the carpenter crew, one by one. The more weight on the trestle, the stronger it became. They were jubilant. It was a tiny victory, really; yet it provided the impetus to begin the detested chore.

Argiento wrote that he could not leave his brother's farm until the crops had been harvested. Neither could Granacci assemble a crew of assistants by mail.

"I'll have to go to Florence and help them finish their commissions. It may take a couple of months, but I promise to bring back everyone you wanted."

"I'll do the drawings. When you get back we'll be ready to start the cartoons."

Summer clamped down. Miasmic vapours moved in from the marshes. No one could breathe. Half the city became ill with clogged heads and pain in the chest. Rosselli, his only companion during these stifling days, fled to the mountains. Michelangelo climbed the ladder to his trestle at dawn, savagely tormented for want of hammer and chisel in his hands. Instead he spent the airless days drawing scale models of the twelve pendentives where the Apostles would be painted, cutting out paper silhouettes of the lunettes and spandrels, which he would also have to fill with what the Pope had called customary decoration. By mid-morning the vault was like a furnace, and he was gasping for breath. He slept as though drugged through the heat of the afternoon, then worked at night in the back garden, evolving designs for the nearly six thousand square feet of sky and stars that had to be replastered and made pretty.

The hot days and weeks passed in lonely suffocation, broken only by the arrival of a former Settignano stonecutter whom his father had found in Florence, Michi by name, who had always wanted to visit Rome. Michi was about fifty, gnarled and pockmarked, sparely spoken, with the chipped, staccato accent of the stonehewer. Michi knew how to cook a few Settignano dishes; before his arrival Michelangelo had gone for days on bread and a thin wine.

In September Granacci returned with a full *bottega* in tow. Michelangelo was amused by how much the former apprentices had aged: Jacopo was still slim, wiry, with darting black eyes to match the remnants of oily dark hair, and deeply etched laugh wrinkles; Tedesco, sporting a bushy beard several degrees more carroty than his hair, had become thickset, with a ponderous manner that made him the natural butt for Jacopo's jokes. Bugiardini, still moonfaced and round-eyed, showed a centre patch of baldness that resembled a tonsure. Sebastiano da Sangallo, newcomer of the group, had developed a serious mien since Michelangelo had last seen him, which earned him the nickname of Aristotle. He wore luxuriant oriental moustaches which he grew in honour of his uncle Giuliano. Donnino, the only stranger to Michelangelo, had been brought by Granacci because " he's a good draughtsman, the best of the lot." He was forty-two, looked like a hawk with a high-bridged thin nose in a long face with negligible slits for eyes and mouth.

That evening, after Granacci had made sure that his mistress, whom he had supported over the summer, was still waiting for him, the new *bottega* held a party. Granacci ordered in flagons of white Frascati wine and a dozen trays of food from the Trattoria Toscana. After three long pulls on the Frascati flagon, Jacopo told the story of the young man who went each evening to the Baptistry in Florence and prayed aloud for St. John to tell him about his wife's behaviour and his son's future.

" I hid behind the altar and called out, ' You're wife's a bawd, and your son will be hanged!' Do you know what he replied? ' You naughty St. John, you always did tell lies. That's why they cut your head off!' "

When the laughter subsided, Bugiardini insisted on drawing Michelangelo's face. When he had finished, Michelangelo exclaimed, " Bugiardini, you still have one of my eyes in my temple!" Next they played the drawing game on Donnino, letting him win so that he would have to buy the next day's dinner.

Michelangelo bought a second large bed in Trastevere. He, Bugiardini and Sangallo slept in the room off the workshop, while Jacopo, Tedesco and Donnino slept in the room down the hall. Bugiardini and Sangallo went out to buy sawhorses and planks, set up a work-table in the centre of the room long enough for all six of them. At ten o'clock Granacci arrived. Jacopo cried, " Careful, everybody, don't let Granacci pick up anything heavier than charcoal, or he'll collapse in a heap."

Officially baptized by this buffoonery, the studio set to work in earnest. Michelangelo laid out on the table before them the scale drawings of the ceiling. The large pendentives at either end of the chapel he reserved for St. Peter and St. Paul ; in the five smaller pendentives on one side would be Matthew, John and Andrew, Bartholomew and James the Great, on the opposite wall James the Less, Judas called Thaddaeus, Philip, Simon and Thomas. He sketched one complete Apostle, sitting on a high-backed throne, pilasters on either side; above were winged caryatids on C-shaped volutes, with medallions in square fields and scroll-like ornaments.

By the first week in October the house had fallen into chaos, for no one thought to make a bed, wash a dish or sweep a floor. Argiento came in from Ferrara, was so delighted to find that he was to have six companions in the house that he washed and scrubbed and polished for days, in addition to cooking the meals, before he got around to being unhappy about Michelangelo's commission.

" I want to work stone. Be a *scultore.*"

" So do I, Argiento. And so we shall, if only you'll be patient and help me get that ceiling splashed with paint."

To each of his six assistants he assigned a division of the vault for decoration: rosettes, *cassettoni,* circles and rectangles, trees and flowers with spreading foliage, wavelike movements of undulating lines, spirals. Michi, he discovered, was adept at grinding colours. He himself would do the final cartoons for most of the Apostles, but Granacci could paint a couple of them, and perhaps Donnino and Sangallo could each do one. He had already spent five months getting to this day, but now that he had them altogether and started, he felt certain he could cover the whole ceiling in seven months. That would be another year out of his life. A total of four since he had first come to Rome to confer with Pope Julius. He would finish by May, and then either go to work on the marble figures for the tomb or return to the Hercules block which Gonfaloniere Soderini had brought to Florence for him.

It did not quite work that way. Donnino, though he was as fine a draughtsman as Granacci said, lacked the courage to venture past his sketches into the coloured cartoons. Jacopo kept them entertained but did no more work at thirty-five than he had at fifteen. Tedesco painted poorly. Sangallo dared anything Michelangelo put him on, but he was still inexperienced. Bugiardini was solidly reliable, but just as at Ghirlandaio's he could paint only flat walls and windows, thrones and pilasters. Granacci's cartoon for his Apostle came out well, but Granacci was having a good time in Rome. Since he had refused to take a salary, how could

Michelangelo oblige him to put in more work hours? Michelangelo worked twice as hard as he had thought he would have to, and made slow progress through the weeks of November.

At last the time arrived, during the first week of December, when they were ready to fresco a major zone of the ceiling. One of the Apostles was his, the St. John on the side ; opposite, Granacci was to paint St. Thomas. The others on the scaffold, led by Bugiardini, were to paint the decorations on the barrel vault between the two Apostles. Piero Rosselli had laid a heavy coat of intonaco on the area the day before, hatching a rough surface on which, this morning, he would plaster the precise area to be painted by dark.

At dawn they set out for the Sistine, Michi driving the donkey, the cart loaded with pails, brushes, tubes of paint, cartoons, bundles of sketches, pointing sticks, pots and bottles for colour, with Rosselli sitting in the midst of sand and lime. Michelangelo and Granacci walked ahead, Bugiardini and Sangallo just behind them, Tedesco, Jacopo and Donnino bringing up the rear. Michelangelo felt hollow at the pit of his stomach, but Granacci was in a gay mood.

"How do you feel, Master Buonarroti? Did you ever imagne you would be walking at the head of your own *bottega* to begin a fresco commission?"

"Not in my wildest nightmares."

"Good thing we were all so patient with you. Remember how the Ghirlandaios taught you to use the instruments for squaring up? How Mainardi showed you to tint flesh in tempera, and David showed you how to make brushes from white pigs . . .?"

"And Cieco and Baldinelli called me a fraud because I wouldn't paint wings on an angel? Oh, Granacci, what have I got myself into? I'm no fresco painter!"

11

The group worked well together, Michi mixing the plaster on the scaffold after hauling the sacks up the ladder, Rosselli expertly laying the daily area to be painted, remaining to watch its drying rate and to keep it sprinkled. Even Jacopo worked hard to copy the cartoon colours into the designs that Bugiardini had outlined with an ivory stick.

After the paint had had time to oxidize and dry, Michelangelo returned alone to study the result. With a seventh of the vault completed, he was able to see what the entire ceiling would be like when they had frescoed the rest. The Pope's objective would be accomplished; no one would be disturbed any more by the projecting spandrels, loomingly empty lunettes or the broken-up vault with its monotonous circles of gold stars. The Apostles on their thrones, the thousands of square feet of brightly coloured designs would conceal and divert.

But what about the quality of the work? It was in the marrow of his bones to create only the finest he could produce; to create far beyond his abilities because he could be content with nothing that was not new, fresh, different, a palpable extension of the whole of the art. He had never compromised with quality; his integrity as a man and an artist was the rock on which his life was built. If he split that rock by indifference, by giving less than the exhausting best of himself, if he were content merely to get by, what was left of him?

He could have done the bronze statue of Pope Julius twice as fast had he been satisfied with a merely adequate statue; no one would have criticized him, since bronze was not his trade, and the commission had been forced upon him. But he had spent energy-draining months determined that his work must bring honour upon himself and his family and all artists. Had he been willing or able to do an immediately conceivable bronze of Julius it would perhaps be easier now to do this conceivable ceiling fresco. He and his group could apply the remaining paint without much trouble. But he could not deny that the quality was mediocre. He told Giuliano da Sangallo so.

" You have done your best under the circumstances," replied his friend.

Michelangelo paced the Sangallo drawing-room, hugging his arms about him, perturbed. " I'm a long way from convinced of that."

" No one will blame you. The Pope gave you a job, and you did as you were told. Who could do otherwise?"

" Me. If I walk away from this ceiling as it is, I'll despise myself."

" Why must you take things so hard?"

" If there is one thing I know for sure it's that, when I hold a hammer and chisel in my hands and start ' Go,' I need my full assurance that I can do no wrong. I need my complete self-respect. Once let me know that I can be content with inferior work . . ." There was agony in his voice, a pleading with Sangallo to affirm this concept. " . . . and as an artist, I'm through."

He kept the *bottega* busy designing the cartoons for the next area of the ceiling. He said nothing of his dilemma. Yet a crisis was impending; he could not take the studio up to the top of the scaffold and cover another area with paint which he knew would not remain. They were only ten days away from blowing up the next cartoons to full size. He would have to reach a decision.

He was temporarily spared by the advent of Christmas. The Rome celebrations, starting considerably in advance, gave him a reason to suspend work without revealing the turmoil going on within him. The studio was overjoyed at the vacation.

He received a note from Cardinal Giovanni. Would Michelangelo join them for dinner on Christmas Day? This was the first word he had heard from Giovanni since his monumental battle with the Pope. He bought himself a handsome brown woollen shirt, the first in several years, a pair of matching hose and a cloak of beige camlet that lightened the colour of his amber eyes. He went to mass at San Lorenzo in Damaso, where his Christmas spirit was shattered at seeing the church so forlorn now that it was stripped of its glorious stone columns.

A groom with Florentine lilies embroidered on his livery admitted him to Cardinal Giovanni's palace on the Via Ripetta. As he passed through the spacious entrance hall with its majestic stairway, and then a drawing-room and music-room, he was able to perceive how greatly Cardinal Giovanni had profited from his benefices. There were new paintings on the walls, ancient sculptures from Asia Minor on pedestals, cabinets of antique coins, carved gems. He moved slowly, studying the recent acquisitions, marvelling that of his father's formidable genius Giovanni should have inherited only this one facet: flawless good taste in the arts.

He came up sharp at the entrance to the smaller of the drawing-rooms. There, sitting before a log fire, her hands exended to the flames, and high colour in her alabaster cheeks, sat Contessina. She looked up.

" Michelangelo."

" Contessina."

" *Come va?* "

" *Non c'è male.* "

" As the Settignano stonecutter says."

" I don't have to ask how you are. You look beautiful."

The colour mounted higher in her cheeks.

" You've never said that before."

" But I've always thought it."

She rose, came close to him. Her scent was the one she had used as a child in the Medici palace. Nostalgia for those happy years swept over him.

" You are a deep part of me. From the days when my life began. In the sculpture garden."

Her eyes filled with pain and joy in equal measure.

" As you have always been a part of me."

He became aware of the others around them, changed his tone.

" Luigi and Niccolò, they are well?"

" They are here with me."

" And Ridolfi?"

" No."

" Then you are not staying?"

" Giovanni has taken me to see the Pope. The Holy Father has promised to intercede with the Signoria for us. But I cannot hope. My husband is committed to the downfall of the Republic. He never loses an opportunity to make his views known . . ."

" I know."

They smiled at each other, wistfully.

" That is not discreet of him, but it is his resolve." She stopped abruptly, studied his face. " I have talked about myself. Now I want to speak of you."

He shrugged his shoulders. " I fight, but always I lose."

" The work does not go well?"

" Not yet."

" It will."

" Are you sure?"

" I'll put my hand in fire."

She held her hand out towards him as though it were already in the searing heat of the flames. He longed to take it in his own, if only for a moment. Then she threw back her head in laughter at the drastic Tuscan phrase of affirmation. Now their laughter joined together, seized

531

each other and held close, harmoniously, intertwined through each other's fabric and substance. This too, he knew, was a kind of possessing; rare, beautiful and sacred.

The *campagna romana* was not Tuscany; it did not fill him with an all-absolving lyrical grace. But it had power, and history: the flat, fertile plains rolling for miles, traversed by the remains of Roman aqueducts that had brought clean water down from the hills; Hadrian's villa, where the Emperor had re-created the glory of Greece and Asia Minor, and where Michelangelo watched the excavators unearth marbles that went back to the generations of Pericles; Tivoli, with its majestic waterfalls, favourite holiday village for the Romans of the Empire; the Castelli Romani, a series of towns located on the lava and tufa slopes of the volcanic Alban Hills, each village on its separate peak in a series of peaks surrounding an enormous crater, with other ranges, covered by dark green forests, rolling back sculpturally as did the mountains beyond Settignano: Frascati, Tusculum, higher into the hills, where he wandered among the ruins of Cicero's villa, the amphitheatre, forum, buried temple; the hills dotted with tiny stone villages whose origins were lost in obscure ages of history: before the Romans, before the Etruscans; the Temple of Fortune at Praeneste, whose walls included an entire village, with a Cave of Destiny and crypts that dated from who knew what distant age of man?

He walked deeper and deeper into the past, circling the enormous rim of the volcano, coming across carved building stones that had been spilled over the ground like milk, beneath which lay ancient settlements. Each night he stopped at a tiny inn or knocked on the door of a *contadino* family to buy his supper and space on a bed to rest, gripping the magnificent mountains between his legs, the irresilient tufa beneath his feet, filled with the delicious pulsating fatigue that beat up from his soles and ankles and calves and knees and thighs into his groin.

The deeper he penetrated into the aeon-old past of the volcanic hills and civilizations, the clearer his own problem became for him. His helpers would have to go. Many marble masters had permitted their apprentices and assistants to hew the marble block to within a safe margin of the central figure, but he had to hammer off the corners, mass the edges, work the four flat sides, remove every last crystal himself. He did not have the nature of a Ghirlandaio, able to do the main figures and focal scenes, allow the *bottega* to do the rest. He had to work alone.

He paid no attention to passing time; the days seemed so infinitesimal among the lost ages of the lava rock. In lieu of time he was conscious of space, trying to fit himself into the core of the Sistine vault as he had into the centre of the Duccio block, so that he would know its weight and mass, grasp what it might hold and what might break off in imbalance. He had cleared the fields, ploughed, seeded, stood with his head in the sun and the rain. Nothing showed; the thin, bright green miracle announcing the beginning of new life remained below the surface of his mind.

On New Year's morning, with his county hosts celebrating the first day of the Year of Our Lord 1509, he left their stone hut in the mountains, mounted higher and higher along the sheep trail until he came to the summit. The air was sharp, clear and cold. As he stood on the peak, muffler wound around his mouth to keep his teeth from freezing, the sun came up behind him, over the most distant range to which his eye could travel. As the sun rose in the sky the *campagna* plains came to life in pale pinks and tawny browns. In the distance stood Rome, sparklingly clear. Beyond and to the south lay the Tyrrhenian Sea, pastel green under a brittle blue winter sky. The whole landscape was flooded with luminosity: forests, the descending ranges beneath him, the hills, towns, the fertile plains, the somnolent farms, the stone-pile villages, the mountain and sea roads leading to Rome, a ship on the ocean. . . .

Reverentially he thought, "What a magnificent artist was God when He created the universe: sculptor, architect, painter: He who originally conceived space, filled it with His wonders." He remembered the lines from the beginning of Genesis:

God, at the beginning of time, created heaven and earth. Earth was still an empty waste, and darkness hung over the deep. . . . Then God said, Let there be light. . . . God said too, Let a solid vault arise amid the waters . . . a vault by which God would separate the waters which were beneath it from the waters above it. . . . This vault God called the Sky. . .

. . . vault . . . God too had been faced with the need to create within a vault! And what had He created? Not merely the sun and moon and heavens of the sky, but a whole teeming world below it. Sentences, phrases, images flooded his mind from the Book of Genesis:

. . . God said, Let the water below the vault collect in one place to make dry land appear . . . the dry land God called Earth, and the water, where it had collected, He called the Sea. . . . Let the earth, He said, yield grasses that grow and seed. . . .

. . . God said, Let the waters produce moving things . . . and winged things that fly above the earth under the sky's vault.

. . . And God said, Let us make man, wearing our own image and likeness; let us put him in command of the fishes in the sea, and all that flies through the air, and the cattle and the whole earth, and all the creeping things that move on earth. So God made man in His own image, made him in the image of God. Man and woman both, He created them. . . .

And Michelangelo knew, just as clearly as he had known anything in his life, that nothing would suffice for his vault but Genesis itself, a re-creation of the universe. What nobler work of art could there be than God's creating of the sun and moon, the water and the earth, the evolving of man, of woman? He would create the world on that Sistine ceiling as though it were being created for the first time. There was a theme to conquer that vault! The only one that could so overwhelm it that all of its ugliness and clumsy architecture would vanish as though it never existed, and in its place would come the glory of God's architecture.

12

He asked Chamberlain Accursio if he might see the Pope alone for a few moments. The chamberlain arranged the meeting for late in the afternoon. Julius was sitting quietly in the small throne room with just one secretary remaining, dictating a letter to Venice, the Vatican's strongest opponent in Italy. Michelangelo kneeled.

"Holy Father, I have come to speak to you about the Sistine vault."

"Yes, my son?"

"I had no sooner painted one section than I realized it would turn out meanly."

" Why so?"

" Because the placing of the Apostles alone will have but a poor effect. They occupy too small an area of the total ceiling and become lost."

" But there are other decorations."

" I have begun these decorations, as you instructed me. They make the Apostles seem poorer than ever."

" This is your last judgment, that at the end we will emerge with a poor effect?"

" I have given the matter a great deal of thought, and that is my honest opinion. No matter how well the ceiling may be painted under the original plan, it can bring little honour to either of us."

" When you speak quietly this way, Buonarroti, I hear truth in you. I can also tell that you have not come to ask permission to abandon the work."

" No, Holy Father. I have a composition that will cover the entire vault with glory."

" I have confidence in you, and so I shall not ask the nature of your design. But I shall come often to the chapel to watch your progress. You are involving yourself in three times as much work?"

" . . . or five or six."

The Pope stirred on his throne, rose, paced up and down the room, then came to a halt before Michelangelo.

" You are a strange one, Buonarroti. You screamed that fresco was not your profession, and almost knocked me down in your rage. Yet now, eight months later, you come back with a plan that will entail infinitely more time and labour. How is one to understand you?"

" I don't know," replied Michelangelo ruefully. " I hardly understand myself. I only know that since I must paint that vault I cannot bring you something mediocre, even if it is all you have asked for."

Julius shook his white-haired, white-bearded head in amused puzzlement. Then he put his hand on Michelangelo's head, blessed him.

" Paint your ceiling as you will. We cannot pay you five or six times the original three thousand ducats, but we will double it to six thousand."

His next task was more delicate and more difficult. He had to tell Granacci that the *bottega* was finished, that the assistants would have to go home. He took him step by step along the tortuous trail.

535

" I will keep Michi to grind the colours, and Rosselli will lay the wet plaster. The rest I simply must do myself."

Granacci was staggered. " I never really thought that you could manage a studio as Ghirlandaio did. But you wanted to try, and so I helped you. . . . But working alone on top of that scaffolding to re-create the story of Genesis will take you forty years!"

" No, closer to four."

Granacci put his arms about his friend's shoulders, quoted softly, " ' If a lion or bear came and carried off one of my rams, I would snatch the prey from their jaws. Did they threaten me, I would catch them by the throat and strangle them.' As an artist, you have David's courage."

" I am also a coward. I can't bear to tell the others. Would you do it for me?"

He returned to the Sistine to look at the vault with sharper eyes. The architectural structure did not accommodate his new vision. He needed a new vault, a completely different ceiling which would appear to have been constructed solely for the purpose of showing his frescoes to their best advantage. But he knew better than to return to the Pope and ask for a million ducats to tear down brick, plaster, soldiers' rooms above, solid roof beyond. Serving as his own architect, he would have to rebuild that tremendous vault with the sole material available to him:

Paint.

Through sheer invention he must transform the ceiling, utilizing its shortcomings even as he had the gouge in the Duccio block, to force his creative powers into channels they might not otherwise have taken. Either he was the stronger, and could displace this vault space, or the force of the vault to resist would crush him.

He was determined to get a teeming humanity up on the ceiling, as well as God Almighty who created it; mankind portrayed in its breathless beauty, its weaknesses, its indestructable strengths: God in His ability to make all things possible. He must project a throbbing, meaningful vitality that would invert the universe: the vault would become the reality, the world of those looking at it would become illusion.

Argiento and Michi built a workbench for him in the centre of the icy marble floor. Now he knew what the vault must say and accomplish; the number of frescoes he could paint would be determined by his architectural reconstruction. He must create the content and the container simultaneously. He stared at the ceiling above him. The centre space running the full length of the vault he would use for his major legends: Dividing the Waters from the Earth. God Creating the Sun, the Moon. God Creating Adam and Eve, Expelling Them from the Garden, the legend of Noah and the Deluge. Now, at long last, he could pay his debt to Della Quercia for the magnificent biblical scenes carved in Istrian stone on the portal of San Petronio.

Architecturally he must frame this crucial middle section; he must also make the long narrow vault visible as a unified whole, with a single impact. For all practical purposes he had not one ceiling to paint, but three. He was going to have to be a magician to achieve a unifying force which would embrace every portion of the walls and ceiling, tie the elements together so that each supported the other, and no figure or scene would be isolated.

It took weeks of concentration, but at length the solution emerged from the severest limitation of the ceiling: the eight heavy, obtruding triangular spandrels, four on each side, their apexes coming a third of the way into the vault, and the four double-sized spandrels at the ends, with their inverted apexes in the corners. He spent a hundred hours trying to design them out, so that they would not dominate the ceiling, before he saw that he had been thinking in reverse. He must transform them into assets by decorating them with rich sculptural designs; then they would constitute a continuous frieze, an outer frame for the whole of his inner design!

Ideas now came tumbling over each other so tumultuously that he could hardly move his hands fast enough to set them down. The twelve pendentives between the apexes of the spandrels on the ends and sides he would preserve for his Prophets and Sibyls, sitting each one on a spacious marble throne. Connecting these twelve thrones would be a marble-like cornice going around all four sides of the chapel; this strong architectural cornice would serve as a cohesive interior frame to encompass his nine central stories. On either side of each throne would be marble-appearing *putti*; above them, enclosing the panels at the corners, would be the glorious male youth of the world, twenty nudes, their figures facing away from the giant panels towards the smaller panels, filling the released corners.

When Rosselli mounted the scaffolding with a claw hammer to tear out the plaster already frescoed, with Michi holding a canvas catchall below, Argiento came to Michelangelo. There were tears in his muddy brown eyes.

" Argiento, what's wrong?"

" My brother is dead."

Michelangelo put a hand on the young man's shoulder.

" I'm so sorry."

" I have to go home. The family farm is mine now. I must work it. My brother left little children. I'll be a *contadino*. I marry my brother's wife, raise the children."

Michelangelo laid down his pen.

" You don't like living on the farm."

" You'll be up on that scaffold a long time. I don't like paint."

Michelangelo rested his head wearily on his hands. " Neither do I, Argiento. But I'm going to paint those figures as though they were carved out of a stone mass. Every one of them will look as though they could move right off that ceiling and come down to earth."

" It's still paint."

" When will you leave?"

" To-day, after dinner."

" I will miss you."

He paid Argiento's back wages, thirty-seven gold ducats. This was almost the last of his funds. He had received no money from the Pope since May, nine months before ; he had bought his furniture and paints, plastered a section of the ceiling and frescoed it, paid the wages and travel expenses of Jacopo, Tedesco, Sangallo, Donnino, Bugiardini, fed them for four months. He could not even consider asking the Pope for more funds until he had an important section of the ceiling finished. Yet how could he paint even one complete panel until he had designed the entire vault? That meant months of drawing before he could start his first fresco. And now, just when he would become most involved, there would be no one to cook a meal, sweep a floor or wash a shirt.

He ate his soup-of-the-country in the silent house, thinking back to the month that it had been so noisy and gay, with Jacopo telling stories, Aristotle giving a lecture on the Bathers, Bugiardini singing love songs about Florence. It would be quiet here now ; but it would be lonelier still, all alone on the scaffolding in the barren chapel.

He began with the Deluge, a large panel towards the entrance of the chapel. By March he had the cartoon blown up and ready to be transferred to the ceiling. Winter had not released its grip on Rome. The Sistine was bitterly cold. A hundred braziers could not heat its lowest areas. He wore his warm wool stockings, *brache* and shirt.

Rosselli, who had left for Orvieto for a profitable commission, had trained Michi in the mixing of the plaster and the method of applying it. Michelangelo helped him carry the sacks of lime, sand and *pozzolana,* volcanic tufa dust, up the steep wall ladders to the top of the scaffolding. Here Michi made his mix. Michelangelo was dissatisfied with the tawny colour caused by the *pozzolana,* adding more lime and ground marble. He and Michi then climbed the series of three receding platforms that Rosselli had built so that they could plaster and paint the top of the rolling vault. Michi laid an area of intonaco, then held the cartoon. Michelangelo used the stick, charcoal bag, red ochre for connecting lines.

Michi descended, set to work grinding colours below. Michelangelo was now on his top platform, sixty feet above the floor. He had been thirteen when he stood for the first time on the scaffolding in Santa Maria Novella, alone on a peak above the chapel and the world. Now he was thirty-four, and now, as then, he suffered vertigo. The Sistine seemed so hollow from up here, with his head just one foot below the ceiling. He smelled the wet plaster, the pungence of his freshly ground paints. He turned from his view of the marble floor, picked up a brush, squeezed it between the fingers and thumb of his left hand, remembering that he would have to keep his colours liquid this early in the morning. . . .

He had watched Ghirlandaio paint enough panels to know that he should begin at the top and work his way downward on either side; but he lacked experience to paint professionally, and so he began at the dominant point, the one that interested him the most: the extreme left end, the last piece of green earth showing above the flood, the trunk of a storm-twisted tree extending towards what would later be Noah's Ark, with the last of perishing humanity climbing the banks: a woman carrying a child in her arms, an older one clutching her leg; a husband carrying his distraught wife on his back; a vanishing trail of heads, old and young, about to be submerged in the rising waters; and above them all, a young man climbing and clutching at the tree trunk in a desperate effort to gain the highest vantage point.

He painted with his head and shoulders pulled sharply back, his eyes staring straight up. Paint dripped on to his face, the moisture of the wet plaster oozed out and dripped in his eyes. His arms and back tired quickly from the strain of the unnatural position. During the first week he allowed Michi to lay only modest areas of intonaco each day, proceeding cautiously, experimenting not only with the contortions of the figures but with a wide variety of flesh tones and the colours of the blue, green and rose robes of those who still retained their clothing. He knew that these small areas caused too many seams, that at this rate Granacci's estimate of forty years would prove more accurate than his own resolution of four. Yet he learned as he went along; this panel of life and death in violent action bore little relation to the Ghirlandaio still lifes. He was content to feel his way slowly until he had mastered his medium.

At the end of the first week a biting north wind arose. Its whistling kept him awake most of the night. In the morning he walked to the Sistine with his scarf wound around his mouth, not sure, even as he climbed the ladder, whether he could get his hands warm enough to hold a brush. But when he reached the top of Rosselli's highest platform he saw that there was no need to do so: his panel was ruined. His plaster and paints were not drying. Instead, there was a moist dripping at the edges of his stormy tree, the man mounting the bank, a bundle of clothes on his shoulder. The oozing moisture was creating a mould which was creeping over the paint, slowly absorbing it. Behind him he heard Michi ask in a choked voice:

" I made the plaster bad?"

It was a long time before he could reply; he felt too sick.

" It was me. I don't know how to mix paints for fresco. It's been too many years since Ghirlandaio's. Granacci and the others did the work on my first prophet; all I did was apply the paint."

540

He stumbled down the ladder, tears in his eyes, made his way blindly to the Papal palace, waited for an interminable time in a cold anteroom. When he was admitted he stood forlornly before Julius.

" What is it, my son? You look ill."

" I have failed."

" In what way?"

" What I have done is spoiled."

" So quickly?"

" I told Your Holiness it was not my art."

" Lift up your head, Buonarroti. I have never seen you . . . crushed. I prefer you storming at me."

" The ceiling has begun to drip. The moisture is causing spots of mould."

" Can't you dry them?"

" I know not how, Holiness. My colours are disappearing into the mould. They are being consumed by the salty edges."

" I can't believe that you would fail. . . ." He turned to a groom. " Go to Sangallo's house, tell him to inspect the Sistine ceiling at once, and bring me his report."

Michelangelo retreated to the cold outer room and the hard waiting bench. This was the worst defeat he had ever suffered. Much as he hated giving his years to fresco, he had nonetheless evolved a masterly conception. He was not accustomed to failure; it was the only thing in his lexicon that was worse than being forced to work in alien mediums. That the Pope would be through with him there could be no doubt, even though his collapse as a fresco painter had nothing to do with his qualities as a marble sculptor. He would certainly not be allowed to carve the tomb. When an artist failed this abjectly, he was finished. The news of his failure would be all over Italy in a matter of days. Instead of returning to Florence in triumph he would creep home like a beaten dog, the tail of his pride between his legs. Florence would not like that. They would consider that he had undermined their position in the art world. Gonfaloniere Soderini would feel let down; he would have been a liability at the Vatican instead of an asset. Again he would have wasted a full year of his productive life.

He was buried so deep in his gloom that he did not see Sangallo come in. He was hustled into the throne room before he had a chance to collect himself.

" Sangallo, what have you found?" the Pope demanded.

" Nothing serious, Holiness. Michelangelo applied the lime

541

in too watery a state, and the north wind caused it to exude."

"But it's the same composition Ghirlandaio used in Florence," Michelangelo cried. "I watched it being prepared. . . ."

"Roman lime is made of travertine. It does not dry as readily. The *pozzolana* Rosselli taught you to mix with it stays soft, and often breaks into an efflorescence while drying. Substitute marble dust for *pozzolana,* use less water with this lime. All will be well."

"What about my colours? Must I tear out that part of the ceiling?"

"No. In time the air will consume the mould. Your colours won't be hurt."

Had Sangallo come back and reported that the ceiling was ruined, he would have been on the road to Florence by noon. Now he could return to his vault, though the events of the morning had given him an excrutiating headache.

The wind died down. The sun came out. His plaster dried. It was Sangallo who travelled the long road of defeat back to Florence. When Michelangelo went to the house on the Piazza Scossacavalli he found the furniture covered with sheets, the family's personal possessions stacked in the downstairs hall. Michelangelo was heartbroken.

"What happened?"

Sangallo shook his head, lips pursed tightly.

"No commissions have come in, not the Palazzo Guiliano, the Mint, the new palaces. Do you know the only assignment I have now? Laying sewers under the main streets! A noble job for a papal architect, no? My apprentices have joined Bramante. He has taken my place, as he vowed he would."

The next morning Sangallo and his family were gone, their departure unnoticed by the Vatican. High on his scaffold, Michelangelo felt more alone in Rome than ever; as though it were he who was lying melancholy and hopeless on the last grey rocks still above the sea, opposite the last bit of green earth.

The Deluge took him thirty-two days of consecutive painting. During the last weeks he was completely out of funds.

"We don't know whether we're rubbing the skin of our belly or the bone of our back," commented Michi.

His former earnings, invested in houses and farms to increase the family income, helped him not a scudo's worth. On the contrary, every letter still brought laments: why wasn't he sending his brothers money to open their shop? Lodovico money to buy fertile farms he had located? Why wasn't he arranging to have Aunt Cassandra's suit transferred to Rome, where he could defend it? At this point he felt like one of the naked men in the centre of his panel, trying to climb into Noah's boat where other agonized men, fearing for the safety of their last refuge, were standing above him with clubs raised.

How was it that only he did not prosper from his papal connections? Young Raphael Sanzio, recently brought to Rome by Bramante, his fellow countryman from Urbino, and an old friend of the Sanzio family, had immediately secured a private commission. The Pope had been so delighted with the grace and charm of the work that he had commissioned Raphael to fresco the *Stanze,* the rooms of his new apartment, into which he was moving from the detested Borgia apartment. The frescoes that had already been started by Signorelli and Sodoma the Pope ordered painted out, so that Raphael's work alone would be seen. Paid a generous retainer by the Pope, Raphael had rented a luxuriously furnished villa, installed a beautiful young mistress and a staff of servants to care for them. Raphael was already surrounded by admirers and apprentices, garnering the ripe fruits of Rome. The Pope included him in his hunting parties and private dinners. He was to be seen everywhere, petted, loved, everyone bringing him new commissions, including the decorating of a summer pavilion for Chigi, the banker.

Michelangelo gazed at the unpainted brick walls of his house, drab, without curtains or carpets, just the few pieces of used furniture he had bought. When Raphael arrived in Rome, Michelangelo had expected him to come and say hello. But Raphael never bothered to walk the few steps to the Sistine or to the house.

One evening when Michelangelo was crossing Piazza San Pietro, returning from the vault with his hair, face and clothes bespattered with paint and plaster, he saw Raphael coming towards him, surrounded by a full train of admirers, apprentices and hangers-on. As they passed, Michelangelo said dryly:

" Where are you going, as surrounded as a rector?"

Raphael did not stop but replied tartly:

" And where are you going, as lonely as an executioner?"

The remark rankled. The fact that his isolation was self-imposed did not help. He went to his draughting table, burying his hunger and loneliness in work, sketching the next fresco, the Sacrifice of Noah. As the figures came alive under his swiftly moving fingers and mind, Noah and his wife, the three nude sons of Noah, their wives, the ram to be sacrificed to the Lord, his workroom filled up with energy and vividness, vitality and colour. His hunger, his sense of isolation receded. He felt secure among his companions in this world of his own creating. To the silent house he murmured:

" I'm never less alone than when alone."

And he sighed, for he knew himself to be a victim of his own character.

14

Pope Julius had been eagerly waiting a chance to see the first fresco, but destitute as he was, Michelangelo took another ten days to paint the Delphic Sibyl and the Prophet Joel on their thrones in the pendentives on either side of the smaller fresco of Noah's Drunkenness. He wanted the Pope to see good examples of the figures with which the central panels would be surrounded.

Julius climbed the ladder, joined Michelangelo on the scaffolding, studied the fifty-five men, women and children, a few showing only heads and shoulders, but most of them fully presented. He commented on the magnificent beauty of the dark-haired Delphic Sibyl, asked questions about the white-maned father carrying his dead son on to the rocks, Noah's Ark in the background looking somewhat like a Greek temple, inquired about what was going to be painted in the other areas. Michelangelo avoided direct answers; he needed freedom to change his ideas as he moved along. Julius was too pleased to mind. He said quietly:

" The rest of the ceiling will be as good?"

" It should be better, Holy Father, for I am still learning about proper perspective at this height."

" It is wholly unlike the frescoes below us."

" The differences will grow greater as I proceed, rather than less."

" I am pleased with you, my son. I shall order the treasurer to pay you another five hundred ducats."

Now he was able to send money home to still the outcries, to buy food for the house, needed supplies for the job; now there would be quiet months ahead, during which he could paint his way towards the Garden of Eden, God Creating Eve, and then the heart of the ceiling, God Creating Adam.

The months proved anything but quiet. Warned by friendly Chamberlain Accursio that his Pietà was being moved out of St. Peter's so that Bramante's army of twenty-five hundred workmen could tear out the south wall of the Basilica to make room for the first of the new piers, he ran up the long flight of stairs to find his Pietà already moved next door to the little chapel of Mary of the Fever, but undamaged. Relieved, he stood watching Bramante's foremen locking cables around the south row of ancient columns; then, unbelieving, and with a sickening sinking of his innards, he saw the ancient marble and granite columns shatter to bits as they fell to the stone floor, be swept up as rubble and hauled away. Monuments built into the south wall were destroyed as the wall collapsed, smashing the antique mosaic tiles of the floor. At so little cost they could have been removed to safety!

Two mornings later a paper was pasted on the door of Bramante's palace, changing his name to Ruinante. A story circulated through the city that Bramante, knocking at the gates of paradise, was refused admission by St. Peter, who asked, "Why did you destroy my temple in Rome?" In reply, Bramante asked whether St. Peter would like him to tear down heaven and rebuild it.

As far as he knew, no one but himself and Chamberlain Accursio had a key to the Sistine. He had insisted upon this, so that no one could spy, or intrude upon his privacy. While painting the Prophet Zacharias on the huge throne over the layman's end of the chapel, he had a feeling that someone was coming at night. He had no tangible evidence, nothing was touched or moved out of place; but he sensed that not everything was quite the way he left it. Someone was mounting the ladder.

Michi hid in a nearby doorway, brought back word that it was Bramante and, he believed, Raphael. Bramante had a key. They came in late, after midnight. Michelangelo was furious: before he could get his vault completed and open to view, his new techniques would be on the walls of

Raphael's *Stanze,* even as Raphael's work now reflected his study of the Bathers. Raphael would have created the revolution, and Michelangelo copying him!

He asked Chamberlain Accursio to arrange a session with the Pope. Michelangelo made the accusation: there would be nothing new, no point of departure that Raphael would not know about. . . .

Bramante stood silent. Michelangelo demanded that the key be taken away from him. The Pope requested Bramante to surrender it to Accursio. Another crisis had been met. Michelangelo returned to the vault.

The next day there came a summons from a niece of Cardinal Piccolomini, who had so briefly been Pope Pius III. The Piccolomini family insisted that he begin carving on the remaining eleven statues for the Siena altar, or return the hundred-florin advance secured for him by Jacopo Galli. He could not spare a hundred florins now. Besides, they still owed him for one of the figures he had already delivered.

Next a letter from Lodovico informed him that, while he was making some repairs to the house in Settignano, Giovansimone had quarrelled with his father, raised his fist and threatened to beat him, then had set fire to the house and barn. The damage was small, since both structures were built of stone, but the experience had made Lodovico ill. Michelangelo sent money to make the repairs, along with a blistering letter to his brother.

The four incidents upset him severely. He had to stop work. A marble hunger seized him with such palpable force that he felt weak. He made for the *campagna,* walked for miles with long ceaseless strides, breathed in heavy gulps of air to prove to himself that he was three-dimensional. In the midst of his despair he received a message from Cardinal Giovanni, summoning him to the Medici palace. What else could have gone wrong? Giovanni was dressed in his red robes and biretta. His pale plump face was freshly shaved, smelled of a familiar Florentine cologne. Giulio stood behind him, dark of face and fiercely serious.

" Michelangelo, as a former companion under my father's roof, I have the warmest feelings for you."

" Your Grace, I have always felt that to be so."

" That is why I want you to become a regular of my household. You must come to dinner, be at my side during my hunting parties, and ride in my train when I cross the city in procession to say mass at Santa Maria in Domenica."

" Why must I do these things?"

" I want Rome to know that you are of my intimate circle."

" Could you not tell Rome that?"

" Words mean nothing. Churchmen, nobility, wealthy merchants come to this palace. When these people see you here they will know you are under my protection. My father would have wanted it."

He blessed Michelangelo, left the room. Michelangelo looked over at Giulio, who stepped forward and spoke with warmth.

" You know, Buonarroti, Cardinal Giovanni never makes enemies."

" That takes genius in Rome to-day."

" Cardinal Giovanni has that genius. He is the most beloved in the College of Cardinals. He feels you need his kindness."

" In what way?"

" Bramante blames you for the Ruinante story. Every day he makes new enemies for you."

" And Cardinal Giovanni wants to fight for me?"

" Not by attacking Bramante. If you become an intimate of this house, the cardinal, without saying one angry word to Bramante, will silence your detractors."

Michelangelo studied Giulio's slender, handsome face; for the first time he felt a liking for Giulio, even as Giulio was manifesting this first friendship towards him.

He climbed the winding trail up the Janiculum, then gazed down on the jagged, tawny rooftops of Rome, the Tiber snaking through the city like a continuous S. He asked himself whether he could join the train of Cardinal Giovanni and paint the Sistine ceiling at the same time. He was grateful to Giovanni for wanting to help him; and he needed help. But even if he were not working night and day, how could he become a hanger-on? He simply had no talent for social amenities, nor any liking for society. Hard as he had striven to raise the status of the artist above that of the artisan, he still believed that the artist was a man who had to work all the time. The years were so short, the frustrations so numerous, that unless he laboured at the top of his capacity he could never achieve a body of work. How could he paint for a few hours in the morning, go to the baths, walk to Giovanni's house, talk charmingly to thirty guests, eat a delicious dinner over several hours . . .?

Cardinal Giovanni listened carefully to his gratitude and his reasons for being unable to accept.

"Why is it impossible for you, when Raphael does it so easily? He too turns out considerable work of high quality, yet he has dinner at a different palace each day, supper with intimate friends, goes to the plays, has just bought a gem of a house in Trastevere for his newest mistress. His is a full life, would you not say? Now commissions come in every day. He refuses none. Why he, and not you?"

"I honestly don't know the answer, Your Grace. For Raphael, the creating of a work of art is a bright spring day in the *campagna*; for me, it is the *tramontana* howling down the valley from the mountain-tops. I work from early morning to dark, then by candlelight or oil lamp. Art for me is a torment, grievous when it goes bad, ecstatic when it goes well; but always it possesses me. When I have finished with a day of work I am a husk. Everything that was inside of me is now inside the marble or the fresco. That is why I have nothing to give elsewhere."

"Not even when it is to your best interest?"

"My best interest can only be my best work. Everything else passes."

15

He returned to his scaffold determined that nothing should further divert him, neither troubles in Rome nor in Florence. His sketches for the vault were fairly complete now, and they called for three hundred men, women and children, all imbued with the potency of life, displacing space as three-dimensional as those who walked the earth. The force to create them must come from within himself. It would take days, weeks, months of demoniacal energy to imbue each individual character with an authentic anatomy, mind, spirit and soul, an irradiation of strength so monumental and out-pouring that few men on the earth below could match them for power. Each one had to be pushed out of his artistic womb, pushed out by his own articulate frenzied force. He must gather within himself his galvanic might; his bur-geoning seed must be generated each day anew within his vitals, hurtled into space, projected on to the ceiling, given life everlasting. Though he was creating God the

Father, he himself was God the Mother, source of a noble breed, half man, half god, inseminated each night by his own creative fertility, carrying until the dawn, and then, on his lonely truckle bed high in the heavens, going through parturition to deliver a race of immortals.

God Almighty creating the sun and the moon, the earth and the water, the plants, the cattle, the crawling things, man and woman, even He had been exhausted from this torrential creativity. " God saw all that He had made, and found it very good." But " On the seventh day, He had come to an end of making, and rested." Why then should he, Michelangelo Buonarroti, a small man, only five feet four, weighing a hundred pounds, no heavier than one of Florence's society girls, labouring for months without adequate food and rest, why should he not be exhausted? When he prayed, " Dear God, help me ! " he was praying to himself, beseeching himself to have fortitude, to be invincible of body and spirit, to have the stamina and will to create mightily in a vision of a more heroic world.

For thirty days he painted from light to darkness, completing the Sacrifice of Noah, the four titanic nudes surrounding it, the Erythraean Sibyl on her throne, and the Prophet Isaiah in the pendentive opposite, returning home at night to enlarge the cartoon of the Garden of Eden. For thirty days he slept in his clothes, without taking off even his boots ; and when at the completion of the section, utterly spent, he had Michi pull his boots off for him, the skin came away with them.

He fed off himself. When he grew dizzy from standing and painting with his head and shoulders thrown back, his neck arched so that he could peer straight upward, his arms aching in every joint from the vertical effort, his eyes blurred from the dripping paint even though he had learned to paint through slits and to blink them shut with each brush stroke as he did against flying marble chips, he had Rosselli make him a still higher platform, the fourth on top of the scaffolding. He painted sitting down, his thighs drawn up tight against his belly for balance, his eyes a few inches from the ceiling, until the unpadded bones of his buttocks became so bruised and sore he could no longer endure the agony. Then he lay flat on his back, his knees in the air, doubled over as tightly as possible against his chest to steady his painting arm. Since he no longer bothered to shave, his beard became an excellent catchall for the constant drip of paint and water. No matter which way he leaned, crouched, lay or knelt, on his feet, knees or back, it was always in strain.

Then he thought he was going blind. A letter arrived from Buonarroto, and when he tried to read it he could see nothing but a blur. He put the letter down, washed his face, ate a few forkfuls of the over-cooked *pasta* Michi had made for him, went back to the letter. He could not decipher a word.

He threw himself on his bed, sorely beset. What was he doing to himself? He had refused to paint the simple commission the Pope had requested, and now he would come out of this chapel a gnarled twisted, ugly, blind dwarf, deformed and aged by his own colossal stupidity. What Torrigiani had done to his face, the vault would do to his body. He would carry its scars to his dying day. Why couldn't he have let well enough alone? He would have made his peace with the Pope, been back in Florence long since, enjoying dinner with the Company of the Cauldron, living in his comfortable house, carving the Hercules.

Sleepless, racked with pain, homesick, lonely, he rose in the inky blackness, lit a candle, and on the back of an old sketch tried to lighten his mood by pouring out his woes:

> *I've grown a goitre by dwelling in this den—*
> *As cats from stagnant streams in Lombardy,*
> *or in what other land they hap to be—*
> *which drives the belly close beneath the chin:*
>
> *My beard turns up to heaven; my nape falls in,*
> *fixed on my spine: my breast-bone visibly*
> *grows like a harp: a rich embroidery*
> *bedews my face from brush-drops thick and thin.*
>
> *My loins into my paunch like levers grind:*
> *my buttock like a crupper bears my weight;*
> *my feet unguided wander to and fro;*
>
> *In front my skin grows loose and long; behind*
> *by bending it becomes more taut and strait;*
> *crosswise I strain me like a Syrian bow: . . .*
>
> *Come then, try*
> *to succour my dead pictures and my fame;*
> *since foul I fare and painting is my shame.*

Word reached him that his brother Lionardo had died in a monastery in Pisa. There was no information as to why he had been moved to Pisa, or whether he had been buried there, or the nature of his illness. But as Michelangelo walked to San Lorenzo in Damaso to have a mass said for the repose of Lionardo's soul, he felt that he knew the answer: his brother had died of an excess of zeal. Might not that also be the cause of his own death?

Michi found a colony of stonemasons in Trastevere with whom he spent his evenings and holidays. Rosselli travelled to Naples in the south, Viterbo and Perugia in the north to build his master walls for frescoing. Michelangelo went nowhere. No one came any more to call or to invite him out. His conversations with Michi were confined to the subjects of grinding the colours and material needed on the scaffold. He was living as monastic and secluded a life as the brothers in Santo Spirito.

He no longer went to the Papal palace to confer with Julius, though the Pope, after a second visit to the ceiling, had sent him a thousand ducats to carry on the work. No one came to the Sistine. When he walked from his home to the chapel and back he did so almost totally blinded, barely able to stagger across the piazza, his head lowered, seeing no one. Passers-by no longer called attention to his paint- and plaster-stained clothes, face, beard, hair. Some thought him crazy.

" Crazed would be the better word," he muttered; " after living up in that valhalla of gods and goddesses all day, how do I make the transition back to this mean earth?"

He did not even try. For himself, he had accomplished his primary objective: the life and the people on the ceiling were real. Those living on earth were phantoms. His close friends, his intimates were Adam and Eve in the Garden of Eden, the fourth majestic panel in the line. He portrayed Adam and Eve not as tiny, timid, delicate creatures, but powerfully built, alert, handsome, as primordial as the boulders which sheltered them from the serpent-entwined apple tree, taking temptation in calm accepting strength rather than weak stupidity. Here was a pair to breed the race of man! And when they were banished from the Garden to the barren earth on the opposite side of the panel, with the archangel's sword pointed at their heads, they were frightened, but not cowed, not destroyed, not reduced to crawling things.

This was the mother and father of man, created by God, and he, Michelangelo Buonarroti, brought them to life in noble mien and proportion.

16

In June 1510, a year and a few weeks after he had shown Julius the Deluge, the first half of the vault was completed. In a small central panel God in His rose-coloured robe had just raised Eve from the rib of the sleeping Adam; in the corners, framing the drama, were four nude sons that would arise from this union, with beautiful faces, powerful bodies carved out of warm flesh-coloured marble; directly below on either side were the Vulcan-like Cumaean Sibyl and the Prophet Ezekiel on their thrones beneath the binding cornices. Half of the vault was now a flood of glorious colour: mustard yellows, pale sea greens, dust rose and azure blues against the mighty parade of sun-flooded flesh tones.

He had not told anyone the vault was half completed, but the Pope knew at once, He sent word to Michelangelo that he would be in the Sistine at midafternoon. Michelangelo helped Julius up the last rungs of the ladder, took him on a tour, pointing out the stories of David and Goliath and Judith and Holofernes, the four stories from the Ancestors of Christ in the side spandrels.

Julius demanded that the scaffold be taken down so that the world could see how great a thing was being executed.

"It is not yet time to take the scaffold down, Holy Father."

"Why not?"

"Because there are so many things to be finished: the children playing behind the thrones of the Prophets and Sibyls, the nudes filling either side of the spandrel apexes . . ."

"But I had heard that the first half was completed."

"The major panels, yes, but there is so much detail still to be done . . ."

"When will it be ready?" insisted the Pope stubbornly.

Michelangelo was irritated. He answered shortly:

"When it is ready!"

Julius went red in the face, satirized Michelangelo's voice harshly as he cried, "When it is ready! When it is ready!" raised his walking stick in a fury and brought it down across Michelangelo's shoulder.

There was a silence while the two antagonists glared at each other. Michelangelo went cold all over, too shocked to feel pain in the shoulder. He bowed, said formally in a voice from which all emotion had been smitten:

" It shall be as Your Holiness desires. The scaffolding will be down by to-morrow, the chapel ready to be shown."

He backed away, leaving the space open for the Pope to descend the ladder.

" It is not for you, Buonarroti, to dismiss your pontiff!" cried Julius. " You are dismissed."

Michelangelo backed down the ladder almost without touching the rungs, left the chapel. So this was the end! A bitter, degrading end, to be beaten with a stick like a *villano*. He who had vowed he would raise the status of the artist from that of skilled labourer to the highest reaches of society, whom the Company of the Cauldron had acclaimed when he defied the Pope, he had now been humiliated and degraded as no other reputable artist he had known!

Waves of nervous revulsion swept over him as he stumbled and jerked his way blindly along unfamiliar streets. He had re-created the world. He had tried to be God! Well, Pope Julius II had put him in his place. Julius was God's viceroy on earth, even as his brother Lionardo had told him; and he, Michelangelo Buonarroti, was a labourer in the fields. Strange, how one blow of a stick could dispel illusion.

" Foul I fare and painting is my shame."

Bramante's triumph was complete.

What did he do now? Julius would never forgive him for inciting him to strike the blow, and he would never forgive Julius for inflicting this ignominy on him. He would never pick up a paintbrush, never again touch that vault. Raphael could decorate the other half.

He made his way home. Michi was waiting for him, silent and owl-eyed.

" Pack your things, Michi," he said. " Get a head start on me. We'd better not leave Rome together. If the Pope orders my arrest, I don't want them taking you too."

" He had no right to hit you. He's not your father."

" He's my Holy Father. He can put me to death if he wants to. Only he'll have to catch me first."

He filled one canvas bag with his drawings, another with his personal things. It took him only a moment to pen a note to Rosselli, bidding him good-bye, and asking him to sell his furniture back to the dealer in Trastevere. Just as he finished there was a knock on the door. He froze. Michi's eyes went to the back door. It was too late for flight. He was caught, before he could get away. What would it be now, what new punishment, humiliation? He smiled grimly. After his fourteen months in the vault, the prison of Sant'Angelo would have its comforts!

There was a second sharp knock. He opened the door, expecting to see soldiers. Instead there was Chamberlain Accursio.

" May I enter, Messer Buonarroti?"

" Have you come to arrest me?"

" My good friend," said Accursio gently, " you must not take these little matters so hard. Do you think the pontiff would bother to strike anyone he was not deeply fond of?"

Michelangelo closed the street door behind Accursio, stood with his palms on the table, staring wide-eyed at the Pope's agent.

" Are you suggesting that the blow was a mark of His Holiness' favour?"

" The Pope loves you. As a gifted, albeit unruly son." He took a purse from his belt, laid it on the worktable. " The pontiff asked me to bring you these five hundred ducats . . ."

" . . . a golden salve to heal my wound?"

" . . . and to convey his apologies."

" The Holy Father sent apologies to me?"

" Yes. The moment he returned to the palace. He did not want this to happen. He says it's because you both have a *terribilità.*"

" Who knows that the Pope sent you to beg my pardon?"

" Is that important?"

" Since Rome will know the pontiff struck me, I can only go on living here if people also know that he apologized."

Accursio rolled his shoulders, subtly. " Who has ever been able to conceal anything in this city?"

Julius chose the week of the Feast of the Assumption to unveil the first half of the vault. Rosselli directed Mottino and his crew in taking down the scaffold and storing it. Michelangelo spent the intervening weeks at home, drawing and making the cartoons for the prophets Daniel and Jeremiah, the Libyan and Persian Sibyls. He did not go near the Sistine or the Papal palace. Julius sent no word. It was an uneasy truce.

He kept no track of time. He knew what season he was in,

and sometimes the month, but little more. When he wrote home he could not date his letters, saying, " I know not what day it is, but I think yesterday was Friday," or " I do not know what the date is to-day, but I know that yesterday was St. Luke's Feast Day." The Pope did not order him to the chapel for the ceremonies. The first he knew of the gathering in the Sistine was when Michi answered a knock at midday, bringing Raphael into the workroom. Michelangelo was crouched over his table sketching Haman and the Brazen Serpent for the spandrels.

He looked up at Raphael, saw that the younger man's face had aged considerably, with dark circles under his eyes, the flesh a little flaccid. He was dressed in expensive mauve satin embroidered with costly jewels. Commissions flooding into his *bottega* included everything from designing a dagger to building great palaces; his assistants completed whatever Raphael had no further time for. Only twenty-seven, he looked ten years older. Even as Michelangelo's hard, gruelling labour had taken its toll of him, so Raphael's fine looks were dissolving in his too-muchness of everything: food, drink, women, pleasure, company, praise.

" Messer Buonarroti, your chapel staggers me," said Raphael with admiration in his voice and eyes. " I came to apologize for my bad manners. I should never have spoken to you as I did in the piazza. You deserved better of me."

Michelangelo remembered going to Leonardo da Vinci to apologize for his own bad manners.

"Artists must forgive each other their sins."

No one else came to congratulate him, no one stopped him on the street, no one approached him with a new commission. He was as solitary as though he were dead. The painting on the ceiling of the Sistine was outside the pale of Rome's life, a private duel between Michelangelo, God and Julius II.

And, suddenly, Pope Julius was deep in war.

Two days after the unveiling, Julius left Rome at the head of his army to drive the French out of northern Italy and to solidify the Papal State. Michelangelo watched him leave, riding a fiery charger, followed in procession by Spanish troops provided by the King of Spain to whom he had given control of Naples; Italian mercenaries under his nephew, the Duke of Urbino; and Roman columns led by his nephew-in-law, Marcantonio Colonna. His first objective was to besiege Ferrara, ally of the French. To help him in his conquest he was to have fifteen thousand Swiss troops, bolstered by the considerable Venetian forces. On the way north there were independent city-states to be reduced: Modena, Mirandola, family seat of the magnificent Pico. . . .

Michelangelo worried; the French were the sole protection of the Republic of Florence. If Julius could drive the French troops out of Italy, Florence would be vulnerable. It would be Gonfaloniere Soderini's and the Signoria's turn to feel the papal stick across their backs. He had also been left stranded; or he had stranded himself. The Pope's chamberlain had brought him money and an apology, but he had not brought him specific permission to put back the scaffolding and commence work on the altar half of the vault. Julius had waited for him to appear at the Vatican. He had waited for Julius to summon him. The Pope could be gone for months. What did he do in the meanwhile?

A letter from his father informed him that his brother Buonarroto was seriously ill. He would have liked to make the trip to Florence to be at his side, but did he dare to leave Rome? He sent money instead, out of Julius' apology purse. He considered seeking a commission, anything in marble or paint that would occupy and support him until the Pope's return. But he had never sought a commission. He did not know how to go about it.

When he heard that the Papal Datary, a Florentine by the name of Lorenzo Pucci, was leaving to join the Pope in Bologna, he sought him out and asked if he would speak to Julius in his behalf, try to collect the five hundred ducats still owed him for the half of the vault he had completed, secure permission to begin the second half, money to erect the scaffold. The Datary said he would try. He would also see if he could find an outside commission for Michelangelo to tide him over.

Then Michelangelo sat down to write a sonnet to the Pope:

> *I am thy drudge and have been from my youth—*
> *Thine, like the rays which the sun's circle fill,*
> *Yet of my dear time's waste thou thinkst no ill.*
> *The more I toil, the less I move thy ruth.*

17

It was not until after the New Year, 1511, that he was able to start painting again. During the intervening months he had added to his fund of aggravation and frustration. Unable to stand the inactivity any longer, he had followed the Pope to Bologna, only to find the Bentivoglios regaining power, Pope Julius too immersed in his troubles to see him. He had gone on to Florence to visit Buonarroti, resolved to take some of his past savings which had been deposited for safe-keeping with the *spedalingo,* business manager of the hospital of Santa Maria Nuova, rebuild his scaffold and return to work without permission or the Pope's money. He found Buonarroto recovered, but too weak to work ; and that his father had received the first political appointment tendered by Florence to a Buonarroti in Michelangelo's lifetime: as *podestà* in the village of San Casciano. Lodovico had taken with him some of the savings from the *spedalingo* without Michelangelo's knowledge or consent, money to which he no longer had a legal right. An apologetic letter from his father explained:

I took them with the hope that I should be able to put them back before your return to Florence. Now I see that I did wrong. I am awfully sorry. I did wrong in following other people's advices.

He had returned to Rome empty-handed. And it seemed that Pope Julius too would return empty-handed. For Julius, the general, everything had gone wrong: though his troops had taken Modena, he had found Bologna meagrely garrisoned and low on food supplies, with the Bentivoglios at one gate, the French army entrenched a few miles away. Ferrara had driven off his army in a serious defeat ; the Swiss troops had been bribed by the French to return home ; he was ready to send Pico della Mirandola's nephew to negotiate his surrender to the French when the Venetian and Spanish troops finally arrived to save him.

Now the Datary returned with the money owed Michelangelo, permission to place his scaffold under the second half of the chapel, across to the Pope's throne at the end, and the money to pay for it. Now Michelangelo could come to grips with God: God Creating Adam, Creating the Sun and Moon, Dividing the Waters from the Earth, Separating Light and Darkness; strive to visualize a God of such transcendence that everyone would cry out, " Yes! That is the Lord God! None other could be!" These four panels were the heart of the vault. Everything depended upon them. Unless he could create God as convincingly as God had created man, his ceiling would lack the focal core from whence sprang its reason for being.

He had always loved God. In his darkest hour he cried out, " God did not create us to abandon us." His faith in God sustained him; and now he must make manifest to the world who God was, what He looked and felt like, wherein lay His divine power and grace. His God must not be special or peculiar or particular; but God the Father to all men, one whom they could accept, honour, adore.

It was a delicate task, yet he did not doubt that he could achieve such a God. He had only to set down in drawings the image he had carried with him since childhood. God as the most beautiful, powerful, intelligent and loving force in the universe. Since He had created man in His own image, He had the face and body of a man. The first human whom God created, Adam, had surely been fashioned in His likeness. By setting forth Adam, the son, true creature of his Father: magnificent in body, noble in thought, tender in spirit, beautiful of face and limb, archetype of all that was the finest in heaven and on earth, there would be reflected God, the Father. God, in clinging white robe which matched His virile white beard, had only to hold out His right arm to Adam, to reach one infinitesimal life-breath more, man and the world would begin.

While Michelangelo remained high in the heavens painting the smaller panel of God Dividing the Waters from the Earth, Julius reversed positions with his fresco painter, plunging into the special inferno reserved for warriors who suffer a rout. He failed in his siege of Ferrara, failed in his efforts to break the alliance between the Holy Roman Empire and France; went down so badly with gout that he had to be carried to Ravenna in an oxcart. His papal and Venetian forces were severely defeated by the rampaging Ferrarese, his funds so exhausted that he had to raise eighty thousand ducats by selling eight new cardinalates at ten thousand ducats each. The French and Ferrarese recaptured Bologna and reinstated the Bentivoglios. Julius lost his armies, artillery, baggage, the last of his resources. Crushed, making his way back to Rome, he found nailed to the cathedral door at Rimini a summons of all rebellious churchmen to a General Council at Pisa to conduct an inquiry into the official behaviour of Pope Julius II.

Julius' defeat was a defeat for Michelangelo, for his life had become inextricably interwoven with his pontiff's. The moment the Bentivoglios returned to power, the Bolognese had thronged into the Piazza Maggiore, torn his bronze statue of Julius from its niche, and thrown it to the paving stones. The triumphant Duke of Ferrara had then melted it down and recast it into a cannon, which he named *Julius*. Fifteen months of his time, energy, talent and suffering now sat on the cobbles of the Piazza Maggiore in the form of a cannon that was the butt of coarse jokes from the Bolognese, and would surely be used against Pope Julius if he were rash enough to lead another army northward. Vincenzo had triumphed.

Here in Rome, it seemed to Michelangelo, the same pattern of overthrow must inevitably continue. During the warm, light days of May and June he spent seventeen consecutive hours on the scaffold, taking food and a chamber pot up with him so that he would not have to descend, painting like a man possessed, the four glorious nude males in the corners of the panels, then the young Prophet Daniel with an enormous book on his lap; opposite, the old Persian Sibyl in her white and rose robes, then the single most powerful portrait on the ceiling, God in deeply dramatic action, creating the golden ball of the sun . . . hoping, praying, striving desperately to complete his Genesis before the collapse of its protector, before outraged successors came in, clerical or military and, wanting to wipe out all traces of Pope Julius II's reign, sent a crew into the Sistine to spread coats of whitewash over its ceiling.

It was a race against death. As a result of his internecine warfare, Julius had returned to Rome the most hated man in Italy, his resources so exhausted that he had to carry the papal tiara to the banker Chigi's house under his robes, ostensibly going to dinner, but actually to borrow forty thousand ducats on the jewels. His enmities extended to all the city-states he had defeated and punished: Venice,

Bologna, Modena, Perugia, Mirandola. . . . Even the Roman nobles, some of whom had led his defeated armies, were now in league against him.

Bound to each other, understanding defeat, Michelangelo felt that he must call on his Pope, the only obligation that could take him off the scaffold.

" Holy Father, I have come to pay my respects."

Julius' face was ravaged by frustration and illness. Their last face-to-face encounter had been a stormy one, yet instinctively Julius sensed that Michelangelo had not come seeking revenge. Julius' voice was friendly, intimate ; they felt strongly drawn to each other.

" Your ceiling, it moves along?"

" Holiness, I think you will be gratified."

" If I am, you will be the first to bring me gratification for a long time."

" It is no simpler in art than in war, Holiness," said Michelangelo firmly.

" I will come to the Sistine with you. This very moment."

He could hardly make it up the ladder. Michelangelo had to haul him the last few rungs. He stood panting at the top ; and then he saw God above him, about to impart the gift of life to Adam. A smile came to his cracked lips.

" Do you truly believe that God is that benign?"

" Yes, Holy Father."

" I most ardently hope so, since I am going to be standing before Him before long. If He is as you have painted Him, then I shall be forgiven my sins." He turned his face towards Michelangelo, his expression radiant. " I am pleased with you, my son."

Basking in the rays of the hot sun and the Pope's hearty acceptance of his labours, Michelangelo was reluctant to relinquish the happy mood. Wanting to hold its warm and tranquillity for a little while longer, he crossed the piazza to where the piers and walls of the new St. Peter's were beginning to rise. As he got closer he was surprised to find that Bramante was not building in the traditional manner for cathedrals, of solid stone and concrete, but was erecting hollow concrete forms and filling them with rubble from the Old Basilica, and other debris. The bulky mass would give the appearance of being solid, but was it not a dangerous way to support so heavy a structure?

This was only the beginning of his astonishment. As he

circled the works and watched the men preparing the concrete, he saw that they were not following the sound engineering precept of one portion of cement to three or four of sand, but were using ten and twelve portions of sand to each one of cement. There was no question in his mind that this mix could be fatal under the best circumstances, but to hold the vast St. Peter's with uncompacted debris between its piers, it could be catastrophic.

He made straight for Bramante's palace, was admitted by a liveried footman into the elegance of the foyer, with its rich Persian carpets, priceless tapestries and furniture. He had not been invited, but the message he had to deliver was urgent. Bramant was working in his library, clad in a silk robe with gold clasps at the throat and waist.

"Bramante, I will pay you the compliment of believing that you do not know what is going on," he began without preamble or salutation. "However, when the walls of St. Peter's crumble, it will make little difference whether you were stupid or merely negligent. Your walls will crack."

Bramante was annoyed at the visit.

"Who are you, a ceiling decorator, to tell the greatest architect in Europe how to build piers?"

"The same one who showed you how to build a scaffold. Someone is cheating you."

"*Davvero?* How?"

"By putting in the mix considerably less cement than the minimum requirements."

"Ah, you're an engineer!"

Michelangelo ignored the remark.

"Bramante, watch your foreman prepare the cement. Somebody is taking advantage . . ."

Bramante went purple with rage, his bull-like shoulders hunched up around his jowls.

"Whom else have you told this to?"

"No one. I hurried here to warn you. . . ."

Bramante rose, clenched both fists in front of his jaw.

"Buonarroti, if you run to the Pope with this scandalmongering I swear I'll strangle you with my bare hands. You're nothing but an incompetent troublemaker . . . Florentine!"

He spat out the last word as though it were a deadly insult. Michelangelo remained calm.

"I shall watch your cement mix for two days. At the

end of that time, if you are not using safe proportions, I shall report it to the Pope and to everyone else who will listen to me."

"No one will listen to you. You command no respect in Rome. Now get out of my house."

Bramante did nothing to change his materials. Michelangelo sweated out the paint from his pores in the Piazza Scossacavalli baths, put on his brown shirt and *calze,* went to the Papal palace. Julius listened for a time, then interrupted. His voice impatient, though not unkind.

"My son, you should not bother yourself with other people's affairs. Bramante has already warned me of your attack on him. I don't know the cause of your enmity, but it is unworthy of you."

"Holy Father, I genuinely fear for the structure. The new St. Peter's grew out of Sangallo's idea for a separate chapel for Your Holiness' tomb. I feel responsible."

"Buonarroti, are you an architect?"

"To the extent that every good sculptor is an architect."

"But you are not as good an architect, or as experienced, as Bramante?"

"No, Holy Father."

"Is he interfering in the way you are painting the Sistine?"

"No, he is not."

"Then why can't you be content to paint your ceiling and let Bramante build his church?"

"If Your Holiness would appoint a commission to investigate . . . I came out of a sense of loyalty."

"I know that, my son," replied Julius. "But St. Peter's is going to take many years to build. If you come running here in hot blood every time you see something you don't like . . ."

Michelangelo knelt abruptly, kissed the Pope's ring, left. The Pope was right. Why could he not mind his own business? Yet he could not be neutral about St. Peter's. It had been the cause of unseating his friend Sangallo, had given Bramante the ascendancy in the Pope's mind which led to the cancellation of the tomb marbles, to his being locked out of the Papal palace, to the months of irresolution in Florence, the more than a year of wasted work in Bologna, and now more years of servitude in the vault.

He was also sorely puzzled. Bramante was too good an architect to put his most important creation in danger.

There must be an explanation. Leo Baglioni knew everything; he knocked on his door.

"It's not hard to explain," replied Leo casually. "Bramante is living beyond his means, spending hundreds of thousands of ducats. He has to have more money . . . from any source. Right now the piers of St. Peter's are paying his debts."

Aghast, Michelangelo cried, "Have you told the Pope this?"

"Assuredly not."

"But how can you be silent in such a matter?"

"You told the Pope the facts. What did it get you, besides an admonition to mind your own business?"

18

In August, while Michelangelo was beginning his panel of the Creation of Eve, Julius went hunting at Ostia, returning home with malaria. He was reported to be at the point of death. The rooms of his private apartment were sacked, down to its linens; the Roman nobles organized to " evict the barbarian from Rome "; from all over Italy the hierarchy hurried to Rome to select a new Pope. The city buzzed with gossip. Would Cardinal Riario at long last have his turn, and Leo Baglioni become the Pope's confidential agent? Meanwhile the French and Spanish hovered on the borders, hoping to conquer Italy during the confusion. Michelangelo became anxious. If Pope Julius died, what happened to his payment for the second half of the Sistine? He had only an oral agreement with Julius, not a written contract which his heirs would have to honour.

The only calm area in Italy seemed to be Florence, thanks to the genius of Gonfaloniere Soderini, who had kept his city-state out of the quarrels, alliances, wars, resolutely holding to the middle ground, offering refuge to both the papal and French soldiers, refusing to house the Pisa Council of protest over Julius, but not attempting to keep it out of Pisa by force. Michelangelo knew that that was where he should be right now, and for ever, out of this capital of chaos.

Julius fooled Rome: he recovered. The nobles fled. The Pope took firm control of the Vatican, money started coming in, he paid Michelangelo another five hundred ducats. Michelangelo sent a modest sum home, but the greater part of the payment he kept in Rome.

"I'm flattered!" cried Balducci when Michelangelo brought in the money. Balducci, grown portly with good and quiet living, had already sired four children. "Didn't you always believe that a dishonest Florentine bank was safer than an honest Roman one?"

"Balducci, I could have saved myself endless aggravation if you had been in charge of my affairs from the beginning. But artists are endlessly inventive in their ways of being stupid about money."

"Now that you're independently wealthy," teased Balducci with his perennial good humour, "Won't you come to dinner on Sunday? We entertain all our biggest depositors."

"Thanks, Balducci, but I'll wait until I'm a part owner."

When Michelangelo made a second sizeable deposit, and again refused Balducci's invitation, the banker walked over to Michelangelo's house late of a Sunday afternoon, bringing a cake his cook had baked. He had not been in the house in two years; he was shocked at its shabby meanness.

"For heaven's sake, Michelangelo, how can you live like this?"

"I can't help it, Balducci. I keep hiring apprentices who swear they want to learn and will take care of the house, but they're lazy and incompetent."

"Then hire a servant, one who knows how to cook and clean, who can give you a few of the amenities of life."

"What would I do with a servant? I'm never here; I don't come home at midday for dinner . . ."

"What would you do with a trained servant? You would live in a clean house, eat decent food; come home at night to a tub of hot water for your bath, have freshly washed linens laid out for you, a bottle of wine properly cooled . . ."

"*Piano, piano,* Balducci, you talk as though I were a rich man."

"You're stingy, not poor! You earn enough to live well. Not like a . . . a . . . You are destroying your health. What good will it do you to be a rich man in Florence if you kill yourself in Rome?"

"I won't kill myself. I am of stone."

"Isn't your life hard enough, up on that scaffold, without making it worse by penury?"

Michelangelo flinched.

"I know you're right, Balducci. I must have some of my

father in me. But right now I have no patience to live well. As long as I'm on that vault, there's nothing I can salvage in terms of pleasure or comfort. The time to live is when one is happy."

"When will that be?"

"As soon as I get back to marble."

He pushed rigorously into the autumn, painting Sundays and religious holidays. A young orphan apprentice by the name of Andrea came to help each afternoon, and to take care of his house. Michelangelo let him paint a few decorative rams' heads and doorframes, flat walls or floor surfaces that Bugiardini had done at Santa Maria Novella. He allowed Michi to fill in some of the exposed surfaces of the thrones and cornices. Young Silvio Falconi, who asked to be considered as an apprentice, and who had a talent for drawing, he permitted to do a few of the colour decorations buried in the end spandrels. All the rest, the entire reach of the vault, he painted himself: every figure, every robe, every face, every limb of every nude, every expression, motion, every *putto,* every child behind the Prophets and Sibyls, the exquisitely beautiful Sibyls, the powerful and glorious Hebrew Prophets, every last touch he did himself: a gigantic lifetime of labour jammed into three apocalyptic years.

There was new trouble abroad. Pope Julius, strong again, turned against Gonfaloniere Soderini, put an interdict on the Republic of Florence for not siding with him, for not providing troops and money when he had been in trouble, for giving refuge to enemy troops, for not crushing the Council at Pisa. Julius appointed Cardinal Giovanni de' Medici as papal legate at Bologna, with an eye to bringing Tuscany under the rule of the Vatican.

Michelangelo was invited to the Medici palace at the end of the Via Ripetta. Cardinal Giovanni, Cousin Giulio and Giuliano were gathered in the drawing-room.

"You have heard that the Holy Father has appointed me papal legate to Bologna, with authority to raise an army."

"Like Piero's?"

There was a strained silence.

"I hope not," replied Cardinal Giovanni. "Everything will be peaceable. We want only to be Florentines again, to have our palace and banks and lands back."

"Soderini must go!" interjected Giulio.

"Is that part of the plan, Your Grace?"

"Yes. Pope Julius is outraged at Florence, and deter-

565

mined to conquer it. If Soderini goes, a few irreconcilables on the Signoria . . ."

"Who is to rule Florence in Soderini's place?" He tried to keep down his rising emotion.

"Giuliano."

Michelangelo looked across the room to Giuliano, saw the colour mount in his cheeks. The choice seemed a stroke of genius: for Giuliano, now thirty-two, tall, with a slight beard and moustache, said to have weak lungs, yet to Michelangelo's glance seeming robust, Giuliano was close to *Il Magnifico* in mind, spirit and temperament. He had put in years of disciplined study, tried to prepare himself in the image of his father. He was handsomer than Lorenzo, though his nose was long and flat, his large eyes heavy-lidded, and had inherited most of Lorenzo's finest qualities: a gentle soul, with a touch of wisdom in him, and no violence. He had a reverence for art and learning, a deep love for Florence, its people and traditions. If Florence had to have a ruler, over and beyond its elected Gonfaloniere, Lorenzo's youngest and most gifted son seemed perfect for the job.

The men in the room knew Michelangelo's affection for Giuliano. They did not know that a fifth person was present, standing in his robes of office in the centre of the floor, his long homely face, wobbly nose, bland eyes and yellow-streaked white hair all corporeally present for Michelangelo: Piero Soderini, elected lifetime Gonfaloniere of the Republic of Florence.

Looking down at his cracked and paint-stained nails, Michelangelo asked, "Why have you told me this?"

"Because we want you on our side," replied Cardinal Giovanni. "You belong with the Medici. Should we need you . . ."

He threaded his way as through the eye of a needle to the Piazza Navona, took a series of right angles to the Piazza Venezia, then went down the street of the ancient Roman forums with their scattered columns standing upright, and entered the Colosseum, brightly lit in the full moonlight, for a thousand years Rome's quarry for home builders needing hand-hewn stone. He climbed to the topmost tier, sat on the parapet of the gallery overlooking the vast theatre from its lowest, darkest pits with its cells where Christians, warriors, slaves, animals had been herded, up to its top section of stone seats where the multitudes of the Roman Empire had sat, screaming for battle and blood.

. . . battle and blood, blood and battle. The phrase kept going through his mind. It seemed to be all that Italy was to know. All that he had known in his lifetime. At this very moment Julius was gathering another army to march north. If Florence resisted, the Pope would send Giovanni's troops against its walls. If Florence did not resist, Gonfaloniere Soderini would be driven out, as would all the members of the Signoria who did not consent to the loss of their independence. Now he too was being asked to become a part of it.

He loved both Gonfaloniere Soderini and Giuliano de' Medici. He felt a strong loyalty to *Il Magnifico*, to Contessina, yes, to Cardinal Giovanni too. But he had a faith in the Republic, which had given him his first recognition. To whom was he to be unfaithful, ungrateful? Granacci would tell him, " If anyone asks what side you're on, answer ' On the side of sculpture.' Be courageous in art, and a coward in the world of affairs."

Could he be?

19

During the grey winter months of 1512, while he painted the lunettes over the tall windows, his eyes became so badly afflicted that he could not read a line unless he threw his head back sharply and held the letter or book high in the air above him. Though Julius had remained in Rome, his wars had started. His armies were commanded by the Spaniard, Cardona of Naples. Cardinal Giovanni left for Bologna, but twice the Bolognese, bolstered by the French, fought off the Pope's troops. Cardinal Giovanni never got into Bologna. The French then chased the Pope's army into Ravenna where, on Easter Day, the decisive battle was fought ; ten to twelve thousand soldiers of the papal troops were reported to have died in the field. Cardinal Giovanni and Cousin Giulio were taken prisoner. The Romagna fell into French hands. Rome was in panic. The Pope took refuge in the fortress of Sant'Angelo.

Michelangelo went on painting his vault.

Again the tide of fortune turned: the winning French

commander was killed. The French fought among themselves. The Swiss came into Lombardy to fight the French. Cardinal Giovanni, having saved Giulio by a ruse, himself escaped and returned to Rome. The Pope returned to the Vatican. During the summer Julius recovered Bologna. The French were driven out of the country. The Spanish general Cardona, an ally of the Medici, sacked Prato, just a few miles from Florence. Gonfaloniere Soderini was forced to resign, fleeing with his family. Giuliano entered Florence as a private citizen. Behind him came Cardinal Giovanni de' Medici with Cardona's army, returning to his old palace in the quarter of Sant'Antonio near the Faenza gate. The Signoria resigned. A Council of Forty-five was appointed by Cardinal Giovanni, a new constitution adopted. The Republic had come to an end.

During all these months the Pope kept insisting that Michelangelo complete his ceiling quickly, quickly! Then one day Julius climbed the ladder unannounced.

" When will it be finished?"

" When I have satisfied myself."

" Satisfied yourself in what? You have already taken four full years."

" In the matter of art, Holy Father."

" It is my pleasure that you finish it in a matter of days."

" It will be done, Holy Father, when it will be done."

" Do you want to be thrown down from this scaffolding?" Michelangelo gazed at the marble floor below.

" On All Saints' Day I shall celebrate mass here," declared the Pope. " It will be two years since I blessed the first half."

Michelangelo had wanted to touch up some draperies and skies *a secco*, in gold and ultramarines, as his Florentine predecessors had done below him. But there would be no time now. He had Michi and Mottino take down the scaffold. The next day Julius stopped by.

" Don't some of the decorations need to be brightened with gold?" he demanded.

Useless to explain that he had wanted to do this. Nor was he going to re-erect the scaffold and go back up into the vault.

" Holy Father, in those times men did not bedeck themselves with gold."

" It will look poor!"

Michelangelo planted his feet stubbornly beneath him, his teeth locked, his chin stiffened. Julius gripped his fist over his walking stick. The two men stood before the altar beneath the heavens and glared at each other.

"Those whom I have painted were poor," said Michelangelo, breaking the silence. "They were holy men."

On All Saints' Day official Rome dressed itself in its finest robes for the Pope's dedication of the Sistine Chapel. Michelangelo rose early, went to the baths, shaved off his beard, donned his blue hose, blue wool shirt.

But he did not go to the Sistine. Instead he walked out under the portico of his house, pulled back the tarpaulin, stood ruminatively before the marble columns he had waited these seven long years to carve. He walked to his work desk, picked up a pen, wrote:

> *The best of artists hath no thought to show*
> *Which the rough stone in its superfluous shell*
> *Doth not include ; to break the marble spell*
> *Is all the hand that serves the brain can do.*

Standing on the threshold of his hard-earned freedom, disregarding his costly hose, the fine wool shirt, he took up his hammer and chisel. Fatigue, memory, bitterness and pain fell away. Sunlight streaming in the window caught the first shafts of marble dust that floated upward.

BOOK EIGHT

THE MEDICI

1

Pope Julius II survived the completion of the Sistine vault by only a few months. Giovanni de' Medici, the first Florentine to be elected to the papacy, was the new Pope.

Michelangelo stood in the Piazza San Pietro among the Florentine nobles who were determined to make this the most lavish procession ever to be seen in Rome. Ahead of him were two hundred mounted spearmen, the captains of the thirteen regions of Rome with their banners flying, the five standard-bearers of the Church carrying flags with the papal arms. Twelve milk-white horses from the papal stables were flanked by a hundred young nobles in fringed red silk and ermine. Behind him were a hundred Roman barons accompanied by their armed escorts, the Swiss guards in uniforms of white, yellow and green. The new Pope, Leo X, mounted on a white Arabian stallion, was shaded from the warm April sun by a canopy of embroidered silk. Next to him, dressed as the standard-bearer of Rhodes, was Cousin Giulio. The lone figure in mourning was the Duke of Urbino, nephew of Julius.

Gazing at Pope Leo X, his heavy bulk perspiring from the weight of the triple tiara and heavily jewelled cope, Michelangelo thought how inscrutable were the ways of God. Cardinal Giovanni de' Medici had been in Florence when Julius died, so ill with ulcers he had had to be carried to Rome on a litter in order to cast his ballot. The College of Cardinals, sealed into the airless Sistine Chapel, had spent nearly a week battling between the forces of Leo Baglioni's Cardinal Riario and Cardinals Fiesco and Serra. The one member who had no enemies was Giovanni de' Medici. On the seventh day the College had unanimously settled on mild-mannered, modest, friendly Giovanni, fulfilling *Il Magnifico's* plan when he had had Giovanni consecrated in the Badia Fiesolana at the age of sixteen.

The trumpeters sounded for the beginning of the march across the city from St. Peter's, where Leo had been crowned in a pavilion in front of the wrecked Basilica, to St. John in Lateran, earliest home of the Popes. The Sant'Angelo bridge was covered with brilliant-hued draperies. At the beginning of the Via Papale, the Papal Way, the Florentine colony had erected a giant triumphal arch bearing the Medici emblems. Throngs lined streets covered with sprigs of myrtle and box.

Riding between his cousin, Paolo Rucellai, and the Strozzi who had purchased his early Hercules, Michelangelo watched Leo, beaming with joy, raising his pearl-encrusted gloved hands in benediction, his chamberlains walking beside him throwing handfuls of gold coins to the crowds. Every house had brocades and velvets hung from its casements. The antique marbles of Rome lined the Via Papale: busts of the emperors, statues of the apostles, saints, the Virgin, placed side by side with pagan Greek sculptures.

At midafternoon Pope Leo descended from his horse by means of a ladder, stood for a moment by the ancient bronze equestrian statue of Marcus Aurelius in front of the Lateran. Then, surrounded by his College of Cardinals, flanked by Cousin Giulio and the Florentine and Roman nobles, he entered the Lateran and seated himself on the Sella Stercoraria, ancient seat of power occupied by the first Popes.

Michelangelo ate little of the elaborate banquet served in the hall of the palace of Constantine, restored for the feast. At sunset he remounted his horse to follow in Pope Leo's train back to the Vatican. By the time they reached the Campo dei Fiori night had fallen. Torches and tapers lit the streets. Michelangelo dropped off his horse at Leo Baglioni's house, handed the reins to a groom. Baglioni had not been invited to ride in the procession; he was alone in the house, unshaven, gloomy. This time he had been certain Cardinal Riario would be elected to the papacy.

" So you made it to the Vatican ahead of me!" he grumbled to Michelangelo.

" I'd be happy never to see the inside of the papal palace again. I cede my place to you."

" This is one game in which the winner can't cede. I'm out; you're in. There'll be glorious commissions."

" I have years of carving ahead for Julius' tomb."

It was late when he returned to his new home which sat in a sea of centuries in the valley between the Capitoline and Quirinal hills, near the foot of Trajan's column where the Macello dei Corvi, Slaughterhouse of the Crows, dribbled into the crowded square. Just before his death Pope Julius had paid him two thousand ducats to settle the Sistine account and to commence carving the tomb marbles. With Gonfaloniere Soderini and the Signoria in exile from Florence, his commission to carve the Hercules for the front of the Signoria had vanished. When this property, consisting of a main building built of yellow firebrick, a shaded veranda along one side, a cluster of wooden sheds in the rear, a stable, tower and overgrown garden with shady laurel trees, had come on the market at a reasonable price, he had bought it and moved his marbles in. Trajan's market, a tiered, abandoned ruin rising just across from him, had once housed hundreds of merchants in separate stalls, attracting buyers from all over the world. Now the piazza was quiet, there were no shops, only a few small wooden houses remained in the shadow of the undomed church of Santa Maria di Loreto. During the day people passed through on their way to the Colonna palace or the Piazza del Quirinale on the one side, or to the Anibaldi palace and San Pietro in Vincoli on the other. At night it was as silent as though he were living deep in the *campagna*.

The house had two front doors, both facing the Macello dei Corvi, for it had formerly been rented as two separate apartments. His living quarters consisted of a good-sized bedroom facing the street, behind it a dining-sitting room, and behind that, feeding out to a garden pavilion, a low-ceilinged kitchen of the same yellow brick. In the second half of the house he had taken out the wall separating its two rooms, making himself as large a workshop as he had built in Florence. He bought a new iron bed for himself, woollen covers, a new mattress stuffed with wool, sent money to Buonarroto for fine Florentine bed sheets, tablecloths and towels which he kept with his store of shirts, handkerchiefs and blouses in a wardrobe standing next to his bed. He acquired a sorrel for travelling the rough cobbled streets of the city, ate his meals at a well-set table, went abroad in warm weather in a cape of black Florentine cloth lined with satin. Silvio Falconi was proving to be a good apprentice-servant.

In the clapboard houses and stone tower at the rear of his garden were assistants helping with the tomb. Michele and Basso, two young stonemasons from Settignano; a foundling and promising draughtsman who had asked permission to call himself Andrea di Michelangelo; Federigo Frizzi and

Giovanni da Reggio, making models for the bronze frieze; Antonio from Pontassieve, who had agreed to bring his crew to Rome to shape and ornament the building blocks and columns.

He felt easy about his future. Had not Pope Leo X announced to the courtiers about him: " Buonarroti and I were educated together under my father's roof "?

For the first time since he had fled from Julius in April of 1505, eight years before, he was carving. Not one marble but three heroic columns, all at once. There was a natural rhythm between the movement of his breath and the movement of his hammer arm as he pounded the chisel across a cutting groove. This tactile joining with marble again made him swell with joy. He recalled the first lesson the Topolinos had taught him:

" Stone works for you. It yields itself to skill and to love."

He threw himself into the three blocks with passion yet with an inner calm and surety. The three white columns surrounded him in his workshop like snow-covered peaks. He desired intensely to breathe the same air his blocks did. He carved for fourteen hours a day, until his legs felt as though they were up in his body; yet he had only to leave the solid image before him, go to the door and gaze restfully into the void of sky to be refreshed.

He was ploughing a straight furrow.

Carving the Moses, mounds of white dust caked in his nostrils like tranquillity settling into the marrow of his bones; he felt a man of substance because his own three-dimensional force became fused with the three-dimensional stone. As a boy on the steps of the Duomo he had been unable to prove that sculpture was superior to painting as an art; here in his studio, moving smoothly from the Moses to the Dying Captive to the Heroic-Rebellious Captive, he could demonstrate the truth with irrefutable crystalline fact.

Moses, holding the stone tablets under one arm, would be eight feet tall and massive even though seated. Yet what he was after was not an awareness of volume but of inner weight and structure. By pushing one leg sharply backward he set into action a dynamics of balance, creating a space-famine which was nourished by the monumentality of the right knee and calf, the outward thrust compensating for the vertigo caused by the withdrawn leg. His chisel hand flew unerringly to the point of entry in the four-foot-thick block: under the sharply pointed horizontal left elbow and

corded forearm. He carved his line of flow through the
wrist to the index finger pointing to the stone tablets under
the opposite arm.

At midnight he reluctantly took off his paper cap with
its goat-tallow candle. There was no sound except the distant
barking of dogs scavenging behind the Colonna kitchens.
Moonlight splashed in through the rear garden window,
enveloping the block with a transcendent light. He pulled
up a bench and sat before the roughed-out mass, musing
about Moses as a human being, a prophet, a leader of his
people who had stood in the presence of God and been
given the Law.

The sculptor who did not have a philosophic mind created
empty forms. What point was there in his knowing precisely
where to enter the marble block if he did not know which
Moses he intended to project? The meaning of his Moses, as
much as the sculptural techniques, would determine its
value. He knew where Moses sat in space; but where did
he stand in time? Did he want to present the passionate
angry Moses, returning from Mount Sinai to find his people
worshipping the Golden Calf? Or the saddened, embittered
Moses, fearing that he had arrived too late with the Law?

As he sat drinking in the almost liquid flow of the issuing
figure he understood that he must refuse to imprison Moses
in time. He was seeking the universal Moses who knew
the ways of man and God; the Lord's servant on earth,
the voice of His conscience. The Moses who had been called
up to the heights of Mount Sinai, had hidden his face
because he dared not look upon the open sight of God,
and received from Him the carved tablets of the Ten Commandments. The fierceness of soul which would burn outward
through the cavernous depths of his eyes could not be moti-
vated by despair, or the desire to punish. What had moved
Moses was the passionate resolve that his people must not
destroy themselves, that they must receive and obey the
Commandments which God had sculptured on the stone tablets, and endure.

His reverie was interrupted when the front door was
unceremoniously thrown open by Balducci, who was advising him on the revision of the tomb contract. Pope Leo
was using his good offices to persuade the Duke of Urbino
and the other Rovere heirs to make the agreement more
equitable for Michelangelo, to allow him more time and more
money. Michelangelo glanced at his friend in amusement as
574

he filled the doorway, for Balducci, who had been exactly Michelangelo's build when they first met on the streets of Rome in 1496, was now double Michelangelo's size in everything but the extremities of head and feet.

"Do you get fat from making profits," Michelangelo teased, "or do the profits come from getting fat?"

"I have to eat for you and for myself," boomed Balducci, patting his big stomach with both palms. "You're just as much a runt as you were when you tried to play football against Doni in Piazzi Santa Croce. Have they agreed to the new terms?"

"They've raised the price to sixteen thousand, five hundred ducats. Seven years to complete, more if I should need it. . . ."

"Let me see the plans for the new tomb."

Reluctantly, Michelangelo dug a batch of papers out of a stained parchment folio. Balducci cried disapprovingly:

"You told me you were reducing the size!"

"So I have. Look here, the front side is a half less in length. I no longer have to build a walk-in chamber . . ."

Balducci had been counting on the sheets.

"How many statues are there?"

"*In toto?* Forty-one."

"What are their sizes?"

"From life size to twice normal."

"How many do you intend to carve yourself?"

"Perhaps twenty-five. All but the angels, *putti . . .*"

Even in the flickering light of the single candle Michelangelo could see Balducci's face turn purple.

"You're *pazzo!*" he cried. "All you've reduced is the structural framework which you weren't going to build anyway. It was bad enough that you didn't listen to Jacopo Galli eight years ago, but you were younger then. What conceivable excuse can you have for contracting a second time to do the impossible?"

"Julius' executors won't settle for less. Besides, I'm getting nearly the price and the time allowance Galli wanted for me."

"Michelangelo," said Balducci softly, "I can't take Jacopo Galli's place as a man of culture, but he respected my talents sufficiently to make me manager of his bank. This is stupid business. Twenty-five giant figures must take you twenty-five years. Even if you live that long, do you want to be chained to this mausoleum for the rest of your days? You'll be more of a slave than these Captives you're blocking out."

"I have a good *bottega* now. Once the new contract is signed I'll bring more stonemasons from Settignano. I have so many of these figures already carved in my mind, not to bring them to life would be a cruel waste. Watch, and you will see marble flying around here like coveys of white doves in the spring."

2

The Sistine ceiling had produced an effect equal to the unveiling of the David in Florence. From artists of every medium, who had flocked to Rome from all over Europe to help Leo celebrate his elevation to the papacy, Michelangelo had rewon the painting title first earned by the Bathers: "Master of the World." Only the group centred around Raphael continued to fight the vault, calling it anatomy rather than artistry, carnal, exaggerated, overwrought. But they were hampered now, for Bramante was no longer art emperor of Rome. Cracks of such serious dimension had shown in his piers of St. Peter's that all work had been stopped and extensive studies undertaken to see if the foundations could be saved. Pope Leo had been too kind to remove Bramante officially as architect; but work on the Belvedere above the Vatican was also in abeyance. Bramante's hands had become so crippled with palsy that he had been obliged to turn over the drawing of his plans to Antonio da Sangallo, nephew of Michelangelo's friend and architectural teacher, Giuliano da Sangallo. Over Bramante's house there now hung the slight odour of decay that had settled over Sangallo's the day Bramante won the prize for his design for St. Peter's.

One dusk Michelangelo answered a knock on his door, impatient with any intrusion. He found himself gazing into the amiable hazel eyes of a young man in an orange silk cloak, with a fair complexion and blond hair that brought Granacci to his mind.

"Master Buonarroti, I am Sebastiano Luciani of Venice. I have come to confess . . ."

"I am not a priest."

". . . that I have been a simpleton and idiot. This knock, these words, are the first time my hand or tongue have made sense I arrived in Rome. I brought my lute so that I could accompany myself while I tell you my bathetic story."

Amused by the Venetian's infectiously light manner, Michelangelo bowed him in. Sebastiano perched on the highest stool in the room and ran his fingers across the strings of the lute.

"Sing and everything passes," he murmured.

Michelangelo dropped into the one padded chair in the workroom, sat with his legs stretched out stiffly before him, hands behind his head. Sebastiano sang a scanned improvisation of how he had been brought to Rome by the banker Chigi to paint his villa, had joined in the idolizing of Raphael by proclaiming that Raphael's brush was "in attune with the techniques of painting, pleasing in colour, ingenious in invention, charming in all its expressions and designed like an angel." Buonarroti? "Admittedly he can draw, but his colourings? Monotonous! His figures? Bumpy anatomy. His scenes? Without grace . . ."

"I have heard these charges before," interrupted Michelangelo. "They weary me."

"As well they might! But Rome shall hear this dirge no more from me. From now on I sing the praises of Master Buonarroti."

"What has brought this change of heart?"

"The eclectic Raphael! He has picked my bones. Absorbed all I learned from Bellini and Giorgione, so that now he is a better Venetian painter than I! And so humbly thanking me for teaching him!"

"Raphael borrows only from the best. He does it well. Why are you abandoning him?"

"Now that he has become a magic Venetian colourist he is getting more commissions than ever. While I . . . I get nothing. Raphael has swallowed me, all except my eyes, which have been feasting on your Sistine ceiling these past days."

Sebastiano lowered his head over his lute, heels locked in the top rung of the stool. His voice filled the room with a robust gondolier's song. Michelangelo studied the Venetian before him, wondering why he had really come.

Sebastiano dropped in often for music and talk. An inveterate pursuer of pleasure and pretty girls, he needed money for the hunt. He was living on portraits while longing for one of the big commissions that brought a steady income. His draughtsmanship was weak, he had no sense of invention. But he was loquacious, full of fun, refusing to be serious even about the illegitimate son who had just been born to him. Michelangelo continued to work while half listening to the amusing chatter.

"My dear *compare*," said Sebastiano, "don't you get mixed up, carving three blocks all at once? How do you remember what you want to do with each of them when you move from figure to figure?"

Michelangelo chuckled. "I wish I could have all twenty-five blocks standing around in a great circle. I would move from one to the other so fast that in five years I'd have all of them completed. Have you any concept of how thoroughly you can hollow out blocks of marble by thinking about them for eight years? Ideas are sharper than chisels."

"I could be a great painter," said Sebastiano in a flat tone. "I have all the techniques. Put a painting in front of me, and I'll copy it so exactly you'll never recognize it from the original. But how do you get the idea in the first place?"

It was a wail, almost of anguish, one of the few times Michelangelo had seen Sebastiano serious. He ruminated while chiselling out the two Tablets of the Law.

"Perhaps ideas are a natural function of the mind, as breathing is of the lungs? Perhaps God puts them there? If I knew the origin of men's ideas, I would have solved one of our deepest mysteries."

He moved upward to Moses' wrist and hand resting on top of the tablets, the fingers leading into the long-flowing, waist-length beard.

"Sebastiano, I'm going to make some drawings for you. Your use of colour and shadow is as fine as Raphael's, your figures are lyrical. Since he has borrowed your Venetian palette, why should you not borrow my designs? Let's see if we can't supplant Raphael."

He enjoyed sketching at night after a full day of carving, thinking up new variations on old religious themes. He introduced Sebastiano to Pope Leo, showed the pontiff scenes from the life of Christ beautifully transformed by Sebastiano. Leo, who cherished all musical entertainers, made him welcome at the Vatican.

Late one night Sebastiano burst in crying, "Have you heard the news? A new rival to Raphael has arisen! The best of the Venetians, equal to Bellini and Giorgione. Paints with the charm and grace of Raphael! But is a stronger, more imaginative draughtsman."

"Congratulations!" said Michelangelo with a wry grin.

When Sebastiano was given the fresco commission for San

Pietro in Montorio, he worked hard to bring Michelangelo's designs to glowing life in his cartoons. Rome assumed that, as part of Michelangelo's *bottega,* Sebastiano was learning to draw with his master's hand.

Only Contessina, newly arived in Rome with her family, thought there was something more involved. She had spent two years of evenings sitting by Michelangelo's side watching him draw; she knew his calligraphy. When he attended her elaborate dinner for the Pope and his court, for Contessina was determined to become Leo's official hostess, she took him into a small study that was so faithful a replica of Lorenzo's *studiolo* with its wood panelling and fireplace, cases of cameos and amulets that it brought nostalgic tears to his eyes. She gazed at him head on, her dark eyes flashing, demanded:

" Why do you allow Sebastiano to parade your work as his?"

" It does no harm."

" Raphael has already lost an important commission to Sebastiano."

" It's a godsend to the overworked, harried man."

" Why should you stoop to a hoax like this?"

He returned her gaze, thinking how much she was still the Contessina, Little Countess, of their youth; but at the same time how greatly she had changed since the election of her brother to the papacy. Now she was the Big Countess, brooking no interference from her two elder sisters Lucrezia Salviati and Maddalena Cibo, who had also moved their families to Rome. Contessina fought for papal appointments, benefices for the members of the Ridolfi family, working hand in glove with Cousin Giulio, who was in control of the business and politics of the Vatican. In her spacious gardens she had a stage built on which were performed plays and musicals for the nobility of the Church and city-states. More and more the laity of the Christian world wanting favours and appointments were coming to Contessina. This grasping for power and the wielding of it was understandable, Michelangelo thought, after the years of exile and poverty; but it had made a change in Contessina which left him uncomfortable.

" Since I finished the Sistine," explained Michelangelo, " certain people have been saying, ' Raphael has grace, Michelangelo has only stamina.' And since I will not stoop to fight the Raphael clique for my position, I find it amusing to have a talented young painter do it for me. Without getting myself involved, Rome is beginning to say, 'Raphael has charm, but Michelangelo has profundity.' Isn't it amusing that fun-loving Sebastiano could have accomplished this transition by improvising verses of praise to my vault, accompanying himself on the lute?"

Contessina clenched her fists at the irony in his voice.

"It is not amusing! I am the Countess of Rome to-day. I can protect you . . . officialy . . . with dignity. I can bring your detractors to their knees. That is the way. . . ."

He reached forward, took her two tightly clenched fists between his stone hewer's hands.

"No, Contessina, it is not the way. Trust me. I am happy now, and working well."

In place of the anger came the lightning-like, radiant smile he remembered from their childhood clashes.

"Very well, but if you do not come to my parties I shall expose you and Sebastiano as a couple of humbugs."

He laughed.

"Who ever got the better of a Medici?"

Without thinking he placed his hands on the puffed shoulders of her silk gown, drew her close, searching for the fragrance of mimosa. She started to tremble. Her eyes grew enormous. Time dissolved: the *studiolo* in the Via Ripetta in Rome became the *studiolo* in the Medici palace in Florence. They were not the great countess and the great artist, with half of their years already gone; but for a fleeting instant, at the threshold of life.

3

Swiss guards in green, white and yellow arrived at his house early in the morning with what amounted to a *breve* from Pope Leo to dine at the Vatican palace that day. It was a hardship to walk away from his work, but he had learned that one did not ignore the summons of a Pope. Silvio laid fresh linens over his arm, Michelangelo went to the baths of the Via de' Pastini, soaked the caked dust out of his pores, and arrived at the Vatican at eleven.

He began to realize why the Romans were complaining that "Rome has sunk to a Florentine colony," for the Vatican was filled with triumphant Tuscans. Moving through the throng of more than a hundred dinner guests assembled in the two throne rooms, he recognized Pietro Bembo, the Vatican Secretary of State and humanist-poet; the poet Ariosto, who was writing his *Orlando Furioso;* the neo-Latinist Sannazaro; Guicciardini, the historian; Vida, author of the *Christiad*; Giovanni Rucellai, writing one of the first blank-verse tragedies, *Rosmunda*; Fracastoro, physician-author; Tommaso Inghirami, diplomat, librarian, classicist and improviser of Latin verses; Raphael, now painting the Stanza d'Eliodoro in the Papal palace, and occupying a place of honour just below Pope Leo; the woodcarver Giovanni Barile of Siena, who was decorating the doors and shutters of the palace with Medici emblems Michelangelo spied Sebastiano and was pleased that his protégé had been invited.

Having bought back from the Republic of Florence most of his father's great library, Leo had experts searching the world for important manuscripts. He had also brought to Rome Lascaris, his father's Greek manuscript hunter, to edit and print the jewels of Greek literature. The Pope was also in process of reorganizing the Roman Academy for classical studies, which had been neglected by Julius, and was giving new hope of learning to the University of Rome. Michelangelo heard this new court of Leo's described as " the most brilliant and cultured since Imperial Rome."

Throughout the long sumptuous dinner, of which the Pope could eat little because he suffered from bad digestion and gaseous disturbances, Leo waved his white, bejewelled, plump hands while he accompanied Gabriel Marin of the remarkably beautiful voice, the master violinist Marone of Brescia, and Raffaelle Lippus, the blind balladier. Between the musical performances buffoons kept Leo amused. His court jester, *Il Magnifico's* former barber, had a fund of anatomical witticisms which he unleashed between bouts of eating forty eggs in a row, and then twenty capons, while nearsighted Leo gazed at him through his magnifying glass, emitting peals of laughter at the gargantuan gorging.

The four-hour dinner seemed endless to Michelangelo. He was incapable of absorbing but the most modest amount of salted trout, roast capon, sweet rice cooked in milk of almonds. He writhed in his seat over the many wasted hours, wondering how soon he would be released. For Pope Leo the dinner was but a preliminary to an afternoon and night of pleasure. Now came some of Italy's finest poets to read their new verses, then a ballet, then a masque, then another buffoonery at the expense of Camillo Querno, called the Arch-Poet, who read from an atrocious epic poem while Leo crowned him with cabbage leaves. The entertainments would continue until Leo could no longer keep his eyes open.

Walking home through the dark and deserted streets, Michelangelo recalled Leo's line to Giulio immediately after his coronation:

" Since God has seen fit to give us the papacy, let us enjoy it."

Italy was more peaceful than it had been for a number of pontificates. True, money was pouring out of the Vatican at an unprecedented rate; several times that day Michelangelo had seen the delighted Leo fling purses containing several hundred florins to singers and performers, which had caused one of his sober neighbours to comment:

" The Pope could no more save a thousand ducats than a stone could fly up into the sky."

Leo was going to need money: millions upon millions of ducats, an even more incredible fortune for the pleasures and the arts than Julius had needed for war. When he begged Cardinal Pucci, in charge of the Vatican's resources, to be sure that nothing was done that would bring dishonour on the Church, no simony, no sale of cardinalates or benefices, the cardinal shrugged and said:

" Holy Father, you have assigned to me the task of financing this world-wide business. My first obligation is to keep it solvent."

Michelangelo reached the Macello dei Corvi as the midnight chimes rang out. He changed into his work clothes, so thick with the accumulation of stone dust and impregnation of sweat from the hot summer sun they had become an extra layer of his own skin. With a sigh of relief he picked up hammer and chisel, juggled them in both hands to feel their accustomed weight. He determined grimly that this was the last time he would be persuaded to waste an entire day. His sympathies went to pale, puffy-faced Raphael, who was summoned at all hours of the night and day for the most trivial of the Pope's errands, to give an opinion of an illuminated manuscript or design a wall decoratation for Leo's new bath chamber. Raphael was always polite, interested, though forced to waste his work hours and to go without sleep.

This was not for him. He was not a charming man. He would be eternally damned if he ever became one!

He could lock out Rome, but the world of Italy was now the world of the Medici, and he was too closely allied to the family to escape. Defeat overcame Giuliano, the only one of *Il Magnifico's* sons he loved. Letters from the family and Granacci told of how magnificently Giuliano was governing Florence: abstemious, gentle, warmhearted, walking the streets unaccompanied, opening the Medici palace to scholar and artist, reviving the Plato Academy, leaving the administration of government and justice in the hands of the elected councils. But these qualities did not appeal to Cousin Giulio or to Pope Leo. Leo recalled his brother from Florence, and now in September Michelangelo was dressing to go to the ceremony in which Giuliano was to be made a Baron of Rome.

The ceremony took place on the ancient Capitoline, just above Michelangelo's house. He sat with the Medici family: Contessina and Ridolfi with their three sons, Niccolò now twelve, and to be named a cardinal on achieving sixteen; the older sisters, Maddalena Cibo, with her husband and five children, including Innocenzo, also to be made a cardinal, and Lucrezia Salviati with her numerous family, and her son Giovanni, in line for a cardinalate. Leo had had a stage built over the ruins where Sangallo had taken Michelangelo sketching to re-create the glories of ancient Rome. The jagged earthen piazza had been covered by a wooden floor and hundred of seats. Michelangelo listened to speeches of welcome to Giuliano from the heads of the Roman Senate, epic poems in Latin, a series of masques and satires in the Florentine tradition, watched as a woman wrapped in cloth of gold, personifying Rome, was carried to Giuliano's throne to thank him for condescending to become commander of the city. After a bawdy comedy by Plautus, Pope Leo bestowed privileges on Rome such as a reduction of the salt tax, to the thunderous applause of thousands of Romans thronging the bare hillsides. Then began a six-hour banquet with a profusion of dishes not seen in Rome since the days of Caligula and Nero.

At the end of the orgy Michelangelo made his way down the Capitoline through the throng that was being fed from the leftovers of the Saturnalia above, and locked both street doors of his house behind him. Neither he nor Giuliano nor Rome had been fooled by this performance, which was designed to conceal the fact that scholarly Giuliano, who loved the Republic of Florence, had been replaced by Lorenzo, twenty-one-year-old son of Piero and the ambitious Alfonsina. Young Lorenzo had been sent to Tuscany with a letter of instructions formulated by Giulio telling him how to control elections, appoint his own Council, absorb the functions of government.

Giulio's power as the figure behind the Pope was growing. A commission appointed by Leo had declared Giulio of legitimate birth, on the grounds that *Il Magnifico's* brother had agreed to marry Giulio's mother, and that only his murder in the cathedral had kept the marriage from taking place. Now that he was legitimate, Giulio was appointed a cardinal; he would have the official power to rule the Church and the Papal States.

Nor was Leo's and Giulio's desire to extend the Medici control throughout Italy remote from Michelangelo's affairs. They had been trying to drive the Duke of Urbino, a Rovere nephew and heir of Pope Julius, out of his dukedom. To-day Pope Leo had deposed the duke as standard-bearer of the Church, in favour of Giuliano. Ultimately Leo would seize his lands. The Duke of Urbino, a violent man, was the one to whom Michelangelo would be responsible for Julius' tomb. The war that had been brought into the open between the Medici and the Roveres could mean nothing but trouble for the Buonarroti.

Over the mild winter he secured a reprieve from Contessina's reception by bringing her to the workshop to see his three emerging figures; and from Leo's entertainments by a series of excuses which amused Leo sufficiently to grant him the high favour of abstinence. His only associates during the long productive work weeks were his assistants in the garden, his solitary diversion an occasional supper with a group of amiable young Florentines whose friendship was based on a nostalgic longing to be within sight of the Duomo.

Only once did he break his fast: when Giuliano came to the studio to urge him to attend a reception for Leonardo da Vinci, whom Giuliano had invited to Rome and installed in the Belvedere.

"You, Leonardo and Raphael are the great masters of Italy to-day," said Giuliano in his quiet way. "I should like the three of you to be friends, perhaps work together. . . ."

"I'll come to your reception, Giuliano, of course," said Michelangelo. "But as for working together . . . We are as different species as are birds, fish and fowl."

"Strange," murmured Giuliano, "I should have thought that all artists would be brothers. Come early. I'd like to show you some of the experiments in alchemy Leonardo is conducting for me."

Entering the Belvedere the next day, Giuliano took him through a series of workrooms extensively renovated for Leonardo's purposes: windows made taller to give higher light, the kitchen built to take care of boiling alchemy pots, a paved terrace overlooking the valley, Papal palace and Sistine, furniture built by the Vatican carpenters, trestle tables, stands for mixing paints. Giuliano had persuaded Pope Leo to give Leonardo a painting commission, but as Michelangelo was led through the workshops, including that of a German ironmonger who was to help Leonardo with his mechanical inventions, he saw that Leonardo had not yet begun to work at his art.

"Look at these concave mirrors," exclaimed Giuliano, "this metal screw-cutting machine, all new. When I took him out on the Pontine marshes he located several extinct volcanoes, and sketched plans for draining the fever-laden area. He won't let anyone see his notebooks, but I suspect he's completing his mathematical studies for the squaring of curved surfaces. His work on optics, his formulations of the laws of botany—amazing! Leonardo feels he will be able to tell the age of trees by counting the rings on the trunk. Imagine!"

"I would rather imagine him painting beautiful frescoes."

Giuliano led him back towards the drawing-room.

"Leonardo is a universal man. Has there been such a scientific mind since Aristotle? I think not. Art he conceives as only one aspect of human creativity."

"It is beyond my comprehension," growled Michelangelo stubbornly. "When a man has such a rare gift he should not spend his days counting the rings on trees."

Leonardo emerged, followed by his lifetime companion, the still exquisite and youthful Salai, dressed in an elaborate red blouse with lacy sleeves. Leonardo himself, Michelangelo thought, looked tired and old, his magnificent flowing beard and shoulder-length hair now white. The two men, who understood each other not at all, exchanged expressions of pleasure at the reunion. Leonardo in his high-pitched voice told Michelangelo of the time he had spent studying the Sistine ceiling.

"After analysing your work I have written corrections to my treatise on painting. You have proved that the study of anatomy is extremely important and useful to the artist." His voice became impersonal. "But I also see a grave danger there."

Nettled, Michelangelo asked. "Of what kind?"

"Of exaggeration. The painter, after he studies your vault, must take care not to become wooden through too strong an emphasis on bone, muscles and sinews; nor to become too enamoured of naked figures which display all their feelings."

"And you think that mine do?" Michelangelo's gorge was rising.

"On the contrary, yours are close to perfection. But what of the painter who tries to go beyond you? If your use of anatomy makes the Sistine so good, then he must use even more anatomy in order to be better."

"I cannot hold myself responsible for later exaggerations."

"Nor are you, except that you have brought anatomical painting to its outside limits. There is no margin for others to perfect. Consequently, they will distort. Observers will say, 'It is Michelangelo's fault; without him we could have refined and improved anatomical painting for hundreds of years.' Alas, you have started it, and you have ended it, on one ceiling."

Other guests began to arrive. Soon there was a hubbub in the rooms. Michelangelo stood alone at a side window overlooking the Sistine, not knowing whether he was perplexed or hurt. Leonardo was astonishing the guests with new contrivances: animals filled with air which sailed over everyone's head; a live lizard to which he had attached wings filled with quicksilver, and whose head he had decorated with artificial eyes, horns and a beard.

"The mechanical lion I made in Milan could walk several steps," he announced to the guests who were congratulating him on his inventiveness. "And when you pressed a button his breast fell open, exposing a bunch of lilies."

To himself Michelangelo muttered, "*Questo è il colmo!* This is the limit!" and rushed home, trembling to get the substantive feel of marble between his hands.

4

In the spring Bramante died. Pope Leo ordered an elaborate funeral for him at which artists spoke of the beauty of his Tempietto, the Cortile of the Belvedere, the Castellesi palace. Pope Leo then sent for Giuliano da Sangallo, his father's favourite architect. Sangallo arrived: his former palace on the Via Alessandrina was returned to him. Michelangelo was there within a matter of minutes to embrace his old friend.

" We meet again! " cried Sangallo, joy shining in his eyes. " I survived dismissal, you the years in the Sistine vault." He paused, knit his brows. " But I found a strange communication from Pope Leo. He asks if I mind making Raphael my assistant at St. Peter's. Is Raphael an architect?"

Michelangelo felt an involuntary twinge. Raphael!

" He has been directing the repairs at St. Peter's, and is seen on the scaffolding at all hours."

" But it is you who should take over my work. After all, I am nearly seventy."

" Thank you, *caro;* let Raphael help you. It gives me freedom with the marbles."

Pope Leo borrowed heavily from the Florentine bankers Gaddi, Strozzi and Ricasoli for the continuation of St. Peter's. Sangallo resumed the building.

Michelangelo allowed few visitors to his studio: former Gonfaloniere Soderini and his wife, Monna Argentina, who had been forgiven by Pope Leo and permitted to live in Rome; three men who offered him his first private commission since Taddeo Taddei had requested the circular Our Lady. Metello Vari dei Porcari, a Roman of ancient blood, and Bernardo Cencio, a canon of St. Peter's, said:

" We would like you to do a Risen Christ for us. For the church of Santa Maria sopra Minerva."

" I am pleased to have the request," declared Michelangelo ; " but I must tell you that my contract with Pope Julius' executors does not permit me to take commissions. . . ."

" This would be a single piece, sculptured at your leisure," exclaimed Mario Scappucci.

" A Christ Risen?" Michelangelo was intrigued by the idea. " Beyond the Crucifixion? How do you envisage the piece?"

"Life size. With a cross in his arms. In an attitude that will be determined by you."

"Could I think about it?"

He had long felt that most Crucifixions did a grave injustice to Jesus, portraying him as crushed and defeated by the weight of the cross. He had never believed that for a single instant: his Christ was a powerful male who had carried the cross on the road to Calvary as though it were the branch of an olive tree. He began to draw. The cross became but a puny thing in Jesus' grasp. Since his commissioners had reversed tradition by asking for a cross after the Resurrection, why could he too not depart from the accepted concept? Instead of the cross crushing Christ, Jesus would stand triumphant. The first rough sketches crosshatched, he gazed intently at his drawing. Where had he seen this Christ before? Then he remembered: it was the figure of a stonemason he had drawn for Ghirlandaio in the first year of his apprenticeship.

Though he managed to keep the peace in Rome, his family in Florence kept his cup of anxiety overflowing. Exhausted by Buonarroto's badgering for money to open his own wool shop, Michelangelo took a thousand ducats from the funds provided by his new Rovere contract and had Balducci send them to Florence. Buonarroto and Giovanisimone opened their shop, promptly running into trouble. They needed more capital. Couldn't Michelangelo send them another thousand? He would soon be earning a profit on his money. . . . In the meanwhile, Buonarroto had found a girl he would not mind marrying, her father having promised a sizeable dowry. Did Michelangelo think he should marry her?

He sent Buonarroto two hundred ducats, which Buonarroto never acknowledged. What had happened to them? For that matter what had happened to the money Lodovico took from Michelangelo's account and had promised to return? What about his funds on deposit at Santa Maria Nuova hospital; why did the *spedalingo* delay in paying out the money as Michelangelo demanded? What was the good of owning five farms if the share tenants were stealing him blind?

A severe blow was word from Buonarroto that Mother Topolino had died. He put aside his work and walked to San Lorenzo in Damaso to say a prayer for the repose of her soul. He sent money to Buonarroto with instructions to ride up to the church in Settignano and have the priest say a mass for her there.

He locked the gates of his mind, as he had locked the gates of the garden. Working the marble was not only a delight, it was a consolation. How rarely a good piece of marble went bad! He spent the ducats advanced to him by the Roveres, hiring additional crews of master carvers, bronze casters, carpenters, all crowding his yard from dawn to dark, building the architectural base and the front façade while he sketched steadily to complete the drawings for the remaining sculptures, turning the Settignano *pietra serena* masons into marble *scultori* who could mass a dozen giant blocks so that he could get to the carving of the Victories.

The months passed. His apprentices brought him the local gossip. Leonardo da Vinci had fallen into serious trouble, spending so much time experimenting with new oils and varnishes for preserving the work that he failed to do any painting on Leo's commission. The Pope had cried mockingly at court:

"Leonardo will never do anything, for he commences by thinking about the end before the beginning of the work."

The courtiers spread the jest. Leonardo, learning that he had become an object of ridicule, abandoned Leo's commission. The Pope heard through informers that Leonardo was dissecting in the hospital of Santo Spirito, and threatened to drive him out of Rome. Leonardo, fleeing the Belvedere to continue his studies in the marshes, came down with malaria. When he recovered he found that his ironmonger had destroyed his mechanical experiments. When his protector, Giuliano, left at the head of the papal troops to drive the invading French out of Lombardy, Leonardo could no longer remain in Rome. Where to go? France, perhaps. He had been invited there years before. . . .

Sangallo too was stricken, with such a severe case of gall-stones that he could do no work at all. For weeks he was bedridden, his eyeballs becoming mustard yellow, his strength ebbing. He was carried back to Florence on a litter. His repatriation had come too late.

Raphael became the architect of St. Peter's, and of Rome.

Michelangelo received an urgent note from Contessina. He hurried to her palace, was received by her son Niccolò, taken upstairs to her bedroom. Though the weather was warm, Contessina was covered by several quilts, her pale face lying exhausted on the pillows, her eyes cavernous.

"Contessina, you are ill."

Contessina beckoned him to her bed, patted a place for him to sit. He took her hand, white and fragile, in his own. She closed her eyes. When she opened them again there were tears moistening the warm brown pupils.

"Michelangelo, I remember the first time we met. In the scupture garden. I asked, 'Why do you work so furiously? Doesn't it exhaust you?' "

"And I answered, 'Cutting stone does not take strength out of you, it puts it back in.' "

"Everyone thought I was soon to die, as my mother and sister had. . . . You put strength in me, *caro*."

"You said, 'When I am near you, I feel strong.' "

"And you answered, 'When I am near you, I feel confused.' " She smiled. "Giovanni said you frightened him. You never frightened me. I saw how tender you were, under the surface."

They stared at each other. Contessina whispered:

"We have never spoken of our feelings."

He ran his fingers gently over her cheek.

"I loved you, Contessina."

"I loved you, Michelangelo. I have always felt your presence in the world."

Her eyes lit for a brief instant.

"My sons will be your friends. . . ."

She was seized with a coughing spell that shook the big bed. As she turned her head away from him, raised a handkerchief to her lips, he saw the red stain. His mind flashed back to Jacopo Galli. This would be the last time he would see Contessina.

He waited, gulping the salt of unshed tears. She refused to turn her head back to him.

He whispered, "*Addio, mia cara,*" wheeled silently, left the room.

The death of Contessina shook him deeply. He concentrated on the head of the Moses, striving to bring it to a state of completion: upward through the beard to the intense, full lower lip, the mouth so expressive that a sound might emerge at any moment; to the sharply protruding nose, the passionate outburst of expression in the forehead, the creased muscles about the cheekbone, and finally, to the eyes set deeply in the head creating dark accents to contrast with the highlights he would file on to the bone and flesh structure of the face.

Then he turned to the exquisitely sensitive, agonized figures of the two Captives, one resisting death, one yielding, pouring into their flesh his own grief and sense of loss. He had known that there could never be a life together for Contessina and himself. But he too had always been aware of her presence, had been nourished and gladdened by it.

Laying aside his hammer and chisel, he made models for the bronze frieze, bought twenty thousand pounds of brass, summoned additional stonecutters from Settignano, speeded up the work of the Pontassieve crew in squaring and decorating the structural stones, wrote a barrage of letters to Florence to locate a marble expert who could go to Carrara and buy him more blocks. He had all the ingredients for a sustained drive to complete in another year the all-important front wall, the Moses and Captives mounted in place, Victories installed in the niches, the bronze frieze set above the first floor. He would work like a man possessed; but since he was to be possessed by marble, it seemed good and natural.

Pope Leo had been determined to reign without war, but that did not mean he could avoid the incessant attempts on the part of his neighbours to conquer the rich country; nor the internecine strife which had been the city-states' history. Giuliano had not been able to subdue the French in Lombardy. He had been taken ill in the attempt, and moved to the monastery of the Badia at Fiesole where, it was rumoured, he was dying, even as had Contessina. . . . The Duke of Urbino had not only refused to help the papal army but had become an ally of the French. Pope Leo himself rushed north to make a treaty with the French, which left him free to attack the Duke of Urbino.

Immediately on his return to Rome he summoned Michelangelo to the Vatican. Leo had been kind to the Buonarroti family while in Florence, naming them counts palatine, a high honour on the road to nobility, and granting them the right to display the Medici crest of six balls.

Leo, sitting at a table in his library with Giulio, was examining through his spyglass a number of gems and carved cameos he had brought back from Florence. His travels seemed to have done him good, for he had lost some of his flatulence, there was colour in his usually chalk-white cheeks.

"Holy Father, you were most generous to my family."

"Not at all," said Leo. "It is many years now that you have been of our house."

"I am grateful, Holiness."

"Good," said Leo, laying aside the spyglass. Giulio also came to attention. "Because we do not want you, a Medici sculptor, spending your time creating statues for a Rovere."

"But the contract! I am obliged . . ."

A silence fell. Leo and Giulio looked at each other for an instant.

"We have decided to present you with the greatest art commission of our age," cried the Pope. "We wish you to undertake a façade for our family church, San Lorenzo . . . as my father thought of it . . . a glorious façade . . ."

Michelangelo stood staring sightlessly out the window, over the chaotic jumble of tawny rooftops. He heard the Pope speaking behind him though he could not discern the words. He forced himself back to the table.

"But, Holy Father, the tomb for Pope Julius! You recall the contract signed only three years ago. I must finish what I have contracted for, or the Roveres will prosecute me."

"Enough time has been given to the Roveres." Giulio's manner was abrupt. "The Duke of Urbino made a treaty to help the French against us. He was partly responsible for the loss of Milan."

"I'm sorry. I did not know. . . ."

"Now you do!" Cardinal Giulio's dark, sharp-featured face became less grim. "A Medici artist should serve the Medici."

"And so it shall be," replied Michelangelo, also relaxing. "Within two years the tomb will be complete. I have everything organized . . ."

"No!" Leo's round face was flushed with anger, a rare and frightening sight. "There will be no two years for the Roveres. You will enter our service at once."

His manner quietened.

"Now Michelangelo. We are your friends. We will protect you against the Roveres, secure a new contract which will give you more time and money. When you have completed the façade for San Lorenzo you can return to Julius' mausoleum. . . ."

"Holy Father, I have lived with this tomb for ten long years. I have every inch of its twenty-five figures carved in my mind. We are ready to construct the front wall, cast the bronzes, mount my three big statues . . ." His voice had been rising; he was shouting now. " You must not stop me. It is a crucial moment for me. I have trained workmen. If I have to dismiss the men, leave the marbles lying about . . . Holiness, on the love I bore your noble father, I implore you not to do this terrible thing to me. . . ."

He dropped on one knee before the Pope, bowed his head.

" Give me time to finish the work that is planned. Then I can move to Florence and to the façade in peace and happiness. I will create a great façade for San Lorenzo, but I must not be tormented in mind and spirit. . . ."

His only answer was a crosshatched silence in which Leo and Giulio, from a lifetime of communication, were expressing to each other by the look in their eyes what they thought of this difficult artist bowed before them.

" Michelangelo," said Pope Leo, shaking his head, " you still take everything so . . . so . . . desperately."

" Or is it," asked Giulio, " that you do not wish to create the San Lorenzo façade for the Medici?"

" I do, Your Grace. But it is a huge undertaking. . . ."

" You are right!" cried Leo. " You must leave for Carrara at once, choose the blocks yourself, supervise the cutting. I will have Jacopo Salviati in Florence send you a thousand florins to pay for them."

Michelangelo kissed the Pope's ring, left Leo's presence, descended the steps of the Vatican palace with the tears streaming down his face. Courtiers, prelates, ambassadors, merchants, entertainers thronging up the stairs to begin their day of merriment, gazed at him in amazement. He did not know that they saw, nor did he care.

That night, lonely, miserable, he found himself walking in the quarter where Balducci had searched among the prostitutes. Coming towards him was a young girl, slender, her blonde hair plucked back to give her a high brow, dressed in a semi-transparent blouse, a string of heavy baubles about her neck causing a deep declivity between her breasts. For a startling instant he thought he caught an image of Clarissa. It passed quickly, for the girl's features were coarse, her movements angular; but even this fleeting memory of Clarissa had been sufficient to awaken his longing.

" *Buona sera. Vuoi venire con me?*"

" I don't know."

" *Sembri triste.*"

593

" I am. Can you cure that malady?"
" *E mio mestiere.*"
" I will come."
" *Non te ne pentirai.*"
But he did, within forty-eight hours. Balducci listened to the
description of his symptoms, cried:
" You've caught the French sickness. Why didn't you tell
me you wanted a girl?"
" I didn't know I wanted one. . . ."
" Idiot! There's an epidemic in Rome. Let me summon my
doctor."
" I contracted this by myself. I'll cure it by myself."
" Not without mercury ointment and sulphur baths, you
won't. It sounds like a light case, you might be able to cure
it quickly."
" I have to, Balducci. Carrara is a rough life."

5

The Apuan Alps loomed like a dark wall beyond his window.
He slipped into his shirt, stockings and hobnail boots for
the climb, left his apartment at the rear of the apothecary
Pelliccia's house, went down the courtyard steps and into
the Piazza del Duomo where an agent and quarry owner
slipped past him in the darkness, the shawls over their shoulders tide at the waist. On the wooden bridge over the
piazza two priests crossed from the sacristy to the choir
loft of the cathedral for early mass. Carrara was asleep inside
its horseshoe-shaped walls, the semicircle of stone closed
towards the sea, open on the steep mountain side. He had
not wanted to leave Rome, but being at the heart of his
source material assuaged the pain.
Tucking his dinner of bread under one arm, he walked up
a narrow street to the Porta del Bozzo, remembering the
proud line of the inhabitants that " Carrara is the only
town in the world that can afford to cobble its squares
with marble." In the ash-grey light he saw the marble houses
with their delicate marble window frames and columns, for
everything that Florence did so superbly with its *pietra
serena* the master masons of Carrara did with their marble
from the quarries in the mountains above.
Michelangelo liked the Carrarini. He felt at home with

them because he was a stone man himself; yet there could be no question but that they were the most inbred, suspicious, insular group he had encountered. They refused to be identified with the Tuscans to their south or with the Ligurians to their north; few left this mountain area, none married outside it; the boys were in the quarries alongside their fathers by the time they were six, and left only at their death. No farmers were permitted to bring their produce to the Carrara markets except those who had been admitted within the walls for generations; when a quarry needed a new man he was selected from the known farming families. Carrara and Massa, the largest of the neighbouring towns, had fought each other since time before memory. Even the tiny surrounding villages were raised in the tradition of *companilismo,* each group for his own tower or town, and against everyone else.

Carrara was a one-crop town: marble. Each day the Carrarino lifted his eyes to the reassuring white slashes in the hills, the patches that resembled snow even in the blinding heat of summer, and thanked God for its sustenance. Their life was communal: when one prospered, all prospered; when one starved, all starved. Their life in the quarries was so dangerous that when they parted from each other they did not say, "Good-bye" but "*Fa a modr,* go carefully."

He wound along the Carrione River. The September air was sharp, good for climbing. Below him he could see the fortress-tower of the Rocca Malaspina and the cathedral spire standing guard over the elbow-to-elbow houses wedged into tight walls that had not been expanded for centuries. Soon the mountain villages began to appear, Codena, Miseglia, Bedizzano, each cluster pouring out its male population, feeding rivulets of quarriers into the human stream flowing upward. These were men more like him than his own brothers: small, wiry, tireless, taciturn, with the primordial power of men who work stubborn stone. They pushed upward, *matalò* or jacket hung on their right shoulder, through Torano, Station of the Bulls.

Sleep had their tongues. As first light sifted beyond the peaks they began speaking in clipped monosyllabic hammer strokes, the compact Carrarino language Michelangelo had had to learn, for the Carrarino dialect broke off words the way chips were chiselled off a block, *casa* becoming *ca*; *mama* becoming *ma*; *brasa,* embers, becoming *bra*; *bucarol,* canvas, becoming *buc*; a swift efficient language of one-syllable words. They were asking him about yesterday's search through the quarries of Grotta Colombara and Ronco.

"You find?"

"Not yet."

"Comes to-day."

"I hope."

"Go to Ravaccione."

"Heard news?"

"Break out new block."

"I try."

Pale yellow sunlight silhouetted the rugged cliffs ahead. The milky ravines of marble chips, dumped for centuries from the *poggio*, or work level below the quarry, emerged like winter drifts of snow. They were up a thousand feet now, moving effortlessly through primeval stands of oak, beech, fir, thorny bushes called *bacon* and then higher up, through a grass for grazing sheep in the summer, called *paleri*. Beyond the trees and San Pellegrino flowers, the trails cut across exposed rock with marble cropping to the surface.

The stream of two hundred quarriers, fathers and sons, split into rivulets again, making their way up the three main canals or marble draws, each of which had its favoured diggings: the Ravaccione, which included the Polvaccio quarry, the Canale di Fantiscritti, which the ancient Romans had opened; and the Canale di Colonnata. As they parted, each murmured:

"*Fa a modr.*"

"*Se Dio 'l vorà.*"

Michelangelo continued with a group on to the Polvaccio where he had found his best marble for Julius' tomb eleven years before. The Polvaccio, at the extreme end of the Poggio Silvestro, produced good statuary white, but the surrounding quarries of Battaglino, Grotta Colombara and Ronco contained ordinary marbles with slanting veins. As the sun edged over Monte Sagro they reached the nearly mile-high *poggio* where the crew dropped their jackets and were at work as swiftly as they could raise a hammer. The *tecchiaioli,* steeplejacks of the quarries, descended their ropes from the precipices above, cleaning the ledges of loose stone, clearing away with their *subbie* and *mazzuoli* as they dangled several hundred feet in the air, to protect those working below from falling debris.

The owner of the quarry, called The Barrel from his enormous round torso, greeted Michelangelo heartily. Though he was as illiterate as his workmen, his contract with buyers from England, France, Germany and Spain had taught him to speak a near-full sentence.

"Ah, Buonarroti, to-day we have your great block."

"Permit me to hope."

The Barrel grasped him by the arm, led him to the area where water-soaked wooden pegs had been driven into a V-shaped incision and, in the natural course of swelling, had forced an opening in the solid marble cliff which the quarriers were now attacking with levers and sledge hammers, driving the pegs deeper to dislodge the marble from its bed. Since marble was quarried vertically, the topmost blocks were being pried out. The foreman cried, "Fall below!" Workmen sawing blocks with sand and water fled to the edge of the *poggio*. The topmost block ripped from its hold with the sound of a falling tree, landed with tremendous impact in the level work space below, splitting according to its *peli*, cracks.

When Michelangelo came forward and studied the huge jagged block he was disappointed. Heavy rains soaking through the bare foot or two of earth that had covered the marble for a millennium had carried with them enough chemicals to vein the pure white. The Barrel, looming in front of him, had cut this particular block hoping Michelangelo would be satisfied.

"A beautiful piece of meat, no?"

"It is good."

"You accept?"

"It is veined."

"The cut is near perfect."

"I must have perfect."

The Barrel lost his temper.

"You cost us cash. A month we quarry for you, and not one *soldo* we see."

"I will pay you much money . . . for statuary marbles."

"God makes marble. Complain to Him."

"Not until I am convinced there are not whiter blocks behind these."

"You want me to cut down my whole peak?"

"I will have thousands of ducats to spend for the façade of San Lorenzo. You will have your share."

The Barrel turned away, a scowl on his face, grumbling something which Michelangelo could not catch, but which sounded as though the owner were calling him "The Big

Noise." Since he had not raised his voice, Michelangelo was sure he had misunderstood.

He picked up his jacket and dinner, struck out for Ravaccione, using an old goat trail that gave him but a few inches of security as he moved down the cliff. He reached the quarry at ten o'clock. On the *poggio* level, teams were two-manning long whipsaws across marble blocks with the *bardi,* apprentices, keeping a stream of sand and water under the teeth. At a chanting call from the foreman, the quarriers who were widening a fault in the stratified marble cliffs above came down to a wooden shed for their dinner. Michelangelo joined them on a plank stretched across two blocks, took out his thick slices of bread flavoured with olive oil, vinegar, salt and berry seed, dipped them into the communal bucket of water and ate hungrily. Monna Pelliccia had offered him *companatico,* a covering for his bread, but he preferred to eat what the quarriers ate.

This was the best way to get along with the Carrarini; for the Carrarini were special. They said proudly of themselves, " So many heads, so many ideas." During his stay in 1505 when he had been gathering blocks for Julius' tomb he had been received with as much reserve as any of the other foreign sculptors who came to buy marble for their commissions. But as he had spent his days in the quarries, detecting intuitively the hollows, bubbles, veining, knots ; as he had worked with the teams to bring his twenty-ton blocks down the steep slopes on rollers with nothing to hold back the oblong cargo but a few ropes tied around nests of wooden stakes, they came to believe that he was not only a sculptor but a quarryman. Now, returning to Carrara, he was accepted as a Carrarino, invited to the taverns on Saturday night where the men gathered to drink the Cinqueterre wine and gamble at *bastoni,* cards with varying numbered sticks, the winners and losers drinking after each hand until the tavern was drunk with fun and wine.

Michelangelo was proud to be accepted at a table where the gambling chairs passed from father to son as a family inheritance. Once, seeing an empty building on a rise above the town where a half dozen marble shops lined the Carrione, the front wall open to the river, he had thought to himself, " Why should I go back to Rome or Florence to carve my statues when here in Carrara it seems natural rather than peculiar if a man wants to give his whole life to sculpture?" Here in Carrara there were expert *smodellatori,* men who did the massing from the model; he would never lack for trained assistants. Crossing Florence or Rome after a day of furious carving, covered from head to foot by marble dust, he had been an object of concern if not derision. Here he looked and felt no different from all the other men returning home from the quarries or marble shops. He belonged.

At Ravaccione he found himself disappointed for a second time that morning: a new cut, ripped out of the white mountain wall and falling to the *poggio* below, showed soft fissures. He could not use it for one of his giant figures.

" A beautiful block," said the owner, hovering near. " You buy?"

" Perhaps. I will try."

Though he had replied courteously, the owner's face set in a grim expression. Michelangelo was about to move on to the next quarry when he heard the sound of the horn coming from the Grotta Colombara, a number of ridges away, echoing up and down the valleys. The quarriers froze in their positions. Then they laid down their tools, draped their jacket over their right shoulder, began a wordless climb down the trail.

One of their numbers had been hurt, perhaps killed. Every quarrier in the Apuan Alps made the hour-long descent to his village, there to await word of the fate of his companion. No further work would be done until the following morning, and none then, if there should be a funeral to attend.

Michelangelo descended by the path along the river, watched the women washing their clothes in water the colour of milk from the marble workshops that swept their dust and chips into the stream. He circled to the bottom of the town, entered the Market of the Pigs, admitted himself to his two-room apartment at the rear of the apothecary's house which sat on a level midway between the shop and the flat of the Pelliccia family above. Apothecary Francesco di Pelliccia, fifty-five, bigger in stature than most of the Carrarini, was the second best-educated man in town, having been trained at the neighbouring University of Pisa. He was one of the few men who had set foot outside Carrara, to buy potions from the Near East, and had seen the David in Florence, as well as the Sistine ceiling and the Moses in Michelangelo's house in Rome. Michelangelo had rented these rooms before; the men had become friends. Pelluccia owned important marble quarries, yet he did not use his friendship as an excuse to press his output upon Michelangelo.

Pelliccia had gone to attend the injured man. There was a doctor in Carrara but few of the quarriers used him, saying, "Nature cures and the doctors collect." When someone fell ill a member of the family came to the apothecary shop, described the symptoms, and then waited while Pelliccia concocted a prescription.

Signora Pelliccia, a busty vigorous woman in her early forties, set the table in the dining-room overlooking the Piazza del Duomo. She had saved Michelangelo some of the fresh fish from their midday dinner. He was finishing the *minestrone* when a groom arrived from the Rocca Malaspina with a note from the Marquis Antonio Alberico II of Carrara, lord of the Massa-Carrara-area, requesting that Michelangelo come at once to the castle.

6

The Rocca was a short walk uphill, a fortress bastion which served as the mountain anchor for Carrara, the opposite wall of the horseshoe fortifications being impregnable because of the Carrione River flowing below it. Built in the twelfth century, the Rocca had crenellated defence towers, a moat and thick stone walls to withstand siege: for that was one reason the Carrarini hated all outsiders, they had been overrun continuously for five hundred years Only lately had the Malaspina family been able to sustain the peace. What had originally been a crude fortress had been converted to an elegant marble palace, with frescoes and furnishings from all over Europe.

The marquis was waiting at the head of a majestic flight of stairs. Even while exchanging greetings Michelangelo could not resist admiring the splendid marble floors and columns ringing the stair well. The marquis was tall, courtly, commanding in mien, with a long thin face, high cheekbones and a luxuriant beard.

"It was kind of you to come, Maestro Buonarroti," the marquis said in his low patriarchal voice. "I thought you might like to see the room where Dante Alighieri slept when he was a guest of my family here."

"Dante was a guest here?"

"Indeed. He wrote some lines of *The Divine Comedy* about our country. This was his bed. And here the plaque with his verses:

That man whose back is close behind his belly
Is Arunas, who once dwelt on Luni's mount,
Near where Carrara's toilers work below;
And from his cave among the snow-white marbles
He could observe the galaxy of stars,
And glimpse the azure of the ocean wave. . . ."

Later, in the panelled library, the marquis got down to business. First he showed Michelangelo a letter from Monna Argentina Soderini, who was also a Malaspina:

Master Michelangelo, a sculptor whom my husband deeply loves, and who is a very honest, polite and kind person, of such a value as to make us think that to-day there is no man in Europe who is similar to him, has gone to Carrara to work a certain quality of marbles. We warmly wish that you offer him every possible benefit and assistance.

The marquis gazed at Michelangelo. "There is some beginning unpleasantness," he murmured.

"Unpleasantness? On what score?"

"Do you remember a name that the owner of the quarry called you?"

"I thought I heard him call me 'The Big Noise.' What can it mean?"

"In Carrarino it means to be a complainer, not to accept what is handed to you. The owners say that you don't seem to know your own mind."

"They're partly right," Michelangelo admitted ruefully. "It has to do with the façade for San Lorenzo. I have a suspicion that Pope Leo and Cardinal Giulio concocted the idea just to take me off the Rovere tomb. They have promised me a thousand ducats to buy marbles, but nothing has arrived. For that matter, I too have been remiss: I promised them scale models, but I have not drawn a line since leaving Rome. A troubled mind, Marquis, makes a poor draughtsman."

"May I make a suggestion? Sign two or three modest contracts for marbles to be delivered in the future. The owners will be reassured. It seems that a number of them who have quarried blocks just for you fear they have cut too much and may have to idle the men. These *gente* have little reserve. A few weeks' beans and flour separate them from hunger. Threaten this thin margin and you become their enemy."

" It is a narrow precipice. I will do as you suggest."

Within the next weeks he signed two contracts, one for eight pieces of marble over eight feet high, plus fifteen smaller ones, with a deposit of a hundred florins; and then bought from Mancino, Left-handed, three pieces of white marble from his quarry at Polvaccio. Two witnesses signed the contract in the Piazza del Duomo. Tension vanished as he promised The Barrel and Pelliccia to buy heavily as soon as money arrived from the Pope.

He had dissipated the tensions for the Carrarini, but he could not do as much for himself. Although the Rovere heirs had buckled under to the Pope's demands, writing a third contract which further cut down the size of the tomb and extended the time limit from seven to nine years, Michelangelo knew that they were outraged. Pope Leo had blandly assured the Roveres that he could continue to carve the tomb marbles while he did those for the façade; but no one, least of all Michelangelo, was fooled by this promise. From now on he would work for the Medici as long as there was a Medici Pope in the Vatican. The unfinished tomb was a canker eating at the lining of his stomach. Sebastiano had promised to keep a careful watch over his house in the Macello dei Corvi; still he worried about his marbles, and the decorated blocks.

News from Florence was equally joyless. The city's pleasure in elevating its first Pope had been soured by the fact that the election had cost the city its freedom. Giuliano had died. The Republic was gone, the elected councils banished, the constitution outlawed. The Florentines did not like being ruled by twenty-four-year-old Lorenzo, son of Piero, whose smallest act was dictated by his Roman mother and by Cardinal Giulio. Nor did the arrival of Giulio in Florence to tighten the Medici control do anything to raise its spirits. Buonarroto's shop was operating at a loss. It was not Buonarroto's fault, these were not good times for a new business venture. Buonarroto needed more money, which Michelangelo could not spare.

His brother had brought his wife, Bartolommea, into the family house to live. He kept expressing the hope that Michelangelo would like her. She was a good woman. She had nursed Lodovico during a recent illness and was managing

602

the house quite well with only the elderly servant, Monna Margherita, who had been caring for Lodovico since *Il Migliore's death*. Michelangelo gathered that she was not especially attracive of face or figure, but had brought a substantial dowry, and had a quiet sweetness.

"I will like her, Buonarroto," Michelangelo told his brother. "Just let us pray that she will produce sons. With Sigismondo living like a nomad, and Giovansimone unwilling to support even a cricket, your good Bartolommea is our only hope to continue the Buonarroti name."

Lodovico had become a real problem. He had grown cantankerous, blaming Michelangelo for squandering his funds on the Rovere tomb without completing it; for taking the Medici façade without a contract or guarantees; for not pouring more funds into Buonarroto's shop; for refusing to buy the additional houses in Florence and farms in the surrounding countryside which Lodovico spent months tracking down. The old man barely let a post go by without demands, reproaches and recriminations.

Winter rains turned the mountain trails into flooding river beds. Then the snows fell. All work stopped in the mountains. The quarriers in their oozing, cold stone houses in the foothills settled down to remain as warm as possible while consuming as little beans and *pasta* as possible. Michelangelo bought himself a wagonload of logs, set up his worktable in front of the fire and surrounded himself by letters from Baccio d'Agnolo, who was going to help him build a wooden model of the façade; from Sebastiano telling him that a dozen sculptors, including Raphael, were trying to take the façade commission away from him; and from Domenico Buoninsegni in Rome, an honest and able man in the tradition of Jacopo Galli, who was devoting time to getting a façade contract negotiated, imploring him to come to Rome because Pope Leo was clamouring to see the designs.

Michelangelo paced the cold room, his hands snuggled under his armpits to keep them warm, saying to himself, "I must get back to that wonderful feeling I had when *Il Magnifico* walked me to San Lorenzo and said, 'One day you will carve a façade that will be the wonder of all Italy.'"

He reached Rome as the city was preparing for Christmas. He went first to his house and was relieved to find everything as he had left it. His Moses seemed nearer to completion than he had remembered. If only he could steal off a month . . .

He received a hearty reception at the Vatican. Cardinal Giulio appeared to have grown surer of his control of the Church. As Michelangelo knelt to kiss the Pope's ring he noted that Leo's double chin was again cascading over the collar of his ermine robe, the fleshy cheeks almost hiding the small sickly mouth.

" It gives me pleasure to see you again, my son," said Leo as he led Michelangelo to the papal library.

The aromatic scents of parchment manuscripts took Michelangelo back to the library in the Medici palace; he saw *Il Magnifico* standing with an illuminated volume bound in purple leather. The sharpness of this vision, as though he were recalling a scene enacted only a week instead of twenty-five years before, enhanced the illusion that he was designing the façade for Lorenzo.

He spread his sheets of paper on a desk. There was an outline of the unfinished brick of San Lorenzo, then the façade, divided into two floors and a tower, the lower floor with a dividing cornice over the three entrances to the church. Flanking the doors he had drawn four large figures representing the saints Lawrence, John the Baptist, Peter and Paul on the ground floor; in the niches of the second floor, larger than life-size statues of Matthew, Luke and Mark; and on the tower, Damian and Cosmas, represented as physicians, which was what the word " medici " meant. He would carve these nine major figures himself; the rest of the façade was architectural. The nine-year plan would afford him the time to complete Julius' marbles. At the end of the contract both the Medici and the Roveres would be happy.

" We are prepared to be generous," said the Pope.

" But one thing must be changed," added Giulio quietly.

" What is that, Your Grace? "

" The marbles must come from Pietrasanta. They have the finest statuary marble in the world."

" Yes, Your Grace, I have heard. But there is no road."

" A matter of labour."

" The Roman engineers were said to have tried to open such a road and failed."

" They did not try hard enough."

There was a look of finality on Cardinal Giulio's hollow, dark face. Michelangelo surmised that something more than

604

the quality of marble was involved. He turned to Leo with a questioning glance.

"You will do better in Pietrasanta and Seravezza," the Pope explained. "The Carraresi are a rebellious lot. They have not co-operated with the Vatican. The people of Pietrasanta and Seravezza consider themselves loyal Tuscans. They have signed over their quarries to Florence. Thus we shall secure the purest statuary marble for only the cost of labour."

"I don't believe it is humanly possible to quarry in Pietrasanta, Holiness," protested Michelangelo. "The blocks would have to come out of stone precipices a mile high."

"You will make the trip to the top of Monte Altissimo and report on what you find."

Michelangelo did not reply.

7

He returned to Carrara, to his rooms behind Pelliccia's apothecary shop. When the Pope's thousand ducats were at last sent to him by Salviati, he put out of his mind any worry about the Pietrasanta quarry and began buying marble almost in a fever: from Jacopo and Antonio three blocks that were on display in the Market of the Pigs, seven blocks from Mancino. He went into partnership with Ragione, Reason, to finance the quarrying of a hundred wagonloads.

That was as far as it went. He rejected the wooden model he had hired Baccio d'Agnola to make, declaring that it "looked like a childish thing." He made one himself . . . which was no better. He paid La Grassa, a *pietra serena* hewer from Settignano, to make a clay model . . . and then destroyed it. When Salviati wrote from Florence, and Buoninsegni from Rome, that the Pope and the Cardinal were disappointed that he had not yet poured his foundations, he made a contract with Francesco and Bartolomeo from Torano for another fifty cartloads of marble, despite the fact that he had designed nothing more than the sizes and shapes of the blocks he wanted the *smodellatori* to mass.

The Marquis of Carrara invited him to Sunday dinner at the Rocca, served the traditional Carrarino cake, *focaccia*, made of sifted wheat flour, eggs, pine nuts and raisins. Afterwards he asked about the Pope's plan for opening quarries, in Pietrasanta, news of which had seeped through from Rome.

"Be assured, *signore*," said Michelangelo. "No work will be done in those mountains."

Then came a stinging letter from Buoninsegni:

> The Cardinal and Pope think you are neglecting the marble at Pietrasanta. They believe you do it on purpose. . . . The Pope wants Pietrasanta marbles.

He told no one of his destination, arranging to have a horse ready at dawn to take him down the coast road. Pietrasanta had once had considerable importance as a boundary stronghold, but unlike the Carrarini, the Pietrasantans no longer enclosed themselves within walls they could not hope to defend. Their houses were build around a spacious square where the markets and festivities were held; the western side was open to a superb view of the Tyrrhenian Sea; the Pietrasanta farmers died in their beds of the incurable malady of old age.

He tarried for a moment at the morning market to buy an orange. Above him towered Monte Altissimo, named Highest Mountain by the people of Pietrasanta and Seravezza because its awesome bastion of sheer rock, jutting jaggedly a mile into the skies, dwarfed and intimidated those who lived in its portentous presence. The Carrarini pointed out disdainfully that Monte Altissimo was not the highest mountain at all; Monte Sagro, Pizzo d'Uccello and Pisanino above Carrara were taller. The Pietrasantans made the rejoinder that the Carrarini could live with their peaks, traverse them, quarry them, but that Monte Altissimo was impregnable. The Etruscan, genius with stone, and the Roman army had not conquered its implacable gorges or precipices.

There was a narrow wagon road between Pietrasanta and the hill town of Seravezza, used for transporting farm products. Michelangelo started up the deeply rutted path to the site of the defending fortress for the hundred families farming the valleys and knolls. Here everything was unrelieved stone, the houses interlocked around a cobbled piazza. He found a room for the night, and a guide in the husky young son of a cobbler. His name was Antonio, called Antò, and he was the possessor of a height of pale pink gums which showed above his stubby teeth when he spoke.

"What you pay? Agreed! We start at first light."

They left Seravezza in the pitch-dark. The first hour's walk in the rising foothills was not difficult, for Antò knew the terrain. But where the trail ended they had to cut through thickets of underbrush with knives taken from the cobbler's shop. They climbed straight up dark stone ranges, rock formations that looked as though they had been made as steps for the gods, half scrambling, half falling down precipitous gullies, keeping from plunging over cliffs by grappling an occasional treetrunk. They descended deep into gorges as dark as Antò's shop in Seravezza, clammy cold from centuries without sun, then climbed on hands and knees up the next range rolling backward, with Monte Altissimo towering in the background still several uncharted miles away.

By midmorning they emerged at the top of a shrub-covered promontory. Between Michelangelo and Monte Altissime was only a sharp hogback, and beyond this a canyon at the foot of the *monte* where they would have to cross a river. Antò took from his leather pouch two loaves of heavy-crusted bread, the soft insides scooped out and refilled with fish in tomato sauce. They ate, then went down into the valley before this next to last hogback, worked their way towards a low division where the cascading ranges sloped downward to expose the wall of Monte Altissimo.

Michelangelo sat on a boulder looking upward at the fearsome Alps.

"With the help of God, and the whole French army, one might get a road built to this point. But how could anyone build a road up that perpendicular wall?"

"Not possible. Why try?"

"To get marbles out."

Antò gazed at Michelangelo, moving his lips up and down incredulously over the field of pink gum.

"You never said marble. That's *pazzesco!* Nobody brings blocks down."

"*E vero.*"

"Then why you come?"

"To make sure. Let's start climbing, Antò. I want to see how good the marbles are that we can't bring down."

The marbles were not only good, they were perfect: out-croppings of purest white statuary. He found a *poggio* where the Romans had dug, fragments of a marble block they had excavated. After the battle to keep their footing up the rocky ravines and gorges until they had passed the snow line, and

607

the struggle to dig the rest of their way up with fingernails and toes, it was clear to Michelangelo why the emperors had used Carrara marble to build Rome. Yet his whole body ached to set hammer and chisel to this shining stone, the purest he had ever seen.

It was dusk by the time he reached Carrara. As he came up the road from Avenza he noted that the farmers in the fields did not appear to see him. When he entered the Porta Ghibellina the townspeople in front of their shops suddenly became busy. In the Piazza del Duomo a group of men talking in a tight circle hunched their shoulders towards each other as he passed. He walked into the apothecary's shop where Pelliccia and his son were grinding medications on a slab of marble.

" What has happened? I left yesterday morning a Carrarino. I return to-night a Tuscan."

Pelliccia said nothing until he had dumped his mixture into the handkerchief of an old woman in black and bade her a " *Fa a modr.*"

" It's your trip up Monte Altissimo."

" So your townspeople have adopted the Roman law that a man is guilty until proved innocent?"

" They are frightened. The opening of quarries in Pietrasanta could destroy them."

" Please report that I was ordered up Monte Altissimo by the Pope."

" They claim it's your doing."

" Mine! How?"

" They trace it to your demand for flawless blocks; say that ' The Big Noise ' was heard in Rome."

" But I have been buying Carrara marbles."

" The Carrarini feel that in your heart you have been searching for the *sanctum sanctorum,* the pure white soul of the mountain ; and that that was why Pope Leo ordered you to open Pietrasanta : to find the perfect marbles that would satisfy you."

For the moment Michelangelo could not answer. He knew that the Pope and Cardinal Giulio had assumed ownership of Monte Altissimo, that they were punishing the Carrarini who were anti-Vatican. But were the Carrarini instinctively right about him? Not once in the past seven months, even after he had paid out good money for their blocks, had he been satisfied that he had secured the best statuary white. Had he been yearning for the Pope to open the Pietrasanta quarries, even while he proclaimed the feat impossible?

"I shall report to His Holiness that no marbles can be brought down from Monte Altissimo."

"They can rely on you?"

"I give them my word of honour."

"That will be good news."

He was more amused than concerned when he learned that Baccio d'Agnolo and Bigio had been granted five hundred ducats to go into the Seravezza mountains and lay out a road. He knew them both; they could not lay out a corpse.

It was a prosperous spring for Carrara, with sculptors coming in to buy marbles, staying in the parish house across the bridge from the Duomo: Bartolomeo Ordoñez from Spain, Giovanni de' Rossi and Maestro Simoni from Mantua, Domenico Garé of France, Don Bernardino de Chivos working for Charles I of Spain. He too felt prosperous, for the Medici had agreed to pay him twenty-five thousand ducats for the façade.

Jacopo Sansovino, apprentice to his old friend Andrea Sansovino from the Medici garden, arrived in Carrara on a rainy afternoon and stood with his back to Michelangelo's fire to get dry. Jacopo was an attractive chestnut-haired man of thirty who had taken his master's family name and appeared to have talent. Michelangelo had seen him at Sansovino's studio on and off for a number of years.

"Jacopo, it's good to see a Florentine face. What brings you to Carrara in this bad weather?"

"You."

"Me? How?"

"Pope Leo has promised me the frieze."

"What frieze?"

"Why, on your façade, of course! I submitted my design to the Pope and he was enchanted."

Michelangelo turned his face away so that Jacopo would not see his astonishment.

"But I have indicated no frieze."

"The Pope opened a competition for anyone wanting to make a contribution. I won. With a continuous bronze band above the three portals, showing scenes from the life of the Medici."

"Suppose your frieze does not fit into my design?"

" You do your work, and I'll do mine."

Jacopo's tone was not insolent, yet it admitted of no argument. Michelangelo said quietly:

" I have never collaborated, Jacopo."

" What the Holy Father says, is done."

" Assuredly. But under my agreement I am bound to correct the faults in anyone else's work."

" There will be no faults. Trust me. You have more to worry about with Baccio and Bigio."

" What about Baccio and Bigio?" Michelangelo felt his spine stiffen.

" They are to do all the decorated stones and columns."

He did not sleep that night. He kept logs on the fire, pacing the two rooms of his apartment while he tried to grapple with the depths of his mind. Why had he let these months go by without completing a model which the Pope and Cardinal Giulio could approve, without designing the major figures, or returning to Florence to lay the foundations? By giving himself a sense of motion, by buying hundreds of marbles, he had created the illusion of direction. The visit of Jacopo Sansovino with the news that the façade was being drained away from him proved he had been wrong. He had been standing still; for an artist, one of the more painful forms of death.

There was no more time to spare. Since he had to carve this façade he might as well start at once and carve the whole of it: squares, columns, cornices and capitals as well as saints.

He wrote to Rome:

I promise you, Holy Father, that the façade of San Lorenzo will be a mirror of architecture and sculpture for all Italy.

8

He returned to Florence in the spring, in time to celebrate the birth of Buonarroto's daughter Francesca, whom he nicknamed Cecca. He invited his friends to the house on the Via Ghibellina for *vin santo* and cake, then went out to buy a piece of land on the Via Mozza, near Santa Caterina, on which to build a studio large enough to house the big blocks for the façade and for Julius' tomb. He had to deal with the canons of the Duomo, who charged him three hundred large gold florins for the land, sixty more than Michelangelo knew it to be worth. When he protested, the canon replied gravely:

"We are sorry, but we cannot deviate from the papal bull concerning sales."

"Then let me have that extra piece at the back for the sixty florins you have overcharged."

"Would you have us go against an order of the Holy Father?"

He worked for several weeks to finish the design from which he would build his wooden model. As he expanded his concept, adding five half-relief histories in square frames, two in circular frames, he expanded his costs so that it would be impossible to create the façade for less than thirty-five thousand ducats. The Pope retorted through Buoninsegni, who wrote:

They like your new plan, but you have raised your price by ten thousand ducats. Is this for extensions of the façade, or a miscalculation of your earlier plans?

Michelangelo replied, "This will be the architectural anc. sculptural marvel of Italy! When will payments be forth-coming?"

Buoninsegni answered:

Money is tight, there is very little available, but do not be suspicious, your contract will be signed. Start work at once on the foundations. His Holiness is disturbed that you have not built them yet.

Jacopo Sansovino, informed by the Vatican that the new model showed no bronze frieze, came to Michelangelo and lanched into a scathing attack.

"May the day be cursed on which you ever said anything good about anybody on earth!"

"Now, Jacopo, I have spoken highly of your work. I tried to tell you in Carrara . . ."

"You tried to tell me that there was no room for anyone but yourself. That's all that was involved."

"Jacopo, don't let us part as enemies. I promise to help you get a commission. Then you will understand that a work of art cannot be a symposium; it must have the organic unity of one man's mind and hands. Anything else is a Livornese fish stew."

Lodovico chose this time to reproach him for not making available to him the *spedalingo* funds at Santa Maria Nuova.

"Father, if you don't stop this eternal nagging, the house will no longer be big enough for the two of us."

By nightfall Lodovico was gone, his room empty. The following evening Buonarroto returned with news that Lodovico was telling everyone he had been driven out of his own house.

"Where is he staying?"

"In the peasant's cottage behind our house in Settignano."

"I'll send a note to him at once."

He sat down at Lodovico's pie-shaped account desk, which looked strange in this conventionally square room, and wrote:

Dearest Father—I hear you are complaining about me and saying that I have driven you from the house. I marvel, for I am quite sure that from the day I was born till now my mind has never harboured a thought, great or small, that was detrimental to you. Every labour I have undertaken has been accepted by me for love of you . . . and you know that I have bestowed all I possess upon you.

You have had thirty years' experience of me, you and your sons, and you are well aware that I have ever thought and acted, when I was able, for your good. How can you go about saying I have turned you out of doors? Do you not see what a character you are giving me? . . . This is all that was wanting to complete my tale of troubles. You repay me well.

But let it be as it may: I am willing to accept the position that I have brought you nothing but shame and disgrace. . . . I implore you to forgive me, like the scoundrel I am. . . .

Lodovico returned to the Via Ghibellina, forgave him.

Florence was depressed, the Florentine pleasure-loving tradition having moved to Leo's court in Rome. His own joylessness was increased when he learned that his cartoon for the Bathers had vanished.

"Destroyed would not be precisely the right word," said Granacci gravely. "Traced, written on, worn out, cut apart, stolen."

"But how? It belonged to Florence. Why wasn't it protected?"

Granacci gave him the details. The cartoon had been sent to the Hall of the Popes near Santa Maria Novella, then to the upper hall of the Medici palace. A hundred artists passing through Florence had worked before it unsupervised, some cutting out portions to take with them. His enemy from the Perugino quarrel, the sculptor Baccio Bandinelli, was alleged to have appropriated a number of sections. The only fragments still in Florence were those purchased by his friends the Strozzi.

"So I join Leonardo," he observed morosely. "My cartoon is gone. Just like my bronze of Julius."

The only one who was able to put his troubles into perspective was Prior Bichiellini, so old and frail now that he was confined to his bed in Santo Spirito.

"Try to think of your whole life as a unity, rather than a series of unrelated fragments," counselled the Father. "That way each period grows out of the last, and you know there will be another to come."

He concentrated on the façade, built a solid model, grooving the columns, decorating the capitals, blocking out the niches which would carry his marbles, making wax figures to represent his final sculptures. Pope Leo signed a contract for forty thousand ducats: five thousand a year for eight years, four thousand forthwith for expenses, and a free dwelling near the church of San Lorenzo. However . . .

"His Holiness wills that all work to be done on the façade of San Lorenzo shall be carried out with marble from Pietrasanta, and no other."

He stood bareheaded in the cemetery of San Lorenzo listening to the last rites of Prior Bichiellini, and feeling that he had lost the dearest and best man on earth. For the saintly prior another period would grow out of the last: his reward in heaven. For Michelangelo, watching his friend being lowered into the grave, the " other period to come " could be pure inferno.

Within an hour of his return to Carrara a crowd began to gather in the Piazza del Duomo, pouring in from the plains below the Market of the Pigs, down the road along the Carrione River and through the Porta del Bozzo, down the mountainsides from Torano, Colonnata, Forestieri, from the quarries in Polvaccio, Fantiscritti, Grotto Colombara, Battaglino. The Carrarini were several hundred strong now, fitting closer and closer in the square beneath the apothecary's windows, spilling under the overhead bridge into the space before the Duomo.

The apothecary's dining-room windows were of floor-to-ceiling height, the centre pair being glass doors. Though there was no balcony, the doors could be opened; outside was a low wrought-iron railing. Michelangelo stood behind the curtained doors listening to the murmur grow in intensity as the quarriers continued to jam into the square. Then someone spied him behind the curtains. A movement went through the crowd. They began shouting.

"Big Noise! Big Noise!"

Michelangelo glanced at his host's distraught face, torn between loyalty to his people and to his guest.

"I'd better go into the square," Michelangelo declared.

"Too dangerous. When they're frightened, they're ugly. They could trample you to death."

"I'll have to talk to them."

He threw open the glass doors, stepped before the two-foot railing. A shout came up from below:

"*Figlio d'un can'!*"

Fists were clenched upwards to him. He held his arms out, trying to quieten them.

"Your words of honour are droppings of sheep."

"This is not my doing. You must believe me."

"*Bastardo!* You have sold us."

"Have I not bought marbles from you? I have new contracts to give. Trust me. I am Carrarino!"

"You are servant of the Pope!"

"I will suffer more from this than you."

A silence fell over the crowd. A man in front cried in ill-suppressed anguish:

"You will not suffer in the belly!"

The cry acted like a signal. A hundred arms were raised. Stones filled the air like hail. Fragments of white marble broke one glass door, then the other.

A large stone struck him on the forehead. He was stunned; more from the impact than the pain. Blood began to trickle down his face. He felt it wet his eyebrow, circle and seep into the corner of his eye.

He made no move to staunch the flow. The crowd saw what had happened. Murmuring swept the piazza.

"*Basta!* We have drawn blood."

The mass began to liquefy, streams flowing past the cathedral out the streets from which they had come. Within a matter of minutes the piazza was deserted, with only the white stones and broken glass to tell what had happened. He rubbed the palm of his hand across his eye, looked at the dark matted ooze. He had bled from marble before:

chips from his too frenzied chiselling had sometimes hit him in the face, pierced the skin. But this was the first time he had been stoned.

9

He rented a house on the sea side of the Pietrasanta piazza, with a view of the mile-wide marsh he was going to have to traverse to make a port, retaining the elderly couple who owned the place to take care of him. Cardinal Giulio had informed him that he must also dig marbles for the building of St. Peter's and for repairs to the Duomo in Florence. The Wool Guild was sending an expert to build his road.

It was March, he had about six months of good weather before snow and ice closed down the mountains. If he could start the marble columns flowing out of the quarries and on to the beach by October, his job would be done . . . if it could be started at all! He would have the first blocks shipped to Florence where he would spend the winter carving them. When good weather came again, a foreman and crew could return to run the quarry.

He listed his needs, set out for Carrara and made directly for the supply shops above the town and outside the walls. He entered a hempstore, the first in the row of provisioners along the river.

" I need stout rope."

The owner did not look up from his cording.

" Have none."

He continued up the street to an ironmonger. The smith was pounding metal on his anvil.

" I want to buy a forge and some iron bars."

" All out."

The tool shop next door was the best in the area.

" Could you sell me some picks, two-man saws . . .?"

" Short supply."

He went into the mountains seeking out the owners with whom he had signed contracts and to whom he had paid big sums of money.

" Come to Pietrasanta with me, Left-handed."

" Big contract. Can't leave."

In the next canal he urged Reason:

" Lend me your foreman for six months. I'll pay you the double."

615

" Can't spare."

He climbed higher, heading for the remote quarries whose men centred around their own campanile instead of Carrara.

" Work my quarry instead of yours. I'll pay you the same profit, plus a contract for blocks from your quarry for next year. What do you say?"

The proprietor's eyes gleamed at the thought of the extra cash; but the enthusiasm quickly faded.

" I don't want the horn to blow for me."

Since he had no chance in the quarries he dropped down the trace quickly to town, entered the apothecary's house through the rear garden and sought out his friend.

" You have been hiring and training men all your life. Send one to me. I need help. Everyone else has refused me."

Pelliccia said sadly, " I know. I am your friend. Friends should not desert each other."

" Then you will help?"

" I can't."

" You mean you won't."

" It's the same. No man would go. They stand by their campanile. This is the gravest danger our commune has faced since the French army overran us. And this shop? It would be as though someone fingered the sign of the plague in ashes on the front door. I ask your forgiveness."

Michelangelo averted his eyes.

" The error was mine, to come."

Feeling more fatigued than if he had carved for twenty hours, he once again went through the marble-paved streets, passing the housewives wrapped in their *scialima*, shawls, until he reached the Rocca Malaspina. The marquis was not only the owner of much of Carrara but the sole government of the marquisate. His word was law. The marquis welcomed him in a manner grave but not hostile.

" The Pope is powerless here," he explained. " He cannot force men to dig marble out of the mountain. Not even if he excommunicates the whole province."

" Then, by implication, neither can you order them to quarry for me?"

The marquis smiled thinly. " A wise prince never issues orders which he knows will not be obeyed."

There was a lacerated silence in the room, until a servant came in to serve wine and *pasmata,* baked rolls, an Easter speciality.

616

"Marquis, I have spent a thousand ducats for marbles that are still sitting in the quarries. What about them?"

"Do your contracts call for the marbles to be taken to the shore?"

"They do."

"Then you may rest assured that they will be delivered. We will fulfil our contracts."

The blocks and columns were brought down from the mountains on marble carts, heavy stones dragging on the rear wheels as brakes. But when they had all been deposited on the beach the Carrarini boatmen refused to transport them to Florence.

"Not in the contract."

"I know that. I'm willing to pay a good fee. I want them taken to Pisa, then up the Arno while it is still high."

"No bottoms."

"Your barges are sitting here, idle."

"Busy to-morrow. No space."

Michelangelo swore, mounted his horse and made the long hard journey through Spezia and Rapallo to Genoa. Here were plenty of shipowners eager for work. They figured out the number of barges that would be necessary. Michelangelo paid in advance, made an appointment to meet them at Avenza to direct the loading.

Two mornings later, when the Genoese barges came into sight, a Carrara rowboat put out to meet them. Michelangelo waited on the beach, chafing at the delay. At last the rowboat returned, carrying the Genoese captain. He glanced at Michelangelo's blocks and columns, said out of one corner of his mouth:

"Can't carry them. Too big."

Michelangelo went white with rage.

"I gave you the number, weights, sizes!"

"Too many."

The captain tossed a money pouch at Michelangelo, departed in the rowboat. The Carrarini on the beach stood expressionless, then turned and trudged up the long plain.

The following day he rode down the coast to Pisa. As he approached the city, saw the tower leaning against its background of blue sky, he remembered his first trip here with Bertoldo when he was fifteen, and his teacher had taken him to the Camposanto to prove that he had not copied the ancient Roman Battle of the Centaurs. Now he was forty-three. Could it be only twenty-eight years since

617

he had studied the marvellous Nocola Pisano sculptures in the Baptistery? The longer he lived the farther he got from Bertoldo's sternest admonition: "You must create a great body of work."

"How?" he wondered, tiredly.

He found a reliable captain, paid a deposit, returned to Pietrasanta. The boats did not come on the agreed day . . . nor the next . . . nor the next. He and his costly, rigidly selected marbles had been abandoned. How was he going to get them off the Carrara beach?

He knew nowhere else to try. He had a quarry to open. He would simply have to leave them there. Later he could try again.

The *pietra serena* quarries of Settignano knew that whatever fame Michelangelo had achieved had been purchased at a high price. They did not envy him as they watched his lean figure trudging up the road. But as he came in view of the open cliff, saw the angled strata of blue-grey stone, the men working the face, his spirits revived, he broke into a broad grin. Below, a crew was sledge-hammering the jagged cuts into saleable sizes. It was time for dinner; small boys arrived with branches across their shoulders, a pot of hot food balancing at either end. The stonemen assembled at the mouth of their cave.

"Anyone know where there's a quarry short on orders?" he asked. "I could use some good men at Pietrasanta."

They would not want it said that they had refused an old companion; yet the quarries were working, and when there was work a man could not leave.

"That is fortunate," he exclaimed. He refrained from adding, But not for me. "Do you think I might try in the neighbourhood? Behind the Pitti palace? At Prato?"

The men gazed at each other in silence.

"Try."

He visited other stone diggings, a *pietra dura* pit, the Cava di Fossato, Coverciano, the *pietra forte* quarry at Lombrellino. The men were working; there was no reason to leave their homes and families; there was serious apprehension about the mountains above Pietrasanta. In desperation he trudged back to Settignano to the Topolinos. The sons were running the yard, with seven mingled grandsons ranging from seven years upward, learning their craft. Bruno, the oldest, with close-cropped, shot-grey hair, negotiated the contracts; Enrico, the middle brother, trained by the grandfather for the most delicate work, columns and lacy carved windows, was the artist of the trio; Gilberto, the most vigorous, squared and bevelled with the speed of three stone hewers. This was his last chance; if his Topolino family would not help him, no one would. He laid out his situation fully, omitting none of the hardships or dangers.

"Could one of you come along? I must have someone I can trust."

He could hear the three of them pool their silent thinking. Finally all eyes rested on Bruno.

"We can't let you go alone," said Bruno slowly. "One must come."

"Which?"

"Not Bruno," said Enrico; "there are contracts to discuss."

"Not Enrico," said Gilberto; "only he does finish work."

The two older brothers looked at Gilberto, said together: "That leaves you."

"That leaves me." Gilberto scratched the bushy hair on his chest while looking at Michelangelo. "I have least skill but most strength. I will do?"

"You will do. I am grateful."

"Do not stir gratitude into family soup," replied Enrico, who had absorbed his grandfather's supply of folk sayings along with his skill at the grinding wheel.

Over the next days Michelangelo assembled a crew: Michele who had worked with him in Rome, the three Fancelli brothers: Domenico, a tiny fellow but a good sculptor, Zara, whom Michelangelo had known for years, and Sandro, the youngest. La Grassa of Settignano, the mason who had made a model for him, agreed to come, as well as a group of assorted stonemen who were tempted by his offer of a double wage. His heart sank when he assembled them to give instructions for leaving in his hired farm wagon the following morning: twelve stonecutters. Not one quarrier in the lot! How could he tackle a savage mountain with this inexperienced crew?

While pondering his way home he passed a group of stone hewers laying new blocks in the Via Sant'Egidio. Among them he was astonished to see Donato Benti, a marble sculptor who had worked in France on successful commissions.

"Benti! In the name of God, what are you doing here?"

Benti, though only thirty, had been born with an old face; he had purple pockets under his eyes, a seamed face with the lines culminating in a crosshatch on his chin. His manner was solemn. He wrung his hands in silent supplication, replied:

"Making small sculptures for people's feet to tread on. While little I eat agrees with me, I still have to swallow some food occasionally."

"I can pay you more in Pietrasanta than you can get in the street. What do you say? I need you."

"You need me," repeated Benti, his owl-eyes batting up and down in disbelief. "Those could be the most beautiful words in the Italian language. I'll come."

"Good. Be at my house in the Via Ghibellina at first light. There'll be fourteen of us going by wagon."

That evening Salviati came to Michelangelo's house with a grey-haired man with thinning hair, whom he introduced as Vieri, a seventh cousin, once removed, of Pope Leo.

"Vieri will go to Pietrasanta with you as your commissary. He will arrange for food, for supplies, for transportation, and keep the records. The Wool Guild will pay his salary."

"I've been worried about who would keep the figures."

Salviati smiled. "Vieri is an artist with accounts. His books will be balanced as perfectly as your David, with never a *baiocco* out of place."

Vieri spoke in the constricted voice of a man who had little liking for words. "It's the columns of figures that are them asters . . . until they balance. Only then have I made them obey."

It was a happy departure, after all, for his sister-in-law Bartolommea was delivered of a healthy boy, whom they named Simone; and at long last the Buonarroti-Simoni name was safe for the future.

Vieri, Gilberto Topolino and Benti moved into the Pietrasanta house with him, Vieri taking one of the bedrooms for his office. Michelangelo then found a larger house in Seravezza for the remaining nine workers. He marked out the most promising route to the quarry area, set the men to work with picks and shovels to cut a trail up which the burros could carry supplies. A number of farm boys came to work under Antò's supervision, wielding sledge-hammers to break out the mountain stone and form a safe ledge for passage.

When it became evident that the one smith in Seravezza could not handle their needs, Benti sent for his godfather, Lazzero, a squat, neckless, bull-torsoed man who set up a forge to serve both the quarry and the road, and to build the special iron-supported wagons for transporting the marble columns down to the sea.

Michelangelo, Michele, Gilberto and Benti went prospecting, found several strata of variegated marbles on the lower levels of Monte Altissimo ; and then, just one jutting crag below the summit, unearthed a formation of pure statuary marble, breathtakingly crystalline white, flawless in colour and composition.

" It's true! " Michelangelo cried to Benti ; " the higher the mountain, the purer the marble."

He summoned his crew, had Antò's men help him carve a level area on the peak from which they could mine. The marble ran straight back in a solid white sheet, an entire cliff of marble to be removed, the surface slightly weathered by snow and wind and rain, but below this outer skin, absolute purity.

" All we have to do now," he exclaimed exultantly, " is strip out great blocks that have been here since Genesis."

" And get them off this mountain," added Benti, gazing downward the five or six miles, past Seravezza and Pietrasanta to the sea. " Frankly, I'm more worried about the road than the marble."

The first weeks of quarrying were a total waste. Michelangelo showed the men how the Carrarini drove in their wet pegs along the seams and faults, how the pegs swelled until the marble cracked, and were then hewn out with giant levers. But marble and its quarriers were like lovers, they knew each other's every mood, transition, disposition to oppose or give in. Marble had always been the temperamental queen of hard mountain formations, yet the most easily shattered because of its delicacy: an obstinate gem demanding devotion and tenderness.

Of these things the Setignano stonemasons knew nothing. Nor did Benti or Domenico, even though they had carved statues. Michelangelo learned by trial and error, leaning heavily on his years of watching the Carrarini work the blocks, trying to absorb generations of skill in a few months. His crew of stonemasons did their best, but they made mistakes. The *pietra serena* on which they had been trained was infinitely more durable. They were not equipped to handle the Shining Stone; it would have been as well if he had brought in a dozen carpenters or blacksmiths.

As foreman, Gilberto Topolino was a volcano of energy; he hustled, bustled, attacked the mountain violently, kept the others going at a fearsome pace; but Gilberto knew only how to fashion *pietra serena* building stones held between his knees. The nature of the marble infuriated him by its arrogant toughness when it should have been as crumbly as sugar, and by dissolving granularly under his *subbia* and *mazzuolo* when it should have had solid substance.

Burly La Grassa complained:

" It's like working in the dark."

After a week of work at a lower outcropping where Domenico said they had found something good, they cut a block which turned out to have swirling circles of dark veins, useless for their purposes.

Vieri proved to be an excellent commissary, getting the lowest possible prices for food and supplies, keeping costs down. He had a receipt to show for every denaro laid out, but at the end of the month the immaculate accounts were of small comfort to Michelangelo. He had not yet quarried one ducat's worth of usable marble.

" You see, Buonarroti, my figures balance beautifully," said Vieri.

" But how much marble have I to balance the one hundred and eighty ducats?"

" Marble? My task is to show where every scudo went."

" And mine is to have marble to show for the expenditures."

By now it was close to June. The Wool Guild had not yet sent a superintendent to build the road. Michelangelo knew from the steepness of the terrain, and the fact that it would have to be cut through solid rock much of the way, that unless it was started immediately it could not be completed before the winter storms shut them down. At last the builder arrived: Bocca, Mouth, an illiterate labourer on the roads of Tuscany in his youth, who had had the extra energy and ambition to learn how to draw maps, to boss road crews, and finally to contract for building roads between farm villages. The Wool Guild had chosen Bocca, a brute, of a man, hairy from his skull to his toes, because of his reputation for pushing through contracts in record time. Michelangelo showed Bocca his drawings for the projected route.

"I see the mountain myself," broke in Bocca. "Where I find a good place I build a good road."

Bocca had trained himself well. Within ten days he had mapped the simplest possible route to the base of Monte Altissimo. The only trouble was that the road was not directed towards those places where the marble was to be found. After Michelangelo had lowered his twenty-ton blocks down the ravines of Monte Altissimo by hand, he would still be a considerable distance from Bocca's road!

He insisted that Bocca accompany him to the topmost quarries, Polla and Vincarella, then down the ravines he would have to use to lower his columns.

"You see, Bocca, I could never get my blocks to your road."

"I took contract to build to Monte. This is where I build."

"What purpose will the road serve if I can't get the marble out?"

"I'm road. You're marble."

"But there is nothing at the other end of your road except marble," cried Michelangelo, exasperated. "I will have a thirty-two-bull team hauling the wagons . . . we are not hauling hay! The road must be the best route from the quarries. Like this, for example. . . ."

When Bocca was agitated he pulled on the inch-long hairs growing out of his nostrils and ears; he took a clump of black tendrils between his thumb and forfinger, massaging them downward.

"You build or I build. Not both."

It was a warm night, the stars hanging low over the sea in brilliant clusters. Michelangelo walked for miles south on the coast road, passing sleeping villages while he wrestled with his problem. What purpose would the road serve if it could not move his marbles? Would it not be considered his fault if he did not get his columns down to the sea? Bocca's route would be worthless, for it went nowhere! What to do about the man?

He could complain to Pope Leo, Cardinal Giulio, Salviati, have another road builder sent in. But what assurance would he have that the second contractor would follow the course he himself thought best? The Pope might even say that this was his *terribilità*, that he could not get along with anyone.

What was his alternative?

He must build the road himself!

A tortured groan racked the warm night air. He looked about him, saw only the dark marsh between himself and the sea. How could he take upon himself the building of a road in some of the wildest country of Italy? He had never built a road. He was a sculptor. What did he know of such matters? It would put him under crushing hardships. It would mean summoning and supervising still another crew as they filled the marsh, cut down trees, blasted a passage through solid walls of rock. He knew what Pope Leo and Cardinal Giulio would say, the same thing that Pope Julius had said when he had fought so bitterly to avoid painting the Sistine vault, and then had conceived a plan which quadrupled his work.

He had cried to Leo and Giulio, " I am not a quarrier!" Now he wanted to be an engineer.

Leo would exclaim:

" How is one to understand you?"

That was one question he could not answer. Though he had not yet brought forth so much as one usable base block, he had seen the glorious meat of Monte Altissimo. He knew that he would eventually quarry its statuary marble. When he did, he had to have a proper road.

Had he not learned over the years that a sculptor had to be an architect and engineer as well? If he could carve the Bacchus, the Pietà, the David, the Moses ; if he could design a mausoleum for Pope Julius and a façade for San Lorenzo, why should a five-mile road be more difficult?

10

He used the rutted farm tracks into Seravezza, swung to the north of the village to avoid the Vezza River and gorge, then mapped the road to make straight for Monte Altissimo despite the fact that huge boulders sat astride his route. He laid out stakes up the valley of the Sera to the cluster of stone houses at Rimagno, crossed the Serra River at a shallow ford and followed the contour of the bank up the steep gorge. At two points he chose to tunnel through solid rock rather than try to push the road up a hogback and then serpentine down into the valley again. For a terminus he chose a spot at the base of the two ravines down which he planned to lower the blocks from Vincarella and Polla.

For two ducats he bought a walnut tree, and had a Massa wagon-maker build a two-wheeled cart with iron fitted over its wheels to carry the cut rock to the marsh between Pietrasanta and the sea. He made sad-faced Donato Benti superintendent of road construction from Pietrasanta to the base of the Monte Altissimo canal; Michele was given charge of the marsh fill; Gilberto Topolino remained as foreman of Vincarella, the quarry some forty-five hundred feet high in the Alps, at the last possible footing in the sheer precipice where a *poggio* could be dug to provide work space for excavation.

By the end of June Vieri presented him with a stern face.

" You'll have to stop building your road."

" Stop . . . but why?"

" There's no more money."

" The Wool Guild is rich. They're paying the costs."

" All I have received is one hundred florins. They have been spent. Here, see how the columns balance."

" The only columns I want to see are those of marble. And I can't get them to the port without a road."

" *Peccato.* Perhaps the money will arrive soon. Until then . . ." Vieri arched both hands outward in an eloquent gesture of defeat. " . . . *finito.*"

" I can't stop now. Use my other money."

" Your private money for marbles? You can't spend it on the road."

" It's the same. No road, no marbles. Pay the bills out of my eight-hundred-ducat account."

" But you may never get them back. You will have no legal hold over the Wool Guild . . ."

" I don't have any hold over anybody," Michelangelo replied hoarsely. " Until I get the marbles out, the Holy Father won't let me be a sculptor. Spend my money for the road. When the Wool Guild sends in cash, pay me back."

From sunrise to dark he was up and down the mountains on a sure-footed mule, watching progress. Benti was doing a fast job on the road, except that he was leaving the heaviest rock work for the end; Gilberto had removed the earth from the Vincarella strata of marble and was driving wet pegs into the faults; the local *carradori,* cart owners, were dumping tons of loose rock into the marsh, slowly building up the base to the beach where Michelangelo planned his harbour. With a hundred long hot workdays of summer ahead, he estimated he would have several columns for the master figures of his façade lowered down the canal to the loading platform by the end of September.

By July, according to Vieri's accounts, he had spent over three hundred of his eight hundred ducats. On Sunday after early mass he sat with Gilberto on the wooden railing of the Ponte Stazzemese, the hot sun beating on their bare backs while they gazed across the hamlet of Stazzema to the sea.

Gilberto glanced sideways at his friend's face.

" I want to tell you . . . so you won't be there when they leave . . ."

" When who leaves?"

" Half the crew: Angelo, Francesco, Bartolo, Barone, Tommaso, Andrea, Bastiano. When Vieri pays them they go back to Florence."

" But why?" Michelangelo was shocked. "They're well paid . . ."

" They're frightened. They think the marble get us, instead we get the marble."

" That's foolishness! We have a good block going. It'll be pried out in a week."

Gilberto shook his head. "A strong veining has shown. The front is waste. We have to drive deeper into the cliff . . ."

" How?" Michelangelo cried. "With half a dozen men who don't know what they're doing?"

Gilberto hung his head. "Forgive me, Michelangelo, I have failed you. Nothing from what I know of *pietra serena* is of any use here."

Michelangelo put an arm about Gilberto's dejected shoulders.

" You're doing the best you can. I'll find new masons. You see, Gilberto, I don't have the privilege of quitting."

By mid-September they were ready to tunnel through the three huge rocks they had by-passsed: one at the edge of Seravezza, the second just beyond Rimagno, and the last where the river ran into an old trail. His road would be finished. He had dumped enough rock into the marsh to fill the whole Tyrrhenian Sea, but the constantly sinking and shifting roadbed was at last secure to the beach. Up in Vincarella, though it had cost an extra six weeks of hewing back into the mountain the whole thickness of the column to avoid the vein, he had at last managed to bring out a magnificent block. He also had a column at the edge of the *poggio*. Though some of the new men had drifted away, grumbling about how hard he worked them, he was happy with the results of the summer.

"I know it has seemed endless to you, Gilberto; but now that we have established a *modus operandi,* we'll get out another three or four columns before the rain closes us down."

The following morning he started to move the enormous column down the ravine, well filled over the months with marble chips to provide a smooth sliding base. The column was roped half a dozen times around its width, several times around its length, crowbarred on to wooden rollers, then pushed and dragged to the edge of the *poggio,* its nose turned over the edge of the canal. Down the length of the draw, on either side, nests of stakes had been driven into the ground, angling outward. The ropes from the column, tied around these stakes, were the only hold the crews would have on the marble.

Down it went, held by some thirty men. Michelangelo, imitating the calls of the Carrara crews, a series of sung and shouted notes, directed the men handling the rollers to run with the one at the rear, when the end of the marble had passed, and put it under the front; and the men at the stake nests, holding the ropes with all their might until the column had slid past them, to run down the trail to the next stakes to tie up their ropes and apply the brake. Hours passed, the sun rose high in the heavens, the men sweated, swore, strained, complained that they were starving.

"We can't stop to eat," Michelangelo cried. "There's no way to secure the marble. It could get away from us."

Down the long steep ravine the column slid, the crew exerting all its strength to hold it back, to slow its movement. It inched forward a hundred yards, two hundred, three, four, five, down almost the entire face of Monte Altissimo, until by late afternoon they were only thirty-five yards from the road. Michelangelo was jubilant; very soon now they would slide the column on to the loading platform, from which it would be moved on to the special wagon drawn by the team of thirty-two bulls.

He never quite knew how the accident happened. An agile young Pisan named Gino, who was running the rollers forward, had just kneeled to put another roller under the front of the column when suddenly there was a cry of alarm, something snapped, and the column started to move on its own.

There were shouts: " Gino! Get out! Quick!"

But it was too late. The column rolled over Gino, swerved towards Michelangelo. He threw himself over the side of the ledge, rolling a number of feet before he could break his fall.

The men stood paralysed as the flawless column picked up speed, smashed its way downward, hit the loading platform and broke into a hundred pieces on the road.

Gilberto was leaning over Gino. Blood stained the marble-choked draw. Michelangelo went on his knees before the boy.

" His neck is broken," said Gilberto.

" He is still alive?"

" No. Killed instantly."

In his mind Michelangelo heard the mournful sound of a horn echoing from peak to peak. He picked up Gino's dead body, stumbled blindly the rest of the descent down the white passage. Someone brought his mule to the loading station. Michelangelo mounted, still holding Gino, while the others led the funeral procession into Seravezza.

11

The death of the boy lay heavy on his conscience. He took to his bed, sick at heart. Torrential rains inundated the piazza. All work was shut down. Vieri closed his books. The crews returned home. Michelangelo's accounting showed that he had spent thirty ducats beyond the eight hundred advanced to him at the beginning of the year for marble. He had loaded not a single block. The lone consolation was the attendance of a group of Carrarini quarriers and owners at Gino's burial. Apothecary Pelliccia linked his arm through Michelangelo's as they left the cemetery.

" We're deeply sorry, Michelangelo. The death of the boy brought us to our senses. We treated you badly. But we too have suffered from the loss of contracts from agents and sculptors waiting to buy the Pope's quarries."

Now the Carrarini boatmen would transport his blocks, still sitting on the beach at Carrara, to the docks in Florence.

For several weeks he lay ill. The future looked blacker

than the slate sky. He had failed in the task assigned to him; spent the monies advanced, used up the year fruitlessly. What happened now? Neither Pope Leo nor Cardinal Giulio had much patience with bunglers.

It took a letter from his friend Salviati, late in October, to set him back on his feet:

I am sorry to hear that you are so distressed about this thing; in such an undertaking you might happen to meet much worse accidents. Believe me that you are going to lack nothing, and God is going to repay you for this accident. Remember when you complete this work, our city will be gratefully obliged to you and to all of your family, and will be under eternal obligation. Great and honest men take more courage in adversities and become stronger.

His fear that the Pope and cardinal might condemn him for the failure was allayed by a letter from Buoninsegni in Rome, who wrote:

The Holy Father and His Lordship are very satisfied that there is a large quantity of marble. They wish the matter hurried as much as possible.

A few days later he made the trip alone on horseback to the end of his road, then climbed Monte Altissimo to Vincarella. The sun had come out, the air was filled with autumnal scents. At the quarry he found tools in the wooden shed, marked vertically with hammer and heavy chisel the four columns to be dug out of the mountain as soon as he could return with quarriers. He returned to Pietrasanta, put his few personal possessions in a saddlebag and made his way down the coast to Pisa, then through the rolling valley of the Arno, the Duomo displacing space on the horizon from miles away.

Florence knew about the accident, but only as a delaying mishap. Though some of the returning workers had complained about his driving them too hard, others praised him for the speed with which he had completed the road and extracted the first marble block ever quarried above Pietrasanta. He was still too shaken to attempt even the simplest carving, and so he settled for a more salutary work, the building of his new studio on the land he had bought on the Via Mozza. This time he did not design a house with a workshop attached, but rather a spacious high-ceilinged studio with a couple of small rooms added for living purposes.

When his plan grew too large for the lot he went to Fattucci, chaplain of Santa Maria del Fiore, and again tried to get the piece of land at the rear. The chaplain replied:

"The Pope has issued a bull saying that all church lands must be sold at the highest possible price."

He returned home, wrote to Cardinal Giulio:

Now if the Pope makes bulls enabling one to steal, I beg Your Lordship have one made for me also.

Cardinal Giulio was amused; but Michelangelo ended by paying the full price for the extra strip. He plunged into the building of his house with hurricane activity, hiring workmen, buying his planks and nails from Puccione, the carpenter, mortar from Ugolino, the kiln man, his roof tiles from Maso, fir trees from Capponi. He hired *contadini* to bring his sand, gravel and stone, remained on the job all day to supervise. At night he kept his accounts as straight as Vieri had kept the books in Pietrasanta, jotting down the names of witnesses who were present when he paid Talosi for putting in the stone window frames, Baggiana, the sandbearer, Ponti for five hundred large bricks, the widow who lived next door for half of her protecting wall.

Trying to be, for once, as good a businessman as Jacopo Galli, Balducci and Salviati would have liked, he took over from the ailing Buonarroto the listings of the modest income from the properties he had bought over the years. . . .

I note hereafter the income I had in three years from the *podere* tilled by Bastiano called Balene (whales), *podere* that I purchased from Piero Tedaldi. In the first year: twenty-seven barrels of wine, eight barrels of oil and four bushels of wheat. In the second year: twenty-four barrels of wine, no oil, eight bushels of wheat. In the third year: ten barrels of oil, thirty-five barrels of wine, five bushels of wheat.

The winter was mild. By February his tile roof had been set, the doors hung, the high northern windows framed, the bronze caster had delivered four bronze pulleys for the studio. He brought half a dozen of his nine-foot Carrara blocks for Julius' tomb from the Arno storehouse, set them upright so that he could study them. His workshop completed, he had only to return to Pietrasanta, excavate the columns he needed for San Lorenzo; then he could settle down on the Via Mozza for years of concentrated work for the Medici and Roveres.

He did not ask Gilberto Topolino to go back to the quarries, that would have been unfair; but most of the others agreed to join him, including a new group of stone-masons. Rather than being frightened by Pietrasanta, the masons felt that with the road completed and the quarries opened the hardest work was already done. He took with him from Florence the needed supplies: heavy-duty rope, cables, sledge hammers and chisels. Still disturbed by the unexplained accident that had killed Gino, he evolved a system of iron lewis rings which could be driven into the surface of the block, giving the crews a surer grip on the marble as it was brought down the ravine. Lazzero said he could make the rings on his forge. Michelangelo sent Benti into Pisa to buy the best iron he could find.

In good time they detached the marble from the mountain vertically, letting the blocks roll on to the *poggio*. The Pope had been rightly informed: there was enough magnificent marble here to supply the world for a thousand years. And now with the white walls exposed, all loose earth, rock, dirt, shale cleaned from above by two *tecchiaioli,* the crystalline cliffs yielded superbly.

He hesitated to take the columns down the slide without the iron grips, but Pelliccia came to the diggings, recommended that he double his nest of outspread stakes along the trail, use heavier rope, and impede the downward movement by lessening the number of rollers.

There were no more accidents. In the ensuing weeks he directed five superb blocks down the canal, on to the wagon, down the road behind the thirty-two bulls, past Seravezza, Pietrasanta, across the marsh, and on to the beach. Here the low barges would be brought up close, their decks filled with sand until they sank low in the water; the columns would be raised on to the sand fill, then the sand washed out through the scuppers until the marble blocks settled down securely on the deck.

At the end of April, Lazzero finished his set of rings. Michelangelo in a state of exultation over the beauty of his glorious white columns, was relieved at this added protection. Now, with the sixth column ready to be moved, he saw to it that the iron rings were firmly attached to hold the massive weight, making it possible to lessen the bulk of rope.

The improvement was his undoing. Halfway down the ravine a ring snapped, the column got away, picking up so much speed that it jumped the bank of the ravine and went crashing down the steepest slope of Monte Altissimo to the river below, breaking to bits on the stony bed.

Michelangelo recovered from his moment of stupefaction, saw that no one was hurt, then examined the broken ring. It had been made of poor iron.

He climbed swiftly up the side of the ravine, took a heavy hammer and hit the iron connections of the hoisting cranes Lazzero had made. They broke under his blows like dry clay. It was a wonder the entire crew had not been killed long before this.

" Benti! "

" Yes? "

" Where was this iron bought? "

" . . . in Pisa . . . like you said . . . "

" I gave you money to buy the best. There is not as much iron in here as there is in the rib of a knife. "

" . . . I . . . I'm sorry, " stuttered Donato Benti, " but I . . . I didn't go. Lazzero went. I had faith in him. "

Michelangelo turned towards the shed where the smith was working a bellows over his forge.

" Lazzero! Why did you not buy the best iron, as I ordered? "

" . . . this was cheaper. "

" Cheaper? You charged me the full price. "

Lazzero shrugged. " *Mah!* What would you? Every man uses a chance to make a few scudi. "

" A few scudi! To smash a column worth a hundred ducats. To endanger the life of every man working here. How could you be so . . . so venal? "

Lazzero shrugged again; he did not know what venal meant.

" What is lost? One column. There are a thousand more just like it. Dig out another.'

As quickly as the news could reach the Vatican, and a letter of instructions be sent to the Board of the Wool Guild, Michelangelo was recalled to Florence. A foreman from the Duomo was sent to replace him.

Michelangelo rode his horse into Florence late the following afternoon. He was to report at once to Cardinal Giulio in the Medici palace.

The palace was in mourning. Madeleine de la Tour d'Auvergne, who had married Piero's son Lorenzo, had died in childbirth. Lorenzo, rising from a sickbed to ride from the Medici villa at Careggi to Poggio a Caiano, caught a fever, and had died only the day before. This removed the last legitimate heir descended from the male side of the Cosimo de' Medici line, though there were now two more illegitimate Medici: Ippolito, son of the dead Giuliano, and Alessandro, rumoured to be the son of Cardinal Giulio.

The palace was also sad because rumour had it that Pope Leo's extravagances had nearly bankrupted the Vatican. The Florentine bankers financing him were in serious trouble.

Michelangelo put on fresh linens, packed his ledger and took the beloved walk through the Florentine streets, up the Via Ghibellina to the Via del Proconsolo, past the Duomo into the Street of the Watermelons with the House of the Five Lamps on the left, into the Via de' Calderai with its coppersmiths and cuirass-makers, across the Via Larga to the Medici palace. Cardinal Giulio, sent by Leo to take over the reins, was saying a requiem mass in the Benozzo Gozzoli chapel. When it was concluded, and everyone had filed out, Michelangelo expressed his regret at young Lorenzo's death. The cardinal did not appear to hear him.

"Your Grace, why have you recalled me? In a matter of months I would have had all nine of my giant columns on the beach of Pietrasanta."

"There is enough marble now."

Michelangelo was unnerved by an undertone of hostility in the cardinal's voice.

"Enough . . .? I don't understand."

"We are abandoning the façade for San Lorenzo."

Michelangelo turned white, speechless.

Giulio continued: "The floor of the Duomo needs repaving. Since the Duomo and Wool Guild Boards paid the cost of the road, they are entitled to the marbles you have excavated."

Michelangelo felt as though the cardinal had walked over his prostrate body in boots covered with dung.

"To pave the Duomo floor? With my marbles? With the finest statuary marbles ever quarried! Why do you humiliate me in this way?"

Cardinal Giulio answered icily, "Marble is marble. It should be used for what is needed next. Right now the cathedral needs paving blocks."

Michelangelo clenched his fists to stop his trembling, gazed at Gozzoli's exquisite portrait of *Il Magnifico* and his brother Giuliano, on the wall of the chapel.

"It is nearly three years now since His Holiness and Your Grace took me off the Rovere tomb. In all that time I have not been able to carve one inch of marble. Of the twenty-three hundred ducats you have sent me, I have spent eighteen hundred on the marbles, quarries and roads. On the Pope's instructions I had the marbles for Julius' tomb shipped here, so that I could carve them while I worked the San Lorenzo façade. To send them to Rome now, the shipment will cost me more than the five hundred ducats' difference! I do not reckon the costs of the wooden model I made; I do not reckon the three years I have wasted in this work; I do not reckon the great insult put upon me by being brought here to do this work, and then having it taken from me; I do not reckon my house in Rome, which I left, and where marbles, furniture and blocked-out statues have suffered upwards of another five hundred ducats. I will not reckon all these things, regardless of the terrible loss to me. I only want one thing now: to be free!"

Cardinal Giulio had listened carefully to Michelangelo's catalogue of complaints. His thin, smooth face grew dark.

"The Holy Father will review these doings at the proper time. You are dismissed."

Michelangelo stumbled down the long hallway, his feet carrying him to what had been *Il Magnifico's studiolo*. He thrust open the door, entered, stared at the room. He cried aloud to the long-departed spirit of Lorenzo:

"I am ruined!"

BOOK NINE

THE WAR

1

Where did a man go when he had been destroyed? Where else but to work, bolting the door of his studio, standing the dozen blocks around the walls as though they were armed soldiers guarding his privacy.

The new studio was a pleasure: ceiling thirty-five feet high, tall windows to the north, spacious enough to allow him to carve several of the tomb figures at the same time. This was where a sculptor belonged, in his workshop.

Since he had signed a contract with Metello Vari in Rome to do the Risen Christ, he decided to do this single piece first. His drawing hand revealed that he could not design a Risen Christ because in his mind Christ had never died. There had been no crucifixion and no entombment; no one could have killed the Son of God; not Pontius Pilate, not all of the Roman legions stationed in Galilee. Christ's corded muscular arms held the cross lightly, its transverse beam too short for man or even child to be nailed to; the symbols were there, the bamboo rod poetically curved, the sponge soaked in vinegar, but in his white marble there would be no sign of anguish, no reminder of the ordeal. He walked to Santa Maria Novella by way of the central market in the Via Sant'Antonio, went to the choir stalls and gazed up at the robust Christ of Ghirlandaio for which he had drawn the sketches. He had never believed that spirituality had to be anæmic or æsthetic.

The small clay model shaped itself easily under his hands, then the studio was christened with the first flying chips, seeming to Michelangelo as pure as holy water. A group of old friends came to celebrate his entering the block: Bugiardini, Rustici, Baccio d'Agnolo. Granacci poured the Chianti, raised his glass and cried:

"I drink to the three late lamented years. *Requiescant in pace.* Now let us drink to the years to come, when all these brave blocks shall spring to life. *Beviamo!*"

"*Auguri!*"

After his three-year fast, the Risen Christ surged out of its column. Having persuaded Vari to contract for a nude figure, his chisel sang out the contours of the standing male in an equilibrium of proportion, the head gazing downward lyrically upon man, the sweet calm tranquillity of Jesus' virile face saying to all who looked upon him:

"Have faith in God's goodness. I have surmounted my cross. I have conquered it. So can you, yours. Violence passes. Love remains."

Because the statue had to be shipped to Rome he left the webbing between the left arm and torso and between the two feet; nor did he attempt to articulate the hair, since it might break off, or give the face a high polish that could be scratched on the journey.

The day it was shipped, Soggi came to visit the studio, fairly bursting out of his own tight red sausagelike skin.

"Michelangelo, I just held a world competition for sculpture."

"Oh. And where did you hold it?"

"In my head. I'm happy to tell you that you won."

"What have I won, Soggi?"

"The right to carve a calf for the front of my new butcher shop."

"Of marble?"

"Certainly."

"Soggi, I promised myself that I would never sculpture a calf unless it was of pure gold. Like the one the Hebrews were worshipping when Moses came down from Mount Sinai."

Soggi's eyes bulged. "Gold! That would be spectacular. How thin a plating could we use?"

"Plating? Soggi, I'm shocked. Do you put only a plating of meat in your sausages? To do your shop justice the calf must be solid gold, from the tip of its nose to the last hair in its tail."

Soggi, his face dripping perspiration, cried:

"Do you know how much a solid gold calf would cost? A million florins."

"But it would make you famous."

Soggi moved his head back and forth mournfully.

"No use to cry over spoiled meat. I'll just have to start a new competition. You're not eligible!"

He would earn little in the coming years, since the Risen Christ netted him less than two hundred ducats, and the figures for Julius' tomb had been paid for in advance. Yet he was still the sole support of his family. His brother Buonarroto now had two children and a third on the way. Buonarroto was sickly, could work little. Giovansimone spent his days in the wool shop but had no business sense. His brother Sigismondo had not been trained for any trade except war. When Lodovici became ill there were constant doctor and apothecary bills. The income from the farms seemed to trickle away. He was going to have to cut his costs.

"Buonarroto, now that I'm back in Florence don't you think your time would be better spent in handling my affairs?"

Buonarroto was crushed. His face went grey.

"You want to close our shop?"

"It's not making money."

"Only because I've been ill. As soon as I'm better I can go to business every day. What would Giovansimone do?"

And Michelangelo realized that the business was necessary to maintain Buonarroto's and Giovansimone's social position. With it they were merchants; without it they were dependants, living off their brother. He could do nothing to hurt his family name.

"You're right, Buonarroto," he said with a sigh. "The shop will make money one day."

The tighter he bolted his studio door against the intrusion of the outside world, the more evident it became that trouble was man's natural state. News reached him that Leonardo da Vinci had died in France, unwanted and unhonoured by his countrymen. A letter from Sebastiano in Rome told him that Raphael was ill and exhausted, obliged to turn more and more of his work over to apprentices. The Medici were beset by difficulties: Alfonsina, suffering from ulcers over the loss of her son and the control of Florence, crept away to Rome to die. Pope Leo's political judgment had prove unsound in the backing of Francis I of France against Charles V, now the newly elected Holy Roman Emperor of Spain, Germany and the Netherlands. In Germany, Martin Luther was challenging papal supremacy by crying:

"I don't know if the Christian faith can endure any other head of the Universal Church on earth . . . save Christ."

After immuring himself for weeks, Michelangelo attended a dinner of the Company of the Cauldron. Granacci came to the studio so that they could walk to Rustici's together. He had inherited the family fortune and was living in austere respectability with his wife and two children in the ancestral home in Santa Croce. When Michelangelo expressed surprise at Granacci's devotion to his business affairs, Granacci replied formally:

"Each generation is the custodian of family property."

"Perhaps you'll become serious about your talent as well, and do some painting?"

"Ah, well . . . talent. You have not neglected your talent, and look what you've been through. I'm still intent on enjoying life. What else is left, after the years have passed? Bitter reflections?"

"If I don't have wonderful sculptures to show that the years have passed, then my memories will be truly bitter."

Rustici still had the same studio in the Via della Sapienza, where they had celebrated the David commission. While passing through the Piazza San Marco, Michelangelo saw a familiar figure. He went faint, grabbed Granacci's arm. It was Torrigiani, talking to a nineteen-year-old goldsmith and apprentice sculptor, Benvenuto Cellini, laughing heartily and throwing his arms wide. They had no sooner arrived at Rustici's than Cellini came in, made straight for Michelangelo:

"That Torrigiani is an animal! He told me that you used to go together to the church of the Carmine to learn drawing from the Masaccios, and that one day when you were bantering him he gave you such a blow on the nose that he felt the bone crumble beneath his knuckles."

Michelangelo's face became grim.

"Why do you repeat his story to me, Cellini?"

"Because his words begat in me such a hatred for the man that although I was considering going to England with him —he's looking for several assistants for a commission there —I know now I could never bear the sight of him."

It was good to have a group of his friends and fellow Florentines about him in the closely knit Company. He had recommended Jacopo Sansovino for an important commission in Pisa, and Jacopo had forgiven him for not being allowed to participate in the now defunct façade. So had Baccio d'Agnolo, who had become famous for the beauty of his inlaid wood mosaics. Bugiardini, with a commission from Palla Rucellai to do an altarpiece of the Martyrdom of St. Catherine for Santa Maria Novella, was having trouble with his drawing. Michelangelo had spent several evenings with his old friend outlining in charcoal a design of nudes, wounded and dead, falling forward and backward, to catch a variety of light and shadow on their strong figures.

The only sour note was Baccio Bandinelli, who would not look in Michelangelo's direction. Michelangelo studied the man who had been fighting him ever since the Perugino quarrel; thirty-one, with a nose that was wire-thin at the bridge but flared wide at the nostrils; heavy-lidded eyes that were deceptively lethargic, and the nimblest, fastest-talking lips in Tuscany. He had been awarded several commissions by the Medici. Cardinal Giulio had recently given him an Orpheus and Cerberus to do.

"What is it that he can't forgive me?" Michelangelo asked Granacci. "The fact that he destroyed my cartoon for the Bathers?"

"That you were born, live, breathe and carve. The very fact that there is such a person as Michelangelo Buonarroti poisons the air for him. If you didn't exist, he believes he would be the first marble master of Italy."

"Would he be?"

"He made an incredible botch of the Hercules and Cacus for the *ringhiera* of the Signoria. But he's a skilled goldsmith, and favourite of the Medici because his father saved their gold plate during the sack. You can become as bad a sculptor as he is, or make him as good as you are. Nothing short of this will ever placate him."

Agnolo Doni, for whom he had painted the Holy Family, had wangled an unofficial membership in the Company by sponsoring a number of their more expensive parties. As Michelangelo's fame had grown, so had the legend of their friendship. Doni had them being an unbeatable combination on the Santa Croce football team; Michelangelo had lived as much in Doni's home as his own; Doni had encouraged him in his art. What Michelangelo now grasped was that, over the fifteen years of expanding and telling, Doni had come to believe his own tall tales. When Doni was relating to Aristotile da Sangallo how he had forced the rear door of a palace late one night and held the candle while Michelangelo sketched from a fresco which the owners had forbidden anyone to copy, Granacci winked at Michelangelo and drawled beguilingly:

"What a wonderful story, Michelangelo. Why did you never tell me?"

639

Michelangelo smiled wryly. He could not call Doni a liar in public. What would it accomplish? Better to regard it as a measure of his success.

As the months passed he broke into four nine-foot blocks simultaneously, creating advanced sculptural forms at one corner of each block, then tipping them over clockwise to work the other side.

These were to be part of his Captive theme for the tomb. Eager to define the muscular body forms, he measured the distances between anatomical areas and drove stubby bronze nails into the outer marble. He walked around the columns with a point in his hand making chips here and there, nicking the planes to familiarize himself with the density of the stone. When he started the detail work on any one section he would know how much marble lay behind it. Only with a hammer and point could he grasp the interior weight, the depth he could bite into.

He knew in his carver's eye the details of the sculptures. In his mind they were not four separate figures but parts of a unified conception: the somnolent Young Giant, trying to free himself from his imprisonment in the stone of time; the Awakening Giant, bursting forth from his mountain chrysalis; the Atlas, full in years and power and wisdom, holding God's earth on his shoulders; and the Bearded Giant, old and tired, ready to pass the world along to the Young Giant in a continuing cycle of birth and death.

He too lived as far outside the realm of time and space as these demigods twisting and spiralling their tortured way out of their encasing blocks. He carved tirelessly through the autumnal and winter days, kept warm by a log fire, eating a little soup or veal when Monna Margherita carried it through the streets in a pot for him, throwing himself on the bed fully clothed when he could no longer follow the tracks of his punch or claw chisel. He awakened after a couple of hours refreshed, put a candle in his cap and continued to work, hewing the fronts of his figures, drilling holes between the legs, modelling the four bodies with pointed chisels, keeping them at the same stage of development.

By spring the four Captive-Giants were viable. Though the Young Giant's body was still embedded in the marble womb from which he was emerging, his feet unformed, and only the outlines of the features suggested in a head shielded beneath the upraised arm, the body lived by its own anatomical weight, the blood coursing through it. The Atlas, his head totally encased in a roughhewn, overhanging cliff-like boulder held up by his gigantic arms, was pulsatingly alive, feeling intensely the bulk of the world he held. The Bearded Giant, his back and buttocks crosshatched, leaned heavily against a base deep-scarred by the vicious pounding of the point. The Awakening Giant's head pushed forcibly to one side, his arms thrown out in an encircling movement, one leg bent violently at the knee, the other still buried in the block.

He stood among his Giants, the nine-foot blocks dwarfing them. Yet all four bowed beneath his superior force, his driving power, the flying hammer and chisel which were creating four pagan gods to hold up the tomb of a Christian pontiff.

Granacci cried:

" You've already made up the three lost years in the quarries. But where do they come from, these mysterious creatures? Are they Olympians from ancient Greece? Or prophets from the Old Testament?"

" Every work of art is a self-portrait."

" They have a tremendous emotional impact; it's as though I must project myself into their unfinished forms, complete them by my own thinking and feeling."

If Granacci did not mean to suggest that Michelangelo leave his four Captives unfinished, Pope Leo and Cardinal Giulio did. They decided to build a sacristy on to San Lorenzo in which to bury their fathers, *Il Magnifico* and his brother Giuliano. The walls of this new sacristy had been started on two earlier occasions. Michelangelo passed the masons without looking up at them, for he had no intention of getting himself involved in another stillborn Medici scheme. Unembarrassed by the fact that they had cancelled his contract for the façade, Pope Leo and Cardinal Giulio, who was back at the Vatican after having left the Cardinal of Cortona in charge of Florence, sent Salviati to Michelangelo with an offer to make sculptures for the new *cappella*.

" I am no longer their sculptor," cried Michelangelo when Salviati appeared at his door. " Baccio Bandinelli now holds that exalted position. By the end of the year I will have these four Captives out of their blocks. Another two years of such work and I can complete Julius' tomb, assemble it, be done with the contract. The Rovere family will owe me some eighty-five hundred ducats. Do you know what that means to a man who has not earned a scudo for four years?"

" You need the good will of the Medici."

" I also need money . . . which I don't get from the Medici. They still think of me as a fifteen-year-old who is left three florins each week on the washstand for spending money."

As the walls of the sacristy rose, so did the Medici pressure on him. The next overture came in a letter from Sebastiano in Rome.

Michelangelo went on carving his Giants, the twisted tension-packed thigh and knee of the Young Giant, the squat trunk-like legs held in bondage by thongs, the expression turned inward. These were the realities of his life during the late spring days, the still, hot summer, the first cool breezes down from the mountain in September.

When his brother Buonarroto, now the father of a second son who was named Lionardo, walked over to the studio to complain that they had not seen him, and ask if he didn't get lonely working night and day without family or friends, he replied:

" The Giants are my friends. They talk not only to me but to each other. In debate . . . like the Athenians used to carry on in their agora."

" Who wins? You, I hope."

" *Dio mio,* no! Sometimes they conspire, and overwhelm me."

" They're so enormous, Michelangelo. If any one of them should drop his arm on your head . . ."

" . . . it would break open like an egg. But there is no violence in them; they are victims, not aggressors, trying to hold up the world rather than tear it down."

Why did he accede? He was not sure. By October the pressure from the Vatican had become intense. By October Buonarroto's accounts showed that he had spent more cash in the past year than he had taken in in rents from the properties in the Via Ghibellina, and from the sale of his wine, oil, barley, wheat, oats, sorghum and straw of his farms. By October he had poured out his strength so prodigiously on the nine-foot Captives that he was vulnerable. The news of Raphael's death had shocked him, made him aware of man's short span, the limited time for creativity. He became sad, thoughtful. The memory of *Il Magnifico* and his untimely death returned to haunt him.

"What would I have been without Lorenzo de' Medici?" he asked himself. "And what have I yet done to repay him? Would it not be ungrateful of me to refuse to carve his tomb?"

Although he again would be saddled with tomb sculptures, he could demand the freedom to carve some highly imaginative pieces, ideas for which began to catch fire in his mind like the autumn burning of the shepherd's *paleri* in the mountains above Carrara.

The final impetus was provided by Pope Leo's open expression of hostility. Sebastiano, striving desperately to get the commission to paint the Hall of Constantine in the Vatican, assured the Pope he could do wonders with the frescoes if only he had Michelangelo's help. Leo cried:

"I do not doubt it, for you all belong to his school. Look at Raphael's work; as soon as he saw Michelangelo's, he left Perugino's style. But Michelangelo has a *terribilità*, and listens to no reason."

Sebastiano wrote:

I said you were only so because you had important works to finish. You frighten everybody, including Popes.

This was the second pontiff in a row who had accused him of having an awesomeness. Even if it were true, who but they had been the cause of it? When he wrote to Sebastiano to complain, Sebastiano replied soothingly:

I do not esteem you terrible, except only in art; that is to say, in being the greatest master who ever lived.

Soon he would complete enough of the figures for Julius' tomb to satisfy the Roveres. Where did he go from there? He could not afford to be in disfavour at the Vatican. It controlled all the churches in Italy; even the nobles and rich merchants would heed its voice. Florence was also governed by the Medici. Either he worked for the Medici, or he might not work at all.

He reassured himself with the fact that since the walls of the new sacristy were almost completed the small, intimate chapel would be a limiting force, restricting the number of sculptures he might envisage. Jacopo Galli would approve of the scope of this commission!

2

Pope Leo and Cardinal Giulio were happy to have him back in the family. Ill feelings over the Pietrasanta quarries and road were forgotten, perhaps because the crews from the Duomo workyard had been unable to get out any additional marble. The quarries were shut down. His five white columns lay neglected on the beach. Salviati, on his way to Rome on Papal business, offered his services in setting up a workable agreement.

"If such a thing is possible," exclaimed Michelangelo resignedly. "Tell the Pope and the cardinal that I will work for them on contract, by the month, by the day, or even as a gift."

Early the next morning he went to the new sacristy, entering through workman's portal. The interior walls were of rough cement. The dome had not yet been added. He thought how delightful it might look if he designed the interior of *pietra serena* from the quarry in Maiano. He could pick the most luminous slabs, convert the cramped chapel into a shrine of white marble against blue-grey *pietra serena*, the two materials he loved best in the world.

Florence was flooded by wind-driven rains. He moved his worktable to the front of the fire and drew exploratory plans. The Pope had now decided that there must also be tombs for the younger Medici, his brother Giuliano, and Piero's son Lorenzo. Michelangelo's first idea of a free-standing tomb with four sepulchres in the centre of the chapel was declined by Cardinal Giulio on the grounds that the chapel was too small to hold the tombs and sculptures as well. The cardinal's idea of a series of arches with a tomb in the walls above each arch, his own sacrophagus to be in the centre, was rejected by Michelangelo as unworkable.

He drew a new concept: one austere sacrophagus on either side of the chapel, each holding two reclining allegorical figures: Night and Day on one, Dawn and Dusk on the other; two male, two female; great brooding figures of intense emotional and physical beauty, which would represent man's cycle within the days of his life.

This plan was accepted.

He thought of his five white columns on the beach of Pietrasanta. But they belonged to the Duomo. Simpler to send the two hundred ducats advanced by the Vatican to his favourite quarry, the Polvaccio in Carrara, providing detailed drawings for their size and massing. When the blocks arrived he was gratified to find that they were of high statuary quality and had been accurately dressed.

He spent the spring and summer months designing the interior walls and dome, drawing for the Night and Day, Dawn and Dusk, the two life-size figures of the young Medici for the niches above the sarcophagi, a Madonna and Child for the wall opposite the altar. Cardinal Giulio came through Florence on his way to Lombardy to join the Pope's army, once again fighting the invading French. He sent for Michelangelo, received him warmly in the Medici palace.

" Michelangelo, how can I see with my eyes and touch with my hands the exact chapel as you will finish it?"

" Your Grace, I will give you actual drawings of the *pietra serena* doors, windows, pilasters, columns, niches, cornices. Then I will build models in wood exactly the size the tombs are to be. Then I will put on them the proposed statues in clay, made to size and finished exactly as they are to be."

" That will take considerable time. The Holy Father is in a hurry."

" No, Your Grace, it will take only a short time and cost little."

" Then it's settled. I will leave with Buoninsegni an order to give you the money as it is needed."

The cardinal did no such thing; but this neither surprised nor diverted Michelangelo. He proceeded to make the models at his own expense. He then turned his attention to the architecture, making sketches and building plans for the dome. He also decided to close in a number of the windows. The only time he stopped work was to celebrate the birth of Buonarroto's third son, Buonarrotino; with three male heirs the name of Buonarroti-Simoni was now secure.

In late November Pope Leo returned from a hunt at his villa at La Magliana and caught a chill. By December 1, 1521, the first Medici Pope was dead in the Vatican. Michelangelo attended the requiem mass in the Duomo, standing next to Granacci, remembering his years with Giovanni in the palace and Giovanni's first big hunt; Giovanni's kindness and loyalty when he had become an influential cardinal in Rome. He joined in the prayer for Leo's soul. Later, he whispered to Granacci:

"Do you suppose that heaven can offer any part of the entertainment Leo provided himself at the Vatican?"

"I doubt it. God would not spend that much money."

The *tramontana* blew icily through the streets. No amount of logs could heat the studio. With Leo dead, the project of the Medici chapel became equally cold and wind-swept. In Rome half a dozen factions of the College of Cardinals fought for supremacy, until they finally compromised on sixty-two-year-old Adrian of Utrecht, a practical-minded Fleming who had been tutor to Charles V.

Cardinal Giulio had fled to Florence, for Pope Adrian was a highly moral churchman who had disapproved of the Medici pontificate and knew Giulio to be responsible for a considerable portion of it. Pope Adrian set out to right the wrongs of Pope Leo and to redress the grievances of all who had been injured. He started by returning sovereignty to the Duke of Urbino, ended by listening sympathetically to the complaints of the Rovere family, agreeing that they should file suit against Michelangelo Buonarroti for failure to fulfil his contract with Pope Julius' heirs.

Michelangelo found himself twitching nervously as he walked through the streets to the house of Raffaello Ubaldini, a notary. Ubaldini had just returned from an audience with Pope Adrian.

"Why should they want to take me into court?" Michelangelo cried. "I haven't abandoned the tomb."

Ubaldini was an intense, serious little fellow with a blue skin where he shaved.

"The Roveres claim you have."

"There are four Captives in my studio . . ."

"In your revised contract you agreed to complete the tomb last May. You agreed not to take any new projects, yet you accepted the Medici sacristy."

"I have only made drawings for the sacristy. . . . Given another year . . ."

"The Duke of Urbino has no more faith in your promises. They showed Pope Adrian that it is seventeen years since you made the agreement, and yet you have delivered nothing."

Quivering with rage, Michelangelo protested, "Did they tell Pope Adrian that it was Julius who stopped me originally by refusing to finance the tomb? By wasting fifteen months of my life forcing me to do his figure in bronze in

Bologna? That Julius stuck me in the Sistine vault for four years of painting . . .?"

"*Piano, piano.* Here, sit down at my desk."

Michelangelo asked hoarsely:

"If Pope Adrian favours their suit, I am defeated?"

"Probably."

"What will they want of me?"

"First, all their money to be returned."

"I'll return it."

"Over eight thousand ducats."

"Eight thou . . .!" He sprang up as though a fire had been started beneath the leather chair. "But I've only had three thousand."

"They have documents, receipts."

Ubaldini showed Michelangelo the accounting. Michelangelo went green.

"The two thousand ducats Julius paid me before he died was for the Sistine."

"Can you prove that?"

". . . no."

"Then the court will grant them eight thousand ducats, plus interest on the money over all these years."

"How much will that be?"

"Not more than twenty per cent. They are also asking monetary damages for your failure to fulfil the contract. That can be any amount the court sees fit to levy. Pope Adrian has no interest in art; he considers this purely a business matter."

Michelangelo blinked hard to force the tears back under his lids.

"What am I to do?" he whispered. "All of my farms and houses put together are hardly worth ten thousand florins. I'll be bankrupt, my life savings swept away . . ."

"Frankly, I don't know. We have to find friends at court. People who admire your work and will intervene with Pope Adrian. In the meanwhile may I suggest that you complete your four Captives and take them to Rome? If you would assemble as much of Julius' tomb as you already have carved . . .?"

He returned blindly to his studio, his body pervaded with nausea. News spread over Florence of the catastrophe hanging over him. Friends began arriving: Granacci and Rustici carrying purses of gold; members of the Strozzi and Pitti families offering to go to Rome in his behalf.

He was trapped. The Roveres did not care about the money, they were out to punish him for abandoning the Rovere tomb in favour of a Medici façade and chapel. When he wrote to Sebastiano offering to come to Rome and complete the tomb, the Duke of Urbino rejected his offer, declaring:

" We no longer want the tomb. We want Buonarroti brought into court and judgment passed on him."

And he learned that there were degrees of being ruined. Three years before, when Cardinal Giulio had recalled him from Pietrasanta and cancelled the façade, he had been seriously hurt, but he had been able to return to work, to carve the Risen Christ and begin the four Captives. Now he faced genuine disaster ; forty-seven years old, he would be stripped of his possessions and publicly discredited as a person unable or unwilling to complete a commission. The Roveres would brand him as a thief for taking their money and giving nothing in return. There would be no work for him as long as Adrian was Pope. As an artist and a man his life was behind him.

He wandered the countryside talking to himself, conjuring up conspiracies against him, the intrigues and machinations of blind fate, often not knowing where he was as his mind veered from one fantasy to another: flight to Turkey with his friend Tommaso di Tolfo, who had invited him a second time ; escape from Italy in disguise to take up life at the French court under another name ; revenge against those who had injured him, diatribes about his tormentors, with visions of doing them violence: all the mental aberrations of the sorely afflicted. He was unable to sleep at night, to sit at table during a meal. His legs moved him to Pistoia or Pontassieve, while his mind was in Rome or Urbino or Carrara or Florence, quarrelling, accusing, shouting, hitting, unable to absorb the injustices and indignities.

He watched the harvests being taken in, the wheat flailed on cobbled farm courtyards, the grapes brought from the vines and squeezed for wine, the hay shaped into ricks and covered for the winter, the olives picked and trees cut back, the trees begin to turn yellow. He became emaciated, could hold down no more food than during his nights of dissection at Santo Spirito. He asked himself over and over again:

" How could it have happened? When I started out so full of love for marble, so consumed to carve, to work at my craft? When I have never wanted anything else in this world? What has happened to me? How have I become displaced?

"What has been my crime, O Lord?" he cried aloud. "Why hast Thou forsaken me? How can I be going through Dante's Inferno if I am not yet dead?"

As he read the *Inferno* he came across passages that made him feel that Dante had written the book to describe his, Michelangelo's life and lot:

Am I a thief, to be tortured by servants?
Must I be part of "that wretched crowd"?

Each one seemed to be most strangely twisted
Between the chin and where the chest begins
The face of everyone turned to his back;
So ever backward they were forced to walk.

I had come among that wretched crew
Which God and all His foes abominate.
These abject cowards who had never lived
Were naked, and were stung incessantly
By monstrous flies and wasps that swarmed about them.

He stayed off the streets during the day, away from the populous piazzas with their noisy, colourful markets and fairs; for it was just as when he had been painting the Sistine ceiling and walked home through the Piazza San Pietro: people seemed to look straight through him as though he were not there. He had the eerie feeling that he was moving like a ghost among the living. He sought out Granacci, demanding:

"What is it that I lack? I have been affiliated with Popes, given stupendous commissions. I have talent, energy, enthusiasm, self-discipline, singleness of purpose. What am I missing? *Fortuna*? Where does one search for the leaven of luck?"

"Last out the bad times, *caro*, then you will be alive to enjoy the good. If you burn yourself out, like a rotted tree trunk set on fire . . ."

"Ah, Granacci, your favourite word: survival. What if one's work is done?"

"How old is your father?"

"Lodovico? Almost eighty."

"You see! Your life is only half spent. So your work is only half done. You just don't have enough faith."

Granacci proved to be right. God alone rescued him. After twenty-two agonizing months He gathered Pope Adrian to his everlasting reward. In the College of Cardinals there followed seven weeks of bargaining, dealing, promises and commitments . . . until Cardinal Giulio de' Medici garnered enough votes to get himself elected. Cousin Giulio!

Pope Clement VII sent word immediately after his coronation: Michelangelo must resume work on the chapel.

He was like a man who has been through a dangerous illness and has gazed into the visage of death. From this vantage point he came to a realization that everything that had happened to him before this had been a journey upward through time, everything that occurred after it a descent. If he could not control his own fate, why be born? The God of the Sistine vault, about to hand on to Adam the spark of life, had implicit in His glorious being the promise of freedom to accompany that life. He began to carve his allegories for the sacristy as creatures who had experienced the hardship and tragedy of life, who knew its wastefulness." its futility. The *contadini* said, "Life is to be lived." Granacci said, "Life is to be enjoyed." Michelangelo said, "Life is to be worked." Dawn, Day, Dusk and Night said, "Life is to be suffered."

His David had been young, knowing he could conquer everything he set out after; Moses was ripe in years, but with the inner strength to move mountains and form nations. These new creatures of his making had an aura of sadness about them, of pity; they were asking the most painful and unanswerable of dilemmas: for what purpose are we put on earth? To live our cycle? To perpetuate it? A continuous chain of living flesh, binding the burden of one generation to another?

Before, his concern had been with the marble and what he could extract from it. Now his concern shifted to human emotion and what he could portray of the philosophic meaning of life. He had been a man with marble; now he achieved an identity of man and marble. He had always wanted his figures to represent something important, but his David, his Moses, his Pietà, all had been solitary pieces, complete within themselves. In this Medici chapel he had an opportunity to portray a unified theme. What his mind evoked about the meaning of the carvings would be more important than the movements of his sculptor's hands over the marble surfaces.

On March 6, 1525, Lodovico gave a dinner at the family home to celebrate Michelangelo's fiftieth birthday. Michelangelo awakened in a melancholy mood, but as he sat down at the table, surrounded by Lodovico, by Buonarroto, his wife and four children, by his brothers Giovansimone and Sigismondo, he was content. He had come into the autumn of his life; a man had his seasons, even as had the earth. Was the harvesting of autumn less important than the seeding of spring? Each without the other was meaningless.

3

He drew, modelled and carved like a man released from prison, to whom the only remaining joy was the freedom to project himself in space. Time was his quarry; from it he would excavate the pure white crystalline years. What else was there to mine in the craggy mountains of the future? Money? It had eluded him. Fame? It had entrapped him. Work was its own reward; there was no other. To create in white marble more glorious figures than had ever been seen on earth or in heaven, to express through them universal truths, this was the payment, the glory of the artist. All else was illusion, vanishing smoke on the horizon.

Pope Clement put him on a lifetime pension of fifty ducats a month, assigned him a house across the piazza from the church of San Lorenzo as a workshop. The Duke of Urbino and the other Rovere heirs were persuaded to drop their lawsuit. He was now to design a single-wall tomb for which he had all the figures except a Pope and Virgin already carved. It had taken him a full twenty years to reach the practical conclusion about Julius' tomb which Jacopo Galli had known from the beginning.

For the sacristy he contracted with the Topolino family to handle the cutting and installing of the *pietra serena* doors, windows, Corinthian columns and architraves which divided the chapel walls into three levels, the giant pilasters of the lower level giving way to the delicate fluted columns and slender niches of the second, the lunettes and pendentives of the third supporting the dome. What he tried to achieve in his dome was a combination of the man-made form of the Duomo and the bulbous form of the ripe fruit all about him. It was somewhat compacted because it had to be set on to walls already erected, but he enjoyed finding out that there was as much sculpture in architecture as there was architecture in sculpture.

Orders and commissions began coming in, everything from windows for palaces to a tomb for Bologna, a villa for Mantua, a statue of Andrea Doria for Genoa, a palace façade for Rome, a Virgin with Archangel Michael for San Miniato. Even Pope Clement offered him a new commission, this time a library to house the Medici manuscripts and books, to be built above the old sacristy of San Lorenzo. He drew some rough plans for the library, again using *pietra serena* for the decorative effects.

His new young apprentice was Antonio Mini, a nephew of his friend Giovan Battista Mini, a long-faced lad with eyes and mouth too round for his thin cheeks, but with a well-modelled bone structure and a serene attitude towards life. He was honest and reliable in delivering models, copying drawings, making and repairing chisels in the forge; as loyal and delightful a helper as Argiento had been, but with considerably more talent. Since Michelangelo now had a woman servant, Monna Agniola, to do the housekeeping in the Via Mozza studio, the romantic Mini was free to spend his spare hours on the Duomo steps with the young boys of the town, watching the girls parade past the Baptistry in their high-necked dresses and puffed sleeves.

Giovanni Spina, merchant-scholar of the noble line of Jacopo Galli, Aldovrandi and Salviati, was named by Pope Clement to handle Michelangelo, the sacristy and Medici library. He was a rangy man, stoop-shouldered, cold even in mild weather, with an intelligent face, and eyes that were not wide but very long. He introduced himself at the studio door by saying:

" I met Sebastiano at court in Rome. He admitted me to your house in the Macello dei Corvi to see the Moses and the two young Captives. I have always worshipped Dona-tello's work. You are like father and son."

" Grandfather and son. I was the heir of Bertoldo, who was the heir of Donatello. We are a continuous Tuscan bloodline."

Spina smoothed the hair which he combed downward over his ears. " When the Pope has no funds in Florence, you can count on me to get them . . . from somewhere." He approached the four unfinished Captives, circling, weaving in and out, studying, eyes opened to their full length in astonishment.

" This Atlas, holding on his shoulders the top of the block where his head will eventually emerge . . . is he saying that every man who carries a head on his shoulders is carrying the full weight of the world?"

They sat on the workbench discussing the Della Quercias in Bologna and the Laocoön in Rome. Spina asked:

" The Rucellai don't acknowledge that you are a cousin, do they?"

" How did you know?"

" I checked the records. Will you come to their palace gardens for our meeting? We are all that's left of the Plato Academy. This Thursday Niccolò Machiavelli is reading the first chapter of his history of Florence, which the Signoria commissioned."

Inside the unfinished sacristy he worked on the blocks of Dawn, Dusk, the Virgin and young Lorenzo. During the warm autumn evenings he sat by the open doors to his yard, making clay models for the River Gods, symbolic of tears and suffering, for the base of the young Medici figures. Later, tired from carving or fashioning clay, but without desire for sleep, he lay wide-eyed hearing the surrounding church bells toll off the hours towards dawn. He saw Contessina's piquant face before him, heard the timbre of her voice; and at the same time felt Clarissa lying by his side, his arms twined tightly about her to hold her close to him; somehow, after the years of lovelessness, the two images merging until they became one, the figure of love itself. He wondered if he would ever know love again, in whatever form or guise. He rose, took sheets of drawing papers covered with crosshatched studies for Dawn and Dusk, arms, hips, breasts, legs, and spent the rest of the night pouring out his feelings in poetry:

LOVE'S FURNACE

So friendly is the fire to flinty stone
That, struck therefrom and kindled to a blaze,
It burns the stone, and from the ash doth raise,
What lives thenceforward binding stones in one;

Kiln-hardened this resists both frost and sun,
Acquiring higher worth for endless days—
As the purged soul from hell returns with praise,

E'en so the fire struck from my soul, that lay
Close-hidden in my heart, may temper me,
Till burned and slaked to better life I rise.

If made mere smoke and dust, I live to-day,
Fire-hardened I shall live eternally;
Such gold, not iron, my spirit strikes and tries.

With the first light he put away the papers, walked to the mirror over his washstand and studied his visage as though it belonged to a characterful model he had hired to pose for him. His entire physiognomy appeared to have deepened: the lines across his flat forehead, the eyes retreating from the world under the bony brows, the nose, which now appeared to be wider than ever, the lips pulled tight as though to lock in word and thought. The eyes were darkly amber. Only his hair had resisted change, remaining rich in colour and texture, curling youthfully across his forehead.

With the return of a Medici as Pope, Baccio Bandinelli was given the commission to carve the Hercules for the front of the Signoria, the one Michelangelo had been offered by Gonfaloniere Soderini some seventeen years before. Knowing that Michelangelo had been upset, Mini ran all the way home, burst into the studio crying:

" The block for the Hercules just arrived . . . and sank in the Arno. People standing on the bank are saying that the marble tried to drown itself rather than be carved by Bandinelli! "

Michelangelo laughed heartily, picked up his chisel and made a long " Go " from the bony knee of the *Crepuscolo*, Dusk, to the groin.

The next morning a canon from Rome brought him a message from Pope Clement.

" Buonarroti, you know the corner of the loggia of the Medici garden, opposite where Luigi della Stufa lives? The Pope asked if you would like to erect a Colossus there, eighty feet high? "

" A marvellous idea," Michelangelo replied sarcastically,

" only it might take up too much of the roadway. Why not put it in the corner where the barbershop stands? We could make the statue hollow inside and rent out the ground floor to the barber. In that way his rent would not be lost."

He went of a Thursday evening to the Rucellai palace to hear Machievelli read his *Mandragola*. The feeling of the group against Pope Clement was bitter; he was referred to as the Mule, Bastard, "the dregs of the Medici." The Plato Academy was at the centre of the plot to restore the Republic. Their hatred was intensified by the fact that the two illegitimate Medici were living in the palace, being groomed to take over the government of Florence.

"That would be the bottom of the trough for us," commented Strozzi, about Clement's son, "to be governed by the mule of a mule!"

Michelangelo heard stories of how Clement was strengthening the cause of the anti-Medici party by making fatal errors of judgment, even as Leo had. In the incessant wars among the surrounding nations he consistently backed the wrong side; his allies, the French, had their armies destroyed by the Holy Roman Emperor, whose overtures Clement had rejected . . . though, truth to tell, Clement changed sides so often that neither Michelangelo nor Europe could keep up with his intrigues. In Germany and Holland thousands of Catholics were abandoning their religion for the reformation which Pope Clement refused to carry out within the Church, and which Martin Luther's ninety-five theses nailed to the door of the castle church at Wittenberg in 1517 had enunciated.

"I am in an awkward position," Michelangelo told Spina as they sat over a supper of roast pigeon served by Monna Agniola. "I long for the return of the Republic, but I am working for the Medici. The whole fate of the sacristy depends on the good will of Pope Clement. If I join a movement to drive out the Medici, what happens to the sculptures?"

"Art is the highest expression of freedom," replied Giovanni Spina. "Let the others fight over politics."

Michelangelo locked himself inside the sacristy, burying his head in marble.

But Cardinal Passerini of Cortona ruled Florence autocratically. A foreigner, he had no love for Florence; nor did Clement seem to have any, for he rejected all appeals from the Signoria and the old families to replace the man whom the Florentines found crude, greedy, contemptuous of their elected councils, bleeding them with excessive taxes. The Florentines were waiting only for an advantageous moment to rise, seize the necessary arms and once again drive the Medici out of the city. When the army of the Holy Roman Empire, sweeping southward to invade Rome and punish Pope Clement, marched thirty thousand strong on Bologna, after which it planned to conquer Florence, the city rose in a mass, stormed the Medici palace and demanded arms to defend itself against the coming invasion, shouting:

"Guns! Guns to the people!"

The Cardinal of Cortona appeared in an upper window and promised arms. But when the cardinal learned that the Pope's army, commanded by Michelangelo's erstwhile opponent, the Duke of Urbino, was approaching Florence, he ignored his promise and rushed out with the two young Medici boys to meet the duke. Now Michelangelo joined Granacci and his friends at the Palazzo della Signoria. In the piazza crowds were calling:

"*Popolo, libertà!*"

Florentine soldiers guarding the Signoria made no attempt to prevent a committee of citizens from entering the government palace. A meeting was held in the Great Hall. Then Niccolò Capponi, whose father had led the earlier movement to drive out Piero de' Medici, stepped on to a balcony and announced:

"The Florentine Republic is re-established! The Medici are banished! All citizens are to be armed and summoned to the Piazza della Signoria!"

Cardinal Passerini arrived with a thousand of the Duke of Urbino's cavalry. The Medici party opened a gate for them. The committee inside the palace bolted the doors. Urbino's cavalry attacked the doors with long pikes. From the two stories of windows, and from the crenellated parapet above, there rained down on the duke's soldiers everything that could be pried loose inside the building: desks, tables, chairs, crockery, armour.

A heavy wooden bench came hurtling down from the parapet. Michelangelo saw that it was headed straight for the David.

"Look out!" he screamed, as though the statue might dodge.

He was too late. The wooden bench struck. The left arm

holding the slingshot snapped off below the elbow. The arm fell to the stone of the piazza, broke.

The crowd drew back. The soldiers turned to stare. All movement from the windows and parapet of the Signoria palace stopped. A hush fell over the throng. He felt himself moving towards the sculpture. The crowd opened, murmuring:

" It is Michelangelo. Let him pass."

He stood below the David, gazing up into the pensive, resolute yet beautiful face. Goliath had not scratched him; but the civil war inside Florence had come within inches of destroying him completely. Michelangelo's arm ached as though it too had been amputated.

Out of the crowd Giorgio Vasari, one of Michelangelo's young apprentices, and Cecchino Rossi sped towards the David, picked up the three marble fragments of the arm and hand and disappeared down the narrow side street.

In the stillness of the night there was a tattooing of finger ends on Michelangelo's door. He opened it to admit Vasari and Cecchino. They began talking at once.

" Signor Buonarroti . . ."

" . . . we have the three pieces hidden . . ."

" . . . in a chest in Rossi's father's house."

" They are safe."

Michelangelo gazed at the two shining young faces before him, thinking:

" Safe?" What was safe in a world of war and chaos?

4

The Holy Roman Emperor's army reached Rome, breached the walls. The horde of mixed mercenaries overran Rome, forcing Pope Clement to flee along the high passageway to the fortress of Sant'Angelo, where he remained a prisoner while the German, Spanish and Italian troops looted, ravaged and burned Rome, destroying sacred works of art, smashing altars, marble statues of Mary, the prophets and saints, melting bronze figures for cannon, stained-glass windows for lead, lighting fires on the inlaid marble floors of the Vatican, putting out the eyes in paintings, dragging a statue of Pope Clement into the streets and hacking it to pieces.

" What of my Pietà? My Sistine ceiling?" groaned Michelangelo. "What of my studio? The Moses and the two Slaves? They can be lying in a thousand pieces."

Spina arrived late at night. He had been to a series of feverish meetings at the Medici palace, and then at the Signoria palace. With the exception of a core of diehard Medici adherents, all Florentines were agreed that the Medici must be deprived of their power. With Pope Clement a prisoner, the Republic could once again be proclaimed. Ippolito, Alessandro and the Cardinal of Cortona would be allowed to leave peacefully.

"And that," concluded Spina thoughtfully, "should be the end of Medici rule for a very long time."

Michelangelo was silent.

"The new sacristy?"

Spina hung his head.

"It must be . . . locked. . . ."

"The Medici are my nemesis," he cried in agony. "All these years of work for Leo and Clements, and what have I to show for them? Six roughhewn blocks, the half-finished interior of a chapel . . . With Clement a prisoner, the Roveres will descend on me again. . . ."

He sat down hard on his workbench. Spina spoke softly.

"I shall recommend you for an office of the Republic. Once our government is secure we can persuade the Signoria that the chapel is for *Il Magnifico,* whom all Tuscans revere. Then we will get permission to unlock the doors and start work again."

He boarded up the house across from San Lorenzo, with its drawings and clay models, returned to the Via Mozza and plunged abruptly into a block to define a Victory, one of the original concepts for Julius' tomb. It emerged as a classic Greek youth, well proportioned though not as muscular as others he had carved. He worked well with his hands, the chisels ploughing the pliant marble; but before long he realized that his head was not working at all.

Victory? Over whom? Over what? If he did not know who was the Victor, how could he determine who was the vanquished? Under the feet of the Victor, defeated and crushed, he carved the face and head of an old man . . . himself? As he might look ten or twenty years from now, with his beard grown full and white. What had defeated him? Age? Was youth the Victor, since it was the only period in which one could imagine that one could be a Victor? The defeated one had experience, a deep knowing and suffering in his face, bent under the knee of the youth. Was that what happened to experience and wisdom? Was it always crushed and destroyed by time in the guise of youth?

Outside his studio the Republic of Florence was triumphant. Niccolò Capponi was elected Gonfaloniere to govern in the Soderini tradition. For its protection the city-state had adopted Machiavelli's revolutionary plan for a militia of citizens trained, armed and equipped to defend the Republic against invaders. Florence was ruled not only by its Signoria but by a Council of Eighty, which represented the old families. Trade was active, the city prosperous, the people happy in their regained freedom. Few cared what happened to Pope Clement, still a prisoner in Sant'Angelo, defended by a few adherents, among them Benvenuto Cellini, the young sculptor who had refused to be apprenticed to Torrigiani. But Michelangelo was vitally interested in Pope Clement. He had put four years of loving work into the sacristy. There were partially finished blocks in the now locked and sealed chapel to whose future he was dedicated. He kept a close watch on Clement's fate.

Pope Clement was in danger from two sides. The Church was being broken up into national units, with power drained away from Rome. It was not merely that the Lutherans were sweeping through mid-Europe. Cardinal Wolsey of England proposed a council of free cardinals in France to set up a new government for the Church. The Italian cardinals were meeting at Parma to establish their own hierarchy. The French cardinals were setting up papal vicars. Charles' German and Spanish troops quartered in Rome were still sacking, destroying, demanding ransom to get out. From Sant'Angelo Clement tried to raise the money, forced to sacrifice hostages to the enemy: Jacopo Salviati was dragged through the streets to the gallows and almost hanged. The months went by, intrigue grew in every country for a new distribution of power, for a new Pope, a council, a reformation.

At the end of the Year of Our Lord 1527 the tide turned. A virulent plague decimated the Holy Roman Emperor's armies. The German troops hated Rome, were desperately anxious to return home. A French army invaded Italy to fight the Holy Roman Empire. Clement agreed to pay the invaders three hundred thousand ducats within three months. The Spanish army was withdrawn from the base of Sant'-

Angelo . . . and after seven months of incarceration Pope
Clement fled, disguised as a merchant, making his way to
Orvieto.

Michelangelo promptly received a communication from
Clement. Was Michelangelo still working for him? Would he
continue to sculpture in the new sacristy? If so, Pope
Clement had five hundred ducats on hand which he would
send to him by messenger to cover the immediate costs.

Michelangelo was deeply moved: the sorely harassed Pope,
without funds or followers or prospects of regaining power,
had sent words of affection and continued trust, as he would
have to any other member of his family.

" I can't take Giulio's money," Michelangelo said to Spina
as they conferred in the Via Mozza studio; " but couldn't
I carve sometimes? If I slipped in unseen, at night? It
could not hurt Florence."

" Patience. In a year or two. . . . The Council of Eighty
is apprehensive about what Clement may do. They would
consider your working on the chapel an act of disloyalty."

With warm weather, the plague struck Florence. People
came down with crushing headaches, pain in the back and
limbs, fever, vomiting, and in three days were dead. If they
dropped in the streets they were left there; if they died in
their houses their families fled. Thousands of Florentines
perished. The city became a morgue. Buonarroto summoned
his brother to the house on the Via Ghibellina.

" Michelangelo, I'm frightened for Bartolommea and the
children. Could I move up to our house in Settignano? We'd
be safe there."

" Certainly. Take Father with you."

" I won't go," growled Lodovico. " When a man is in his
mid-eighties he has a right to die in his own bed."

Fate was waiting for Buonarroto at Settignano, in the room
where he had been born. By the time Michelangelo reached
there Buonarroto was delirious, his tongue was swollen and
covered with a dry yellowish fuzz. Giovansimone had
moved Buonarroto's wife and children to safety the day before.
The servants and *contadini* had fled.

Michelangelo drew a chair up to his brother's bed, thinking
how much alike they still looked. Buonarroto's eyes lit in
alarm at the sight of his brother.

" Michelangelo . . . don't stay . . . the plague . . ."

Michelangelo wet his brother's parched lips with a damp

cloth, murmured, "I will not leave you. You're the only member of our family who has loved me."

"I always loved you. . . . But I've been . . . a burden. Forgive me. . . ."

"There's nothing to forgive, Buonarroto Had I kept you by my side all during the years I would have been much better off."

Buonarroto managed a weary smile.

"Michelangelo . . . You always were . . . good."

By sundown Buonarroto was dying. Michelangelo encircled him with his left arm, his brother's head resting on his chest. Buonarroto woke only once, saw Michelangelo's face held close to his own. The pain-caused furrows eased, resignation spread its calm unguent. In a few moments he was dead.

Michelangelo carried his brother in a blanket to the graveyard behind the church. There were no coffins, no diggers. He dug a grave, lowered Buonarroto into the hole, summoned the priest, waited until Buonarroto had been sprinkled with holy water and blessed; then he shovelled earth into the grave, filled it.

He returned to the Via Mozza, burned his clothes in the back yard, scrubbed himself in his wooden tub in water hot as he could stand. He did not know whether this helped against the plague, nor did he greatly care. Word was brought to him that Simone, his oldest nephew, was also dead of the plague. Michelangelo thought:

"Perhaps Buonarroto is the fortunate one?"

If he had caught the disease he had but a few hours to put his affairs in order. He drew up a paper paying back to Buonarroto's wife the dowry she had brought with her; a young woman, she would need it to get a second husband. He arranged for his eleven-year-old niece, Cecca, to be put into the Convent of Boldrone, providing for her keep and education by assigning produce from two of his farms. He set aside assets to pay for the education of his nephews Lionardo and little Buonarrotino. When Granacci banged on the locked door Michelangelo cried:

"Go away. I've been exposed to the plague. I may have caught it."

"Don't be *sciocco*. You're too crusty to die. Open up, I've got a bottle of wine to ward off evil spirits."

"Granacci, go home and drink by yourself. I'm not going

to be the cause of killing you. Maybe if you stay alive you'll paint one more good picture."

"Now isn't that an inducement!" laughed Granacci. "*Alora*, if you're still alive to-morrow, come finish your half of the Chianti."

The plague abated. People filtered down from the surrounding hills. Shops reopened. The Signoria returned to the city. One of its first resolutions was to commission Michelangelo Buonarroti to carve the Hercules which Soderini had ordered twenty years before, out of the block that Bandinelli had massed up to its navel.

Once again Pope Clement interfered. Having returned to the Vatican by making an alliance with the Holy Roman Emperor, he resumed power over the renegade Italian, French and English cardinals, formed an army out of the forces of the Duke of Urbino, the Colonna and Spanish troops. This army was being sent against independent Florence to wipe out the Republic, punish the enemies of the Medici and once again restore the family to power. Spina had underestimated Pope Clement and the Medici. Michelangelo was summoned before the Signoria, where Gonfaloniere Capponi sat at Soderini's desk, surrounded by his Eight-in-Office.

"Since you are a sculptor, Buonarroti," he said in a rushing voice, "we assume you can also be a defence engineer. We need walls that cannot be breached. Since they are of stone, and you are a man of stone . . ."

Michelangelo gulped. Now he would really be involved on both sides!

"Confine yourself to the south of the city. We are impregnable from the north. Report at the quickest possible moment."

He explored along the several miles of wall that began on the east with the hillside church of San Miniato, and snaked its way westward before returning to the Arno. Neither the walls nor defence towers were in a good state of repair, nor were there ditches on the outside to make the enemy approach more hazardous. Stones were loose, badly baked bricks were crumbling, more towers for cannon were needed, additional height to make scaling a longer task. The anchor of the defence line would have to be the campanile of San Miniato, from whose height the defenders could command most of the ground over which the enemy troops would have to charge.

He returned with his report to Gonfaloniere Capponi and the Signoria, laying out before them the number of stonemasons, brick-makers, carters, peasants he would need to make the walls defensible. The Gonfaloniere cried impetuously:

" Do not touch San Miniato. There is no need to fortify a church."

"There is every need, Excellency, for if we do not the enemy will not need to break down the walls. They will turn our flank here, east of the San Miniato hill."

He was given permission to prove that his plan was the best one possible. He pressed everyone into service: Granacci, the Company of the Cauldron, the masons from the Duomo workyard. Where before he had scoured the countryside seeking a figure, or face, a husky arm or elongated sunburnt throat for a statue or painting, now he searched for stonemasons, quarriers from Maiano and Prato, carpenters, brickmakers, mechanics, to stem a war. Work went ahead at full speed, for the Pope's army was reported moving on Florence from several directions, a formidable force of trained men and weapons, Michelangelo built a road up from the river for his men and supplies, began his bastions at the first tower outside the gate of San Miniato towards San Giorgio, closing in the vital defence hill with high walls of brick made of pounded earth mixed with flax, or tow, and cattle dung, a hundred *contadini* working in teams, throwing up the walls as fast as they could get the bricks squared. The stonemasons cut, chipped, shaped, shoring up weak stretches, adding height to the walls and towers, erecting new areas at the more vulnerable spots.

When the first phase of his work was completed the Signoria made an inspection. The next morning when he entered the corner office overlooking the Piazza della Signoria and the tight-knit roofs of Florence, he was greeted with smiles.

" Michelangelo, you have been elected to the *Nove della Milizia,* the Militia Nine, as Governor General of the Fortifications."

" It is a great honour, Gonfaloniere."

" And a greater responsibility. We want you to make an inspection trip to Pisa and Livorno, to make sure our defences from the sea are secure."

There was no further thought of sculpture. Nor could he cry, " War is not my trade." He had a specific job to do. Florence had called on him in its time of crisis. He had never imagined himself a commander, an organizer, but now he found that evolving intricate works of art had taught him how to co-ordinate each mounting detail to accomplish a finished result. He might even wish he had a little of Leonardo da Vinci's inventiveness with machines.

On his return from Pisa and Livorno he began a series of ditches as deep as moats, using the excavated earth and rock to form a further series of barricades. His next move was to secure permission to level all buildings between the defence walls and base of the encircling foothills a mile to the south, terrain over which the papal army would have to attack. The militia used battering rams of the kind the ancients used, to knock down the farmhouses and village homes. The farmers helped to level houses that had been in their families for hundreds of years. The wealthy protested against the wrecking of their palaces; not without reason, Michelangelo acknowledged, since they were so beautifully built. Only a few of the soldiers could be induced to level the several small chapels. When he himself came to the refectory of San Salvi and saw Andrea del Sarto's Last Supper shining in all its brilliance on the half-razed walls, he cried out:

" Let it be. It is too great a work of art to be destroyed."

The levelling job was just finished when he received word that the Via Mozza studio had been broken into. Models were thrown to the floor, folios of drawings and sketches scattered in wild confusion, many missing, as well as four models in wax. He saw the glitter of metal on the floor. Leaning over, he picked up a chisel from among a pile of papers. It was the kind used in a goldsmith's shop. He walked to the home of his friend Piloto, who knew the local goldsmiths.

" Do you recognize this chisel?"

" Yes. It belongs to Bandinelli."

Very discreetly the sketches and wax models were returned; Michelangelo instructed Mini to see that the studio was kept guarded.

The Signoria dispatched him to Ferrara to study the Duke of Ferrara's new fortifications. The note he carried with him read:

We send to Ferrara our celebrated Michelangelo Buonarroti, as you are aware a man of rare endowments, for certain purposes which he will explain to you by word

664

of mouth. We greatly desire that he should be recognized as a person highly esteemed by us and cherished as his merits deserve.

The Duke of Ferrara, a cultivated man of the Este family, and an enthusiast of painting, sculpture, poetry, the theatre, urged him to be a guest at the palace. Michelangelo graciously declined, staying at an inn where he enjoyed an uproarious reunion with Argiento, who brought in his nine children to kiss Michelangelo's hand.

"Well, Argiento, have you become a good farmer?"

Argiento grimaced. "No. But the earth makes things grow, no matter what I do to it. Children are my main crop."

"And mine is trouble, Argiento."

When Michelangelo thanked the Duke of Ferrara for revealing his defence structures, the duke said:

"Make me a painting. Then I shall be rewarded."

Michelangelo grinned. "As soon as this war is over."

Back in Florence he found that General Malatesta of Perugia had been brought to Florence to serve as one of the commanding generals. He quarrelled immediately with Michelangelo's plan to throw up stone supports in the manner he had learned in Ferrara.

"You have already burdened us with too many walls. Take your peasants away, and let my soldiers defend Florence."

Malatesta seemed cold, devious. That night Michelangelo roamed the base of his ramparts. He came upon the eight pieces of artillery that had been given to Malatesta to defend the San Miniato wall. Instead of being placed inside the fortifications, or on the parapets, they lay outside the walls, unguarded. Michelangelo awoke the sleeping general.

"What do you mean by exposing your artillery pieces that way? We guarded them with our lives until you arrived. They could be stolen or destroyed by anyone who stumbled upon them."

"Are you the commander of the Florentine army?" demanded Malatesta, livid.

"Just the defence walls."

"Then go make your cow-dung brick, and don't tell a soldier how to fight."

Returning to San Miniato, Michelangelo encountered General Mario Orsini, who demanded:

" What has gone wrong, my friend? Your face is on fire."
Michelangelo told him. When he had finished, Orsini
replied sadly:

" You must know that the men of his house are all traitors.
In time he will betray Florence."

" Have you reported this to the Signoria?"

" I am a hired officer, like Malatesta, not a Florentine."

In the morning Michelangelo waited in the Great Hall of the
palace until he could be admitted to the Gonfaloniere's
office. The Signoria was not impressed.

" Stop concerning yourself over our officers. Confine
yourself to your new plans for the walls. They must not be
breached."

" They won't need to be with Malatesta guarding them."

" You are overwrought. Get some rest."

He returned to the walls, continued to work under
the broiling September sun, but he could not put Malatesta
out of his mind. Everywhere he went he heard stories against
the general: he had yielded Perugia without a battle; his
men would not fight the Pope's troops at Arezzo; when the
armies reached Florence, Malatesta would surrender the
city . . .

In his mind he went back time and again to the Signoria,
pleading that Malatesta be removed, seeing his labours in
building impregnable walls going for nothing as Malatesta
opened the gates to the Pope's army. Or was it really to
Gonfaloniere Capponi that he was protesting? . . . Wasn't it to
Pope Julius . . . about Bramante's walls for St. Peter's . . .
which were made of weak cement and would crumble? . . .
Had Malatesta demanded, " Are you the commander of the
army?" Wasn't it Pope Julius who had asked, " Are you
an architect?" . . .

He became agitated. He envisaged the Pope's troops
destroying Florence even as Rome had been, sacking, pillag-
ing, smashing the works of art. Sleepless, unable to eat or to
concentrate on directing his stone crews, he began to over-
hear shards of sentences which convinced him that Malatesta
had gathered the officers on this south wall in a conspiracy
against Florence.

He went six days and nights without rest or nourishment,
unable to control his anxieties. One night a voice spoke to
him. He whirled about on the parapet:

" Who are you?"

" A friend."

" What do you want?"

" To save your life."

" Is it in danger?"

" Of the worst kind."

" The Pope's army?"

" Malatesta."

" What is he going to do?"

" Have you killed."

" Why?"

" For exposing his treason."

" No one believes me."

" Your corpse will be found at the base of the bastion."

" I can protect myself."

" Not in this mist."

" What should I do?"

" Flee."

" That is treason."

" Better than being dead."

" When must I go?"

" Now."

" I'm in charge here."

" You haven't a moment."

" How can I explain?"

" Hurry!"

" My command . . . the walls . . ."

" Hurry! Hurry!"

He descended from the parapet, crossed the Arno, took a back route to the Via Mozza. Figures emerged from the thick fog half formed, like massed marble blocks. He ordered Mini to put clothes and money in their saddlebags. He and Mini mounted their horses. At the Prato gate they were challenged. A guard cried:

" It is Michelangelo, of the Militia Nine. Let him by."

He headed for Bologna, Ferrara, Venice, France . . . safety.

He was back after seven weeks, humiliated and in disgrace. The Signoria fined him, and barred him from the Council for three years. But because the papal armies were now camped thirty thousand strong on the hills beyond his southern defence walls they sent him back to his command. He had Granacci to thank for his reprieve; when the Signoria outlawed him, along with others who had taken flight.

Granacci had secured a temporary commutation for him and sent Bastiano, who had helped Michelangelo repair the walls, in pursuit.

" I must say the Signoria was lenient," commented Granacci sternly, " considering that you have returned a full five weeks after the Rebel Exclusion Act. You could have lost all your property in Tuscany, and your head too, as Ficino's grandson lost his life for stating that the Medici seemed more entitled to rule than anyone else, considering their contribution to the city. You had better take a blanket up to San Miniato and enough victuals for a year's siege. . . ."

" Don't worry, Granacci, I can't be that stupid twice."

" What possessed you?"

" I heard voices."

" Whose?"

" My own."

Granacci grinned.

" I was helped by the rumours of your reception at the court in Venice, the offer from the Doge to design a bridge over the Rialto, and the French ambassador's efforts to get you to the French court. The Signoria thought you were an idiot, which you are, but great artist, which you are. They weren't happy about your settling in Venice or Paris. Just thank your stars that you know how to chip marble, or you might never again have lived in sight of the Duomo."

Michelangelo looked out of the third-floor window of Granacci's study to where Brunelleschi's glorious red tile dome stood in its spatial majesty against a stormy sunset.

" The finest architectural form in the world is the bowl of the sky," he mused, " and do you know, Brunelleschi's dome is equally beautiful!"

5

He settled his effects in the tower of San Miniato, gazed through the powdery light of a full moon at the hundreds of enemy tents with their pointed cones set up a mile away, beyond the ground he had cleared on the hills that formed a semicircle to enclose his protective line.

He was awakened at dawn by artillery fire. As he had expected, the attack was concentrated against the tower of

San Miniato. If it could be knocked down, the Pope's forces would pour into the city. One hundred and fifty pieces of artillery fired steadily. Whole sections of brick and stone were blasted out by the exploding cannon balls. The attack lasted for two hours. When it was finished Michelangelo let himself out by a tunnel and stood at the base of the bell tower, surveying the damage.

He asked for volunteers among those who knew how to handle stone and cement. Bastiano directed the work inside, Michelangelo took a group outside and in full view of the papal troops refitted the fallen, shattered stone into the walls. For some reason beyond his comprehension, perhaps because they did not know how much damage they had inflicted, the enemy troops remained in camp. He ordered his carters to bring in Arno sand and sacks of cement, sent out runners to collect the crews of masons and quarriers, at dusk set them to rebuilding the tower. They worked all night; but it took time for cement to harden. If the enemy artillery opened fire too soon, his defence would be levelled. He gazed up at the campanile, its crenellated cornice wider by four feet all around than th shaft of the tower. If there were a way to hang something from those parapets, something that could absorb the impact of the iron and stone cannon balls before they could strike the tower itself . . .

He made his way down the hill, crossed the Ponte Vecchio, obliged the guards to awaken the new Gonfaloniere, Francesco Carducci, explained his device, obtained a written order and a company of militia. By first light they were beating on the doors of the wool shops, the warehouses and the customs sheds where wool was held for taxing purposes. Next they hunted the city for mattress covers, in shops and in private homes, then requisitioned carts to carry the material. He worked fast. By the time the sun was up he had dozens of his stoutest covers stuffed with wool and suspended by ropes across the face of the tower.

When the Pope's officers learned what was going on and turned their artillery on the campanile, it was too late. Their cannon balls struck the heavy padding which, although they gave with the impact, had four feet of leeway before reaching the wet stone walls. The mattresses served as a shield for Michelangelo's newly cemented blocks. The cannon balls fell harmlessly into the ditch below. After firing until noon, the enemy abandoned the attack.

The success of his ingenious wool buffers won him repatriation. He returned to his studio, had his first night of peaceful sleep in months.

Heavy rains began to fall. The open mile of cleared fields between his walls and the enemy became a bog. There could be no attack now. Michelangelo began to paint in tempera a Leda and the Swan for the Duke of Ferrara. Though he worshipped the physical aspect of beauty, his art had been permeated with a sexual purity. Now he found himself indulging in a robust carnality. He portrayed Leda as a ravishingly beautiful woman, lying on a couch, with the swan nestled between her legs, the " S " of his long neck cupping one breast, his lips on hers. He enjoyed portraying the lusty fable.

The raw overcast continued. He spent the days on the parapets, at night waited his opportunity to slip into the sacristy and carve by candlelight. The chapel was cold, full of shadows; but he was not alone. His figures were familiar friends: the Dawn, the Dusk, the Virgin: for although they were not fully born, they were alive in the marble, thinking, telling him what they felt about the world, just as he spoke to them and through them, of art as man's continuity, the eternality that ties together the future and the past; a means of conquering death: for as long as art lives, man does not perish.

In the spring the war was resumed, but none of the battles except the one against starvation took place in Florence. Restored to his position on the Militia Nine, Michelangelo received reports each evening. By capturing small fortresses on the Arno, the papal army had cut off supplies from the sea. Spanish troops arrived from the south and Germans from the north to swell Pope Clement's troops.

Food grew scarce. Meat vanished first, then oil, greens, flour, wine. Famine took its toll. Michelangelo gave his own daily ration to Lodovico to keep his father alive. People began eating the city's asses, dogs, cats. Summer heat baked the stones, the water supply failed, the Arno dried up, the plague struck again. Men panted for air, dropped and never rose. By mid-July five thousand were dead within the city.

Florence had only one chance to survive, through its heroic general Francesco Ferrucci, whose army was near Pisa. Plans were laid for him to attack by way of Lucca and Pistoia and lift the siege. The last sixteen thousand men within the walls who were able to fight took the sacrament, vowing to storm the enemy camps on both sides of the city, while General Ferrucci struck from the west.

General Malatesta betrayed the Republic. He refused to help Ferrucci. Ferrucci hit hard, was on the verge of victory, when Malatesta treated with the Pope's generals. Ferrucci was defeated and killed.

Florence capitulated. Malatesta's troops opened the gates. Pope Clement's representatives entered the city to take control in the name of the Medici. Florence agreed to hand over eighty thousand ducats as back pay to the papal armies. Those members of the government who could, fled; others were hanged from the Bargello or thrown into the Stinche. All members of the Militia Nine were condemned.

"You'd better get out of the city this very night," Bugiardini urged Michelangelo. "The Pope will show no mercy. You built the defences against him."

"I can't run again," replied Michelangelo wearily.

"Take refuge in the attic in my house," offered Granacci.

"I will not endanger your family."

"As official architect, I have the keys of the Duomo. I can hide you there," cried Baccio d'Agnolo.

Michelangelo was thoughtful. "I know a tower on the other side of the Arno. No one will suspect it. I'll take refuge there until Malatesta clears out with his troops."

He bade his friends farewell and made his way by back passages to the Arno, crossed the river and slipped silently to the bell tower of San Niccolò, knocking at the house next door, which belonged to the stonemason sons of old Beppe of the Duomo workyard, to let them know he was taking refuge. Then he locked the door of the tower behind him, climbed its circular wooden staircase and spent the rest of the night staring over the hills at the deserted enemy camp. At sunrise he was still leaning against the stone walls gazing sightlessly at the terrain he had levelled to protect the city-state.

Looking inward and backward, his own fifty-five years seemed as torn down, and uselessly so, as the mile of levelled ground below him. He reckoned the account of the years since Pope Leo had forced him to abandon the work on Julius' tomb. What did he have to show for those fourteen years? A Risen Christ which, Sebastiano had tearfully reported from Rome, had been injured by the inept apprentice who had removed the webbing between the legs and feet, and who had idiotically overlicked the face while polishing. A Victory which to-day, even more than the day he finished it, seemed confused. Four Giants still writhing in their blocks in the Via Mozza. A Moses and two Young Slaves in a house in Rome that had been plundered by an invading army.

Nothing. Nothing finished, nothing put together, made whole, delivered. And a one-armed, crippled David standing as a symbol of the vanquished Republic.

Not only cities were besieged and sacked. Man too was beleaguered.

Lorenzo had said that the forces of destruction were everywhere, overtaking everything and everybody within their range. That was all he had known since the days of Savonarola: conflict. Perhaps his father and Uncle Francesco had been right to try to beat some sense into him. Whom had he enriched or made happy? He had spent a lifetime tearing himself apart, enduring the *terribilità* of his own nature in an attempt to create beautiful marbles, meaningful statues. He had loved the sculptor's art since he was born. He had wanted only to revive it, re-create it, bring to it newer, greater conceptions. Had he wanted too much? For himself, and for his time?

So very long ago his friend Jacopo Galli had told Cardinal Groslaye of San Dionigi, " Michelangelo will make you the most beautiful marble to be seen in Rome to-day, such that no master of our own time will be able to produce a better."

And here he was, a self-incarcerated prisoner cowering in an ancient bell tower, afraid to come down for fear he would be hanged from the Bargello as he had seen so many hanged during his youth. What an inglorious end for the pure bright fire that had burned in his bosom.

Between midnight chimes and cockcrow he walked along the upper marshes of the Arno, returning to find that food and water had been left for him, and the news of the day jotted down by Mini. Gonfaloniere Carducci had been decapitated in the courtyard of the Bargello. Girolami, who had succeeded him as Gonfaloniere, had been taken to Pisa and poisoned. Fra Benedetto, a priest who had sided with the Republic, had been taken to Rome to be starved to death in Sant'Angelo. All who had escaped were outlawed, their property confiscated.

Florence knew where he was hiding, but the somnolent

hatred for Pope Clement, his generals and troops was so intense that he was not only safe from exposure but had become a hero.

Lodovico, whom Michelangelo had sent to Pisa with Buonarroto's two sons during the worst stage of the siege, returned without Buonarrotino. The boy had died in Pisa.

On a mid-November day he heard someone calling his name, loud and clear. Gazing downward from the bell tower, he saw Giovanni Spina huddled in a huge fur coat, hands cupped to his mouth as he cried upward:

" Michelangelo, come down!"

He took the circular wooden stairs three at a time, unbolted the door, saw Spina's long narrow eyes gleaming.

" The Pope has pardoned you. He sent word through Prior Figiovanni that if you were found you were to be treated kindly, your pension restored, and the house by San Lorenzo . . ."

" . . . why?"

" The Holy Father wants you to return to work in the sacristy."

While Michelangelo gathered his things Spina surveyed the tower.

" It's freezing up here. What did you use to keep warm?"

" Indignation," said Michelangelo. " Best fuel I know. Never burns out."

As he walked through the streets in the late autumn sun he let his fingers trail over the *pietra serena* blocks of the houses; slowly they imparted their warmth to him. His breath came fast at the thought of returning to the *cappella*.

His studio in the Via Mozza had been thoroughly ransacked by the papal troops who had searched for him; even the chimney and chests had been looked into. Nothing had been stolen. In the chapel he found the scaffolding removed, probably to keep the clergy of San Lorenzo warm; but none of his marbles had been disturbed. After three years of war he could resume work. Three years . . .! As he stood in the centre of his allegorical blocks he divined that time too was a tool: a major work of art required months, years for its emotional elements to solidify. Time was a yeast; many aspects of the Day and Dusk, the Madonna, which had eluded him before now seemed clear to him, their form matured, their definition resolved. A work of art meant growth from the particular to the universal. To a work of art, time brought timelessness.

After a light supper with Lodovico he returned to the Via Mozza studio. Mini was out. He lit an oil lamp, walked about the studio touching familiar pieces of furniture. It was good to be home again, among his few possessions: the Battle of the Centaurs and his Madonna of the Stairs hanging on the back wall; the four unfinished Captives still facing each other in an intimate circle in the centre of the studio. He took out his folios of drawings, leafed through them approvingly, or made a stabbing correction line with a stubby pen. Then he turned over a drawing-sheet and wrote with deep emotion:

Too much good luck no less than misery
May kill a man condemned to mortal pain,
If, lost to hope and chilled in every vein,
A sudden pardon comes to set him free.

Beauteous art, which, brought with us from heaven,
Will conquer nature; so divine a power
Belongs to him who strives with every nerve.

If I was made for art, from childhood given
A prey for burning beauty to devour,
I blame the mistress I was born to serve.

Baccio Valori, new governor of Florence for Pope Clement, sent for him to come to the Medici palace. Michelangelo wondered: Valori had helped drive Soderini out of Florence in 1512. But Valori was all smiles as he sat behind the desk from which *Il Magnifico* had guided the destinies of Florence.

" Buonarroti, I need you."

" It is always good to be needed, *signore*."

" I want you to design a house for me. So I can build at once! And along with it, one of your great marble sculptures for the courtyard."

" You do me too much honour," muttered Michelangelo as he descended the broad staircase. But Granacci was delighted.

" It's your turn to woo the enemy. Valori loathes the Company. He knows we were anti-Medici. If you do as he asks we'll all be reprieved."

Michelangelo walked to the house on the Via Ghibellina. In a wool-padded storage bin in the kitchen stood the experimental David he had carved from the marble Beppe had bought for him, the David whose foot rested on Goliath's black, bloody head. With a litle chiselling the head of Goliath would disappear, and in its place would be a round sphere . . . the world. David would become a new Apollo.

The family home seemed empty and forlorn. He missed Buonarroto. Sigismondo, who had been part of the Florentine army for the past three years, asked permission to live on the family farm in Settignano. Giovansimone was determined to have Michelangelo finance the reopening of the wool shop. Lodovico had grown feeble, so stricken by the death of his young grandchild Buonarrotino that he was unable to recount what had happened to the boy. Eleven-year-old Lionardo was the remaining hope and satisfaction of the Buonarroti family, inheritor of the family name. Michelangelo had paid for his three years of education.

" Uncle Michelangelo, could I be apprenticed to you?"

" As a sculptor?" Michelangelo was aghast.

" Aren't you a sculptor?"

" Yes. But it is not a life I would wish on my only nephew. I think you would be happier apprenticed to the Strozzi for the wool trade. Until then, suppose you come to the studio and take over your father's account books. I need someone to make the entries."

The boy's brown eyes, with the amber flecks so similar to Buonarroto's and his own, lighted.

Returning to the Via Mozza, he found Mini entertaining a lavishly gowned emissary from the Duke of Ferrara.

" Maestro Buonarroti, I have come to collect the painting you promised to my duke."

" It is finished."

When he brought out the Leda and the Swan, the emissary stared at it in silence. After a moment he said:

" This is but a trifle. My duke expected a masterpiece."

Michelangelo studied the tempera, gazing with satisfaction at the voluptuous Leda.

" May I ask what your business is, *signore*?

" I am a merchant." Haughtily.

" Then your duke will find you have made a bad bargain for him. Be so kind as to remove yourself from my studio."

6

He resumed work in the chapel, again hiring brickmasons and cement men. Instead of working his Allegories on turntables to catch the changing light, he had them propped with wooden blocks at the angle at which the figures would rest on the sarcophagi, and in the position in the chapel they would ultimately occupy. In this way he would make the most effective use of the actual light and shadow they would absorb.

In designing the four reclining figures for the two tombs his problem was to hold the visual attention and not let it drain downward off the arc of the curved tomb cover. To this end he created a countercurve in the torso, with one leg of each figure bent upward in high projection, the other with outstretched toes extending to the farthest edge of the block. The abrupt upward thrust into space of the leg would hold his shoulder-to-shoulder figures on their precarious ledges.

It was cold in the chapel from the outside rains, and penetratingly damp from the water oozing out of the slow-drying cement of the bricked-up windows. He sometimes felt his teeth chattering even when moving with high speed through the marble. At night when he returned to his own studio he found his head filled with mucus, his throat raw. He ignored the difficulties, grimly determined that this project must not become another Julius' tomb.

Sebastiano continued to write from Rome: the Pietà had been exposed to danger in its chapel, but no man had dared injure the dead Jesus on his mother's lap. The Bacchus had been buried by Jacopo Galli's family in the orchard outside his old workshed and had now been set up again. He, Sebastiano, had been appointed the Pope's Keeper of the Seals, become a friar, with a handsome salary, and was now known as Sebastiano del Piombo. As for the house on the Macello dei Corvi, the plaster of the walls and ceilings was crumbling, most of the furnishings had vanished, the buildings round the edge of the garden had been torn down for firewood. His marbles were safe, but the house was in desperate need of attention. Couldn't Michelangelo send money to have the repairs made?

Michelangelo had no money to send. Florence had not recovered from the war; food and materials were scarce, trade was so poor that his outlay for the family shop was lost each month. Valori ruled with a harsh hand. Pope Clement kept the various factions of Florence at each other's throats. The city had hoped that Ippolito, the gentle, sweet-natured son of Giuliano, would replace Valori; but Pope Clement had other plans. Ippolito was made a cardinal, against his strongest wishes, and sent to Hungary as commander of the Italian forces against the Turks. Clement's own son, known as Alessandro the Moor because of his swarthy skin and thick lips, was brought to Florence with great ceremony and made sovereign of the city-state for life. A dissolute, ugly youth of low intelligence and rapacious appetites, with his father's troops on hand to enforce his slightest wish, Alessandro murdered his opponents in broad daylight, raped and debauched the youth of the city, wiped out its last semblances of freedom, and quickly brought it to a state of anarchy.

Equally quickly, Michelangelo fought with Alessandro. When Alessandro asked him to design a new fort above the Arno, Michelangelo declined. When Alessandro sent word that he wished to show the chapel to the visiting Viceroy of Naples, Michelangelo locked the sacristy.

"Your conduct is dangerous," cautioned Giovanni Spina.

"I'm safe until I complete the tomb. Clement has made that clear, even to his thick-skulled son . . . or I would have been dead long ago."

He laid down his chisels, wiped the marble dust from his face and eyebrows, looked about him and exclaimed with gratification:

"This chapel will outlive Alessandro, even if I don't."

"You won't, I'm sure of that. You are emaciated, you have a racking cough. Why don't you walk in the hills in the warm sun, cure your cold, put some merciful flesh on your bones?"

Michelangelo sat on the edge of a plank placed between the two sawhorses, answered thoughtfully:

"There is nothing left of the good in Florence, of order, except its art. When I stand before this marble Day with a hammer and chisel in my hands I feel that I am fulfilling the law of Moses through an art form, to compensate for the spiritual degradation of Alessandro and his bullies. Which will survive, these marble sculptures or the debauchery?"

677

"Then at least let me move the marbles to a warm, dry room."

"I have to carve them here, Spina, where the light is exactly what it will be when they are on the sarcophagi."

In the studio that evening he found a request from Giovan Battista, Mini's uncle: the boy had fallen hopelessly in love with an impoverished widow's daughter and wanted to marry her. His uncle thought he ought to be sent out of the country. Could Michelangelo help?

When Mini returned from the night's diversion Michelangelo asked him, "Do you love this girl?"

"Passionately!" said Mini.

"Is it the same girl you loved passionately last summer?"

"Of course not."

"Then take this painting of Leda and the Swan. And these drawings. The money from them will set you up in a studio in Paris."

"But the Leda is worth a fortune!" exclaimed Mini, astonished.

"Then see that you get a fortune for her. Write to me from France."

Mini had no sooner headed north than a young man of about twenty presented himself at the door of the studio, introducing himself as Francesco Amadore.

"Though I am called Urbino," he added in a quiet voice. "The priest at San Lorenzo told me you needed someone."

"What kind of job are you looking for?"

"I seek a home, Signor Buonarroti, and a family, for I have none. Later, I should like to marry and have a family of my own; but I must work for many years first. I come of humble people and have only these clothes on my back."

"You wish to become a sculpture apprentice?"

"An art apprentice, *messere*."

Michelangelo studied the man standing before him, his clothes threadbare but neat, lean to the point of boniness, with a convex stomach that had never known its fill; steady grey eyes, dust-grey teeth and light, ash-grey hair. Urbino needed a home and employment, yet his manner had dignity, an inner quietude. Apparently he respected himself; and this Michelangelo liked.

"Very well, let us try."

Urbino had a nobility of spirit which illuminated everything he did. He was so overjoyed to belong somewhere that he filled the house with his own happiness, treating

678

Michelangelo with the reverence due a father. Michelangelo found himself growing attached to the young man.

Pope Clement again urged Julius' heirs to negotiate a release. The Roveres, though they felt insulted and put upon, agreed orally to accept the single-faced wall tomb, ornamented by the figures which Michelangelo had already carved. He was to relinquish the Moses and two Slaves, finish the four Captives, and ship them with the Victory to Rome. All that remained for him to do was make drawings for the other figures and raise two thousand ducats to return to the Roveres, who would pay it over to another marble master to complete the sepulchre. After twenty-seven years of worry, and eight major sculptures for which he was not to receive one scudo of wage, he would be freed from his self-imposed hell.

He could not sell any one of his farms or houses for the necessary two thousand ducats. No one in Tuscany had any money. The only building for which he could get a fair offer was the Via Mozza studio.

" I'm heartbroken," he cried to Spina. " I love this *bottega*."

Spina sighed. " Let me write to Rome. Perhaps we can arrange to have the money payment postponed."

Giovansimone chose this moment to come to the Via Mozza for one of his rare visits.

" I want the big house in the Via di San Proculo," he announced.

" For what?"

" To set myself up in style."

" It's rented."

" We don't need the rent money."

" Perhaps you don't, but I do."

" For what? You're rich enough."

" Giovansimone, I'm struggling to pay a debt to the Roveres . . ."

" That's just your excuse. You're stingy, like Father."

" Have you ever lacked for anything?"

" My proper place in life. We are noble burghers."

" Then act nobly."

" I haven't the money. You keep hoarding it."

" Giovansimone, you're fifty-three years old, and you have never supported yourself. I have supported you for thirty-four years, ever since Savonarola's death."

" You get no praise for doing your duty. You speak as though we were vulgar artisans. Our family is as old as the

Medici, Strozzi or Tornabuoni. We have been paying taxes in Florence for three centuries!"

"You sound like Father," replied Michelangelo wearily.

"We have the right to display the Medici crest. I want to set it up in front of the Via di San Proculo house, hire servants. You're for ever protesting that everything you do is for our family. Well then, prove it, dig out the words and fill the hole with gold."

"Giovansimone, you couldn't see a black crow in a bowl of milk. I don't have the resources to make a Florentine nobleman out of you."

He heard that Sigismondo had moved into the peasant's quarters in Settignano and was working the land. He rode up the hill to find Sigismondo behind a plough guiding two white oxen, his face and hair under a straw hat wet with perspiration, manure caked on one boot.

"Sigismondo, you're working like a *contadino*."

Sigismondo took off his hat, wiped his forehead with a heavy clublike movement of his forearm.

"I just plough the field."

"But why? We have tenants here to do the manual labour."

"I like to work."

"But not as a labourer. Sigismondo, what can you be thinking of? No, Buonarroti has worked with his hands for three hundred years."

"Except you!"

Michelangelo flushed. "I am a sculptor. What will people in Florence say when they hear my brother is working like a peasant? After all, the Buonarroti have been noble burghers; we have a coat of arms . . ."

". . . coat of arms won't feed me. I'm too old to fight now, so I work. This is our land, I raise wheat and olives and grapes. . . ."

"Do you have to walk in dung to do it?"

Sigismondo looked down at his crusted boot.

"Dung fertilizes the field."

"I've worked all my life to make the Buonarroti name honoured throughout Italy. Do you want people to say that I have a brother in Settignano who tends oxen?"

Sigismondo gazed at his two handsome white animals, replied with affection, "Oxen is nice."

"They are beautiful animals. Now go take yourself a

bath, get into clean clothes, and let one of our renters plough the furrows."

He lost both arguments. Giovansimone spread the word in Florence that his brother Michelangelo was a miser and a vulgarian who refused to allow his family to live according to their high rank in Tuscan society. Sigismondo spread the word in Settignano that his brother Michelangelo was a snob and aristocrat who thought his family had become too good for honest labour. As a result both brothers got what they wanted : more money for Giovansimone to spend ; the land for Sigismondo to tend.

He concentrated on the two female figures, Dawn and Night. Except for the Madonnas, he had never sculptured a woman. He had no desire to portray young girls at the threshold of life, he wanted to carve fertility, the bounteous body which brings forth the race of man, mature women who had laboured and been in labour, with bodies fatigued but indomitable. Did he have to be androgynous to create authentic women? All artists were androgynous. He carved Dawn as not yet awake, caught in the transition between dream and reality, her head still resting wearily on her shoulder ; a band drawn tight under the breasts to emphasize spatially their bulbous quality ; the stomach muscles sagging, the womb exhausted from bearing, the whole arduous journey of her life in the half-closed eyes and half-open mouth ; the left arm bent and suspended in air, ready to fall as soon as she lifted her head from her shoulder to face the day.

He moved the few steps across the chapel to work on the sumptuously voluptuous figure of Night: still young, fertile, desirable, cradle of men ; the exquisite Greek head resting on its delicately arched neck, eyes closed in resigning to sleep and darkness; tension reflected through the long-limbed figure in plastic manipulations of flesh to give a quality of sensuality which he would heighten with a high polish. Light moving freely on the contours of the milky marble would intensify the female forms: the hard ripe breasts, fount of sustenance, the magnificently robust thigh, the arm pulled sharply behind the back to turn the breast proudly outward: every man's dream of the beauteous, bounteous female body, ready for sleep? love? fecundation?

He polished the figure with straw and sulphur, remembering how his ancestors, the Etruscans, had carved reclining stone figures for the lids of their sarcophagi.

He finished Dawn in June, and Night in August, two heroic marble carvings in the nine months since he had left his tower, pouring out his inner power over the hot dry summer, then turned to the male figures of Day and Dusk, leaving strong calligraphic textures about the head, doing no filing or polishing because the tool markings in themselves denoted vigorous masculinity. With Day, a wise, strong man who knew every aspect of life's passing pain and pleasure, he carved the head sweeping out over its own massive shoulder and forearm, reflecting in its muscled torso a back that had lifted and carried the weights of the world.

Dusk was a portrait of his own sunken-eyed, bony-nosed, bearded face, the head diagonally reclining like the sinking sun as it dipped towards the horizon, the gnarled expression of the features reflected in the laboured hands, the strong-modelled knees raised and crossed, leg extending outward on its thin shelf of marble beyond the tomb itself.

He had studied anatomy to acquaint himself with the inner physical workings of man; now he treated the marble as having an anatomy of its own. In this chapel he wanted to leave something of himself, something which time itself could not erase.

He finished Dusk in September.

The rains started, the chapel became cold and raw. Again his flesh vanished, he was down to bone and gristle, under a hundred pounds as he picked up hammer and chisel to siphon the blood of his veins, his marrow and calcium into the veins and bones of the Day, the Virgin and Child, the statue of a seated, contemplative Lorenzo. As the marbles grew throbbingly alive, vibrant, powerful, lusty, he became correspondingly drained; it was from his own inner storehouse of will, courage, daring and brain that the marbles were infused with their eternal energies. His last ounce of strength he poured into the immortality of the marbles.

" It won't do, you know." This time it was Granacci who reproved him, a Granacci who himself had grown lean over the misfortunes of his city. " Death from overindulgence is a form of suicide, whether it's from work or wine."

" If I don't work twenty hours a day I'll never finish."

" It's the other way around. If you would have the good sense to rest you could live for ever."

" It's been for ever."

Granacci shook his head. " At fifty-seven you have the *forza* of a man of thirty. Me, I'm worn out . . . from pleasure.

With your luck, why should you think that dying is going to be any easier than living?"

Michelangelo laughed for the first time in weeks.

"Granacci *mio*, how poor my life would have been without your friendship. It's your fault . . . this sculpturing . . . you took me to Lorenzo's garden, you encouraged me."

Granacci chuckled.

"You never wanted to do tombs, yet you've spent most of your life on marbles for tombs. All your years you said you would never do portraits, and here you are stuck with two of them, life size."

"You're dreaming."

"You're not going to carve the portraits for the niches?"

"Assuredly not. Who will know a hundred years from now whether my marbles are good likenesses of young Lorenzo and Giuliano? I'm going to carve universal figures of action and contemplation. They will be nobody, yet everybody. A subject is a farm wagon to carry a sculptor's ideas to market."

Urbino had been taught to read and write by the priests at Castel Durante; slowly he slipped into the position of steward of both the household and the studio. Now that his nephew Lionardo was doing well as an apprentice to the Strozzi, Michelangelo gave Urbino the books to keep. Urbino paid the wages and bills, assumed the role Buonarroto had played when he was young, became a protector who could make Michelangelo's life smoother, take the petty annoyances off his shoulders. Michelangelo came to have a feeling of permanence about the relationship.

He rested by moving into clay models, mixing in cloth frayings to make the clay fatter so that it would be more responsive to his manipulation, kneading the composition to adhere to the armature. The dampness of the clay was so similar to the dampness of the chapel that he felt he was shaping the wet raw interior space of the sacristy. Transferring from the clay to the marble block, he carved the statue of young Lorenzo for the niche above Dawn and Dusk, using an architectonic approach, designing this figure of contemplation to be static, tight, withdrawn, involved in its own interior brooding. For contrast he evolved an action-composition of Giuliano for over the tomb holding the Day and Night on the opposite wall: loose, with a circulation of tension and a continuous state of motion. Lorenzo's head was well set and compressed into his shoulders; Giuliano sat with a sudden thrust of the neck into space.

It was the Madonna and Child from which he took his joy. He longed to the very fibres and roots of his soul to give her a divine beauty: her face glowing with love and compassion, the birth-place and the resurgent future, instrument of the godhead through which the human race, in the face of its adversities and tragedies, endures.

He saw the mother-and-child theme all fresh and shining, as though he had never carved it before: intense desire and intense fulfilment: the child twisted about on his mother's lap, vigorously seeking nourishment; the elaborate folds of the mother's gown heightening the agitation, externalizing her feeling of fulfilment and pain as the greedy, earthy child sucked. He felt lightheaded, somehow as though he were back in his first studio, carving the Madonna for the merchants of Bruges . . . back in his period of grace.

It was only a high fever. When it passed he was so weak his legs could barely hold him.

The Pope sent a carriage and driver to Florence, ordering Michelangelo to come to Rome to recuperate in the warmth of the more southerly sun, and to hear about an exciting new project he had envisaged. Clement invited Michelangelo's friends in the Florentine colony for dinner at the Vatican, had several comedies played to amuse him. Clement's solicitude for his health was genuine, almost like that of a beloved brother. Then the Pope revealed his desire: would Michelangelo like to paint a Last Judgment on the vast altar wall of the Sistine Chapel?

At the dinner Michelangelo met a young man of singular beauty, like that of the Greek youths he had painted behind the Holy Family he had made for Doni. He had eyes of a luminous *pietra serena* grey-blue; a classical nose and mouth carved out of flesh-coloured marble by Praxiteles; a high, rounded forehead in perfect plumb with the big-boned, curved chin; chestnut hair; long, symmetrically carved cheeks with high cheekbones; and the rose-bronzed skin of the youths who competed in the Stadia of Greece.

Tommaso de' Cavalieri, twenty-two, well educated, serious, was the heir of a patrician Roman family. Ambitious to become a first-rate painter, he asked eagerly if he might become an apprentice. The admiration in Tommaso's eyes amounted almost to idolatry. Michelangelo replied that he must return to Florence to finish the Medici chapel, but there was no reason why they could not spend some part of his time in Rome drawing together. The young man's intense concentration as he watched Michelangelo achieve his volatile effects was enormously flattering. Michelangelo found Tommaso to be a talented, conscientious worker, delightful and *simpatico*. Tommaso had the welcome faculty of making the thirty-five year difference between their ages dissolve, so that in Tommaso's presence he felt young, was able to laugh, to be taken out of himself. When they parted they agreed to write to each other. Michelangelo volunteered to send special drawings from which Tommaso could study, and to send word when he had arrived at his decision for the Pope.

Back in Florence he returned to the sacristy refreshed. By spring he had forgotten about dying. In achieving his skin finishes on the two male figures he used the crosshatching method first taught him by Ghirlandaio with a pen: one set of calligraphic lines made by a two-toothed chisel superimposed over a set of *ugnetto* lines, at right angles so that the finer tooth marks of the chisel would not fall into the heavier and more prominent tracks of the *ugnetto*. He emerged with textures of skin that had all the tension and pull of living tissue. On the Madonna's cheeks he achieved a soft, pebbly texture.

The beauty of her face was sublime.

7

Time was not a mountain but a river; it changed its rate of flow as well as its course. It could become swollen, overflow its banks, or dry to a trickle; it could run clean and pure along its bed or become laden with silt and throw up debris along the shore. When Michelangelo was young, every day had been particularised; it had had body, content, shape, stood out as an individual entity to be numbered, recorded and remembered.

Now time was a soluble: the weeks and months merged in a continuous flow at an ever accelerated speed. He was getting as much work done but the very texture of time had altered for him, its arbitrary boundaries become indistinct. The years were no longer individual blocks but Apuan Alps which man in his need broke into separate peaks. Were

the weeks and months really shorter in duration, or had
he stopped counting, adopted a different measure? Formerly
time had had a hard brittle quality, been a solid. Now it was
a fluid. Its landscape had become as different for him as
was the Roman *campagna* from Tuscany. He had imagined
time to be absolute, the same always, everywhere, to all men ;
now he saw that it was as variable as human nature or
the weather of the skies. As 1531 became 1532, as 1532 began
contracting and converging on 1533, he asked himself :

" Where does time go? "

The answer was plain enough : it had been transmuted from
the amorphous to the substantive by becoming part of the
life force of the Madonna and Child, of the Dawn and
Dusk and Night, the young Medici. What he had not
understood was that time became foreshortened, just as space
did. When he stood on a hill looking across a Tuscan valley
the front half was visible in all its lucid detail ; the more
distant half, though as wide and broad, was compacted,
compressed, jammed up, seeming to be a narrow belt instead
of widely extensive fields. This happened to time in the
more distant area of a man's life as well ; no matter how
closely he peered at the hours and days as they went by,
they seemed shorter when compared to the wideflung first
portion of his life.

He carved the two lids of the sarcophagi in severely pure
lines, the descending curves ending in a chaste convolute,
a few simple leaves sculptured at the top of the supporting
columns. He did nothing about the River Gods or about
symbols of Heaven and Earth, ideas he had developed in a
preliminary stage. He carved a mask below the outward
shoulder of Night, and put an owl in the right angle
formed by her raised knee ; that was all. For him the
beauty of man had always been the beginning and the end
of art.

Word of what he was essaying in the chapel spread through
Italy and then Europe. He welcomed serious artists, who
sketched and made notes while he worked, but the increasing
flow of sightseers got under his skin. One elaborately gowned
nobleman demanded :

" How did you come to make that astonishing figure of
Night? "

" I had a block of marble in which was concealed that
statue which you see there. The only effort involved is

686

to take away the tiny pieces which surround it and prevent it from being seen. For anyone who knows how to do this, nothing could be easier."

" Then I shall send my servant to look for statues in the stones."

He made a journey to San Miniato al Tedesco to visit Pope Clement, who was on his way to solemnize the marriage of Caterina de' Medici, daughter of Piero's son Lorenzo, to the Dauphin of France. He had a happy time with Cardinal Ippolito, now attached to the Pope, and with Sebastiano del Piombo, still a favourite of Clement's.

For the rest, he remained within the quadrangle formed by the Medici sacristy where he carved, the house across the street where he made his models, and the Via Mozza studio where he lived and was cared for by Urbino. As drained of suet and sinew as he knew himself to be, he considered himself fortunate in having surrounded himself with good sculptors who were helping him conclude the chapel: Tribolo, who was to carve the marble Heaven and Earth from Michelangelo's models; Angelo Montorsoli, who was going to do a St. Cosmas; Raffaello da Montelupo, son of his old friend Baccio, clown of the Medici sculpture garden who had finished his two Piccolomini Popes. Sometimes at night he refreshed himself by picking up drawing materials and surveying his mind to see what it might have to say about a Last Judgment.

Bandinelli finished his Hercules for Clement. Duke Alessandro gave the order to have it installed opposite the David, in front of the Palazzo della Signoria, which he had renamed the Palazzo Vecchio because Florence was to have no more ruling council. The public outcry against the statue was so great that Bandinelli had to go to Rome to get a papal order to have it set up. Michelangelo walked with Urbino through the Piazza della Signoria to see the Hercules, the pieces of paper stuck to it during the night fluttering in the wind. He winced as he looked up at Bandinelli's meaningless muscle-bulges. After reading a few of the verses he commented with a grimace:

" Bandinelli is going to be unhappy when he reads these tributes."

Then he remembered Leonardo da Vinci's prophecy in the Belvedere:

" The painter, after he studies your ceiling, must take care

687

not to become wooden through too strong an emphasis on bone, muscle and sinews. . . . What do painters do, when they try to go beyond you?"

He understood now what Leonardo had been trying to tell him.

"Don't complete your own revolution. Leave something for those who follow you." But even if he had understood Leonardo earlier, what could he have done about it?

Like the Carrarini, he had been a *campanilista*, rallying around the base of Giotto's bell tower as though it were the centre of the universe. But Florence was supine now, its freedom strangled by Alessandro. Since art was being strangled in the same bloody bed with political liberty, most of the Company of the Cauldron had moved to other cities. The Florence of the early Medici had vanished. The Orcagna and Donatello marbles still stood majestically in the niches of Orsanmichele, but Florentines walked the streets with their heads bowed; after the interminable wars and defeats, the "mule of the mule," the "Moor," was the final blow. When he passed the Marzocchi in the Piazza della Signoria, Michelangelo turned his head away. He could not even bring himself to repair David's broken arm; not until the Republic, the greatness of Florence as an art and intellectual centre, the Athens of Europe, had been restored.

Lodovico's ninetieth birthday fell on an exhilarating day in June 1534. The air was warm but piercingly clear. Florence glistened like a precious stone in its prong of mountains. Michelangelo gathered the remnants of the Buonarroti family. At the dinner table there were Lodovico, so feeble that he had to be propped with pillows, Giovansimone, wan and thin from a protracted illness, silent Sigismondo, living his life alone on the family farm where they had all been born; Cecca, Buonarroto's seventeen-year-old daughter, and young Lionardo, who was completing his apprenticeship to the Strozzi.

"Uncle Michelangelo, you promised you would reopen my father's wool shop as soon as I was ready to manage it."

"So I shall, Lionardo."

"Soon? I'm fifteen now, and I've learned the business quite well."

"Yes, soon, Lionardo, as soon as I can get my affairs straightened out."

Lodovico ate only a few spoonfuls of the soup carried to

his lips with trembling hands. In the middle of dinner he asked to be taken to his bed. Michelangelo picked his father up in his arms. He weighed no more than the tied bundles of sticks Michelangelo had used to protect his walls at San Miniato. He put his father in bed, tucked a blanket around him. The old man turned his head slightly so that he could see the pie-shaped desk with its account books, neatly stacked. A smile came over his ash-grey lips.

" Michelagnolo."

The pet name. Lodovico had not used it for years.

" *Messer padre?*"

" I wanted . . . to live . . . to be ninety."

" And so you have."

" . . . but it was hard. I have . . . worked . . . every minute . . . just to stay alive."

" It's as good a work as any I know."

" But now . . . I'm tired . . ."

" Rest. I'll close the door."

" Michelagnolo . . .?"

" Yes, Father?"

" . . . you will take care of . . . the boys . . . Giovansimone . . . Sigismondo?"

Michelangelo thought, " The boys! In their middle fifties!" Aloud he replied, " Our family is all I have, Father"

" You'll give . . . Lionardo . . . his shop?"

" When he is ready?"

" And Cecca . . . a dowry?"

" Yes, Father."

" Then all is well. I have kept my family . . . together. We have prospered . . . gained back . . . the money . . . my father lost. My life . . . has not been lived . . . in vain. Please call the father from Santa Croce."

Lionardo brought the priest. Lodovico died quietly, surrounded by his three sons, grandson and granddaughter. There was so much colour left in his cheeks, and his face looked so peaceful, that Michelangelo could not believe his father was dead.

He felt strangely alone. He had been without a mother all his life; and without love from his father, without affection or understanding. Yet none of that mattered now; he had loved his father, just as in his flinty Tuscan way Lodovico had loved his son. The world would seem empty, even forlorn, without him. Lodovico had caused him endless anguish, yet it had not been Lodovico's fault that only one of his five sons had been an earner. That was why he had had to work Michelangelo so hard, to make up for the other four who had added nothing to the account books on the pie-shaped desk. Michelangelo was proud that he had been able to fulfil Lodovico's ambition, enable his father to die a success.

That night he sat in his studio, the big doors open to the garden, writing under an oil lamp. Suddenly the garden and his room were invaded by thousands of small white moths, called " Manna from the Hebraic Desert," weaving a net around the lamp and his head, flying in patterns like birds. In a few moments they were dead, leaving the studio and garden looking as though a light snow had fallen. He brushed the thick layer of ephemera off his workbench, picked up a pen and wrote:

> Death is less hard to him who wearily
> Bears back to God a harvest fully ripe,
> Than 'tis to him in full and freshest mind.
>
> But cruel were the heart that did not weep,
> That he should see no more about this earth
> Him who gave being first, and then support.
>
> Our grief's intensity, our weight of woe,
> Are less no more, according as each feels;
> And all my utter weakness, Lord, thou knowest.

He stood alone in the sacristy under the dome he had designed and built, surrounded by the *pietra serena* and marble walls so lovingly co-joined. Lorenzo, the Contemplative, was in his niche; Giuliano was sitting on the floor, not quite finished. Day, the last of the seven figures, was propped under the shoulders with wooden blocks, the back of the powerful male body unfinished where it would stand against the wall. The face, poised behind the high-raised shoulder, was that of an eagle, gazing stonily at the world through deep-sunk eyes, the hair, nose and beard rough-chiselled, as though cut out of granite, a strange, primordial contrast to the highlighted skin of the massive protective shoulder.

Was the chapel finished? After fourteen years?

Standing midst his exquisitely carved sarcophagi on either side, each to hold its two giant figures, Dawn and Dusk,

Day and Night, the beauteous Madonna and Child sitting on her ledge against the spacious side wall, he felt that he had carved everything he had wanted to carve, and said everything he had wanted to say. For him the Medici chapel was complete. He believed that *Il Magnifico* would have been gratified, that he would have accepted this chapel and these marble sculptures in place of the façade he had envisaged.

He picked up a piece of drawing-paper, wrote instructions for his three sculptors to mount Day and Night on their sarcophagus, Dusk and Dawn opposite. He left the note on the plank table under a piece of scrap marble, turned and went out of the door without looking back.

Urbino packed his saddlebags.

" Do you have everything, Urbino?"

" All except the folios of drawings, *messere*. They will be ready in a few moments."

"Wrap them in my flannel shirts for protection."

They mounted their horses, crossed the city and went out of the Porta Romana. At the top of the rise he stopped, turned to look back at the Duomo, Baptistry and Campanile, at the tawny tower of the Palazzo Vecchio glistening in the September sunlight, at the exquisite city of stone nestled under its red tile roof. It was hard to take leave of one's city ; hard to feel that, close to sixty, he could not count on returning.

Resolutely he turned the horses south towards Rome.

" Let us push on, Urbino. We'll stay the night at Poggi-bonsi, at an inn I know there."

" And will be in Rome by the following nightfall?" Urbino asked excitedly. "What is Rome like, *messere*?"

He tried to describe Rome, but his heart was too heavy. He had no idea what the future held for him, though he was certain that his own interminable war was at last over. If the astrologists who centred around the Porta Romana had cried out to him as he passed that he still had before him a third of his years, two of the four loves of his life, the longest, bloodiest battle, and some of his finest sculpture, painting and architecture, he would have remembered *Il Magnifico's* contempt for their pseudo science, and he would have laughed, tiredly.

But they would have been right.

BOOK TEN

LOVE

1

He rode his horse through the Porta del Popolo. Rome, after its latest warfare, seemed in a worse state of ruin than when he had first seen it in 1496. He walked through his own dilapidated premises on the Macello dei Corvi. Most of the furniture had been stolen, along with the mattresses and kitchen utensils, and some of the base blocks for Julius' tomb. The Moses and the two Captives had not been injured. He surveyed the rooms, looked around the overgrown garden. He would have to plaster and paint the walls, put in new flooring, refurnish the entire house. Of the five thousand ducats he had earned over the past ten years for the Medici chapel he had managed to save and bring to Rome only a few hundred.

"We must put our house in order, Urbino."

"I can handle the repairs myself, *messere.*"

Two days after Michelangelo reached Rome, Pope Clement VII died in the Vatican. The city poured into the streets in a paroxysm of joy. The hatred of Clement, which continued to manifest itself during the elaborate funeral ceremonies, was based on his responsibility for the sack of Rome. Only the day before Michelangelo and Benvenuto Cellini had visited Clement. He had been in good spirits, discussing with Cellini a new medal he was to strike, and with Michelangelo the design for the Last Judgment. Although Cousin Giulio had sometimes caused him suffering, he felt a considerable sense of loss for his childhood friends from the Medici palace.

During the two weeks it took for the College of Cardinals to assemble and elect a new Pope, Rome stood still. But not the Florentine colony. When Michelangelo reached the Medici palace he found that only the outside was draped in mourning cloth. Inside, the *fuorusciti,* exiles, were jubilant. With Clement dead there would be no one to protect his son Alessandro; he could be replaced by Ippolito, son of the beloved Giuliano.

Twenty-five-year-old Cardinal Ippolito stood at the head of the Medici steps to receive Michelangelo, an affectionate smile lighting his pale countenance with its patrician features and jet-black hair. He was wearing a dark red velvet coat and cap, a band of bold gold buttons across his chest. An arm was placed about Michelangelo's shoulder; he turned to find Contessina's son, Cardinal Niccolò Ridolfi, with his mother's slight figure and flashing brown eyes.

" You must stay with us here in the palace," said Ippolito, " until your house is repaired."

" My mother would have wanted it," added Niccolò.

A dozen of his old friends thronged to greet him: the Cavalcanti, Rucellai, Acciajuoli, Olivieri, Pazzi, Baccio Valori, Clement's Commissary of Florence, Filippo Strozzi and his son Roberto, Cardinal Salviati the elder, Cardinal Giovanni Salviati, son of Jacopo, Bindo Altoviti. The Florentine colony in Rime had been swollen by those families from whom Alessandro had stripped all property and power.

With Clement dead there was no further need to be discreet. What had formerly been an underground plot to get rid of Alessandro was now an open movement.

" You'll help us, Michelangelo?" asked Cardinal Giovanni Salviati.

" Most certainly. Alessandro is a wild beast."

There was a sharp murmur of approval. Niccolò said, " There is only one further obstacle: Charles V. With the Emperor on our side, we could march on Florence and overwhelm Alessandro. The citizens would rise and join us."

" How can I help?"

It was Florence's historian, Jacopo Nardi, who replied: " The Emperor cares little about art. However we have heard reports that he has expressed interest in your work. Would you carve or paint something for him, if it would help our cause?"

Michelangelo assured them that he would. After dinner Ippolito said, " The stables that Leonardo da Vinci designed for my father are completed. Would you like to see them?"

In the first stall, under the high-ceilinged beams, was a white Arabian steed. Michelangelo stroked the animal's long neck, warm under his hand.

" He's a beauty. I've never seen so perfect a piece of horse-flesh."

" Please accept him as a gift."

" Thank you, no," said Michelangelo quickly. " Only this

morning Urbino tore down the last of our old barn. We would have no place to keep him."

But when he reached home he found Urbino standing in the garden gingerly holding the animal by the reins. Michelangelo again patted the horses' elegant white neck, asked:

" Do you think we should keep him?"

" My father taught me never to accept a gift that eats."

" But how can I turn back such a beautiful animal? We must buy some lumber and build a new barn."

He asked himself over and over again whether he was relieved to have the crushing burden of the Last Judgment off his shoulders. The altar wall of the Sistine would have required a minimum of five years to paint, for it would be the largest wall in Italy ever essayed in a single fresco. Yet as his ducats poured out for the repairs and refurbishing of his house he saw that he would soon be in need of money.

Balducci, as wide as he was tall, but of hard flesh and red cheeks, now raising grandchildren in profusion, exploded:

" Of course you're in trouble! Spending all those years in Florence without my financial wizardry. But you're in safe hands now. Turn over to me the money you earn, and I'll invest it so that you'll be independently wealthy."

" Balducci, there is something about me that seems to alienate money. Ducats say to themselves, ' This man will not give us a secure home in which we can multiply. Let us go elsewhere.' Who is going to be the next Pope?"

" You guess."

From Balducci's he went on to Leo Baglioni, in his same house on the Campo dei Fiori. Leo, with a leonine mane and unwrinkled face, had flourished as confidential agent to Popes Leo and Clement, a job Michelangelo had helped secure for him.

" I'm ready to retire now," Leo confided to Michelangelo over a dinner in the exquisitely furnished dining room. " I have had nearly all the money, women and adventure any man could ask. I think I will let the next Pope run his own errands."

" Who is that Pope going to be?"

" Nobody knows."

Early the next morning the Duke of Urbino came to call, folowed by a servant with a box containing the four contracts for Julius' tomb. The duke was a ferocious-looking man, with a trench-lined battlefield for a face. He carried a lethal dagger at his side. It was the first time since Leo's coronation twenty-one years before that the two antagonists had met. The duke informed Michelangelo that the wall had been prepared for Julius' tomb in San Pietro in Vincoli, which had been Julius' church when he was Cardinal Rovere. He then took from the top of the leather box the latest agreement, that of 1532, which "freed, liberated and absolved Michelangelo from all contracts made previously," and flung it at Michelangelo's feet.

"There will be no more Medici to protect you. If you do not complete this last contract by May of next year, as specified in the agrement, I shall force you to fulfil the 1516 contract: twenty-five statues, larger than life. The twenty-five we have paid for."

The duke stormed out, right hand clasped on the handle of his dagger.

Michelangelo had not arranged for the four unfinished Giants or the Victory to be brought from Florence. He had welcomed the release afforded by the change from the original walk-in monument to a single-wall tomb; nevertheless he had been disturbed because these enormous statues would now be out of proportion on the marble façade. For the additional three carvings he owed the Roveres, he decided to sculpture a Virgin, Prophet and Sibyl, the blocks for which were stored in the garden. These figures would be neither large nor difficult. He was certain the Roveres would be as well pleased; in any event his own sense of design demanded the change. By next May, as specified in the contract, he would be finished with the three smaller figures and his workmen could assemble the wall in San Pietro in Vincoli.

In the matter of completing the Rovere tomb the fates were as much against the Duke of Urbino as against Michelangelo. On October 11, 1534, the College of Cardinals elected Alessandro Farnese to the papacy. Farnese had been educated by Lorenzo, but he had already left the palace for Rome before Michelangelo's time. From *Il Magnifico* he had acquired a lifelong love of art and learning. When his ravishingly beautiful sister Giulia had been taken by Pope Alexander VI as his mistress, Farnese had been made a cardinal, and entered into the dissolute life of the Borgia court, siring four illegitimate children by two mistresses. Rome had satirically called him the "petticoat cardinal," because he had received his appointment through his sister's position. However in 1519 when he was ordained a priest he renounced the pleasures of the flesh and began to live an exemplary life.

Pope Paul III sent a courier to the house on the Macello dei Corvi: would Michelangelo Buonarroti come to the Vatican palace that afternoon? The Holy Father had something of importance to communicate. Michelangelo went to the baths in the Via de' Pastini, where a barber trimmed his beard, washed and brushed his hair forward over his brow. Gazing at himself in the mirror of his bedroom as Urbino helped him into a mustard-coloured shirt and cloak, he noted with surprise that the amber flecks in his eyes were beginning to fade, and that the crushed declivity at the bridge of his nose no longer seemed so deep.

" It's odd," he groused, " now that it no longer matters to me, I'm not as plain as I used to be."

" If you're not careful," said Urbino, observing the self-appraisal with a grin, " you'll grow to look like a Michelangelo sculpture."

When Michelangelo entered the small throne room of the Vatican he found Pope Paul III talking vivaciously to Ercole Gonzaga, Cardinal of Mantua, son of the cultivated Isabella d'Este, and a man of superb taste. Michelangelo knelt, kissed the Pope's ring, his eyes quickly sketching the new Pope's face: the narrow head, eyes incisively shrewd, the long thin nose jutted over the snowy white moustache; the hollow cheeks and thin-lipped mouth speaking of the voluptuary turned æsthete. It was a strong face.

" My son, I consider it a good omen that you will be working in Rome during my pontificate."

" Your Holiness is kind."

" It is a matter of self-interest. Several of my predecessors will be remembered largely because of the art works they commissioned you to create."

Michelangelo bowed humbly before the compliment. The Pope added warmly:

" I wish you to enter our service."

Michelangelo paused for the stonemason's rest count of one two three four.

" How can I serve Your Holiness?"

" By continuing your work on the Last Judgment."

" Holy Father, I cannot take so large a commission."

" Why not?"

" I am bound by contract to the Duke of Urbino to

696

complete Pope Julius' tomb. He has threatened me with disaster if I do not labour exclusively to that end."

" Is the Holy See to be intimidated by a war lord? Put the tomb out of your mind. I wish you to complete the Sistine Chapel for the glory of our pontificate."

" Holy Father, for thirty years now I have been tortured for the sin of signing that contract."

Paul rose on his throne, his slight body trembling under the bright red velvet, ermine-trimmed cape.

" It is thirty years for me, also, that I have desired to have you in my service! Now that I am Pope, am I not to be allowed to satisfy that desire?"

" Holines, it is your thirty years against mine."

With a fiery gesture Paul pushed the red velvet skullcap back off his eyebrows and cried:

" I am determined to have you serve me, come what may."

Michelangelo kissed the Pope's ring, backed out of the small throne room. Returning to his house, he sank into an old leather chair. A sharp knock on the door straightened him up from his collapsed position. Urbino admitted two Swiss guards, tall blond giants in identical yellow and green costumes, who announced that Michelangelo Buonarroti would receive, the following midmorning, a visit from His Holiness Paul III.

" I will find charwomen, *messere*," announced the imperturbable Urbino. " What refreshment does one serve the Holy Father and his train? I have never seen a Pope before, except in procession."

" I wish that that was the only place I had ever seen one," grumbled Michelangelo. " Buy *passito* and *biscotti*. Use our best Florentine tablecloth."

The Pope arrived with his cardinals and attendants, causing considerable excitement in the Piazza del Foro Traiano. Paul smiled benignly on Michelangelo, went quickly to the Moses. The cardinals surrounded the figure in a field of red cassocks. It was obvious from the glance Pope Paul stole at Ercole Gonzaga that the Cardinal of Mantua was the acknowledged art authority of the Vatican. Gonzaga drew back from the Moses with his head cocked forward, eyes blazing with excitement. He declared in a voice compounded of awe, pride and gratification:

" This Moses alone is sufficient to do honour to Pope Julius. No man could want a more glorious monument."

Pope Paul said wistfully, " Ercole, I wish I had said that."

Then, turning to Michelangelo, he added, "You see, my son, I was not being unreasonable. Paint the Last Judgment for me. I will arrange for the Duke of Urbino to accept the Moses and these two Captives from your hand."

Michelangelo had not lived through four pontificates without learning when he was outmanœuvred.

2

When he was young his mind had leaped to herculean projects. Once in Carrara he had wanted to carve a whole marble peak to guide the sailors on the Tyrrhenian Sea. But as he twisted restlessly in his bed that night he demanded of himself, "Where am I to get the strength to cover a wall larger than the Sistine panels of Ghirlandaio, Botticelli, Rosselli and Perugino put together?" He would not have to lie on his back and paint above him on the ceiling; but the wall would take as long and drain him as utterly. How to summon at sixty the cyclonic powers he had enjoyed at thirty-three?

Haggard from sleeplessness, he rose and went to early mass at San Lorenzo in Damaso. He bumped into Leo Baglioni, *en route* to his house on the corner. After each had confessed his sins and taken communion, they left the church and stood in the Campo dei Fiori with the pale November dawn on their faces.

"Leo, you've been out carousing, and I've been wrestling with my immortal soul; yet it took you less time to confess than it did me."

"My dear Michelangelo, to me anything that gives pleasure is good, while anything that brings pain is sinful. Ergo, my conscience is clear. From your wan look I would say you had put yourself through much suffering last night; ergo, you had much transgression to be forgiven. Come inside for a cup of hot milk, we'll toast Cardinal Gonzaga's tribute to your Moses. Rome is talking of little else."

The hour of comradeship was relaxing. He left Baglioni's, walked slowly through the empty streets to the Pantheon, circled its majestic dome, then along the Via Recta to the Tiber and up the Via Alessandrina to St. Peter's. Antonio da Sangallo, nephew of Giuliano da Sangallo, and Bramante's assistant, had inherited the title of Architect of St. Peter's.

As far as Michelangelo could tell, little had been accomplished in the eighteen years since he had left Rome except the repair of the giant piers and the building of the lowest foundation walls. Two hundred thousand ducats from all over Christendom had been poured into the concrete; but mostly, Michelangelo had learned, into the pockets of a ring of contractors who were erecting St. Peter's as slowly as was humanly possible. At the present rate, Michelangelo mused, St. Peter's would have trouble getting itself completed by Judgment Day.

The tiny chapel of Mary of the Fever had not yet been removed to make way for the transept. He entered, stood before his own Pietà. How beautiful Mary was. How exquisite and tender. And the son on the mother's lap, how sensitive the face.

He fell to his knees. For a moment he wondered if it were wrong to pray before his own creation; but he had carved these figures so long ago, when he was only twenty-four. Though there flooded over him waves of emotion from those distant days when he had first become a marble sculptor, he could not remember any of the actual detail of carving the block. It was as though someone he had known ages ago had done the work.

Rome was in the streets in holiday clothes, for to-day was a feast day in which twelve triumphal carts would start from the Capitoline hill and be driven ceremoniously to the Piazza Navona. This year it was to be a race between buffalo and horses, then twenty bulls would be attached to carts at the top of Mount Testaccio and driven down the steep slope to where they would be slaughtered as a spectacle, even as had the little pigs he had watched with Balducci.

Without knowing that he had so directed his steps, he found himself before the residence of the Cavalieri family. The palace was in the Rione di Sant'Eustachio, facing its own piazza and surrounded by extensive gardens. Square-cut, battlemented, the Cavalieri mansion had served for several hundreds of years as the centre of continuous generations of Cavalieri "Conservators," Roman citizens who volunteered to conserve the Roman antiquities, old Christian churches, the fountains and statuary of the city.

It had taken him three weeks to achieve what could have been a ten-minute walk from his house in the Macello dei Corvi, along the narrow Via di San Marco and Via delle

Botteghe Oscure, to the Cavalieri palace. As he dropped the heavy clapper against its metal base on the ponderous front door he wondered why it had taken him so long to call on Tommaso de' Cavalieri when in the back of his mind, during that last exhausting year in Florence, he had known that one of the reasons he looked forward to returning to Rome was the presence there of this charming young friend.

A servant opened the door, led Michelangelo into the high-ceilinged salon on the left which contained one of the best private collections of antique marble sculptures in Rome. As Michelangelo walked from a faun with a bunch of grapes to a child sleeping on a rock with some poppies in his hand, to a sea horse in half relief with a woman sitting on it surrounded by dolphins, he recalled the affectionate letters that had passed between himself and Tommaso, and the drawings of Ganymede and Tityos which he had made for Tommaso to study.

He heard footsteps behind him, turned . . . and gasped aloud. In the two years since he had seen Tommaso, he had made the transition from an attractive youth to the most magnificent male figure Michelangelo had ever laid eyes on: more beautiful even than the ancient marble Greek discus thrower that stood between himself and Tommaso: with broad, muscular shoulders, slim waist, straight slender legs.

"You've come at last," said Tommaso in a quiet voice, so surprisingly grave and courtly for a twenty-four-year-old.

"I had not wished to bring you my troubles."

"Friends can share troubles."

They met halfway across the salon, gripped each other's arms in a tense welcoming salute. Tommaso's eyes had deepened to a cobalt blue, his features slimmed to a finer mould.

"Now I know where I've seen you before," cried Michelangelo. "On the ceiling of the Sistine!"

"And just how did I get up on to the ceiling of the Sistine?"

"I put you up there myself. Adam, about to receive the spark of life from God. Even to the way your light chestnut hair tumbles back on to your neck."

"You painted Adam a long time ago."

"About twenty-four years. Just as you were being born. You have made my portrait come true."

"Do you see to what extent I will go for my friends?" said Tommaso with a chuckle. "I will even believe in miracles."

"Miracles may not be impossible. I came through your front door heavy-footed and heavy-hearted. I spend ten minutes with you, and ten years drop off my life."

"As your drawings have added ten years to my maturity as a craftsman."

"How wonderful that an old man and a young one can exchange years, as though they were gifts on Befana's Day."

"Do not call yourself old," cried Tommaso. When he grew angry his eyes became dark as ink. "I am shocked to find you thinking so conventionally. A man is as old as the creative force within him."

A warm smile spread over Michelangelo's features. The knots in his head and chest came untied.

"You know I am to do the Last Judgment for Pope Paul."

"I heard at mass this morning. It will be a grand completion for the Sistine, to match the vault."

Michelangelo turned his back on Tommaso to conceal the upsurge of emotion, stood running his hands over the exquisite posterior cheeks of an undraped marble Venus. A wave of happiness swept over him. He turned back to his friend.

"Tommaso, up to this moment I had not thought I could summon the courage to create a Last Judgment. Now I know I can."

They climbed a broad flight of stairs. On the balustrade the Cavalieri had mounted some of their smaller and more subtle carvings: the head of a woman with a basket on it, a Roman sculpture of the Emperor Augustus, an open sea shell inside of which was a nude figure. Tommaso de' Cavalieri spent half of his day working for the tax commission and as curator of public works, and the other half drawing. His workshop was at the back of the palace, overlooking the Torre Argentina, a room stripped bare except for long planks on wooden horses. On the wall above the table were the drawings Michelangelo had made two years before, as well as those he had sent from Florence. Spread out over the planks were dozens of sketches. Michelangelo studied them, exclaimed:

"You have a fine talent. And you work hard."

Tommaso's face clouded.

'In the past year I have fallen into bad company. Rome is full of temptations, as you know. I have drunk and whored too much, worked too little . . ."

Michelangelo was amused at the sombre seriousness of his friend's self-reproach.

"Even St. Francis was wild as a young man, Tomao," he said, using the diminutive to cause a smile.

"May I work with you, if only for two hours a day?"

"My studio is yours. What could bring me greater happiness. See what your faith and affection have done for me already. I am now eager to start drawing for the Last Judgement. I shall serve not only as your friend but as your master. In return you shall help me blow up the drawings, share my models. We will develop you into a great artist."

Tommaso went pale, his eyes fading to the luminous powder-grey. He replied stiffly:

"You are the personification of art. The affection you show me is that which you would show to those who love art and wish to devote themselves to it. I can tell you this: never have I loved a man more than you, never have I desired a friendship more."

"It is an infinite sorrow to me not to be able to give you my past as well as my future.'

"I have so little to give in return."

"Ah," said Michelangelo softly, "there you are wrong. As I stand opposite you at this worktable I feel neither age nor the fear of death. Do you know anything more precious that one man can bring another?"

They became inseparable. They walked arm in arm around the Piazza Navona for a breath of air, sketched on the Capitoline or in the Forum on Sundays, had supper in each other's homes after the day's work, then spent the evenings in stimulating hours of drawing and conversation. Their joy in each other gave off a radiance that made others happy in their presence; and now that they were acknow-ledged companions, they were invited everywhere together.

How did he define his feeling for Tommaso? Assuredly, it was an adoration of beauty. Tommaso's physical being had a strong impact on him, gave him a hollow feeling at the pit of his stomach. He realized that what he felt for Tommaso could only be described as love; yet he was hard-pressed to identify it. Of the loves of his life, where did this one fit? To which did it compare? It was different from his dependent love for his family, from the reverence and awe he felt for *Il Magnifico*, his respect for Bertoldo; his enduring though tenuous love for Contessina; the unforgotten passion for Clarissa; his friendly love for Granacci, the fatherly love he felt for Urbino. Perhaps this love, coming so late in his life, was undefinable.

"It is your lost youth you revere in me," said Tommaso.

"Not even in my dreams did I look anything like you," replied Michelangelo scoffingly. They were sketching at a table before a log fire. He was blocking out his first plan for the Sistine wall: using counterbalancing figures for the side portions, some floating upward towards heaven, others falling downward towards hell.

"You speak of your outer shell," retorted Tommaso. "My inner visage is plain. I would gladly exchange my features for your genius."

"You would be foolish, Tommaso; physical beauty is one of the rarest gifts of God."

The colour faded from Tommaso's face.

"And one of the most useless," he added in something of anguish.

"No, no," cried Michelangelo. "It brings joy to all people. Why do you think I have given my life to creating a race of glorious creatures in marble and paint? Because I worship human beauty as God's most divine attribute."

"Your people are beautiful because you have imbued them with souls. Your Pietà and Moses and Sistine characters, they feel and think, they know compassion. . . . That is why they live and have meaning for us."

Michelangelo was humbled by the passionate outburst.

"You have spoken with the wisdom of a man of sixty, while I have uttered the foolishness of a youth of twenty-four."

He was up at first light, eager to get to his drawing-board. By the time the sun hit the top of Trajan's Column, Tommaso had come with a packet of freshly baked rolls for his midmorning refreshment. Each day a different model arrived, hired by Urbino in his search for the types designated by Michelangelo: labourers, mechanics, scholars, noblemen, peoples of all races and all sizes. Since there would be many women in the Last Judgment they had female models, the women from the baths, the bordellos, some of the more expensive hetæræ who posed in the nude for the adventure.

He did a portrait of Tommaso, the only time he had paid

anyone such a compliment: in black chalk, with his smooth cheeks, the finely modelled bone structure, dressed in ancient costume and holding a medallion in one hand.

"Do you recognize yourself, Tommaso?"

"The drawing is superb. But it is not me."

"It is you, as I see you."

"It discourages me . . . it proves what I have suspected from the beginning: I have taste, I can recognize good work from bad, but I do not have the creative fire."

Michelangelo stood above Tommaso, who was sitting hunched over a bench. His love for Tommaso made him feel fifteen feet tall.

"Tommaso, did I not make Sebastiano a fine painter, and secure him important commissions? You have a thousand times his talent."

Tommaso set his jaw squarely. He had his own convictions.

"From your teaching I gain a deeper understanding of what is involved in this art; but no greater power to produce it myself. You waste your time thinking about me. I should not come here any more."

After supper Michelangelo sat at his long table and began writing. By morning he had completed two sonnets:

LOVE THE LIGHT-GIVER

With your fair eyes a charming light I see,
For which my own blind eyes would peer in vain;
Stayed by your feet, the burden I sustain
Which my lame feet find all too strong for me;

Wingless upon your pinions forth I fly;
Heavenward your spirit stirreth me to strain;
E'en as you will, I blush and blanch again,
Freeze in the sun, burn 'neath a frosty sky.

Your will includes and is lord of mine;
Life to my thoughts within your heart is given;
My words begin to breathe upon your breath:

Like to the moon am I, that cannot shine
Alone; for lo! our eyes see nought in heaven
Save what the living sun illumineth.

When Tommaso arrived at the studio Michelangelo handed

him the first sonnet. As Tommaso read, his face flushed. Michelangelo took the second sheet from his workbench, said, "This is the second poem I wrote."

I saw no mortal beauty with these eyes
When perfect peace in thy fair eyes I found;
But far within, where all is holy ground,
My soul felt Love, her comrade of the skies. . . .

Tommaso stood with his head bowed, remaining that way for a long moment. Then he raised eyes that were clear and radiant.

"I am unworthy of such a love; but I shall do everything possible to deserve it."

"Let us not get our just deserts," said Michelangelo with a gentle smile, "or Judgment Day will be unbearable."

3

He stood alone in the Sistine Chapel, the tumultuous array from Genesis overhead, making a detailed survey of the altar wall. Jonah, presiding at the end of the ceiling on a marble throne, would sit as an Old Testament prophet over the judgments of the New Testament Christ.

The fifty-five-foot-high wall, forty feet wide, was busy and chopped up; in the bottom zone were painted tapestries similar to the ones on the long side walls; above the table-altar were two Perugino frescoes, the Finding of Moses and Birth of Christ; in the next area were the two tall windows corresponding to those on the side walls, with portraits of the first two Popes, St. Linus and St. Cletus; and then, in the topmost, or fourth compartment, his own two lunettes in which he had painted the early ancestors of Christ.

The wall was fire-blackened at the bottom, pitted and broken at the second height; above, there was spoilage from damp, and an over-all soiling of dust, grime and smoke from the candles burned on the altar. He disliked destroying the Perugino frescoes, but since he was also obliterating two of his own lunette paintings no one could think him vengeful. He would seal up the two diverting windows, build a new baked-brick wall which he would engineer to slant outward a foot from ceiling to floor so that dust, dirt and smoke would no longer adhere.

Pope Paul readily gave his consent to Michelangelo's building plans. Michelangelo found himself liking the Farnese Pope more and more, developing a feeling of friendship for him. Having lived through the excesses of youth, Paul had become a Latin and Greek scholar, a fine speaker and writer. He intended to avoid the wars of Julius, the orgies of Leo, the international blunders and intrigues of Clement. He also was blessed with an astute sense of humour, as Michelangelo learned when he called at the Vatican. Noting the pontiff's good colour and bright gleam of the eyes, he remarked:

"Your Holiness is looking well to-day."

"Not so loud," said Paul with mock whisper, "you'll disappoint the College of Cardinals. They only elected me because they thought I was on my deathbed. But the papacy agrees with me, and I shall outlive them all."

He was happy during these months of steady drawing in the studio that Urbino had redone with a touch of colour in the walls. Drawing, like food, drink and sleep, puts strength back into a man. Through the medium of his drawing hand he was beginning to catch the tail of some germinal ideas. The Last Day had been promised by the Christian faith to coincide with the end of the world. Could that be? Could God have created the world in order to abandon it? The decision to create man had been God's alone. Then was not God powerful enough to sustain the world for ever in spite of wickedness and evil? Would He not want to? Since every man judged himself before death, either in confessing his sins or dying unrepentant, could not the Last Judgment be a concept of a millennium which God held for ever in reserve, with Christ just arriving among the nations of men, about to begin judgment? He did not believe he could paint the Last Judgment as something that had already happened, but only at the moment of inception. Then he might portray man's agonizing appraisal of himself. There could be no evasions, deceits. He believed that each individual was responsible for his conduct on earth, that there was a judge within. Could even a blazingly angry Christ inflict greater retribution? Could Dante's Charon in his rowboat on the river Acheron whip the miscreants into a deeper, more everlasting hell than man's unvarnished verdict on himself?

From the moment his pen touched the paper he sought the contour of the human form, a single line for each figure, nervous in quality to denote the desperate urgency behind its movements. Repeatedly he dipped the quill in the ink, impatient to have to interrupt the continuity of his linear passage, wanting to achieve a simultaneity of form and space. Inside the contour lines he used a system of parallel blocking and crosshatching to describe the play of muscles in their various states of stress as affected by the nervous tensions of the contours. What he sought was a sharp delineation of the human body from the crisp air about the figure; this he achieved by probing into the bare nerves of space. Every man, woman and child was to stand out in stark clarity, to achieve his full human dignity; for each was an individual and had worth. This was the key to the rebirth of human learning and freedom that had been sired in Florence, after the darkness of a thousand years. Never would he, Michelangelo Buonarroti, a Tuscan, be responsible for reducing man to an indistinguishable part of an inchoate mass, not even *en route* to heaven or hell!

Though he would not have admitted it, his arms were weary after the ten years of continuous carving on the Medici chapel. The more he studied his vault in the Sistine, the more he came to think that painting might become a noble and permanent art, after all.

He found himself the centre of a group of young Florentines who met in the refurbished studio of the Macello dei Corvi house each afternoon to implement their plans for the conquest of Alessandro. The leaders were the brilliant, vital Cardinal Ippolito, who was sharing with Cardinal Ercole Gonzaga the leadership of Rome's high society of artists and scholars; the gentle and lovable Cardinal Niccolò; Roberto Strozzi, whose father had helped Michelangelo put Giovansimone and Sigismondo in the wool business, and whose grandfather had bought Michelangelo's first sculpture; the sons and grandsons of the long-established Florentine colony into whose homes he had been invited on his first visit to Rome, while Cardinal Riario was keeping him dangling. When he went visiting of a Sunday evening he found himself the focus of an attentive and excited group of young people: Pierantonio, the sculptor; Pierino del Vaga, most popular stucco worker and decorator in Rome, and his disciple, Marcello Mantovano; Jacopino del Conte, a young Florentine pupil of Andrea del Sarto, who had followed Michelangelo to Rome; Lorenzetto Lotti, an architect of St. Peter's and son of the bell caster who had worked for Michelangelo in Bologna. The young people believed him a man of courage who had stood up to Popes; a worthy son of Lorenzo the Magnificent. At a time when Florence had descended to the depths, when its children despaired, they took comfort from the idea that Michelangelo towered above Europe like a Monte Altissimo. He made them proud to be Tuscans; singlehanded he had created more works of pure genius than all other artists combined. If Florence could create a Michelangelo it could survive an Alessandro.

Michelangelo realized with a pang that he had never enjoyed this kind of acceptance before; nor, for that matter, would he have been receptive if it had happened.

"My nature is changing," he commented to Tommaso. "While I was painting the vault I talked to no one but Michi."

"Was it a period of unhappiness for you?"

"An artist working at the top of his powers exists in a realm beyond human happiness."

He knew that this change in his nature had been brought about, in part, by his feeling for Tommaso. He admired Tommaso's handsomeness and nobility of spirit as though he were a young man falling in love with his first girl. He had all the symptoms: an overwhelming joy when Tommaso came into the room, a sense of forlornness when he left, pain-fraught hours until he could see him again. He gazed over at Tommaso, who was drawing concentratedly with charcoal. He dared not tell him how he felt, and so late at night he wrote sonnets instead:

> *Love is not always harsh and deadly sin:*
> *If it be love of loveliness divine,*
> *If it leaves the heart all soft and infantine*
> *For rays of God's own grace to enter in. . . .*

News reached Rome that Charles V planned to marry his illegitimate daughter Margaret to Alessandro; that would mean an alliance between the Emperor and Alessandro, which would keep Alessandro in power. The hopes of the Florentine colony were dashed. A more personal disappointment for Michelangelo was Friar Sebastiano, round as a butterball, just returned after a journey.

"My dear *compare,* how wonderful to see you again! You must come to San Pietro in Montorio to see how well I transformed your drawings to oils."

708

"Oils? You were supposed to work in fresco."

Sebastiano's blush flooded downward through a large quantity of jowl.

"Fresco is for you, dear master, who never make a mistake. Oil is better for my temperament: if I make a dozen mistakes, I can wipe them off and start over."

The mounted to San Pietro in Montorio, which over-looked Rome. The air was pellucid, the waters of the Tiber as it wove through the tile roofs a clear blue under the winter sky. In the courtyard they passed Bramante's Tempietto, a jewel of architecture which always wrung an exclamation of praise from Michelangelo. Inside the church, Sebastiano proudly led Michelangelo to the first chapel on the right. He saw that Sebastiano had done a masterly job of blowing up his, Michelangelo's drawings: that the colours had remained fresh and unchanged. Former artists who had painted with oil on walls, even such masters as Andrea del Castagno, Antonio and Piero Pollaiuolo, frequently had had their figures fade or turn black.

"It's a new method I invented," explained Sebastiano proudly. "I use a rough cast of lime mixed with mastic and resin, melt them together over a fire, then smooth them on the wall with a white-hot trowel. Aren't you proud of me?"

"What else have you painted since this chapel?"

". . . not much . . ."

"But if you were so proud of perfecting a new method?"

"When Pope Clement appointed me Keeper of the Seals I no longer needed to work. I had all the money I wanted."

"That was the only reason you painted?"

Sebastiano turned on Michelangelo and stared, as though his benefactor had suddenly been bereft of his senses.

"What other reason could there be?"

Michelangelo started to grow angry, then realized that he was dealing with an amiable child.

"Sebastiano, you're entirely right. Sing, play your lute, amuse yourself. Art should be practised only by those poor wretches who can't help themselves."

The halting of St. Peter's was a more bitter potion. Though hundreds of men had been employed and tons of cement mixed during the months since his arrival in Rome, his experienced eye told him that no progress had been made in the body of the construction, or fabric of the church. The Florentine colony knew about the waste of money and time; but not even his three young cardinal friends could tell him whether Pope Paul suspected. Antonio da Sangallo had become so firmly entrenched during his twenty years as architect of St. Peter's that no one dared attack him. Michelangelo realized that it was the better part of discretion to keep still. Yet he burned inwardly, for he had never got over the feeling that St. Peter's was his own project because he had been part of the cause of its inception. When he could be silent no longer he found a moment to tell the Pope what was going on.

Pope Paul listened patiently, smoothing down his long white beard.

"Did you not make the same charge against Bramante? The court will say that you are jealous of Antonio da Sangallo. It puts you in a bad light."

"I've been in a bad light most of my life."

"Paint the Last Judgment, Michelangelo, and let Antonio da Sangallo build St. Peter's."

When he reached home, frustrated, he found Tommaso waiting for him with Cardinals Ippolito and Niccolò. Each was pacing his own orbit of floor.

"You look like a delegation."

"We are," replied Ippolito. "Charles V is coming through Rome. He will visit with only one private person, Vittoria Colonna, the Marchesa di Pescara. He is a long-time friend of her husband's family in Naples."

"I do not know the marchesa."

"But I do," replied Tommaso. "I have asked her to invite you to her gathering, this Sunday afternoon. You'll go, of course?"

Before Michelangelo could ask, "But how do I fit in?" Niccolò, with Contessina's sombre brown eyes, said, "It would mean a great deal to Florence if you became friends with the marchesa and could be introduced by her to the Emperor when he comes to Rome."

When the two cardinals had gone Tommaso said, "Actually I have wanted you to meet Vittoria Colonna. In the years since you last lived here she has become the first lady of Rome. She is a rare poet, one of the finest minds in Rome. She is beautiful. She is also a saint."

"Are you in love with the lady?" asked Michelangelo.

Tommaso laughed good-naturedly. "Oh no, she is a woman of forty-six, has had a wonderful romance and marriage, and has been widowed for the past ten years."

"Is she a Colonna from the palace on the Quirinal, above me?"

"Yes, a sister of Ascanio Colonna, though she rarely uses the palace. Most of the time she stays at a convent where they have the head of St. John the Baptist. She prefers the austere life of the mothers and sisters."

Vittoria Colonna, daughter of one of the most powerful families in Italy, had been engaged to Ferrante Francesco d'Avalos of Naples, the Marchese di Pescara, when each had been four years old. They were married in a lavish wedding in Ischia when they were nineteen. The honeymoon was short-lived, for the marchese was a general in the service of the Holy Roman Emperor, Maximilian, and had had to leave for the wars. In the sixteen years of their marriage Vittoria had seldom seen her husband. In 1512 he had been wounded in the Battle of Ravenna. Vittoria had nursed him back to life, but he had returned to his command, and thirteen years later was killed at the Battle of Pavia in Lombardy after heroic action on the field. The lonely Vittoria had spent the long years of separation in a disciplined study of Greek and Latin, and had become one of the best scholars of Italy. At her husband's death she had attempted to take the veil, but Pope Clement had forbidden it. She had spent the last ten years giving her service and fortune to the poor, and to the building of convents, thereby enabling the innumerable young girls who were without dowries, and hence could not find husbands, to enter the nunnery. Her poems were considered to be among the most important literary events of the time.

"I've seen only one saint walking around in shoe leather," commented Michelangelo; "that was Prior Bichiellini. I shall be interested to see what the female version looks like."

That was the last he thought about Vittoria Colonna, Marchesa di Pescara, until late Sunday afternoon when Tommaso called for him and they walked up the Via de' Cavalli past the Colonna gardens on one side and the Baths of Constantine on the other, to the top of Monte Cavallo, named after the two marble Horse Tamers which Leo Baglioni had taken him to see on his first day in Rome. The gardens of the convent of San Silvestro al Quirinale were filled with warm spring sunlight, there were laurels for shade, and old stone benches against walls covered with green ivy.

Vittoria Colonna, sitting in the midst of half a dozen men, rose to greet him. Michelangelo found himself considerably surprised. After Tommaso's description of her deprivation and sorrow, of her saintliness, he had expected to meet an old lady in black, showing the ravages of tragedy on her face. Instead he found himself gazing into the deep green eyes of the most vitally lovely woman he had ever seen, with high colour in her cheeks, warm lips parted in welcome, the expression of a young woman enormously excited by life. She had a regal bearing, though without hauteur. Beneath the lightweight cloth of her simple robe he envisaged a ripe figure to complement the large expressive eyes, the long braids of honey-gold hair looped low on her neck, the strong white teeth between full red lips, the straight Roman nose, slightly and amusingly turned up at the end, and the finely modelled chin and cheekbones which lent her face strength to match its beauty.

He felt so ashamed at undressing the defenceless woman, as though she were a hired model, that there was a roaring in his ears, and he could not hear her greeting. He thought:

"What a dreadful thing to do to a saint!"

His repentance caused the noise in his ears to abate; but he could not take his eyes from her. Her beauty was like the noonday sun, filling the garden with its light but at the same time blinding him. With an effort he acknowledged an introduction to Lattanzio Tolomei, a learned Sienese ambassador; the poer, Sadoleto; Cardinal Morone; the papal secretary Blosio, whom Michelangelo knew from court; and a priest who was discoursing to the group on the Epistles of Paul.

Vittoria Colonna spoke in a richly melodious voice:

"I welcome you as an old friend, Michelangelo Buonarroti, for your works have spoken to me for many years."

"My works were more fortunate than I, Marchesa."

Vittoria's green eyes clouded.

"I had heard that you were a blunt man, *signore*, who knew no flattery."

"You heard correctly," replied Michelangelo.

His tone left little room for argument. Vittorio Colonna hesitated for a moment, then continued:

"I have been told that you knew Fra Savonarola."

"No. But I heard him preach many times. In San Marco and the Duomo."

"I could covet that experience."

"His voice thundered through the vast spaces of the cathedral and bounded off the walls against my ears."

"It is too bad the words did not strike Rome. Then we would have had our reforms inside the Mother Church. We would not now be losing our children in Germany and Holland."

"You admired Fra Savonarola?"

"He died a martyr to our cause."

Listening to the intensity about him, Michelangelo realized that he was in the midst of a revolutionary group, highly critical of the practices of the Church and seeking a means to begin its own reformation of the clergy. The Inquisition in Spain and Portugal had taken thousands of lives on charges far less serious. He turned back to the marchesa, admiring her courage; her face was shining with dedication.

"I do not mean to sound disrespectful, *signora*, but Fra Savonarola martyred a good deal of fine art and literature on what he called 'a bonfire of the vanities' before he himself came to grief."

"I have always regretted that, Signor Buonarroti. I know one does not cleanse the human heart by wiping clean the human mind."

The conversation became general. They spoke of Flemish art, which was highly respected in Rome, and its sharp contrasts to Italian painting; then of the origins of the concept of the Last Judgment. Michelangelo quoted from Matthew 25:31-33:

When the Son of Man comes in his glory, and all the angels with him, he will sit down upon the throne of his glory, and all nations will be gathered in his presence, where he will divide men one from the other, as the shepherd divides the sheep from the goats; he will set the sheep on his right, and the goats on his left.

As they walked down Monte Cavallo watching the sunset deepen the colours of the city below them, Michelangelo asked:

"Tommaso, when can we see her again?"

"When she invites us."

"We have to wait until then?"

"We have to wait; she goes nowhere."

"Then I will wait," cried Michelangelo, put out, "like a silent supplicant, until the lady deigns to send for me again."

An amused smile twitched the corners of Tommaso's lips.
" I thought you would be impressed."

That night it was Vittoria Colonna's face that glowed in
the room. It was many years since a woman's presence had
so completely taken possession of him. The poet's lines
that had been roaming through his skull replaced Tommaso
de' Cavalieri with the Marchesa di Pescara; and at cockcrow he rose to write:

Well may these eyes of mine both near and far
Behold the beams that from thy beauty flow;
But, lady, feet must halt where sight may go:
We see, but cannot climb to clasp a star. . . .

Clogged with mortality and wingless, we
Cannot pursue an angel in her flight:
Only to gaze exhausts our utmost might.

Yet, if but heaven like earth incline to thee,
Let my whole body be one eye to see,
That not one part of me may miss thy sight!

4

It was two weeks before he received a second invitation.
Somehow in the interval he had begun to identify the
sculptural beauty of her figure, the strong but tender face,
with his marble statue of Night in the Medici chapel. It
was a warm May Sunday when the marchesa's servant,
Foao, arrived with the message from the marchesa.

" My mistress bade me tell you, *messere*, that she is in the
chapel of San Silvestro al Quirinale; that the church
is closed and pleasant. She asks whether you would care
to come and lose a little of the day with her so that she
might gain it with you."

He was excited as he refreshed himself in a tub of cold
water which Urbino set out on the garden porch, then
dressed in a dark blue shirt and stockings he had bought
against just such an invitation, and made his way up the
hill.

He had hoped to be alone with her, but as Vittoria Colonna
came to greet him, gowned in pure white silk, with a white
lace mantilla over her head, he saw that the chapel was filled.

He recognized illustrious members of the Vatican court and the university faculty. A Spanish painter was complaining that there was no good art in Spain because the Spaniards considered painting and sculpture of little worth and refused to pay for it. The men began speaking of the art of their own city-states: in Venice the portraits by Tiziano; in Padua the frescoes of Giotto; the singular painting of the municipal chamber in Siena; in Ferrara the works in the castle; in Pisa, Bologna, Parma, Piacenza, Milan, Orvieto . . .

Michelangelo knew most of these works, and only half listened, for he was watching Vittoria, sitting motionless beneath a stained-glass window which threw a sheen of variegated colour over her flawless skin. He found himself wondering about her; if her marriage to the Marchese di Pescara had been such a great love match, why had they been together only a few months out of the sixteen years? Why had the marchese remained in the north of Italy during the long rainy winters when no war could be waged? And why had an old friend looked away when he had asked under what heroic circumstances the marchese had been killed?

Suddenly he became aware of a silence in the chapel. All eyes were turned on him. Cardinal Ercole Gonzaga politely repeated the question: would Michelangelo tell them of his favourite works of art in Florence? With his face slightly flushed, and his voice a little off key, Michelangelo spoke of the beauties of the sculptures of Ghiberti, Orcagna, Donatello, Mino da Fiesole; of the painting of Masaccio, Ghirlandaio, Botticelli. When he had finished, Vittoria Colonna said:

"Knowing Michelangelo to be a modest man, we have all refrained from speaking of the art of Rome. In the Sistine he has done the work of twenty great painters. Surely all of mankind will one day see and understand the Creation through his painting?"

Her enormous green eyes engulfed him completely. Now when she spoke, it was directly to him; quietly, chastely, yet her voice had a peculiarly throaty quality, her lips seemed only a few inches from his.

Michelangelo, do not think that I overpraise you. In point of fact, it is not you I praise at all, except as a faithful servant. For I have long thought that you have a divine gift and were chosen by God for your great tasks."

He searched his mind for an answer but no words formulated themselves. He wanted to speak only of how he felt about her.

"His Holiness has done me the favour of allowing me to build a nunnery for young girls at the foot of Monte Cavallo," continued Vittoria. "The site I have chosen is by the broken portico of the Tower of Maecenas, where it is said that Nero watched Rome burning. I would like to see the footprints of such a wicked man wiped out by those of holy women. I do not know, Michelangelo, what shape or proportion to give the house, whether some of the old work may be adopted to the new."

"If you would care to descend to the site, *signora,* we could study the ruins."

"You are indeed kind."

He had no idea of being kind, he had merely hoped that he and Vittoria could descend to the old temple alone and spend an hour together while going over the piles of stones. Vittoria invited the entire group to accompany them down the hill. Michelangelo salvaged the right to walk by her side, churned by her closeness, the physical, spiritual and intellectual emanation that engulfed his senses. He emerged from his emotional cloud long enough for the architect to break through, to make an estimate of where the convent could best be placed.

"Marchesa, I think this broken portico might be converted into a campanile. I could make you some drawings for the convent."

"I did not dare to ask for so much."

The warmth of her gratitude reached out like two arms to embrace him. He congratulated himself on his stratagem in breaking down the impersonal barrier which Vittoria kept high between herself and the others.

"I will have some sketches in a day or two. Where may I bring them to you?"

Vittoria's eyes turned opaque. When she spoke her voice was constrained.

"There is much work to do at my convent. Could Foao bring you word when I am free? In a week or two?"

He returned to his studio in a fury, began knocking things about. What kind of game was this woman playing? Was she paying him these extraordinary compliments merely to bring him to her feet? Did she admire him, or did she not? If she wanted his friendship, why was she refusing it? Shunting him off . . . for another two weeks! Could she not tell how completely he was taken by her? Did she not have human blood in her veins, and human feelings in her breast?

"You must understand," Tommaso explained when he saw that Michelangelo was disturbed. "She is dedicated to the memory of her husband. For all these years, since his death, she has loved only Jesus."

"If the love of Christ prevented a woman from loving mortal man, the Italian people would have died out long ago."

"I have brought you some of her poems. Perhaps you will learn more about her from them. Listen to this one:

'Since a chaste love my soul has long detained
In fond idolatry of earthly fame;
Now to the Lord, who only can supply
The remedy, I turn.

'Me it becomes not, henceforth, to invoke
Of Delos, or Parnassus; other springs,
Far other mountaintops, I now frequent
Where human steps unaided cannot mount.

And this from another:

'Would that a voice impressive might repeat,
In holiest accents to my inmost soul,
The name of Jesus; and my words and works
Attest true faith in Him, and ardent hope. . . .'"

Michelangelo chewed on the words for a few moments, running his index finger through the furrows of his brow.

"She sounds like a woman deeply hurt."

"By death."

"Permit me to doubt."

"What then?"

"My instinct tells me something is wrong."

When Tommaso had departed, Michelangelo asked Urbino to refill the oil lamp, and sat quietly before the sheaf of papers, studying their content. He read from the poem written to her husband:

Thou knowest, Love, I never sought to flee
From thy sweet prison, nor impatient threw
Thy dear yoke from my neck; never withdrew
What, that first day, my soul bestowed on thee."

Time hath not changed love's ancient surety;
The knot is still as firm; and though there grew

717

Moment by moment fruit bitter as rue,
Yet the fair tree remains as dear to me.

And thou hast seen how that keen shaft of thine,
'Gainst which the might of Death himself is vain,
Smote on one ardent, faithful breast full sore.

Now loose the cords that fast my soul entwine,
For though of freedom ne'er I recked before,
Yet now I yearn my freedom to regain.

He was puzzled. Why had Vittoria described her love as a prison and a yoke? Why would she " yearn my freedom to regain " from a love to which she had devoted the whole of her life? He had to have the answer: for he knew now that he loved her, had loved her from that first blinding moment he had laid eyes on her in the garden of San Silvestro.

" There are ways of getting information," resourceful Leo Baglioni assured him, " among the Neapolitans in Rome, particularly those who fought alongside the marchese. Let me see who among them owe me favours."

The material took five days to assemble; when Leo came to the studio he seemed weary."

" The facts started raining on me as though someone had pulled a stopper in heaven. But what tires me, even in my cynical old age, is the amount of myth that passes for truth."

" Urbino, be so good as to bring Signor Baglioni a bottle of our best wine."

" First of all, this was no lyrical love affair. The marchese never loved his wife, and fled from her a few days after the wedding. Secondly, he wenched the whole way from Naples to Milan. Third, he used every excuse known to inventive husbands never to get into the same city with his wife. And fourth, the noble marchese pulled one of the most dastardly double treasons in history, betraying both his own Emperor and his fellow conspirators. Rumour has it that he died by poison, a very long way from anybody's battlefield."

" I knew it," cried Michelangelo. " Leo, you have just made me the happiest of men."

" Permit me to doubt."

" What the devil do you mean?"

" Knowledge will make your life harder, rather than

easier. I feel that if Vittoria Colonna learned that you knew the truth about her marriage . . ."

"Do you think I'm an idiot?"

"A man in love will use any weapon against a woman he is importuning . . ."

"Importuning! I have yet to get an hour alone with her."

He was drawing at his long table piled high with paper, pens, charcoal, a copy of Dante's *Inferno* opened to the story of Charon, when Vittoria's servant Foao entered to invite Michelangelo for the following afternoon to the gardens of the Colonna palace on the hill above his house. The fact that she had summoned him to her ancestral home rather than a church garden or chapel led him to believe that they might be alone. In a fever of expectancy he wrestled with a stub pen:

> *Nay, prithee tell me, Love, when I behold*
> *My lady, do mine eyes her beauty see*
> *In truth, or dwells that loveliness in me*
> *Which multiplies her grace a thousandfold?* . . .

The Colonna gardens occupied an important part of the slope of Monte Cavallo, thickly planted with trees whose greenery Michelangelo could see from his house. A servant led him along a trail heavy with jasmine in bloom. From a distance he heard a babble of voices and was keenly disappointed. He came in sight of a summerhouse shaded by plane trees, with a waterfall and lily pond to keep the air cool.

Vittoria came to meet him. He nodded to the men in the pavilion and sat down abruptly in one corner, leaning against the lacy white latticework. Vittoria sought his eyes, tried to bring him into the discussion, but he declined. Into his mind there flashed the thought:

"That is why she refuses to love again. Not because the first love was so beautiful, but because it was so ugly! That is why she gives her love only to Christ."

He looked up, gazing at her with an intensity that could have pierced the tissue of her brain and the marrow of her bone. She stopped in the middle of a sentence, turned to ask solicitously:

"Is something wrong, Michelangelo?"

Then he sensed something else:

"She has never known a man. Her husband never consummated that marriage, either on their honeymoon or when

719

he returned injured from the wars. She is as virginal as the young girls she takes into her nunneries."

He ached with compassion for her. He would have to accept the legend of the immortal love, and from that starting point try to persuade this courageous and desirable woman that he had a love to offer that could be as beautiful as the one she had invented.

5

His love for Vittoria in no way changed his feelings for Tommaso Cavalieri, who continued to arrive early each morning carrying a jug of cool milk or a basketful of fruit to get in his two hours of drawing under Michelangelo's critical eye before the sun grew hot. Michelangelo made him do his sketches over a dozen times, never appearing satisfied, but in truth well pleased with Tommaso's progress. Pope Paul had accepted Tommaso at court and appointed him Conservator of the Fountains of Rome.

Tommaso looked up from the draughting table, his expression intent, the blue eyes serious.

" Michelangelo, there's not an engineer in Rome who knows how the ancients brought all that water down! Or would dare to rebuild the aqueducts. How can a people so completely lose their talents? I think I no longer want to become a painter. I should like to become an architect. My family have been Romans for eight hundred years. The city is in my blood. I want not only to conserve it but to help rebuild it. Architects are what the city needs most."

The over-all design for the Sistine wall was now complete. He was able to count more than three hundred characters he had integrated from his original drawings, all of them in motion, no one still: a tumultuous horde of humans surrounding Christ in inner intimate circles and outer remote ones; vertical shafts of bodies rising upward on one side, descending on the other, the clouds below Christ presenting the only emptiness. On the bottom to the left was the yawning cave of hell, with the burial ground of the ages; the river Acheron was on the right. He set himself a schedule of painting one normal-size figure on the wall each day, with two days allotted to those larger than life.

The Virgin emerged as a harmonious blend of his mother, the Pietà and Medici madonnas, his own Eve, six panels down the ceiling, taking the apple from the serpent, and Vittoria Colonna. Like Eve, she was a young, robust, life-containing female; like the others, she was glorious of face and figure. Mary was tactfully turned away from her son's merciless judgment of mankind, since she herself was not being judged. Was she also withdrawn in compassion because man must be judged, however just his fate might be? Did God judge the sheep, the oxen, the cattle, the birds? As a mother, would she not feel pain for the doomed souls cowering under her son's arm upraised in righteous wrath? Could she free herself from responsibility for him, even though he were the son of God? She had carried him in her womb for nine months, given him the breast, healed his wounds. Her son was judging other mothers' sons! The good would be saved, the saints return to heaven; but the elect seemed so few in comparison to the endless hordes of sinners. Everything her son did was perfection; yet she could not help but be anguished at the awful suffering that must follow.

Charles V did not come to Rome, but instead prepared a fleet to sail from Barcelona against the Barbary pirates. The Florentine exiles sent a delegation to him, urging him to appoint Cardinal Ippolito as ruler of Florence. Charles received the delegation in encouraging terms . . . but delayed his decision until he should have returned from the wars. When Ippolito heard the news he decided to join Charles in his expedition and fight by the Emperor's side. At Itri, where he was waiting to board ship, he was poisoned by one of Alessandro's agents and died instantly.

The Florentine colony was plunged into the profoundest gloom. For Michelangelo the loss was especially poignant; in Ippolito he had found everything he had loved in Ippolito's father, Giuliano. It left him with only Contessina's son to carry on the continuity of his love for the Medici. Niccolò seemed to feel the same way, for they sought each other's company during the dread-filled days.

By autumn, one year after he had reached Rome, his Sistine wall was re-bricked and dried; his cartoon of more than three hundred " men of all races," as Matthew had put it, ready to be blown up to wall size. Pope Paul, wishing to give him security, issued a *breve* which declared Michelangelo Buonarroti to be the *Sculptor, Painter and Architect of All the Vatican, with a lifetime pension of a hundred* ducats a month, fifty from the papal treasury, fifty from the benefice of the ferry over the Po River at Piacenza. Sebastiano del Piombo stood with him before the scaffold in the Sistine, asking eagerly:

"Would you like me to put the intonaco on, *compare*? I'm an expert."

"It's a tedious job, Sebastiano. Are you sure you want to?"

"I would be proud to say that I had a hand in the Last Judgment."

"All right. But don't use Roman *pozzolana*, it stays soft; put in marble dust instead, and not too much water with the lime."

"I will lay you a flawless surface."

So he did, structurally; but the moment Michelangelo approached the altar he smelled something wrong: Sebastiano had mixed mastic and resin with the lime, brewed them together, applied the plaster with a mason's trowel heated over fires.

"Sebastiano, you have prepared this wall for oil paints!"

"Isn't that what you wanted?" Sebastiano asked innocently.

"You know I work in fresco!"

"But you didn't tell me, Godfather. I did our San Pietro in Montorio wall in oil."

Michelangelo surveyed the Venetian from the crown of his bald head through the middle layers of his now frightened fat.

"And that made you qualified to paint part of this wall . . .?"

"I only wanted to help."

". . . to paint the Last Judgment?" Michelangelo's voice was rising. "Since you know how to work only in oil, you prepared an oil wall so that you could collaborate with me. What else have you done?"

"Well, I . . . I spoke to Pope Paul. He knows I am of your *bottega*. You've been complaining that I don't paint any more. Here is your opportunity . . ."

"To throw you out!" shouted Michelangelo. "I ought to pull the entire plaster down over your ungrateful head."

But even as Sebastiano scurried away, Michelangelo knew that the surface would take days, weeks to scrape off. Then the brick wall would have to be allowed to dry again before a genuine fresco base could be laid. It, too, would take time to dry. Sebastiano had wasted months of his time.

The wall would be repaired by the capable Urbino; but the breach caused between Michelangelo and Antonio da Sangallo by Pope Paul's *breve* would last for the rest of his life.

Antonio da Sangallo, now fifty-two years old, decorated his thin face with a replica of his uncle Giuliano's luxuriant oriental moustache. He had joined Bramante as an apprentice on St. Peter's and, after Bramante's death, had worked as an assistant to Raphael. He had been part of the Bramante-Raphael clique that had attacked the Sistine vault. Since Raphael's death, with the exception of a few years when Baldassare Peruzzi of Siena had been forced on him as co-architect by Pope Leo, Sangallo had been the architect of St. Peter's, and of Rome. For fifteen years, while Michelangelo was working in Carrara and Florence, no one had risen to challenge his supremacy. . . . The Pope's *breve* made him raving mad.

Tommaso first brought the warning that Sangallo was growing increasingly violent.

"It's not so much that he fights your being named the official sculptor and painter of the Vatican palace. He laughs that off as a colossal piece of bad judgment. It's the appointment as official architect that has him half out of his mind."

"I didn't ask Pope Paul to put that in the *breve*."

"You could never convince Sangallo of that. He claims you're conniving to take St. Peter's away from him."

"What St. Peter's? Those piers and foundations he's been pouring for fifteen years?"

Sangallo showed up that very night, accompanied by two of his apprentices who lighted him across the Piazza del Foro Traiano. Michelangelo invited them in, tried to propitiate Sangallo by recalling memories of their early days together in his uncle's house in Florence. Sangallo refused to be placated.

"I should have come here the very day I heard you had made accusations against me to Pope Paul. It was the same kind of wicked slander you used against Bramante."

"I told Pope Julius that Bramante's mix was bad and that the piers would crack. Raphael spent years repairing them. Is that not true?"

"You think you can turn Pope Paul against me. You

demanded that he declare you the Vatican architect. You want to push me out!"

"That is not true. I am concerned for the building. The fabric has already been paid for, and no part of the church proper is yet apparent."

"Listen to the great architect talk! I've seen that miserable dumpy dome you inflicted on the Medici chapel." Sangallo pressed his clenched fists against his bosom. "Get your bashed-in nose out of St. Peter's. You've been a meddler in other people's affairs all your life. Even Torrigiani couldn't teach you any better. If you value your life: *St. Peter's is mine!*"

Angry for the first time, distressed at the mention of Torrigianni's name, Michelangelo compressed his lips, replied coldly:

"Not quite. It was mine in its inception, and it may very well be mine in its completion."

Now that Sangallo had announced open warfare, Michelangelo decided he had better see Sangallo's walk-in model. Tommaso arranged to take him to the office of the commissioners of St. Peter's where it was lodged. They went on a religious holiday when no one would be there.

Michelangelo was aghast at what he saw. Bramante's interior in the form of a simple Greek cross had been clean and pure, full of light and isolated from its surroundings. Sangallo's model included a ring of chapels which deprived Bramante's concept of all its light and provided none of its own. There were so many ranges of columns one upon the other, so many innumerable projections, pinnacles and subdivisions that the former serene tranquillity was lost. Sangallo had been building fortresses and defence walls; he had no sense whatever of how to create a spiritual church, one that was envisaged as the Mother Church of Christendom. If Sangallo were allowed to continue, he would erect a heavy monument, cluttered and in bad taste.

Walking home, Michelangelo said ruefully to Tommaso:

"I was wrong to tell the Pope about the waste of money. That is the least of the danger."

"Then you will say nothing?"

"It's clear from your voice, Tommaso, that you hope I won't. In point of fact, the Pope would tell me, 'This puts you in a bad light.' So it would. But St. Peter's will be as dark as a Stygian cave."

6

All the Last Judgments he had seen had been sentimenal, unrealistic child's tales, rigid, without movement, stratified as much in space as in spiritual category, with an aloof still-life Christ sitting on a throne, his Judgment already passed. Michelangelo had always searched for the moment of decision, which was for him the eternal womb of truth: David, before the battle with Goliath; God, before giving the spark of life to Adam; Moses, before sustaining the Israelites. Now too he sought a Last Judgment not yet made, with Christ arriving on the scene in a burst of force, while all the nations of earth and time made their way towards him wondering in the starkest fear:

"What is to happen to me?"

This would be the most powerful of all his Christs; he made him Zeus and Hercules, Apollo and Atlas, while realizing it was he, Michelangelo Buonarroti, who would be judging the nations of men. He pulled back into space the right leg of Christ, even as he had the Moses, to cause an imbalance of weight and set the whole figure in a state of tension. The wall would be dominated by Christ's *terribilità*, his terrifying awesomeness.

On the vault he had painted his Genesis in bright, dramatic colours; the Last Judgment would be confined to quieter monotones, flesh tones and brown. On the ceiling he had worked in sharply delineated panels; with the Last Judgment he would have to perform the magician's trick of making the wall vanish and infinite space appear.

Now, ready to begin the fresco itself, all feeling of spent years, of fatigue and uncertainty about the future, vanished. Comfortable and warmed by his love for Tommaso, confident in the pursuit of his love for Vittoria, he tackled the wall with vigour.

"Tommaso, how can a man be happy painting the judgment of the world when so pitifully few will be saved?"

"Because it's not the damnation itself that your happiness derives from. Ecclesia supporting the young girl in her lap, and this condemned sinner, are as fine as anything you painted on the vault."

He was attempting to capture naked truth through nakedness, to express everything the human figure could articulate.

His Christ would wear a wisp of a loincloth, the Virgin a pale lilac robe; yet as he painted her beautiful legs he could bring himself to veil them with only the sheerest of lilac-coloured silk. All the rest, men, women, children, angels, were nude. He was painting them as God made them . . . and as he had wanted to paint them from the age of thirteen. He eschewed conventional iconography to achieve his emotional responses; there was little of the ritualistic vocabulary of religious painting. He did not conceive of himself as a religious painter, or of the Last Judgment as a religious fresco. It was spiritual, having to do with the eternality of the human soul, with the power of God to make man judge himself and hold himself accountable for his sins. He portrayed a single naked humanity struggling with the same fate, the peoples of all races. Even the Apostles and saints, holding forth their symbols of martyrdom, frightened lest they not be recognized, seemed stunned by this image of Christ, the "most high Jupiter," as Dante described him, about to cast fierce thunderbolts at the guilty.

By day he locked himself into the world of the Sistine, with only Urbino by his side on the high scaffold, painting first in the lunettes from which he had obliterated his early work. Just below was the figure of Christ, on the rock of heaven, the golden sun for a throne behind him. Standing on the floor of the chapel, looking upward, he felt a need to impart greater visual impact to Christ's raised arm. He ascended the scaffold, added more volume by extending the paint beyond the outline delineated in the wet plaster. Then he painted Mary beside Christ, the hordes of humans on either side.

At night he read the Bible, Dante, and Savonarola's sermons sent to him by Vittoria Colonna; all fitted together as parts of a whole. He could hear Savonarola's voice as he read sermons he had heard the friar preach forty years before. Now, even as Vittoria had told him, the martyred priest stood forth in his glory as a prophet. Everything that Fra Savonarola had predicted had come true: the division within the Church; the setting up of a new faith within the framework of Christianity; the low estate of the papacy and the clergy; the decay of morals, the increase of violence:

> Rome, a mighty war shall strip thee of thy pomp and pride, a mighty pestilence make ye cast aside your vanities.

Behold, O Florence, thy fate, if thou wouldst have a tyrant. Thy tongue enslaved, thy person subject to him, thy goods at his disposal . . . debased in all ways.

On the outside, it looked as though Judgment Day had arrived for Pope Paul. Cardinal Niccolò, now one of the most influential cardinals at court, brought the news to Michelangelo: Charles V of Spain and Francis I of France had once again declared war on each other. Charles was travelling north from Naples with his army, the one that had sacked Rome and crushed Florence. Pope Paul had no army or means of resistance; he was preparing to flee.

"But where?" demanded Tommaso hotly. "To Sant'-Agnolo, while Charles's troops pillage again? We cannot stand another sack; we will become just another pile of stones, like Carthage."

"What will he fight with?" Michelangelo asked. "I watched the Emperor's army beyond the San Miniato walls. They have cannon, cavalrymen, lancers. . . . What would you use to defend yourselves?"

"Our bare hands!" Tommaso was livid with rage, the first time Michelangelo had ever seen him this way.

Pope Paul decided to fight . . . with peace and grandeur. He received the Emperor on the steps before St. Peter's, surrounded by the hierarchy of the Church in their splendid robes, and three thousand valiant young Romans. Charles behaved graciously, accepted the Pope's spiritual authority. The following day he called on Vittoria Colonna, Marchesa di Pescara, friend of his family, who summoned her friend, Michelangelo Buonarroti, for the meeting in the garden of San Silvestro al Quirinale.

The Holy Roman Emperor, a formal and haughty monarch, acknowledged Vittoria's introduction with considerable sanguinity. Michelangelo pleaded with Charles for the removal of Alessandro as the tyrant of Florence. The Emperor did not appear to be greatly interested but, when Michelangelo had concluded, leaned towards him and said with unaccustomed heartiness:

"I can promise you one thing when I get to Florence."

"Thank you, Excellency."

"That I shall pay a visit to your new sacristy. People of my court, returning to Spain, have declared it one of the marvels of the world."

Michelangelo looked towards Vittoria to see if he might continue. Vittoria's face was calm; she was willing to risk the Emperor's displeasure to allow Michelangelo to speak for his country.

"Excellence, if the sculptures of the new sacristy are good, they are so because I was raised in the art capital of Europe. Florence can continue to create noble works of art only if you rescue her from under the boot of Alessandro."

Charles maintained his pleasant mien, murmuring, "The Marchesa di Pescara says that you are the single greatest artist since the beginning of time. I have seen your Sistine Chapel ceiling; in a few days I shall see your Medici chapel sculptures. If they are all that I have heard, you have our royal promise . . . something shall be done."

The Florentine colony ran wild with joy. Charles V kept his word; he was so deeply stirred by his visit to the new sacristy that he ordered the wedding ceremonies of his daughter Margaret to Alessandro to be held in Michelangelo's chapel. The prospect made Michelangelo so ill he could not work. He walked in the *campagna* along the tomb-lined Via Appia, revulsion sweeping over him as he tried to vomit forth the noxious nature of the existing world.

The marriage proved to be short-lived; Alessandro was murdered in a house next to the Medici palace by a Popolano cousin, Lorenzino, when he thought he was keeping a tryst with Lorenzino's chaste sister. Florence was freed of its rapacious tyrant; but not Michelangelo. Alessandro's body, loathsome to all of Tuscany, was clandestinely dumped in the dark of night into the chastely sculptured sargophagus under Dawn and Dusk.

"All Florentines are rid of Alessandro . . . except me," he said to Urbino morosely. "Now you see what a marble carver is good for: to provide tombs for tyrants."

Revulsion passes, as joy does. Each bad blow kept him out of the Sistine for a week or two. Such good news as the marriage of his niece, Cecca, to the son of the famous Florentine historian, Guicciardini, or the election of Vittoria Colonna's father confessor and teacher, Reginald Pole, to the cardinalate, which gave a strong boost to the reform faction, sent him back renewed to paint the compact group of saints pictorially beyond Christ's wrath: Catherine, with part of a wheel, Sebastiano, with a handful of arrows, attenuated forms wafting upward in the firmament, glorious female figures among the intermeshed maze of males. He used his spare energies to propitiate the still outraged Duke of

Urbino by making a model of a bronze horse for him, as well as a richly decorated salt cellar. He took comfort from the fact that Cosimo de' Medici, a descendant of the Popolano branch of the Medici, a humble, decent seventeen-year-old, was in the Medici palace, and many of the exiles were returning home, the young sons of his friends coming to bid him an affectionate *A rivederci.*

He was shattered when the malign fates which had begun the enveloping of Florence since the untimely death of Lorenzo, *Il Magnifico,* moved on inexorably to inflict a culminating tragedy: Cosimo, though well behaved morally, was developing into a tyrant, reducing the newly elected councils to impotence. The young men of Florence organized an army, bought arms, appealed to Francis I of France to lend them troops to defeat Cosimo's supporters. Charles V did not want a republic; he loaned his army to Cosimo, who crushed the uprising. The leaders were executed, hundreds of the finest minds and spirits of Tuscany, with every family suffering severe losses: Filippo Strozzi run through with a sword, his son killed; Baccio Valori and his son put to death; a dozen more of the young exiles who had thronged his studio, who had been bold and eager to return and fight for their city-state, dead, dead in the beauty and glory of their youth.

" What was their sin?" Michelangelo cried. " For what were they judged, that they had to be murdered in cold blood? What kind of jungle do we live in that such brutal, senseless crime can be committed with impunity?"

How right he had been to put up on that wall a fierce and wrathful Jesus on Judgment Day!

He redrew the lower right-hand corner of his cartoon, opposite the dead arising from their graves on the left; and for the first time pictured a group already condemned, being driven by Charon into the mouth of hell. Now man seemed just another form of animal life cropping his way along the surface of the earth. Was he possesssed of an immortal soul? Precious little good it had done him: it was just another appendage he was going to have to carry down to the inferno with him. Perhaps this soul would help him to climb back up to purgatory, and eventually even to paradise. At the moment he would have said, " Permit me to doubt " . . . for Vittoria Colonna too had come into troubled times.

Giovanni Pietro Caraffa, long suspicious of her activities

as an inquirer into new doctrines and a challenger of the faith, had been elected a cardinal. A religious fanatic, Cardinal Caraffa began his efforts to bring the Inquisition into Italy to wipe out the heretics, the freethinkers, the unbelievers . . . and in the case of Vittoria Colonna, those who were working from outside the Church to oblige the Church to reform itself from within. He made it plain that he considered her, and the little group around her, dangerous. Though they rarely had more than eight or nine at their meetings, there was an informer in their midst; Cardinal Caraffa had a complete record by Monday morning of the Sunday afternoon discussions.

" What will this mean to you?" Michelangelo asked Vittoria anxiously.

" Nothing, so long as some of the cardinals are in favour of reform."

" But if Caraffa gains control?"

" Exile."

Michelangelo was shocked. He stared at her alabaster face, himself turning pale.

" Should you not be careful?"

The thought had made his voice harsh. Was he asking it for her, or for himself? She knew how important her presence in Rome was to him.

" It would do no good. I might issue the same warning to you." Her voice too seemed sharp. Was she asking it for herself, for him? Had she not shown him that she wanted him near? " Caraffa does not like what you are painting in the Sistine."

" How could he know? I keep it locked."

" The same way he knows what we say here."

Though he had allowed no one but Urbino, Tommaso and the Cardinals Niccolò and Giovanni Salviati into his studio since he had begun blowing up his cartoon, and not a solitary soul but Urbino into the Sistine, Cardinal Caraffa was not the only one who knew what he was putting on the wall. Letters began to arrive from all over Italy, commenting on it. The strangest came from Pietro Aretino, whom Michelangelo knew by reputation as a gifted writer and unscrupulous wretch who lived by blackmail, obtaining the most astounding favours and sums of money, even from princes and cardinals, by showing them how much damage he could do by flooding Europe with evil letters about them, couched in such vivid and witty terms that the courts of Europe repeated his slanders as amusing anecdotes. Sometimes cast down by his greed and concupiscence into poverty and disgrace, he was at the moment a man of importance in Venice, intimate friend of Titian and consort of kings.

The purpose of Aretino's letter was to tell Michelangelo exactly how he should paint the Last Judgment:

> I see in the crowd the Antichrist with features which you alone could imagine: I see terror on the countenance of the living. I see the signs of the extinction of the sun, moon and stars; I see the elements melt and disappear, and I see exhausted Nature become sterile. . . . I see life and death scared by the fearful anarchy. . . . I see the arrowy flight of the words of judgment, issuing from the mouth of the Son of God, amidst tremendous thunderings. . . .

Aretino ended his long letter with the comment that, although he had vowed never to return to Rome, his resolve was broken by the desire to pay honour to Michelangelo's genius. Michelangelo answered satirically, thinking to rid himself of the interloper:

> Do not change your decision not to come to Rome just for the sake of seeing my work. That would be asking too much! When I received your letter I rejoiced; yet I grieved at the same time because, since I have completed a large section of my story, I cannot put to use your conception.

Aretino began a barrage of letters which importuned drawings, sections of cartoons, models: "Does not my devotion deserve that I should receive from you, the prince of sculpture and of painting, one of those cartoons which you fling into the fire?" He even sent missives to Michelangelo's friends, to young Vasari whom he had known in Venice, and others who frequented the studio on the Macello dei Corvi, determined to have their help in getting some of the sketches which he could then sell. Michelangelo answered evasively, grew bored and ignored Aretino completely.

It was an error: Aretino saved his venom until the Last Judgment was completed, then struck with two inky ejaculations, one of which almost destroyed his five years of painting, the second, his character.

7

Now time and space became identical. He could not swear how many days, weeks, months passed as 1537 gave way to 1538, but before him on the altar wall he could tell precisely how many figures he had floating upward through the lower cloud levels to the rocky crags on either side of the Madonna and Son. Christ with his arm raised above his head in outraged denunciation was not here to listen to special pleading. No good for sinners to cry for mercy. The wicked were already damned, and terror was in the air.

Yet never were the forms of the human body more lovingly and pulsatingly portrayed. How could so mean a spirit live in so noble a castle? Why was the flesh so much more perfect in structure, power, beauty, than anything these frightened mortals had been able to accomplish with their minds and souls?

Each morning Urbino laid the needed field of intonaco ; by nightfall Michelangelo had filled it with a body tumbling downward towards hell, or the portraits of the now elderly Eve and Adam. Urbino had become as expert as Rosselli at joining each new day's plaster so that the lines could not be seen. Each day at noon he had the woman servant, Caterina, bring hot food which he reheated on a brazier on the scaffold before serving Michelangelo.

"*Mangiate bene*. You need your strength. It is a *torta*, like your stepmother used to bake, chicken fried in oil and ground into sausage with onions, parsley, eggs and saffron."

"Urbino, you know I'm too wrought up to eat in the middle of a day's work."

". . . and too tired to eat at the end of one. Look what I have here, a salad that sings in the mouth."

Michelangelo chuckled. To indulge Urbino, he ate, and was surprised at how good it was, how like *Il Migliore's*. Urbino was pleased with the success of his stratagem.

When Michelangelo began to falter, after months of intensive work, it was Urbino who made him stay at home, rest, divert himself by massing the blocks for the Prophet, Sibyl and Virgin for the Roveres. When the Duke of Urbino died, Michelangelo was immensely relieved even though he knew he would have to confess the sin of rejoicing over another man's death. Before long the new Duke of Urbino arrived at the studio on the Macello dei Corvi. Michelangelo took one look at him standing in the doorway in his father's face.

"*Dio mio*," he thought, "I inherit the sons of my enemies as well as my friends."

But he was wrong about the young duke.

"I have come to put an end to the strife," he said quietly. "I have never agreed with my father that your failure to complete my granduncle's tomb was totally your fault."

"You mean that I can now call the Duke of Urbino my friend?"

"And admirer. I often told my father if you had been allowed to continue your work you would have completed that tomb even as you did the Sistine Chapel and the Medici chapel. You shall be harassed no more."

Michelangelo sank into a chair. "My son, do you know from what you have just delivered me . . .?"

"But by the same token," continued the young man, "you will readily understand our earnest wish to see you finish the holy monument to my uncle, Pope Julius. Because of the reverence we bear Pope Paul, we shall not interrupt you while you are completing your fresco; but, being finished, we ask that you give yourself to the monument, doubling your diligence to remedy the loss of time."

"With all my heart! You shall have your tomb!"

During the long winter nights he made drawings for Vittoria: a Holy Family, a Pietà, exquisitely conceived; while she returned his feelings by presenting him with a first copy of her published poems, *Rime*. For Michelangelo, desiring to pour out the whole of his passion, it was an incomplete relationship, yet his love for her, and his conviction that she felt deeply for him, kept his creative powers at the flood while he painted husky *contadini* angels on a floating bastion several clouds below Christ, blowing their trumpets with such hell-let-loose loudness that all the dead below would hear and rise from their graves.

His brothers, his nephew Lionardo and his niece Cecca kept him posted on family affairs. Lionardo, approaching twenty, was showing the first profit at the family wool shop. Cecca presented him with a new nephew each year. Occasionally he had to write irritated letters to Florence, as when he received no acknowledgment of money sent, or when Giovansimone and Sigismondo quarrelled over who should get how much wheat from which farm; or Lionardo, requested to send him some fine Florentine shirts, chose three which proved to be " so coarse a peasant couldn't wear them."

When Lionardo sent good pears or *trebbiano* wine, Michelangelo took a portion to the Vatican to give to Pope Paul as a present. They had become fast friends. If a long period went by without Michelangelo's visiting him, Paul summoned him from his work to come to the throne room, asking in an injured tone:

" Michelangelo, why do you never come to see me?"

" Holy Father, you do not need my presence here. I believe that I serve you better by remaining at work than do others who stand before you all day."

" Painter Passenti presents himself here every day."

" Passenti has an ordinary talent that can be found without a lantern in the market places of the world."

Paul was proving to be a good Pope; he appointed honourable and able men as cardinals, was dedicated to reform within the Church. Though he found it necessary to pose the authority of the Church against Charles's military power, he brought neither wars nor invasions down upon himself. He was devoted to the arts and learning. Nevertheless his heritage from the Borgia regime held over, making him a target for attack. As sentimentally attached to his sons and grandsons as the Borgia Pope had been to Cæsar and Lucrezia, there was almost no piece of chicanery he considered despicable if it helped found the fortune of his son Pier Luigi, for whom he was determined to carve out a duchy. He appointed his fourteen-year-old grandson, Alessandro Farnese, a cardinal, and another young grandson he married to Charles V's daughter, the widow of Alessandro de' Medici, creating a place for him by taking the Duchy of Camerino away from the Duke of Urbino. Because of these acts his enemies called him base and ruthless.

By the end of 1540, when Michelangelo had completed the upper two third of the fresco, he hired the carpenter Ludovico to lower the scaffolding. Pope Paul heard the news, arrived at the locked Sistine door unannounced. He had given up the use of his personal chapel so that Michelangelo might have privacy. Urbino, who answered the banging on the door, could not refuse to admit the pontiff.

Michelangelo came down from the new, low scaffold,

greeted Pope Paul and his Master of Ceremonies, Biagio da Cesena, with cordial words. The Pope stood facing the Last Judgment, walked stiffly towards the wall without removing his eyes. When he reached the altar he sank to his knees and prayed.

Not so Biagio da Cesena, who stood glaring up at the fresco. Paul rose to his feet, made the sign of the cross over Michelangelo and then the Last Judgment. There were tears of pride and humility on his cheeks.

" My son, you have created a glory for my reign."

" It is disgraceful . . .!" spat out Biagio da Cesena.

Pope Paul was astounded.

" And totally immoral! I cannot tell the saints from the sinners. There are only hundreds of nudes showing their private parts. It is shameful."

" You think the human body shameful?" asked Michelangelo.

" In a *bagno,* no. But in the Pope's chapel! *Scandaloso!* "

" Only if you wish to create a scandal, Biagio," replied Paul firmly. " On Judgment Day we shall all stand naked before the Lord. My son, how do I express my overwhelming gratitude?"

Michelangelo turned to the Master of Ceremonies with a conciliatory gesture, for he wanted to make no enemies for his fresco. Biagio da Cesena broke in roughly.

" One day this sacrilegious wall will be annihilated, even as you destroyed the beautiful Peruginos beneath it."

" Not while I live," cried Pope Paul, furious. " I will excommunicate anyone who dares touch this masterpiece!"

They left the chapel. Michelangelo stood rubbing a sorely painful area under his left breast. He asked Urbino to mix some intonaco and lay it on the blank spot on the extreme right-hand corner of the wall. This done, he painted a caricature of Biagio da Cesena, representing him as the judge of the shades of Hades, with the ears of an ass, and a monstrous snake coiled around the lower part of the torso: a lethal likeness, the pointed nose, lips drawn back over buck teeth. It was a poor revenge, he knew, but what other was open to an artist?

Word leaked out somehow. Biagio da Cesena demanded a second meeting before the fresco.

" You see Holy Father," cried the Master of Ceremonies, " the report was true. Buonarroti has painted me into the fresco. With some kind of repulsive serpent for my genitalia."

"It's a covering," replied Michelangelo. "I knew you would not want to be portrayed wholly naked."

"A remarkable likeness," observed the Pope, his eyes twinkling. "Michelangelo, I thought you said you could not do portraiture?"

"I was inspired, Holiness."

Biagio da Cesena hopped up and down on either foot as though it were he instead of his picture standing over the fires of hell.

"Holiness, make him take me out of there!"

"Out of hell?" the Pope turned surprised eyes on the man. "Had he placed you in purgatory, I should have done everything in my power to release you. But you know that from hell there is no redemption."

The following day Michelangelo learned that no one ever got the last laugh. He was on the lowered scaffolding painting Charon with the protruding eyes and horns for ears, whipping the damned out of his boat and into the fiery depths, when he felt dizzy, tried to grasp a support rail, fell to the marble floor. There was a moment of excruciating pain. He revived to find Urbino splashing cold, sandy water from the bucket on to his face.

"Thanks to God, you're conscious. How badly are you hurt? Is anything broken?"

"How would I know? If I'm so stupid, I should have broken every bone in my body. For five years I work on this scaffold, and at the very end I fall off."

"Your leg is bleeding where it struck this piece of lumber. I will find a carriage."

"You'll find nothing of the sort. Nobody is going to know what an idiot I am. Help me up. Now put an arm under my shoulder. I can ride the horse home."

Urbino put him to bed, pressed a glass of *trebbiano* to his lips, then washed out the wound. When he wanted to go for a doctor Michelangelo stopped him.

"No, doctor. I'd be the laughingstock of Rome. Bolt that front door."

Despite all that Urbino could do by way of hot towels and bandaging, the wound began to fester. Michelangelo developed a fever. Urbino was frightened and sent word to Tommaso.

"If I let you die . . ."

"The thought has its compensations, Urbino. I wouldn't have to go climbing scaffolds any more."

"How can you tell? Perhaps in hell a man has to do for ever the thing he most hated to do in life?"

Tommaso went for Dr. Baccio Rontini. When Michelangelo refused to allow them to enter the front door they forced a back door of the house. Dr. Rontini was irate.

"For sheer perverse idiocy, no one can rival a Florentine." He probed the infected wound. "Another day or two . . ."

It took a week to get him back on his feet; he felt like a bag of meal. Urbino helped him up the scaffolding, laid a patch of intonaco in the sky just below St. Bartholomew. Michelangelo painted a caricature of his own drained, woebegone face and head, suspended in the middle of an empty skin, and held aloft by the hand of the saint.

"Now Biagio da Cesena doesn't have to feel too badly," he observed to Urbino as he gazed at his empty hanging carcass. "We've both been judged, and recorded."

He painted the bottom third of the wall, the simplest part since there were fewer figures: the symbolic graveyards and hell, with the long dead rising from their tombs, one of them a skeleton trying to join those in the sky; and the too long alive, being driven into the fires.

It was at this moment that Vittoria's troubles came to a crisis. The most influential and talented of women, praised by the great Ariosto for her poetry, by the Pope for her saintliness; the closest friend of Emperor Charles V in Rome, a member of the wealthy Colonnas, and the D'Avalos by marriage, she was nonetheless about to be driven into exile by Cardinal Caraffa. It seemed impossible that a woman of such high position could be so persecuted.

Michelangelo called on Cardinal Niccolò at the Medici palace to ask for help. Niccolò tried to reassure him.

"Everyone in Rome now acknowledges the need for reform. My uncles Leo and Clement were too highhanded, they tried to bring the dissenters back by disciplining them. But Paul is sending the marchesa's friend, Cardinal Contarini, to negotiate with the Lutherans and Calvinists. I think we shall succeed in time."

Cardinal Contarini was on the verge of a brilliant success at the Diet of Ratisbon when Cardinal Caraffa had him recalled, accused him of collusion with Emperor Charles V, and had him exiled to Bologna.

Vittoria sent Michelangelo a message; could he come at once? She wished to say "Farewell."

It was an intoxicating April day, the buds bursting forth in the Colonna gardens, the wild scents of spring enclosed within the walls. Michelangelo had expected to find her alone for so personal a moment, but the garden was full of people. She rose, greeting him with a sombre smile. She was dressed in black, a black mantilla covering the golden hair; her face seemed carved out of Pietrasanta statuary marble. He went close to her.

"It was good of you to come, Michelangelo."

"Let us not waste time on the formalities. You have been exiled?"

"I have been given to understand that it would be advisable to leave Rome."

"Where are you going?"

"To Viterbo. I lived in the convent of St. Catherine there. I consider it one of my homes."

"When will I see you again?"

"When God wills."

They stood in silence, probing deep into each other's eyes, trying to communicate.

"I'm sorry, Michelangelo, that I shall not be able to see your Last Judgment."

"You will see it. When do you leave?"

"In the morning. You will write to me?"

"I will write, and send you drawings."

"I will answer, and send you poems."

He turned abruptly and left the garden; locked himself in the studio of his house, bereft. It was dark by the time he roused himself from his torpor and asked Urbino to light him to the Sistine. In the Florentine district oil lamps were glowing in the windows of the houses. The Castel Sant'-Angelo loomed up at the other end of the bridge like a cylindrically carved stone mountain. Urbino unlocked the Sistine door, went ahead with the taper to let warm wax drip on to the scaffolding and make a base for the two candles he was carrying.

The Last Judgment sprang cyclonically to life in the flickering half-world of the chapel. Judgment Day became Judgment Night. The three hundred men, women, children, saints, angels and demons, many of whom had been submerged in the full light of day, pressed forward to be recognized and to play out their portentous drama in the open spaces of the chapel itself.

Something drew his attention to the ceiling. Looking upward, he saw God creating the universe. Lines from Genesis came into his mind:

The earth yielded grasses that grew and seeded, each according to its kind, and trees that bore fruit, each with the power to propagate its own kind. And God saw it, and found it good.

God made the two great luminaries, the greater of them to command the day, and the lesser to command the night; then he made the stars. All these he put in the vault of the sky, to shed their light on the earth, to control day and night, and divide the spheres of light and darkness. And God saw it, and found it good.

So God made man in his own image, made him in the image of God. Man and woman both, he created them.

And God saw all that he had made, and found it very good.

Michelangelo turned his attention back to his painting on the altar wall. He saw all that he had made, and he found it very good.

BOOK ELEVEN

THE DOME

1

On All Saints' Eve, exactly twenty-nine years after Pope Julius had consecrated the ceiling with a special ceremony, Pope Paul said high mass to celebrate the completion of the Last Judgment.

On Christmas Day, 1541, the chapel was thrown open to the public. Rome streamed through the Sistine, terrified, shocked, awe-stricken. The studio in the Macello dei Corvi was thronged with Florentines, cardinals, courtiers, artists and apprentices. When the last of the guests had disappeared Michelangelo realized that two groups had not been represented: Antonio da Sangallo and the artists and architects who centred around him, remnants of the Bramante-Raphael coterie; and Cardinal Caraffa and his followers.

Very soon war was declared. An unfrocked monk, Bernardino Ochino, censured Pope Paul by demanding:

"How can Your Holiness allow such an obscene painting as that of Michelangelo's to remain in a chapel where the divine office is sung?"

But when Michelangelo returned to the Sistine the following day he found half a dozen artists sitting on low stools sketching and copying. The Pope rallied to his support by asking him to fresco two virtually twenty-foot-square walls of the chapel named after him, the Pauline, designed and recently completed by Antonio da Sangallo between the Sistine and St. Peter's. The chapel was ponderously top-heavy, the two overhead windows affording insufficient light, but the walls were attractively set off by reddish Corinthian pillars. Pope Paul wanted a Conversion of Paul on one wall, a Crucifixion of Peter on the opposite.

While thinking through the imagery of the Conversion, Michelangelo spent his days with hammer and chisel. He sculptured a head of Brutus, which the Florentine colony had been urging. He articulated the thick curls on Moses' head, carving at the forefront the two horns, or rays of light, which the Old Testament attributed to Moses. With the heat of midsummer, he moved two marbles out to the bricked garden terrace from which to carve a Rachel and a Leah, Contemplative and Active Life, for the two niches alongside the Moses; niches which, in his redesigning of Julius' single-wall tomb, had become too small to hold the Heroic Captive and Dying Captive. He finished the sketches for the Virgin, Prophet and Sibyl which would complete the monument, then sent for Raffaelo da Montelupo, who had carved the St. Damian for the Medici chapel, to sculpture them. With the two Captives no longer part of the design, and the four unfinished Giants and Victory still in Florence, it was Ercole Gonzaga who was proving to be the prophet. The Moses alone would be the majesty of Julius' tomb, and represent his best carving. Was it, as the Cardinal of Mantua had said, "sufficient monument for any man"?

Michelangelo wondered what Jacopo Galli would have said about his finishing the tomb with only one major work of the original forty he had contracted for.

He decided that Urbino had earned his independence.

"Urbino, you're past thirty now, and it's time you began making money for yourself. The Pope has agreed to pay you eight ducats a month for grinding the colours when I paint his chapel. Would you like also to contract for the construction of the tomb wall?" ·

"Yes, *messere*, for I must begin putting away money against my marriage. The family that bought my parental home in Urbino, they have a little girl . . . in about ten years she will make a good wife. . . ."

He sorely missed Vittoria Colonna. In the deep of night he wrote her long letters, frequently sending a sonnet or a drawing. At first Vittoria replied promptly, but as his letters became too urgent she answered less frequently. To his anguished cry of "Why?" she replied:

Magnificent Messer Michelangelo:
I did not reply earlier to your letter, because it was, as one might say, an answer to my last: for I thought that if you and I were to go on writing without intermission, according to my obligation and your courtesy, I should have to neglect the chapel of St. Catherine here, and be absent at the appointed hours for company with my sisterhood, while you would have to leave the chapel of St. Paul and be absent from morning through the day. . . . Thus we should both of us fail in our duty.

He felt crushed, chagrined, as though he were a small boy who had been reproved. He continued to write passionate poems to her . . . but did not send them, contenting himself with scraps of news brought by travellers from Viterbo. When he learned that she was ill and rarely left her room, his sense of mortification turned to anxiety. Did she have good medical attention? Was she taking proper care of herself?

He was depleted, tired, at loose ends; yet all the loose ends had to be tied together securely. He laid a new plaster wall in the Pauline chapel; deposited fourteen hundred ducats in the bank of Montauto to be paid out to Urbino and Raffaelo da Montelupa as they made progress with the tomb. He drew a modest design for the Conversion of Paul, with some fifty figures and an additional number of faces surrounding Paul as he lay on the ground, having been struck by a shaft of yellow light coming down from heaven, the first New Testament miracle he had ever painted. He carved the Rachel and Leah, two tender, lovely young women, heavily swathed in robes, symbolic figures; and for the first time since the Piccolomini statues he was carving marbles in which he had no genuine interest. They appeared to him watered down in emotional intensity, without the throbbing, self-contained core of energy to grip and dominate the space about them.

His studio and garden had been turned into a busy workshop, with half a dozen young people helping Urbino and Raffaelo da Montelupo to finish the tomb. He was delighted to find a number of the Jews of Rome, some of whom reported that they were the sons or grandsons of the men who had posed for his first Pietà, asking permission to come to the studio to see the Moses. They stood before their great teacher caught between pride and wonder, their lips silently murmuring something which Michelangelo knew could not be prayers, since the Ten Commandments forbade it.

The present and future had shape for him only in terms of work to be done. How many more works of art could he live? The Conversion of St. Paul would take so many years, the Crucifixion of St. Peter so many more. Better to count the projects ahead than the days; then he would not tick off the years one by one as though they were coins he was counting into the hands of a wary merchant. Simpler to think of time as creativity: the two Pauline frescoes, then a

Descent from the Cross he wanted to carve for his own pleasure from the last of his magnificent Carrara blocks . . . God would not be inclined to interrupt an artist in the midst of begetting.

He consumed time as smoothly as he drank a cup of water: a few days represented a servant trying to restrain Paul's frightened horse; a week involved a wingless angel, a month conceived Paul, stricken by the light from Christ's hand; a year meant the massing of figures on one side of Paul, soldiers and companions, some terrorized, some trying to flee, some gazing upward in their consternation. What better way to tell time than through the body of content?

A Committee of Inquisition had been established in Rome. Cardinal Caraffa, who had lived a morally upright life as a priest in the corrupt court of the Borgia Pope, Alexander VI, had attracted power against the will and wishes of those who served him. Though he boasted that he never made himself agreeable to anyone, that he turned away roughly everyone who asked favours; though he was choleric in temperament and painfully thin of face and body, his burning zeal for the dogma of the Church was making him the most influential leader of the College of Cardinals; respected, feared and obeyed. His Committee of Inquisition had already established an Index which said what books could be printed and read.

Vittoria Colonna returned to Rome and entered the convent of San Silvestro in Capite near the Pantheon. Michelangelo did not think she should have left the safety of Viterbo. He pressed for a meeting. Vittoria refused. He accused her of cruelty; she replied that it was a kindness. Finally, from sheer persistence, he gained her assent . . . only to find that her strength and her beauty had been ravaged. Her illness and the pressure of the accusations against her had aged her twenty years. She had passed from a lovely, robust, vibrant woman to one whose face was lined, lips dry and pale, the green eyes sunk in their sockets, the rich copper gone from her hair. She was sitting alone in the convent garden, her hands folded in her lap, her head veiled. He was overcome.

" I tried to save you from this," she murmured.

" You think my love so shallow?"

" Even in your kindness there is a cruel revelation."

" Life is cruel, never love."

743

"Love is the cruellest of all. I know . . ."

"You know only a fragment," he interrupted. "Why have you kept us apart? And why have you returned to this dangerous atmosphere?"

"I must make my peace with the Church, find forgiveness for my sins against her."

"Sins?"

"Yes. I disobeyed, indulged my own vain opinions against the divine doctrine, harboured dissenters. . . ."

His throat locked. Another echo from the past. He remembered the anguish with which he had listened to the dying Lorenzo de' Medici pleading for absolution from Savonarola, the man who had destroyed his Plato Academy. He heard again his brother Lionardo's disavowal of Savonarola's disobedience to the Borgia Pope. Was there no unity between living and dying?

"My last desire is to die in grace," Vittoria was saying, quietly. "I must return to the bosom of the Church, like a child to the bosom of its mother. Only there can I find redemption."

"Your illness has done this to you," he cried. "This Inquisition has tortured you."

"I have tortured myself, inside my own mind. Michelangelo, I worship you as God-given among men. But you too, before your death, will have to seek salvation."

He listened to the noise of the bees as they buzzed in the cups of the flowers. His heart ached for her despair. They were still alive on the face of the earth. She spoke as though they were already dead. He said:

"My feelings for you, which you would never allow me to express, have not changed. Did you think I was a young boy who had fallen in love with a pretty *contadina*? Do you not know how great a place you occupy in my mind . . .?"

Tears flooded her eyes. She began breathing rapidly.

"Thank you, *caro*," she whispered. "You have healed wounds that go . . . very far back."

And she was gone, into a side door of the convent, leaving him on the stone bench which suddenly was cold beneath him, in a garden cold about him.

2

When Antonio da Sangallo began pouring his foundations for the ring of chapels on the south side of the tribune of St. Peter's, the long smouldering feud between them became full-blown. According to Michelangelo's measurements, the corresponding wing to the north, towards the Papal palace, would of necessity replace the Pauline chapel and part of the Sistine.

"I simply cannot believe my eyes," cried Pope Paul when Michelangelo drew him a plan of what was going on. "Why would Sangallo want to tear down a chapel he designed and built himself?"

"His plans for St. Peter's keep expanding."

"How much of the Sistine would his chapels replace?"

"Approximately the area covered by the Deluge, the Drunkenness of Noah, the Delphic Sibyl and Zacharias. God would survive."

"How fortunate for Him," murmured Paul.

The Pope suspended work on St. Peter's on the grounds that there was insufficient money to continue. But Sangallo knew that Michelangelo was the cause. Sangallo did not attack direcly. He entrusted this to his assistant, Nanni di Baccio Bigio, with a long tradition of hostility to Michelangelo absorbed from his father, who had been excluded from the architectural work on the abortive façade of San Lorenzo, and from his long-time Florentine friend, Baccio Bandinelli, Michelangelo's most vocal opponent in Tuscany. Baccio Bigio, who aspired to succeed Sangallo as the architect of St. Peter's, had an inexhaustible set of vocal cords which he now employed in a retaliatory attack on the Last Judgment as giving comfort to the enemies of the Church and causing converts to Luther. Sangallo and Bigio succeeded in getting a statement issued through Cardinal Caraffa that all works of art, like all books, must first be approved by his committee.

Yet travellers coming into the Sistine fell on their knees before the fresco, even as Paul III had, repenting of their sins; such a dissolute poet as Molza of Modena underwent conversion. Michelangelo grumbled to Tommaso.

"When it comes to me, there is no middle ground. I am

either the master or the monster of the world. The Sangallo crowd have formed an image of me out of the stuff of which their own hearts are made."

"Mice," replied Tommaso reassuringly, "trying to undermine the Great Wall of China."

"More like flies," retorted Michelangelo; "they bite deep enough to draw blood."

"You have blood to spare."

Bindo Altoviti, who had served on the last Florentine Council and was a leader of the exiles in Rome, chose this moment to declare at court that Michelangelo's defence walls of San Miniato had been "a work of art." Pope Paul sent for Michelangelo to join a conference on the defences of the Vatican with the already appointed commission. His son Pier Luigi was president, Antonio da Sangallo architect; it included Alessandro Vitelli, an officer experienced in warfare, and Montemellino, an artillery officer and engineer.

Sangallo glared. Michelangelo kissed the Pope's ring, was introduced to the others. The Pope pointed to Sangallo's model, said:

"Michelangelo, we seek your opinion. We have a serious problem here, since our defences proved so inadequate against Charles V."

A week later, having studied the terrain, Michelangelo was back in the Pope's study. The commission assembled to hear his verdict.

"Holiness, I have spent the days analysing approaches to the Vatican. My opinion is that Sangallo's walls could not be defended."

Sangallo jumped to his feet.

"Why can't they be defended?"

"Because they are drawn to protect too large an area. Some of your positions in the hills behind us, and the walls going to Trastevere along the Tiber, could be breached."

"May I remind you," replied Sangallo, coldly sarcastic "that people call you a painter and sculptor?"

"My bastions in Florence were never breached."

"They were never attacked."

"The Emperor's armies respected them too much to attack."

"And on the basis of one small wall at San Miniato you are an expert who will replace my fortifications!" shouted Sangallo.

"That will do," said Pope Paul sternly. "The meeting is adjourned."

Michelangelo left behind him his criticism of Sangallo's plan, along with detailed drawings to show what alterations should be made to give the Leonine City, or Vatican area, adequate protection. Pier Luigi Farnese and Montemellino agreed with the analysis. The Pope permitted a few of Sangallo's curtain walls to the river to be completed, as well as his lovely Doric gateway. The rest of the work was suspended. Michelangelo was appointed consulting architect to the defence commission, not to succeed Sangallo but to work alongside him.

The next foray came when Sangallo submitted his design for the third-floor windows and cornice of the Farnese palace which he had been building in sections over a long period of years for Cardinal Farnese before he became Pope Paul. Michelangelo had frequently seen the palace under construction, for it faced a piazza just a block from Leo Baglioni's house. He had thought the design ponderous, belonging to the fortresslike bastions of another age, with stubborn strength in its solid stone bulk but without the soaring beauty that such a formidable pile required to give it wings. Now Pope Paul asked Michelangelo to write him a candid criticism of the palace. Michelangelo marked a chapter in Vitruvius' book on architecture, sent it to the Vatican with Urbino, then wrote several blistering pages to prove that the Farnese palace had "no order of any kind; for order is a quaint suitability of the elements of the work separately and universally placed, coherently arranged." Neither did it have disposition, elegance, style, convenience, harmony, propriety or "a comfortable apportionment of places."

If designed brilliantly, he concluded, this top row of windows and cornice could be its saving grace.

As a result of his letter the Pope threw open to competition the design of the top floor and the decorative cornice. A number of artists, Giorgio Vasari, Pierino del Vaga, Sebastiano del Piombo and Jacopo Meleghino, announced that they were setting to work. And so did Michelangelo Buonarroti.

"It is beneath you to compete against the kind of artist one finds without a lantern in the market places of the world," protested Tommaso. "Suppose you were to lose? The humiliation would be a blow to your prestige."

"I won't lose, Tommaso."

His cornice was sculpture, carved and brilliantly decorated. the arches and slender columns of the windows gave the palace the elegance it needed to carry its ponderous body of stone.

Pope Paul studied the designs side by side on his breakfast table in the presence of Sangallo, Vasari, Sebastiano, Del Vaga. He looked up and announced:

"I wish to praise all of these drawings as ingenious and very beautiful. But surely you would agree that it is most true of the divine Michelangelo?"

Michelangelo had saved the Farnese palace from mediocrity and dullness, but gossip had it that he had done it to replace Sangallo as architect of St. Peter's; that now all he had to do was to walk into Pope Paul's throne room and announce that he wanted to take over the fabric.

"I shall do nothing of the sort," Michelangelo told Cardinal Niccolò at the Medici palace, when he had ridden there of a Sunday afternoon on his white Arabian stallion.

Cardinal Caraffa's Commission for the Inquisition began rewriting the classics and preventing new books from being printed. Michelangelo was astonished to find his poetry being regarded as serious literature, his sonnets on Dante, Beauty, Love, Sculpture, Art and the Artist being copied and passed from hand to hand. Some of his madrigals were set to music. Reports reached him of lectures being given about his poetry in the Plato Academy of Florence, and by the professors at the universities of Bologna, Pisa and Padua.

Urbino assembled the single-wall tomb of Pope Julius in San Pietro in Vincoli. He placed the Leah and Rachel in the lower niches, the Virgin, Prophet and Sibyl of Raffaelo da Montelupo in the wall above. Michelangelo considered the monument a failure; but the Moses sitting in the central bay of the marble wall dominated the church with a power equalled only by that of God in the Genesis and Christ in the Last Judgment.

He set up an architectural office in a spare room of the house and put Tommaso de' Cavalieri in charge of the working drawings for the Farnese palace.

He completed the Conversion of St. Paul, Christ leaning downward from the sky, cleaving the heavens, with a multitude of wingless angels on either side of him. Paul, fallen from his horse, was dazed and terrified by the revelation, some of his company trying to raise him up, others fleeing in panic. The strong figure of the horse divided the two groups of travellers and soldiers on the ground, as Christ divided the angels above.

He had Urbino lay a fresh coat of intonaco for the Crucifixion of Peter. While it was drying he closed out the world, massing for the Descent, a Christ supported on one side by the Virgin, on the other by Mary Magdalene, and behind a portrait of himself as Nicodemus, who had helped take Christ down from the cross.

Reputations in Rome were made and broken in the time it took a man to crack a walnut. When Michelangelo refused to take advantage of his victory to force Sangallo out of St. Peter's, the city forgave him for criticizing the Farnese palace.

Then a leter arrived from Aretino, sent from Venice. Though he had never laid eyes on the man, Michelangelo had received a dozen letters from him during the past years, in which Aretino had coupled obsequious flattery with threats of destruction if Michelangelo continued to deny him a gift of drawings. He was about to throw this new epistle unopened into the fire when something wild in the way Aretino had splashed his name across its face arrested his attention. He broke the seal.

The letter began with an attack on the Last Judgment. It was too bad Michelangelo had not take Aretino's advice to represent the world and paradise and hell with the glory, honour and terror sketched in his earlier letters. Instead " You, who are a Christian, you so subordinate belief to art that you have made the violation of modesty among martyrs and virgins into a spectacle, such as we should only venture to contemplate with half-averted eyes in houses of evil repute."

From there he went on to call Michelangelo " avaricious " for agreeing to build a tomb for an unworthy Pope, and then a fraud and a thief for having taken " the heaps of gold which Pope Julius bequeathed you," and given the Roveres nothing in return. " That is robbery!"

Repulsed but fascinated by the violent ranting and alternate begging tone of the long letter, Michelangelo then read: " It would certainly have been well if you had fulfilled your promise with due care, had it been only to silence the evil tongues who assert that only a Gherardo or a Tommaso know how to allure favours from you!"

Michelangelo was swept by a cold chill. What evil tongues? What favours? Drawings were his to give where he liked. They had not been " allured " from him.

He dropped the sheets from Aretino's pen, began to feel ill. In his seventy years he had been accused of many things, of being cantankerous, arrogant, unsociable, snobbishly unwilling to associate with any but those who had the greatest talent, intellect, excellence. But never had such an insinuation been made as this one. Gherardo was a former Florentine friend to whom he had given a few black chalk drawings more than twenty years ago. Tommaso de' Cavalieri was as noble a soul, as finely intelligent and well bred a person as there was in Italy! It was unbelievable. For fifty-odd years, since Argiento had come to him, he had taken apprentices, assistants and servants into his home; there had been at least thirty young men who had lived and worked with him, grown up with him in this traditional relationship. Never in his association with young art apprentices, starting with Ghirlandaio's *bottega*, had there been a word breathed against the propriety of his conduct. What a target for blackmail he would have been had he ever put himself at anyone's mercy!

The charge of blasphemy in his concept of the Last Judgment, the accusation that he had defrauded the Rovere family, could be simply fought. But to be confronted at this time of his life with this false imputation, a charge not unlike the one for which Leonardo da Vinci had been publicly proscuted in Florence so long ago, seemed to him as devastating a blow as he had received in all his stormy years.

It did not take long for Aretino's poison to seep into Rome. A few days later Tommaso arrived with his face pale, his lips compressed. When Michelangelo insisted on knowing what was wrong he brushed the fingers of his right hand across the palm of his left, as though to rid his hands of offal.

" I heard last night," he said, more in sadness than anger, " from a bishop at court, about Aretino's letter."

Michelangelo slumped into a chair.

" How does one deal with such a creature?" he asked hoarsely.

"One doesn't. One accedes to his demands. That's how he has prospered in the world."

"I'm sorry, Tommaso. I never meant to cause you embarrassment."

"It is you I am worried about, Michelangelo, not myself. My family and companions know me well; they will scoff at this canard and ignore it. . . . But you, my dear friend, are revered all over Europe. It is you that Aretino means to hurt, your work and position. . . . The last thing in the world I want is to hurt you."

"You could never hurt me, Tomao. Your love and admiration fed me. With Marchesa Vittoria ill, it is the only love I can count on to sustain me. I also will ignore Aretino. As one should all blackmailers. If he can destroy our friendship he will already have achieved some part of his purpose of inflicting injury on me."

"Rome's tongue would rather wag over a fresh scandal than a *scaloppina*," warned Tommaso.

"Let us continue with our lives and our work. That is the proper answer to scandalmongers."

3

In his drawings for the Crucifixion of St. Peter he struck out boldly to find a new expression for painting. In the centre of the design he pictured a hole being dug to hold the heavy cross. Peter was nailed to it, upside down, while it lay angled across a giant boulder. Unharmed as yet by his impaling, Peter glared out at the world, his elderly bearded face fiercely eloquent in its condemnation not merely of the soldiers about him who were directing the crucifixion, or of the labourers who were helping to raise the cross upward, but of the entire world beyond: an indictment of tyranny and cruelty as piercing as that of the Last Judgment.

As he was completing the sketch of the two Roman centurions and wishing he could draw their horses with the genius that Leonardo da Vinci had had with them, church bells started tolling mournfully over the city. His servant woman burst into the studio, crying:

"*Messere*, Sangallo is dead!"

" . . . dead? He has been building in Terni. . . ."

" He caught the malaria. They just brought his body back."

Pope Paul gave Antonio da Sangallo a spectacular funeral. His coffin was carried through the streets with great pomp, followed by the artists and craftsmen who had worked with him over the years. In church, Michelangelo stood with Tommaso and Urbino listening to the eulogizing of Sangallo as one of the greatest architects since the ancients who had built Rome. Walking home, Michelangelo commented:

" That eulogy is word for word the one I heard for Bramante; yet Pope Leo had stopped all of Bramante's work, just as Pope Paul had halted Sangallo's on the Farnese palace, the defence walls . . St. Peter's . . ."

Tommaso stopped in his tracks, turned to look sharply at Michelangelo. " Do you think . . .?"

" Oh no, Tommaso!"

The superintendent of the fabric suggested that Giulio Romano, sculptor and architect, disciple of Raphael, be called from Mantua and appointed architect of St. Peter's. Pope Paul cried:

" It shall be Michelangelo Buonarroti. None else!"

Michelangelo was summoned by a groom, rode his stallion to the Vatican. The Pope was surrounded by a contingent of his cardinals and courtiers.

" My son, I am herewith appointing you architect of St. Peter's."

" Holiness, I cannot assume the post."

There was a twinkle in Paul's fading but still shrewdly discerning eyes.

" Are you going to tell me that architecture is not your trade?"

Michelangelo flushed. He had forgotten that Pope Paul, then the Cardinal Farnese, had been in this same throne room when Julius commissioned him to decorate the Sistine vault, and he had cried in anguish, " It is not my trade."

" Holy Father, I might have to tear down everything Sangallo has built, dismiss Sangallo's contractors. Rome would be solidly against me. I have the Crucifixion of St. Peter to complete. I am over seventy years old. Where will I find the vital force to build from the ground up the mightiest church in Christendom? . . . I am not Abraham, Holy Father, who lived one hundred and seventy-five years. . . ."

Pope Paul was singularly unaffected by Michelangelo's tale of woe. His eyes gleamed.

" My son, you are but a youth. When you reach my august age of seventy-eight you will be allowed to speak of your years. Not before! By that time you will have St. Peter's well on its way."

Michelangelo's smile was on the wan side.

He left the Vatican grounds by the Belvedere gate, made the long climb to the top of Monte Mario, and after resting and watching the sunset, descend the opposite side of St. Peter's. The workmen had gone home. He went over Sangallo's foundations, the lower walls for the ring of chapels extending to the south. The numerous and heavy piers, on which Sangallo had meant to build a nave and two aisles, would have to be levelled. The huge cement bases for the two steeples, or bell towers, would have to go, as would the supports being built for the heavy dome.

His tour of inspection ended just as night closed down. Finding himself in front of the chapel of Mary of the Fever, he went in and stood in the dark before his Pietà. He was torn by inner conflict. Every move he had made since he had first denounced Bramante's cement mix to Pope Julius had pushed him towards the inevitability of his taking over this task. He truly wanted to rescue St. Peter's, make it a glorious monument to Christianity. He had always felt that it was his church; that if not for him, it might never have been conceived. Then was he not responsible for it?

He also knew the dimension of the task, the depth of the opposition he would meet, the years of gruelling labour. The end of his life would be harder driven than any portion that had gone before.

An old woman came into the chapel, placed a lighted taper before the Madonna. Michelangelo reached into the long basket of candles, selected one, lit it, placed it beside the other.

Of course he must build St. Peter's! Was not life to be worked, and suffered, right to the end?

He refused to accept any pay for his services as architect, even when Pope Paul sent his Keeper of the Wardrobe to the Macello dei Corvi with a packet of one hundred ducats. He painted from first light until dinnertime in the Pauline chapel, then walked the few steps to St. Peter's to watch the levelling. The workmen were sullen and ill disposed towards him . . . but they followed the schedule he set. To his dismay he found that Bramante's four major piers, which had been repaired over a period of years by Raphael, Peruzzi and Sangallo, were still defective and would not support the tribune and dome until more tons of concrete were poured into them. The disclosure of this still evident weakness further infuriated the superintendent of the fabric and the contractors who had worked under Sangallo. They put so many obstacles in his path that Pope Paul had to issue a decree declaring Michelangelo superintendent as well as architect, ordering everyone employed on St. Peter's to follow his orders implicitly. Those contractors and artisans who remained unfriendly, Michelangelo dismissed.

From that moment the fabric began to grow with a momentum that startled and then amazed Rome as people came to look at the two spiral ramps he had built on either side of the slope so that both animals, carrying materials, and men on horseback, carrying supplies across their saddles, could climb to the top, speeding up the provisioning process fiftyfold over the workmen walking up and down with materials on their backs.

A committee of Roman Conservators, impressed, came to ask if he would rescue the Capitoline hill and downslope called the Campidoglio, which had been the seat of religion and government of the Roman Empire, with its Temples of Jupiter and of Juno Moneta. This glorious spot, just above his own house, where he had sat with Contessina to watch Pope Leo declare Giuliano de' Medici a Baron of Rome, was a shambles, the old temples reduced to piles of stone, the Senate building an archaic fortress, animals feeding off the site, the level area a sea of mud in winter and of dust in summer. Would Michelangelo undertake to restore the Campidoglio to its former grandeur?

"Would I?" cried Michelangelo to Tommaso, when the Conservators had left him to consider their offer. "If only Giuliano da Sangallo could know! This was his dream. You shall help me, Tomao. We can make your hope of rebuilding Rome come true."

Tommaso's eyes were dancing like stars on a windy night.

"Thanks to your training, I can do the job. You will see that I shall become a good architect."

"We will plan big, Tomao, set up work for the next

fifty years. When I am gone, you will complete everything according to our plans."

Now that he was working as a fully-fledged architect, he appointed Tommaso as his assistant, assigning additional architectural work space in the house. Tommaso, a meticulous draughtsman, was rapidly developing into one of the ablest of the city's young architects.

Vittoria Colonna's brother Ascanio had become involved in a quarrel with the Pope over the salt tax, and his private army attacked by the papal forces. Ascanio had been driven out of Rome, all of the Colonna family properties confiscated. Cardinal Caraffa's antagonism to Vittoria was heightened. Several of her former associates fled to Germany and joined the Lutherans . . . which further convicted her in the eyes of the Committee of Inquisition. She now took refuge in the convent of Sant'Anna de' Funari, buried deep within the gardens and colonnades of the ancient Theatre of Pompey. When Michelangelo visited her of a Sunday afternoon, she sometimes did not utter a word. He brought sketches with him, trying to interest her in the works he had projected, but she came alive only when she told him of the special permission she had received to visit the Sistine Chapel and stand before the Last Judgment, and when he spoke of the dome for St. Peter's, still vague and illusive in his mind. She knew of his abiding love for the Pantheon, and the Duomo of Florence.

" Because they are pure sculpture," he said.

" And what of St. Peter's dome? Will that be only a top to keep out the rain?"

" Vittoria, it is good to see you smile, and hear you tease me."

" You must not think me unhappy, Michelangelo. I await with trembling joy my reunion with God."

" *Cara,* I should be angry with you. Why are you so eager to die, when there are those of us who love you dearly? Is it not selfish of you?"

She took his hand between hers. In the early flood of his love this would have been a portentous moment; now he could only feel how sharp her bones were beneath the skin. Her eyes burned as she whispered:

" Forgive me for failing you. I can forgive myself only because I know you have no real need of me. A new Descent from the Cross in marble, a regal staircase for the Campidoglio, a dome for St. Peter's: these are your loves. You created majestically before you met me, and you will create majestically after I am gone."

Before there was time for another Sunday meeting he was summoned to the Cesarini palace, home of a Colonna cousin who had married a Cesarini. He crossed beyond the Torre Argentina, was met at a gate and led into a garden.

"The marchesa?" he asked of the doctor who came out to greet him.

"She will not see the sunrise."

He paced the garden while the heavens moved in their cycle. At the seventeenth hour he was admitted to the palace. Vittoria lay on her pillow, her faded copper hair enclosed in a silk hood, dressed in a shirt of finest linen, with a lace collar fastened at the throat. She looked as young and beautiful as the first time he had met her. Her expression was one of sublimity, as though she had already gone beyond all earthly troubles.

Speaking in a low voice, Donna Filippa, Abbess of Sant'-Anna de' Funari, ordered in the coffin. It was coated with tar. Michelangelo cried:

"What is the meaning of the tar-covered coffin? The marchesa has not died of an infectious disease."

"We fear reprisals, *signore,*" the abbess murmured. "We must get the marchesa back to the convent and buried before her enemies can claim the body."

Michelangelo longed to lean over and kiss Vittoria on the brow. He was restrained by the knowledge that she had never offered him anything but her hand.

He returned home, aching in every joint of his body and cranny of his skull. He sat down at his workbench to write:

If being near the fire I burned with it,
Now that its flame is quenched and doth not show,
What wonder if I waste within and glow,
Dwindling away to cinders bit by bit?

Vittoria in her will had directed the abbess to select her grave. Cardinal Caraffa forbade burial. For almost three weeks the coffin was left unattended in a corner of the convent chapel. Michelangelo was at last informed that she had been buried in the chapel wall, but when he went to the church he could find no sign of the immurement. The abbess looked about cautiously, then answered to his question:

" The marchesa was removed to Naples. She will lie next to her husband, in San Domenico Maggiore."

Michelangelo trudged wearily homeward, chewing on the bitter herb of irony: the marchese, who had fled his wife during his married life, would now have her by his side for all eternity. And he, Michelangelo, who had found in Vittoria the crowning love of his life, had never been permitted to fulfil it.

4

He did not lack for projects. In the eyes of the world he was truly the " Master." He was assigned yet another task by Pope Paul, who asked him to undertake the design and building of the defence works which would give him greater security within the Leonine City, and to engineer the erection of the obelisk of Caligula in the Piazza San Pietro. Duke Cosimo urged him to return to Florence to create sculptures for the city. The King of France deposited money in a Roman bank in his name against the day when he would carve or paint for him. The Sultan of Turkey offered to send an escort party to bring him to Constantinople to work there. Whereever an art commission was to be granted, in Portugal a Madonna della Misericordia for the king, in Milan a tomb for one of the distant Medici, in Florence for the ducal palace, Michelangelo was consulted about the theme, design, the proper artists for the job.

He spent the better part of the daily hours in the Pauline, painting the amazed and terror-stricken faces of women who were watching Peter on the cross, then the portrait of the elderly bearded soldier, grief-stricken over his part in the execution. Tiring of paintbrushes, he returned home to pick up hammer and chisel, glorying in the sheer freedom of being able to carve to satisfy his inner needs. Only marble carving gave him a sense of his own three-dimensional fullness. He had been unhappy about the Leah and Rachel, ashamed of presenting second-rate work to the world; he had been afraid that he had grown too old for the vigorous art of marble sculpture. But now his

chisel sang through the shining stone in a continuous "Go!",
creating the collapsed Christ and behind him Nicodemus
with his own white beard, deep-sunk eyes, flattened nose,
a cowl over his head, the mouth sensitive, poetic.

He allowed no one in the Pauline chapel while he painted,
but his studio was thronged with artists from all over Europe
whom he employed, encouraged, taught and found commissions for.

Then, after weeks and months of lavishly outpoured energy,
he would suddenly fall ill, with what he could not tell: a
pulling in his thighs, a piercing pain in the groin, a weakness in the chest that kept him from breathing, a kidney
ailment. At such times he would feel his brain shrink, he
would grow cranky, fractious with his closest friends and
relatives, accuse his nephew Lionardo of making a trip
to Rome during his illness to make sure he would inherit
all the properties, and his manager of selling copies of an
engraving to make money for himself. Realdo Colombo,
Italy's greatest anatomist, who was writing the first book
on the subject, spent his spare hours in the Macello dei
Corvi, flushing Michelangelo with spring water from Fiuggi.
He would recover, his brain seem to expand, and he would
cry to Tommaso:

"Why do I behave so cantankerously? Because my
seventies are fleeing so fast?"

"Granacci said you were already crusty at twelve, when
he first met you."

"So he did. Bless his memory."

Granacci, his oldest friend, had died; so had Balducci,
Leo Baglioni and Sebastiano del Piombo. With each passing
month he seemed closer to the vortex of the birth and death
cycle. A letter from Lionardo brought him the news that
his brother Giovansimone had died and been buried in
Santa Croce. He reproached his nephew for not sending the
details of Giovansimone's illness. He also broached the
subject of his nephew's marriage, suggesting that since
Lionardo was approaching thirty it was time he sought
a wife, and had sons to carry on the Buonarroti name:

I believe in Florence there are many noble but poor
families with whom it would be a charity to form a
union, and it would be well there should be no dowry for
there would then be no pride. You need a wife to
associate with, and whom you can rule, and who will
not care about pomps and run about every day to parties

758

and marriages. It is easy for a woman to go wrong who does these things.

Nor is it to be said by anyone that you wish to ennoble yourself by marriage, for it is well known we are as ancient and noble citizens of Florence as any other house.

Tommaso de' Cavalieri was married. Tommaso had waited until he was thirty-eight, then proposed to the young daughter of a noble Roman family. They were married in a sumptuous wedding, attended by the Pope and his court, the entire roster of Roman nobility, the Florentine colony, the artists of Rome. Within the year Signora Cavalieri presented her husband with his first son.

The birth was quickly followed by a death: that of Pope Paul, grieving over the incorrigibility of his grandson, Ottavio, and the murder of his son, Pier Luigi, whom he had foisted on the Duchy of Parma and Piacenza. In contrast to Clement's funeral, the people of the city showed genuine grief over the loss of Paul.

When the College of Cardinals met there was expectant joy in the hearts of the Florentine colony, for they believed it was the turn of Cardinal Niccolò Ridolfi, Contessina's son, to become Pope. He had no enemies in Italy except the small group sharing power with Duke Cosimo of Florence. However, Niccolò had a powerful enemy outside of Italy: Charles V, the Holy Roman Emperor. During the conclave in the Sistine Chapel, with the election all but settled in favour of Niccolò, he became suddenly and violently ill. By morning he was dead. Dr. Realdo Colombo performed an autopsy. At its completion he came to the house on the Macello dei Corvi. Michelangelo looked up with dazed eyes.

" Murder?"

" Beyond any doubt."

" You found proof?"

" If I myself had administered the poison I could not be more sure of the cause of Niccolò's death. Lottini, Duke Cosimo's agent, could have had the opportunity."

Michelangelo lowered his head, stricken.

" Once again it is the end of our hopes for Florence."

As always, when he was made desolate by the events of the outside world, he turned to marble. Now in the Descent, which he was carving in the hopes that his friends would place it on his own tomb after his death, he encountered

759

a strange problem: Christ's left leg was hampering the design. After careful consideration he cut the leg off in its entirety. Christ's hand, extending downward and clasped in the Madonna's, adroitly hid the fact that there was only one leg left.

The College of Cardinals elected sixty-two-year-old Giovan Maria de' Ciocchi del Monte, who become Pope Julius III. Michelangelo had known him at court for countless years; he had helped to rewrite the contract for Julius' tomb several times. Three times during the siege of 1527 Cardinal Ciocchi del Monte had been seized by the Emperor's army and taken to the gallows in front of Leo Baglioni's house in the Campo dei Fiori; three times he had been reprieved at the last moment. His main interest in life was pleasure.

" He should have taken the name Leo XI," Michelangelo confided to Tommaso. " He will probably paraphrase Leo's statement by saying, ' Since God saved me three times from the gallows just to make me Pope, let me enjoy it.' "

" He will be good for artists," Tommaso replied. " He likes their company best. He plans to enlarge his small villa near the Porta del Popolo into a sumptuous palace."

Very quickly Michelangelo was summoned to dinner at the Villa di Papa Giulio, already filling up with ancient statues, columns, paintings; and with artists in all media, most of whom already had commissions, including Michelangelo's friends Giorgio Vasari, the new architect for the villa, and Cecchino Rossi, who, with Vasari, had saved the David's arm; Guglielmo della Porta, successor to Sebastiano, Annibale Caracci. As yet the new Pope had not discussed the continuation of St. Peter's. Michelangelo waited anxiously.

Julius III had a long nose that drooped downward, about the only feature to emerge from a matted grey beard. He was a prodigious eater, stuffing large quantities of food into an opening in the beard which seemed to entrap it. Suddenly the Pope called for silence. The diners became still.

" Michelangelo," he cried in his rough, hearty voice, " I have not asked you to work for me out of respecct for your age."

" It is a mere twelve years' difference, Holiness," replied Michelangelo with mock humility. " Since we all know how hard you are going to strive to make your pontificate outstanding, I do not think I dare claim exemption on that score."

Julius enjoyed the sarcasm.

"You are so valuable to us, dear Master, that I would gladly give years off my life if they could be added to yours."

Michelangelo watched the Pope dispatch a plate of richly stuffed goose, thought. "We Tuscans are lean eaters, that is why we live so long."

Aloud, he said, "I appreciate your offer, but in all fairness to the Christian world I cannot let you make the sacrifice."

"Then, my son, if I survive you, as is probable in the natural course of life, I shall have your body embalmed, and keep it near me, so that it shall be as lasting as your work."

Michelangelo's appetite vanished. He wondered if there were some way to be excused. But Julius was not through with him.

"There are a few things I would like you to design for me: a new staircase and fountain for the Belvedere, a façade for a palace at San Rocco, monuments for my uncle and grandfather. . . ."

But no word of St. Peter's.

The Pope gathered his company in the vineyard for music and plays. Michelangelo slipped away. All he wanted from Julius was to be confirmed as architect of St. Peter's.

The Pope procrastinated. Michelangelo kept his designs and plans secret, providing the contrators only with those specifications for the next segment of the job. He had always had this need for privacy with work in progress. Now he had a valid reason for working in secrecy; but it got him into trouble.

A group of the ousted contractors, led by the persuasive Baccio Bigio, interested Cardinal Cervini, in charge of the bookkeeping for the fabric, in their claims. A written document was presented to the Pope. Michelangelo was summoned to the Villa di Papa Giulio.

"You are not afraid to face your critics?" asked Julius.

"No, Holiness, but I want the meeting to take place inside the fabric itself."

It was a large crowd that assembled in what was to become the new chapel of the Kings of France. Baccio Bigio opened the attack by exclaiming:

"Buonarroti has pulled down a more beautiful church than he is capable of building."

"Let us proceed to your criticism of the present structure," replied the Pope amiably.

761

An official cried, "Holy Father, immense sums are being spent without our being told why. Nor has anything been communicated to us of the manner in which the building is to be carried on."

"That is the responsibility of the architect," replied Michelangelo.

"But, Holiness, Buonarroti treats us as if the matter did not concern us at all. We are completely useless!"

The Pope repressed a half-formed quip. Cardinal Cervini threw his arms upward to indicate the arches that were being built.

"Holiness, as you can see, Buonarroti is building three chapels at each end of these transverse arches. It is our opinion that this arrangement, particularly in the southern apse, will permit too little light to reach the interior . . ."

The Pope's eyes peered over the edge of the matted beard.

"I'm inclined to agree with the criticism, Michelangelo."

Michelangelo turned to Cervini, replied quietly, "Monsignor, above those windows in the travertine vaulting there are to be three other windows."

"You never gave a hint of that."

"Nor was I bound to do so."

"We have a right to know what you are doing." Cardinal Cervini was now furious. "You are not infallible."

"I will never bind myself to give Your Lordship, or anyone else, information of my intentions. Your office is to furnish money and take care that it is not stolen. The building plan concerns me alone."

A bruised silence adumbrated through the vast construction, its walls, piers, arches reaching to the open sky. Michelangelo turned back to the Pope.

"Holy Father, you can see with your own eyes how much excellent building I am getting for the money. If all this work does not tend to the saving of my soul, since I have refused to accept any pay, I shall have expended considerable time and trouble in vain."

The Pope placed his hand on Michelangelo's shoulder.

"Neither your eternal nor your temporal welfare shall suffer. You are the supreme architect of St. Peter's." Turning to the ring of accusers, he said sternly, "And so shall he remain, as long as I am Pope!"

It was a victory for Michelangelo. In the process he had incurred a new enemy, Cardinal Marcello Cervini.

5

To placate Baccio Bigio, Pope Paul took away from Michelangelo the reconstruction job he had started on the Ponte Santa Maria. Bigio removed the ancient travertine supports to lighten the bridge, finished it with cement and pebbles. Michelangelo, riding over the bridge on horseback with Vasari, said:

"Giorgio, this bridge is shaking under us. Let us spur our horses or it may fall while we are on it."

Vasari spread the quip around Rome. Biglio was livid with rage.

"What does Buonarroti know about bridges?"

At the beginning of 1551 Julius III finally issued his *breve* making Michelangelo official architect of St. Peter's; but in a few months he had to shut down all work on the fabric. Julius was pouring such a vast fortune into the Villa di Papa Giulio and entertaining himself on such a lavish scale that he used up the income stipulated for St. Peter's.

It was now Michelangelo's turn to be livid. He demanded of Tommaso, as they hunched over their drawing boards:

"How can I go to Julius and cry, 'Holiness, your insatiable appetite for pleasure is bankrupting us. Restrain yourself so that we can complete St. Peter's'?"

"He would have you thrown into a dungeon of Sant'-Angelo."

"Then I will keep silent, painful as it may be."

He was still agitated when he began to carve on the Descent later in the day. He struck emery in Christ's forearm. The sparks flew under his chisel. Angrily he struck the forearm a series of harsh blows . . . only to have it shatter and fall to the floor. He put down his hammer and chisel and left the house.

He walked past the stalls of Trajan's market like black holes in a cliff as they climbed the hill, towards the Temple of Mars. Unhappy about smashing the arm, he decided to start all over again. This time on an Entombment. He entered a stoneyard just beyond Cæsar's forum, came across an ancient block that had been part of a cornice, a marble-coloured limestone from the Palestrina area. Despite the fact that the stone had deep hollows he had it sent to the studio, began searching his mind for a concept. In his new version there would be no Nicodemus; Christ would be a giant head and arms and torso with foreshortened legs falling away, crushed under their burden, only Mary's head and hands visible as she tried desperately to hold up the weight of her massively dead son.

Relaxed and refreshed, he returned to the Macello dei Corvi. Urbino was waiting for him with a worried expression.

"*Messere*, I do not like to bring you further problems, but I must now leave you."

Michelangelo was too astonished to answer.

"Leave me?"

"You remember the girl I chose, in Urbino, ten years ago? . . ."

Michelangelo shook his head in disbelief. Was it already ten years?

"She is eighteen to-day. It is time for us to marry."

"But why go? Bring your wife here, Urbino, we'll fix up an apartment for you, buy furniture. Your wife can have her own maid . . ."

Urbino's eyes were round as Giotto's O.

"Are you sure, *messere*? For I am forty now, and I should have children as quickly as possible."

"This is your home. I am your family. Your sons will be my grandsons."

He gave Urbino two thousand ducats in cash so that he could be independent, then an additional sum to fix up a room for his bride and to buy a new bed. In a few days Urbino returned with his wife, Cornelia Colonelli, a sympathetic girl who took over the management of the household and ran it well. She gave Michelangelo the affection she would have brought to her husband's father. Nine months later they named their first son Michelangelo.

He urged his nephew in Florence to "purchase a handsome house in town, to cost from fifteen hundred to two thousand ducats, in our quarter. As soon as you have found it, I shall forward the money." Once Lionardo had settled in a proper house, he was to find a wife, and go about the serious business of having sons.

Lionardo chose Cassandra Ridolfi, a distant member of the family into which Contessina had married. Michelangelo was so delighted that he sent Cassandra two rings, one diamond and the other ruby. Cassandra sent Michelangelo eight lovely shirts as a return gift. They named their first-born son Buonarroto, after Lionardo's father. The next son they named Michelangelo, but he died very quickly, and Michelangelo grieved.

To re-create the Campidoglio he took the ancient Roman stone salt tax office, which a few hundred years before had been turned into a bastionlike Senatorial building, and converted it into a regal official palace with lyrical flights of steps rising from either end to a centre entrance. He then planned two palaces, identical in design, for either side of the square which for centuries had been a market. He levelled the piazza, paved it with patterned stones, searched his mind for a flawless work of art for the middle of the square. He thought of the Laocoön, the Belvedere torso, the gigantic stone head of Augustus. None of these seemed right. Then he remembered the bronze equestrian statue of the Emperor Marcus Aurelius which had stood unharmed in front of St. John in Lateran all through the centuries because the Christians had believed it to be Constantine, the first Christian Emperor. He placed it on such a low platform that the gloriously lifelike statue would appear to be on eye level with the people coming in and out of the palaces on either side; Marcus Aurelius seemed to have just come down the Senatorial steps and mounted his horse to ride across Rome.

In March 1555, Tommaso, Vasari, Raffaelo da Montelupo, Ammanati and Daniele da Volterra gave him a party for his eightieth birthday. The walls of the studio were lined with drawing and projects for another eighty years ahead. . . .

Two weeks later Pope Julius III died, unable to spare any years off his life for his friend Michelangelo. To Michelangelo's consternation, Cardinal Marcello Cervini, erstwhile accountant for the fabric, was elected Pope. He took the title of Marcellus II.

And that, reasoned Michelangelo quite calmly, was the end for him. He had told Cardinal Cervini that the plan of St. Peter's was none of his business. As Pope, it would now be very much his business!

He spent no time in bemoaning his fate. Instead, he began winding up his affairs in Rome, making arrangements to transfer his bank account and marbles to Florence. He was leaving Urbino in the house, since his wife Cornelia was again pregnant. He burned his early drawings for St.

Peter's and the dome, was about to pack his saddlebags when, after a three-week reign, Pope Marcellus died.

Michelangelo went to Church, offered thanks to God for giving him the strength not to rejoice over Cervini's death. After another three weeks he decided that it might have been just as well for him to have returned to Florence: Cardinal Giovanni Pietro Caraffa became Pope Paul IV.

No one knew quite how he had been elected. He was a thoroughly disagreeable man, violent of nature, intolerant of all about him. Pope Paul IV, knowing how completely he was hated, said:

" I do not know why they elected me Pope, so I am bound to conclude that it is not the cardinals but God who makes the Popes."

Announcing that it was his ambition to wipe out all heresy in Italy, he unleashed on the Roman people the horrors of the Spanish Inquisition. In a fortresslike structure near the Vatican his Board of Inquisition tortured and condemned accused people without trial, locked them in dungeons in the cellars, burned others in the Campo dei Fiori . . . at the same time the Pope was making a corrupt nephew a cardinal and establishing duchies for others of his relatives. Michelangelo considered he would be fit fuel for the fires burning outside Leo Baglioni's house; but he made no attempt to flee. The Pope did not molest him . . . until the day of reckoning.

Pope Paul IV received him in a small, monastic room with white-washed walls and a minimum of uncomfortable furniture. His expression was as severe as his robe.

" Buonarroti, I respect your work. But it is the implicit will of the Council of Trent that heretical frescoes such as your altar wall be destroyed."

" . . . the Last Judgment?"

He stood before the Pope's wooden chair feeling as though he were a corpse in the dead room of Santo Spirito and a dissector had just chiselled off his skull, lifted out his brain, and let it slip to the floor. He half slid to the corner of a bench, sat staring blindly at the whitewashed wall before him.

" Many in our hierarchy feel that you have blasphemed; they are confirmed by an article written by Aretino of Venice . . ."

" A blackmailer! "

" . . . a friend of Titian, of Charles V, Benvenuto Cellini,

the late Francis I of France, Jacopo Sansovino. . . . Here is
one of the copies passing from hand to hand in Rome.
I'm convinced the Council of Trent has also studied it."

Michelangelo took the paper from the Pope, began to
read:

Is it possible that you can have represented in the sacred
temple of God, above the altar of His Son, in the greatest
Chapel in the world, where Cardinals and Bishops and
the Vicar of Christ, with Catholic ceremonial and sacred
ritual, confess, contemplate and adore the body and
blood of Jesus . . so lofty a subject, with angels and
saints without a remnant of modesty and denuded of
all celestial ornament!

He jerked his head up abruptly.

"Holiness, this attack was written when I refused to
send Aretino some of my drawings and cartoons. It was
his way of striking at me . . ."

"Decent people are shocked by the nakedness of saints
and martyrs, of hundreds of men and women fully exposed . . ."

"They are the narrow-minded, Holy Father, ignorant of
the true nature of art."

"Would you call your Holy Father narrow-minded, Michelangelo? And ignorant? For I am one of them."

"The fresco is not evil. Never has there been a wall
more permeated with a love of God."

"Very well, I will not demand that the wall be torn down.
We will simply give it a coat of whitewash. Then you can
paint something over it, a theme that will make everyone
happy. Something simple and devout, that you can do
quickly."

He was too crushed to fight back. Not so, Rome. His
friends, adherents, his old associates at court, including a
number of Cardinals led by Ercole Gonzaga, began a campaign to save the wall. Tommaso brought him daily reports
of new friends gained: an ambassador from France, a bishop
from Venice, a noble Roman family.

Then an anonymous intermediary came up with what
Rome believed to be a brilliant compromise. Daniele da
Volterra, trained in painting under Sodoma and in architecture under Peruzzi, now one of Michelangelo's most
enthusiastic followers, came to the studio with high colour
in his cheeks.

"Master, the Last Judgment is saved."

" I can't believe it. The Pope has agreed?"

" . . . not to destroy it. There will be no coat of white-wash."

Michelangelo collapsed on to his leather chair, breathing hard.

" I must go out and thank personally every last person who helped me. . . ."

" Master," interrupted Daniele, with eyes averted, " we have had to pay a price."

" What price?"

" . . . well, to mollify the Pope . . . he agreed not to destroy the wall providing breeches were put on everybody's nakedness."

" Breeches? You mean . . . *calzoni*?"

" And petticoats on the females. We must cover every erogenous zone. Only a few women may remain bare above the waist. All must be clothed from the hips to the knees, particularly those whose bottoms are facing the chapel. His favourite saints must be robed, as well as St. Catherine, the Virgin's skirt made heavier . . ."

" If in my earlier years I had given myself to make sulphur matches," swore Michelangelo, " I should now suffer less."

Daniele shivered, as though struck.

" Master, let us try to be sensible about this. The Pope was going to call in a court painter . . . but I persuaded him to let me do the job. I will injure the wall as little as possible. If we let some stranger . . ."

" ' Adam and Eve sewed fig leaves together, and made themselves girdles.' "

" Don't be angry with me. I am not at the Council of Trent."

" You are right, Daniele. We must offer up these private parts to the Inquisition. I have spent a lifetime portraying the beauty of man. Now he has become shameful again, to be burned in a new bonfire of vanities. Do you know what that means, Daniele? We are returning to the darkest, most ignorant centuries of the past."

" Look here, Michelangelo," said Daniele placatingly, " I can blend in gauze, bits of cloth to match your flesh tones. I will use so thin a paint that the next Pope can have all the breeches and robes removed without harming anything beneath . . ."

Michelangelo shook his head.

" Go then, and wrap their winding sheets about them."

"Trust me. I shall outwit the Pope at every point. This task is so delicate that it will be months, years before I even dare begin." Daniele was a hard worker, without originality, and so painstakingly slow that he had earned the reputation of never completing a commission during the patron's lifetime. "Perhaps by that time Caraffa will be dead, the Inquisition over. . . ."

The best way to shut out terror was to pick up hammer and chisel and start carving. He had recently bought an irregular column, protruding at top and bottom. Instead of straightening the block, he decided to make use of this odd shape to achieve a crescent profile. He started massing inside the centre, wondering if the block could tell him what he wanted to create. The marble remained aloof, unyielding, silent. It was asking too much of raw material, even though it was shining stone, to create a work of art all by itself; but the challenge of the characterful column excited new energy in him.

It was just as necessary to survive at eighty as at thirty-five; but a little more difficult.

6

Sigismondo died in Settignano, the last of his brothers. He had outlived his generation. Equally sad was the illness of Urbino, who had been with him for twenty-six years. The nobility of Urbino's spirit shone forth when he whispered to Michelangelo:

"Even more than dying, it grieves me to leave you alone in this treacherous world."

Urbino's wife, Cornelia, gave birth to her second son at the moment her husband was being buried. Michelangelo kept them with him until Urbino's will was settled. He was named guardian and tutor of the two boys; when their mother left with them for her parents' home in Urbino, the house seemed desolate.

He pushed ahead the work of the rising tribune of St. Peter's; he carved his new Pietà; he bought another farm for Lionardo, sent Cornelia Urbino seven spans of a light-weight black cloth she had asked for; began searching for worthy poor whom he could help for the salvation of his soul. Then he had to let the work on St. Peter's grind to a halt once again because of the threatened invasion of the Spanish army.

The eighties, he decided, were not the most pleasant decade in the span of man. When he left Florence at sixty he had feared that his life might be over; but love had made him young again, and the sixties had flown by. During his seventies he had been so deeply immersed in the Pauline chapel frescoes, the carving of the Descent, his new architectural career, and St. Peter's, that no day had been long enough to accomplish his tasks.

But now, as he became eighty-one, and moved towards eighty-two, the hours were like hornets, each stinging as it passed. He could no longer see as well as he used to; his step was not as firm; stamina was giving way to a series of minor disturbances, sapping his strength, interfering with his drive to finish St. Peter's, to create a glorious dome for it.

Then he went down with a severe attack of kidney stones. Dr. Colombo pulled him through with the aid of Tommaso's untiring care; but he was confined to his bed for several months and was obliged to turn over the designs for one of the chapels to a new superintendent. When he recovered, and laboriously climbed the scaffolding, he found that the new superintendent had misread his plans, making serious errors in construction. He was overcome with shame and remorse; this was his first failure in the ten years of building. And at last he had handed Baccio Bigio a fulcrum on which to rest a new attack: an error of grave proportions which he could neither excuse nor explain away.

He called on the Pope at once; but quick as he was, Bigio had been there before him.

"It is true?" Pope Paul asked as he saw Michelangelo's face. "The chapel will have to be pulled down?"

"Most of it, Holiness."

"I am saddened. How could such a thing happen?"

"I have been ill, Holy Father."

"I see. Bigio claims you are too old to carry such a heavy responsibility. He feels that for your own sake you should be relieved of the crushing burden."

"His solicitude touches me. He and his associates have been trying to get this 'crushing burden' off my shoulders and into their own hands for a lot of years now. But didn't Bigio's Ponte Santa Maria just collapse in the flood? Can you believe that Baccio Bigio is better on his good days than I am on my bad?"

"No one is questioning your ability."

Michelangelo was silent for a moment, thinking backward.

"Holiness, for thirty years I watched good architects pour foundations. They never got St. Peter's off the ground. In the ten years I have been the architect, the church has risen upward like an eagle. If you dismiss me now, it will be the ruin of the edifice."

The Pope's lips twitched.

Michelangelo, as long as you have the strength to fight back, you shall remain the architect of St. Peter's."

That night there was a meeting in the house on the Macello dei Corvi. Because he had nearly died, Tommaso, a group of his oldest friends, and the Cardinal of Carpi, who had become his protector at court, insisted that he build a complete model of the dome. Up to now he had made only fragmentary sketches.

"If we had lost you last week," said Tommaso flatly, "how would anyone have known what kind of dome you envisaged?"

"I have heard you say," added the cardinal, "that you wanted to progress the fabric so far that no one could change its design after your death."

"That is my hope."

"Then give us the dome!" cried Lottino, an artist disciple. "There is no other way."

"You are right," replied Michelangelo with a sigh. "But I have not yet conceived the final dome. I shall have to find it. Then we shall build a wooden model."

Everyone left except Tommaso. Michelangelo walked to his drawing table, pulled up a wooden chair. He mused aloud, as his pen roamed over a fresh sheet of paper. The Pantheon and the Duomo in Florence had two domes, one inside the other, interlaced structurally to give each other support. The interior of his dome would be sculpture, the exterior architecture. . . .

A dome was not a mere covering; any roof would serve that utilitarian purpose. A dome was a major work of art, the perfect blending of sculpture and architecture in displacing space and adding to the firmamment. It was a vault of man, created in the image of the vault of heaven. The perfect dome went from horizon to horizon in man's mind, covering it with grace. It was the most natural of all architectural forms, and the most celestial, for it aspired to re-create the sublime form under which humanity spent the days of its years.

A dome of a church was not in competition with the dome of the sky; it was the same form in miniature, as a son to his father. Some people said the earth was round; for a man like himself whose travels had been confined between Venice and Rome, that was hard to prove. In Master Urbino's school of grammar he had been taught that the earth was flat, ending where the dome of heaven came down to its circular boundaries. Yet he had always observed a peculiar facet of that supposedly anchored-down horizon: as he walked or rode to reach it, it receded at an equal pace. . . .

Just so, his dome. It could not be finite. No man standing beneath it must ever feel that he could reach its boundaries. The sky was a perfect creation; whoever stood on the earth, wherever he might be, was centred at its heart, with the dome of heaven spread equidistant about him. Lorenzo, *Il Magnifico,* the Plato Four, the humanists had taught him that man was the centre of the universe; and this was never more demonstrable than when he stood looking upward and found himself, a lone individual, serving as the central pole holding up the tarpaulin of sun and clouds, moon and stars, knowing that, lone or abandoned as he might feel, without his support the heavens would fall. Take away the dome as a shape, an idea, the symmetrical roof which sheltered man, and what was left of the world? only a flat plate, the kind on which his stepmother, *Il Migliore,* had sliced her breads, hot out of the oven.

No wonder man had placed heaven in the sky! It was not because he had ever seen a soul ascend thereto, or caught a glimpse of the vistas of paradise above; but because heaven simply had to be housed in the most divine form known to man's mind or senses. He wanted his dome too to be mystical, not a protection from heat or rain, thunder or lightning, but of a staggering beauty that would reassure man of His presence . . . a sentient form which man could not only see and feel but enter. Under his dome a man's soul must soar upward to God even as it would in the moment of its final release from his body. How much closer could man come to God, while still on earth? With his vast cupola he meant to paint His portrait just as surely as when he had painted Him on the Sistine ceiling.

The saving of his own soul became part of the creation of the dome for St. Peter's. For his last great work he had assumed the most difficult task of the sixty-eight years since Granacci had taken him past the Street of the Painters, to the studio on the Via dei Tavolini, and said, "Signor Ghirlandaio, this is Michelangelo, about whom I told you."

His mind and fingers were moving with force and clarity. After drawing for hours he turned for refreshment to his crescent-shaped block. He changed his original concept of a Christ with head and knees turned in opposite directions for a version in which the head and knees concurred, but were contraposed to the Virgin's head above Christ's shoulder, affording a more dramatic contrast. He hollowed out a large figure from the crescent of the block before faltering. Then he returned to his dome.

7

He was after absolute balance, perfection of line, curve, volume, mass, openness, density, elegance, the profundity of endless space. He aspired to create a work of art that would transcend the age through which he had lived.

He laid aside his charcoal and drawing pens, started modelling, thinking that the manœuvrability of the damp clay might bring him more freedom than the rigidity of the drawn line. Over the weeks and months he made a dozen models, destroying them, moving on to new designs. He felt he was coming closer to revelation, for he first achieved monumentality, then dimension, then majesty, then simplification ; yet the results still derived from artistry rather than spirituality.

At last it came, after eleven years of thinking, drawing, praying, hoping and despairing, experimenting and rejecting : a creature of his imagination, compounded of all his arts, staggering in size, yet as fragile as a bird's egg in a nest ; soaring, lilting heavenward, constructed of gossamer which carried effortlessly and musically upward its three-hundred-and-five-foot height, pear-shaped, as was the breast of the Medici Madonna. . . . It was a dome unlike any other.

"It has arrived," murmured Tommaso ecstatically, when he saw the completed drawings. "Where did it come from?"

"Where do ideas come from, Tomao? Sebastiano asked

that same question when he was young. I can only give you the answer I gave him, for I am no wiser at eighty-two than I was at thirty-nine: ideas are a natural function of the mind, as breathing is of the lungs. Perhaps they come from God."

He hired a carpenter, Giovanni Francesco, to build the model. He made it of linden wood, one fifteen-thousandth of the projected size. The giant dome would rest on the piers and on the arches that the piers supported, and on a circular drum, or wide cement base. The drum would be built of brick with a sheathing of travertine; the external ribs of the dome would be of Tivoli travertine, the buttresses held to the drum by a framework of wrought iron, while the columns and horizontal entablatures would also be of travertine. Eight ramps along the lower drum would afford a means of carrying materials on the backs of donkeys up to the dome walls. The engineering plans took months to draw, but Michelangelo had the skill, Tommaso had become an expert.

All work was done at the Macello dei Corvi studio, in the strictest privacy. The interior dome Michelangelo moulded himself; the exterior one he let Francesco indicate with paint. The festooned carvings and decorations were made of clay mixed with sawdust and glue. He called in a reliable Carrara woodcarver by the name of Battista to cut out the statuettes and capitals, the bearded faces of the Apostles.

Pope Paul IV died suddenly. Rome burst into the most violent insurrection Michelangelo had yet seen at the death of any pontiff. The crowd knocked down a newly erected statue of the former Cardinal Caraffa, dragged its head through the streets for hours while the citizenry heaped imprecations upon it, then threw the head into the Tiber before storming the headquarters of the Inquisition to release all prisoners and destroy the mass of papers and documents assembled to convict the accused of heresy.

Wearied of strife and bloodshed, the College of Cardinals elected sixty-year-old Giovanni Angelo Medici, from an obscure Lombardy branch of the Medici family. Pope Pius IV had been trained as a lawyer, was judicious of temperament. As a professional advocate he was a brilliant negotiator and soon came to be trusted in Europe as a man of integrity. The Inquisition, foreign to the Italian character, was ended. Through a series of legalistic conferences and

774

contracts the Pope brought peace to Italy and the surrounding nations; and to the Lutherans as well. Guided by diplomacy, the Church achieved peace for itself at the same time that it reunited Catholicism in Europe.

Pope Pius IV reconfirmed Michelangelo's position as architect of St. Peter's, providing him with funds with which to push the arches upward to the drum. He also commissioned him to design a gate for the city walls, to be called Porta Pia.

It was clearly a race against time. He was approaching his mid-eighties. With a maximum of money and workmen he could reach the drum in perhaps two or three years. It was not possible for him to estimate just how long it would take to complete the dome, with its windows, columns and decorative frieze; but he thought he could do it in ten to twelve years. That would bring him to a round century mark. Nobody lived that long; but despite his attacks of the stone, pains in the head, a colic which brought disorders of the stomach, occasional aches in the back and loins, intermittent bouts of dizziness and weakness when he had to lie abed for a few days, he did not feel any true diminishing of his power. He still took walks in the *campagna*.

As he gazed into the mirror he saw that there was good colour in his face. He had a vigorous shock of black hair on his head, albeit generously streaked with white, as was his forked beard. His eyes were clear and penetrating.

He would get that dome built. Had not his father, Lodovico, achieved ninety? Was he not a better man than his father, by at least ten years?

He had to go through yet one more ordeal by fire. Baccio Bigio, who had worked himself up to a high administrative position in the superintendent's office, had a documented set of figures to prove how many ducats Michelangelo's illness had cost the fabric because of the faulty chapel. He used his information to its fullest advantage, even convincing Michelangelo's friend, the Cardinal of Carpi, that St. Peter's was going badly. Bigio was putting himself into position to succeed to the job on the day Michelangelo took to his bed.

When Michelangelo no longer had the strength to climb the scaffolding each day, one of his able young helpers, Pier Luigi Gaeta, was appointed as assistant to the Clerk of the Works. Gaeta brought Michelangelo detailed reports each night. When the Clerk of the Works was murdered,

Michelangelo proposed that Gaeta be promoted. Instead Baccio Bigio got the appointment. Gaeta was dismissed entirely. Bigio began to remove structural beams, take down scaffolding, and prepare the fabric for a new design.

Michelangelo, crawling painfully up the scaffolding of time, past eighty-seven towards eighty-eight, was too stricken by the news to get out of his bed, which he had had moved into his studio.

" But you must," cried Tommaso, trying to wake him from his lethargy, " or Bigio will undo the work you have done."

" He who contends with the worthless achieves no great victory."

" Forgive me, but this is not a time for Tuscan adages. It is a time for action. If you cannot go to St. Peter's to-day, you must send a deputy in your place."

" Would you go, Tommaso?"

" People know that I am as a son to you."

" Then I will send Daniele da Volterra. He has so long outwitted the court with the breeches for the Last Judgment, he should be able to handle the conspirators in the superintendent's office."

Daniele da Volterra was turned away. Baccio Bigio was given full building powers at the fabric. When Michelangelo encountered the Pope crossing the Campidoglio at the head of his train, he shouted crustily:

" Holiness, I insist that you make a change! If you do not, I shall return to Florence for ever. You are letting St. Peter's be torn down."

In his astringent courtroom manner Pope Pius IV replied:

" *Piano, piano,* Michelangelo, let us go into the Senatorial palace where we can talk."

The Pope listened carefully.

" I shall summon the members of the fabric who have been opposing you. Then I shall ask my relative, Gabrio Serbelloni, to go to St. Peter's and investigate their charges. Come to the Vatican palace to-morrow."

He arrived too early to be received by the Pope, wandered into the Stanza della Segnatura which Raphael had painted during the years when he himself was up in the Sistine vault. He gazed at the four frescoes, first the School of Athens, then Parnassus, then the Dispute and Justice. He had never before allowed himself to look at Raphael's work without prejudice. He knew that he could never have conceived or painted these idealized still lifes; yet seeing how exquisitely they were done, with what integrity of craftsmanship, he realized that for lyricism and romantic charm Raphael had been the master of them all. He left the Stanza in a philosophic frame of mind.

When he was ushered into the small throne room he found the Pope surrounded by the fabric committee which had dismissed Gaeta and refused to accept Daniele da Volterra. In a few minutes Gabrio Serbelloni entered.

"Holiness, I find not an iota of truth in this report written by Baccio Bigio. It is fabricated . . . but unlike the great fabric of Buonarroti, it is pasted together maliciously, with no discernible purpose except self-interest."

In the voice of a judge handing down a decision Pope Pius decreed:

"Baccio Bigio is herewith dismissed from St. Peter's. In the future the plans of Michelangelo Buonarroti may not be altered in the smallest detail."

8

While the cathedral structure rose through its giant columns, arches and façades, Michelangelo spent his days in his studio completing the designs for the Porta Pia and, at the Pope's request, converting part of the ruins of the stupendous Baths of Diocletian into the lovely church of Santa Maria degli Angeli.

Several years had passed since he had carved on his crescent-shaped marble. One afternoon while resting on his side in bed, the idea dawned on him that what he needed to mature the block was not merely a new form for the figures but a new form for sculpture itself.

He rose, picked up his heaviest hammer and chisel and removed the head of Christ, carving a new face and head from what had been the Virgin's shoulder. He then dissected Christ's right arm from the body, just above the elbow, though the detached arm and hand remained as part of the supporting marble that went down to the base. What had previously been the left shoulder and part of the chest of Christ he converted into the left arm and hand of the Virgin. Christ's magnificent long legs were now out of proportion, constituting three-fifths of the entire body. The new attenuation created an emotional effect of limpidity, youth and grace. Now he began to be satisfied. Through the distortion of the elongated figure he felt that he had achieved a truth about man: the heart might tire but humanity, carried on its ever young legs, would continue to move across the face of the earth.

"If only I had another ten years, or even five," he cried to the statues standing about him, "I could create a whole new sculpture."

Suddenly darkness flooded over him. After a lapse of time he regained consciousness; but he was confused. He picked up his chisel, gazed at the limpid Christ. All continuity of thought was gone. He could not remember just what he had been doing with the marble. He knew that something had happened, but he could not collect his thoughts. Had he dropped off to sleep? Was he not quite awake? Then why did he feel a numbness and weakness in the left arm and leg? Why did the muscles on one side of his face feel as though they were sagging?

He called his servant. When he asked her to summon Tommaso, he noticed that his speech was slurred. The elderly woman gazed at him, wide-eyed.

"*Messere*, are you all right?"

She helped him into bed, then put on a shawl to go through the streets. Tommaso returned with the Cavalieri doctor. Michelangelo could see by their expressions that something serious had occurred though they pretended that he had just overtired himself. Dr. Donati gave him a warm drink, stirring in a foul-tasting medicine.

"Rest cures everything," said the doctor.

"Except old age."

"I've been hearing about your old age too long now to take it seriously," replied Tommaso, putting an extra pillow under his head. "I'll stay here until you sleep."

He awakened to find deep night outside his window. He lifted himself gingerly. The headache was gone, and he could see all too clearly the work that was still required on the crescent Pietà. He rose, put a goat candle in his cap, returned to his carving. The confusion was gone from his mind. It was good to have the feel of marble at his fingertips. He blinked his eyes to stave off the flying chips as he made a slashing "Go!" up the right side and around the shoulder, his calligraphic strokes pulsating on the marble torso and melting into space.

At dawn Tommaso opened the street door cautiously, burst into laughter.

"Why, you rogue! You pretender! I left you at midnight, deep enough asleep to stay for a week. I come back a few hours later, and find a snowstorm."

"Delicious smell, isn't it, Tomao? When the white dust cakes inside my nostrils, that's when I breathe the best."

"Dr. Donati says you need rest."

"In the next world, caro. Paradise is already replete with sculpture. There'll be nothing for me to do but rest."

He worked all day, had supper with Tommaso, then drew himself on the bed for a few hours of sleep before rising to fix another candle in his cap and begin polishing, starting with pumice and sulphur, then going to straw, giving the elongated legs of Christ a finish like satin.

He forgot all about the attack.

Two days later, as he stood before his marble, deciding that it was now safe to cut away the superfluous arm and hand to further release the elongated figure in space, he was struck again. He dropped his hammer and chisel, stumbled to the bed, fell on his knees, with his face sideways on the blanket.

When he awaked the room was full of people: Tommaso, Dr. Donati and Dr. Fidelissimi, Gaeta, Daniele da Volterra, a number of Florentine friends. Facing him was the disembodied forearm of the statue which throbbed with a life all its own. On the inside of the elbow was a vein, bulging with blood and life; though suspended in space, it existed. He had not been able to destroy it, any more than the centuries of being buried and trod upon had destroyed the Laocoön. Gazing at his own vein on the inside of his elbow, he saw how flat and withered it appeared. He thought:

"Man passes. Only works of art are immortal."

He insisted on sitting in a chair before the fire. Once when he was left alone he slipped a robe over his shoulders and started walking in the rain in the direction of St. Peter's. One of his newer apprentices, Calcagni, met him in the street, asked:

"Master, do you think it right to be about in such weather?"

He allowed Calcagni to take him home, but at four the next afternoon he dressed and tried to mount his horse for a ride. His legs were too weak.

Rome came to bid him farewell. Those who could not be admitted left flowers and gifts on the doorstep. Dr. Donati tried to keep him in bed.

"Don't hurry me," he said to the doctor. "My father lived to his ninetieth birthday, so I still have two weeks to enjoy this salubrious life."

"As long as you're feeling so intrepid," commented Tommaso, "what about a carriage ride in the morning? The last work on the drum is complete. To celebrate your ninetieth birthday, they're going to start the first ring of the dome."

"*Grazie a Dio*. No one will ever be able to change it now. But all the same, it's sad to have to die. I would like to start all over again, to create forms and figures I have never dreamed of." His amber-speckled eyes were unwavering. "I like best to work in white marble."

"You've had your *divertimento*."

That night, as he lay sleepless in bed, he thought, "Life has been good. God did not create me to abandon me. I have loved marble, yes, and paint too. I had loved architecture, and poetry too. I have loved my family and my friends. I have loved God, the forms of the earth and the heavens, and people too. I have loved life to the full, and now I love death as its natural termination. *Il Magnifico* would be happy: for me, the forces of destruction never overcame creativity."

He was swept by a massive wave of darkness. Before he lost consciousness he said to himself, "I must see Tommaso. There are things to be done."

When he next opened his eyes Tommaso was sitting on the edge of the bed. He put an arm under Michelangelo and raised him up, holding his chest.

"Tomao . . ."

"I am here, *caro*."

"I want to be buried in Santa Croce with my family . . ."

"The Pope wants you buried in your own church, St. Peter's."

"It is not . . . home. Promise you will take me back to Florence . . .?"

"The Pope will forbid it, but the Florentine merchants can smuggle you out of the Porta del Popolo in a caravan of goods. . . ."

"My will, Tomao." His strength was ebbing. "I commit my soul into the hands of God . . . my body to the earth, and my substance to my family . . . the Buonarroti . . ."

"It will all be done. I shall finish the Campidoglio, exactly as you planned. With St. Peter's at one end, and the Capitol at the other, Rome will forevermore be Michelangelo's as much as Cæsar's or Constantine's."

"Thank you, Tommaso. . . . I am tired . . ."

Tommaso kissed Michelangelo on the brow, withdrew weeping.

Dusk was falling. Alone in the room, Michelangelo began to review the images of all the beautiful works he had created. He saw them, one by one, as clearly as the day he had made them, the sculptures, paintings and architecture succeeding each other as swiftly as had the years of his life:

The Madonna of the Stairs and the Battle of the Centaurs he had carved for Bertoldo and *Il Magnifico*, with the Plato group laughing at him because he had made them "pure Greek"; Sts. Proculus and Petronius that he had made for Aldovrandi in Bologna; the wooden Crucifix for Prior Bichiellini; the Sleeping Cupid with which he had tried to fool the dealer in Rome; the Bacchius he had carved in Jacopo Galli's orchard; the Pietà that Cardinal Groslaye di Dionigi had commissioned for St. Peter's; the Giant David for Gonfaloniere Soderini and Florence; the Holy Family teased out of him by Agnolo Doni; the cartoon for the Battle of Cascina, called the Bathers, to compete with Leonardo da Vinci's; the Madonna and Child for the merchants of Bruges, carved in his own first studio; the ill-fated bronze portrait of Pope Julius II; Genesis, painted for Julius II on the vault of the Sistine; the Last Judgment for Pope Paul III to complete the chapel; the Moses for Julius' tomb; his four unfinished Giants in Florence; the Dawn and Dusk, Night and Day for the Medici chapel; the Conversion of Paul and the Crucifixion of Peter for the Pauline chapel; the Campidoglio, Porta Pia, the three Pietàs sculptured for his own pleasure . . . and as the picture came to a stop and stood still in his mind's eye, St. Peter's.

St. Peter's. . . . He entered the church through its front portal, walked in the strong Roman sunshine down the wide nave, stood below the centre of the dome, just over the tomb of St. Peter's. He felt his soul leave his body, rise upward into the dome, becoming part of it: part of space, of time, of heaven, and of God.

BIBLIOGRAPHY

The amount of material published about Michelangelo Buonarroti is probably the most extensive on any single artist. The authoritative bibliography, printed in 1927, lists over 2100 published works (of which five per cent were written in English, and another three per cent translated into English), including monographs, theses and articles as well as books. There have been several hundred new publications added between 1926 and 1961. The dates given after the titles are those of the editions we found available, and actually used in our studies and translations.

Only those titles are listed from which specific materials were used for this book. I was able to work in the French references myself; translations from the Latin, Italian and German were made by my assistants in Italy. All of this research material, comprising some five thousand typewritten pages, as well as the many drafts of the manuscript, has been deposited in the library of the University of California at Los Angeles.

BIBLIOGRAPHIESH *La Bibliografia di Michelangelo Buonarroti e gli Incisori delle sue Opere* (1875); Ernst Steinmann and Rudolf Wittkower, *Michelangelo-Bibliographie* (1927).

CHRONOLOGIES: Aldo Fortuna, "Cronologia Michelangiolesca," *Il Vasari*, II, Nuova Serie, Fasc. I (1958).

GENEALOGIES OF THE BUONARROTI: Senator Filippo Buonarroti, *Descrizione dell'Albero Genealogico della Nobilissima Famiglia de' Buonarroti*, pub. in Condivi, Gori edit. (1746) and in Vasari-Milanesi (vol. vii, 1881); Karl Frey, *Denunzia dei Beni della Famiglia de' Buonarroti* (1885; Karl Frey, *Michelagniolo Buonarroti—Quellen und Forschungen zu seiner Geschichte und Kunst* (1907).

BIOGRAPHIES OF MICHELANGELO: Ascanio Condivi, *Life of Michelangelo Buonarroti* (1553) translated into English by Herbert P. Horne (1904); Giorgio Vasari, "Michelangelo," *Lives of the Most Eminent Painters, Sculptors*
782

and Architects (1550, 1568); John Harford, *Life of Michelangelo Buonarroti* (1858); Herman Grimm, *Life of Michelangelo* (1869); *Aurelio Gotti, Vita di Michelangelo Buonarroti* (1875); Charles Heath Wilson, *Life and Works of Michelangelo Buonarroti* (1876); John A. Symonds, *The Life of Michelangelo Buonarroti* (1893); Henry Thode, *Michelangelo* (6 vols.) (1902-13); Charles Holroyd, *Michael Angelo Buonarroti* (1903); Gerald S. Davies, *Michelangelo* (1909); Robert Carden, *Michelangelo (A Record of His Life as Told in His Own Letters and Papers)* (1913); Wilhelm Valentiner, *The Late Years of Michel Angelo* (1914); Hans Mackowsky, *Michelangelo* (1919); Romain Rolland, *Michelangelo* (1927); Donald L. Finlayson, *Michelangelo, the Man* (1935); Jean Davray, " Michel-Ange," *Essai*, Paris (1937); Marcel Brion, *Michelangelo* (1940); Friedrich Kriegbaum, *Michelangelo Buonarroti* (1940); Leo Lerman, *Michelangelo* (1942); Michele Saponaro, *Michelangelo* (1950); Charles de Tolnay, *Michelangiolo* (Italian edition in one vol., 1951); Giovanni Papini, *Michelangelo, His Life and His Era* (1952); Agnes Allen, *The Story of Michelangelo* (1953); Adrian Stokes, *Michelangelo* (1956); Charles H. Morgan, *The Life of Michelangelo* (1960).

BIOGRAPHIES OF OTHER PEOPLE: Giorgio Vasari, *Lives of the Most Eminent Painters, Sculptors and Architects* (10 vols.) (1550, 1568); *Notizie Inedite della Vita d'Andrea del Sarto* (1831); BACCIO BANDINELLI: A. Colasanti, " Il Memoriale di Baccio Bandinelli," *Repertorium für Kunstwissenschaft*; BACCIO DA MONTELUPO: B. Filippini, *Dedalo* (1927); LUCREZIA BORGIA: Maria Bellonci, *The Life and Times of Lucrezia Borgia* (1953); BRAMANTE: Luca Beltrami, " Alcune Osservazioni sopra Recenti Studi Intorno a Bramante e Michelangelo Buonarroti," *Rassegna d'Arte* (1901); TOMMASO DE' CAVALIERI: Ernst Steinmann, *Sixtinische Kapelle* (1905); VITTORIA COLONNA: Christopher Hare (Mrs. Marian Andrews), *Most Illustrious Ladies of the Italian Renaissance* (1940); IL CRONACA: C. de Fabriczy, " Simone del Pollaiuolo detto il Cronaca," *Jahrbuch der Königlich Preuszischen Kunstsammlungen* (1906); DANTE: Paget Toynbee, *Dante Alighieri* (1900); GHIRLANDAIO: Henri Hauvette, *Ghirlandaio* (1907); LEONARDO DA VINCI: Adolf Rosenberg, *Leonardo da Vinci* (1903); Sigmund Freud, *Leonardo da Vinci* (1921); Rachel Taylor, *Leonardo the Florentine* (1928); Antonina Vallentin, *Leonardo da Vinci* (1938); THE MEDICI: Enrico Barfucci, *Lorenzo de' Medici e la Società Aristica del suo Tempo* (1945); Von Bode, " Bertoldo und Lorenzo de' Medici," *Die Werke seiner Lieblingskünstler* (1925); I. del Lungo, " Gli Amori del Magnifico Lorenzo," *Nuova Antologia* (1913); William Roscoe, *Life of Lorenzo de' Medici* (1796); Niccolò Valori, *Laurentii Medicis Vita* (1749); G. F. Young, *The Medici* (2 vols.) (1909); Herbert Vaughan, *The Medici Popes* (1908); Yvonne McGuire, *The Women of the Medici* (1927); THE MEDICI COURT: E. Müntz, *Les Collections d'antiques formées par les Médicis au XVI siècle* (1895); Philippe Monnier, *Le Quattrocento, Essai sur l'histoire littéraire du XV siècle italien* (1901); I. del Lungo, *The Women of Florence* (1908); PICO DELLA MIRANDOLA: Count of Mirandola, his nephew, *Giovanni Pico della Mirandola* (1496, tr. 1510); POLIZIANO: Alan Moorehead, *The Villa Diana* (1951); RAPHAEL: R. Duppa and Q. de Quincy, *The Lives and Works of Michel Angelo and Raphael* (1861); F. A. Gruyer, *Raphael peintre de portraits* (1881); J. D. Passavant, *Rafael von Urbino und sein Vater Giovanni Santi* (1839-58, French edition 1860); Vasari, " Raphael," *Lives of the Most Eminent Painters, etc.* (1550, 1568); Oskar Fischel, *Raphael* (2 vols.) (1948); SANGALLO: Gustave Clausse, *Les Sangallo* (1902); SAVONAROLA: Pasquale Villari, *Life and Times of Girolamo Savonarola* (1888); Joseph Schnitzer, *Savonarola* (2 vols.) (1924); Enrico Barfucci, " The Garden of San Marco," *Illustrazione Toscana*, Oct. 1940; R. Ridolfi, *Life of Girolamo Savonarola* (1952); M. de la Bedoyère, *The Meddlesome Friar* (1957); SAVONAROLA, MACHIAVELLI, CASTIGLIONE, ARETINO: Ralph Roeder, *The Man of the Renaissance* (1933); " Savonarola, Machiavelli and Guido Antonio Vespucci," *Political Science Quarterly*, LXIX, No. 2; VASARI: Robert Carden, *The Life of Giorgio Vasari* (1910).

HISTORY

GREECE: G. Grote, *History of Greece*; J. B. Bury, *The History of Greece*; *The Cambridge Ancient History*, V, VI, VII (1927-28); *The Greek Historians*, ed. by F. Godolphin (2 vols.) (1942); C. M. Bowra, *The Greek Experience* (1957); E. Hamilton, *The Echo of Greece* (1957).

Homer, *The Iliad* and *The Odyssey*, A. Pope (1720 and ЕВТРЕ; *The Dialogues of Plato and The Works of Aristotle*, Oxford University Press (1871 and 1908); Plutarch, *Twelve Lives*, J. Dryden, revised by Clough (1864).

R. Richardson, *A History of Greek Sculpture* (1911); C. Bluemel, *Greek Sculptors at Work* (1955); E. Pfuhl, *Masterpieces of Greek Drawing and Painting* (1955); G. Richter, *Handbook of Greek Art* (1959).

ROMAN EMPIRE: Pliny, *Natural History* (tr. 1857); Suetonius, *The Twelve Cæsars*, R. Graves (1957); E. Gibbon, *The History of the Decline and Fall of the Roman Empire*, ed. by J. B. Bury (1909-13); T. Mommsen, *Roman History* (1854-56); Quarenghi, *Mura di Roma* (1880); M. W. Porter, *What Rome Was Built With* (1907); Blake, *Ancient Roman Construction* (1947); M. Sherer, *Marvels of Ancient Rome* (1955); *Rome of the Cæsars*, Phaidon edit. (1956).

ITALY: Mrs. H. M. Vernon, *Italy from 1494 to 1790* (1909); Jamison, Ady, Vernon and Terry, *Italy, Mediæval and Modern* (1917).

PAPACY: M. Creighton, *A History of the Papacy* (6 vols.) (1897).

BOLOGNAH *Francesco d'Agostino, Della Nobilità di Bologna*, Cremona (1588); Pompeo Dolfi, *Cronologia delle Famiglie Nobili di Bologna* (1670); J. J. Berthier, *Le Tombeau du Saint Dominique* (1895); F. Filippini, *Nota agli Scultori del Sarcofago di San Domenico, Archi-ginnasio* (1914); Supino Benvenuto, "Michelangelo a Bologna," *Atti e Memorie della Deputazione di Storia Patria per le Provincie della Romagna,* Serie IV, Vol. IX (1919); *Guide to the Basilica of St. Domenic in Bologna,* Provincial Tourist Board (1950); U. Beseghi, *Chiese di Bologna* (1953) and *Palazzi di Bologna* (1956); P. Gigli, *Per le Vie e le Piazze di Bologna* (1957); Balacci, De Toni, Frati, Ghigi, Gortani, etc., *Sulla Vita e le Opere di Ulisse Aldovrandi* (1907); L. Frati, *La Vita Privata in Bologna dal Secolo XIII al XVII,* Zanichelli (1928).

CAPRESE AND CASENTINO: Ing. Luigi Mercanti, *Illustrazione del Castello di Caprese* (1875); G. Chinali, *Carpete e Michelangelo* (1904); C. Beni, *Guida Illustrata del Casentino.*

CARRARA: C. Lazzoni, *Carrara and Her Villas* (1880) and *Riassunto Storico sopra Carrara e la sua Accademia di Belle Arti* (1880).

FLORENCE: Goro Dati, *History of Florence* (1410); Giov. Cambi, "Historie," *Delizie degli Eruditi Toscani* (1785); Jacopo Nardi, *Istorie della Città di Firenze* (1584); Francesco Guicciardini, *Storia Fiorentina a Tempi di Cosimo de' Medici a quelli del Gonfaloniere Soderini* (1859 edit.); N. Machiavelli, *History of Florence and the Affairs of Italy* (1528); P. Mini, *Difesa della Città di Firenze,* Lione (1577); Aurelio Gotti, *Storia del Palazzo Vecchio in Firenze* (1889); André Perate, "Le Musée de Santa Maria del Fiore," *Gazette des Beaux Arts* (1892); P. Villari, *The Two First Centuries of Florentine History* (1893-94); G. Poggi, *Catalogo del Museo dell'Opera del Duomo* (1904); J. Ross, *Florentine Palaces and Their Stories* (1905); G. Poggi, *Il Duomo di Firenze* (1909); A. Lensi, *Il Palazzo Vecchio* (1929); Guccerelli, *Stradario Storico di Firenze* (1929); C. Botto, "L'Edificazione della Chiesa di S. Spirito in Firenze," *Rivista d'Arte* (1931) n. 4, and (1932) n. 1; C. de Tolnay, "Michel-Ange et la Façade de S. Lorenzo," *Gazette des Beaux Arts* (1934); G. Carocci, *I Dintorni di Firenze* (1906-7); E. Pieraccini, *La Stirpe dei Medici di Cafag-*

giolo (1924); P. Bargellini, *The Medici Palace and the Frescoes of Benozzo Gozzoli*, Del Turco Editore (1954).

LOMBARDY: E. Hutton, *The Cities of Lombardy* (1912).

ROME, MEDIEVAL AND RENAISSANCE: Ademollo, *Alessandro VI, Giulio II, Leone X, nel Carnevale Romano* (1886); F. Gregorovius, *Rome in the Middle Ages*, tr. by G. Hamilton (13 vols.) (1894); Rodocanachi, *La Rome de Jules II et Léon X* (1912); Callari, *I Palazzi di Roma* (1943); P. Paschini, "Storia di Roma," *Roma nel Rinascimento*, Vol. XII; L. Morandi, "Pasquino e Pasquinate," *Nuova Antoligia* (1889).

TUSCANY: E. Repetti, *Dizionario Georgrafico Fisico Storico della Toscana* (1833); Von Borsig and Bianchi-Bandinelli (n.d.).

HISTORY OF ITALIAN PEOPLE: G. Mecatti, *Storia Genealogica della Nobilità e Cittadinanza di Firenze* (1754); J. P. Trevelyan, *A Short History of the Italian People* (1920 edit.); M. Pallottino, *The Etruscans*, tr. by J. Cremona (1955).

CUSTOMS, MANNERS: W. Scaife, *Florentine Life during the Renaissance* (1893); M. Besso, *Roma e il Papa nei Proverbi e nei Modi di Dire* (1904); *Costumi, Musica, Danze e Feste Popolari Italiane*, Opera Nazionale Dopolavoro (1931); G. DeVoto, *Storia della Lingua di Roma* (1940); I. Origo, *The Merchant of Prato* (1957).

HUMOUR, STORIES: *Facezie, Motti e Burle di Diversi Signorie Persone*, Private Coll., L. Domenichi (1574); F. Sacchetti, *Trecentonovelle* (1724).

COSTUMES: P. Lacroix, *Manners, Customs and Dress during the Middle Ages and during the Renaissance Period* (1876); I. Brooke, *Western European Costume* (1939); M. Davenport, *The Book of Costume* (1949).

RENAISSANCE: N. Machiavelli, *The Prince* (1513); J. Burckhardt, *The Civilization of the Renaissance in Italy* (also under ART HISTORIES) (1860); J. A. Symonds, *The Renais-*

sance in Italy (7 vols.) (1875-86); Georg Voigt, *Die Wiederbelebung des classischen Altertums* (2 vols.) (1893); J. Klaczko, *Rome and the Renaissance* (1903); R. Lanciani, *Golden Days of the Renaissance* (1906); H. B. Cotterill, *Italy from Dante to Tasso* (1919); *R. Taylor, Invitation to Renaissance Italy* (1930); P. Kristeller, *The Philosophy of Marsilio Ficino* (1943); E. Garin, *The Italian Humanism* (1952); M. Gilmore, *The World of Humanism* (1952); W. Durant, *The Renaissance* (1953); "The Renaissance," *The New Cambridge Modern History* (1957).

ART HISTORIES: Crowe-Cavalcaselle, *A History of Painting in Italy*, VI; Jacob Burckhardt, *The Civilization of the Renaissance in Italy* (1860); L. Viardot, *Wonders of Sculpture* (1872); C. Perkins, *Historical Handbook of Italian Sculpture* (1883); L. Scott, *Sculpture, Renaissance and Modern* (1886); Marquand and Frothingham, *A Textbook of the History of Sculpture* (1904); K. Cox, *Old Masters and New* (1905); G. F. Hill, *One Hundred Masterpieces of Sculpture* (1911); E. Faure, *History of Art: Renaissance Art* (1923, 1937); C. Holmes, *Old Masters and Modern Art* (1923); E. L. Seeley, *Artists of the Italian Renaissance* (1925); A. Venturi, *Storia dell'Arte Italiana* (1925); C. Morey, *Mediæval Art* (1942); Bernard Berenson, *The Italian Painters of the Renaissance* (1952); H. Wölfflin, *Classic Art* (1952); Manfred Ferbach, *Das Chaos in der Michelangelo-Forschung* (1957); C. Gould, *An Introduction to Italian Renaissance Painting* (1957); J. Pope-Hennessy, *Italian Gothic Sculpture* (1955) and *Italian Renaissance Sculpture* (1958); Charles de Tolnay, *Michelangelo* (5 vols.) (1943-60).

ART TECHNIQUES

THE ARTS: Sigmund Freud, "The Moses of Michelangelo," *Coll. Papers* (1959 edit.; first pub. anon. in *Imago*, 1914); André Malraux, *The Voices of Silence* (1953).

ART OF SCULPTURE: A. Hildebrand, *The Problem of Form*

(1907) ; Auguste Rodin, *Art* (1912) ; K. Clark, *The Nude* (1956) ; H. Read, *The Art of Sculpture* (1956).

TECHNIQUES OF SCULPTURE: *The Book of Art of Cennino Cennini* (first pub. c. 1396-1437) ; *Vasari on Technique* (first pub. with Vasari's *Lives*, 1550, 1568) ; *Vasari on Technique*, transl. by Louisa S. Maclehose (1907) ; Francesco Carradori, *Istruzione Elementare per gli Studiosi della Scultura* (1802) ; M. Hoffman, *Sculpture Inside and Out* (1939).

ARCHITECTURE: Victor Hafner, *The Dome of St. Peter's Cathedral at Rome* (1924).

FRESCO PAINTING: Cennini and Vasari (*see* TECHNIQUES OF SCULPTURE); Raffaello Borghini, *Il Riposo* (1584) ; G. Hale, *Fresco Painting* (1933) ; M. Merrifield, *The Art of Fresco Painting* (1952) ; W. G. Constable, *The Painter's Workshop* (1954).

PAINTERS' STUDIOS IN FIFTEENTH CENTURY: J. Mesnil, " L'Education des peintres florentins au 15ème siècle," *Revue des idées*, Sept. 15, 1910 ; Martin Wackernagel, *Der Lebensraum des Künstlers in der florentinischen Renaissance* (1938).

FRESCOES AT SANTA MARIA NOVELLA: Giuseppe Marchini, " The Frescoes in the Choir of Santa Maria Novella," *The Burlington Magazine*, XCV, 607, Oct. 1953.

MICHELANGELO'S WORKS: Hercules: F. Ramorino, *Mitologia Classica* (1940) ; Tolnay's reply to Weinberger, *Art Bulletin*, June 1945 ; PICCOLOMINI ALTAR: F. Kriegbaum, " Le Statue di Michelangelo nell'Altare dei Piccolomini a Siena," *Michelangelo Buonarroti nel IV Centenario del Giudizio Universale* (1952) ; W. R. Valentiner, " Michelangelo's Statuettes of the Piccolomini Altar in Siena," *The Art Quarterly*, V (1942) ; DAVID: G. de Nicola, " La Giuditti di Donatello e la Madonna Panciatichi di Desiderio," *Rassegna d'Arte* (1917) ; BRONZE DAVID: Ducerceau, *Les Plus Excellents Bâtiments de France* (1576) ; F. Reiset, " Un Bronze de Michel Ange," *L'Athenaeum Français*, II (1853) ; Courajod, " Le David

de Bronze du Château de Bury," *Gazette archéologique,*
X (1885) ; BRONZE DAVID AND TWELVE APOSTLES: " La
Vie et l'œuvre de Michel-Ange," *Gazette des Beaux Arts*
(1897) ; DONI HOLY FAMILY: " Michelangelo Madonna
Doni in den Uffizien," *Jahresbericht des Kunsthistorischen
Instituts* (1906-7) ; BRUGES MADONNA: Prof. G. Poggi,
La Madonna di Bruges di Michelangelo (1954) ; CASCINA
CARTOON: A Foratti, " Il Cartone di Michelangelo per
la Battaglia di Cascina," *Rassegna d'Arte,* VII (1920) ;
MEDICI CHAPEL: C. de Tolnay, " Studi sulla Cappella
Medicea," *L'Arte,* Anno XXXVII (1934) ; George
Gronau, *Jahrbuch der Preuszischen Kunstsammlungen*
(1911) ; MODELS: L. Goldscheider, *Michelangelo's
Bozzetti for Statues in the Medici Chapel* (1957).

BOOKS OF REPRODUCTIONS: *Old Italian Masters,* engraved
by T. Cole, notes by W. J. Stillman (1888) ; K. Frey,
Die Handzeichnungen Michelagniolos Buonarroti (1909) ;
Dr. P. Garnault, *Les Portraits de Michelangelo* (1913) ;
E. Steinmann, *Die Portraitdarstellungen des Michelangelo*
(1913) ; F. Knapp, *Michelangelo* (1923) ; B. Berenson,
The Drawings of the Florentine Painters (1938) ; *Dona-
tello,* Phaidon (1941) ; *Raphael,* Phaidon (1941); *Leo-
nardo da Vinci,* Phaidon (1943) ; Roberto Hoesch,
Michelangelo (1945) ; L. Goldscheider, *Ghiberti* (1949) ;
" Michelangelo's Sistine Ceiling," *Life,* Dec. 26, 1949 ;
R. Bacchelli, *Per la Traslazione della Pietà Rondanini di
Michelangelo* (1952) ; *Italian Drawings: Michelangelo
and His Studio,* pub. by Trustees, British Museum (1953) ;
L. Goldscheider, *Michelangelo* (1953) ; *Firenze Nell'-
Incisione di G. Zocchi,* Edizioni Ponte Vecchio (1955) ;
J. de Toth, *Vatican Grottoes* Fabric of St. Peter (1955) ;
The Bible in Art: The Old Testament, Phaidon (1956) ;
L. Goldscheider, *Leonardo da Vinci: Life and Work,
Paintings and Drawings* (1959) ; *Parla Michelangelo,*
a cura di Aldo L. Cerchiari, Ediz. Toninelli (1946).

ORIGINAL SOURCES

LETTERS: *Le Lettere di Michelangelo Buonarroti coi Ricordi
ed i Contratti Artistici,* ed. by Gaetano Milanesi (1875);
Die Briefe des Michelagniolo Buonarroti, ed. by K. Frey

(1907); *Les Correspondants de Michel-Ange*, I, *Sebastiano del Piombo*, par Gaetano Milanesi, tr. in French by A. Le Pileur (1890); *Carteggio Inedito di Aristi dei Secoli XIV, XV, XVI*, ed. by Giov. Gaye (3 vols.) (1839-40); *Lettere di Artisti*, ed. by N. Guanlandi (1844); *Tre Libri di Lettere* (1552).

RICORDI: *Die Aufzeichnungen des Michelangelo Buonarroti in British Museum in London und im Vermächtnis Ernst Steinmann in Rome*, ed. by Wolf Maurenbrecher (1938); " Spogli agli Strozzi di un Libro di Memorie e Ricordi," *Memorie*, IV (1849).

JOURNALS: *Notebooks of Leonardo da Vinci*, tr. by E. McCurdy; " Dialogues of Francisco d'Ollanda " (Appendix of *Michael Angelo Buonarroti* by C. Holroyd); Francisco de Hollanda, *Four Dialogues on Painting*, transl. by A. F. G. Bell (1928).

ARCHIVES: *Il Codice Magliabechiano*, ed, by K. Frey (1897); *Archivio Storico Italiano*, Serial III, XIX (Lorenzo and Piero de' Medici's ricordi); *Inventory of Palazzo Medici*, 1512, pub. by R. Archivio di Stato di Firenze.

AUTOBIOGRAPHIES: *Memoirs of Angelus Politianus, Joannes Pico of Mirandula, etc.*, tr. and notes by Rev. W. Parr Greswell (1805); *The Life of Benvenuto Cellini*, tr. by J. A. Symonds (1889).

BOOKS AND ARTICLES: *The Florentine Fior di Virtù of* 1491 tr. by Nicholas Fersin, pub. by Lib. of Cong. (1953); S. Fornari, *La Sposizione di Messer Simone Fornari da Reggio sopra L'Orlando Furioso di Messer Lodovico Ariosto*; Donato Giannotti, *De' Giorni che Dante Consumò nel cercare l'Inferno e 'l Purgatorio*, Florence (1859).

ENCYCLOPEDIAS: *Enciclopedia Italiana*, pub. by Istituto Giovanni Treccani (1931); *Encyclopædia Britannica* (1929); *Catholic Encyclopedia*, Robert Appleton and Co. (1911); *Enciclopedia Storico-Nobiliare Italiana*, V. Spreti (1932); *The Encyclopedia of Painting*, ed. by B. Myers (1955); *Dizionario Enciclopedico*, by Sansoni (1954); *Dictionary of the Artists*, by Thieme-Becker; *Dictionnaire d'Orfèvrerie*, by Texier (1857); *Dictionnaire des sculpteurs, dessinateurs et graveurs*, by Du Benezit (1911); *Dizionario delle Opere* by Bompiani (1955); *Vocabolario degli Accademici della Crusca* (7 vols.), (1806).

RELIGIOUS REFERENCES: *The Holy Bible*, tr. by Msgr. Ronald Knox (1944); *The Holy Scriptures*, according to the Masoretic Text (1917); George Ferguson, *Signs and Symbols in Christian Art* (1954).

TRAVEL GUIDES, MAPS, ETC.: " Italy," *Hachette World Guides* (1956); " Quattro Mappe di Bologna del XVII e XVIII Secolo," compiled by C. Casamorata, Istituto Geografico Militare, Bologna; " Florence " (map), Credito Italiano, Florence; *How to Visit Florence* by Francesco Bigliazzi (1949); *Roma Prima di Sisto V* (commentary with map), by Francesco Ehrle (1908); *Rome, The Eternal City*, pub. by Lozzi (1949); *The Roman Forum and the Palatine*, ed. by Dr. G. Bardi (1956).

MYTHOLOGY: Ovid, *The Metamorphoses*, tr. by H. Gregory (1958); Thomas Bulfinch, *Mythology*; Robert Graves, *The Greek Myths* (2 vols.) (1955).

POETRY: Michelangelo, *Rime*, pref. by G. Papini (1928); *The Sonnets of Michelangelo*, tr. by J. A. Symonds (1950); *The Complete Poems of Michelangelo*, tr. by Joseph Tusiani (1960); *The Divine Comedy* by Dante Alighieri, tr. by Lawrence White (1943); *The Sonnets, Triumphs and Other Poems of Petrarch*, tr. by various hands, with Life of the Poet by Thomas Campbell (1909); Karl Frey, *Die Dichtungen des Michelagniolo Buonarroti* (1897).

NOVELS: Dmitri Merezhkovsky, *The Romance of Leonardo da Vinci*, tr. by Bernard Guerney (1938); George Eliot, *Romola* (1862-63).

GLOSSARY of Italian words and phrases used most frequently in this book. The endings sometimes change for
gender, singular or plural, or verb form, but the meanings
remain clear. Sometimes the more modern usage is slightly
different. All are also translated when they first appear in
the body of the text.

The various titles include: *Messer* or *signor,* sir or mister.
There is the *podestà* or mayor, *gonfaloniere* or governor,
signoria or council. *Padrone* is a proprietor, and *buonuomini*
are noblemen; *padre* is a priest.

The personal relationships include *madre* or mother, *padre*
or father. *Figlio* is a son, *nonno* a grandfather, *compare* a
godfather, *bambino* a child. *Monna* is a general term, short
for *madonna,* woman.

Madre mia and *mamma mia* are endearing terms, mother
mine; as are also *amico* for friend, and *amico mio.* With love
and affection there is *caro, carissimo* for *dear.*

Gente are people.

A *palazzo* is a palace, a *piazza* a square, *ringhiera* a balcony.
A *casino* is a small house, *stanza* a room, *studiolo* a small
library, *bagno* a bath. The *Signoria* is the city Hall; *Stinche*
the prison. The *calcio* is a football game, and the *palio*
a horse race. *Bastoni* is a card game.

The countryside is the *campagna,* a *podere* the farm;
paleri, grass for grazing. The *contadino* is a farmer or farm
worker, or peasant.

The men wear *farsetti* or doublets, *calzoni* or *calze,* which
are long stockings; the *camicia* a long shirt or tunic, *brache,*
short outer drawers. For the woman there is the *gonnella*
or skirt, *gamurra* the long gown, *scialima* or shawl, *ghirlanda,*
wreath for the hair. The *berretto* is a soft cap, beret.
The *biretta* is worn by the Pope or a cardinal. The *sarta*
is the dressmaker, and the *sarto* a tailor.

Among the foods are the various kinds of *pasta,* or dough
products, in various shapes and sometimes filled: *cannelloni,
ravioli, lasagne, tortellini*; also *pane* and *panini* for bread and
rolls. A *pasmata* is an Easter cookie, *biscotti,* cookies in

general. *Carne* or meat includes the veal of *scaloppine*, the *bistecca* or beefsteak, the *salame* or sausage meat. A *stufato* is a stew, *cacciucco* of fish, *bramangiere* of fowl. There is the *alla cacciatora* or hunter's style, and the elaborate casserole preparation of a *torta*; *pappardelle alla lepre* is noodles with hare sauce, a *fritto misto* a mixed fry. *Galinga* is a spice, *piselli*, peas. *Trebbiano* and *chianti* are both wines, as are *vin santo* a dessert wine, and *passito* a raisin wine. The *damigiana* is a demijohn. A *trattoria* is a small restaurant, as is an *osteria*, which is usually in an inn. *Parmigiano* is a cheese, the one most frequently grated and used with the *pasta* or *minestrone*, soup. *Mangiate bene!* is Eat well!

Within the *bottega*, studio or artist's workshop, are the various craftsmen: *scultori*, sculptors, the *statuario* or statue maker. In Carrara the *bardi* are apprentices. The tools include the claw-toothed *gradina*, the *subbia*, a scalpel, the *scribbus*, *calcagnuolo*, *ugnetto*, *scarpello*, *mazzuolo*, various degrees of punch and point which the sculptor or stonehewer uses. The *colpo vivo*, or *ferrata*, is the live blow, or series of strikes in a single run. *Trementina* is a turpentine, *pozzolana* a grit ingredient in the plaster, or intonaco, for fresco, *a secco*, a dry touch-up. The *sagoma* is the outline or silhouette.

Putti are small angels or cherubs, and with *cassettoni*, sunken panels, decorate practically everything.

The stones are *pietra serena*, for the serene stone of Florence, the *ardita*, *dura* or *forte* for the hard stone; the volcanic *peperino* is of Rome. The stone men are *scalpellini*.

As concerns *marmo*, marble: there are the Carrara and Seravezza white marbles, the *cipollino*, *breccia*, *verdaccio*, *bardiglio*, all with some colour. The marble workmen are the *smodellatori* or marble blockers; the *tecchiaiolo*, steeplejack cliff sweeper, the *carradori*, cart owners. A *poggio* is a level work area.

Soldi, *scudi*, *denari* are money; a *baiocco* the smallest of coins. Most of the city-states minted their own. The *spedalingo* is the financial business manager.

A list of most frequently used expressions includes those for good day, evening or night: *buon dì'*, *buon giorno*, *buona sera*, *buona notte*. Good-bye is *A riverderci* or *Addio*. Until to-morrow is *A domani*, and in Carrara, *Fa a modr* or Go carefully.

There is *Ben venuto* or *Ben trovato* for Welcome. *Beviamo!*

means Drink up! *Auguri,* Good Wishes, *Salve* or *Salute,* Good Health! *Come va* asks How goes it? and *Non c' é male* answers Not too bad.

Buona fortuna is good luck, and *peccato,* what a pity! *Finito* is finished, and *il colmo,* the limit! *Dio* or *Dio mio,* my God!

Basta is Stop, I've had enough; *bene* is good! and *Bavissimo* wonderful! *Il migliore* is the best. *Ecco* points out, Here it is, or That's it! *Allora* means Well then!

Non importa shrugs, It's not important. *E vero* or *davvero* echoes How true! *Senz' altro* is Without question. *Uguale* or *lo stesso* mean the same, the same. *Ammesso* is Admitted! *Permette,* Allow me. *Grazie* or *grazie mille,* thanks.

Pazienza! means Have patience; *calma,* be calm; *piano, piano,* take it easy.

Divertimento is fun or diversion; *scandaloso,* scandalous. *Ma* is a big But, or What can one do about it? *Ma che!* Of course not!

Comprendo or *capisco* means I understand.

Among the derisions are: *pazzo, pazzesco* for You're crazy; *sciocco,* silly, *stupido* and *idiota,* plain dumb. *Putana* is a whore, *villano* an ill-bred, *bastardo* a bastard; *figlio d'un can,* son of a . . . dog, *Va all' inferno* is Go to hell.

Simpatico is charming, a *rigorista* is a strict or narrow-minded person, *terribilità* is awesomeness. A *campanilista* is a provincial who cares only about his own tower; *campanilismo,* chauvinism; *fuorusciti,* exiles, *paesano* a countryman.

Il cronaca is the storyteller.

A *riposo* is a rest or nap, a *festa* a holiday, *ferragosto* a mid-August vacation.

Amore is love; *viva forza,* human strength; *incinta,* pregnant.

Monte is a mountain, *tramontana* the north wind; *volgare* is the vulgate; *budelli e sangue,* blood and guts.

A *breve* is a Pope's brief, or declaration, *cappella* a chapel, *sanctum sanctorum* the holy of holies, or holiest place.

PRESENT LOCATION

OF MICHELANGELO'S WORKS

TITLE	YEAR	LOCATION
Madonna of the Stairs	1491	Casa Buonarroti, Florence
Battle of Centaurs	1492	Casa Buonarroti, Florence
Sts. Petronius and Proculus, and the Angel	1495	San Domenico, Bologna
Bacchus	1497	Bargello, Florence
Pietà	1498–1500	St. Peter's, Vatican City
Bruges Madonna	1501–4	Church of Notre Dame, Bruges, Belgium
Statues for Piccolomini Altar	1501	Cathedral, Siena
David	1501–4	Accademia, Florence
Doni Holy Family	1503	Uffizi, Florence
Pitti Madonna	1504	Bargello, Florence
Taddei Madonna	1504–5	Royal Academy, London
St. Matthew	1505–6	Accademia, Florence
Tomb of Pope Julius II	1505–45	San Pietro in Vincoli, Rome
Sistine Ceiling	1508–12	Vatican Palace, Vatican City
Heroic and Dying Captives	1513–16	Louvre, Paris
Moses	1513–42	San Pietro in Vincoli, Rome
The Risen Christ	1518–21	Santa Maria sopra Minerva, Rome
The Four Unfinished Captives (Giants)	c. 1519	Accademia, Florence
The Medici Chapel	1620–34	Florence
The Laurentian Library	1524–34	Florence
Dawn	1524–31	Medici Chapel, Florence
Dusk	1524–31	Medici Chapel, Florence
Madonna and Child	1524–34	Medici Chapel, Florence
Duke Lorenzo	1524–34	Medici Chapel, Florence
Night	1526–31	Medici Chapel, Florence
Duke Giuliano	1526–34	Medici Chapel, Florence
Day	1526–34	Medici Chapel, Florence
Victory	c. 1526–30	Palazzo Vecchio, Florence
David-Apollo	1502, 1531	Bargello, Florence
The Last Judgment	1536–41	Sistine Chapel, Vatican City
Brutus	c. 1539	Bargello, Florence

TITLE	YEAR	LOCATION
Rachel	1542	San Pietro in Vincoli, Rome
Leah	1542	San Pietro in Vincoli, Rome
Conversion of Paul	1542–45	Pauline Chapel, Vatican City
Crucifixion of Peter	1546–50	Pauline Chapel, Vatican City
St. Peter's	1547–64	Vatican City
Farnese Palace: third story, cornice and courtyard	1547–50	Rome
The Capitol	1547–64	Rome
Pietà (Deposition from the Cross)	1548–55	Duomo, Florence
Palestrina Pietà (Entombment)	c. 1550–56	Accademia, Florence
Rondanini Pietà	1555–64	Castello Sforzesco, Milan
Porta Pia	1561–64	Rome
Santa Maria degli Angeli	1563–64	Rome

The Following works by Michelangelo have been lost: Mask of a Faun, 1490; Santa Spirito Crucifix, 1494; Hercules, 1494; Little St. John, 1496; The Sleeping Cupid, 1496; Cupid for Jacopo Galli, 1497; Bronze David, 1502-8; Battle of Cascina cartoon, 1504-5; Bronze Statue of Julius II, 1506-8; Leda and the Swan, tempera panel, 1529-30.

Of Michelangelo's many wax and clay models, only a few have survived, and there is disagreement about the authenticity of some of these. Five models are generally accepted: the clay River God in the Accademia in Florence; the clay Victory group or Hercules and Cacus, a clay male nude, and a clay of the Awakening Giant in the Casa Buonarroti in Florence; the clay Giant, repaired with red wax, in the British Museum, London.

The following are disputed and doubtful, although several critics accept them as Michelangelo's work: a clay allegorical female figure, and a clay Giant in the Casa Buonarroti; a red wax Young Giant at the British Museum, London; a clay Night and Dawn in the collection of Dr. Alejandro Pietri in Caracas, Venevuela. Less authenticated are two wax Captives at the Casa Buonarroti.

The major collections of Michelangelo's drawings are to be found in the Casa Buonarroti and Uffizi in Florence; the British Museum in London; the Louvre in Paris; the Ashmolean Museum in Oxford, and the Royal Library at Windsor Castle.

NOTE

This biographical novel is documented by several years of living and researching in the source materials of Florence, Rome, Carrara and Bologna. The work actually began six years ago when I had the entire body of Michelangelo's four hundred and ninety-five letters, as well as his records and art contracts (Milanesi edition, Florence, 1875), translated into English, a task not before attempted, by Dr. Charles Speroni, professor of Italian at the University of California at Los Angeles, to create a solid base for the novel. A considerable amount of material is here published for the first time. The sources are now on record at the library of the University of California at Los Angeles.

I am deeply indebted to the scholars in the Renaissance field. The late, great Bernard Berenson afforded me expert counselling on the Michelangelo bibliography, and opened his magnificent library at I Tatti, in his own words, "night or day." Ludwig Goldscheider, the British authority, gave warmheartedly of his precious time and materials. Aldo Fortuna, the Florentine archivist, shared his lifetime of Renaissance documentation. Cardinal Tisserant made available the superb Michelangelo collection in the Vatican Library. Professor Giovanni Poggi unlocked the Buonarroti family record books, which go back many years before Michelangelo's birth. Dr. Ulrich Middeldorf, director of the Kunsthistorisches Institut in Florence, facilitated our work in his library, as did the directors of the Bibliotheca Hertziana in Rome.

In Carrara, I am grateful to Bruno and Mario Taverelli for the opportunity to study the quarries at close range, and for their indefatigable efforts to document the Carrarino dialect and mores. In Bologna, I am indebted to Professor Umberto Beseghi for leading me to the best of the Bolognese source materials; in Siena, I am grateful to the descendants of Vittoria Colonna, Marchesa Pace Misciatelli and Donna Ginevra Bonelli, for helping me with the story of the Marchesa di Pescara. Stanley Lewis, the Canadian sculptor, was my guide in Florence to Michelangelo's techniques; there he also taught me to carve marble. He has answered an unending stream of questions about the thinking and feeling of the sculptor at work. Charles and Carmela Speroni corrected manuscript and galleys, as a labour of love.

Lastly, I want to acknowledge my considerable indebtedness to Charles de Tolnay, whose monumental five volumes constitute the definitive art history on Michelangelo's work. Michelangelo's sonnets are quoted from the J. A. Symonds translation. The quotation from Ovid's *The Metamorphoses* is from the Horace Gregory version. Quotations from Dante's *The Divine Comedy* are from the Lawrence Grant White translation.

Fontana Books

Fontana is best known as one of the leading paperback publishers of popular fiction and non-fiction. It also includes an outstanding, and expanding, section of books on history, natural history, religion and social sciences.

Most of the fiction authors need no introduction. They include Agatha Christie, Hammond Innes, Alistair MacLean, Catherine Gaskin, Victoria Holt and Lucy Walker. Desmond Bagley and Maureen Peters are among the relative newcomers.

The non-fiction list features a superb collection of animal books by such favourites as Gerald Durrell and Joy Adamson.

All Fontana books are available at your bookshop or newsagent; or can be ordered direct. Just fill in the form below and list the titles you want.

FONTANA BOOKS, Cash Sales Department, G.P.O. Box 29, Douglas, Isle of Man, British Isles. Please send purchase price, plus 6p per book. Customers outside the U.K. send purchase price, plus 7p per book. Cheque, postal or money order. No currency.

NAME (Block letters)

_____

ADDRESS

_____

_____

_____